Mr Holmes

Mitch Cullin is the author of ten books, including the novel *Tideland*, the film adaptation of which was directed by Terry Gilliam, and the novel-in-verse, *Branches*. He lives in California's San Gabriel Valley, and as a teenager was featured in *USA Today* in 1984 as one of the foremost Holmes fans in the world.

ALSO BY MITCH CULLIN

Mr Holmes

MITCH CULLIN

CANONGATE
Edinburgh · London

This paperback edition published by Canongate Books in 2015

First published in Great Britain as *A Slight Trick of the Mind* in 2014 by
Canongate Books Ltd, 14 High Street, Edinburgh EH1 1TE

www.canongate.tv

1

First published in the United States in 2005 by Nan A. Talese,
an imprint of Doubleday, a division of Random House, Inc.

British Library Cataloguing-in-Publication Data
A catalogue record for this book is available on
request from the British Library

ISBN 978 1 78211 331 7

Book design by Caroline Cunningham.

Printed and bound in Great Britain by Clays Ltd, St Ives Plc

For my mother, Charlotte Richardson,

a fan of mysteries and life's scenic routes;

and for the late John Bennett Shaw,

who once left me in charge of his library

I was sure, at least, that I'd finally seen a face which played an essential part in my life, and that it was more human and childlike than in my dream. More than that I didn't know, for it was already gone again.

—Morio Kita, *Ghosts*

What is this strange silent voice that speaks to bees and no one else can hear?

—William Longgood, *The Queen Must Die*

ACKNOWLEDGMENTS

With gratitude to the following for support, information, advice, friendship, and inspiration: Ai, John Barlow, Coates Bateman, Richard E. Bonney, Bradam, Mike and Sarah Brewer, Francine Brody, Joey Burns, Anne Carey and Anthony Bregman and Ted Hope, Neko Case, Peter I. Chang, the Christians (Charise, Craig, Cameron, Caitlin), John Convertino, my father, Charles Cullin, Elise D'Haene, John Dower, Carol Edwards, Demetrios Efstratiou, Todd Field, Mary Gaitskill, Dr. Randy Garland, Howe and Sofie Gelb (www.giantsand.com), Terry Gilliam, Jemma Gomez, the Grandaddy collective, Tony Grisoni, Tom Harmsen, the Haruta family (whose help with this book was most appreciated), lovely Kristin Hersh, Tony Hillerman, Robyn Hitchcock, Sue Hubbell, Michele Hutchison, Reiko Kaigo, Patti Keating, Steve and Jesiah King, Roberto Koshikawa, Ocean Lam, Tom Lavoie, Patty LeMay and Paul Niehaus, Russell Leong, Werner Melzer, John Nichols, Kenzaburo Oe, Hikaru Okuizumi, Dave Oliphant, the Parras (Chay, Mark, Callen), Jill Patterson, Chad and Jodi Piper, Kathy Pories, Andy Quan, Michael Richardson, Charlotte Roybal, Saito Sanki, Daniel Schacter, Marty and Judy Shepard, Peter Steinberg, Nan Talese, Kurt

Wagner and Mary Mancini, Billy Wilder and I. A. L. Diamond, Lulu Wu, and William Wilde Zeitler.

An extra-special nod goes to William S. Baring-Gould and his excellent *Sherlock Holmes of Baker Street* (Bramhall House, 1962), which has been a favorite since childhood and proved invaluable during the writing of this novel. Mycroft's mention of his "old friend Winston" was taken directly from this edition.

PART

I

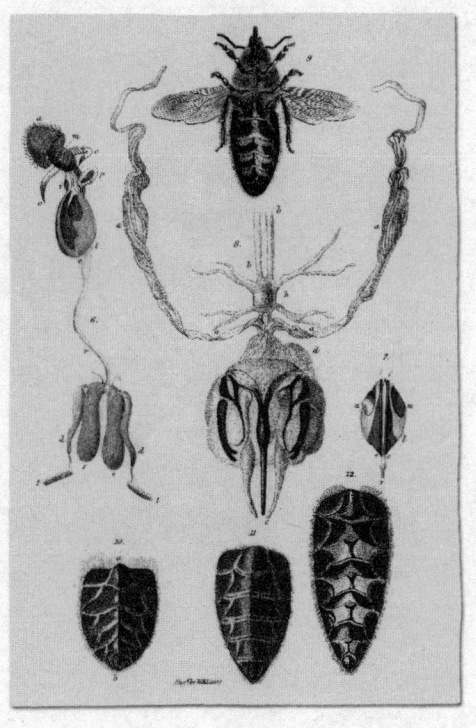

1

UPON ARRIVING from his travels abroad, he entered his stone-built farmhouse on a summer's afternoon, leaving the luggage by the front door for his housekeeper to manage. He then retreated into the library, where he sat quietly, glad to be surrounded by his books and the familiarity of home. For almost two months, he had been away, traveling by military train across India, by Royal Navy ship to Australia, and then finally setting foot on the occupied shores of postwar Japan. Going and returning, the same interminable routes had been taken—usually in the company of rowdy enlisted men, few of whom acknowledged the elderly gentleman dining or sitting beside them (that slow-walking geriatric, searching his pockets for a match he'd never find, chewing relentlessly on an unlit Jamaican cigar). Only on the rare occasions when an informed officer might announce his identity would the ruddy faces gaze with amazement, assessing him in that moment: For while he used two canes, his body remained unbowed, and the passing of years hadn't dimmed his keen gray eyes; his snow-white hair, thick and long, like his beard, was combed straight back in the English fashion.

"Is that true? Are you really him?"

"I am afraid I still hold that distinction."

"You are Sherlock Holmes? No, I don't believe it."

"That is quite all right. I scarcely believe it myself."

But at last the journey was completed, though he found it difficult to summon the specifics of his days abroad. Instead, the whole vacation—while filling him like a satisfying meal—felt unfathomable in hindsight, punctuated here and there by brief remembrances that soon became vague impressions and were invariably forgotten again. Even so, he had the immutable rooms of his farmhouse, the rituals of his orderly country life, the reliability of his apiary—these things required no vast, let alone meager, amount of recall; they had simply become ingrained during his decades of isolation. Then there were the bees he tended: The world continued to change, as did he, but they persisted nonetheless. And after his eyes closed and his breaths resonated, it would be a bee that welcomed him home—a worker manifesting in his thoughts, finding him elsewhere, settling on his throat and stinging him.

Of course, when stung by a bee on the throat, he knew it was best to drink salt and water to prevent serious consequences. Naturally, the stinger should be pulled from the skin beforehand, preferably seconds after the poison's instantaneous release. In his forty-four years of beekeeping on the southern slope of the Sussex Downs—living between Seaford and Eastbourne, the closest village being the tiny Cuckmere Haven—he had received exactly 7,816 stings from worker bees (almost always on the hands or face, occasionally on the earlobes or the neck or the throat: the cause and subsequent effects of every single prick dutifully contemplated, and later recorded into one of the many notebook journals he kept in his attic study). These mildly painful experiences, over time, had led him to a variety of remedies, each depending on which parts of his body had been stung and the ultimate depth to which the stinger had gone: salt with cold water, soft soap mixed with salt, then half of a raw onion applied to the irritation; when in extreme discomfort, wet mud or clay sometimes did the trick, as long as it was reapplied hourly, until the swelling was no longer apparent; however, to cure the smart, and also prevent inflammation, dampened tobacco rubbed immediately into the skin seemed the most effective solution.

Yet now—while sitting inside the library and napping in his armchair beside the empty fireplace—he was panicked within his dreaming, unable to recall what needed to be done for this sudden sting upon his Adam's apple. He witnessed himself there, in his dream, standing upright among a stretching field of marigolds and clasping his neck with slender, arthritic fingers. Already the swelling had begun, bulging beneath his hands like a pronounced vein. A paralysis of fear overtook him, and he became stock-still as the swelling grew outward and inward (his fingers parted by the ballooning protuberance, his throat closing in on itself).

And there, too, in that field of marigolds, he saw himself contrasting amid the red and golden yellow beneath him. Naked, with his pale flesh exposed above the flowers, he resembled a brittle skeleton covered by a thin veneer of rice paper. Gone were the vestments of his retirement—the woolens, the tweeds, the reliable clothing he had worn daily since before the Great War, throughout the second Great War, and into his ninety-third year. His flowing hair had been shorn to the scalp, and his beard was reduced to a stubble on his jutting chin and sunken cheeks. The canes that aided his ambling—the very canes placed across his lap inside the library—had vanished as well within his dreaming. But he remained standing, even as his constricting throat blocked passage and his breathing became impossible. Only his lips moved, stammering noiselessly for air. Everything else—his body, the blossoming flowers, the clouds up high—offered no perceptible movement, all of it made static save those quivering lips and a solitary worker bee roaming its busy black legs about a creased forehead.

2

H OLMES GASPED, waking. His eyelids lifted, and he glanced around the library while clearing his throat. Then he inhaled deeply, noting the slant of waning sunlight coming from a west-facing window: the resulting glow and shadow cast across the polished slats of the floor, creeping like clock hands, just enough to touch the hem of the Persian rug underneath his feet, told him it was precisely 5:18 in the afternoon.

"Have you stirred?" asked Mrs. Munro, his young housekeeper, who stood nearby, her back to him.

"Quite so," he replied, his stare fixing on her slight form—the long hair pushed into a tight bun, the curling dark brown wisps hanging over her slender neck, the straps of her tan apron tied at her rear. From a wicker basket placed on the library table, she took out bundles of correspondence (letters bearing foreign postmarks, small packages, large envelopes), and, as instructed to do once a week, she began sorting them into appropriate stacks based on size.

"You was doing it in your nap, sir. That choking sound—you was doing it, same as before you went. Should I bring water?"

"I don't believe it is required at present," he said, absently clutching both canes.

"Suit yourself, then."

She continued sorting—the letters to the left, the packages in the middle, the larger envelopes on the right. During his absence, the normally sparse table had filled with precarious stacks of communication. He knew there would certainly be gifts, odd items sent from afar. There would be requests for magazine or radio interviews, and there would be pleas for help (a lost pet, a stolen wedding ring, a missing child, an array of other hopeless trifles best left unanswered). Then there were the yet-to-be-published manuscripts: misleading and lurid fictions based on his past exploits, lofty explorations in criminology, galleys of mystery anthologies—along with flattering letters asking for an endorsement, a positive comment for a future dust jacket, or, possibly, an introduction to a text. Rarely did he respond to any of it, and never did he indulge journalists, writers, or publicity seekers.

Still, he usually perused every letter sent, examined the contents of every package delivered. That one day a week—regardless of a season's warmth or chill—he worked at the table while the fireplace blazed, tearing open envelopes, scanning the subject matter before crumpling the paper and throwing it into the flames. The gifts, however, were put aside, set carefully into the wicker basket for Mrs. Munro to give to those who organized charitable works in the town. But if a missive addressed a specific interest, if it avoided servile praise and smartly addressed a mutual fascination with what concerned him most—the undertakings of producing a queen from a worker bee's egg, the health benefits of royal jelly, perhaps a new insight regarding the cultivation of ethnic culinary herbs like prickly ash (nature's far-flung oddities, which, as he believed royal jelly did, could stem the needless atrophy that often beset an elderly body and mind)—then the letter stood a fair chance of being spared incineration; it might find its way into his coat pocket instead, remaining there until he found himself at his attic study desk, his fingers finally retrieving the letter for further consideration. Sometimes these lucky letters beckoned him elsewhere: an herb garden beside a ruined abbey near Worthing, where a strange hybrid of burdock and red dock thrived; a bee farm outside of Dublin, bestowed by chance with a slightly acidic, though not unpalatable, batch of honey as a result of moisture covering the combs one particularly warm season; most recently, Shimonoseki, a Japanese town that offered specialty cuisine made from prickly ash, which, along with a diet of miso paste and fermented soybeans, seemed to afford the locals sustained longevity (the need for documentation and firsthand knowledge of such rare, possibly life-extending nourishment being the chief pursuit of his solitary years).

"You'll live with this mess for an age," said Mrs. Munro, nodding at the mail stacks. After lowering the empty wicker basket to the floor, she turned to him, saying, "There's more, too, you know, out in the front hall closet—them boxes was cluttering up everything."

"Very well, Mrs. Munro," he said sharply, hoping to thwart any elaboration on her part.

"Should I bring the others in? Or should I wait for this bunch to be finished?"

"You can wait."

He glanced at the doorway, indicating with his eyes that he wished for her withdrawal. But she ignored his stare, pausing instead to smooth her apron before continuing: "There's an awful lot—in that hall closet, you know—I can't tell you how much."

"So I have gathered. I think for the moment I will focus on what is here."

"I'd say you've got your hands full, sir. If you're needing help—"

"I can take care of it—thank you."

Intently this time, he gazed at the doorway, inclining his head in its direction.

"Are you hungry?" she asked, tentatively stepping onto the Persian rug and into the sunlight.

A scowl halted her approach, softening a bit as he sighed. "Not in the slightest" was his answer.

"Will you be eating this evening?"

"It is inevitable, I suppose." He briefly envisioned her laboring recklessly in the kitchen, spilling offal on the countertops, or dropping bread crumbs and perfectly good slices of Stilton to the floor. "Are you intent on concocting your unsavory toad-in-the-hole?"

"You told me you didn't like that," she said, sounding surprised.

"I don't, Mrs. Munro, I truly don't—at least not your interpretation of it. Your shepherd's pie, on the other hand, is a rare thing."

Her expression brightened, even as she knitted her brow in contemplation. "Well, let's see, I got leftover beef from the Sunday roast. I could use that—except I know how you prefer the lamb."

"Leftover beef is acceptable."

"Shepherd's pie it is, then," she said, her voice taking on a sudden urgency. "And so you'll know, I've got your bags unpacked. Didn't know what to do with that funny knife you brought, so it's by your pillow. Mind you don't cut yourself."

He sighed with greater effect, shutting his eyes completely, removing her from his sight altogether: "It is called a *kusun-gobu,* my dear, and I appreciate your concern—wouldn't want to be stilettoed in my own bed."

"Who would?"

His right hand fumbled into a coat pocket, his fingers feeling for the remainder of a half-consumed Jamaican. But, to his dismay, he had somehow misplaced the cigar (perhaps lost as he disembarked from the train earlier, as he stooped to retrieve a cane that had slipped from his grasp—possibly the Jamaican had escaped his pocket then, falling to the platform, only to get flattened underfoot). "Maybe," he mumbled, "or maybe—"

He searched another pocket, listening while Mrs. Munro's shoes went from the rug and crossed the slats and moved onward through the doorway (seven steps, enough to take her from the library). His fingers curled around a cylindrical tube (nearly the same length and circumference of the halved Jamaican, although by its weight and firmness, he readily discerned it wasn't the cigar). And when lifting his eyelids, he beheld a clear glass vial sitting upright on his open palm; and peering closer, the sunlight glinting off the metal cap, he studied the two dead honeybees sealed within—one mingling upon the other, their legs intertwined, as if both had succumbed during an intimate embrace.

"Mrs. Munro—"

"Yes?" she replied, about-facing in the corridor and coming back with haste. "What is it?"

"Where is Roger?" he asked, returning the vial to his pocket.

She entered the library, covering the seven steps that had marked her departure. "Beg your pardon?"

"Your boy—Roger—where is he? I haven't seen him about yet."

"But, sir, he carried your bags inside for you, don't you remember? Then you told him to go wait for you at them hives. You said you wanted him there for an inspection."

A confused look spread across his pale, bearded face, and that puzzlement that occupied the moments when he sensed the failing of his own memory also threw its shadow over him (what else was forgotten, what else filtered away like sand seeping between clenched fists, and what exactly was known for sure anymore?), yet he attempted to push his worries aside by inducing a reasonable explanation for what confounded him from time to time.

"Of course, that is right. It was a tiring trip, you see. I haven't slept much. Has he waited long?"

"A good while—didn't take his tea—can't imagine he minds a bit, though. Since you went, he's cared more for them bees than his own mother, I can tell you."

"Is that so?"

"Yes, sadly it is."

"Well, then," he said, situating the canes, "I suppose I won't keep the boy waiting any longer."

Easing from the armchair, the canes bringing him to his feet, he proceeded for the doorway, wordlessly counting each step—one, two, three—while ignoring Mrs. Munro uttering behind him, "Want me at your side, sir? You got it all right, do you?" Four, five, six. He wouldn't conceive of her frowning as he trudged forward, or foresee her spotting his Jamaican seconds after he exited the room (her bending before the armchair, pinching the foul-smelling cigar from the seat cushion, and depositing it in the fireplace). Seven, eight, nine, ten—eleven steps brought him into the corridor: four steps more than it took Mrs. Munro, and two steps more than his average.

Naturally, he concluded when catching his breath at the front door, a degree of sluggishness on his part wasn't unexpected; he had ventured halfway around the world and back, forgoing his usual morning meal of royal jelly spread upon fried bread—the royal jelly, rich in vitamins of the B-complex and containing substantial amounts of sugars, proteins, and certain organic acids, was essential to maintaining his well-being and stamina; without its nourishment, he felt positive, his body had suffered somewhat, as had his retention.

But once outside, his mind was invigorated by the land awash in late-afternoon light. The flora posed no quandary, nor did the shadows hint at the voids where fragments of his memory should reside. Everything there was as it had been for decades—and so, too, was he: strolling effortlessly down the garden pathway, past the wild daffodils and the herb beds, past the deep purple buddleias and the giant thistles curling upward, inhaling all the while; a light breeze rustled the surrounding pines, and he savored the crunching sounds produced on the gravel from his shoes and canes. If he glanced back over his shoulder just now, he knew the farmhouse would be obscured behind four large pines—the front doorway and casements bedecked with climbing roses, the molded hoods above the windows, the exposed brick mullions of the outer walls; most of it barely visible among that dense crisscrossing of branches and pine needles. Ahead, where the path ended, stretched an undivided pasture enriched with a profusion of azaleas, laurel, and rhododendrons, beyond which loomed a cluster of freestanding oaks. And beneath the oaks—arranged on a straight-row plan, two hives to a group—existed his apiary.

Presently, he found himself pacing the beeyard as young Roger—eager to impress him with how well the bees had been tended in his absence, roving now from hive to hive without a veil and with sleeves rolled high—explained that after the swarm had been settled in early April, only a few days prior to Holmes's leaving for Japan, they had since fully drawn out the foundation wax within the frames, built honeycombs, and filled each hexagonal cell. In fact, to his delight, the boy had already reduced the number of frames to nine per hive, thereby allowing plenty of space for the bees to thrive.

"Excellent," Holmes said. "You have summered these creatures admirably, Roger. I am very pleased by your diligence here." Then, rewarding the boy, he removed the vial from his pocket, presenting it between a crooked finger and a thumb. "This was meant for you," he said, watching as Roger accepted the container and gazed at its contents with mild wonder. "*Apis cerana japonica*—or perhaps we will simply call them Japanese honeybees. How's that?"

"Thank you, sir."

The boy gave him a smile, and, gazing into Roger's perfect blue eyes, lightly patting the boy's mess of blond hair, Holmes smiled in turn. Afterward, they faced the hives together, saying nothing for a while. Silence like this, in the beeyard, never failed to please him wholly; from the way Roger stood easily beside him, he believed the boy shared an equal satisfaction. And while he rarely enjoyed the company of children, it was difficult avoiding the paternal stirrings he harbored for Mrs. Munro's son (how, he had often pondered, could that meandering woman have borne such a promising offspring?). But even at his advanced age, he found it impossible to express his true affections, especially toward a fourteen-year-old whose father had been among the British army casualties in the Balkans and whose presence, he suspected, Roger sorely missed. In any case, it was always wise to maintain emotional self-restraint when engaging housekeepers and their kin—it was, no doubt, enough just to stand with the boy as their mutual stillness hopefully spoke volumes, as their eyes surveyed the hives and studied the swaying oak branches and contemplated the subtle shifting of the afternoon into the evening.

Soon, Mrs. Munro called from the garden pathway, beckoning for Roger's assistance in the kitchen. Then, reluctantly, he and the boy headed across the pasture, doing so at their leisure, stopping to observe a blue butterfly fluttering around the fragrant azaleas. Moments before dusk's descent, they entered the garden, the boy's hand gently gripping his elbow—that same hand guiding him onward through the farmhouse door, staying upon him until he had safely mounted the stairs and gone into his attic study (navigating the stairs being hardly a difficult undertaking, though he felt grateful whenever Roger steadied him like a human crutch).

"Should I fetch you when supper's ready?"

"Please, if you would."

"Yes, sir."

So at his desk he sat, waiting for the boy to aid him again, to help him down the stairs. For a while, he busied himself, examining notes he had written prior to his trip, cryptic messages scrawled on torn bits of paper—*levulose predominates, more soluble than dextrose*—the meanings of which eluded him. He glanced around, realizing Mrs. Munro had taken liberties in his absence. The books he had scattered about the floor were now stacked, the floor swept, but—as he had expressly instructed—not a thing had been dusted. Becoming increasingly restless for tobacco, he shifted notebooks and opened drawers, hoping to find a Jamaican or at least a cigarette. After the hunt proved futile, he resigned himself with favored correspondence, reaching for one of the many letters sent by Mr. Tamiki Umezaki weeks before he had embarked on his trip abroad: *Dear Sir, I'm extremely gratified that my invitation was received with serious interest, and that you have decided to be my guest here in Kobe. Needless to say, I look forward to showing you the many temple gardens in this region of Japan, as well as—*

This, too, proved elusive: No sooner had he begun reading than his eyelids closed and his chin gradually sagged toward his chest. Then sleeping, he wouldn't feel the letter slide through his fingers, or hear the faint choking emanating from his throat. And upon waking, he wouldn't recall the field of marigolds where he had stood, nor would he remember the dream which had placed him there again. Instead, startled to find Roger suddenly leaning over him, he would clear his throat and stare at the boy's vexed face and rasp with uncertainty, "Was I asleep?"

The boy nodded.

"I see—I see—"

"Your supper will be served soon."

"Yes, my supper will be served soon," he muttered, readying his canes.

As before, Roger gingerly assisted Holmes, helping him from the chair, sticking close to him when they exited the study; the boy traveled with him along the corridor, then down the stairs, then into the dining room, where, at last slipping past Roger's light grasp, he went forward on his own, moving toward the large Victorian golden oak table and the single place setting that Mrs. Munro had laid for him.

"After I'm finished here," Holmes said, addressing the boy without turning, "I would very much like to discuss the business of the apiary with you. I wish for you to relate all which has transpired there in my absence. I trust you can offer a detailed and accurate report."

"I believe so," the boy responded, watching from the doorway as Holmes propped his canes against the table before seating himself.

"Very well, then," Holmes finally said, staring across the room to where Roger stood. "Let us reconvene at the library in an hour's time, shall we? Providing, of course, that your mother's shepherd's pie doesn't finish me off."

"Yes, sir."

Holmes reached for the folded napkin, shaking it open and tucking a corner underneath his collar. Sitting upright in the chair, he took a moment to align the flatware, arranging it neatly. Then he sighed through his nostrils, resting his hands evenly on either side of the empty plate: "Where is that woman?"

"I'm coming," Mrs. Munro suddenly called. She promptly appeared behind Roger, holding a dinner tray that steamed with her cooking. "Move aside, son," she told the boy. "You're not helping nobody like that."

"Sorry," Roger said, shifting his slender body so that she could gain entrance. And once his mother had rushed by, hurrying to the table, he slowly took a step backward—and another, and another—until he had removed himself from the dining room. However, there would be no more loitering about on his part; otherwise, he knew, his mother might send him home or, at the very least, order him into the kitchen for cleanup duty. Avoiding that eventuality, he made his escape quietly enough, doing so while she served Holmes, stealing away before she could leave the dining room and summon him by name.

But the boy didn't head outside, fleeing toward the beeyard like his mother might expect—nor did he go inside the library and prepare for Holmes's questions concerning the apiary. Instead, he crept back upstairs, entering that one room in which only Holmes was allowed to sequester himself: the attic study. In truth, during the weeks that Holmes was traveling abroad, Roger had spent long hours exploring the study—initially taking various old books, dusty monographs, and scientific journals off the shelves, perusing them as he sat at the desk. When his curiosity had been satisfied, he had carefully placed them again on the shelves, making sure they looked untouched. On occasion, he had even pretended that he was Holmes, reclining in the desk chair with his fingertips pressed together, gazing at the window, and inhaling imaginary smoke.

Naturally, his mother was oblivious to his trespassing, for if she had found out, he would have been banished from the house altogether. Yet the more he explored the study (tentatively at first, his hands kept in his pockets), the more daring he became—peeking inside drawers, shaking letters from already-opened envelopes, respectfully holding the pen and scissors and magnifying glass that Holmes had used on a regular basis. Later on, he had begun sifting through the stacks of handwritten pages upon the desktop, mindful not to leave any identifying marks on the pages while, at the same time, trying to decipher Holmes's notes and incomplete paragraphs; except most of what was read was lost on the boy—either due to the nature of Holmes's often nonsensical scribbling or as a result of the subject matter being somewhat oblique and clinical. Still, he had studied every page, wishing to learn something unique or revealing about the famous man who now reigned over the apiary.

Roger would, in fact, discover little that shed new light on Holmes. The man's world, it seemed, was one of hard evidence and uncontestable facts, detailed observations on external matters, with rarely a sentence of contemplation pertaining to himself. Yet among the many piles of random notes and writings, buried beneath it all as if hidden, the boy had eventually come across an item of true interest—a short unfinished manuscript entitled "The Glass Armonicist," the sheaf of pages kept together by a rubber band. As opposed to Holmes's other writings on the desk, this manuscript, the boy had immediately noticed, had been composed with great care: The words were easy to distinguish, nothing had been scratched out, and nothing was crammed into the margins or obscured by droplets of ink. What he then read had held his attention—for it was accessible and somewhat personal in nature, recounting an earlier time in Holmes's life. But much to Roger's chagrin, the manuscript ended abruptly after only two chapters, leaving its conclusion a mystery. Even so, the boy would dig it out again and again, rereading the text with a hope that he might gather some insight that had previously been missed.

And now, just as during those weeks when Holmes had been gone, Roger sat nervously at the study desk, methodically extracting the manuscript from underneath the organized disorder. Soon the rubber band was set aside, the pages placed near the glow of the table lamp. He studied the manuscript in reverse, briefly scanning the last few pages, while also feeling certain that Holmes had not yet had a chance to continue the text. Then he started at the beginning, bending forward as he read, turning one page over onto another page. If he concentrated without distractions, Roger believed, he could probably get through the first chapter that night. Only when his mother called his name would his head momentarily lift; she was outside, shouting for him from the garden below, searching for him. After her voice faded, he lowered his head once more, reminding himself that he didn't have much time left—in less than an hour, he was expected at the library; before long the manuscript would need to be concealed exactly as it had originally been found. Until then, an index finger slid below Holmes's words, blue eyes blinked repeatedly but remained focused, and lips moved without sound as sentences began conjuring familiar scenes within the boy's mind.

3

THE GLASS ARMONICIST

A Preface

On any given night should a stranger climb the steep stairs which conclude here in this attic, he will wander a few seconds in darkness before reaching the shut door of my study. Yet even in such pitch, a dim hue of light will steal past the closed doorway, just as it does now, and he might stand there in thought, asking himself, What sort of preoccupation keeps a man awake well after midnight? Who is it, exactly, that exists within as the majority of his countrymen slumber? And if the knob is then tried so that his curiosity could be satisfied, he will find the door locked and his entrance forbidden. And if, at last, he resigns an ear against the doorway, a faint scratching sound will likely reach him, signifying the quick movement of pen upon paper, the preceding words already drying as the following symbols arrive watery from the blackest of ink.

But, of course, it is no secret that I remain elusive at this time in my life. Nor has the chronicling of my past exploits, while apparently of infinite fascination to the reading public, ever been a gratifying endeavour for me. During the years in which John was inclined to write about our many experiences together, I regarded his skilful, if somewhat limited, depictions as exceedingly overwrought. At times, I decried his pandering to popular tastes and asked that he be more mindful of facts and figures, especially since my name had become synonymous with his often superficial ruminations. In turn, my old friend and biographer urged me to write an account of my own. "If you imagine I have done an injustice to our cases," I recall him saying on at least one occasion, "I suggest you try it yourself, Sherlock!"

"Perhaps I will," I told him, "and perhaps then you will read an accurate story, one lacking the usual authorial embellishments."

"Best of luck to you there," he scoffed. "You are going to need it."

Yet only retirement afforded me the luxury and inclination finally to engage myself with John's suggestion. The results of which, though hardly impressive, were nonetheless enlightening on a personal level, if simply to show me that even a truthful account must be presented in a manner which should entertain the reader. Realising such an inevitability, I abandoned John's form of storytelling after publishing just two stories, and, in a brief note sent to the good doctor later on,

offered a sincere apology for the derision I had heaped upon his earlier writings. His response was swift and cleverly to the point: *No
apology required, my friend. The royalties absolved you ages ago, and
continue to do so, despite my protests. J. H. W.*

As John is now once again in my thoughts, I would like to take
this opportunity to address a current irritation of mine. It has come
to my attention that my former helpmate has recently been cast in an
unfair light by both dramatists and so-called mystery novelists. These
individuals of dubious repute, whose names are not worthy of mention here, have sought to portray him as little more than an oafish,
blundering fool. Nothing could be further from reality. The very notion that I would burden myself with a slow-witted companion might
be humourous in a theatrical context, but I regard such forms of in-
sinuation as a serious insult to John and to me. It is possible that
some error of representation could have stemmed from his writings,
for he was always generous in overstating my abilities, while, at the
same time, treating his own remarkable characteristics with tremendous modesty. Even so, the man I worked beside displayed a native
shrewdness and an innate cunningness which was invaluable to our
investigations. I do not deny his sporadic inability to grasp an obvious conclusion or to choose the best course of action, but rarely was
he unintelligent in his opinions and conclusions. Above that, it was
my pleasure to spend my younger days in the company of one who
could sense adventure in the most mundane of cases, and who, with
his customary humour, patience, and loyalty, indulged the eccentrici-

ties of a frequently disagreeable friend. Therefore, if the pundits are honestly inclined to pick the most foolish of the pair, then I believe, without question, they should bestow the dishonour upon me alone.

Lastly, it should be noted that the nostalgia which the reading public maintains for my former Baker Street address does not exist in me. I no longer crave the bustle of London streets, nor do I miss navigating through the tangled mires created by the criminally disposed. Moreover, my life here in Sussex has gone beyond pure contentment, and the majority of my waking hours are spent either in the peaceful solitude of my study or amongst the methodical creatures who inhabit my apiary. I will admit, however, that my advanced age has diminished my retentive abilities somewhat, but I am still fairly agile in both body and mind. Almost every week, I manage an early-evening walk down to the beach. In the afternoons, I am usually seen wandering about my garden pathways, where I tend to my herb and flower beds. But as of late, I have been consumed with the significant task of revising the latest edition of my *Practical Handbook of Bee Culture,* while alternately putting the finishing touches on my four volumes of *The Whole Art of Detection.* The latter is a rather tedious, labyrinthine undertaking, although it should stand as an indispensable collection when published.

Nevertheless, I have felt compelled to set my masterwork aside, and, at this moment, I find myself beginning the chore of transferring the past to paper, lest I forget the specifics of a case which, by whatever inexplicable rationale, sprang to mind on this night. It might come about that some of what is to be said or described henceforth is not as it was actually spoken or seen, so I shall apologise beforehand for any licence that is used to fill out the gaps and grey areas of my memory. Yet even if a degree of fiction should prevail in the following events, I guarantee that the overall account—as well as those individuals who were involved in the case—is as accurately rendered as I can make possible.

I.

The Case of Mrs. Ann Keller
of Fortis Grove

I recall that it was in the spring of the year of '02, just one month after Robert Falcon Scott's historic balloon flight in Antarctica, that I received a visit from Mr. Thomas R. Keller, a stooped, narrow-shouldered, well-dressed young man. The good doctor had yet to take up his own rooms on Queen Anne Street, but, as it happened, he was away on holiday, lazing at the seaside with the woman who would soon become the third Mrs. Watson. For the first time in many months, our Baker Street flat was all mine. As was my usual custom, I sat with my back to the window and invited my visitor into the opposite armchair, where—from his vantage point—I became obscured by the brightness of the outside light, and he—from mine—was illuminated with perfect clarity. Initially, Mr. Keller appeared uncomfortable in my presence, and he seemed at a loss for words. I made no effort to ease his discomfort, but used his awkward silence instead as an opportunity to observe him more closely. I believe that it is always to my advantage to give clients a sense of their own vulnerability, and so, having reached my conclusions regarding his visit, I was quick to instil such a feeling in him.

"There is a great deal of concern, I see, about your wife."

"That is correct, sir," he replied, visibly taken aback.

"Still, she is an attentive wife, for the better part. I gather, then, it is not her fidelity which is at issue."

"Mr. Holmes, how do you know this?"

His squinting and perplexed expression tried to discern me. And as my client awaited a response, I took it upon myself to ignite one of John's fine Bradley cigarettes, a fair number of which I had pilfered from the stash he kept hidden in his top desk drawer. Then having let the young man dangle long enough, I deliberately exhaled my fumes into the sun's rays while revealing what was so plainly evident to my eye.

"When a gentleman enters my room in an apprehensive state, and when he toys absently with his wedding ring as he sits before me, it is not hard to imagine the nature of his problem. Your clothes are new and adequately fashioned, but not professionally tailored. You have surely noticed a slight unevenness at your cuffs, or, perhaps, the dark brown thread used at the bottom of your left pants leg, the black thread upon the right. But have you observed the middle button there on your shirt which, while very similar in colour and design, is negligibly smaller than the others? This suggests that your wife has done the job for you, and that she has been diligent enough to do her best even when lacking the proper materials. As I have said, she is attentive. Why do I think it is your wife's handiwork? Well, you are a young man of modest means, clearly married, and your card has already shown me that you are a junior accountant at Throckmorton & Finley's. It would be a rare thing to meet a starting accountant with a maid and a housekeeper, would it not?"

"Nothing escapes you, sir."

"I possess no unseen powers, I can assure you, but I have learned to pay attention to what is obvious. Even so, Mr. Keller, you did not call upon me this afternoon to ponder my talents. What event transpired Tuesday last and sent you here from your home at Fortis Grove?"

"This is incredible—" he ejaculated, and again a startled look came over his hollow face.

"My dear fellow, calm yourself. Your personally delivered letter arrived on my door yesterday—a Wednesday—with your return address, yet it was dated by your own hand on Tuesday. No doubt the letter was written in the night; otherwise, you would have delivered it the same day. As you urgently requested this appointment for to-day—a Thursday—it would seem that something troublesome and pressing had likely occurred on Tuesday afternoon or evening."

"Yes, I wrote the letter on Tuesday night after reaching my end with Madame Schirmer. Not only is she given to meddling in my marriage but she also threatened to have me arrested—"

"To have you arrested, really?"

"Yes, those were her last words to me. She is rather an imposing woman, that Madame Schirmer. A talented musician and teacher by all accounts, but with a manner that is intimidating. I would have summoned a constable myself if it weren't for my dear Ann's sake."

"Ann is your wife, I take it."

"Quite so."

The young man took from his waistcoat a cabinet photograph and, thrusting his hand forwards, offered it for my inspection.

"This is she, Mr. Holmes."

I leaned up in my armchair. With a quick, all-comprehensive glance, I saw the features and figure of a woman of twenty-three—a single cocked eyebrow, a reluctant half smile. Yet the face was stern, giving her the appearance of one who was older than her years.

"Thank you," I said, looking up from the photograph. "She has a most unique quality about her. Now pray explain, from the beginning, what it is exactly that I should know about your wife's relationship with this Madame Schirmer."

Mr. Keller frowned miserably.

"I will tell you what I know," he said, returning the photograph to his waistcoat, "and I hope that you will be able to find reason in it.

You see, since Tuesday my brain has been muddled with this problem. I haven't slept very well the past two days, so please be patient with me if my words are unclear."

"I shall attempt to be as patient as possible."

It was wise of him to forewarn me; for if I had not expected my client's narrative to be, mostly, a rambling and inconsequential statement, then I fear my irritation would have cut him short. As it was, I readied myself by reclining into my armchair while bringing my fingertips together, and tilted my head towards the ceiling so as to listen with the greatest concentration of attention.

"You may begin."

He inhaled deeply before proceeding.

"My wife—Ann—and I were married just over two years ago. She was the only daughter of the late Colonel Bane—her father having died while she was still an infant, killed in Afghanistan during Ayub Khan's uprising—and she was raised by her mother in East Ham, where we met as children. You cannot envision a lovelier girl, Mr. Holmes. Even then I was taken with her, and, in time, we fell in love—the kind of love which is based on friendship and partnership and a desire to share both lives as if they were one. We were married, of course, and soon moved into the house at Fortis Grove. For a while, it seemed that nothing could disrupt the harmony of our little home. I do not exaggerate by saying ours was an ideal, joyful union. Obviously, there came a few rough periods, such as the protracted illness of my own dying father and the unexpected passing of Ann's mother, but we had each other, and that made all the difference. Our happiness increased when we learned of Ann's pregnancy. Then six months later, she had a sudden miscarriage. Five months after that, she was pregnant again, but soon miscarried once more. This second time, there was an excessive amount of bleeding, a haemorrhage, which nearly took her from me. While in hospital, our doctor informed her that she was probably incapable of having a baby and that any further attempts at childbirth would likely kill her. Thereafter, she began to change. These miscarriages upset and occupied her obsessively. At home, she turned somewhat morose, Mr. Holmes, despondent and indifferent, and, she told me, losing our babies was her greatest trauma.

"My antidote for her malaise was the therapeutic activity of a new preoccupation. For mental and emotional reasons alike, I thought she should take up a hobby to fill the void in her life—which I feared was growing deeper. Among my recently deceased father's possessions was an antique glass armonica. It had been a gift from his great-uncle, who, my father claimed, had purchased the instrument from Etienne-Gaspard Robertson, the famous Belgian inventor. In any case, I took the armonica home for Ann, and, with a fair amount of reluctance on her part, she finally agreed to at least give the instrument a try. Our upstairs attic is quite roomy and comfortable—we had once talked of making it the bedroom for our child—and so it was a natural environment for a tiny music den. I even polished and refurbished the armonica's casing, replaced the old spindle so the glasses would nest more securely inside each other, and fixed the foot treadle, which had been damaged years earlier. But what little interest Ann had summoned for the instrument waned almost completely from the start. She didn't like being alone in the attic, and she found it difficult creating music on the armonica. She was also bothered by the curious tones produced by the glasses as her fingers slid across their brims. The resonance of them, she explained, made her all the more sad.

"Except I wouldn't have it. You see, I believed that the advantages of the armonica were in its tones, and that these tones far surpassed the beauty of any other instrument's sound. If performed properly, its music can increase and diminish at ease by just the pressure of fingers, and its wondrous tones can be sustained for any length. No, I wouldn't have it, and I knew that if Ann could only hear the instrument played by another—a person with training and skill—then she might feel differently towards the glasses. As it happened, an associate of mine remembered attending a public recital of Mozart's Adagio and Rondo for Armonica, Flute, Oboe, Viola, and Cello, but he could only say for certain that the performance was held in a small flat above a bookstore on Montague Street, somewhere near the British Museum. Of course, I didn't need a detective to help track down the place, and so, without much footwork, I found myself inside Portman's Booksellers & Map Specialists. The proprietor then directed to me a flight of stairs which led to the very flat where my friend had heard the armonica played. I have since regretted climbing those stairs, Mr. Holmes. At the time, however, I was rather excited about who might greet me after I knocked on the door."

Mr. Thomas R. Keller looked like the sort of man who it would be tempting to bully for fun. His boyish manner was sheepish and his wavering, soft voice carried a slight lisp as he spoke.

"And here, I take it, is where your Madame Schirmer is introduced," I said before lighting up another cigarette.

"Quite. It was she who answered the door—a very solid, manly woman, although not really corpulent—and while she is German, my first impression of her was still rather favourable. Without asking my business, she invited me into her flat. She had me sit in her drawing room, and I was given tea. I believe she just assumed I was seeking music instruction from her, for the room itself was lined with instruments of all kinds, including two beautiful, fully restored armonicas. I knew then that I'd found the right place—I was charmed by Madame Schirmer's graciousness, her obvious love of the instrument—so I made my reasons for coming there known: I explained about my wife, the tragedy of the miscarriages, how I had taken the armonica into our house to help ease Ann's suffering, and how the enchantment of the glasses had proved elusive to her, et cetera. Madame Schirmer listened patiently, and when I was finished, she suggested I bring Ann in for lessons. I couldn't have been more pleased, Mr. Holmes. All I had wanted, truly, was for Ann to hear the instrument played well by someone else, so this suggestion of hers exceeded my hopes. Initially, we agreed on ten lessons—twice a week, Tuesday and Thursday afternoons, full payment in advance—with Madame Schirmer offering a reduced fee because, she told me, my wife's situation was a special one. This was on a Friday. The following Tuesday, Ann would begin her lessons.

"Montague Street isn't terribly far from where I live. Instead of taking a carriage, I decided to walk home and give Ann the good news. But we ended up in a minor row, and I would have cancelled the lessons that day if I hadn't believed they might be beneficial for her. I arrived, to find the house quiet and the curtains drawn. When I called out for Ann, there was no reply. After searching the kitchen and our bedroom, I went into the study, and that's where I discovered her—dressed entirely in black, as if in mourning, with her back turned away from the door, staring idly at a bookcase while remaining perfectly still. The room was so dim, she appeared like a shadow, and when I spoke her name, she did not move to face me. I became very concerned, Mr. Holmes, that her mental state was worsening at an accelerated pace.

" 'You're home already,' said she in a tired voice. 'I wasn't expecting you this soon, Thomas.'

"I explained that I had left work early that afternoon for personal reasons. Then I told her where I'd gone, and I gave her the news about the armonica lessons.

" 'But you shouldn't have done that on my account. Naturally, you have not asked me if I wish to take these lessons.'

" 'I assumed you wouldn't mind. It can only do you good; I'm sure of it. It certainly can't be any worse than staying indoors like this.'

" 'I assume I have no choice.'

"She glanced at me, and in the darkness, I could just barely see her face.

" 'Am I not allowed any say in the matter?' she asked.

" 'Of course, you are, Ann. How can I make you do something you don't wish to do? But will you at least attend one lesson and hear Madame Schirmer play for you? If afterwards you'd rather not continue, I won't insist.'

"This request silenced her for a moment. She slowly pivoted around towards me and then lowered her head to stare at the floor. When she at last looked up, I saw the faint expression of someone who felt defeated by all, and who would acquiesce to anything, regardless of her true feelings.

" 'All right, Thomas,' said she, 'if you want me to take a lesson, I won't fight you on it, but I hope you won't expect much from me. It is you, after all, who loves the sound of the instrument, not I.'

" 'I love you, Ann, and I want you to be happy again. We both deserve at least that.'

" 'Yes, yes, I know. I am awfully troubling of late. I must tell you, however, that I no longer believe that something like happiness exists for me. I fear every individual has an inner life, with its own complications, which sometimes cannot be articulated, regardless of how one might try. So all I ask is that you be tolerant of me, and allow me the time I need to better understand myself. Meanwhile, I shall take that single lesson, Thomas, and I pray my doing so will satisfy me as much as I know it will satisfy you.'

"Fortunately—or unfortunately now—I was proven right, Mr. Holmes. After one lesson from Madame Schirmer, my wife began seeing the armonica in a more favourable light. How delighted I was with her newfound appreciation for the instrument. In fact, it seemed that by her third or fourth lesson she had made a miraculous transformation of spirit. Gone was her morbidity, as well as the listlessness which had often kept her bedridden. I admit it: During those days, I regarded Madame Schirmer as something of a godsend, and my esteem for her was unequalled. So several months later, when my wife asked if the lessons could be increased from one hour to two hours, I agreed without hesitation—especially since she had greatly improved on the glasses. Moreover, I was pleased at the many hours— afternoons and nights, sometimes an entire day—she devoted to mastering the armonica's varying tones. Besides learning Beethoven's 'Melodrama,' she developed an incredible ability to improvise her own pieces. These compositions of hers, however, were the most unusual, melancholic music I have ever heard. They were imbued with a sadness which, as she practised alone in the attic, permeated the entire house."

"This is all very interesting, in a roundabout way," I interjected, stopping his narrative, "but what—if I may kindly press you—are your exact reasons for calling upon me today?"

I could see that my client was dismayed by the sharpness of my interruption. I stared at him in an emphatic fashion, and then I composed myself, with my lids drooping and fingertips once more together, to hear the relevant facts of his problem.

"If you will allow me," he stammered, "I was just getting to that, sir. As I said, since beginning with Madame Schirmer, my wife's state of mind bettered—or at least it appeared so at first. Yet I began to sense a certain detachment in her manner, a kind of absentmindedness and an inability to engage in any prolonged conversation. In short, I soon realised that while Ann seemed to be doing well on the surface, there was something still amiss within her. I believed it was simply her preoccupation with the armonica which had distracted her, and, I hoped, she would eventually come around. But this was not to happen.

"Initially, it was just a few things I noticed—plates waiting to be washed, meals half-cooked or badly burnt, our bed left unmade. Then Ann began spending the majority of her waking hours in the attic. Often I stirred to the sound of glasses being played from above, and when I returned from work, I was welcomed home by the same noise. By that point, I had come to detest those tones which I had once enjoyed. Then, aside from our meals together, there were days that passed when I rarely caught sight of her—she would join me in our bed once I had fallen asleep, leaving at dawn, before I arose—but there was always that music, those plaintive, unending tones. It was enough to drive me mad, Mr. Holmes. The preoccupation had, in effect, become an unhealthy obsession, and I blame Madame Schirmer for that."

"Why is she responsible?" I asked. "Surely she isn't privy to the domestic problems of your household. She is, after all, only the music teacher."

"No, no, she is more than that, sir. She is, I fear, a woman with dangerous beliefs."

" 'Dangerous beliefs'?"

"Yes. They are dangerous to those who are desperately seeking hope of some sort, and who are susceptible to ludicrous falsehoods."

"And your wife falls into such a category of person?"

"I'm sorry to say she does, Mr. Holmes. To a fault, Ann has always been a very sensitive, trusting woman. It's as if she was born to feel and experience the world more acutely than the rest of us. It is both her greatest strength and weakness; if recognised by someone with devious intentions, this delicate quality can be easily exploited—and that's what Madame Schirmer has done. Of course, I didn't realise it for a long while—I was oblivious, in fact, until recently.

"You see, it was a typical evening. As is our custom, Ann and I dined quietly together, and, having swallowed a scant few bites, she promptly excused herself to go practise in the attic—this, too, had become customary. But something else was to occur soon thereafter: For earlier that day at my office—as a gift for resolving some complications with his private account—a client of mine had sent me a precious bottle of Comet wine. My intention was to surprise Ann with the wine during our supper, except, as I mentioned, she went quickly from the table before I could retrieve the bottle. So, instead, I decided to take the wine to her. With the bottle and two wineglasses in hand, I proceeded up the attic stairs. By then, she had already started playing the armonica, and its sound—extremely low tones, monotonous and sustained—transmitted its way into my body.

"When I approached the attic door, the wineglasses I was holding began vibrating, and my ears began to ache. All the same, I could hear well enough. It wasn't a musical piece she was performing, nor was she idly experimenting with the armonica. No, this was a deliberate exercise, sir—an incantation of some unholy fashion. I say *incantation* because of what I then heard next: my wife's voice addressing someone, speaking almost as lowly as the tones she was creating."

"Am I to understand that it wasn't singing you heard?"

"I wish to God it had been, Mr. Holmes. However, I assure you she was talking. Most of her utterances escaped me, but what I did hear was enough to produce a feeling of horror in my mind.

" 'I am here, James,' said she. 'Grace, come to me. I am here. Where are you hiding? I wish to see you again—' "

I raised a hand, silencing him.

"Mr. Keller, my patience is truly a limited resource, and it can withstand just so much. In attempting to put colour and life into your statement, you have continually erred by prolonging the arrival of the very issue which you wish to be resolved. If at all possible, do confine yourself to the notable features, as those will likely be the only things of any use to me."

My client said nothing for a few seconds, knitting his brows and averting his eyes from mine.

"If our child had been born a boy," he finally said, "James was to be his name—or Grace if it had been a girl."

Overcome by strong sentiment, he suddenly paused.

"Tut tut!" I said. "There is no need for displays of emotion at this juncture. Pray continue from where you left off."

He nodded, setting his lips tightly. Then he passed a handkerchief over his brow and turned his gaze to the floor.

"After setting the bottle and wineglasses down, I threw open the door. Startled, she stopped playing at once and looked upon me with wide, dark eyes. The attic was lit by candles, which were placed in a circle around the armonica, casting her in a flickering glow. In that light, with such deathly pale skin, she looked as if she might be a ghost. There was an otherworldly quality about her, Mr. Holmes. But it wasn't merely an effect of the candles which gave me this impression. It was her eyes—the way in which she stared at me, suggesting the absence of something essential, something human. Even as she spoke to me, her voice was hushed and lacked emotion.

" 'What is it, dear?' she asked. 'You frightened me.'

"I went towards her.

" 'Why you are doing this?' I cried. 'Why are you talking as if they are here?'

"She rose slowly from the armonica, and when I went to her, I saw a faint smile upon her white face.

" 'It's all right. Thomas, it's all right now.'

" 'I cannot understand,' I said. 'You were saying the names of our unborn. You spoke as if they were alive and in this very room. What is all this about, Ann? How long has this been going on?'

"She gently took hold of my arm and began moving us both away from the armonica.

" 'I must be alone when I play. Please respect that about me.'

"She was leading me to the door, but I wanted answers.

" 'Look here,' I said. 'I won't leave until you explain yourself. How long has this been going on? I insist. Why are you doing this? Is Madame Schirmer aware of what you are up to?'

"She could no longer meet my eyes. She was like a woman who had been caught in a terrible lie. It was an unexpected and cold answer that finally passed her lips.

" 'Yes,' she said, 'Madame Schirmer is fully aware of what I am doing. She's helping me, Thomas—you saw to it that she would. Good night, dear.' And with that, she shut the door on me and locked it from the inside.

"I was livid, Mr. Holmes. You can imagine that I returned downstairs in an agitated state. My wife's explanation—vague as it was—led me to one conclusion: Madame Schirmer was teaching Ann something other than music lessons, or, at the very least, she was encouraging her to perform that unnatural ritual in the attic. It was a vexing situation, especially if what I believed was correct, and I knew that only from Madame Schirmer herself could the truth be learned. My intention was to go directly to her flat that evening and discuss the matter. However, in an effort to steady my nerves, I drank far too much of the Comet wine, almost the entire bottle. Therefore, I couldn't properly call on her until the following morning. But once I did arrive at her flat, Mr. Holmes, I was as sober and determined as a man could be. Madame Schirmer had hardly opened the door when I confronted her with my concerns.

" 'What rubbish have you been teaching my wife?' I demanded. 'I want you to tell me why she talks to our unborn children—and please don't pretend you know nothing, because Ann has already told me enough.'

"There was an awkward silence, and she was some little time before speaking. Then she asked me inside and sat with me in the drawing room.

" 'Your wife, Herr Keller, is this bothered, unhappy woman,' said she. 'These lessons she has from me, they don't really interest her. She keeps her thoughts always on the babies—no matter what, always the babies—and the babies are the problem, no? But, of course, you want her to play, and she wants the babies—so I do something for both of you, right? And now she plays most beautifully. I think she is happier, don't you?'

" 'I don't understand. What is it that you've done for the both of us?'

" 'It is nothing too difficult, Herr Keller. It is the nature of the glasses, you know—the echoes of the divine harmony—I teach her about this thing.'

"You cannot fathom the nonsense that she went on to explain to me."

"Oh, but I can," I said. "Mr. Keller, I have some basic knowledge regarding the unusual history surrounding this particular instrument. There was a time when certain disturbances were attributed to glass music. This produced panic in the general population of Europe, and led to the armonica's decline in popularity. That is why encountering one—let alone hearing one performed—is a unique opportunity indeed."

"What sort of disturbances?"

"Everything from nerve damage to nagging depression, as well as domestic disputes, premature births, any number of mortal afflictions—even convulsions in household pets. No doubt your Madame Schirmer is familiar with the police decree that once existed in various German states, a proclamation which banned the instrument altogether for the sake of public order and health. Naturally, as your wife's melancholy antedates her usage of the instrument, we can likely rule it out as the source of her troubles.

"However, there is another side to the armonica's story, one which Madame Schirmer was hinting at by mentioning 'the echoes of the divine harmony.' There are some—those adhering to the idealistic musings of men like Franz Mesmer, Benjamin Franklin, and Mozart—

who feel glass music promotes a kind of human harmony. Others hold the fervent belief that listening to the sounds produced on glasses can cure maladies of the blood, while others—and I suspect this Madame Schirmer is among them—maintain that the sharp, penetrating tones travel swiftly from this world into the hereafter. They are of the opinion that an extremely gifted player of glass can readily summon the dead, and that, as a result, the living might again communicate with their departed loved ones. This is what she explained to you, is it not?"

"It is exactly so," my client said with a rather surprised air.

"And at that point you released her from your employment."

"Yes—but how—"

"My boy, it was an inevitability, wasn't it? You believed she was responsible for your wife's occultist behaviour, so the intention, surely, was already there before you went to see her that morning. In any event, if she were still kept in your service, she would hardly have threatened you with arrest. Now please forgive these occasional interruptions. They are needed to expedite what might otherwise prove redundant to my mind. Proceed."

"What else, I ask you, could I have done? I had no other choice. Imagining myself to be fair, I didn't insist she refund the fee for the remaining lessons, nor did she make an offer to do so. Nonetheless, I was shocked at her composure. As I told her that she was no longer needed, she smiled and nodded in agreement.

" 'My dear sir, if you think it is the best for Ann,' said she, 'then I, too, think it is the best for Ann. You are the husband, after all. I wish you both live a long, happy life together.'

"I should have known better than to accept her at her word. When I went from her flat that morning, I believe she knew well enough that Ann was under her influence, and that my wife wasn't about to walk away from her. I realize now that she is a conniving woman of the worst sort. It's all quite evident in hindsight: the way she had initially offered me a discount rate and then—once poor Ann had been taken in by her rubbish—suggested extending the hourly lessons in order to get more from my pocket. I worry, too, that she has designs on the inheritance left by Ann's mother, which—while not greatly substantial—is still a rather tidy sum. I am absolutely positive of this, Mr. Holmes."

"It had not occurred to you at the time?" I asked.

"No," he answered. "My only concern was how Ann might respond to the news. I spent an uneasy day pondering the situation at work and debating the appropriate words with which to tell her. After returning home that evening, I asked Ann into my study, and, as she sat before me, I calmly spoke my mind. I pointed out that she had been neglecting her chores and responsibilities of late, and that her obsession with the armonica—it was the first time I had ever classified it as such—was putting a strain on our marriage. I told her that each of us had certain obligations to the other: Mine was to provide a secure, sound environment for her; hers was to maintain the duties and upkeep of the household for me. Moreover, I said, I was deeply bothered by what I had discovered going on in the attic, but that I didn't blame her for mourning the loss of our unborn. Then I discussed my visit with Madame Schirmer. I explained that there would be no more armonica lessons, and that Madame Schirmer had agreed that it was probably for the best. I took her hand, and I stared directly into her inexpressive face.

" 'You are forbidden to see that woman again, Ann,' I said, 'and tomorrow I am removing the armonica from the house. It is not my intention to be cruel or unreasonable in this matter, but I need my wife back. I want you back, Ann. I want us to be like we once were. We must restore order to our life.'

"She began weeping, but they were tears of remorse and not anger. I knelt beside her.

" 'Forgive me,' I said, and put my arms around her.

" 'No,' she whispered in my ear, 'it is I who should ask your forgiveness. I am so confused, Thomas. I feel as if I can do nothing right anymore, and I don't understand why.'

" 'You mustn't give in to that, Ann. If you will just trust me, you will see that everything is all right.'

"She promised me then, Mr. Holmes, that she would strive to be a better wife. And she seemed to honour that promise. In fact, I had never seen her make such a prompt turnabout before. Of course, there were moments when I sensed those deeper currents raging quietly within her. On occasion, her mood grew sombre—as if something oppressive had entered her thoughts—and, for a while at least, she did devote an inordinate amount of attention to cleaning the attic. But by then the armonica was gone, so I wasn't overly concerned. And why should I have been? The chores were all completed by my return from work. After supper, we enjoyed each other's company, just as we had during better times, sitting together and talking for hours in the front room. It was as if happiness had returned to our home."

"I am delighted for you," I said blandly, lighting my third cigarette. "Yet I remain perplexed as to why you have chosen to consult me. It is an intriguing story on some level, to be sure. But you appear agitated about something else, and I do not understand why. You seem well capable of handling matters for yourself."

"Please, Mr. Holmes, I need your help."

"I can't help you without knowing the true nature of your problem. As it is, there is no puzzle here."

"But my wife keeps disappearing!"

" 'Keeps disappearing'? Am I to gather, then, that she keeps reappearing, as well?"

"Yes."

"How often has this happened?"

"Five times."

"And when did her disappearing act commence?"

"Just over a fortnight ago."

"I see. On a Tuesday, more than likely. Then again on the subsequent Thursday. Speak up if I am mistaken, but the following week it would be the same—and Tuesday last, of course."

"Precisely."

"Excellent. Now we are getting somewhere, Mr. Keller. Clearly, your story concludes at Madame Schirmer's front door, but do tell it to me anyway. There may be one or two particulars that I have yet to glean for myself. If you will be so kind as to begin with the first disappearance, although it really is inaccurate to describe her waywardness as such."

Mr. Keller looked sadly at me. Then he glanced at the window, shaking his head solemnly.

"I have thought too much on this," he remarked. "You see, as my midday tends to be rather busy, the errand boy usually brings in my meal. But my work was less consuming that day, so I decided to go home and join Ann for lunch. When I found her missing, I wasn't terribly concerned. In fact, of late I have encouraged Ann to get out of the house on a regular basis, and, taking my advice, she has begun enjoying afternoon walks. I assumed this was where she had gotten off to, so I wrote her a note and headed to my office."

"And where does she claim these walks lead her?"

"To the butcher, or the marketplace. She has also grown quite fond of the public park at the Physics and Botanical Society, and says she spends hours there reading amongst the flowers."

"Indeed, it would be an ideal place for that sort of leisurely pursuit. Continue with your statement."

"I returned home that evening, only to discover she was still gone. The note I had put on the front door remained, and there wasn't any trace of her having been back. At that point, I became worried. My first thought was to go in search of her, but no sooner had I stepped outside than Ann wandered through the gate. How tired she looked, Mr. Holmes, and the very sight of me seemed to produce some hesitation in her. I asked why she was so late coming in, and she explained that she had fallen asleep at the Physics and Botanical Society. It was an unlikely but hardly implausible answer, and I refrained from pressing her further. Frankly, I was just relieved to have her home again.

"Two days later, however, the same thing occurred. I arrived home and Ann was gone. She arrived shortly thereafter, explaining that she had once more napped underneath a tree in the park. The following week, it happened again, exactly as before—on Tuesdays and Thursdays only. Had the days been different, my doubts would not have arisen so readily, nor would I have sought to verify my suspicions this past Tuesday. Knowing that her previous armonica lessons began at four and concluded at six, I departed work early and took up an inconspicuous position across the street from Portman's. At almost a quarter past four, a vague feeling of relief impressed itself upon me, but just as I was about to vacate my position, I spotted her. She was walking nonchalantly along Montague Street—on the other side of the road—holding high the parasol I had given her for her birthday. My heart sank at that moment, and I continued standing there, not going after her or calling her name, only watching as she shut the parasol and then stepped into Portman's."

"And does your wife make a habit of arriving late for appointments?"

"On the contrary, Mr. Holmes. She believes punctuality is a virtue—until recently, that is."

"I see. Do go on, by all means."

"You might well imagine the upset that finally stirred within me. Seconds later, I was racing up the stairs to Madame Schirmer's flat. Already I could hear Ann playing the armonica—those awful, disagreeable tones of hers—and the very sound of it simply furthered my ire, and I struck with all my fury at the door.

" 'Ann!' I cried. 'Ann!'

"But it wasn't my wife who met me. It was Madame Schirmer. She opened the door and gazed upon me with the most venomous expression I have ever witnessed.

" 'I wish to see my wife, immediately!' I exclaimed. 'I know she is in there!' Just then, the music abruptly ceased from inside her flat.

" 'Go home to see this wife of yours, Herr Keller!' said she in a low voice, stepping forwards and shutting the door behind herself. 'Ann is my student no more!' She kept one hand on the doorknob, and her massive body blocked the doorway, preventing me from rushing past her.

" 'You deceived me,' I told her, speaking loudly enough for Ann to hear me. 'Both of you have, and I won't stand for it! You are a vile, wicked person!'

"Madame Schirmer had grown fierce with anger, and, indeed, I was so angry myself that my own words slurred from me as if I were intoxicated. Looking back, I realise now that my behaviour was somewhat irrational, yet this awful woman had betrayed me and I was fearful for my wife.

" 'I just do my teaching,' she said, 'but you make this trouble for me. You are a drunk man, so you think about this tomorrow and feel mad over yourself! I will talk to you no more, Herr Keller, so you never knock like this on my door again!'

"At this, my temper erupted, Mr. Holmes, and I am afraid that I raised my voice beyond reason.

" 'I know she has been coming here, and I am certain that you are continuing to sway her unduly with your devilish notions! I have no idea what you hope to gain by doing so, but if it is her inheritance you seek, I can assure you that I shall do all that is humanly possible to prevent you from touching it! Let me warn you, Madame Schirmer, that until my wife is free of your influence, you shall be hindered by me at every turn, and I won't allow myself to be fooled any further by whatever you might say to appease me!'

"The woman's hand slid from the knob, her fingers curling into a fist, and she seemed on the verge of striking me. As I have said, she is a large, sturdy German, and I have no doubt that she could easily overtake most men. Nevertheless, she restrained her hostility and said, 'The warning is mine, Herr Keller. You go and never come again.

If you bring the trouble around another time, I can have you arrested!" Then she turned upon her heels and entered her flat, slamming the door on me.

"Badly shaken, I left at once and headed home, with the full intention of castigating Ann upon her return. I was sure she had heard me arguing with Madame Schirmer, and I was rather upset that she had remained hiding in that woman's drawing room instead of showing herself. For my part, I had no reason to deny I was spying on her; she was, by that afternoon, fully aware of that fact. However, to my complete and thorough amazement, she was already home when I arrived there. And this is what I cannot figure out: It would have been impossible for her to leave Madame Schirmer's before I did, especially since the flat itself is on the second floor. Yet even if she had managed it somehow, she would hardly have been able to have my supper cooking by the time I arrived. I was, and still am, baffled by how she pulled it off. During our meal, I waited for her to make some mention of my argument with Madame Schirmer, but she said absolutely nothing about it. And when I asked what she had done that afternoon, she replied, 'I started a new novel, and earlier I took a brief stroll through the Physics and Botanical Society's grounds.'

" 'Again? Haven't you tired of it by now?'

" 'How could I? It's such a lovely spot.'

" 'You haven't encountered Madame Schirmer on these strolls of yours, have you, Ann?'

" 'No, Thomas, of course not.'

"I asked her if she might be mistaken, and, seemingly annoyed by my assertion, she insisted otherwise."

"Then she is lying to you," I said. "Some women have a remarkable talent for making men believe what they already know to be false."

"Mr. Holmes, you do not understand. Ann is incapable of uttering a meaningful lie. It isn't in her nature. And if she had, I would have seen right through her and confronted her at that moment. But, no, she wasn't lying to me—I saw it in her face, and I am convinced she has no knowledge of my row with Madame Schirmer. How that is possible is beyond me. Yet I am positive that she was there—just as I am positive that she has told me the truth—and I am at a loss to make sense of any of it. This is why I urgently wrote to you that night and asked for your advice and assistance."

Such was the puzzle which my client had presented me. Trifling as it was, however, there were several points about it which I found engaging. Drawing then upon my well-established method of logical analysis, I began eliminating rival conclusions, until only one remained, for it seemed very few possibilities could determine the reality of the matter.

"At this book and map shop," I asked, "did you, to the best of your belief, notice any other employees aside from the proprietor?"

"I recall just the old proprietor, no one else. I am of the feeling that he runs the place by himself, although he doesn't appear to be getting on well."

"How so?"

"I meant to say that he appears in poor health. He has an incessant cough, which sounds rather severe, and his eyesight is clearly failing him. When I first went there and asked the whereabouts of Madame Schirmer's flat, he used a magnifying glass to view my face. And this last time, he didn't even seem to realise I had entered his shop."

"Too many years hunched over texts by lamplight, I suspect. All the same—while I am extremely knowledgeable of Montague Street and its environs—I will admit that this particular shop is unfamiliar to me. Is it an amply stocked place, do you know?"

"Indeed I do, Mr. Holmes. It is a small place, mind you—I believe it was a family's household once—but each room contains row upon row of books. The maps, it appears, are kept elsewhere. A sign at the front of the shop requests that customers take their map enquiries to Mr. Portman personally. In fact, I don't remember seeing a single map in the shop."

"By chance, did you ask Mr. Portman—for I assume that is the proprietor's name—if he had seen your wife enter his shop?"

"There was no need to. As I said, the man's eyesight is quite horrid. In any case, I observed her entering the place myself, and my eyesight is more than adequate."

"I do not question your vision, Mr. Keller. Still, the matter itself is unremarkable, yet there are a couple of things which should be settled in person. I will go with you to Montague Street at once."

"At once?"

"It is Thursday afternoon, is it not?" Tugging at my watch chain, I soon determined the time to be approximately half past three. "And I see that if we depart now, we might make it to Portman's before your wife does." Rising to fetch my overcoat, I added, "We must be circumspect from this point on, for we are dealing with the emotional complexities of at least one troubled woman. Let us hope that your wife is as reliable and consistent in her actions as my watch here. Although it may weigh in to our advantage if she chooses once again to be late upon arrival."

Then with some haste, we ventured out from Baker Street, and promptly found ourselves mixing amidst the crowded din of London's busy thoroughfares. And while making our way towards Portman's, I became keenly aware that the problem which Mr. Keller had offered me was, upon pondering its details, of little or no importance. Indeed, the case would surely fail to stir even the literary musings of the good doctor. It was, I realise now, the sort of minor affair which I would have jumped at in my formative years as a consulting detective, but which, by the twilight of my career, I mostly saw fit to send elsewhere; more often than not, I referred these sorts of matters to a choice few of the younger upstarts—usually Seth Weaver, or Trevor of Southwark, or Liz Pinner—all of whom displayed a degree of promise in the consulting detective trade.

I must confess, however, that my own regard for Mr. Keller's dilemma was not found at the conclusion of his long-winded account, but instead rested solely on two unrelated and yet private fascinations: the musical wonderment generated from the ill-famed glass armonica—an instrument which I had often wished to experience for myself—and that alluring, curious face I had glimpsed in the photograph. Suffice it to mention, I can explain the appeal of one better than I can the other, and I have since decided that my short-lived predisposition for the fairer sex was aroused by John's oft-stated belief concerning the health benefits derived from female companionship. Aside from assuming such about those irrational feelings of mine, I remain truly at a loss to make sense of the attraction which was summoned by the common, unremarkable photograph of a married woman.

4

WHEN ASKED by Roger how the two Japanese honeybees came into his possession, Holmes stroked the length of his beard and then—after some thought—mentioned the apiary he had discovered at the center of Tokyo: "Pure luck finding it—would have missed seeing the place if I had gone by car with my luggage, but being cooped up at sea, I needed the exercise."

"Did you walk far?"

"I believe so—yes, in fact, I am certain I did, although I cannot accurately recall the exact distance."

They were in the library, seated across from each other—Holmes reclining with a glass of brandy, Roger leaning forward with the vial of honeybees sandwiched between his clasped hands.

"You see, it was an excellent opportunity for a stroll—the weather was ideal, very pleasant—and I was eager for a look around the city." Holmes's manner was relaxed and effusive, his gaze on the boy as he recounted that morning in Tokyo. He would, of course, omit the embarrassing details—such as the fact he had gotten lost in the Shinjuku business district while searching for the railroad station, and that as he wandered the narrow streets, his normally infallible sense of direction abandoned him altogether. There was no point in telling the boy that he had almost missed the train for the port city of Kobe, or that, until finding relief at the apiary, he had observed the worst aspects of postwar Japanese society: men and women living in makeshift huts and packing crates and corrugated iron lean-tos in the busiest parts of the city; housewives with babies on their backs lined up to purchase rice and sweet potatoes; individuals crammed into packed cars, sitting on coach roofs, clinging to engine cowcatchers; the countless hungry Asian bodies moving past him on the street, those ravenous eyes glancing every so often at the disoriented Englishman walking among them (carried forward by two canes, his muddled expression impossible to read beneath the long hair and beard).

Ultimately, Roger learned only of the encounter with the urban bees. The boy remained thoroughly fascinated by what he heard nonetheless, his blue-eyed stare never once straying from Holmes; his visage passive and accepting, his eyes open wide, Roger's pupils stayed fixed on those venerable, reflective eyes, as though the boy were seeing distant lights shimmering along an opaque horizon, a glimpse of something flickering and alive existing just beyond his reach. And, in turn, the gray eyes that focused sharply on him—piercing and kind at the same instant—endeavored to bridge the lifetime that separated the two of them, attempting to do so as brandy was sipped, and the vial's glass grew warmer against soft palms, and that seasoned, well-lived voice somehow made Roger feel much older and more worldly than his years.

As he journeyed deeper and deeper into Shinjuku, Holmes explained, his attention was drawn to worker bees foraging here and there, buzzing around the limited patches of flowers beneath street trees and in the flowerpots left outside of residences. Then, attempting to pursue the workers' route, sometimes losing track of one but soon spotting another, he was led to an oasis within the city's heart: twenty colonies by his count, each capable of producing a sizable amount of honey every year. What shrewd creatures, he found himself thinking. For surely the foraging sites of the Shinjuku colonies varied from season to season. Perhaps they flew greater distances in September, when flowers were rare, while traveling much less distance while the summer and spring flowers bloomed, for once the cherry blossoms came out in April, they would be hemmed in by a food-rich environment. Better still, he told Roger, the shorter foraging range increased the colonies' foraging efficiency; thus, considering the decreased competition for nectar and pollen from poor urban pollinators like syrphid, flies, butterflies, and beetles—more profitable food sources were evidently located and exploited at a closer range in Tokyo than in the outlying areas.

Yet Roger's initial query regarding the Japanese honeybees was never addressed (the boy being far too polite to press it). Even so, Holmes hadn't forgotten the question. The answer, however, wasn't forthcoming, lingering instead like a name suddenly caught at the tip of the tongue. Yes, he had brought the honeybees back from Japan. Yes, they were intended as a gift for the boy. But the manner in which they had come into Holmes's possession was unclear: maybe at the Tokyo apiary (though highly unlikely, since he was preoccupied with finding the railroad station), or maybe during his travels with Mr. Umezaki (for they had covered a lot of ground once he had arrived in Kobe). This apparent lapse, he feared, was a result of changes in his frontal lobe due to aging—how else could one explain why some memories stayed intact, while others were substantially impaired? Strange, too, that he could recall with complete clarity random moments from his childhood, like the morning he entered the fencing salon of Maître Alphonse Bencin (the wiry Frenchman stroking his bushy military mustache, gazing warily at the tall, lean, shy boy standing before him); whereas now, on occasion, he might check his pocket watch and find it impossible to account for previous hours of his day.

Still, as opposed to whatever knowledge was forfeited, he believed a greater degree of recollection always prevailed. And on subsequent evenings following his return home, he sat at the attic desk and—alternating between work on his unfinished masterwork (*The Whole Art of Detection*) and revising his thirty-seven-year-old *Practical Handbook of Bee Culture* for a new printing from Beach & Thompson—invariably turned his mind toward where he had been. Then it wasn't impossible that he might find himself there, waiting on the railroad platform in Kobe after the long train ride, looking for Mr. Umezaki, glancing at those moving about him—a smattering of American officers and soldiers wandered among Japanese locals, businessmen, families; the cacophony of dissimilar voices and swift footsteps resonated across the platform, heading off into the night.

"Sherlock-san?"

As if materializing from nowhere, a slender man wearing an alpine hat, a white open-necked shirt, shorts, and tennis shoes appeared beside him. In his company was another man, somewhat younger, dressed in exactly the same attire. Both identical men stared at him through wire-rimmed glasses, and the older of the two—possibly in his mid-fifties, Holmes assumed, although it was difficult saying for sure with Asian men—stepped in front of him, bowing; the other promptly did likewise.

"I suspect you must be Mr. Umezaki."

"I am, sir," said the older one, remaining bowed. "Welcome to Japan, and welcome to Kobe. It is our honor to meet you at last. We are also honored to have you as a guest in our home."

And while Mr. Umezaki's letters had revealed a keen grasp of English, Holmes was pleasantly surprised by the man's British-tinged accent, suggesting an extensive education beyond the Land of the Rising Sun. Yet all he really knew of the man was that they shared a passion for prickly ash, or, as it was called in Japanese, *hire sansho*. It was this equal interest that had initiated their lengthy correspondence (Mr. Umezaki having first written after reading a monograph Holmes had published years ago, entitled *The Value of Royal Jelly, with Further Comment Upon the Health Benefits of Prickly Ash*). But because the shrub thrived mostly near the sea of its native Japan, he hadn't actually experienced it firsthand, or tasted the cuisine made with its leaves. Furthermore, during the travels of his youth, the opportunities to visit Japan were never seized. When Mr. Umezaki's invitation came, he realized time might not afford him another chance to explore those glorious gardens he had only read about—or, for once in his life, to behold and sample the unusual sprawling plant that had long fascinated him so, an herb whose qualities he suspected might prolong one's life in the same manner as his beloved royal jelly.

"Let us say a mutual honor, shall we?"

"Yes," said Mr. Umezaki, becoming upright. "Please, sir, let me introduce my brother. This is Hensuiro."

Hensuiro continued bowing, his eyes half-closed: "*Sensei*—hello, you are very great detective, very great—"

"Hensuiro is it?"

"Thank you, *sensei,* thank you—you are very great—"

How puzzling the pair suddenly seemed: One brother spoke English without effort, while the other brother could barely speak the language. Shortly thereafter, as they went from the railroad station, Holmes noticed a peculiar sway in the younger brother's hips—as though the weight of the luggage Hensuiro now toted had somehow given him a feminine swagger—and concluded it was of a natural disposition, rather than an affectation (the luggage, after all, wasn't that heavy). When finally reaching a tram stop, Hensuiro put the bags down and offered up a pack of cigarettes: "*Sensei*—"

"Please," Holmes said, taking a cigarette, bringing it to his lips. Illuminated beneath the streetlight, Hensuiro lit a match, cupping the flame. Leaning toward the match, Holmes saw the delicate hands flecked with red paint, the smooth skin, the trimmed fingernails, which were dirty around the edges (the hands of an artist, he decided, and the fingernails of a painter). Then savoring the cigarette, he peered down the dark street, spotting in the distance the shapes of people strolling an intimate quarter aglow with neon signs. Somewhere jazz music was playing, faint but lively, and between drags on the cigarette, he breathed in the fleeting scent of charred meat.

"I imagine you're hungry," said Mr. Umezaki, who, since their going from the station, had kept silently beside him.

"Indeed," Holmes said. "I am rather tired, as well."

"If that's the case, why don't we get you settled in at the house. We'll have supper served there tonight, if you'd like."

"An ideal suggestion."

Hensuiro began talking, speaking in Japanese to Mr. Umezaki; those dainty hands gestured wildly—for a moment touching his alpine hat, then repeatedly indicating a shape like a small tusk near his mouth—as a cigarette bounced precariously on his lips. Afterward, Hensuiro smiled broadly, nodding at Holmes, bowing slightly.

"He wonders if you brought your famous hat," said Mr. Umezaki, looking slightly embarrassed. "The deerstalker, I believe it's called. And your big pipe—did you bring it along?"

Hensuiro, still nodding, pointed simultaneously at his alpine hat and his own cigarette.

"No, no," Holmes replied, "I am afraid I never wore a deerstalker, or smoked the big pipe—mere embellishments by an illustrator, intended to give me distinction, I suppose, and sell magazines. I didn't get much say in the matter."

"Oh," said Mr. Umezaki, his face registering disillusionment—the expression quickly mirrored by Hensuiro when the truth was relayed (the younger man promptly bowing, seemingly ashamed).

"Really, there is no need for that," said Holmes, who was accustomed to such questions and, truth be known, derived a modicum of perverse satisfaction in dispelling the myths. "Tell him it is quite all right, quite all right."

"We had no idea," Mr. Umezaki explained, before calming Hensuiro.

"Few do," Holmes said lowly, exhaling smoke.

Soon the tram appeared, rattling toward them from where the neon signs glowed, and, as Hensuiro took up the luggage, Holmes found himself gazing down the street once again. "Do you hear music?" he asked Mr. Umezaki.

"Yes. In fact, I hear it often, throughout the night sometimes. There're not many tourist sights in Kobe, so we make up for it in nightlife."

"Is that so," Holmes said, squinting, trying without success for a better glimpse at the bright clubs and bars beyond (the music now becoming lost with the tram's clamorous approach). Eventually, he found himself riding farther from the neon signs, going through a district of closed shops, empty sidewalks, and darkened corners. Seconds later, the tram entered a realm of ruins, of burned-out sites ravaged during the war—a desolate landscape lacking streetlights, the crumbling silhouettes made clear only by the full moon above the city.

Then, as if Kobe's forsaken avenues deepened his own fatigue, Holmes's eyelids shut and his body slumped on the tram seat. The long day had finally consumed him, and, minutes later, what little energy he had left would be used for stirring in his seat and hiking up a hillside street (Hensuiro leading the way, Mr. Umezaki gripping him by the elbow). As his canes tapped along the ground, a warm buffeting wind from the sea pressed over him, carrying with it the essence of salt water. Breathing in the night air, he envisioned Sussex and the farmhouse he'd nicknamed "La Paisible" (*My peaceful place,* he'd once called it in a letter to his brother Mycroft), and the coastline of chalk cliffs visible through the attic study's window. Wishing for sleep, he saw his tidy bedroom at home, his bed with the sheets pulled back.

"Nearly there," said Mr. Umezaki. "You see before you my inheritance."

Ahead, where the street ended, stood an unusual two-story house. Anomalous in a country of traditional *minka* dwellings, Mr. Umezaki's residence was clearly of the Victorian style—painted red, encircled by a picket fence, the front yard approximating an English garden. Whereas blackness loomed behind and around the property, an ornate cut-glass fixture cast light across the wide porch, presenting the house like a beacon underneath the night sky. But Holmes was far too exhausted to comment on any of it, even when following Hensuiro into a hallway lined with impressive displays of Art Nouveau and Art Deco glass objects.

"We collect Lalique, Tiffany, and Galle, among others," said Mr. Umezaki, guiding him forward.

"Evidently," Holmes remarked, feigning interest. Thereafter, he felt ethereal, as if drifting through a tedious dream. In hindsight, he could recall nothing else of that first evening in Kobe—not the meal he ate, or the conversation they shared, or being shown to his room. Nor could he remember meeting the sullen woman known as Maya, though she had served him supper, had poured his drink, had no doubt unpacked his luggage.

Yet there she was the next morning, drawing the curtains, waking him. Her presence wasn't startling, and while having been half-conscious when they'd met previously, he regarded her immediately as a familiar face, albeit a dour one. Is she Mr. Umezaki's wife? Holmes wondered. Maybe a housekeeper? Wearing a kimono, her graying hair done in a more Western fashion, she appeared older than Hensuiro, but not much older than the refined Umezaki. Still, she was an unattractive woman, rather homely, with a round head, flat nose, and eyes slanted into two thin slits, giving her a myopic, mole-like quality. Without question, he concluded, she must be the housekeeper.

"Good morning," he uttered, watching her from his pillow. She didn't acknowledge him. Instead, she opened a window, letting the sea air waft inside. Then she exited the room, promptly entering again with a tray, upon which steamed a cup of breakfast tea beside a note written by Mr. Umezaki. Using one of the few Japanese words he actually knew, he blurted out *"Ohayo"* as she set the tray on the bedside table. Once again, she ignored him, this time going into the adjacent bathroom and running him a bath. He sat up, chagrined, and drank the tea, doing so while reading the note:

> Must do some business.
> Hensuiro awaits downstairs.
> Back before dusk falls.
>   Tamiki

"Ohayo," he said to himself, speaking with disappointment and with the concern that his being there had possibly disrupted the household (perhaps the invitation wasn't meant to be accepted, or perhaps Mr. Umezaki was disappointed by the less than vibrant gentleman he had found waiting at the station). He felt relief when Maya had gone from the room, but it was overshadowed by the thought of Hensuiro and an entire day without proper communication, and by the notion of gesticulating whatever was important—food, drink, lavatory, nap. He couldn't explore Kobe alone, lest insulting his host when it was realized he had sneaked out on his own. As he bathed, the rumbling of unease gained momentum. Though worldly by most standards, he had spent almost half his life sequestered on the Sussex Downs, and now he felt ill-equipped to function within such an alien country, especially without a guide who spoke proper English.

But after dressing and meeting Hensuiro downstairs, his worries vanished. "Good more-knee-eng, *sensei,*" Hensuiro stammered, smiling.

"Ohayo."

"Oh, yes, *ohayo*—good, very good."

Then, as Hensuiro repeatedly nodded with approval at his chopsticks abilities, Holmes ate a simple breakfast consisting of green tea and a raw egg stirred into rice. Before midday, they were walking together outside, enjoying a beautiful morning canopied by a clear blue sky. Hensuiro, like young Roger, gripped him at the elbow, casually directing him along, and, having slept so well, invigorated, too, from his bath, he felt as if he were experiencing Japan anew. In daylight, Kobe was entirely different from the desolate place he had viewed through the tram window: The ruined buildings were nowhere in sight; the streets teamed with foot traffic. Vendors occupied the central square, where children ran about. Chatter and boiling water erupted inside a multitude of noodle shops. On the northern hills of the city, he spied an entire neighborhood of Victorian and Gothic homes, which, he suspected, must have originally belonged to foreign traders and diplomats.

"What, if I might ask, does your brother do, Hensuiro?"

"*Sensei*—"

"Your brother—what does he do—his job?"

"This—no—I not understand, just a little understand, not many."

"Thank you, Hensuiro."

"Yes, thank you—thank you very much."

"You are excellent company on this pleasant day, regardless of your deficiencies."

"I think so."

However, as the walk progressed, as they turned corners and crossed busy streets, he began recognizing signs of hunger all around. The shirtless children in the parks didn't run like the other children; rather, they stood inert, as if languishing, their pronounced rib cages framed by bone-defined arms. Men begged in front of the noodle shops, and even those who looked fed—the shopkeepers, the patrons, the couples—wore similar expressions of yearning, although less obvious. Then it seemed to him that the flux of their daily lives masked a noiseless despair: Behind the smiles, the nods, the bows, the general politeness, there lurked something else that had grown malnourished.

5

DURING HIS TRAVELS, every now and then, Holmes would again sense an immense want permeating human existence, the true nature of which he couldn't fully comprehend. And while this ineffable longing had skirted his country life, it still saw fit to visit him on occasion, becoming more and more evident among the strangers who continually trespassed upon his property. In earlier years, the trespassers were usually a mixed assortment of drunken undergraduates wishing to laud him, London investigators seeking help with an unsolved crime, the occasional young men from the Gables—a well-known coaching establishment some half a mile away from Holmes's estate—or holidaying families, there in the hope of catching a glimpse of the famous detective.

"I am sorry," he told them without exception, "but my privacy must be respected. I will ask you to please leave the grounds now."

The Great War brought him some peace, as fewer and fewer people knocked on his door; this occurred, too, while the second Great War raged across Europe. But between both wars, the encroachers returned in force, and the old conglomeration was gradually replaced by another assortment: autograph seekers, journalists, reading groups from London and elsewhere; those gregarious individuals contrasted sharply with the crippled veterans, the contorted bodies confined forever to wheelchairs, the various breathing mutations, or the literal basket cases appearing like cruel gifts on his front steps.

"I am sorry—I truly am—"

What was sought by one group—a conversation, a photograph, a signature—was easy to deny; what was desired by the other, however, was illogical but harder to rebuke—just the laying on of his hands, perhaps a few words whispered like some healing incantation (as if the mysteries of their ailments might at last be solved by him and him alone). Even so, he remained firm with his refusals, often admonishing the caretakers who had inconsiderately pushed the wheelchairs past the NO TRESPASSING signs.

"Please go this instant. Otherwise, I will inform Anderson of the Sussex Constabulary!"

Only recently had he begun to bend his own rules, sitting for a while with a young mother and her infant. She had first been seen by Roger, crouched beside the herb garden, her baby wrapped in a cream-colored shawl and its head cradled at her exposed left breast. As the boy led him to her, Holmes pounded his canes along the pathway, grumbling so she might hear, saying aloud that entry into his gardens was strictly prohibited. Upon seeing her, his anger dissipated, but he hesitated before going any closer. She gazed up at him with wide, sedated pupils. Her dirty face betrayed loss; her unbuttoned yellow blouse, muddied and torn, hinted at the miles she had walked to find him. Then she held the shawl out toward him, offering her infant with soiled hands.

"Get to the house," he ordered Roger in a low voice. "Call Anderson. Tell him it is an emergency. Say that I am waiting in the garden."

"Yes, sir."

He had observed what the boy had not: the tiny corpse held by its mother's trembling hands, its purple cheeks, its blue-black lips, the numerous flies crawling on and encircling the handwoven shawl. Once Roger was on his way, he put the canes aside and, with some effort, sat down by the woman. Again she thrust the shawl toward him, so he gently accepted the bundle, holding the baby against his chest.

By the time Anderson arrived, Holmes had given the infant back to her. For a while, he stood beside the constable there on the pathway, both men watching as the bundle was held at the woman's breast, her fingers repeatedly pressing a nipple against the baby's rigid lips. Coming from the east, ambulance sirens rang out, drawing nearer, eventually ceasing near the gate of the property.

"Do you think it's a kidnapping?" whispered Anderson, stroking his slightly curled mustache, remaining openmouthed after he spoke, his gaze frozen on the woman's chest.

"No," answered Holmes, "I believe it is something far less criminal than that."

"Really," the constable replied, and Holmes detected displeasure in his tone: For a great mystery wasn't presenting itself after all, nor would the constable be involved in working a case with his childhood hero. "So what are your thoughts, then?"

"Look at her hands," Holmes told him. "Look at the dirt and mud underneath her fingernails, on her blouse, on her skin and clothing." She has been in the earth, he figured. She has been digging. "Look at her muddy shoes—fairly new and showing few signs of wear. Still, she has walked a distance, but no further than Seaford. Look at her face and you'll recognize the grief of a mother who has lost her newborn. Contact your associates in Seaford. Ask about a child's grave that was dug up during the night, the body taken—and ask if the child's mother has gone missing. Ask if the infant's name might be Jeffrey."

Anderson looked swiftly at Holmes, reacting as if he'd been slapped. "How do you know this?"

Holmes shrugged ruefully. "I don't—at least not for certain."

Mrs. Munro's voice carried from the farmhouse yard, instructing the ambulance men where to go.

Appearing forlorn in his uniform, Anderson cocked an eyebrow while tugging his mustache. He said, "Why'd she come here? Why'd she come to you?"

A cloud passed over the sun, casting a long shadow across the gardens.

"Hope, I suspect," said Holmes. "It seems I am known for discovering answers when events appear desperate. Beyond that, I wouldn't care to speculate."

"And what about it being called Jeffrey?"

Holmes explained: He had asked the infant's name while holding the shawl. "Jeffrey," he thought he'd heard her say. He asked how old. She stared miserably at the ground, saying nothing. He asked where the child had been born. She said nothing. Had she traveled far?

"Seaford," she had muttered, brushing a fly off her forehead.

"Are you hungry?"

Nothing.

"Would you like something to eat, dear?"

Nothing.

"I believe you must be quite famished. I believe you need water."

"I believe it's a stupid world," she finally said, reaching for the shawl.

And if he had then addressed her forthrightly, he would have been inclined to agree.

6

I N K O B E A N D, subsequently, on their travels westward, Mr. Umezaki sometimes inquired about England, asking—among other things—if Holmes had seen the Bard's birthplace in Stratford-upon-Avon, or strolled within the mysterious Stonehenge circle, or visited Cornwall's scenic coastline, which had inspired so many artists over the centuries.

"Indeed," he usually answered before elaborating.

And had the great Anglican cities survived the devastation of the war? Had the spirit of the English people remained intact throughout the Luftwaffe's aerial bombings?

"For the most part, yes. We have an indomitable character, you know."

"Victory tends to underscore that, wouldn't you say?"

"I suppose so."

Then returning home, it was Roger posing questions about Japan (although asking in a less specific manner than Mr. Umezaki had). Following an afternoon of removing overgrown grass from around the hives, of pulling weeds so that the bees could come and go without obstruction, the boy escorted him to the nearby cliffs, where, minding every step, they proceeded down a long, steep path that eventually ended at the beach below. There, in either direction, stretched miles of scree and shingles, interrupted only by shallow inlets and tide pools (filled afresh with each flow, existing as ideal watering places). In the distance, on a clear day, the little cove that held the village of Cuckmere Haven was seen.

Presently, their clothing lay neatly on the rocks, and both he and the boy eased into a favored tide pool, reclining while the water rose to their chests. Once settled—their shoulders just above the currents, the afternoon sunlight shimmering off the sea beyond—Roger glanced toward him and, shadowing his eyes with a hand, said, "Sir, does the Japanese ocean look anything like the Channel?"

"Somewhat. At least what I saw of it—salt water is salt water, is it not?"

"Were there lots of ships?"

Shielding his own eyes, Holmes realized that the boy was now staring at him inquisitively. "I believe so," he said, unsure if the numerous tankers, tugboats, and barges drifting through his memory had been seen in a Japanese or an Australian port. "It is an island nation, after all," he reasoned. "They, like us, are never far from the sea."

The boy let his feet float up, absently wiggling his toes in the surface foam.

"Is it true? Are they a little people?"

"It's quite true, I'm afraid."

"Like dwarves?"

"Taller than that. On average about your height, my boy."

Roger's feet sank, the wiggling toes disappearing.

"Are they yellow?"

"What do you mean exactly? Skin or constitution?"

"Their skin—is it yellow? Do they have big teeth, like rabbits?"

"Darker than yellow." He pressed a fingertip into Roger's tanned shoulder. "Closer to this color, you see?"

"What about their teeth?"

He laughed and said, "I cannot say with certainty. On the other hand, I surely would recall a predominance of lagomorph incisors, so I suspect it is safe to say they have teeth much like yours and mine."

"Oh," Roger muttered, but he said no more for the moment.

The gift of the honeybees, Holmes figured, had sparked the boy's curiosity: those two creatures in the vial, similar to yet different from the English honeybees, suggesting a parallel world, where everything was comparable but not quite the same.

Only later, when they began climbing the steep path, did the questioning resume. Now the boy wanted to know if the Japanese cities still bore traces of Allied bombing. "In places," Holmes answered, aware of Roger's preoccupation with airplanes and attack and fiery death—as if some resolution regarding the father's untimely fate might be found in the sordid details of war.

"Did you see where the bomb got dropped?"

They had stopped to rest, sitting for a while on a bench that marked the path's middle point. Stretching his long legs toward the cliff edge, Holmes gazed out at the Channel, thinking, the Bomb. Not the incendiary variety, nor the antipersonnel model, but the atomic kind.

"They call it *pika-don*," he told Roger. "It means 'flash-bang'—and yes, I saw where one was dropped."

"Did everyone look ill?"

Holmes continued to stare at the sea, observing the gray water now reddened by the sun's descent. He said, "No, most didn't look visibly ill. However, quite a few seemed so—it is a difficult thing to describe, Roger."

"Oh," the boy replied, looking at him with a slightly puzzled expression, but he said nothing more.

Holmes found himself considering that most unfortunate event in the life of a hive: the sudden loss of the queen, when no resources were available from which to raise a new one. Yet how could he explain the deeper illness of unexpressed desolation, that imprecise pall harbored en masse by ordinary Japanese? It was hardly perceptible upon such reticent people, but it was always there—roaming the Tokyo and Kobe streets, visible somehow on the solemn young faces of repatriated men, within the vacant stares of malnourished mothers and children, and hinted at by a popular saying from the previous year. *"Kamikaze mo fuki sokone."*

On his second evening with his Kobe hosts, while sharing sake inside a cramped drinking establishment, Mr. Umezaki translated the saying: " 'The Divine Wind didn't blow'—that's basically what it means." He had said this after a drunken patron—dressed shabbily in former military attire, staggering wildly from table to table—was escorted outside, yelling as he went, *"Kamikaze mo fuki sokone! Kamikaze mo fuki sokone! Kamikaze mo fuki sokone!"*

As it happened, just prior to the drunk's outburst, they had been discussing postsurrender Japan. Or rather, Mr. Umezaki, straying abruptly from a conversation regarding their travel itinerary, asked Holmes if he, too, found the Allied occupation rhetoric of freedom and democracy at odds with the continual suppression of Japanese poets, writers, and artists. "Don't you find it somewhat baffling that many are starving, yet we aren't allowed to criticize the occupation forces openly? For that matter, we can't grieve as a whole for our losses and mourn together as a nation, or even create public eulogies for our dead, in case such an evocation is perceived as a promotion of militaristic spirit."

"Frankly," Holmes admitted, bringing his cup to his lips, "I know little about it. I am sorry."

"No, please, I'm sorry for mentioning it." Mr. Umezaki's already-flushed face burned brighter, then slackened with fatigue and a presentiment of intoxication. "Anyway, where were we?"

"Hiroshima, I believe."

"That's right, you were interested in visiting Hiroshima—"

"Kamikaze mo fuki sokone!" the drunk began yelling, startling everyone except Mr. Umezaki. *"Kamikaze mo fuki sokone!"*

Unfazed, Mr. Umezaki poured himself another drink, and one for Hensuiro, who had repeatedly downed his sake in one swallow. Following the drunk's shouting and prompt removal, Holmes found himself studying Mr. Umezaki, and Mr. Umezaki—his demeanor becoming increasingly somber with each drink—stared thoughtfully at the tabletop, the downcast glower on his face protruding like the pout of a scolded child (an expression appropriated by Hensuiro, whose normally cheerful appearance took on a grim, withdrawn look). At last, Mr. Umezaki glanced toward him. "So, where were we again? Ah, yes, our journey west—and you wanted to know if Hiroshima might be on our way. Well, I can tell you it is."

"I very much wish to see the place, if you are agreeable."

"Certainly, I'd like to see it, too. To be honest, I haven't been there since before the war—other than passing through by train."

But Holmes detected apprehension in Mr. Umezaki's voice, or possibly, he second-guessed, it was simply weariness saturating his host's tone. After all, the Mr. Umezaki who had greeted him that afternoon appeared run-down from his business dealings elsewhere, as opposed to the attentive and affable fellow who had met him at the railroad station the day before. Now, having taken a satisfying nap after exploring the city alongside Hensuiro, it was his turn to be wide-awake during the evening, whereas Mr. Umezaki conveyed a heavy and deep-rooted exhaustion (a lassitude made less burdensome with a steady intake of alcohol and nicotine).

Holmes had recognized the signs earlier that day, when opening the door to Mr. Umezaki's study, finding him standing there beside his desk, lost in thought, a thumb and index finger pressing against his eyelids, an unbound manuscript held loosely at his side. Because Mr. Umezaki still wore his hat and jacket, it was evident he had just come home.

"Pardon me," Holmes said, feeling suddenly intrusive. However, he had stirred within a silent house, where the doors were shut and no one else was seen or heard. Still, without intending to, he had violated his own code: Throughout his life, he had believed a man's study was hallowed ground, a sanctuary for reflection and a retreat from the outside world, meant for important work, or, at least, the private communion with the written texts of others. Therefore, the attic study of his Sussex home was the room he cherished the most, and while he never made it explicitly known, both Mrs. Munro and Roger understood they wouldn't be welcomed inside if the door was closed. "I didn't mean to interrupt you. It appears my advancing years usher me into rooms for no obvious reason."

Mr. Umezaki glanced up, showing little surprise, and said, "On the contrary, I'm glad you're here. Come in, please."

"Really, I'll not bother you any further."

"Actually, I thought you were asleep. Otherwise, I'd have invited you to join me. So do come in, have a look around. Tell me what you think of my library."

"Only if you insist," Holmes said, advancing toward the teak bookshelves, which covered an entire wall, noticing Mr. Umezaki's activities while going forward: the manuscript being placed at the center of the uncluttered desk, the hat then removed and set carefully over it.

"I apologize about my business obligations, but I trust my comrade took good care of you."

"Oh, yes, we had a pleasant day together—language obstacles aside."

Just then, Maya called from down the hallway, her voice sounding somewhat irritated.

"Excuse me," Mr. Umezaki said. "I won't be a minute."

"Take your time," Holmes said, now standing before the extensive rows of books.

Again, Maya called out, and Mr. Umezaki walked hurriedly in her direction, forgetting to close the door as he went. For a few moments after he had gone, Holmes gazed at the books, his eyes roving from shelf to shelf. Most of the books were fine hardbound editions, the majority of which had Japanese characters on the spines. Even so, one shelf held nothing but Western works, organized thoughtfully into separate categories—American literature, English literature, plays, a large portion devoted to poetry (Whitman, Pound, Yeats, various Oxford textbooks regarding the Romantic poets). The shelf below it was devoted almost exclusively to Karl Marx, although several volumes by Sigmund Freud were squeezed in at the end.

As Holmes turned and looked around, he saw that Mr. Umezaki's study, though small, was arranged efficiently: a reading chair, a floor lamp, a few photographs, and what appeared to be a framed university diploma hung high behind the desk. Then he caught the incomprehensible banter of Mr. Umezaki and Maya, their discussion fluctuating from heated debate to sudden quiet, and he was about to go and peep into the hallway, when Mr. Umezaki returned, saying, "We've had some confusion regarding the supper menu, so I fear we'll be eating later than usual. I hope you don't mind."

"Not at all."

"In the meantime, I believe I would like a drink. There's a bar not too far, rather comfortable, probably as good a place as any to discuss our travel schedule—if that's all right."

"Sounds delightful."

So out they'd gone for a while, walking leisurely to the cramped drinking establishment as the sky darkened, staying at the bar much longer than was intended, then headed back only after the drinking crowd grew too large and too loud. Then it was a simple supper consisting of fish, some vegetables, steamed rice, and miso soup—each dish served unceremoniously in the dining room by Maya, who refused any offer to join them. But the joints of Holmes's fingers ached from working the chopsticks, and no sooner had he lowered them than Mr. Umezaki suggested they retire to his study. "If you will, there's something I wish to show you." And with that, the two went from the table, going together into the hallway, leaving Hensuiro alone with what remained of their meal.

His recollection of that night in Mr. Umezaki's study remained quite vivid, even though, at the time, the alcohol and the food had tired him. Yet, as opposed to earlier, Mr. Umezaki was the enlivened one, smiling as he offered Holmes his reading chair, then producing a lit match before a Jamaican could be retrieved. Once comfortable in the chair—the canes across his lap, the cigar burning at his lips—Holmes watched as Mr. Umezaki opened a desk drawer and removed a slender hardbound book from within.

"What do you make of this?" Mr. Umezaki asked, coming forward, the book held out for him to take.

"A Russian edition," Holmes said, accepting the volume, immediately noting the imperial crests adorning the otherwise bare cover and spine. With further inspection—his fingers touching the reddish binding and gold inlay around the crests, his eyes momentarily scanning the pages—he concluded it was an extremely unique translation of a very popular novel. *"The Hound of the Baskervilles—*a one-off printing, I suspect."

"Yes," said Mr. Umezaki, sounding pleased. "Fashioned exclusively for the Czar's private collection. I understand he was a great follower of your stories."

"Was he?" said Holmes, handing the book back.

"Very much so, yes," Mr. Umezaki replied, crossing back over to his desk. Depositing the rare volume inside the drawer, he added, "As you can imagine, this is the most valuable item in my library—though well worth the price I paid for it."

"Indeed."

"You must own a good many books regarding your adventures—different printings, numerous translations, various editions."

"Actually, I possess none—not even the flimsy paperbacks. Truthfully, I've only read a handful of the stories—and that was many years ago. I couldn't instill in John the basic difference between an induction and a deduction, so I stopped trying, and I also stopped reading his fabricated versions of the truth, because the inaccuracies drove me mad. You know, I never did call him Watson—he was John, simply John. But he really was a skilled writer, mind you—very imaginative, better with fiction than fact, I daresay."

Mr. Umezaki's gaze was on him, and there was a touch of bewilderment in his eyes. "How can that be?" he asked, lowering himself to his desk seat.

Holmes shrugged, exhaling smoke, saying, "Simply the truth, I am afraid."

But it was what occurred thereafter that remained clear in his mind. For Mr. Umezaki—still flushed from drinking, drawing a long breath, as though he, too, were smoking—paused thoughtfully before asserting himself. Then grinning, he confessed he wasn't too surprised to learn the stories weren't entirely accurate. "Your ability—or perhaps I should say the character's ability—to draw definitive conclusions from often tenuous observations always struck me as fanciful, don't you think? I mean, you don't seem anything like the person I've read so much about. How do I say it? You seem less extravagant, less colorful."

Holmes sighed reproachfully, briefly waving a hand, as if clearing the smoke. "Well, you are referring to the arrogance of my youth. I am an old man now, and I have been retired since you were but a child. It is rather shameful in hindsight, all the vain presumption of my younger self. It really is. You know, we bungled a number of important cases—regrettably. Of course, who wants to read about the failures? I certainly don't. But I can tell you this with a fair degree of certainty: The successes may have been exaggerated; however, those fanciful conclusions you mention were not."

"Really?" Mr. Umezaki paused again, taking another long breath. Then he said, "I wonder what you know of me. Or is your talent retired, as well?"

It was possible, Holmes considered upon reflection, that Mr. Umezaki did not use those exact words. Nevertheless, he remembered tilting his head back, bringing his stare to the ceiling. With the cigar fuming in one hand, he began slowly at first: "What do I know of you? Well, your command of English suggests a formal education abroad—from the old Oxford editions on the bookshelves, I would say you studied in England, and the diploma on the wall there should prove me correct. I submit that your father was a diplomat with strong preferences for all things Western. Why else would he favor such a nontraditional dwelling as this—your inheritance, if memory serves—or, for that matter, send his son to study in England, a country where he no doubt had dealings?" He closed his eyes. "As for you specifically, my dear Tamiki, I can easily gather that you are a man of letters and well read. Actually, it is amazing how much can be learned about people from the books they own. In your case, there is an interest in poetry—especially Whitman and Yeats—which tells me you have an affinity for verse. However, not only are you a reader of poetry but you often write it, too—so frequently, in fact, that you probably didn't realize that the note you left me this morning was actually in haiku form—the five-seven-five variety, I believe. And while I have no way of knowing unless I look, I imagine the manuscript sitting on your desk contains your unpublished work. I say *unpublished* because you were careful to conceal it beneath your hat earlier. Which brings me to your business trip. If you came home with your own manuscript—somewhat dispirited, I should add—then I suspect you took it with you this morning. But what sort of business requires a writer to take along an unpublished text? And why would he come home in such a mood, the text still in hand? Likely a meeting involving a publisher—which didn't go favorably, I gather. So while one could assume it was the quality of your writing preventing publication, I believe otherwise. I submit that it is the content of your writing that is in question, not the quality. Why else would you express indignation over the continual suppression of Japanese poets, writers, and artists by Allied censors? But a poet who devotes a large portion of his library to Marx is hardly a champion of the emperor's militaristic spirit—in all likelihood, sir, you are something of an armchair Communist—which, of course, means you are deemed worthy of censorship by both the occupying forces and those who still hold the emperor in high regard. The very fact that you referred to Hensuiro as your comrade this evening—a strange word for one's own brother, I think—hints at your ideological leanings, as well as your idealism. Of course, Hensuiro isn't your brother, is he? If he were, your father would undoubtedly have sent him in your footsteps to England, giving him and me the luxury of better communication. Curious, then, that the two of you share this home, and dress so alike, and that you continually substitute *we* for *I*—in much the same manner as married couples do. Naturally, this is none of my concern, although I'm convinced you were raised as an only child." A mantelpiece clock began chiming, and Holmes opened his eyes, fixing his stare on the ceiling. "Lastly—and I pray you won't take offense—I have wondered how you manage to survive so comfortably during these troubled days. You show no signs of poverty, you maintain a housekeeper, and you are quite proud of your expensive collection of Art Deco glassware—all of this being a notch or two above the bourgeoisie, wouldn't you agree? On the other hand, a Communist dealing goods in the black market is slightly less hypocritical—especially if he is offering his bounty at a fair price and at the expense of the capitalist hordes occupying his country." Sighing deeply, Holmes fell silent. Finally, he said, "There are other particulars, I am sure, but they escape me at the moment. You see, I am not as retentive as I once was." At this point, he lowered his head, brought the cigar to his mouth, and gave Mr. Umezaki a weary glance.

"It's remarkable." Mr. Umezaki shook his head with a gesture of disbelief. "Absolutely incredible."

"No need, really."

Mr. Umezaki attempted to appear unfazed. He fished a cigarette from a pocket, holding it between his fingers without bothering to light it. "Aside from one or two errors, you've completely undressed me. Still, I've had minor involvement in the black market, but only as an infrequent buyer. In truth, my father was a very wealthy man and made sure his family was taken care of, but that doesn't mean I can't appreciate Marxist theory. Also, it isn't exactly accurate to say I maintain a housekeeper."

"Mine is hardly an exact science, you know."

"It's impressive nonetheless. I will say your observations about me and Hensuiro aren't terribly surprising. Without being too blunt—you are a bachelor who lived with another bachelor for many years."

"Purely platonic, I assure you."

"If you say so." Mr. Umezaki continued looking at him, momentarily awestricken. "It really is remarkable."

Holmes's expression became puzzled: "Am I mistaken—the woman who cooks your meals and tends your house—Maya—she is your housekeeper, correct?" For clearly Mr. Umezaki was a bachelor by choice, yet it struck him odd just then that Maya behaved more like a put-upon spouse than hired help.

"It's semantical, if that's what you mean—but I don't like to think of my mother as such."

"Naturally."

Holmes rubbed his hands together, puffing blue fumes, hoping to mask what was, in reality, a bothersome oversight on his part: the forgetting of Mr. Umezaki's relation to Maya, something he had surely learned when introductions were made. Or perhaps, he entertained, the oversight was his host's—perhaps he was never told to begin with. Regardless, it wasn't worth fretting over (an understandable mistake, as the woman appeared too young to be Mr. Umezaki's mother anyway).

"Now if you will excuse me," Holmes said, holding the cigar a few inches from his mouth. "I have become rather tired—and we are starting early tomorrow."

"Yes, I'll be turning in shortly myself. May I say first that I'm truly grateful for your visit here."

"Nonsense," Holmes said, standing with his canes, the cigar at one side of his mouth, "it is I who is grateful. Sleep well."

"You, too."

"Thank you, I will. Good night."

"Good night."

With that, Holmes made his way into the dim corridor, stepping where the hall lights were extinguished and everything ahead of him was steeped in shadow. Yet some illumination prevailed amid the darkness, spilling past an ajar door up ahead. Toward the light he ambled, bringing himself to stand before that brightened doorway. And peeking inside the room, he observed Hensuiro at work: shirtless within a sparsely furnished parlor, stooping in front of a painted canvas that—from Holmes's vantage point—depicted something like a bloodred landscape littered with a multitude of geometric shapes (straight black lines, blue circles, yellow squares). Peering closer, he saw finished paintings of various sizes stacked along the barren walls—primed in red, and, of those he could see plainly, bleak (crumbling buildings, pale white bodies surfacing lengthwise through the crimson, twisted arms, bent legs, grasping hands, and faceless heads presented as a visceral pile). Dotting the wooden flooring, sprinkled haphazardly around the easel, were countless drops and splashes of paint, appearing like the spattering of blood loss.

Later, when settled in bed, he would ponder the poet's suppressed relationship with the artist—the two men posing as brothers, yet living as a couple beneath the same roof, no doubt within the same sheets, judged by the critical glare of the disapproving but loyal Maya. To be sure, it was a clandestine life, one of subtlety and complete discretion. But he suspected there were other secrets as well, possibly one or two delicate matters soon to be imparted—for Mr. Umezaki's letters, he now suspected, had further motives beyond what was written. So an invitation had been offered, and it had been accepted. Come the next morning, he and Mr. Umezaki would begin their travels, leaving Hensuiro and Maya alone in the big house. How deftly you've lured me here, he thought before sleeping. Then, at last, he drifted off with eyes half-open, eventually dreaming as a familiar low, buzzing suddenly pricked up his ears.

PART
II

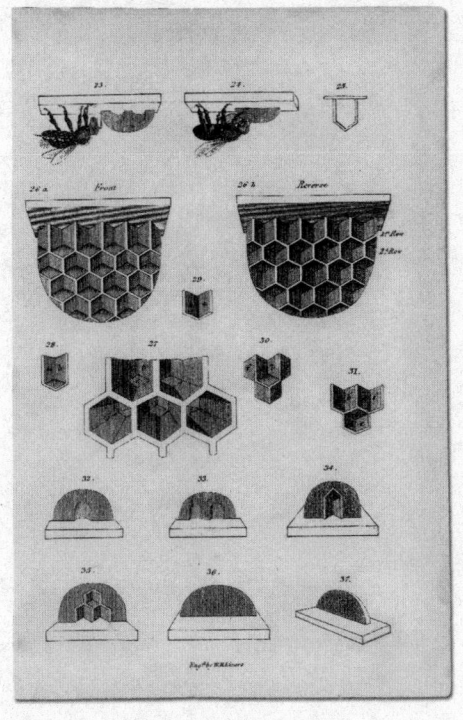

7

HOLMES WOKE, gasping. What had happened?

Seated at his desk, he glanced toward the attic window. Outside, the wind was blustering, monotonous and steadfast, humming against the panes, billowing through the gutters, swaying pine limbs in the yard, no doubt ruffling the blooms of his flower beds. Other than the gusts beyond the closed window and the emergence of night, everything in his study remained as it had been prior to his drifting off. The shifting hues of dusk framed between the parted curtains were replaced now by pitch-blackness, yet the table lamp cast the same glow across his desktop; and there, spread haphazardly before him, were the handwritten notes for *The Whole Art of Detection*'s third volume—page after page of various musings, the words often scrawled into the margins—scattershot from line to line, and, in a way, lacking any conceivable order. Whereas the first two volumes had proved a rather effortless undertaking (both written concurrently over a fifteen-year period), this latest endeavor was hampered by an inability to concentrate fully: He would sit down and promptly fall asleep, pen in hand; he would sit down and find himself staring out the window instead, sometimes for what seemed hours; he would sit down and begin writing an erratic series of sen-

83

tences, most unrelated and free-flowing, as if something palpable might evolve from the mess of ideas.

What had happened?

He touched his neck, rubbing his throat lightly. Only the wind, he thought. That swift humming at the window, filtering into his sleep, startling him awake.

Just the wind.

His stomach grumbled. And then he realized supper had been missed again—Mrs. Munro's Friday usual of roast beef and Yorkshire pudding with side dishes—and that he was sure to find a tray in the hallway (the roasted potatoes having grown cold beside the locked attic door). Kind Roger, he thought. Such a good boy. Because during the past week—while he had remained sequestered within the attic, forgoing supper and his normal activities in the beeyard—the tray had always found its way up the stairs, waiting to be encountered whenever he stepped into the hallway.

Earlier that day, Holmes had felt some degree of guilt about having neglected his apiary, so following breakfast he had wandered toward the beeyard, catching sight of Roger ventilating the hives from afar. Anticipating hot weather and with the nectar flow at its most vigorous, the boy was wisely offsetting the upper supers on each hive, allowing an air current to push through the entrance and out the top, thereby aiding the fluttering wings, which, aside from also helping cool the hives, could better evaporate the nectar stored in the supers. Then whatever guilt Holmes had felt vanished; for the bees were being properly tended, and it was evident that his casual, if not deliberate, tutelage of Roger had reached fruition (the beeyard considerations, he was pleased to observe, were in the boy's capable, attentive hands).

Soon enough, Roger would start harvesting the honey on his own—gingerly removing the frames one at a time, calming the bees with a puff of smoke, using an uncapping fork to lift the wax covers off the cells—and in the days to come a small amount of honey would flow through a double strainer into a honey bucket, followed thereafter by larger amounts. And from where he stood on the garden pathway, Holmes could imagine himself again in the beeyard with the boy, instructing Roger about the simplest method in which a novice could produce comb honey.

After placing a super on a given hive, he had previously told the boy, it was better to use eight extracting frames rather than ten, doing so only when the nectar flow was in progress. Then the remaining two frames should be set in the middle of the super, making sure that unwired comb foundation was used. If everything was done properly, the colony would draw the foundation, filling the two frames with honey. Once the comb-honey frames became filled and capped, they should be immediately replaced with more comb foundation—providing, of course, that the flow was proceeding as expected. In the event that the flow appeared less profuse than what was desired, it was wise, then, to replace the unwired comb foundation with a wired extracting foundation. Obviously, he pointed out, the hives must be inspected frequently in order to best decide which method of extraction was appropriate.

Holmes had walked Roger through the entire regimen, showing the boy each step of the process, feeling positive that—as the honey was ready for harvest—Roger would heed his instruction by the letter. "You understand, my boy, that I am entrusting this task to you because I believe you are fully capable of managing it without error."

"Thank you, sir."

"Do you have any questions?"

"No, I don't think so, no," replied the boy, speaking with a gentle enthusiasm, which somehow gave the false impression that he was smiling—even though his expression was serious and mindful.

"Very good," Holmes said, shifting his gaze from Roger's face to the surrounding hives. He didn't realize that the boy remained staring at him, didn't notice that he was being looked upon with the same kind of quiet reverence that he himself reserved only for the beeyard. Instead, he pondered the comings and goings of the apiary's inhabitants, the busy, diligent, active communities of the hives. "Very good," he repeated, whispering to himself on that afternoon in the recent past.

Turning around on the garden pathway, returning slowly to the house, Holmes knew Mrs. Munro would eventually do her part, filling jar after jar with the honey surplus, delivering a batch to the vicarage, to the charity mission, to the Salvation Army when running her errands in town. By providing these gifts of honey, Holmes believed he was also doing his part—making available the viscid material from his hives (something which he regarded as a wholesome by-product of his true interests: bee culture and the benefits of royal jelly), giving it to those who would fairly disburse the many unlabeled jars (on condition that his name would never become associated with what was given), and providing a beneficial sweetness to the less fortunate of Eastbourne and, hopefully, elsewhere.

"Sir, it's God's blessed work you're doing," Mrs. Munro had once told him. "Sure enough, it's His will you're following—the ways you help them who've been living without."

"Don't be ludicrous," he'd replied disdainfully. "If anything, it is you following my will. Let us remove God from the equation, shall we?"

"As you like," she'd said in a humoring tone. "But if you ask me, it's God's will, that's all."

"My dear woman, you were never asked to begin with."

What could she know about God anyway? The personification of her God, Holmes figured, was surely the popular one: a wrinkled old man sitting omnisciently upon a throne of gold, reigning over creation from within puffy clouds, speaking both graciously and commandingly at the same instant. Her God, no doubt, wore a flowing beard. For Holmes, it was amusing to think that Mrs. Munro's Creator probably looked somewhat like himself—except her God existed as a figment of imagination, and he did not (at least not entirely, he reasoned).

However, sporadic references to a divine entity aside, Mrs. Munro proclaimed no open affiliation with a church or a religion, nor had she made any obvious effort toward insinuating God into her son's thoughts. The boy, it was clear, held very secular concerns, and, truth be known, Holmes found himself gladdened by the youngster's pragmatic character. So now on that windy night, there at his desk, he would jot several lines for Roger, a few sentences he wanted the boy to read sometime later.

Placing a clean sheet of paper before him and bringing his face to hover just above the desktop, he began writing:

> Not through the dogmas of archaic doctrines will you gain your greatest understandings, but, rather, through the continued evolution of science, and through your keen observations of the natural environment beyond your windows. To comprehend yourself truly, which is also to comprehend the world truly, you needn't look any farther than at what abounds with life around you—the blossoming meadow, the untrodden woodlands. Without this as mankind's overriding objective, I don't foresee an age of actual enlightenment ever arriving.

Holmes put his pen down. Twice, he considered what was written, speaking the words aloud, changing nothing. Afterward, he folded the paper into a perfect square, pondering an acceptable location in which to store the note for the time being—a place where it wouldn't be forgotten, a place where he could retrieve it with ease. The desk drawers were out of the question, as the note would soon become lost among his writings. Likewise, the disorganized, overstuffed file cabinets would be too risky, and so would the confounding enigmas that were his pockets (often small items went in without much thought—bits of paper, broken matches, a cigar, stems of grass, an interesting stone or shell found upon the beach, those unusual things gathered during his walks—only to vanish or appear later as if by magic). Someplace reliable instead, he decided. Someplace appropriate, memorable.

"Where then? Think . . . "

He surveyed the books stacked along one wall.

"No . . ."

Pivoting the chair, he glanced at the bookshelves beside the attic doorway, narrowing his gaze to a single shelf reserved solely for his own published editions.

"Perhaps . . ."

Moments later, he stood before those early volumes and various monographs of his, an index finger pushing a horizontal line across the dust-coated spines—*Upon Tattoo Marks, Upon the Tracing of Footsteps, Upon the Distinction Among the Ashes of 140 Tobacco Forms, A Study of the Influence of a Trade Upon the Form of the Hand, Malingering, The Typewriter and Its Relation to Crime, Secret Writings & Ciphers, Upon the Polyphonic Motets of Lassus, A Study of the Chaldean Roots in the Ancient Cornish Language, The Use of Dogs in the Work of the Detective*—until arriving at the first magnum opus of his latter years: *Practical Handbook of Bee Culture, with Some Observations Upon the Segregation of the Queen.* How immense the book felt when taken off the shelf, the hefty spine cradled by his palms.

Between chapter 4 ("Bee Pasturage") and chapter 5 ("Propolis"), Roger's note was stuck like a bookmark—because, Holmes had decided, the rare edition would be a fitting gift for the boy's next birthday. Of course, being one who seldom acknowledged such anniversaries, he needed to ask Mrs. Munro when the auspicious day was celebrated (had the occasion come already, or was it imminent?). Still, he envisioned the surprised look spreading on Roger's face as the book was presented, then the boy's fingers slowly turning the pages while reading alone in his cottage bedroom—where, eventu-

ally, the folded note would get discovered (a more prudent, less offi-
cious manner in which to deliver an important message).

Confident that the note now resided within an assured location,
Holmes placed the book on the shelf. When turning and going
toward the desk, he was relieved that his attention could again focus
on work. And once settled in his chair, he stared intently at the
handwritten pages covering the desktop, each filled with a multitude
of hastily conceived words, inked characters like a child's scrawl—
but just then the strands of his memory began unwinding, leaving
him unsure of what those pages might actually pertain to. Soon the
receding threads floated away, disappearing into the night like leaves
whisked from the gutters, and for a spell, he remained staring at the
pages, while not questioning or recalling or thinking anything.

Yet his hands kept busy even as his mind was at a loss. His fingers roamed about the desktop—sliding over the many pages before him, randomly underlining sentences—ultimately rummaging
through the stacks of papers without any apparent reason. It was as
if his fingers were operating of their own accord, searching for something that had recently been forgotten. Pages and pages were set
aside, one upon another—creating an entirely new stack near the
center of the desk—until, at last, his fingers lifted that unfinished
manuscript that was held together by a single rubber band: "The
Glass Armonicist." Initially, he gazed blankly at the manuscript, appearing indifferent to its rediscovery; nor did he discern in any way
that Roger had repeatedly studied the text, the boy sneaking into the
attic on occasion to check if the story had been elaborated or finished.

But it was the manuscript's title that finally eased Holmes from
his stupor, producing a curious, modest smile within his beard; for if
the words had not been written clearly at the top, appearing above
the first section, he might have put the manuscript into the new
stack, where the text would once more become obscured beneath
subsequent and unrelated jottings. Now his fingers removed the rubber band, letting it drop to the desktop. Thereafter, he reclined in

his chair, reading the incomplete story as if it had been written by someone else. Nevertheless, the recollection of Mrs. Keller suddenly persisted with a certain amount of clarity. He could behold her photograph. He could easily summon her upset husband sitting across from him at Baker Street. Even when pausing for a few seconds, glancing upward at the ceiling, he could still place himself back in time—venturing out from Baker Street with Mr. Keller, mixing amid the crowded din of London's thoroughfares as they made their way toward Portman's. He could, on that night, occupy the past better than the present, doing so as the wind murmured ceaselessly against the attic panes.

8

II.

A Disturbance at Montague Street

At precisely four o'clock, my client and I were positioned beside a lamppost, waiting across the street from Portman's, but Mrs. Keller had not yet arrived. As it happened, we were also loitering within sight of the shuttered rooms I had leased on Montague Street when I first came up to London in 1877. Clearly, there was no reason to share such personal information with my client, or to impart that—during my youthful tenure within that terrace development—Portman's shop was once a female boardinghouse of some dubious repute. Even so, the area itself had changed little since I lodged there, and consisted mostly of identical common-walled dwellings, the ground floors dressed in white stone, the upper three levels showing brick.

And yet standing there, my eyes travelling from those windows of the past to the present locale before me, I was touched by a degree of sentiment for what had escaped me over the years: the anonymity of my formative consulting detective practice, the liberty of coming and going without recognition or diversion. So while the street endured as it always had, I understood that my older incarnation differed somewhat from the man I had been when living there. Early on, disguises were previously donned only as a means for infiltration and observation, a way in which to blend effortlessly into various parts of the city while gaining information. Amongst the numerous roles I assumed, there was a common loafer, a rakish young plumber named Escott, a venerable Italian priest, a French *ouvrier,* even an old woman. However, towards my career's end, I had resorted to carrying upon me at all times a fake moustache and a pair of eyeglasses, doing so for the sole purpose of evading the widespread followers of John's accounts. No longer could I go about my business unidentified, nor could I sup in public without strangers accosting me midmeal, wishing to converse with me and shake my hand, asking intolerable questions regarding my calling. Therefore, it might seem an imprudent oversight—as I quickly realised while hurrying with Mr. Keller from Baker Street—that I was able to start forth on the case while forgetting to bring along my facade. For as we rushed to

Portman's, we found ourselves engaged by a workman of the amiable and simpleminded variety, to whom I would offer a few curt words.

"Sherlock Holmes?" said he, suddenly joining us as we made our way along Tottenham Court Road. "Sir, it is you, is it not? I have read all your stories, sir." My reply was given with the gesturing of a hand, which I waved briskly in the air, as if to cast him aside. But the fellow was not to be deterred; he set his senseless gape upon Mr. Keller, saying, "And I should think this is Dr. Watson."

Surprised by the workman, my client glanced at me with an uneasy expression.

"What an absurd notion," I said demurely. "If I am Sherlock Holmes, then pray explain how it is possible for this much younger gentleman to be the doctor?

"I don't know, sir. But you are Sherlock Holmes—I ain't easily flat, I can tell you that."

"Perhaps a touch glocky?"

"No, sir, I wouldn't say I am." Sounding a tad doubtful and confused, the workman paused in his tracks as we continued onwards. "Are you on a case?" he soon called after us.

Again I gestured my hand in the air, addressing him no more. This was how I usually dealt with the unwanted attention of strangers. Moreover, had the workman truly been accustomed to the narratives of John, he would have surely known that I never wasted words or disclosed my thoughts while a case was under consideration. Yet my client seemed dismayed by my abruptness, although he said nothing of it, and the two of us continued silently together on our journey to Montague Street. Then having taken up our position near Portman's, I began to ask something which had crossed my mind earlier while en route: "A final question regarding payment of—"

My remark was cut in on by Mr. Keller, who spoke with urgency as his thin white fingers gripped at his lapel.

"Mr. Holmes, it is true that I exist on a modest wage, but I will do whatever is necessary to reward you for your services."

"My dear boy, my profession is its own reward," I said, smiling. "Should I be put to any expenses—which I do not foresee in this matter—you are free to defray them at a time which best suits your modest wage. And now if you can contain yourself for a moment, I beg you to let me finish the question I was attempting to ask: How is it that your wife could pay for these clandestine lessons?"

"I cannot tell," he answered. "Nevertheless, she has her own means."

"You are referring to her inheritance."

"I am."

"Very good," I said, surveying the human traffic on the other side of the street—my view obstructed every so often by four-wheelers, hansoms, and, what was becoming a less singular apparition by those days, at least two clamorous transporters of the upper class: the automobile.

Believing my case to be almost complete, I waited expectantly for

Mrs. Keller's approach. When, after the passing of several minutes, she failed to materialise, I found myself wondering if she might not have entered Portman's ahead of schedule. Or perhaps she was, in reality, completely aware of her husband's suspicions and had decided against showing herself. As I was about to suggest the latter possibility, my client's gaze narrowed; nodding his head, he said lowly, "There she is," and with that his body was eager for pursuit.

"Steady," I said, bracing a hand upon his shoulder. "At the moment, we should maintain our distance."

And then I, too, glimpsed her as she walked idly toward Portman's, a slower form moving gradually amidst swifter currents. The bright yellow parasol floating above her was at odds with the woman beneath it; for Mrs. Keller, a diminutive wisp of a creature, was in the conventional costume of a grey day dress—the austere pigeon-breast look and the waist line dipping in front to accentuate the S curve of her corset shape. She wore white gloves, and one of those adorned hands cradled a rather small brown-covered book. Upon reaching the entrance of Portman's, she brought the parasol down and tugged it shut, tucking it then under an arm before venturing inside.

My client's shoulder resisted my grip, but I prevented his rushing ahead of me by asking, "Is your wife in the habit of applying perfume?"

"Yes, she is."

"Excellent," I said, releasing my hold and stepping past him into the street. "Let's see what all this is about, shall we?"

My senses are—as my friend John certainly noted—remarkably attuned perceivers, and I have long upheld the belief that the prompt outcome of a given case often relies on the immediate recognition of perfumes; therefore, criminal experts would be well advised to learn how to distinguish them. Regarding Mrs. Keller's scent of choice, it was that sophisticated blend of roses complemented by a hint of spice, the lingering of which was first detected in the entryway of Portman's shop.

"The fragrance is Cameo Rose, is it not?" I whispered after my client. But as he had already charged beyond me in haste, no reply was forthcoming.

Still, the farther we went, the stronger the odour became, until, pausing briefly to discern its course, I felt that Mrs. Keller was some-where very close to us. My eyes darted around the cramped, dusty establishment—rickety bookcases tilting unevenly from one end of the shop to the other, with volumes filling the shelves and, as well, stacked haphazardly along the dim aisles; yet she was nowhere to be seen, nor was the elderly proprietor, who I had imagined would be sitting behind the counter by the entryway, his face peering down at some obscure text. In fact, devoid of both staff and patrons, Portman's gave the eerie impression of having been vacated; no sooner had that thought crossed my mind than, as if to underscore the unusual aura of the place, I caught the faint sound of music coming from upstairs.

"It's Ann, Mr. Holmes. She's at it now; she's playing!"

I suppose truly to claim such ethereal abstraction as being music was inaccurate; for the delicate sounds which reached my ears lacked form, arrangement, or simple melody. However, the magnetism of the instrument had its effect: the varying tones converged into a single sustained harmony which was at once discordant and captivating; enough so that my client and I were drawn in its direction. With Mr. Keller leading the way, we passed between bookcases and reached a flight of stairs near the back.

But while climbing upwards towards the second story, I realized that the odour of Cameo Rose had not travelled beyond the ground floor. I glanced back, surveyed the shop below, again saw no one about, stooped for a better view, and, with no success, contrived to bring my stare over the tops of bookcases. This hesitation on my part prevented me from stopping the fervour of Mr. Keller's fist upon Madame Schirmer's door, a short-lived pounding which resonated along the corridor and silenced the instrument. Nonetheless, the case was, to a certain degree, finished by the time I joined him there. Without a doubt, I knew Mrs. Keller had gone elsewhere, and whoever was practising on the armonica would prove to be someone other than she. Ah, that I should reveal so much when attempting my own narrative. I cannot hide the truth as John could, nor do I possess his talent of withholding the relevant points in order to fashion a superficially significant conclusion, alas.

"Calm yourself, man," said I, admonishing my companion. "By no means should you display yourself so."

Mr. Keller frowned gravely and held his gaze at the door. "You must forgive me," said he.

"There is nothing to forgive. But as your furore may impede our progress, I shall speak on your behalf from here on."

The silence which ensued in the wake of my client's angry knocking was then vanquished by the quick, equally pounding steps of Madame Schirmer. The door was thrown open and she appeared then with inflamed features and ruffled demeanour, as brawny a woman as I have ever encountered. Before she could utter a heated word, I stepped forwards and handed her my calling card, saying, "Good afternoon, Madame Schirmer. Could you be so gracious as to grant us a little of your time?"

Considering me momentarily with a questioning glance, she proceeded to shoot her formidable stare to my companion.

"I promise we shan't keep you but a few minutes," I continued, tapping my finger against the card she was holding. "Perhaps you are familiar with me."

Disregarding my presence altogether, Madame Schirmer spoke harshly: "Herr Keller, don't come here like this again! I won't have this interruption! Why must you come and create these problems for me? And for you, sir," she added, fixing her stare upon me, "the same goes, too. That's right! You are his friend, no? So you go away with him and never come back to me like this! I have no more patience for these people like you!"

"My dear woman, please," said I, extracting the card from her hand and lifting it in front of her face.

To my surprise, the sight of my name provoked an adamant shaking of her head. "No, no, you are not this person," said she.

"I assure you, Madame Schirmer, that I am none other than he."

"No, no, you are not him. No, I have seen this person often, you know."

"And pray tell me when the acquaintance was made?"

"In the magazine, of course! This detective is much taller, right? With the black hair, and the nose, and the pipe. You see, it was never you."

"Ah, the magazine! It is a somewhat intriguing misrepresentation. On that we can agree. I fear I do my caricature an injustice. If only the majority of people I meet could perceive me as wrongly as you do, Madame Schirmer, then my liberty might be less hampered."

"You are ridiculous!" With that, she crushed the card and threw it at my feet. "So you go from me now, or the constables are coming for you!"

"I cannot leave here," said Mr. Keller firmly, "until I see Ann with my very own eyes."

Our inconvenienced antagonist suddenly stomped on the floor, doing so repeatedly, until the noise of it reverberated beneath us.

"Herr Portman," she cried out afterwards, her emphatic voice echoing past us into the corridor, "there is trouble with me now! Go for the constables! There are two burglars at the door! Herr Portman—"

"Madame Schirmer, it is of no use," said I. "It seems Mr. Portman has gone out for a while." Then I turned to my client, who looked deeply chagrined. "You should also be aware, Mr. Keller, that Madame Schirmer is completely within her rights and that we have no legal status to go within her flat. However, she must understand that your action is governed solely by concern for your wife. I venture to hope that if we were allowed to have just two minutes inside with Madame Schirmer, we could certainly put this issue to rest."

"The wife is not here with me," said the displeased woman. "Herr Keller, I have told you this enough. Why do you come here and give me your problems? I can ring up the police on you, you know!"

"There is no reason for that," I said. "I am fully conscious of the fact that Mr. Keller has accused you unjustly, Madame Schirmer. But any interference by the police would only complicate what is, in truth, a rather sad affair." I leaned forwards and whispered several words into her ear. "You see," I then said when moving back from her, "your assistance would be most valuable."

"How could I know this?" she gasped, her expression transforming from annoyance to regret.

"Indeed," I answered sympathetically. "My trade, I am sorry to say, is sometimes a woeful business."

As my client's face focused on me with confusion, Madame

Schirmer stood in thought for a moment, her massive arms akimbo. Then she nodded and stepped aside, gesturing for us to enter: "Herr Keller, I think it is not your fault. Come inside, if you wish to see for yourself, poor man."

We were shown into a bright, sparsely decorated drawing room, with a low ceiling and half-opened windows. An upright piano was in one corner, a harpsichord and a good many percussion instruments in another, and, put side by side, two impressively refurbished armonicas sat nearest the windows. These instruments, with a number of small wickerwork chairs placed at or around them, were the only objects in what was an otherwise-barren room. Save for a square of Wilton in the centre, the discoloured brownish slats of the floor remained exposed; the white-painted walls were also unadorned, allowing for the sound waves to reflect in such a way as to produce a distinct echoing timbre.

It was not, however, the contrivances of the drawing room which immediately caught my attention, nor was it the scent of spring flowers wafting through the open windows; rather, it was the fidgeting, slight form sitting before an armonica: a boy of no older than ten, with red hair and freckled cheeks, turning nervously in his seat to view us as we came into the room. Seeing the child, my client stopped in his steps; his eyes then darted about while Madame Schirmer watched from the entryway, her arms folded at her waist. I, on the other hand, proceeded towards the boy, addressing him with the warmest of intonations: "Hello there."

"Hello," said the child shyly.

Glancing back at my client, I smiled and said, "I take it that this young man is not your wife."

"You know he isn't" was my client's bristling reply. "But I cannot understand it. Where is Ann?"

"Patience, Mr. Keller, patience."

I drew up one of the chairs to the armonica and sat beside the boy, while my eyes travelled round and over the instrument, taking in every detail of its design.

"Pray what is your name, child?"

"Graham."

"Now then, Graham," said I, noting that the old glasses were thinner in the treble and thus were easier to make sing, "is Madame Schirmer teaching you well?"

"I believe so, sir."

"Hum," said I thoughtfully, lightly running a fingertip across the brims of the glasses.

The opportunity to inspect an armonica—especially a model in such pristine condition—had never before presented itself. What I had known previously was that the instrument was played upon when sitting directly in front of the set of glasses, spinning them by means of a foot treadle, and wetting them on occasion with a moistened sponge. I was also aware that both hands were required, allowing different parts to be performed simultaneously. However, while actually looking closely at the armonica, I observed that the glasses were blown into the shape of hemispheres, with each having an open socket in the centre. The largest and highest pitched of the glasses was G. To distinguish the glasses, each—save the semitones, which were white—was painted inside with one of the seven prismatic colours: C, red; D, orange; E, yellow; F, green; G, blue; A, indigo; B, purple; and C, red again. The thirty or so glasses varied in size from about nine inches in diameter to no more than three inches; fixed upon a spindle, they sat within a three-foot-long case, which—tapered in its length to adapt to the conical shape of the glasses and fastened to a frame with four legs—lifted on hinges from the middle of its height. The spindle was cast of hard iron, and, made to turn on brass gudgeons on either end, it crossed the case horizontally. On the widest side of the case was a square shank, upon which a mahogany wheel was fixed. It was the wheel which served as a fly to make the motion steady, doing so when the spindle and the glasses were rotated by the action of the foot. With a strip of lead concealed near its circumference, the wheel appeared to be some eighteen inches in diameter, and, approximately four inches from the axis, an ivory pin was fixed to its face; around the neck of the pin was placed a loop of string, which travelled up from the moveable treadle to provide its motion.

"It is a remarkable contraption," said I. "Am I to understand that the tones are best drawn out when the glasses turn from the ends of the fingers, not when they turn to them?"

"Yes, it is so," Madame Schirmer replied from behind us.

Already the sun was angling for the horizon, its light reflecting off the glasses. Graham's wide-eyed stare had slowly become a squint, and the sound of my client's restless sighs took advantage of the room's acoustics. Carried from outside, the bouquet of daffodils tingled in my nostrils, an onionlike smell, hinting of mould; I am not alone in my dislike of the flower's subtle qualities, as deer, too, are repelled by it. Then giving the glasses a final touch, I said, "If circumstances were different, I should ask you to play for me, Madame Schirmer."

"Of course, this we can always arrange, sir. I am available for the private performance; that is what I do sometimes, you know."

"Naturally," said I, rising from the seat. Gently patting the boy's shoulder, I continued: "I believe we have monopolised enough of your lesson, Graham, so we shall now leave you and your teacher in peace."

"Mr. Holmes!" my client ejaculated in protest.

"Really, Mr. Keller, there is nothing else for us to learn here, aside from what Madame Schirmer offers at a price."

And with that, I pivoted upon my heels and set across the drawing room, where I was followed by the woman's dumbfounded stare. Mr. Keller rushed to join me in the hallway, and as we exited the flat, I called back to her while shutting the door: "Thank you, Madame Schirmer. We won't bother you again, although I suspect you might be engaged by me at a later date for a lesson or two. Good-bye."

But once we had started down the corridor, the door was flung open and her voice chased after me: "Is this true, then? Are you him in the magazine?"

"No, my dear lady, I am not him."

"Ha!" said she, and the door slammed shut.

It wasn't until my client and I had reached the bottom of the stairs that I paused to calm him; for his face had become flushed and darkened from encountering the boy instead of his wife. His brows were drawn into two crooked, thick lines, while his eyes shone out beneath them with an almost irrational pall. His nostrils, too, flexed with the deepest of vexations, and his mind was so absolutely confounded by the whereabouts of his wife that the whole of his expression conveyed a significant question mark.

"Mr. Keller, I assure you that all is not as grave as you imagine it to be. In fact, while granting some deliberate omissions on her part, your wife has been mostly honest in her account to you."

The grimness of his expression lessened somewhat. "You have evidently seen more upstairs than was visible to me," said he.

"Perhaps, but I wager that you saw exactly what I did. However, I may have discerned a little more. Even so, you must allow me one week to bring the matter to a satisfactory conclusion."

"I am in your hands."

"Very good. I ask now that you promptly return to Fortis Grove, and when your wife arrives, you should mention nothing of what has occurred here today. It is very essential, Mr. Keller, that you should adhere to my advice in every respect."

"Yes, sir. I shall endeavour to do so."

"Excellent."

"I wish to know something first, Mr. Holmes. What was it you spoke in Madame Schirmer's ear which gained us entrance into her flat?"

"Oh, that," I remarked, with a flick of the hand. "It is a simple but effective untruth, one I have used previously in similar instances; I told her that you were a dying man, and I said your wife had abandoned you in your time of need. The very fact that it was whispered should have revealed it as a lie—yet it rarely fails as a skeleton key of sorts."

Mr. Keller stared at me with a look of slight distaste.

"Tut, man," said I, and turned from him.

Then going to the front of the shop, we at last happened upon the elderly proprietor, a little wrinkled fellow, who had resumed his place behind the counter. Sitting there in a soil-stained gardening smock, hunched over the text of a book, the man clutched a magnifying glass in a trembling hand and was using it to read. Near him were brown gloves, which he had apparently just shuffled off, laying them on the counter. Twice, the man rattled out a cough of the harshest kind, startling us both. But I lifted a finger to my lips so that my companion would remain silent. Still, as Mr. Keller had mentioned earlier, the man seemed oblivious to anyone being in the shop, even as I came within two feet of him, peering down at the large book which held his attention: a volume on the art of topiary. The pages I could see were illustrated with carefully rendered drawings of shrubs and trees trimmed into the shapes of an elephant, a cannon, a monkey, and what appeared to be a canopic jar.

We soon made our way outside as quietly as possible, and in the waning sunshine of late afternoon, I requested one last thing of my client before departing. "Mr. Keller, you have something which may prove useful to me for the time being."

"You have but to name it."

"Your wife's photograph."

My client nodded reluctantly.

"Certainly, if you need it."

He reached inside his coat and retrieved the photograph, offering it to me while appearing wary to do so.

Without hesitation I slipped the photograph into my pocket, saying, "I thank you, Mr. Keller. Then there is no more to be done today. I wish you a very pleasant evening."

And that was how I left him. With his wife's image upon me, I wasted not a moment in taking my retreat. Along the road moved buses and traps, hansoms and four-wheelers, bearing the figures of those riding home or elsewhere, while I weaved around fellow pedestrians on the paved walk, strolling in a deliberate pace towards Baker Street. A few country carts rolled past, displaying what remained of the vegetables which had been carried into the metropolis at dawn. Shortly, I knew well enough, the thoroughfares surrounding Montague Street would become as hushed and inanimate as any village after nightfall; and I, by then, would be leaning back in my chair, watching as the blue smoke from my cigarette floated to the ceiling.

9

B Y S U N R I S E , the note for Roger had escaped Holmes's consciousness altogether; it would stay inside the book until, several weeks later, he retrieved the volume for research purposes and found the folded sheet flattened between the chapters (a curious message in his own hand, yet one he couldn't fathom having written). There were other folded sheets as well, all hidden throughout his many attic books and ultimately lost—urgent missives never sent, odd reminders, lists of names and addresses, the occasional poem. He wouldn't recall concealing a personal letter from Queen Victoria, or a playbill kept since his brief engagement with the Sasanoff Shakespearean Company (playing Horatio in an 1879 London stage production of *Hamlet*). Nor would he remember putting away for safekeeping a crude but detailed drawing of a queen bee among the pages of M. Quinby's *Mysteries of Beekeeping Explained*—the picture having been done by Roger when the boy was twelve, and slipped beneath the attic door two summers ago.

Regardless, Holmes wasn't unaware of his memory's increasing fallibility. He believed he was capable of incorrectly revising past events, especially if the reality of those events were beyond his grasp. But, he wondered, what was revised and what was true? And what was known for certain anymore? More importantly, what exactly had been forgotten? He couldn't say.

Even so, he adhered to the consistent tangibles—his land, his home, his gardens, his apiary, his work. He enjoyed his cigars, his books, a glass of brandy sometimes. He favored the evening breezes, and the hours after midnight. Without a doubt, he knew that Mrs. Munro's chatty presence often annoyed him, yet her soft-spoken son had always been a dear, welcomed companion; but here, too, his mental revisions had changed what was, in fact, the truth: For he hadn't taken kindly to the boy upon first sight—that shy, awkward youngster peeking sullenly at him from behind his mother. In the past, he had made it an unwavering rule never to hire a housekeeper with children, except that Mrs. Munro, recently widowed and in need of steady employment, had come highly recommended. Moreover, finding reliable help had become quite difficult—particularly when being isolated in the country—so, he had told her plainly that she could stay as long as the boy's activities were restricted to the guest cottage, as long as his work wasn't disrupted by whatever ruckus her child might produce.

"No worries there, sir, I promise. My Roger won't cause you trouble. I'll see to that."

"It is understood, correct? I may be retired—however, I am still a very busy man. Needless distractions of any sort are simply not tolerated."

"Yes, sir, I understand that well enough. Don't concern yourself a bit over the boy."

"I won't, my dear, although I suspect you should."

"Yes, sir."

Then almost a year passed before Holmes saw Roger again. One afternoon while strolling about the west corner of his property, near the guest cottage where Mrs. Munro dwelled, he glimpsed the boy at a distance, watching as Roger entered the cottage with a butterfly net in hand. Thereafter, he spotted the solitary boy more frequently—traversing the meadows, doing schoolwork in the gardens, studying the scree upon the beach. But it wasn't until encountering Roger in the beeyard—finding the boy facing the hives, one hand holding the wrist of the other, inspecting a single sting at the center of his left palm—that Holmes at last dealt with him directly. Seizing the boy's stung hand, he used a fingernail to brush the stinger off, explaining, "It was wise you resisted grasping the stinger; otherwise, you would have surely emptied the entire poison sac into your wound—so use your fingernail, brush it away like this, and don't compress the sac, understand? You were saved just in time— see, here, it has hardly begun swelling. I have had much worse, I assure you."

"It doesn't hurt too bad," said Roger, looking at Holmes with his eyes screwed up, as if the sun shone brightly on his face.

"It will soon—but only a little, I expect. Should it get worse, try soaking your hand in salt water or onion juice—that usually cures the smart."

"Oh."

And while Holmes expected tears from the boy (or, at the very least, some embarrassment at having been caught in the beeyard), he was impressed by how quickly Roger's attention then went from his wound to the hives—transfixed, it seemed, with apiary life, the light clustering of bees roaming before or after flight near the hive entrances. Had the boy cried once, had he shown even the slightest lack of courage, Holmes would never have urged him forward, leading him to a hive and lifting the top so Roger could see the world within (the honey chamber with its white wax cells, the larger cells that housed the drone brood, the darker cells below where the worker brood lived); he would never have given the child a second thought, or considered the boy to be of a like mind. (It is often the case, he had thought, that exceptional children usually come from mundane

parents.) Nor would he have invited Roger to return the next afternoon, allowing the boy to witness firsthand the March chores: checking the hive's weekly weight, combining colonies when a queen
ceased functioning in one, making sure enough food was available to
the brood nests.

Subsequently, as the boy went from curious spectator to valued
helper, Roger was given the clothing Holmes no longer wore—
light-colored gloves and a veiled beekeeper's hat—which were then
dispensed with once he grew comfortable handling the bees. Soon it
became an effortless, innate association. After school, on most afternoons, the boy joined Holmes in the beeyard. During the summer,
Roger awoke early and was busy at the hives when Holmes arrived
there. While they tended the hives—or sometimes sat quietly in the
pasture—Mrs. Munro brought them sandwiches, tea, perhaps something sweet she had created that morning.

On the hottest of days—following whatever work was done,
when the refreshing waters of the tide pools beckoned—they hiked
the winding cliff trail, where Roger walked beside Holmes, picking
rocks off the steep path, peering repeatedly at the ocean below,
stooping every so often to study something found along the way
(broken bits of seashells, or a diligent beetle, or a fossil embedded
within the cliff wall). A warm salty smell increased with their descent, as did Holmes's delight at the boy's inquisitiveness. It was one
thing to take notice of an object, but an intelligent child, like Roger,
had to inspect and touch carefully those things that drew his attention. Holmes was positive there was nothing too remarkable on the
path, yet he was inclined to pause with Roger, contemplating all that
enticed the boy.

When first traveling the trail together, Roger gazed up at the expansive rugged folds towering above and asked, "Is this cliff only
chalk?"

"It is made of chalk, and it is made of sandstone."

Within the strata beneath the chalk was gault clay, greensand, and Wealden sands in successive order, explained Holmes as they continued downward; the clay beds and the thin layer of sandstones were covered with chalk, clay, and flint added throughout the aeons by countless storms.

"Oh," said Roger, absently veering toward the path's rim.

Dropping a cane, Holmes pulled him back. "Careful, my boy. You must mind your step. Here, take my arm."

The trail itself was barely wide enough for a full-grown adult, let alone an elderly man and a boy walking side by side. The path was about three feet across, and in places erosion had narrowed its width considerably; the pair, however, managed together without much trouble—Roger keeping mostly near the sheer edge, Holmes moving inches from the cliff wall as the boy gripped his arm. After a while, the path broadened in a spot, providing an overlook and a bench. Although it had been Holmes's intention to continue to the bottom (for the bathing pool could only be reached during daylight; otherwise, the evening tide swallowed the entire shore), the bench suddenly felt a more convenient location in which to rest and converse. Sitting there with Roger, Holmes dug a Jamaican from his pocket but soon realized he had no matches; instead, he chewed on the cigar, savoring the sea air, eventually following the boy's stare to where seagulls circled and swooped and cried out.

"I've heard the nightjars, have you? I heard them last night," Roger said, his memory stirred by the seagulls' squalling.

"Did you? How fortunate."

"People call them goatsuckers, except I don't believe they feed on goats."

"Insects, for the most part. They catch their prey on their wings, you know."

"Oh."

"We have owls, as well."

Roger's expression brightened. "I've never seen one. I'd like one for a pet, but my mother doesn't think birds are good pets. I think they'd be nice to have around the house, though."

"Well then, perhaps we can catch you an owl some night. We have plenty on the property, so one won't be missed, surely."

"Yes, I'd like that."

"Of course, we had best keep your owl in a place where your mother won't find it. My study is a possibility."

"Wouldn't she look there?"

"No, she wouldn't dare. But if she did, I would tell her it belonged to me."

A mischievous grin formed on the boy's face: "She'd believe you, too. I know she would."

Letting on that he wasn't being serious about the owl, Holmes gave Roger a wink. All the same, he appreciated the boy's confidence—the sharing of a secret, the covert alliances inherent to a friendship—and this pleased Holmes so much that he found himself offering what he'd ultimately forgotten to say: "In any case, Roger, I will speak with your mother. I suspect she will allow you a parakeet." Then to further their camaraderie, he promised that they would start earlier the next afternoon and reach the tide pools well before dusk approached.

"Should I fetch you?" asked Roger.

"Indeed. You will find me at the hives."

"When, sir?"

"Three is early enough, don't you imagine? That should allow ample time for the hike and a bathe and the stroll back up. I fear we started off too late today to complete the journey."

Already the waning sunlight and the burgeoning ocean breeze enveloped them. Holmes inhaled deeply, squinting his eyes against the setting sun. With his sight blurred, the ocean beyond appeared like a blackened expanse fringed with a massive fiery eruption. We should begin heading up the cliff, he thought. But Roger seemed to be in no hurry. Neither was Holmes, who glanced sideways at the boy and beheld that intent young face tilted toward the sky, those clear blue eyes fixed on a seagull circling high overhead. A little while longer, Holmes told himself, smiling as he observed Roger's lips parting in strange fascination, the boy somehow undaunted by the sun's brilliant glare or the wind's persistent rush.

10

MANY MONTHS afterward, Holmes would find himself alone within Roger's cramped bedroom (the first and last time he ever set foot among the boy's few possessions). On an overcast, gray morning—with no other soul present at the guest cottage—he unlocked Mrs. Munro's gloomy living quarters, going inside to where the impermeable drapes remained drawn, and the lights were kept off, and the woodsy barklike smell of mothballs obscured whatever else he inhaled. Every three or four steps, he paused, peering ahead into the darkness, and readjusted his grip on the canes, as if anticipating some vague, unimaginable form to emerge out of the shadows. Then he continued forward—the taps of his canes falling less heavily and wearily than his footsteps—until making his way past Roger's open doorway, entering the only cottage room that wasn't sealed wholly from daylight.

It was, in fact, a very tidy room, far from what Holmes had expected to discover—the careless, random droppings of a boy's vibrant life, that clutter. A housekeeper's son, he concluded, was surely more inclined than most children to maintain an ordered space—unless, of course, his bedroom was also tended by the housekeeper. Still, as the boy was rather fastidious by nature, Holmes felt positive it was

Roger who had organized his things so dutifully. Furthermore, the pervasive mothball smell hadn't yet filtered into the bedroom, suggesting the absence of Mrs. Munro's bearing; instead, a musty but not unpleasant, somewhat earthy aroma was evident. Like dirt during a good rain, he thought. Like fresh soil on the hands.

For a while, he sat at the edge of the boy's neatly made bed, taking in the general surroundings—the walls painted baby blue, the windows covered by transparent lace curtains, the various oak furnishings (nightstand, single bookcase, chest of drawers). Peering through the window directly above a student's writing desk, he noticed the crisscrossing of slender branches just outside, which appeared somewhat ethereal behind the gauze of lace, scraping almost noiselessly against the panes. And then his attention turned toward the personal, those things Roger had left there: six textbooks stacked on the writing desk, a sagging schoolbag hung from the closet doorknob, the butterfly net propped upright in a corner. Eventually, he stood, wandering slowly about, moving from wall to wall like one respectfully surveying a museum exhibit, then stopping briefly to take closer looks, resisting the urge to touch certain belongings.

But what he observed didn't surprise him, or offer any new insights into the boy. There were books about bird-watching and bees and warfare, several tattered science-fiction paperbacks, a good many *National Geographic* magazines (spanning two shelves, arranged chronologically), and there were rocks and seashells found at the beach, assorted by size and likeness, lined up in equal-numbered rows on the chest of drawers. Aside from the six textbooks, the writing desk displayed five sharpened pencils, drawing pens, blank paper, and the vial containing the Japanese honeybees. Everything had been ordered, given a proper place, aligned; so, too, were the objects occupying the nightstand—scissors, a bottle of rubber cement, a large scrapbook with an unadorned black cover.

Nevertheless, the most revealing items, it seemed, had ended up either taped or hung on the walls: Roger's colorful drawings—

nondescript soldiers firing brown rifles at one another, green tanks exploding, violent red scribbles bursting like explosions from chests or the foreheads of cross-eyed faces, yellow antiaircraft fire streaming upward toward a blue-black bomber fleet, massacred stick figures strewn about a bloodied battlefield as an orange sun rose or set on the pink horizon); three framed photographs, sepia-toned portraits (a smiling Mrs. Munro holding her infant son while the young father stood proudly beside her, the boy posing with his uniformed father on a train platform, toddler Roger running into his father's out-stretched arms (each photograph—one near the bed, one near the writing desk, one near the bookcase—showed a stocky, strong-looking man, a square, ruddy face, sandy hair combed straight back, the benevolent eyes of someone who was now gone and someone who was terribly missed).

Yet, of all the things there, it was the scrapbook that, in the end, held Holmes's attention the longest. Returning to the boy's bed, he sat and stared at the nightstand, considering the scrapbook's black cover, the scissors, the rubber cement. No, he told himself, he wouldn't pry into the pages. He wouldn't snoop any more than he already had. Best not, he warned himself, reaching for the scrapbook—and with that, he left his better thoughts unheeded.

Thereafter, he leisurely perused the pages, his gaze lingering for a while on a series of intricate collages (photographs and words clipped from assorted magazines, then glued together shrewdly). The first third of the scrapbook betrayed the boy's interest in nature, in wildlife and foliage. Upright grizzly bears roamed forests near spotted leopards that lounged within African trees; cartoon hermit crabs hid with snarling pumas amid a cluster of Van Gogh sunflow-ers; an owl and a fox and a mackerel lurked beneath an aggregate of fallen leaves. What soon followed, however, was increasingly less sce-nic, although similar in design: The wildlife became British and American soldiers, the forests became the bombed-out ruins of cities, and the leaves became either corpses or single words—DEFEATED, FORCES, RETREAT—scattered across the pages.

Nature complete in and of itself, man forever at odds with man— the yin-yang of the boy's worldview, Holmes believed. For he assumed the initial collages—those at the front of the scrapbook—had been done years earlier, while Roger's father was still alive (the curled, yellowed edges of the cut images suggested this, as did the lack of odor from the rubber cement). The rest, he decided after sniffing at the pages, examining the seams of three or four collages, had been fashioned little by little over the recent months, and appeared more complicated, artful, and methodical in their layout.

Even so, the final piece of Roger's handiwork was unfinished; in actuality, with only one image centered on the page, it appeared to have been just begun. Or, Holmes wondered, had the boy intended it to be seen as such—a desolate monochromatic photograph floating in a void of blackness; a stark, puzzling, yet emblematic conclusion to all that had preceded it (the vivid overlapping imagery, the fauna and wilderness, those grim, determined men of war). The photograph itself was no mystery; Holmes knew the place well enough, had glimpsed it with Mr. Umezaki in Hiroshima—that former prefectural government building reduced to skeletal remains by the atomic blast ("the Atom Bomb Dome," Mr. Umezaki had called it).

But alone on the page, the building resonated utter annihilation, much more so than when seen in person. The photograph had been taken weeks, possibly days, after the bomb was dropped, revealing an immense city of rubble—no humans, no tramcars or trains, nothing recognizable save the ghostly shell of the prefectural building existing above the flattened, burned landscape. Then what preceded the final piece—unused scrapbook paper, page after page of black—simply underscored the disquieting impact of that sole image. And suddenly, when closing the scrapbook, Holmes was overcome by the weariness he had carried into the cottage. Something has gone amiss with the world, he found himself thinking. *Something has changed in the marrow, and I'm at a loss to make sense of it.*

"So what is the truth?" Mr. Umezaki had once asked him. "How do you arrive at it? How do you unravel the meaning of something that doesn't wish to be known?"

"I don't know," Holmes uttered aloud, there in Roger's bedroom. "I don't know," he said again, lowering himself to the boy's pillow and shutting his eyes, the scrapbook held against his chest: "I haven't a clue. . . ."

Holmes drifted away after that, though not into the sort of sleep that came from total exhaustion, or even a restless slumber in which dreams and reality were interlaced, but rather a torpid state submerging him into a vast stillness. Presently, that expansive, downreaching sleep delivered him elsewhere, tugging him from the bedroom where his body rested.

11

HAVING CARRIED the shared suitcase Holmes and Mr. Umezaki would be taking aboard the morning train (the two men having packed lightly for their sight-seeing journey), Hensuiro saw them off at the railroad station, where, tightly clasping Mr. Umezaki's hands, he whispered fervently in his companion's ear. Then before they entered the coach, he stepped in front of Holmes, bowing deeply, and said, "I see you—again—very again, yes."

"Yes," Holmes said, amused. "Very, very again."

And when the train departed the station, Hensuiro remained on the platform, his arms raised and waving amid a crowd of Australian soldiers, his swiftly receding but stationary figure eventually diminishing altogether. Soon the train gathered its westward momentum, and both Holmes and Mr. Umezaki sat rigidly in their adjacent second-class seats, watching with sidewise stares as Kobe's buildings gradually gave way to the lush terrain that moved and shifted and flashed beyond the window.

"It's a lovely morning," Mr. Umezaki remarked, a comment he would repeat several times throughout their first day of travel (the lovely morning becoming a lovely afternoon and, finally, a lovely evening).

"Quite," was Holmes's consistent reply.

Yet during the start of the trip, the men spoke hardly a word to each other. They sat quietly, self-contained and remote in their respective seats. For a while, Mr. Umezaki occupied himself by writing inside a small red journal (further haiku, Holmes figured), while Holmes, fuming Jamaican in hand, contemplated the blurs of scenery outside. It was only after departing the station at Akashi— when the jarring start of the train's movement shook the cigar from Holmes's fingers, sending it rolling across the floor—that real conversation ensued (initiated by Mr. Umezaki's general curiosity, and ultimately encompassing a number of subjects preceding their arrival at Hiroshima).

"Allow me," said Mr. Umezaki, rising to fetch the cigar for Holmes.

"Thank you," said Holmes, who then, having already lifted himself some, eased back down, placing the canes lengthwise over his lap (but at an angle so as to avoid bumping Mr. Umezaki's knees).

Once settled again in their seats, with the countryside sweeping past, Mr. Umezaki touched the stained wood of one cane. "They're finely crafted, are they not?"

"Oh, yes," said Holmes. "I have had them at least twenty years, quite possibly longer. They are my durable companions, you know."

"Have you always walked with both?"

"Not until recently—recently for me, that is—actually, about the last five years, if memory serves."

Then Holmes, feeling the desire to elaborate, explained: In fact, he really required only the support of the right cane while walking; the left cane, however, had an invaluable dual purpose—to give him support should he lose hold of the right cane and find himself stooping to retrieve it, or to stand in as a quick replacement should the right cane ever become irretrievable. Of course, he went on, lacking the sustained nourishment of royal jelly, the canes would serve him no useful function whatsoever, as he was convinced he'd surely be confined to a wheelchair.

"Is that so?"

"Unquestionably."

With that, their mutual exchange began in earnest, for both were eager to discuss the benefits of royal jelly, especially its effects in halting or controlling the aging process. Mr. Umezaki had, as it turned out, interviewed a Chinese herbalist before the war regarding the beneficial qualities of that viscous milky white secretion: "The man was clearly of the opinion that royal jelly could cure menopause and male climacteric, as well as liver disease, rheumatoid arthritis, and anemia."

"Phlebitis, gastric ulcer, various degenerative conditions," Holmes interjected, "and general mental or physical weakness. It also nourishes the skin, erases facial blemishes, wrinkles, while also preventing the signs of normal aging or even premature senility." How amazing it was, Holmes mentioned, that such a powerful substance, the chemistry of which was still not completely known, could be produced by the pharyngeal glands of the worker bee—creating queens from ordinary bee larvae, healing a multitude of mankind's ills.

"Though try as I may," said Mr. Umezaki, "I've found little or no evidence to support the claims of its therapeutic usefulness."

"Ah, but there is," replied Holmes, smiling. "We have studied royal jelly a long, long while, haven't we? We know it is full of protein and lipids, fatty acids and carbohydrates. That said, neither of us has come close to discovering all it contains, so I rely on the only evidence I truly possess, which is my own good health. But I take it you are not a regular user."

"No. Aside from writing one or two magazine articles, my interest is purely casual. I'm afraid, however, that I lean toward the skeptic's side on the matter."

"What a shame," said Holmes. "I was quite hoping you might spare a jar for my journey back to England—I have gone awhile without, you know. Nothing that can't be remedied upon my arrival home, although I do wish I had remembered to pack a jar or two— at least enough for a daily dose. Fortunately, I have brought more than enough Jamaicans, so I am not completely lacking in what I require."

"We might still find you a jar along our way."

"Such bother, don't you think?"

"It's hardly a bother."

"That is quite all right, really. Let us just consider it the price I must pay for forgetting. It seems even royal jelly cannot prevent the inevitable loss of retention."

And here, too, was another springboard in their conversation, because now Mr. Umezaki, scooting closer to Holmes, speaking lowly, as if his question was of the utmost importance, could ask him about his renowned faculties; more specifically, he wanted to know how Holmes had mastered the ability to perceive so easily what others often missed. "I'm aware of your belief in pure observation as a tool for achieving definitive answers—except I'm puzzled by the way in which you actually observe a given situation. From what I've read, as well as experienced firsthand, it appears that you don't merely observe, but you also use recall effortlessly, almost photographically— and somehow this is how you arrive at the truth."

" 'What is truth? asked Pilate,' " Holmes said, sighing. "Frankly, my friend, I've lost my appetite for any notion of truth. For me, there simply is what is—call that truth, if you must. Better put—and I am understanding this with a fair amount of hindsight, mind you— I am drawn toward that which is clearly seen, gathering as much as I can from the external, and then synthesizing whatever is gathered into something of immediate value. The universal, mystical, or long-term implications—those places where truth, perhaps, resides—are of no interest."

Yet what of recall? Mr. Umezaki wondered. How was it used?

"In terms of forming a theory, or reaching a conclusion?"

"Yes, exactly."

As a younger man, Holmes would then tell him, visual recall was fundamental to his capacity for solving certain problems. For when he examined an object or investigated a crime scene, everything was instantaneously converted into precise words or numbers corresponding with the things he observed. Once the conversions formed a pattern in his mind (a series of particularly vivid sentences or equations that he could both utter and visualize), they locked themselves into his memory, and while they might stay dormant during those times when he was caught up with other considerations, they would immediately emerge whenever he turned his attention to the situations that had generated them.

"Over time, I have realized my mind no longer operates in such a fluid manner," Holmes continued. "The change has been by degrees, but I sense it fully now. My means for recall—those various groupings of words and numbers—aren't as easily accessible as they were. Traveling through India, for example, I stepped from the train somewhere in the middle of the country—a brief stop, a place I had never seen before—and was promptly accosted by a dancing, half-naked beggar, a most joyous fellow. Previously, I would have observed everything around me in perfect detail—the architecture of the station building, the faces of people walking by, the vendors who were selling their goods—but that rarely happens anymore. I don't remember the station building and I cannot tell you if there were vendors or people nearby. All I recall is a toothless brown-skinned beggar dancing before me, an arm outstretched for a few pence. What matters to me now is that I possess that delightful vision of him; where the event took place is of no account. Had this occurred sixty years ago, I would have been quite distraught for being unable to summon the location and its minutiae. But now I retain only what is necessary. The minor details aren't essential—what appears in my mind these days are rudimentary impressions, not all the frivolous surroundings. And for that I'm grateful."

For a moment, Mr. Umezaki said nothing, his face taking on the distracted, thoughtful look of someone processing information. Then he nodded and his expression softened. When he spoke again, his voice sounded almost tentative. "It's fascinating—how you describe it."

But Holmes was no longer listening. Down the aisle, the passenger car door had opened and a slender young woman with sunglasses on had entered the carriage. She wore a gray kimono and held an umbrella at her side. She headed waveringly in their direction, pausing every few steps as if to steady herself; then, still standing in the aisle, she gazed at a nearby window, drawn for a while by the fast-moving landscape—her profile suddenly displaying a broad, disfiguring keloid scar, which slithered like tentacles from underneath her collar (up her neck, over her jawline, across the right side of her face, vanishing into her immaculate black hair). When at last she came forward, passing them without notice, Holmes found himself thinking, You were once an enticing girl. Not so long ago, you were the most beautiful vision someone had ever seen.

12

THEY ARRIVED at Hiroshima Station in the early afternoon, and found themselves departing the train and entering a crowded, boisterous area of black-market stalls—the banter of haggling, the passing of illicit goods, the occasional tantrum thrown by a weary child—but after the monotonous rumble and steady vibrations inherent to railway travel, such human clamor was a welcome relief. They were, as Mr. Umezaki pointed out, entering a city newly reborn on the principles of democracy—where, just that month, a mayor had been chosen by popular vote during the first postwar election.

But when glimpsing Hiroshima's outskirts from within the passenger car, Holmes had seen very little that indicated a bustling city was nearby; instead, he had noticed clusters of temporary wooden shacks, like impoverished villages existing at close proximity to one another, separated only by wide fields strewn with tall horseweeds. When the train slowed on its approach to the dilapidated station, he realized that the horseweeds—sprouting thickly over a dark, uneven terrain of charred earth and concrete slabs and debris—were, in fact, thriving upon the burned-out land in which office buildings, entire neighborhoods, and business districts had stood.

The normally detested horseweed, Holmes then learned from Mr. Umezaki, was an unexpected blessing following the war. In Hiroshima, the plants' sudden emergence—offering a sense of hope and rebirth with its budding—had dispelled the widely accepted theory that the city would remain an infertile place for at least seventy years. There and elsewhere, its abundant growth had prevented mass death through starvation: "The leaves and flowers became a main ingredient in dumplings," Mr. Umezaki said. "Not too appetizing—believe me, I know—but those who couldn't continue on an empty stomach ate them to relieve the hunger."

Holmes had continued to look out the window, searching for a more definitive sign of the city, but, as the train moved into the rail yard, he could see just the wooden shacks—increasing in number, with some of the vacant lots around them transformed into modest vegetable gardens—and the Enko River, which ran parallel to the tracks. "As my stomach is a bit empty at the moment, I wouldn't mind sampling the dumplings myself—sounds like a most singular concoction."

Mr. Umezaki had nodded in agreement. "They are singular, it's true—except hardly in the best sense."

"Seems intriguing nonetheless."

But while Holmes had hoped for a late lunch of horseweed dumplings, it was another local specialty that eventually appeased him—a Japanese-style pancake covered in a sweet sauce, stuffed inside with whatever the customer chose from the menu list, and sold by any number of street vendors or makeshift noodle shops around Hiroshima Station.

"It's called *okonomi-yaki*," Mr. Umezaki explained later, while he and Holmes sat at a noodle shop counter, watching the cook create their lunch with great skill upon a large iron plate (their appetites further aroused by the sizzling fragrances wafting toward them). He went on to mention that he had first tried the dish when he was a boy, doing so while he vacationed in Hiroshima with his father. Since that childhood trip, he had visited the city a handful of times, usually staying only long enough to exchange trains, but sometimes an *okonomi-yaki* vendor would be at the station. "It's always impossible for me to resist it—the very smell conjures up that weekend with my father. You see, he had brought us to visit Shukkei-en Garden. Except rarely do I think of him and me being here together—or together at all, for that matter—unless *okonomi-yaki* is in the air."

Then during their meal, Holmes paused between bites, poking the interior pocket of the pancake with a chopstick and eyeing that mixture of meat, noodle, and cabbage, then said, "It is an uncomplicated creation, though rather exquisite, don't you agree?"

Mr. Umezaki looked up from the pancake piece held by his chopsticks. He appeared preoccupied with chewing and did not reply until he had swallowed. "Yes," he said at last. "Yes—"

Afterward, having been given hasty, vague directions by the busy cook, they headed for Shukkei-en Garden, a seventeenth-century refuge that Mr. Umezaki knew Holmes would enjoy seeing. Toting their suitcase at his side, leading the way along sidewalks teeming with foot traffic, ambling by crooked telephone poles and bent pine trees, he painted a vivid portrait, the details being extracted from his boyhood memories of the place. For the garden, he told Holmes, was a landscape in miniature, with a pond based on China's famous Xi Hu lake, and consisted of streams, islets, and bridges that appeared much larger than they actually were. An unimaginable oasis, Holmes realized when trying to envision the garden—impossible to conceive of, it seemed, in a flattened city struggling with reconstruction (the noises of which surrounded them—the beating of hammers, the groan of heavy equipment, the workmen moving down the street with lumber on their shoulders, the patter of horses and cars).

In any case, Mr. Umezaki readily admitted, the Hiroshima of his youth no longer remained, and he feared the garden had probably been badly damaged by the bomb. All the same, he believed something of its original charm might still remain intact—possibly the small stone bridge crossing a clear pond, maybe the stone lantern built in the image of Yang Kwei Fei.

"I suppose we will know soon enough," said Holmes, eager to leave the sun-drenched streets for a serene, relaxing environment, somewhere he could pause awhile amid the shade of trees and wipe the sweat from his forehead.

But when nearing a bridge that went across the Motoyasu River, at the city's barren center, Mr. Umezaki sensed a wrong turn had been made along the way, or that he had somehow misheard the cook's swiftly spoken instructions. Yet neither stopped, compelled instead to go forward toward what loomed ahead: "The Atom Bomb Dome," said Mr. Umezaki, pointing at the reinforced-concrete dome that had been stripped bare by the blast. His index finger climbed up past the building, indicating the hard blue sky. And there, he revealed, was where the great flash-bang had occurred, that inexplicable *pika-don,* engulfing the city in a massive firestorm; its wake then bringing days of black rain—fast-falling radioactivity mixed with the ashes of homes, trees, and bodies that had been obliterated by the blast and were sent swirling into the atmosphere.

As they approached the building, the breeze off the river started to blow more freely and the warm afternoon suddenly felt cooler. The sounds of the city, muted by the breeze, were less bothersome as they paused for a smoke—Mr. Umezaki setting the suitcase at their feet before lighting Holmes's cigar, both then sitting on a fallen concrete column (a convenient ruin, around which grew various weeds and wild grass). Other than what appeared to be a smattering of newly planted trees, the area provided little else in the way of shade; it was mostly an open stretch of land, which—absent of anyone else other than an elderly woman accompanied by two younger women—resembled a deserted, hurricane-swept shore. A few yards away, at the fence that encircled the Atom Bomb Dome building, they could see the women, each one kneeling and dutifully placing a paper crane necklace among the thousands of necklaces that were already there.

Then inhaling and releasing smoke between pursed lips, they sat mesmerized by the sight of the reinforced-concrete structure—a ravaged symbol standing close to ground zero, a forbidding memorial to the dead. After the blast, it was one of the few buildings not reduced to melted rubble—the skeletal steel frame of the dome arching above the ruins and prominent against the sky—while almost everything else below it had fragmented and burned and disappeared. Inside, there were no floors, as shock waves had collapsed the interior material into the basement, leaving only the vertical walls in place.

Yet, for Holmes, the building conveyed a kind of hopefulness, although he wasn't exactly sure why. Perhaps, he mused, the hope manifested from the sparrows perched along the building's rusted girders and the patches of blue sky present within the hollowed dome—or perhaps, in the aftermath of unfathomable destruction, the building's defying perseverance was in and of itself a harbinger of hope. But several minutes earlier—as he had first glimpsed the building—the very propinquity of the dome, suggesting so much violent death, filled him with profound regrets for where modern science had ultimately brought mankind: this uncertain age of atomic alchemy. He'd recalled the words of a London physician he'd once interrogated, an intelligent, thoughtful individual who, without any conceivable motive, had killed his wife and three children with strychnine, and who, subsequently, had set his own house on fire. When repeatedly asked about the reasons for his crime, the physician, refusing to speak, finally wrote three sentences on a sheet of paper: *There is a great weight beginning to push down on all sides of the earth at once. Because of it, we must stop ourselves. We must stop; otherwise, the earth will reach a complete standstill and cease to go round from all we have pressed upon it.* Only now, many years since, could he attach some modicum of meaning to that cryptic explanation, however tenuous it might be.

"We haven't much time," said Mr. Umezaki, dropping the butt

of his cigarette, then crushing it underfoot. He consulted his watch. "No, I'm afraid not much time at all. If we want to see the garden and catch the ferry for Miyajima, we should probably be going—that is, if we want to make the spa near Hofu by evening."

"Of course," said Holmes, situating his canes. As he rose off the column, Mr. Umezaki excused himself, wandering over to the women so he could get proper directions for Shukkei-en Garden (his friendly greeting and inquisitive voice carrying in the breeze). Still savoring his cigar, Holmes watched Mr. Umezaki and the three women, all standing beneath the somber building, smiling together in the afternoon sunlight. The elderly woman, whose creased face he could see quite plainly, was smiling in an unusually blissful manner, betraying the childlike innocence that sometimes reemerged with old age. Then, as if on cue, the three bowed, and Mr. Umezaki, after doing the same, about-faced sharply and walked quickly away from them, his smile promptly dissolving behind a stoic, somewhat grim expression.

13

A s at the Atom Bomb Dome, a high fence surrounded Shukkei-en Garden, put there in order to prevent entrance. Mr. Umezaki, however, was undeterred, and, as had apparently been done by others, he found a fissure in the fence (mangled open with wire cutters, Holmes suspected, and pulled back with gloved hands, creating a wide-enough gap for a body to squeeze through). Presently, they found themselves strolling on the interconnected, circuitous footpaths, which were powdered with a grayish soot and wound around dark, lifeless ponds or the sticklike remains of charred plum and cherry trees. Maintaining a leisurely pace, they often stopped to look off the paths, taking in the burned, fragile remnants of the historical garden—the blackened vestiges of tea-ceremony rooms, a meager grouping of azaleas where once hundreds, possibly thousands, had flourished.

But Mr. Umezaki kept silent about all they observed and—much to Holmes's dismay—ignored whatever questions were asked regarding the garden's previous splendor; moreover, he showed an infuriating hesitation to stay beside Holmes—sometimes walking ahead, or abruptly lagging behind on the paths while Holmes, unaware, went forward. In fact, after getting directions from the women, Mr. Umezaki's mood had turned rather sullen, suggesting some unwanted information had been passed on. Most likely, Holmes imagined, that the garden of his memory had become an inhospitable, restricted domain—a place where public access was now forbidden.

Except, as was soon evident, they were not the only trespassers there. Coming toward them on a path was a sophisticated-looking man—in his late forties or early fifties, shirtsleeves rolled to his elbows—holding the hand of a cheerful small boy, who skipped alongside him in blue shorts and a white shirt. As the two approached, the man nodded politely at Mr. Umezaki and spoke something in Japanese, and when Mr. Umezaki replied, he nodded politely again. It seemed the man wished to say more, but the boy tugged at his hand, urging him on, so the man simply continued nodding and walked by.

When Holmes asked what the man had said, Mr. Umezaki shook his head and shrugged. The brief encounter, Holmes realized, had had an unsettling effect upon Mr. Umezaki. Repeatedly glancing over his shoulder, Mr. Umezaki appeared distracted and, walking close to Holmes for a while, gripping the suitcase handle with whitened knuckles, looked as if he had met an apparition. Then, before once more hurrying ahead, he said, "How odd. . . . I believe I have just passed myself with my father, though my younger brother—my actual brother, not Hensuiro—is nowhere to be seen. As you were convinced I was an only child, and having lived the majority of my life without a sibling, I didn't see any point in mentioning him to you. You see, he died of tuberculosis—in fact, he died only a month or so after we strolled this very pathway together." He glanced back while quickening his steps. "How very strange, Sherlock-san. It was many years ago, and yet now it doesn't seem so distant at all."

"It is true," Holmes said. "The disregarded past has sometimes startled me with vivid and unexpected impressions—moments I had scarcely remembered until they revisited me."

The footpath brought them to a larger pond and curved toward a stone bridge that arched over the water. With several tiny islands dotting the pond—each bearing traces of tearooms and huts and other bridges—the garden suddenly felt vast and far from any city. Farther ahead, Mr. Umezaki had stopped, waiting for Holmes to join him; then both men stared for a time at a monk sitting cross-legged on one of the islands, his robed body upright and perfectly still, like a statue, his shaved head lowered in prayer.

Holmes stooped near Mr. Umezaki's feet, taking a turquoise-colored pebble from the path and dropping it into a pocket.

"I don't believe there is such a thing as fate in Japan," Mr. Umezaki eventually said, his gaze fixed on the monk. "Following my brother's death, I saw less and less of my father. He traveled a lot in those days, mostly to London and Berlin. With my brother gone— his name was Kenji—and my mother's grief pervading our household, I wanted terribly to accompany him on his trips. But I was a schoolboy, you see, and my mother needed me near her more than ever. My father was encouraging, though: He promised if I learned English and did well in school, then someday I might travel abroad with him. So, as you can imagine an eager child doing, I spent my free hours learning to read and write and speak English. I suppose, in a way, that kind of diligence fostered the resolve I needed for becoming a writer."

When they began walking again, the monk lifted his head, tilting it to the sky. He chanted lowly under his breath, a guttural, droning sound that drifted across the pond like ripples.

"A year or so later," Mr. Umezaki continued, "my father sent me a book from London, a fine edition of *A Study in Scarlet*. It was the first novel I read from start to finish in English, and it was my introduction to Dr. Watson's writings concerning your adventures.

Regrettably, I wouldn't read the English editions of his other books for quite a while—not until I'd gone from Japan to attend school in England. You see, because of my mother's state of mind, she refused to allow any books dealing with you—or England—to be read in our home. In fact, she got rid of that edition my father sent me—finding where I'd hidden it, disposing of it without asking my permission. Luckily, I'd already finished the last chapter the night before."

"A rather harsh reaction on her part," said Holmes.

"It was," said Mr. Umezaki. "I was angry at her for weeks. I refused to speak to her, or to eat her meals. It was a difficult period for everyone."

They came to a range of hillocks on the pond's northern shore, where—past the garden property—a neighboring river and distant hills provided a pleasant backdrop. A deliberately placed boulder was nearby, functioning as a kind of natural bench, its upper half having been leveled and smoothed. So Holmes and Mr. Umezaki sat, enjoying a good overview of the garden grounds from their vantage point.

Sitting there, Holmes felt as worn down as that age-old boulder, resting by hillocks, somehow remaining present when everything else that had been previously recognized was receding or gone. Across the pond, beyond the opposite bank, were the curious shapes of fallow trees—the crooked, unproductive limbs of which no longer shielded the garden from the city's houses and busy streets. For a while, they stayed there, saying very little and contemplating the view, until Holmes—pondering what Mr. Umezaki had told him—said, "I pray I am not being too inquisitive, but I take it your father is no longer living."

"My mother was less than half his age when they married," Mr. Umezaki said, "so I'm quite sure he's dead, though I have no idea where or how he passed on. To be honest, I was hoping you could tell me."

"How exactly do you propose I do that?"

Bending forward, Mr. Umezaki pressed his fingertips together; then he glanced at Holmes with intent eyes. "During our correspondence, was my name not familiar to you?"

"No, I cannot say that it was. Should it have been?"

"My father's name, then—Umezaki Matsuda, or Matsuda Umezaki."

"I am afraid I don't understand."

"It appears you had some dealings with my father while he was in England. I've been uncertain on how to broach the subject with you, because I feared you might question my reasons for inviting you here. I suppose I assumed you'd make the connections on your own and somehow be more forthcoming."

"And when would these dealings have occurred? For I assure you I possess no memory of them."

Nodding gravely, his fingers now unlatching the traveling bag at his feet, Mr. Umezaki proceeded to open the suitcase on the ground, digging deliberately through his own clothing, and retrieving a letter, which he unfolded and handed to Holmes. "This arrived with the book my father sent. It was for my mother."

Holmes brought the letter near his face, scrutinizing what he could.

比処倫敦に於て著名なる探偵
シーロック・ホームズ氏に相談致したる
結果相応の期間吾英国に留まる事を
以て最も吾らの利を得るものと確信致し候
貴殿此の本を読まばお分かりになるが如く
ホームズ氏は真実勝れた頭脳と知性の
持主にて候 依て斯る重大事件に関し
彼の言ばすや軽々に扱わるべからずと
心得候 吾既に吾が資産と財務を民樹
成人し責任を負得る時に至る迄貴殿に
委託すべく諸手続を終了致し候

"It was written forty, maybe forty-five years ago, correct? See how the paper has yellowed considerably along the edges, and how the black ink has turned bluish." Holmes gave the letter to Mr. Umezaki. "The contents, unfortunately, are lost on me. So if you will please do me the honor—"

"I'll do my best." With his expression remote and transfigured, Mr. Umezaki began translating: "After consulting with the great detective Sherlock Holmes here in London, I realize that it is in the best interest of all of us if I remain in England indefinitely. You will see from this book that he is, indeed, a very wise and intelligent man, and his say in this important matter should not be taken lightly. I have already made arrangements for the property and my finances to be placed in your care, until such a time as Tamiki can take over these responsibilities in adulthood." Then Mr. Umezaki began folding the letter, adding as he did so, "The letter was dated March twenty-third. The year was 1903—which means I was eleven and he was fifty-nine. We never heard from him again—nor was any further information discovered as to why he felt compelled to stay in England. In other words, this is all we know."

"That is regrettable," said Holmes, watching as the letter was placed back inside the suitcase. It was not possible, at that moment, to tell Mr. Umezaki that he believed his father was a liar. But he could address his own mystification, explaining that he wasn't sure if a meeting with Matsuda Umezaki had ever happened. "It is conceivable that I may have met him—then again, I may not have. You have no idea how many people came to us during those years, literally thousands. Yet very few stand out in my mind, although I think a Japanese man in London certainly would, don't you? Still, one way or the other, it really does escape me. I am sorry, for I know that isn't very helpful."

Mr. Umezaki waved his hand, a dismissive gesture, which, as if by choice, caused him suddenly to cast off his serious demeanor. "It's hardly worth the trouble," he said, his voice becoming casual in tone.

"I care little about my father—he disappeared so long ago, you understand, and he's buried in my childhood, along with my brother. It's for my mother that I had to ask you—because she has always wondered. To this day, in fact, she continues to agonize. I realize I should have discussed this with you earlier, but it was difficult bringing it up in her presence, so I chose our travels to do so."

"Your discretion and your devotion to your mother," Holmes said genially, "are commendable."

"I appreciate that," said Mr. Umezaki. "And please, this small matter mustn't cloud the true reasons for why you're here. My invitation was sincere—I want that made clear—and we have much to see and talk about."

"Naturally," said Holmes.

Except nothing of substance was said for a good while after that exchange, aside from brief generalities spoken mostly by Mr. Umezaki ("I fear we should be going. We don't want to miss our ferry."). Nor did either man feel inclined to prompt a conversation—not as they left the garden, not even when they found themselves on a ferry bound for Miyajima Island (keeping silent even when glimpsing the huge red torii that stood above the sea). Then their awkward silence would only increase, staying with them as they rode the bus to Hofu, and as they settled in for the evening at Momiji-so Spa (a resort where, according to legend, a white fox had once nursed its wounded leg in the healing hot springs, and where, while sinking into a tub of the famed water, one might spy the fox's face floating amid the steam. It dissipated only just before supper, when Mr. Umezaki looked straight at Holmes and smiled broadly, saying, "It's a lovely evening."

Holmes smiled in return, though without enthusiasm. "Quite" was his concise reply.

14

B U T I F Mr. Umezaki had, with a slight raising of his hand, discarded the issue of his father's disappearance, then it was Holmes who was preoccupied by the quandary of Matsuda. For the man's name, he later became convinced, had a vaguely recognizable ring (or was this sense, he wondered, based solely on the already-familiar surname?). And so during their second overnight stay—while eating fish and drinking sake at a Yamaguchi inn—he inquired further about the father, his initial question being met with a lingering, uncomfortable stare from Mr. Umezaki. "Why are you asking me this now?"

"Because my curiosity has gotten the better of me, I am sorry to say."

"Is that so?"

"I am afraid it is."

Thereafter, all questions received thoughtful answers, with Mr. Umezaki growing increasingly effusive as his cup was repeatedly emptied and refilled. Though by the time both men reached intoxication, Mr. Umezaki occasionally stopped in midsentence, unable to complete what he had been saying. For a while, he stared hopelessly at Holmes, his fingers tightening around his cup. Soon he ceased talking altogether, and it would be Holmes, for once, helping him to stand, to walk from the table, to go unsteadily forward. Presently, they would retire into their respective rooms, and the next morning—when sight-seeing at three nearby villages and shrines—no mention was made of the previous evening's discussion.

That third day of travel would stay with Holmes as the highlight of his entire trip. Both he and Mr. Umezaki, while feeling the disagreeable aftereffects of having drunk too much, were in great spirits, and it was a glorious spring day. Sitting on buses, bumping through the countryside, their conversation drifted from subject to subject in a natural, lighthearted manner. They talked of England, and they talked of beekeeping; they talked of the war, and they talked of travels both had undertaken in their youth. Holmes was surprised to hear that Mr. Umezaki had visited Los Angeles and shaken hands with Charles Chaplin; in turn, Mr. Umezaki was fascinated by Holmes's account of his adventures in Tibet, where he had visited Lhasa and spent some days with the Dalai Lama.

Their amicable, easy exchange carried on through the morning and into the afternoon—while exploring goods at a village bazaar (Holmes purchasing an ideal letter opener: a *kusun-gobu* short sword), and witnessing an unusual spring fertility festival in another village, the two chatting surreptitiously as a procession of priests, musicians, and locals dressed like demons paraded down the street: the men hoisting erect wooden phalluses, the women embracing smaller carved penises swathed in red paper, the spectators touching the tips of passing phalluses to ensure good health for their children.

"How remarkable," commented Holmes.

"I thought you might find this of interest," said Mr. Umezaki.

Holmes grinned slyly. "My friend, I suspect this is much more to your liking than mine."

"You're probably right," agreed Mr. Umezaki, smiling while his fingertips reached out for an oncoming phallus.

But the ensuing evening was like the one before: another inn, supper together, rounds of sake, cigarettes and cigars, and more questions regarding Matsuda. Since it was impossible for Mr. Umezaki to know everything concerning his father—especially after the questioning went from the general to the specific—his replies were often indefinite, or answered simply with a shrug, or by saying, "I don't know." Still, Mr. Umezaki didn't begrudge the probing, even if Holmes's inquiries brought back unhappy memories of childhood and the agony of his mother's grief. "She destroyed so much—almost anything my father had touched. Twice, she set fire to our house, and she also tried persuading me to join her in a suicide pact. She wanted us to walk together into the sea and drown ourselves; it was her idea of avenging my father's wrong against us."

"I take it, then, that your mother has a distinct dislike for me. The woman can hardly contain her contempt—I sensed it early on."

"No, she isn't very fond of you—but, honestly, she isn't very fond of anyone, so you needn't take it too personally. She hardly acknowledges Hensuiro, and she dislikes the path I've taken in life. I haven't married; I live with my companion—she blames these things on my father's abandonment of us. In her mind, a boy can never become a man unless he has a father to teach him what it means."

"Was I not, supposedly, decisive in that choice of abandonment?"

"She thinks so."

"Well, I must take it personally. How could I not? I pray you don't share her feelings."

"No, not at all. We are different creatures of reason, my mother and I. I hold nothing against you. You are—if I may say—a hero of mine, and a newfound friend."

"You flatter me," said Holmes, proffering his cup for a toast. "To newfound friends—"

Then surfacing on Mr. Umezaki's face throughout the evening was a trusting, attentive expression. Indeed, Holmes perceived the expression as one of faith: that Mr. Umezaki—in speaking of his father, in relating what he knew—believed the retired detective might shed some welcome light on the disappearance, or, at the very least, provide a few insights once the questioning had concluded. Only later, when it was clear Holmes had nothing to reveal, did a separate expression become evident—a sorrowful face, somewhat morose. Canker and melancholy, thought Holmes, after Mr. Umezaki berated a waitress who had accidentally spilled fresh sake on their table.

Subsequently, on the last leg of their trip, there came long periods of introspection between the two, punctuated only by the exhalations of tobacco smoke. On board the train headed for Shimonoseki, Mr. Umezaki kept busy by writing inside his red journal, and Holmes—his thoughts now preoccupied with what he had learned of Matsuda—stared out the window, following the course of a slender river that curved alongside steep mountains. At times, the train wound near country residences, each house having a single twenty-gallon barrel set beside the river's bank (the words on the side of the barrels, Mr. Umezaki had explained earlier, meant "Fire-Prevention Water"). Along the way, Holmes observed various small villages, with mountains towering beyond them. To reach the summits of those mountains, he imagined, was to stand above the prefecture and command a breathtaking view of everything below—the valleys, the villages, the distant cities, maybe the entire Inland Sea.

While surveying that scenic terrain, Holmes mulled over all Mr. Umezaki had told him concerning his father, forming in his mind a basic portrait of the vanished man—someone whose presence he could almost summon from the past: the thin features and the tall stature, the distinctive shape of his gaunt face, the goatee of a Meiji intellectual. Yet Matsuda was also a diplomat-statesman, serving as one of Japan's leading foreign ministers, before disgrace shortened his term. Even so, he endured as an enigmatic character, known for his skill with logic and debate, and for his vast understanding of international policies. Most notable among his many accomplishments was a book documenting Japan's war with China, written while he was residing in London and detailing, among other things, the secret diplomacy that occurred prior to the war's outbreak.

Ambitious by nature, Matsuda's political aspirations began during the Meiji Restoration, when he entered government service despite his parents' wishes. Considered an outsider because he wasn't associated with any of the favored four Western clans, his abilities were impressive enough that eventually the governorship of a number of prefectures was offered to him, and while in that post, he made his first visit to London in 1870. On the heels of resigning his gubernatorial position, he was selected to join the expanding Foreign Ministry, but his promising career ended three years later as his dissatisfaction with the clan-dominated government found him plotting its overthrow. The failed conspiracy led to a lengthy imprisonment, where—rather than languishing behind bars—he continued doing important work, such as translating Jeremy Bentham's *Introduction to the Principles of Morals and Legislation* into the Japanese language.

After his prison release, Matsuda married his girl-like wife, and in time she gave him two sons. Meanwhile, he spent several years traveling abroad, frequently coming and going from Japan, making London his European home base, while journeying often to Berlin and Vienna. This was a long period of study for him, his main interest being constitutional law. And while he was widely considered to be a scholar with a profound knowledge of the West, his beliefs were always those of an autocrat: "Make no mistake," Mr. Umezaki had said on that second evening of questioning, "my father believed a single, absolute power should rule its people—I think this is why he preferred England to America. I also think his dogmatic beliefs made him too impatient to be a successful politician, let alone a good father and husband."

"And you imagine he remained in London until his death?"

"It's more than likely."

"And you never sought him out while attending school there?"

"Briefly, yes—except it proved impossible to find him. Frankly, I didn't try hard enough, but I was a young man and taken with my new life and new friends—and felt no urgent need to contact the man who had abandoned us long ago. In the end, I deliberately gave up on any effort to locate him, feeling somehow liberated in that decision. He was, after all, of another world by then. We were strangers."

Yet decades later, Mr. Umezaki confessed, he would come to regret that decision. Because now he was fifty-five—only four years younger than his father had been when they last saw each other—and he fostered a growing emptiness inside himself, a black space where the absence of his father dwelled. Moreover, he was convinced that his father must have shared the same empty place for the family he'd never see again; with Matsuda's passing, that murky, vacuous wound had somehow found its way into his surviving son, eventually festering within as a frequent source of bewilderment and distress, existing as an unresolved problem of an aging heart.

"Then it is not just for your mother's sake that you require some answers?" Holmes had asked, his words suddenly tainted by intoxication and weariness.

"No, I suppose it's not," answered Mr. Umezaki with a degree of despair.

"You are really seeking the truth for yourself, correct? It is—in other words—important to grasp the facts of the matter for your own well-being."

"Yes." Mr. Umezaki reflected for a moment, peering into his sake glass before glancing again at Holmes. "So what is the truth? How do you arrive at it? How do you unravel the meaning of something that doesn't wish to be known?" He kept his eyes on Holmes, in the expectation that such questioning would produce a definitive starting point; if Holmes responded, the disappearance of his father and the greatest pain of his childhood might begin to be dealt with.

But Holmes was quiet, seemingly lost in thought; his inward

expression as he sat thinking generated an optimistic twinge in Mr. Umezaki. Without a doubt, Holmes was sorting through the vast index of his memory. Like the contents of a file buried deep inside a forgotten cabinet, the once-known specifics surrounding Matsuda's forsaking of his family and homeland would, when at last retrieved, give way to an invaluable amount of information. Soon Holmes's eyes would close (the old detective's ruminating mind, Mr. Umezaki felt certain, was already reaching into that cabinet's darker recesses), and almost imperceptibly, a faint snoring would then be heard.

PART

III

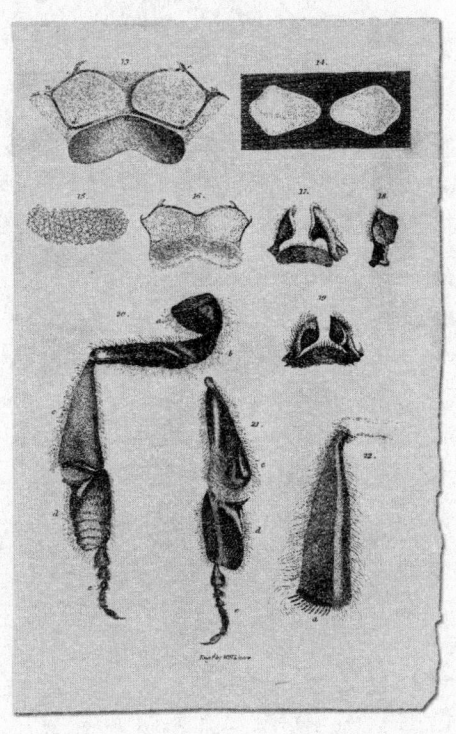

15

IT WAS HOLMES—after waking at his desk with numbed feet, and then taking a stroll outside to bolster his circulation—who discovered Roger on that late afternoon, finding him very near the beeyard and partially concealed amid the adjacent pasture's higher grass. The boy was stretched out upon his back, arms along his sides, lounging there and gazing upward at the slow-moving clouds far above. And before stepping any closer or saying Roger's name, Holmes, too, pondered those clouds, wondering what it was exactly that held the boy's attention so rigidly—for nothing extraordinary could be spotted, nothing at all save the gradual evolving of cumulus and the expansive cloud shadows that periodically muted sunlight and swept across the pasture like waves rushing over a shoreline.

"Roger, my boy," Holmes eventually said, lowering his stare while wading forward through the grass, "your mother has, unfortunately, requested your help in the kitchen."

As it happened, Holmes had had no intention of venturing into the beeyard. He'd simply planned a brief walk around the gardens, checking the herb beds, yanking the occasional weed, patting down loose soil with a cane. Except Mrs. Munro had caught him as he went past the kitchen doorway, wiping flour on her apron, asking if he might be good enough to fetch the boy for her. So Holmes agreed, although not without reluctance, because there was still unfinished work awaiting him in the attic, and because a hike beyond the gardens inevitably became a protracted but welcome distraction (once setting foot within the beeyard, he was sure to remain at the apiary until dusk, peeking into hives, rearranging the brood nest, removing unneeded combs).

Some days later, however, he'd realize that Mrs. Munro's request was a dismally fortuitous one: Had she gone for the boy herself, she'd never have looked any farther than the beeyard, at least not initially; she'd never have observed the high grass trampled into a fresh trail in the pasture, or—then traveling alongside that narrow, curving course—noticed Roger resting motionless, facing such massy white clouds. Yes, she'd have shouted his name from the garden pathway, but with no answer forthcoming, would have imagined him being elsewhere (reading at the cottage, chasing butterflies in the woods, maybe picking shells off the beach). She wouldn't have grown suddenly concerned. A troubled expression wouldn't have spread on her face—as her legs parted the grass, as she went to him and repeated his name.

"Roger," said Holmes. "Roger," he whispered while standing over the boy, pressing a cane gently against his shoulder.

Ultimately, when locked again inside his study, he'd recall only the boy's eyes—those dilated pupils transfixed on the sky, somehow conveying rapture—and he'd think little more of what had been quickly fathomed there amid the gently shuddering grass: Roger's swollen lips and hands and cheeks, the countless weltlike stings that formed irregular patterns on the boy's neck, face, forehead, ears. Nor would Holmes ponder the few words he had then uttered while crouched by Roger, such gravely spoken words that, if heard by another, would have rung impossibly cold, unimaginably callous.

"Quite dead, my boy. Quite dead, I fear. . . ."

But Holmes was well acquainted with death's unwelcome arrival—or at least he wished to believe so—and hardly did its sudden visitations surprise him anymore. During the long expanse of his life, he'd knelt near a multitude of corpses—women, men, children, and animals alike, often complete strangers, though sometimes acquaintances—observing the conclusive ways in which quietus had left its calling card (blue-black bruises along one side of a body, discolored skin, curled fingers frozen with rigor, that sickly sweet smell inhaled into the nostrils of the living: any number of variations but always the same undeniable theme). *Death, like crime, is commonplace,* he'd once written. *Logic, on the other hand, is rare. Therefore, maintaining a logical mental inclination, especially when facing mortality, can be difficult. However, it is always upon logic rather than upon death that one should dwell.*

And so, too, amid the high grass was logic brought out like a shield of sterling armor to repel the heartbreaking discovery of the boy's body (forget the slight dizziness Holmes felt taking hold, or the trembling of his fingers, or the befuddling anguish that was starting to blossom in his mind). Roger being gone was of no importance at the moment, he convinced himself. What mattered now was how Roger had reached his end. But without even examining the body—without even bending, studying that inflamed, swollen face—the scenario of Roger's demise was understood.

The boy had been stung, of course. Stung repeatedly, Holmes knew upon first glance. Before Roger had succumbed, his skin had become flushed, accompanied by a burning pain, generalized itching. He'd fled his attackers, perhaps. In any case, he'd wandered from the hives into the pasture, likely disoriented, pursued by the swarm. There was no indication of vomit on his shirt or around his lips and chin, although the boy had surely ached from abdominal cramps, nausea. His blood pressure would have dropped, creating a feeling of weakness. The throat and mouth had no doubt swelled, preventing him from swallowing or calling for help. Alterations of heart rate would have followed, as well as difficulty breathing, and probably a notion of impending doom (he was an intelligent child, so he would've sensed his fate). Then, as if slipping past a trapdoor, he had collapsed in the grass and become unconscious—dying, remarkably, with eyes wide open.

"Anaphylaxis," Holmes muttered, brushing dirt flecks off the boy's cheeks. Severe allergic reaction, he concluded. One sting too many. The extreme end of the allergic spectrum, a relatively immediate and uncomfortable death. He brought his forlorn stare to the sky, watching as the clouds progressed overhead, aware of dusk's increasing eminence at day's end.

What mishap occurred? he finally asked himself, struggling with his canes to stand upright. What did the boy do—what provoked the bees so? For the beeyard appeared as serene as it usually did; when crossing the apiary earlier, searching for Roger and speaking the boy's name, Holmes had witnessed no swarm, no agitated activity at the hives' entrances, nothing out of the ordinary. Furthermore, not a single bee hovered in proximity to Roger now. Regardless, the apiary deserved closer consideration; the hives required proper inspection. Overalls, gloves, a hat, and a veil needed to be worn, lest a similar fate as the boy's await Holmes. But first the authorities had to be informed, and Mrs. Munro told, and Roger's body carried away.

Already the sun was dipping toward the west, and behind the fields and woods, the horizon glowed faintly white in the distance. Going unsteadily from Roger, Holmes made his way across the pasture, forging his own crooked trail in order to avoid the beeyard altogether, stepping through the grass until reaching the gravel of the garden pathway; there, he paused, looking back at the tranquil beeyard and the grassy spot where the boy lay unseen, both places now awash in golden sunlight. Just then, he spoke beneath his breath, flustered at once by the insignificance of his own silent words.

"What are you saying?" he suddenly said aloud, pounding his

canes on the gravel. "What—are you—" A worker bee whizzed by, trailed by another, restraining him with their buzzing.

The blood had drained from his face, and his hands shook while clutching at the cane handles. Attempting to regain composure, he inhaled deeply and then turned quickly to the farmhouse. But he couldn't yet proceed, because everything ahead of him—the garden rows, the house, the pine trees—was only vaguely tangible. For a moment, he remained perfectly still, confounded by all around and before him: How is it possible, he questioned, that I've blundered into someplace that isn't mine? How did I lead myself here?

"No," he said, "no, no—you are mistaken—"

He shut his eyes, inhaling air into his chest. He had to concentrate, not just to recover himself but also to vanquish the sense of unfamiliarity, for the pathway was his design, the garden, too—there were wild daffodils nearby; even closer at hand were purple buddleias. If his eyes were to open, Holmes was positive, he'd certainly recognize his giant thistles; he'd see his herb beds. And at last parting his eyelids, he saw the daffodils, the buddleias, the thistles, the pine trees farther on. Then he urged his legs forward, doing so with a fair degree of grim determination.

"Of course," he mumbled, "of course—"

That night, Holmes would stand at the attic window, looking out into the darkness. As if by choice, he'd fail to examine the previous moments that had sent him up into the study, the specifics of all that was said and explained—the brief conversation with Mrs. Munro after he entered the farmhouse, her voice calling to him from the kitchen: "Did you find him?"

"Yes."

"Is he on his way?"

"I am afraid so—yes."

"About time, I'll say."

Or the hushed phone call notifying Anderson of the boy's passing, telling the constable where the body could be found, and a warning to Anderson and his men to keep clear of the apiary: "There is something amiss with my bees, so be careful. If you will tend to the boy and inform his mother, I will tend to the hives and then reveal tomorrow what was learned."

"We'll be right there. And I'm sorry for your loss, sir. I truly am."

"Do hurry, Anderson."

Or his self-reproach for having avoided Mrs. Munro, rather than dealing with her directly—his inability to convey his own remorse, to share something of his agony with her, to stand at her side when Anderson and his men entered the house. Instead, stupefied by Roger's death and the very idea of facing the boy's mother with the truth, he had climbed upstairs to his study, shutting and locking the door, forgetting to return to the apiary as planned. Then he had sat at his desk, jotting note after note, scarcely cognizant of the meanings of his hastily written sentences, paying some mind to the comings and goings outside, the impromptu sorrow of Mrs. Munro rising from down below (her guttural wails, the breathless sobs—a profound grief that coursed through the walls and floors, echoed along the corridors, and soon ended as abruptly as it had begun). Minutes later, Anderson had knocked on the study door, saying, "Mr. Holmes—Sherlock—" So Holmes had reluctantly allowed him entrance, though only for a short while. Nonetheless, the particulars of their discussion—the things Anderson had suggested, the things Holmes had agreed upon—were inevitably lost on him.

And in the silence thereafter—once Anderson and his men had left the house, taking Mrs. Munro in one vehicle and the boy in an ambulance—he went to the attic window, seeing nothing beyond except complete darkness. But still he perceived something, that disquieting image he couldn't shake completely from memory: Roger's blue eyes out there in the pasture, those wide pupils seemingly intent in their upward gaze, yet unbearably vacuous.

Going again to his desk, he rested for a while in his chair, hunched forward, with thumbs pressed against his shut eyelids. "No," he muttered, shaking his head. "Is that so?" he then said aloud, raising his head. "How can that be?" He opened his eyes, glancing about as if expecting to find someone else nearby. But, as always, he was alone in the attic, seated at his desk, a hand now reaching absently for his pen.

His stare fell on the work before him, the stacks of pages, the clutter of notes—and that unfinished manuscript bound by a single rubber band. In the subsequent hours preceding dawn, he wouldn't think much more of Roger, nor would he ever conceive of the boy sitting in the same chair, poring over the case of Mrs. Keller and wishing for the story's completion. And yet, on that night, he suddenly felt compelled to finish the story anyway—to reach for fresh sheets of writing paper, to begin fashioning a kind of closure for himself where previously none had existed.

Then it was as if the words were arriving well ahead of his own thoughts, filling the pages with ease. The words propelled his hand forward while also taking him back, back, back—past the summer months in Sussex, past his recent trip to Japan, past both great wars—to a world that thrived in the flux of one century's conclusion and another century's outset. He wouldn't cease his writing until sunrise. He wouldn't stop until the ink had almost been emptied.

16

III.

In the Gardens of the
Physics and Botanical Society

As documented in John's short sketches, I was often not above the unscrupulous when working on a case, nor was I always selfless in my actions; for, in that regard, to be honest about my intentions concerning the need for the photograph of Mrs. Keller is to confess that I had no real need of it whatsoever. Indeed, the case was finished before going from Portman's on that Thursday evening, and I might have revealed all to Mr. Keller then had the woman's face ceased to beguile me so. Yet by prolonging the outcome, I knew I could again witness her in person, but from a better vantage point. The photograph, too, was wanted for my own reasons, with some desire for it to remain among my possessions in lieu of payment. And later that night, sitting alone near the window, the woman continued to stroll effortlessly through my thoughts—her parasol held high against the sun as if to shield the alabaster whiteness of her skin—while her diffident image gazed up from my lap.

But several days passed before I was afforded the opportunity to consign my full attention to her. During the intervening time, my energies were spent on a matter of supreme importance which the French government had engaged me to settle—a sordid affair revolving around an onyx paperweight stolen from a diplomat's desk in Paris and, eventually, stashed beneath the floorboards of a West End stage. Even so, the woman persisted in my mind, manifesting in an increasingly fanciful manner, which, while being almost wholly of my invention, was as enticing as it was disconcerting. I did not, however, lack the insight of realising that my ruminations were based on fantasy and, therefore, were probably inaccurate; yet I cannot deny the complicated impulses which arose when I was preoccupied by such foolish reverie—for the tenderness I felt was, for once, extending beyond my sense of reason.

So it was to be on the subsequent Tuesday that I disguised myself accordingly, giving a fair amount of consideration towards the persona which might best suit the ineffable Mrs. Keller. I settled on Stefan Peterson, an unattached middle-aged bibliophile with a kind-natured, if not somewhat effeminate, disposition; a myopic, bespectacled character, attired in well-worn tweed, who had the habit of nervously running a hand across his unkempt hair while tugging absently at his blue ascot.

"Begging your pardon, miss," I said, squinting at my reflection in the mirror, assuming what I believed would be my persona's polite and shy first words to Mrs. Keller. "I'm sorry, miss—begging your pardon—"

Adjusting the ascot, I realised that his predisposition for flora was to rival her love of all things which bloomed. Tousling my hair, I was positive that his fascination for romance literature was unsurpassed. He was, after all, an avid reader, preferring the detached solace of a book above most human interaction. Yet at his core he was a lonely man, existing as someone who, as he had grown older, had begun to contemplate the value of steady companionship. To this end, he studied the subtle art of palmistry, more as a way to make contact with others than as a means for divulging future events; if the correct palm were to rest briefly within his hand, he imagined that the fleeting warmth of it could sustain him in the months thereafter.

And now it is here that I cannot envision myself concealed behind my own creation—rather, when recalling the moments of that afternoon, I am removed from the proceedings altogether. Instead, it was Stefan Peterson walking into the declining light of day, his head lowered and his shoulders drawn toward his chest, a floundering and pitiable figure gingerly ambling in the direction of Montague Street. The sight of him garnered no lingering glances, nor was his presence notable by any manner. He was, to those who brushed beside him, an imminently forgettable soul.

Yet he was resolute upon his mission, bringing himself to Portman's prior to Mrs. Keller's arrival. Entering the shop, he went silently past the counter, where, as before, the proprietor gazed at a book—magnifying glass in hand, face hovering near the text—and was unaware of Stefan's fleeting proximity; only then, as he roamed down an aisle, did the proprietor's hearing come into question, for the old fellow had not been stirred by the shop door squeaking on its hinges, or by the OPEN placard bumping against the glass after the door was shut. He wandered along the veiled corridors of bookcases, crossing through the dust motes which swirled amidst the scant rays of sunlight; the farther one went within the shop, he discerned, the darker it became ahead—until everything to the fore of him was blanketed by shadow.

Reaching the stairwell, he climbed seven steps and crouched there, then, so that he might clearly observe Mrs. Keller's entrance without being noticed. And, in due course, events would at last commence thusly: the armonica's mournful vibrations began from above—the boy's fingers sliding upon the glasses; moments later, the shop door swung back and, as she had done on previous Tuesdays and Thursdays, Mrs. Keller came in off the street with her parasol slipped under an arm and a book held in a gloved hand. Paying the proprietor no mind—nor he her—she drifted into the aisles, pausing at times to survey the shelves, occasionally touching the spines of various volumes as though her fingers were impelled to do so. For a while, she remained visible, yet her back was kept away from him; he watched her glide slowly towards the darker recesses, becoming less and less apparent. Finally, she moved from his view completely, but not before he saw her place the book she was carrying on a top shelf, trading it, then, for another volume, which she seemingly chose at random.

You are hardly a thief, he told himself. No, you are, in truth, a borrower.

Once she had passed from sight, he could only surmise her exact location—somewhere close, yes, as he caught the scent of her perfume; surely somewhere amidst the near pitch, if only for a few seconds. As it happened, what followed next was expected and offered little surprise, although his eyes were not quite prepared: a sudden bright white flash illuminated from the shop's rear, flooding the aisles momentarily with its brilliance, vanishing as swiftly as it had erupted. He promptly descended the steps, seeing still the afterglow upon his pupils of that light which had swept inside and, he knew, now enveloped Mrs. Keller.

He travelled along a narrow passage between the double row of bookcases, inhaling the powerful, guiding fumes of her fragrance, and stopped within the shadows by the far wall. As he stood facing the wall, his eyes began adjusting to the surroundings, and he whispered lowly, "Right here, and nowhere else." The muted sounds of the armonica continued falling quite distinctly upon his ear. He glanced to the left—precarious stacks of books; then to the right—more piles of books. And there, directly in front of him, was the portal of Mrs. Keller's departure—a back exit, a shut door framed by the same brightness which had stunned his vision. He took two steps forwards and pushed at the door. It took all his self-control to prevent himself from rushing after her. With the door swinging wide, the light again spilled into the shop. Yet he hesitated in going past the threshold, and cautiously, as he squinted outside at the trellis screens forming an enclosed walkway, gradually eased onwards with a shuffling, reserved gait.

Soon her perfume became obscured by the even richer odours of tulips and daffodils. Then he could compel himself no farther than the walkway's end, where he peered through the vine-covered lattice-work and beheld a tiny landscaped garden of the most elaborate design: Herb beds thrived beside a somewhat oblique topiary pruned from dense hedging plants, and perennials and roses cloaked the walled perimeter; such an ideal oasis the proprietor had fashioned in the heart of London, one which was barely glimpsed from Madame Schirmer's window. The old man had, likely in the years preceding his failing eyesight, tailored his garden to the differing microclimates of his backyard: Where the roof of the building kept sunlight from reaching long into places, the proprietor had planted variegated foliage in order to highlight the darkened areas; elsewhere, the perennial beds hosted foxglove, geraniums, and lilies.

A path of river stone curved towards the garden's centre and concluded at a square patch of turf which was encircled by a formal boxwood hedge. Upon the turf was a small bench, and near it was a large
terra-cotta urn, painted with copper patina; and upon the bench—
her parasol across her lap, the book she had taken gripped by both
hands—sat Mrs. Keller within the building's shade, reading while the
armonica's sound drifted from the window above and down into the
garden like an enigmatic breeze.

Of course, he thought, of course—thinking this when she glanced
up from the book, cocking her head to one side, listening intently as
the playing slackened for a moment and, eventually, then swelled into
a refined, less dissonant performance. Madame Schirmer, he was certain, had now taken Graham's place at the armonica, showing the boy
how the glasses should be properly manipulated. And while those
masterful fingers pulled exquisite tones from the instrument, transforming the very air with its lulling textures, he studied Mrs. Keller
from afar, observing the subtle rapture in her expression—the gentle
exhaling of her breath between parted lips, the loosening of her rigid
posture, the slow closing of her eyes—and the hidden presence of
something pacific about her which emerged, if but for a scant few
minutes, in accord with the music.

It is difficult to remember how long he remained there, face at the
trellis screen, watching her; for he, too, was captivated by all that had
come to enrich the garden. Yet his concentration would at last be broken with the squeaking of the rear door, followed thereafter by the

violent cough, which hastened the proprietor across the threshold. Wearing the soiled smock and brown gloves, the old man entered into the walkway, a hand clutching the handle of a watering can; soon enough, the proprietor would lumber past the figure pressed nervously against the trellis screen, stepping into the garden while never once giving heed to its trespassers, then reaching the flower beds just as the last strains of the armonica ebbed away, the watering can slipping from the hand and landing upon its side and emptying most of its contents.

At that instant it was over: The armonica had fallen silent; the proprietor was stooping by his rose beds, feeling upon the lawn for what had escaped his grasp. Mrs. Keller gathered her belongings and stood from the bench, going towards the old man with that by-now-familiar manner of leisure; her form cast over him as she bent in front of his outstretched hands, righting the watering can, and the proprietor, without having fathomed her ghostlike presence, promptly seized hold of its handle and coughed. Then like a cloud shadow passing easily upon the earth, she moved off in the direction of a little ironwork gate at the back of the garden; there, she turned the key which sat within the lock, allowing the gate to swing wide enough for her to leave—the gate opening and closing with the same mixture of rattles and scrapes. And then it seemed, to him, that she had never been in the garden or in the shop; she was, in a way, immediately nebulous to his mind, receding into nothingness like the final tones spun from Madame Schirmer's instrument.

Rather than hurrying after her, however, he found himself turning away, returning instead through the bookstore, and out upon the street; and, by dusk, he was mounting the steps leading to my flat. Yet while en route, he cursed the paralysis of his will, which had held him back, keeping him bound to the garden even as she ventured from sight. Only later—once the attributes of Stefan Peterson had been removed, folded neatly, and put within my chest of drawers—did I contemplate the very nature of one so deficient in resolve. How, I wondered, could a man as versed and knowledgeable as he become discomposed by such an unassuming wisp of a woman? For Mrs. Keller's passive countenance betrayed little that was unbridled or exceptional about her. So had the gap of isolation and detachment which surrounded his lifetime of study—the solitary hours spent absorbing all manner of human behaviour and thought—given him no amount of insight into what was required of him then?

You must be strong, I wished to impress upon him. You must think more as I do. She is real, yes, but she is also a figment, a longing formed out of your own need. In your loneliness, you have settled on the first face which has caught your eye. It might have been anyone, you know. You are, after all, a man, my dear fellow; she is only a woman, and there are thousands like her scattered throughout this great city.

I had a single day in which to plot Stefan Peterson's best course of action. On the forthcoming Thursday, I decided, he would keep himself outside of Portman's and watch from afar as she entered the shop—at which point, he would make his way into the alley behind the proprietor's garden and wait, out of range, for the back gate eventually to open. Without fail, my plan was realized on the next afternoon: At approximately five o'clock Mrs. Keller exited through the back gate with her parasol raised and a book in one hand. She began walking immediately, and he went after her, maintaining his distance. Even when he wished to draw closer, something kept him at bay. Still, his eyes discerned the hairpins in her thick black hair and the minute bustling of her hips. Every so often, she would pause and tilt her head to the sky, allowing him to catch sight of her profile—the outline of her lower jaw, the almost transparent smoothness of her skin. Then it would appear as if she was speaking beneath her breath, and her mouth mumbled without sound. Once her utterances were finished, she would stare ahead again and continue forwards. She moved through Russell Square, journeyed down Guilford Street, turned left upon Gray's Inn Road, headed across the intersection at King's Cross, and travelled for a short time on a side street, where, soon deviating from the footpath, she proceeded alongside railway tracks near St. Pancras Station. It was an undirected, circuitous route; yet from the deliberate movement of her steps, he understood that this was no mere stroll for Mrs. Keller. And when, finally, she passed through the large iron gates of the Physics and Botanical Society, the late afternoon had begun its transformation into early evening.

The park in which he found himself as he followed her beyond the high redbrick walls presented as great a contrast to the area as there could be: Outside, on a wide artery which conveyed the city's traffic, the roadway was packed with commerce streaming in either direction, while the footpaths were swarming with pedestrians; but past the iron gates, where olive trees stood amidst winding gravel pathways and beds of vegetables and herbs and flowers, was 6.4 acres of lush, pastoral terrain surrounding a manor house which, in 1772, had been bequeathed to the society by Sir Philip Sloane. There, in the shade of those trees, she went on ahead while lazily rotating the parasol; veering right from the main pathway, she took a slender trail, going past echium and *Atropa belladonna,* past horsetail and feverfew, stopping on occasion to touch the flowers lightly, whispering as she did. He, too, was there with her, but he was not yet willing to close the distance between them, even as he became aware that they were the only two people walking upon the trail.

They continued past irises, past chrysanthemums—one before the other—until, for a moment, he lost sight of her where the trail wound behind a tall hedgerow, seeing only the parasol, which floated above the foliage. Then her parasol dipped from view, and her footsteps on the gravel fell quiet. And when he rounded the corner, she was much closer than he expected her to be. Settling herself upon a bench which marked a fork in the trail, she placed the shut parasol across her lap and opened the book. Quite soon, he knew, the sun would angle below the park's walls, casting everything in darker hues. Now you must act, he told himself. Now, while light persists.

Tucking in his ascot, he nervously approached her, saying, "Pardon me." For he wanted to enquire about the volume she was holding, politely explaining that he was a collector of books, an avid reader, and was always interested to learn about what others were reading.

"I've only just begun it," she said, glancing at him warily when he sat down beside her.

"How wonderful," he said, speaking enthusiastically, as if to hide his own awkwardness. "It certainly is a pleasant location in which to enjoy something new, wouldn't you agree?"

"It is," she answered in a composed voice. Her eyebrows were very thick, almost bushy, giving her blue eyes a stern appearance. She seemed annoyed by something—was it the imposition of his presence, or simply the guarded reticence of a cautious, withdrawn woman?

"If I may—" he said, nodding at the book. A reluctant moment transpired before she offered it to him, and, marking her page with his index finger, he looked at its spine. "Ah, Menshov's *Autumn Vespers*. Very good. I, too, have a fondness for Russian writers."

"I see," said she.

There was a long silence, broken only by the measured tapping of his fingertips upon the book's cover. "A fine edition—the binding is well stitched." Her stare lingered on him as he gave her back the book, and he was struck by her odd, asymmetrical face—the cocked eyebrow, that forced half smile he had also seen in the photograph. Then she rose and reached for her parasol.

"You will excuse me, sir, but I must be going."

She had found him unappealing—how else to explain her need to depart after having just arrived at the bench?

"Forgive me. I have disturbed you."

"No, no," said she, "not at all. But it's getting rather late, and I'm expected at home."

"Of course," said he.

There was something otherworldly in her blue eyes, and her pale skin, and her overall demeanour—the slow, meandering movements of her limbs as she left him, the way she drifted like an apparition on the trail. Yes, something aimless and poised and unknowable, he was sure, as she went away from him and moved back around the hedgerow. Now with dusk creeping over the grounds, he felt at a loss. It was not meant to end so suddenly; to her, he was supposed to have been interesting, unique—a kindred spirit, perhaps. So what was that inability, that lacking in himself? Why, when it seemed every molecule within him pulled towards her, had she been quick to leave him? And what was it, just then, that made him go after her on the trail, even while it appeared that she regarded him as a nuisance? He could not say, nor could he fathom why it was that his mind and body were, at that moment, in disagreement: One knew better than the other did, yet the more rational of the two remained less determined.

Still, a chance of reprieval awaited him beyond the hedgerow, for she had not hurried on like he'd believed; instead, she was crouched beside the irises, the hem of her grey dress brushing against the gravel, and had set the book and parasol aside on the ground. Cupping one of the large showy flowers in her right hand, she was unaware of him coming near, nor, in the decreasing light, did she realise his shadow when it fell across her. And while standing over her, he watched intently as her fingers pressed gently against the linear leaves. Then as she withdrew her hand, he observed that a worker bee had strayed onto her glove. But she did not flinch, shaking the creature free, or crush it in her fist. A slight grin spread upon her face as she pondered the bee closely, doing so with apparent reverence, and for a while affectionate whispers were uttered. The worker bee, in turn, stayed upon her palm—not busying itself, or burying its stinger into her glove—as if regarding her the same. How unusual a communion, he thought, the likes of which he had never witnessed before. At last, she saw fit to release the creature, setting it loose on the very flower from whence it had come, and reached for the parasol and book.

"*Iris* means 'rainbow,' " he stammered, yet she was not startled to discover him there. As she rose up, assessing him with a dispassionate stare, he heard the waver of desperation in his voice but could not prevent himself from speaking. "It's easy to understand why, as they grow in so many colours—blues and purples, whites and yellows—like these—and pinks and oranges, browns and reds, even blacks. It is a resilient flower, you know. With enough light, they will grow in desert regions, or in the cold of the far north."

Her absent expression turned into one of permissiveness, and, going forth, she left space for him to stroll alongside her, listening as he told her everything he knew about the flower. Iris was the Greek goddess of the rainbow, the messenger of Zeus and Hera, whose duty it was to lead the souls of dead women to the Elysian fields. As a result, the Greeks planted purple irises on the graves of women; ancient Egyptians adorned sceptres with an iris, which represented faith, wisdom, and valour; the Romans honoured the Goddess Juno with the flower, and used it during purification ceremonies. "Perhaps you are already aware that the Iris Florentina—*Il Giaggiolo*—is the official flower of Florence. And if you have ever visited Tuscany, you have no doubt also inhaled the purple irises which are cultivated amongst the many olive trees there—a scent very much like that of violets."

Glancing at him, she was now attentive and fascinated, as if this sudden encounter had highlighted an uneventful afternoon. "It does sound rather pleasing, the way you describe it," said she. "But, no, I haven't visited Tuscany—or Italy, for that matter."

"Oh, you must, my dear, you really must. There is no place better than its Hill Country."

Then, in that instant, he could think of nothing else to say. The words, he feared, had all dried up, and there was little else for him to impart. She looked away, staring ahead. He hoped that she would offer something, yet he was sure that she would not. So it was as though, out of frustration or out of pure impatience with himself, he decided to dispense with the endless weighing of his own thoughts and, instead, speak without first considering the actual meaning of what would be said.

"I wonder—might I ask—what attracts you to such a thing as an iris?"

She drew a deep breath of temperate spring air and, for no clear reason, shook her head. "What attracts me to such a thing as an iris? It is something I have never really examined." She breathed deeply again and smiled to herself, finally saying, "I suppose a flower thrives during even the worst of times, does it not? And an iris endures: After it has withered, there comes another just like it to take its place. In that regard, flowers are short-lived yet persistent, so I suspect they are less affected by all which is great or awful around them. Does that answer your question?"

"Somewhat, yes."

They had reached the point where the trail verged with the main pathway. He slowed his steps, glancing at her, and when he stopped walking, she did, too. But what was it he wanted to tell her, then, as he searched her face? What was it, in the faint glow at dusk, which stirred his desperation once more? She gazed up into his unblinking eyes, waiting for him to continue.

"I possess a gift," he heard himself tell her. "I would like to share it with you, if you will allow me."

"A gift?"

"More of a hobby, really, although one which has proven rather beneficial for others. You see, I am somewhat of an amateur palmist."

"I don't understand."

He extended an arm towards her, showing her his palm: "From this, I can discern future events with a fair degree of accuracy." He could gaze upon any stranger's hand, he explained, and decipher the course of his or her life—the potential for true love, for a happy marriage, the ultimate number of offspring, various spiritual concerns, and whether one might expect a long life. "So if you can spare me a moment, I would very much like to give you a taste of my talent."

How despicable he felt, how manoeuvring he must have seemed to her. And the puzzled expression which she displayed made him confident that a polite rebuke was forthcoming; except—while the expression remained upon her—she knelt instead, depositing the parasol and book at her feet, then stood again to face him. Without a trace of hesitation, she tugged off the right glove and, fixing her eyes upon him, presented her bare hand, palm up.

"Show me," said she.

"Very well."

He took her hand into his hand, yet it was difficult to see anything in the evening light. Bending for a closer look, he could only make out the whiteness of her flesh—the pale skin muted by shadows, obscured at the day's end. Nothing distinguished its surface—no obvious lines, no deep-set grooves. It was nothing but a smooth, pure layer; all he could perceive about her palm, then, was its lack of depth. It was unblemished beyond measuring, and devoid of the telltale marks of existence, as if, in fact, she had not been born at all. A trick of the light, he reasoned. A trick of vision. But still came a voice from within himself which troubled his thoughts: This is someone who will never grow into an old woman, who will never become wrinkled or dodder from one room into the next.

Even so, there was another kind of clarity revealed upon her palm, and it contained both the past and the future. "Your parents are gone," said he. "Your father when you were but an infant, your mother rather recently." She did not move, nor did she reply. He spoke of her unborn, her husband's concerns for her. He told her that she was loved, that she would regain hope, and that, in time, she would find great happiness in her life. "You are correct to believe you are part of something larger," he said, "something benevolent, like God."

And there, in the shade of gardens and parks, was the affirmation she sought. There she was free, sheltered from the busy lanes where carriage after carriage rolled by, where the potential for death was always lurking, and where men swaggered about, throwing their long, dubious shadows behind them. Yes, he could see it upon her skin: She felt alive and intact when sequestered with nature.

"I cannot say any more, as it is getting too dark. But I would be more than willing to resume on some other day."

Her hand had begun trembling, and, shaking her head with consternation, she unexpectedly retracted it as if flames grazed her fingers. "No, I'm sorry" was her flustered reply, spoken while she knelt to collect her belongings. "I must be going, I really must. Thank you."

Then, as if he were not standing beside her, she promptly turned and hurried along the main pathway. Yet the warmth of her hand lingered; the fragrance she wore persevered. He did not attempt to call after her, or try to leave the grounds in her company. It was only right that she should go without him. It was foolish expecting anything else from her on that evening. Surely it is for the best, he thought, watching her drift onwards, her body receding from his. What happened next, however, was scarcely to be believed; he would, later on, insist that it had not occurred as it was remembered, and yet he would envision it so: For before his eyes, she vanished upon the pathway, dissolving within a cloud of whitest ether. But what remained— fluttering down at that instant like a leaf—was the glove which had held the bee. In astonishment, he ran to the spot where she had disappeared, stooping for the glove. Again, when returning to Baker Street, he questioned the accuracy of his memory, even while he was sure that the glove had moved farther away from him, like a mirage— until it, too, slipped beyond his grasp and was no more.

And soon, just like Mrs. Keller and the glove, Stefan Peterson would also swiftly dematerialise, forever lost with the shifting of limbs, the change of facial characteristics, the unbuttoning and folding of clothing. Once his removal was complete, an immense burden felt taken from my shoulders. Yet I was not fully satisfied, for there was much about the woman which continued to engage me. When a preoccupation stayed upon my mind, I would often go for days without sleep, mulling the evidence over and considering it from every angle. So with Mrs. Keller loitering in my thoughts, I realised that any kind of rest would elude me for a while.

That night, I wandered about in my large blue dressing gown, gathering pillows from my bed and cushions from the sofa and armchairs. In the drawing room, then, I fashioned a makeshift Eastern divan, upon which I placed myself, along with a fresh supply of cigarettes, a box of matches, and the woman's photograph. By the flickering of the lamp, I eventually saw her there; coming through the veil of blue smoke, her hands reached for me, her eyes locked upon mine, and I sat motionless, cigarette fuming between my lips, as the light shone over her softly defined features. Then it was as if her appearance resolved whatever intricacies were plaguing me; she had come, she had touched my skin, and, in her presence, I was lulled easily into a restful slumber. Sometime thereafter, I awoke, to discover the spring sun illuminating the room. The cigarettes were all consumed, and the tobacco haze still floated at the ceiling—but there was no lingering trace of her to be found, other than that remote, pensive face sealed behind a veneer of glass.

17

MORNING CAME.

His pen was nearly out of ink. The clean sheets of writing paper had been exhausted, and the desk was blanketed with Holmes's feverish nocturnal endeavor. Though as opposed to the mindless jotting of notes, it was a more focused undertaking that had spurred his hand until dawn—that continuation of the story regarding a woman he'd met once decades ago, and who, for some apart reason, had compelled herself into his thoughts during the nighttime, coming to him as a vivid, fully formed specter while he rested at his desk, thumbs pressed against his closed eyelids: "You haven't forgotten me, have you?" said the long-dead Mrs. Keller.

"No," he whispered.

"Nor I you."

"Is that so?" he asked, raising his head. "How can that be?"

She, too, like young Roger, had walked alongside him among flowers and on gravel pathways, often saying very little (her attention roving here and there, to the curious objects she encountered upon her way)—and, like the boy, her existence in his life was an ephemeral one, leaving him quietly distraught and senseless after their parting. Of course, she never knew anything factual regarding his true self, had no idea he was a renowned investigator following her in disguise; instead, she forever knew him as a timid book collector, a shy man sharing an equal love for flora and Russian literature—a stranger met in the park one day, but a kind soul all the same, nervously approaching her as she sat on a bench, inquiring politely about the novel she was reading: "Pardon me—I couldn't help noticing—is that Menshov's *Autumn Vespers* you've got there?"

"It is," she said in a composed voice.

"The writing is remarkable, wouldn't you agree?" he continued, speaking enthusiastically, as if to hide his own contrived awkwardness. "Not without its flaws—except in a translation, the mistakes are expected and, I suppose, somewhat forgivable."

"I haven't seen any. Actually, I've only just begun—"

"Still, you must have," he said. "Possibly you didn't realize it—they're easy to miss."

She glanced at him warily when he sat down beside her. Her dark eyebrows were very thick, almost bushy, giving her blue eyes a stern appearance. She seemed annoyed by something—was it the imposition of his presence, or simply the guarded reticence of a cautious, withdrawn woman?

"If I may—" he said, nodding at the book in her hands. After a silent moment, she gave it to him, and, marking the page with his index finger, he searched toward the front of the book, eventually saying, "See, here for example: Early in the story the gymnasium students were shirtless, for Menshov wrote: 'The imposing man stood the bare-chested boys in a line, and Vladimir, feeling exposed with Andrei and Sergei, hung his long arms at his side.' Later, however—on the next page—he writes: 'Upon hearing the man was a general, Vladimir discreetly fastened his cuffs behind his back, then straightened his narrow shoulders.' You can find many instances of this sort of thing in Menshov's writing—or at least in the translations of his writing."

Yet in his account of her, Holmes had failed to recall the exact conversation that had prompted their acquaintance, noting only that he'd asked about the book and that he had then been struck by the lingering stare she gave him (the odd, asymmetrical allure of her face—the one cocked eyebrow, that reluctant half smile he'd first studied in a photograph—was of the impassive-heroine type). There was something otherworldly in her blue eyes, and her pale skin, and her overall demeanor—the slow, meandering movements of her limbs, the way she drifted like a ghost on the garden pathways. Something aimless and poised and unknowable—something resigned and fatalistic, apparently.

Setting his pen aside, Holmes returned to the sharp reality of his study. Since dawn, he'd been ignoring his physical needs, but now he'd go from the attic (however much he dreaded the idea) and empty his bladder, and drink water, and, prior to stomaching a meal, investigate the apiary in the light of day. Carefully, he gathered up the pages on his desk, sorting them, organizing them into a stack. Afterward, he yawned, arching his spine. His skin and clothes smelled of cigar smoke, musty and pungent, and he felt light-headed from having worked through the night, his head and shoulders bent over the desktop. With canes in place, he pushed himself off the seat, gradually coming to his feet. Pivoting around, he began inching toward the door, oblivious to the popping of leg bones, the gentle cracking of joints put in motion.

Then as impressions of Roger and Mrs. Keller commingled in his mind, Holmes exited his smoke-filled workplace, reflexively checking for the supper tray usually left by the boy in the hallway, yet knowing even before crossing the threshold that it wouldn't be there. He proceeded along the hallway, tracing the route that had brought him miserably upstairs. However, his stupor of the previous evening was gone; the horrible black cloud that had stunned his senses and turned a pleasant afternoon to the darkest of nights had dissipated, and Holmes was ready for the task ahead: the descending into a house absent of any soul other than himself, the donning of suitable attire, the sluggish journey beyond the garden—where he'd approach the beeyard like a phantom concealed behind a veil, going forward in clothes of white.

But for a long time, Holmes stood at the top of the stairs, waiting as he did when Roger was coming to assist him downward. His tired eyes closed, and the boy moved swiftly up the stairs. Subsequently, the boy materialized elsewhere, too, appearing in places Holmes had seen him in the past: easing his slender form into the tide pool, the cool water producing goose pimples on his chest as it engulfed his body; running through high grass with his butterfly net outstretched, wearing an untucked cotton shirt, its sleeves rolled to his elbows; hanging a pollen feeder near the hives, positioning it in a sunny spot for the creatures he'd grown to love so. Curiously, each fleeting glimpse of the boy was in the spring or the summer. Still, Holmes could feel winter's cold, could suddenly imagine the boy underground, entombed beneath the frigid earth.

Mrs. Munro's words found him then: "He's a good boy," she'd said when taking the job of housekeeper. "Keeps to himself, rather shy—very quiet, more like his father was. He won't be a burden on you, I promise."

Except, Holmes knew now, the boy had become a burden, a most painful burden. All the same, he told himself, whether it was Roger or anyone else, every life had a finish. And every one of the dead he'd knelt beside had had a life. He set his sights on the stairs below, and while beginning his descent, he repeated within the questions he'd pondered to no avail since his youth: "What is the meaning of it? What object is served by this circle of misery? It must tend to some end, or else the universe is ruled by chance. But what end?"

Upon reaching the second floor—where he'd use the lavatory, and enliven his face and neck with cold water—Holmes heard, for a moment, the faint hum of what he imagined to be an insect or bird singing, and thought of the thick stems that likely guarded it. For neither stems nor insects took part in the misery of mankind.

Perhaps, he mused, this was why—as opposed to people—they could return again and again. Only later, when arriving on the ground floor of his house, would he realize that the humming was originating indoors—a soft drone, sporadic and human, brightening the kitchen; it was a woman's, or a child's voice, to be sure—although clearly not Mrs. Munro's, and, with certainty, not Roger's.

Taking half a dozen nimble steps, Holmes brought himself to the kitchen doorway, catching sight of steam rising from a boiling pot on the stove. Then moving inside, he spotted her at the cutting board, her backside to him as she sliced a potato and thoughtlessly hummed. But it was the long, waving black hair that at once unsettled him—the floating black hair, the pink-and-white skin of her arms, that diminutive form he associated with the unfortunate Mrs. Keller. How speechless he stood there, incapable of addressing such an apparition—until, finally, he parted his lips, desperately saying, "Why have you come here?"

With that, the humming ceased, and the head pivoting sharply to meet his stare revealed a plain-looking girl, a child no older than eighteen—large, mild eyes and a kind, possibly stupid, expression.

"Sir . . ."

Holmes ambled forward, looming in front of her.

"Who are you? What are you doing here?"

"It's me, sir" was her earnest answer. "I'm Em—I'm Tom Anderson's daughter—I thought you knew."

There was silence. The girl lowered her head, avoiding his glare.

"Constable Anderson's daughter?" asked Holmes quietly.

"Yes, sir. I didn't think you'd be taking your breakfast—I was getting your lunch ready."

"But what are you doing here? Where is Mrs. Munro?"

"She's asleep, poor dear." The girl didn't sound glum about this, but happy to have something to relate. She kept her head lowered, addressing the canes near her feet, and as she talked, she made a slight whistling noise, as if she were blowing the words between her lips. "Dr. Baker was with her through the night—except she's sleeping now. I don't know what he gave her."

"She is at the cottage?"

"Yes, sir."

"I see. And Anderson sent you here?"

She seemed bewildered. "Yes, sir," she said. "I thought you knew—I thought my father told you he'd send me."

Then Holmes recalled Anderson knocking on the study door the night before—the constable asking questions, saying some trivial things, placing a hand gently on his shoulder—but it was all a blur.

"Of course," he said, glancing at the window above the sink, the sunlight illuminating the countertop. He breathed rather hard, then looked again, with a hint of disarray, at the girl. "I am sorry—it's been a very trying few hours."

"No apologies, sir, really." Her head rose up. "Something to eat is what you need."

"Just a glass of water, I should think."

Listless from lack of sleep, Holmes scratched at his beard and yawned, watching as the girl promptly fetched his drink, frowning as she ran her hands on her hips upon filling the glass from the tap (the glass being delivered to him with a pleased, somewhat grateful smile).

"Anything else?"

"No," he said, hanging a cane on his wrist, freeing a hand so he could accept what she held for him.

"Got the pot boiling for your lunch," she told him, crossing back to the cutting board. "But if you change your mind about breakfast, you let me know."

The girl lifted a paring knife from the counter. She slouched carelessly forward, slicing at a potato piece, clearing her throat as the blade diced. And after Holmes emptied the glass, placing it in the sink, she resumed humming. So he left her, going from the kitchen without saying any more—along the corridor, out the front door—

listening to that wavering, tuneless hum, which stayed with him for a while—into the yard, toward the garden shed—even when it could no longer be heard.

But as he approached the shed, the girl's drone fluttered away like the butterflies around him, becoming replaced in his thoughts by the beauty of his own garden: the blooms aimed at the clear sky, the scent of lupine in the air, the birds twittering from the nearby pines—and the bees hovering here and there, alighting on petals, vanishing within the cups of flowers.

You wayward workers, he thought. You mercurial insects of habit.

Looking from the garden, facing the wooden shed directly before him, the centuries-old advice of a Roman writer on agriculture found Holmes at that moment (the name of the author eluding him, yet the man's antiquated message eased readily through his mind): *Thou must not come puffing or blowing unto them, neither hastily stir among them, nor resolutely defend thyself when they seem to threaten thee; but softly moving thy hand before thy face, gently put them by; and lastly, thou must be no stranger to them.*

He unlatched and pulled open the shed door fully so that sunshine could precede him into the shadowy, dust-rich hut—the rays irradiating the crowded shelves (bags of soil and seeds, gardening spades and claws, and empty pots, and the folded clothing of a once-novice beekeeper), those places where his hands now reached. On a rake standing upright in a corner, he'd hung his coat, leaving it there as he managed to slip on the white overalls, the light-colored gloves, the wide-brimmed hat, and the veil. Soon he emerged transformed, surveying his garden from behind the veil's gauze, shuffling onward—down the pathway, across the pasture, to the beeyard—with his canes as the only visible signatures of his identity.

Yet when Holmes wandered about his apiary, everything immediately appeared ordinary there, and suddenly he felt ill at ease in the confining clothing. Peering into the dark interior of one hive, then another, he saw the bees among their cities of wax—cleaning their antennae, rubbing forelegs vigorously around their compound eyes, readying themselves for departure into the air. On initial observation, all was customary in the bees' world—the machinelike life of such social creatures, that steady, harmonious murmur—with no clue of any rebellion brewing amid the ordered routine of their insect commonwealth. The third hive was the same, as were the fourth and fifth (whatever reservations he'd harbored quickly evaporated, replaced instead by more familiar feelings of humility and awe for the complex civilization of the hive). Taking his canes from where he'd propped them during an inspection, a sensation of invulnerability claimed him: You won't harm me, was his calming thought. There is nothing here for either of us to fear.

However—while hunched over, removing the cover of the sixth hive—an ominous shadow fell upon him, giving him a start. Glancing sideways through the veil, he first noticed black clothing (a woman's frock, fringed in lace), then a right hand, the thin fingers gripping a red gallon canister. But it was the stoic face gazing at him that provided the greatest vexation—those wide, sedated pupils, the grief conveyed only by the insensible absence of emotion—recalling the young woman who had come to his garden holding her dead infant, yet belonging now to Mrs. Munro.

"I am not sure it's safe, you know," he told her, becoming upright. "You probably should go back at once."

She didn't alter her gaze, or respond with as much as a blink.

"Did you hear me?" he said. "I cannot say for sure if you are at peril, but you might be."

Her eyes kept firmly on him, except her lips moved, imparting nothing for a moment, until asking in a whisper, "Will you kill them?"

"What's that?"

She spoke a little louder: "Will you destroy your bees?"

"Certainly not" came his emphatic reply, even as he felt sympathy for her, and suppressed a growing sense that she was intruding.

"I think you must," she said, "or I'll do it for you."

He already understood it was petrol she was carrying (for the canister belonged to him, its contents used on the dead wood in the nearby forest). In addition, he'd just seen the box of matches held in her other hand, although in her state he couldn't envision her mustering the vigor to ignite the hives. Still, there was something determined in the flatness of her voice, something resolute. The grief-stricken, he knew, were occasionally possessed by a powerful, ruthless indignation—and the Mrs. Munro before him (unflinching, cool, somehow impassive) was a far cry from that chatty, gregarious housekeeper he'd known for years; this Mrs. Munro, unlike the other, made him hesitant, and timid.

Holmes raised the veil, showing an expression as restrained as her own. He said, "You are upset, my child—and confused. Pray go to the cottage and I will have the girl send for Dr. Baker."

She didn't budge. She didn't take her stare from him. "I'm burying my son in two days," she told him plainly enough. "I'll be going tonight—he's going with me. He's going to London in a box—it isn't right."

A deep gloom settled on Holmes. "I am sorry, my dear. I am so sorry—"

And with the softening of his expression, her voice rose above his, saying, "You didn't have the decency to tell me, did you? You hid in your attic and refused seeing me."

"I am sorry—"

"I think you're a selfish old man, it's true. I think you are responsible for my son's death."

"Nonsense," he uttered, but all he felt was her anguish.

"I blame you as much as I blame these monsters you keep. If it weren't for you, he wouldn't have been here, would he? No, it'd be you that got stung dead, not my boy. It wasn't his job anyway, was it? He didn't have to be here alone—he shouldn't have been here, alone like that."

Holmes studied her austere face—the hollow cheeks, the blood-shot eyes—and searched for words, finally telling her, "But he wanted to be here. You must know that. Could I have foreseen the danger, do you imagine I would have let him tend the hives? Do you know how I ache from his loss? I ache for you, as well. Can't you see?"

A bee circled her head, landing briefly on her hair; yet, pinning Holmes with those glaring pupils, she paid the creature no mind. "Then you'll kill them," she said. "You'll destroy them all, if you care anything about us. You'll do what's right to do."

"I won't do that, my dear. It would serve no one to do so, not even the boy."

"Then I'll do it now. You can't stop me."

"You will do nothing of the sort."

She remained motionless, and for several seconds, Holmes con-templated his course of action. If she toppled him, he could do little to prevent her havoc. She was younger; he was frail. But if the attack was his, if he could swing a cane into her chin or neck, she might fall to the ground—and if she fell to the ground, he could strike her again, repeatedly. He glanced at his canes, both propped against the hive. His stare returned to her. Moments passed in silence, neither shifting an inch. At last she relented, shaking her head, saying with a trembling voice, "I wish I'd never met you, sir. I wish I'd never made your acquaintance in this world—and I'll shed no tears on your passing."

"Please," he implored her, reaching for his canes, "it isn't safe for you. Go back to the cottage."

But already Mrs. Munro had turned, going sluggishly away, as if walking in her sleep. By the time she reached the edge of the bee-yard, the canister had been dropped, followed shortly thereafter by the box of matches. Then as she traveled across the pasture, where presently she went from view, Holmes heard her weeping, her sobs becoming more severe, yet fainter and fainter along the cottage pathway.

Stepping in front of the hive, he continued looking at the pasture, at the high grass swaying in Mrs. Munro's wake. She had disrupted the equanimity of the beeyard, now the tranquil grass. There's important work to be done, he wanted to shout out, but stopped himself, for the woman was ravaged by sadness, and he could think only of the business at hand (inspecting the hives, finding a degree of peace within the apiary). You are right, he thought. I am a selfish man. The reality of this notion produced a frown on his troubled face. Propping his canes once more, he sank to the ground, sitting there as a feeling of emptiness swelled up inside. His ears registered the low, concentrated murmur of the hive—the sound of which, in that moment, refused to summon his isolated, content years cultivating the beeyard, but, rather, conveyed the undeniable and deepening loneliness of his existence.

How thoroughly the emptiness could have consumed him then, how easily he might have begun sobbing like Mrs. Munro—if not for the lone yellow-and-black-winged stranger landing on the side of the hive, drawing Holmes's attention, pausing long enough for him to speak its name *"Vespula vulgaris"*—before taking flight again, zigzagging overhead and off in the direction of Roger's death place. Absently, he went for his canes, his brow creasing with puzzlement: What of the stingers? Were there stingers on the boy's clothing, on his skin?

But try as he did—conjuring Roger's body, seeing just the boy's eyes—he couldn't say for sure. Even so, he had probably warned Roger about wasps, mentioning the danger they posed to the apiary. He would, most certainly, have explained that the wasp was the natural enemy of the bee, capable of crushing honeybee after honeybee with its mandibles (some species killing as many as forty bees per minute), wiping out an entire hive, and robbing the larvae. Surely, he would have told the boy the differences between a bee's stinger and a wasp's stinger—the heavily barbed organ of the bee fixing into skin, disemboweling the creature; the wasp's lightly barbed needle barely penetrating flesh, getting withdrawn and used many times.

Holmes climbed to his feet. Hastily, he crossed the beeyard, and as his legs brushed through high grass, he began trampling down a parallel trail alongside the one that Roger had previously created, hoping to chart the boy's journey from the beeyard to his death place. (No, you weren't fleeing the bees, he reasoned. You weren't running from anything, not yet.) Roger's trail curved sharply at its halfway point and veered toward the spot that had obscured the corpse, dead-ending where the boy had fallen—a small clearing of limestone encircled by the grass. There, Holmes saw two more man-made trails, stretching from the distant garden pathway, circumventing the beeyard altogether, each leading to or from the clearing (one fashioned by Anderson and his men, the other by Holmes after finding the body). Then he wondered if he should simply continue forging his own trail farther into the pasture, pursuing what he knew he would likely find. But when turning and staring at the flattened grass, noting the curve that had sent the boy to the clearing, he began retracing his own steps.

Stopping near the curved area, he looked ahead at Roger's trail. The grass was crushed deliberately and evenly, suggesting the boy, like himself, had walked slowly from the beeyard. He glanced to the clearing. The grass was flattened only intermittently, telling him that the boy had been running there. He set his sights on the curve, that changing of course, that abrupt departure. To this point you walked, he thought, and from here you ran.

He moved forward, bringing himself to stand on the boy's trail, where he peered into the grass just beyond the curve. Several yards away, he saw a glint of silver among the thick stems. "What's this?" he said to himself, searching for the glint again. No, he was not mistaken: Something was gleaming dully there in the high grass. He pushed onward for an improved view, departing the boy's trail but soon discovering he had entered another, less obvious path—a detour that had taken the boy step by gradual step into the pasture's densest overgrowth. Pressed with impatience, Holmes quickened his pace, crushing the spots the boy had been careful to tread upon, unaware of the wasp riding on his shoulder—or the other wasps skimming above his hat. Half-crouching, he took a few more steps and found the source of the strange gleaming. It was a watering can, one belonging to his garden, resting on its side, the spout still wet and dripping and obliging the thirst of three wasps (the black-and-yellow workers bustling around the sprinkler, scurrying about for a fuller drop).

"A grave decision, my boy," he said, nudging the watering can with a cane, watching as the startled wasps gave flight. "A terrible miscalculation—"

He lowered the veil before proceeding, feeling little concern about the wasp who then roamed along the beekeeper's gauze like a sentinel. For he knew he was close to their nest, and, he knew, they could do nothing to defend themselves. He was, after all, better suited for their destruction than the boy had ever been, so he would finish what Roger had attempted but ultimately failed to do. Yet as he scanned the ground below, minding every step he took, he was filled with regret. In teaching the boy much, he had apparently not taught him a most vital fact: that pouring water into a wasps' nest only hastened the insects' wrath; it was—Holmes wished he had told him—like using petrol to quell a fire.

"Poor boy," he said, spying a hole in the ground formed curiously like a gaping, filthy mouth. "My poor boy," he said, dipping a cane just past the lips of the hole, extracting it then, bringing the inserted end in front of the veil and studying the wasps that were now clinging to it (seven or eight of the creatures, agitated by the cane's violation, angrily probing the offender's circumference). He shook the cane, scattering the wasps. Then he gazed into the hole, its lips muddy from where the water had spilled, and saw the darkness inside taking shape, writhing upward as wasp after wasp began scrambling from the opening—a good many going straight into the air, some landing on the veil, others swarming around the hole. So this was how it happened, he thought. This, my boy, was how you were taken.

Without panic, Holmes retreated, heading woefully to the beeyard. In time, he would phone Anderson, uttering exactly what the local coroner was in the process of recording, something Mrs. Munro would hear related at the afternoon's inquest: There were no stingers protruding from the boy's skin or clothing, indicating that Roger was the victim of wasps, not bees. Moreover, Holmes would make clear, the boy was trying to protect the hives. Roger had no doubt observed wasps in the apiary, had then found their nest, and, attempting to eradicate the creatures by drowning them, provoked the brood into a full-scale attack.

There was more Holmes would share with Anderson, various minor details (the boy fleeing in the opposite direction of the beeyard while getting stung, perhaps intending to steer the wasps away from the hives). Before calling the constable, however, he would retrieve the dropped petrol canister and find the matches Mrs. Munro had discarded. Leaving one cane at the apiary, his fingers grasping the canister's handle, he'd journey again to the pasture, eventually pouring petrol into the hole as doused wasps struggled helplessly outward. A single match would complete his task, the flame cutting like a fuse across the ground, igniting the gaping mouth with a hiss, producing a slight eruption, which momentarily belched fire past the earthen lips (nothing escaping from within afterward save a single twisting ribbon of smoke that dissipated above the undisturbed grass), eliminating in an instant the queen and the fertile eggs and the throng of workers trapped inside their colony: a vast and intricate empire encased by the yellowish paper of the nest, gone in a flash, like young Roger.

Good riddance, mused Holmes while weaving through the high grass. "Good riddance," he said aloud, his head arched to the cloudless sky, his vision disoriented by the expanse of blue ether. And upon speaking those words, he was overcome by an immense melancholy for all enduring life, everything that had and did and would someday rove beneath such perfect, ever-present stillness. "Good riddance," he repeated, and began weeping noiselessly behind the veil.

18

WHY HAD the tears come? Why—while resting in bed, then pacing the study, then going to the beeyard the next morning, and the morning after that—did Holmes find his head touched by his own hands and his fingertips wetted from brushing his whiskers, even as no crippling sob or mighty lament or paralysis transfigured him? Somewhere else—he imagined a small cemetery on the outskirts of London—stood Mrs. Munro and her relatives, everyone dressed in clothes as bleak as the gray clouds brooding over the sea and land. Was she crying, too? Or had Mrs. Munro shed all her tears during the lonely trip to London, sustaining herself in the city with the strength of family, the comfort of friends?

It's unimportant, he told himself. She is elsewhere, and I am here—and I can do nothing for her.

Still, he had made some effort toward helping her. Prior to her departure, he'd sent Anderson's daughter to the cottage twice, the girl carrying an envelope with more than enough money for travel and funeral expenses; both times, the girl returned, her features demure yet pleasant, informing him that the envelope had been refused.

"She won't take it, sir—won't talk to me, either."

"It is all right, Em."

"Should I try again?"

"Best not—I don't think it will accomplish much."

Now facing the apiary alone, his expression was abstracted and strict and frozen in dismay, as if he were also standing with the mourners at Roger's graveside. Even the hives—the white rows of boxes, the unadorned rectangular shapes rising from the grass— seemed like burial monuments to him. A small cemetery not dissimilar to the beeyard, he hoped was the case. A simple place—well tended and green, no weeds, no buildings or roadways visible nearby, no motorcars or human bustle disrupting the dead. A peaceful place aligned with nature, a good location for the boy to rest and for the mother to say good-bye.

But why was he weeping so effortlessly, yet without emotion, the tears impelled by their own accord? Why couldn't he cry out loud, sobbing into his palms? And why—on the occasion of other deaths, when the pain was equal to what he felt now—had he shunned the funerals of loved ones and never once spilled a single tear, as if sorrow itself was something to be frowned upon?

"No matter," he muttered. "It's pointless."

He wouldn't strive for any answers (at least not on this day), nor would he ever believe that his tearfulness might be the concentrated sum-total result of everything he had seen, known, cared for, lost, and kept stifled throughout the decades—the fragments of his youth, the destruction of great cities and empires—those vast, geography-changing wars—then the slow atrophy of fond companions and one's own health, memory, personal history; all of life's implicit complexities, each profound and altering moment, condensed to a welling salty substance in his tired eyes. Instead, he sank downward without dwelling any more, lowering himself to the ground, sitting there like some stone figure that had inexplicably been set in the shorn grass.

He'd sat there previously, on the very same spot—near the apiary, the location marked off by four rocks carried up from the beach eighteen years earlier (black-gray stones made smooth and flat by the tide, fitting perfectly into his palm), placed exactly apart—one in front of him, one behind, one to the left, one to the right—forming a discreet, unassuming patch, which had, in the past, contained and muted his despair. It was a slight trick of the mind, a game of sorts, though often beneficial: Within the rocks' domain, he could meditate, thinking warmly of those who were gone—and later, when stepping beyond the patch, whatever grief he'd brought into the space was kept there, if only for a short while. *"Mens sana in corpore sano"* was his incantation, spoken once inside the patch, repeated afterward when stepping from it. "Everything comes in circles, even the poet Juvenal."

First in 1929, and then again in 1946, he'd regularly used the spot to commune with the dead, subduing his woes in the unanimity of the beeyard. But 1929 was almost his undoing, producing a far more grievous period than the current upset, for elderly Mrs. Hudson—his housekeeper and cook since his London days, the only person who had accompanied him to the Sussex farmhouse upon his retirement—fell to the kitchen floor with a broken hip, cracking her jaw, losing teeth and consciousness (the hip, it was learned, had likely fractured just prior to the lethal fall, her bones having become too brittle to support her overweight body); in hospital, she eventually succumbed from pneumonia. (*A mild enough ending,* Dr. Watson wrote to Holmes, after being notified of her passing. *Pneumonia is, as you well know, a blessing to the feeble, a light touch for the aged.*)

But no sooner had Dr. Watson's letter been filed away—and Mrs. Hudson's belongings collected by her nephew, and an inexperienced housekeeper hired for the farmhouse chores—than that companion of many seasons, the good doctor himself, died unexpectedly of natural causes late one night (he'd enjoyed a nice supper with his visiting children and grandchildren, drunk three glasses of red wine, laughed at a joke his eldest grandson whispered in his ear, wished everyone good night before ten, and was dead before midnight). The heartbreaking news came in a telegram sent from Dr. Watson's third wife, delivered unceremoniously into Holmes's hands by the young housekeeper (the first of many women who would pass wretchedly through the farmhouse, quietly tolerating their irascible employer, usually quitting inside a year's time).

In the days thereafter, Holmes wandered the beach for hours, from dawn till dusk, contemplating the sea and, for long periods, the many rocks beneath his feet. He hadn't seen or spoken directly to Dr. Watson since the summer of 1920, when the doctor and his wife spent a weekend with him. Yet it had been an awkward visit, more so for Holmes than for his guests; he wasn't particularly friendly toward the third wife (finding her rather dull and overbearing), and, aside from rehashing some of their earlier adventures together, he realized he shared little in common with Dr. Watson anymore; their evening conversations inevitably faded into uncomfortable silences, broken only by the wife's inane need to mention her children, or her love of French cuisine—as if silence was somehow her ultimate foe.

All the same, Holmes regarded Dr. Watson as someone who had passed beyond his kin, so the man's sudden death, coupled with the recent loss of Mrs. Hudson, felt like a door slamming abruptly shut on everything that had previously shaped him. And while strolling along the beach, pausing to watch the waves curl in on themselves, he understood how adrift he'd become: Within that month, the purest connections to his former self had dwindled to almost no one, but he remained. Then on his fourth day of walking the shore, he began considering rocks—holding them to his face, discarding one in favor of another, finally settling on the four that pleased him the most. The tiniest of pebbles, he knew, held the secrets of the entire universe. Moreover, the rocks he soon carried up the cliff in his pockets had preceded his lifetime; they had—as he was conceived, as he was born and educated and made old—waited on the shore, unchanged. Those four common rocks, like the others he had tread upon, were infused with all the elements that then formed the great sweep of humanity, every possible creature and imaginable thing; without question, they possessed rudimentary traces of both Dr. Watson and Mrs. Hudson, and, obviously, much of himself as well.

So Holmes gave the rocks a specific area, sitting among them with legs crossed, clearing his mind of what troubled him—the muddle caused by the permanent absence of two people he cared deeply about. Yet, he had determined, to feel someone's absence was, in a way, also to feel his or her presence. Breathing the beeyard's autumn air, exhaling his remorse *(tranquillity of thought* was his unspoken mantra—*tranquillity of the psyche,* just as he'd been taught by the Lamaists of Tibet), he sensed the beginnings of closure for himself and the dead, as if they were ebbing away gradually, attempting to depart from him in peace, finally allowing him to rise and go forward, his transient sorrow bridled between the venerable rocks. *"Mens sana in corpore sano."*

During the latter half of 1929, he occupied the spot on six different occasions, each subsequent meditation growing shorter in duration (three hours and eighteen minutes, one hour and two minutes, forty-seven minutes, twenty-three minutes, nine minutes, four minutes). By the new year, his need to sit among the rocks had abated, and whatever attention he then afforded the spot was for its tending (the removal of weeds, the trimming of grass, the rocks pressed firmly into the earth like the stones lining the garden pathway). Almost two hundred and one months would transpire before he lowered himself there again, doing so several hours after being informed of his brother Mycroft's passing—his breath streaming outward in puffs on a frigid November afternoon, dissipating beyond like some half-glimpsed, ethereal vision.

But it was an inward vision that engaged him, already taking shape within his mind, welcoming him into the Strangers' Room of the Diogenes Club four months earlier—where Holmes had a final meeting with his only surviving sibling (the two enjoying cigars while sipping brandy). Mycroft looked well, too—clear-eyed, with a hint of color in his plump cheeks—although his health was failing and he was prone to exhibiting a loss of mental faculties; yet on that day, he was incredibly lucid, reliving stories of his wartime glories, seemingly delighted with his younger brother's company. And while Holmes had just recently begun sending jars of royal jelly to the Diogenes Club, he believed the substance was already bettering Mycroft's condition.

"Even with your imagination, Sherlock," Mycroft had said, his massive body verging on laughter, "I do not think you could picture me clambering ashore from a landing barge with my old friend Winston. 'I'm Mr. Bullfinch,' Winston said—for that was the code name agreed upon—'and I've come to see for myself how things are going in North Africa.' "

However, Holmes suspected that the two great wars had, in fact, been a terrible strain on his brilliant sibling (Mycroft having continued in service well past the retirement age, rarely leaving his Diogenes Club armchair, yet indispensable to the government nonetheless). As the most mysterious of men, an individual poised at the very top of the British Secret Service, his elderly brother had often functioned for weeks without proper sleep—fueling his energy by eating voraciously—while single-handedly overseeing a multitude of intrigues, both domestically and abroad. It came as no surprise to him that—at the conclusion of the Second World War—Mycroft's health was declining rapidly; nor was Holmes astounded to observe an improvement in his brother's vigor, brought about, he was sure, by the sustained use of royal jelly.

"It's good to see you, Mycroft," said Holmes when standing to go. "You have become the antithesis of lethargy once more."

"A tramcar coming down a country lane?" said Mycroft, smiling.

"Something like that, yes," said Holmes, reaching for his brother's hand. "It has been too long between meetings, I fear. When shall we do it again?"

"We won't, I'm sorry to say."

Holmes bent forward at his brother's chair, clutching Mycroft's heavy, soft hand. He would have laughed at that moment, except he saw those eyes contrasting his brother's smile. Irresolute and precarious with resignation, they suddenly fixed and held his stare, communicating as best they could: Like you, they seemed to say, I have dipped my toes into two centuries, and my race is about run.

"Now, Mycroft," said Holmes, lightly tapping a cane against his brother's shin, "I wager you are mistaken on that count."

But as had always been the case, Mycroft was never wrong. And soon the last thread to Holmes's past was severed by an unsigned letter sent from the Diogenes Club (the contents offering no condolences, stating simply that his brother had died quietly on Tuesday, November 19, and—in keeping with the final wishes—the body had been interred anonymously and unceremoniously). How very Mycroft, he thought, folding the letter, putting it among the other papers on his desk. How right you were, he considered later when sitting among the rocks—staying there into the chilly night, unaware of Roger spying on him from the garden pathway at dusk, or Mrs. Munro finding the boy, speaking with an admonishing tone: "You leave him be, son. He's in a queer mood today—Lord knows why."

Of course, Holmes said nothing of Mycroft's death to anyone, nor did he openly acknowledge that second delivery from the Diogenes Club: a small package following the letter by exactly a week, discovered on the front doorsteps and nearly crushed underfoot as he went outside for a morning walk. Beneath the brown wrapping, he found a worn edition of Winwood Reade's *The Martyrdom of Man* (the same copy his father, Siger, had given him while he was a convalescent boy, languishing for months in the attic bedroom of his parents' Yorkshire country house), with a short note from Mycroft attached. What a depressing book it was, but one that had made a great impression on Holmes as a youngster. And in reading the note, in holding the volume once again, a memory he'd long since suppressed revealed itself—for he had loaned the book to his older brother in 1867, insisting Mycroft read it: "When finished, you must share your impressions—I wish to know what you think." *Many interesting ruminations,* was Mycroft's brief assessment some seventy-eight years later, *although a bit too meandering for my tastes. Took me ages to get through it.*

It wasn't the only time that the departed offered their words to him. There were the notes Mrs. Hudson had apparently written for herself, possible reminders jotted on scraps of torn paper and tucked away—in kitchen counters, in the broom closet, scattered throughout the housekeeper's cottage—only to be chanced upon by her initial replacement, who gave them to Holmes with always the same perplexed expression. For a while, he kept the notes, contemplating each one as if it might piece together what seemed a nonsensical puzzle. But in the end, he could gather no definitive meaning from Mrs. Hudson's messages, all of which consisted of two nouns: *Hatbox Slippers; Barley Soapstone; Girandole Marzipan; Hound Cheapjack; Ordo Planchet; Carrot Housecoat; Fruitlet Prelibation; Tracheid Dish; Pepper Scone.* The library fireplace, he concluded without sentiment, was where the notes belonged (Mrs. Hudson's cryptic scraps igniting on a winter's day, smoldering into nothing, along with various letters sent to him by complete strangers).

A similar fate had previously befallen three of Dr. Watson's unpublished journals, and for good reason. From 1874 until 1929, the doctor had recorded the minutiae of his daily life, producing countless volumes, which lined his study bookshelves. But the three journals he bequeathed to Holmes—covering Thursday, May 16, 1901, through late October 1903—were more sensitive in nature. For the most part, however, the journals chronicled hundreds of minor cases, a few notable exploits, as well as a particularly humorous anecdote concerning stolen racehorses ("A Case of the Trots"); yet mixed with the trivial and the noteworthy were a handful of sordid, potentially damaging affairs: various indiscretions by relatives of the royal family, a foreign dignitary with a palate for small Negro boys, and a prostitution scandal that had threatened to expose fourteen parliamentary members.

So it was prudent of Dr. Watson to bestow the three journals to him, lest they fall into the wrong hands. Moreover, Holmes had decided, it was important for the volumes to be destroyed; otherwise, after his own passing, the doctor's texts might become public. What would get lost, he figured, was either already published as fictional accounts, likely inconsequential, or worthy of perishing to maintain the secrets of those who had sought his confidentiality. And with that—avoiding even a flip through the pages, resisting even a brief glimpse at all that Dr. Watson had written down—the volumes ended up in the library fireplace, the paper and binding smoking profusely, suddenly bursting into orange-blue flames.

But many years later, while traveling across Japan, Holmes recalled the destruction of the journals with some misgivings. According to Mr. Umezaki's story, he had supposedly advised the man's father in 1903, which meant—if the story had any truth value—the details of that encounter had surely been reduced to ashes. Then resting at an inn in Shimonoseki, he again envisioned Dr. Watson's journals blazing on the hearth—those glowing cinders once etched with days gone by, breaking apart gradually and soaring up the chimney like ascending souls and becoming irretrievable as they floated off into the sky. The remembrance blunted his mind; stretched on a futon, eyes closed, he experienced a sensation of emptiness, of inexplicable loss. Such an acute, hopeless sensation returned to him months thereafter, finding him while he sat among the rocks on that overcast, gray morning.

And as Roger was being buried elsewhere, Holmes could neither perceive nor understand a single thing, nor could he push aside the suffocating feeling of his self somehow stripped bare (his diminished faculties now navigating an uninhabited region, exiled from the familiar, bit by bit, without a way back into the world). Yet it was a lone tear that revived him—sliding into his whiskers, coursing toward his jawline—a tear then dangling on a chin hair, hastening fingers. "All right," he said with a sigh, opening his inflamed eyes to the beeyard, his fingers lifting from the grass, rising to catch a tear before it fell.

19

THERE, near the apiary—then there, somewhere else: The sunlight increased; the overcast summer morning shifted backward to a windy spring day—to another shore, to that far-off land. Yamaguchi-ken, the extreme western tip of Honshu, the island of Kyushu visible across the narrow strait. *"Ohayo gozaimasu,"* said the round-faced hostess as Holmes and Mr. Umezaki sat on tatami mats (both wearing gray kimonos, seated at a table with a garden view). They were staying at the Shimonoseki Ryokan, a traditional inn where every guest was loaned a kimono and given an opportunity to sample, upon request, regional famine food with each meal (a variety of soups, rice balls, and dishes using carp as the main ingredient).

The hostess went from the morning room to the kitchen, from the kitchen to the morning room, carrying trays. She was a heavy woman. Her stomach bulged against the sash around her waist; the tatamis vibrated on her approach. Mr. Umezaki wondered aloud how she stayed so fat, with the country's shortage of food. But she continually bowed at her guests without ever understanding Mr. Umezaki's English, coming and going from the morning room like a well-fed, obedient dog. Then as bowls, plates, and steaming dishes were set on the table, Mr. Umezaki wiped his glasses, replacing them while reaching for chopsticks. And Holmes—studying their breakfast, gingerly taking up chopsticks—yawned away what had been a fitful sleep (a vagrant wind having shaken the walls until dawn, its frightful whine keeping him half-awake).

"If you don't mind, what is it you dream in the night?" Mr. Umezaki abruptly asked, picking at a rice ball.

"What do I dream in the night? I am sure I dream nothing whatsoever."

"How is it possible? You must dream sometimes—doesn't everyone?"

"As a boy I did—I am fairly certain of that. I cannot say when it stopped—possibly after adolescence, or later on. In any case, I don't recall the details of whatever dreams I may have once had. Such hallucinations are infinitely more useful to artists and theistic minds, wouldn't you agree? For men like me, however, they are rather an unreliable nuisance."

"I've read about people who claim they are dreamless, but I've never believed it. I just assumed they felt the need to suppress them for some reason."

"Well, if indeed the dreams do come, then I have grown accustomed to ignoring them. But now I ask you, my friend: what is it that plays in your head at night?"

"Any number of things. It can be very specific, you see—places I've been, everyday faces, often mundane situations—other times it's remote, disconcerting scenes that are seen—my childhood, dead friends, people whom I know well but who look nothing like themselves. Sometimes I awake confused, unsure of where I am or what I've glimpsed—it's like I'm caught somewhere between the real and the imagined, though only for a short moment."

"I know the feeling." Holmes smiled, glancing to the window. Beyond the morning room, in the garden outside, a breeze swayed the red and yellow chrysanthemums.

"I regard my dreams as frayed pieces of my memory," Mr. Umezaki said. "Memory itself is like the fiber of one's existence. Dreams, I think, are like broken strands of the past, little ragged edges that veer from the fiber but remain a part of it. Maybe that's a fanciful notion—I don't know. Still, don't you think dreams are a kind of memory, an abstraction of what was?"

For a while, Holmes continued gazing out the window. Then he said, "Yes, it is a fanciful notion. As for me, I have shed my skin and regenerated for ninety-three years now, so those ragged strands you speak of must be many—yet I am positive I dream nothing. Or maybe it is that the fibers of my memory are extremely durable; otherwise—judging from your metaphor—I would likely be lost in time. Anyway, I don't believe dreams are an abstraction of the past— they could easily be symbols for our fears and desires, like the Austrian doctor was so fond of suggesting." With chopsticks, Holmes took a pickled cucumber slice from a bowl and Mr. Umezaki watched as he moved it carefully toward his mouth.

"Fears and desires," Mr. Umezaki said, "are products of the past as well. We simply carry them with us. But there's a lot more to dreaming than that, isn't there? Don't we seem to occupy another region in sleep, a world built on the experiences we've had in this one?"

"I haven't the foggiest."

"What are your fears and desires, then? I myself have plenty."

Holmes did not reply, even as Mr. Umezaki paused and waited for a response. Keeping his eyes fixed on the bowl of pickled cucumbers, a deeply troubled expression appeared on his face. No, he would not answer the question, nor would he say that his fears and desires were, at some point, one and the same: the forgetfulness increasingly plaguing him, startling him awake, gasping, a sense of the familiar and safe turning against him, leaving him helpless and exposed and struggling for air; the forgetfulness also subduing the despairing thoughts, muting the absence of those he could never see again, grounding him in the present, where all he might want or need was at hand.

"Forgive me," Mr. Umezaki said. "I didn't mean to pry. We should've spoken last night, after I came to you—but it seemed the wrong moment."

Holmes lowered his chopsticks. Using his fingers, he picked two slices from the bowl, eating them. When finished, he rubbed his fingers on his kimono. "My dear Tamiki, do you suspect I dreamt something about your father last night? Is this why you are asking me these questions?"

"Not exactly."

"Or were you dreaming of him, and now you wish to relate the experience to me over breakfast, in a somewhat roundabout fashion."

"I have dreamt of him, yes—although it's been a long while."

"I see," said Holmes. "So pray tell me: What is the pertinence of this?"

"I'm sorry." Mr. Umezaki bowed his head. "I apologize."

Holmes realized he was being needlessly short, but then it was irksome to be pressed repeatedly for answers he didn't possess. Besides, he was already annoyed that Mr. Umezaki had entered his room during the previous night, kneeling near the futon while he slept restlessly; when he was stirred by the wind—a plaintive, mournful whir at the windows—the shadowy presence of the man must have taken his breath away (hovering just above him like a black cloud, asking with a hushed voice, "Are you all right? Tell me. What is it?"), because he couldn't utter anything, couldn't move his arms, his legs. How difficult it was at that moment to remember where exactly he was, or to comprehend the voice addressing him through the darkness: "Sherlock, what is it? You can tell me."

Only as Mr. Umezaki left him, silently crossing the floor, opening and shutting the sliding wall panel between their rooms, did

Holmes regain himself. Turning on his side, he listened to the wind's melancholy din. He touched the tatami beneath the futon, pushing his fingertips against the mat. Then closing his eyes, he pondered what Mr. Umezaki had asked, the words at last registering: *Tell me. What is it? You can tell me.* For, in truth, despite all the man had said earlier about enjoying their trip together, Holmes knew that Mr. Umezaki was determined to learn something of his lost father, even if it meant holding a vigil at his bedside (why else would Mr. Umezaki enter his room—what other explanation could bring him there?). Holmes, too, had questioned sleepers—thieves, opium addicts, suspected murderers—in a similar manner (whispering into their ears, gathering information from the breathless mumbles of dreamers, those drowsy confessions, which later surprised the perpetrators with their accuracy). So he didn't begrudge the method, yet he wished Mr. Umezaki would let the mystery of his father rest, at least until their trip was finished.

Such concerns are long in the past, Holmes wanted to tell him, and little will be gained by fretting over them now. Matsuda's motives for fleeing Japan were possibly justifiable, and maybe the family's better interests were very much a factor. Even so, without a father ever really present for Mr. Umezaki, he understood how the man could feel like an incomplete person. And whatever else Holmes convinced himself of during that night, he never pretended Mr. Umezaki's search was irrelevant. On the contrary, he'd always believed that the conundrums of one's own life were worthy of tireless investigation, but in the case of Matsuda, Holmes knew that any clues he might offer—if indeed they existed—had been destroyed on the hearth ages ago; the recollection of Dr. Watson's incinerated journals then preoccupied him, eventually dulling his mind, and soon he could envision nothing. Nor could he hear the wind anymore—while awake upon the futon—rampaging along the streets, tearing slits in latticed paper-covered windows.

"It is I who should apologize," said Holmes at breakfast, reaching across the table to pat Mr. Umezaki's hand. "I had a rather rough night, what with the weather and all, and feel worse for it today."

Mr. Umezaki, his head kept bowed, nodded. "It's just that I'm worried. I thought you cried out in your sleep—it was a horrible sound."

"Of course," said Holmes, humoring him. "You know, I have wandered moors where the wind gave the distinct impression of someone yelling, a distant shout or wail, almost like a cry for help. A tempest can easily fool your ears; I have been fooled myself, I assure you." Grinning, he retracted his hand, moving his fingers into the bowl of cucumbers.

"You believe I was mistaken, then?"

"It is possible, isn't it?"

"Yes," said Mr. Umezaki, bringing his head up with a gesture of relief. "It is possible, I suppose."

"Very good," said Holmes, holding a slice before his lips. "That puts an end to it. Shall we begin the day anew? And what is on the agenda this morning—another stroll along the beach? Or should we pursue our purpose for coming here—the quest for the elusive prickly ash?"

But Mr. Umezaki looked perplexed. How often had they discussed Holmes's reasons for visiting Japan (the desire to taste prickly-ash cuisine, and also witness the shrub growing in the wild), and their destination, which would lead them, later that day, into the rustic *izakaya* by the sea (a Japanese version of a pub, Holmes would realize when stepping past the doorway)?

When they entered the *izakaya,* there was a cauldron boiling inside and fresh prickly-ash leaves being cut by the proprietor's wife, and the local faces looked up, some with mistrust, from glasses of beer or sake. Yet since Holmes's arrival, how often had Mr. Umezaki spoken of the special cake sold at the *izakaya,* created with the roasted ground fruits and seeds of prickly ash, the ingredients kneaded into flour as a flavoring? And how often had they mentioned the letters sent back and forth over the years, the contents always touching on their interest in the slow-growing, mounding, perhaps life-enhancing shrub (nourished by salt-spray exposure, full sun, and drying winds)? Not once, it seemed.

The *izakaya* smelled of peppercorns and fish, and they sat at a table, sipping tea and listening to the boisterous conversations around them. "Those two are fishermen," said Mr. Umezaki. "They are arguing about a woman."

Presently, the proprietor passed through a back-room curtain, revealing his toothless grin as he did so, addressing each patron in an overbearing, comical voice, laughing with those he knew, then eventually making his way to their table. The man appeared amused at the sight of the elderly Englishman and his refined companion, happily patting Mr. Umezaki on the shoulder, winking at Holmes as if they were all close friends. Sitting down at the table, the proprietor glanced at Holmes while saying something to Mr. Umezaki in Japanese—a remark that made everyone in the *izakaya* laugh, except Holmes. "What did he say?"

"It's rather funny," Mr. Umezaki told him. "He thanked me for bringing my father here—he said we're the spitting image—but he thinks you're more pleasing on the eye."

"I would agree with the latter statement," said Holmes.

Mr. Umezaki translated the message to the proprietor, who then burst out laughing, nodding his head in agreement.

Then upon finishing his tea, Holmes said to Mr. Umezaki, "I should like a look at that cauldron. Will you ask our new friend if I may? Will you tell him that I would very much like to see how the prickly ash is stewed?"

When the request was conveyed, the proprietor promptly stood. "He'll gladly let you," said Mr. Umezaki. "But his wife does the cooking. She alone can show you the process."

"Delightful," said Holmes, rising. "Are you coming?"

"In a moment—I still have my tea."

"It is a rare chance, you know. I hope you won't mind if I don't wait for you."

"No, not at all," said Mr. Umezaki, even though he stared sharply at Holmes, as if he were somehow being deserted.

Soon, however, they would both be at the cauldron, holding the shrub's leaves in their hands and watching as the wife stirred the broth. Afterward, they were directed to where the prickly ash thrived—farther along the beach, somewhere among the dunes.

"Should we go tomorrow morning?" asked Mr. Umezaki.

"It isn't too late in the day to go now."

"It's a good distance, Sherlock-san."

"Shall we go part of the way—at least until dusk?"

"If you wish."

They took a last, curious look around the *izakaya*—at the cauldron, the soup, the men with their glasses—before stepping outside, hiking across the sand, moving gradually into the dunes. By dusk, they had found no sign of the shrub and so decided to head back for supper at the inn, both feeling exhausted from the hike, each retiring early, instead of taking the usual evening drinks. But that night—the second evening of their stay in Shimonoseki—Holmes awoke around midnight, stirring from another fitful sleep. What struck him initially was that he could no longer hear the wind as on the previous night. Then he remembered what had preoccupied him in the minutes prior to sleep: the run-down *izakaya* by the sea, the prickly-ash leaves boiling in a cauldron of carp soup. He lay under the covers, staring at the ceiling in the dim light. After a while, he felt sleepy once more and closed his eyes. Except he didn't drift off; instead, he thought of the toothless proprietor—Wakui was his name—and how his humorous comments had delighted Mr. Umezaki, among them a rather tasteless joke at the emperor's expense: "Why is General MacArthur the belly button of Japan? Because he is above the prick."

Yet no comment had pleased Mr. Umezaki more than Wakui's playful remark about Holmes being his father. In the late afternoon, as they had walked the beach together, Mr. Umezaki had brought up the remark again, saying, "It's strange to think of it—if my father was living, he would be just a bit older than you are."

"I suppose so," Holmes had said, peering ahead at the dunes, surveying the sandy soil for signs of the prickly, sprawling shrub.

"You're my English father—how's that?" Mr. Umezaki had unexpectedly taken hold of Holmes's arm, his hand remaining firmly on him as they went forward. "Wakui is a funny fellow. I'd like to visit him tomorrow."

Only then had Holmes perceived of himself as having been chosen—perhaps not consciously—as Matsuda's surrogate. It was already obvious that behind Mr. Umezaki's mature, circumspect demeanor lurked the psychic wounds of childhood. The rest did not become apparent until Wakui's remark had been repeated and Mr. Umezaki's needful fingers had grabbed him on the beach. Then how clear it had suddenly become: The last time you heard word from your father, Holmes had thought, was the first time you heard of me. Matsuda vanishes from your life, and I arrive in the form of a book—one replaces the other, as it were.

So there were the letters postmarked in Asia, the subsequent invitation following months of genial correspondence, the eventual trip through the Japanese countryside, the days spent together—like father and son making quiet amends after living many years estranged. And if Holmes could provide no concrete answers, then maybe—by traveling a vast distance to join Mr. Umezaki, in sleeping at the family's Kobe house, finally embarking on the journey westward and visiting the Hiroshima garden where Matsuda had taken Mr. Umezaki as a boy—his very nearness might provide some resolution. What had also become clear was that Mr. Umezaki really cared little for prickly ash, or royal jelly, or anything else that those intelligent letters had discussed in detail. A simple ruse, Holmes had realized, yet effective—each topic well researched, articulated on stationery, and likely forgotten.

These children with missing fathers, Holmes had mused, imagining Mr. Umezaki and young Roger when trekking into the dunes. This age of lonely, searching souls, he'd thought as the fingers tightened on his arm.

But as opposed to Mr. Umezaki, Roger understood his own father's fate and harbored a belief that the man's death—while tragic on a personal level—was truly heroic in the grand scheme. Mr. Umezaki, however, could claim nothing of the sort, relying instead on the frail old Englishman he had accompanied into the sandy hills by the beach, clutching at his bony elbow, clinging to him, in reality, rather than guiding him along: "Should we turn back?"

"Have you tired of the search?"

"No, I was more concerned for you."

"I believe we are too close to turn back now."

"It's getting dark."

Holmes opened his eyes now and looked again at the ceiling, weighing the problem's solution; for to appease Mr. Umezaki was to reveal something that must be conceived of as the truth beforehand (like Dr. Watson working out the plot of a story, he reasoned—the mixing of what was and what never had been into a single, undeniable creation). Yes, his association with Matsuda wasn't an impossibility—and, yes, the man's disappearance could be explained, though not without careful elaboration. And where had they first been introduced? Perhaps in the Strangers' Room of the Diogenes Club, at Mycroft's urging. But why?

"If the art of the detective began and ended in the reasoning from this room, Mycroft, you would be the greatest criminal agent who ever lived. Yet you are absolutely incapable of working out the practical points that must be gone into before a matter can be decided upon. I gather that is why you have called me here once again."

He pictured Mycroft in his armchair. Nearby sat T. R. Lamont (or was it R. T. Lanner?)—a dour, ambitious man of Polynesian descent, a London Missionary Society member who had lived on the Pacific island of Mangaia and, as a spy for the British Secret Service, kept rigid police supervision over the indigenous population in the name of morality. Hoping to aid New Zealand's expansionist ambitions, Lamont, or Lanner, was under consideration for a more important role, that of British resident—a position which included negotiations with the Cook Islands' chiefs to pave the way for New Zealand's annexation of the islands.

Or was he known as J. R. Lambeth? No, no, recalled Holmes, he was a Lamont, surely a Lamont. In any case, it was 1898—or 1899, or was it 1897?—and Holmes had been summoned by Mycroft to give an opinion on Lamont's character (*As you know, I can return an excellent expert opinion,* his brother had written in a telegram, *but gathering the details of someone's true value is not my métier*).

"We must have our cards in the game," explained Mycroft, well aware of France's influence on Tahiti and the Society Islands. "Naturally, Queen Makea Takau wants her islands annexed to us, but our government remains a reluctant administrator. New Zealand's prime minister, on the other hand, has his sights set—so we are obligated to be as helpful as we can—and seeing how Mr. Lamont is acquainted with the natives—and shares more than a few common physical traits—we believe he will be quite useful toward that end."

Holmes eyed the short, uncommunicative fellow seated at his brother's right (looking down through his spectacles, hat in his lap, dwarfed by the huge form to his left). "Aside from you, Mycroft, who are the *we* you speak of?"

"That, my dear Sherlock—like everything else mentioned in my company—is of the utmost secrecy and is of no issue at present. What is required, however, is your counsel on our colleague here."

"I see. . . ."

Except it wasn't Lamont, or Lanner, or Lambeth, that Holmes now saw beside Mycroft, but, rather, the tall stature, the long face, the goatee of Matsuda Umezaki. In that private room, they had been introduced, and almost immediately Holmes could tell he matched the position's proviso; from the dossier Mycroft had given him, it was evident that Matsuda was an intelligent man (the author of several notable books, one of which dealt with covert diplomacy), capable as an agent (his background in the Japanese Foreign Ministry attesting to that fact), an Anglophile disenchanted by his own country (willing to travel, whenever needed, from Japan to the Cook Islands, then to Europe, and then back to Japan).

"You think he's our man for the job?" asked Mycroft.

"Indeed," said Holmes, grinning. "*We* think he is the perfect man."

Because like Lamont, Matsuda would be discreet in all maneuvering and politicking—mediating the Cook Islands' annexation even as his own family imagined him researching constitutional law in London.

"Best of luck to you, sir," said Holmes, shaking Matsuda's hand when the interrogation was finished. "I am sure your mission will go smoothly."

As it happened, they would meet once more—in the winter of 1902—or, better still, in early 1903 (some two years after New Zealand's formal occupation of the islands began)—when Matsuda would seek Holmes's advice about the troubles in Niue, an island previously associated with Samoa and Tonga but seized a year following the annexation. Again, Matsuda was being sought for another influential position, although now on behalf of New Zealand and not England: "It's a most lucrative opportunity, Sherlock, I'll admit it—staying among the Cook Islands indefinitely, quelling Niue's protests and working to place the rebellious island under separate administration, while also managing the upgrading of the other islands' public facilities."

They were sitting in Holmes's Baker Street drawing room, talking over a bottle of claret.

"Yet you fear your doing so will be viewed as a betrayal of White-hall?" asked Holmes.

"Somewhat, yes."

"I shouldn't worry, my good fellow. You have fulfilled what has been asked of you, and you have done your job admirably. I suspect you are now free to apply your talents elsewhere, and why shouldn't you?"

"Do you really think so?"

"I do, I do."

And just like Lamont, Matsuda would thank Holmes, asking thereafter that their conversation stay between them. Then he'd finish his glass before departing, bowing as he stepped out the front door and into the street. He would return to the Cook Islands forthwith, traveling routinely from island to island, meeting the five head chiefs and the seven lesser ones, outlining his ideas for a future Legislative Council, then eventually extending himself to Erromango in the New Hebrides, where he was last seen journeying into its deepest region (a locale rarely visited by outsiders, an isolated, densely overgrown realm known for its large totems erected from skulls and its necklaces fashioned from human bone).

Of course, it was hardly an airtight story. If pressed by Mr. Umezaki, Holmes feared he might confuse details, names, dates, various historical specifics. Furthermore, he could give no proper explanation as to why Matsuda had abandoned his family to live on the Cook Islands. Yet as desperate for answers as Mr. Umezaki was, Holmes felt certain the story would suffice. Whatever other unknown reasons had impelled Matsuda into a new life, he figured, were of no concern to him (such reasons were, without doubt, based on personal or private considerations, ones that resided beyond his knowledge). Still, what Mr. Umezaki would learn about his father was not insignificant: Matsuda had played a pivotal role in preventing a French invasion of the Cook Islands, as well as suppressing Niue's revolt, and, prior to his vanishing within the jungle, had sought to rally the islanders into someday forming their own government. "Your father," he would tell Mr. Umezaki, "was highly respected by the British government, but for the elders of Rarotonga—and those on the surrounding islands old enough to remember—his name is legendary."

Finally, aided by the soft glow of a lantern burning by the futon, Holmes gripped at his canes and rose. After donning his kimono, he made his way across the room, taking care not to trip over his own feet as he went. When he came to the wall panel, he remained standing before it for a while. Beyond, in Mr. Umezaki's room, he could hear snoring. As he continued staring at the panel, he tapped the floor lightly with a cane. Then he heard what sounded like a cough from within, followed by slight movements (Mr. Umezaki's body shifting, the ruffling of sheets). He listened for some time but heard nothing else. Eventually, he found himself feeling for a handle, finding instead a hollowed groove, which helped him slide the panel open.

The adjoining room was a duplicate of where Holmes had slept—cast in the dim yellowish light of a lantern, a single futon centered on the floor, the built-in desk, and, leaning against a wall, the floor cushions used for sitting or kneeling. He approached the futon. The sheets had been kicked away and he could barely see Mr. Umezaki sleeping half-naked on his back, motionless and now silent, not appearing to breathe. To the left of the mattress—by the lantern—a pair of slippers had been placed, one aligned evenly with the other. And as Holmes lowered himself to the floor, Mr. Umezaki suddenly awoke, speaking apprehensively in Japanese, peering at the shadowed figure looming beside him.

"I must talk," said Holmes, setting the canes lengthwise upon his lap.

Mr. Umezaki, still peering forward, sat up. Reaching for the lantern, he raised it, illuminating Holmes's stern face. "Sherlock-san? Are you all right?"

Holmes squinted in the lantern's glare. He rested a palm on Mr. Umezaki's raised hand, gently pushing the lantern downward. Then, from the shadows, he spoke: "I ask that you only listen—and when I am finished, I ask that you press me no further on the subject." Mr. Umezaki gave no reply, so Holmes continued. "Over the years, I have made it a rule never—under any circumstances—to discuss those cases that were of the strictest confidence or involved national affairs. I hope you understand—making exceptions to the rule could risk lives and jeopardize my good standing. But I realize now that I am an old man, and think it's fair to say that my standing is beyond re-proach. I think it's also fair to say that the people whose confidences I have kept for decades are no longer of this world. In other words, I have outlived everything that has defined me."

"That isn't true," Mr. Umezaki remarked.

"Please, you mustn't speak. If you just say nothing, I will be forthcoming about your father. You see, I wish to explain what I know of him before I forget—and I want you to simply listen. And when I am finished and have left you here, I ask that it never be dis-cussed with me again—because tonight, my friend, you receive the first exception to the rule of a lifetime. Now please let me attempt to put both our minds at rest, as best as I possibly can."

With that, Holmes began relating his story, doing so in a low, whispering tone, which had a vaguely dreamlike quality. Once his whispering concluded, they remained facing each other for a while, neither moving or saying a word—two indistinct forms sitting there like each other's obscure reflection, their heads hidden by shadow, the floor glowing beneath them—until Holmes stood without a sound, shuffling then toward his room, heading wearily for bed as his canes thumped along the mats.

20

SINCE HIS return to Sussex, Holmes had never dwelled much on what he had told Mr. Umezaki that night in Shimonoseki, nor had he reflected on his trip as having been hampered by the enigma of Matsuda. Instead—when locked inside the attic study, his mind suddenly carrying him there—he pictured the far-off dunes where he and Mr. Umezaki had strolled; more specifically, he saw himself heading to them again, walking the beach with Mr. Umezaki, both pausing along the way to survey the ocean or the few white clouds hanging above the horizon.

"Such beautiful weather, isn't it?"

"Oh, yes," agreed Holmes.

It was their last day visiting Shimonoseki, and while neither had slept very well (Holmes slipping in and out of sleep before going to Mr. Umezaki's bedside, Mr. Umezaki then staying awake long after Holmes had gone from him), they proceeded in good spirits, resuming the search for prickly ash. That morning, the wind had ceased altogether and a perfect spring sky presented itself. The city, too, was vivified as they departed the inn following a late breakfast: People emerged from their homes or shops and swept the ground of what the wind had scattered; at the bright vermilion shrine of Akamajingu, an elderly couple chanted sutras in the sunshine. Then moving along the seaside, they spotted beachcombers farther down the shore—a dozen or so women and old people rummaging through the flotsam, collecting shellfish or whatever useful items had drifted in with the currents (some lugging bundles of driftwood on their backs, others wearing thick strands of wet seaweed about their necks like ragged, filthy boas). Soon they had wandered beyond the beachcombers, stepping onto the slender trail that led into the dunes and then gradually widened, until becoming just the radiant, pliable terrain all around them.

The dunes' wind-rippled surface, dotted by wild grass, flecks of seashells or stones, obscured any view of the ocean. The sloping hills seemed to stretch endlessly from the coastline, ascending and falling toward a distant mountain range to the east, or toward the sky to the north. Even on such a windless day, the sand shifted as they trudged onward, swirling in their wake, dusting their cuffs with a salty powder. Behind them, the impressions of their footsteps slowly vanished, as if covered over by an invisible hand. Ahead, where the dunes met the sky, a mirage shimmered like vapors rising from the earth. Yet they could still hear the waves breaking against the shore, the beachcombers shouting to one another, the gulls crying above the sea.

To Mr. Umezaki's surprise, Holmes pointed to where they had searched on the previous evening, and to where he believed they should look now—north, near those dunes that sloped closest to the water. "You will see that the sand is damp there, creating an ideal breeding place for our shrub."

They continued without stopping—screwing up their eyes from the glare, blowing sand from their lips—their shoes occasionally swallowed by deeper pockets within the dunes; at times, Holmes struggled to maintain his balance, only to be rescued by Mr. Umezaki's steadying grip. Finally, the sand hardened underfoot, the ocean appeared several yards away, and they came to an open area comprised of wild grass, various mounds of foliage, and a single bulky piece of driftwood, likely having belonged to a fishing vessel's hull. For a while, they stood together, catching their breath, brushing sand off their trouser legs. Then Mr. Umezaki took a seat on the driftwood—dabbing himself with a handkerchief, wiping the sweat that dripped from his brow and down his face and chin—while Holmes, having stuck an unlit Jamaican between his lips, began exploring the wild grass in earnest, studying the surrounding foliage, stooping at last beside an expansive shrub set upon by flies (the pests swarming the plant, gathering in large numbers on the blooms).

"So here you are, my lovely," Holmes half-exclaimed, setting his canes aside. He gently touched the twigs, which were armed with short paired spines at the base of the leaves. He noted the male and female flowers on separate plants (inflorescent axillary clusters; flowers unisexual, greenish, minute—a tenth of an inch long, petals five-seven, white)—the male flowers with about five stamens, the female ones with four or five free carpels (each containing two ovules). He peered at the seeds, round and shiny black. "Exquisite," he said, addressing the prickly ash as if it were a confidant.

Presently, Mr. Umezaki crouched beside the shrub, dragging on a cigarette, blowing smoke at the flies and scattering them. But it wasn't the prickly ash that held his attention; rather, it was Holmes's enchantment with the plant—those nimble fingertips stroking the leaves, the mumbled words uttered like a mantra ("Odd-pinnately compound, one to two inches long—the main axis narrowly winged, prickly, leaflets three-seven pairs, plus a terminal leaflet, glossy—"), the pure contentment and wonder made evident by the old man's slight grin and beaming eyes.

And when Holmes glanced at Mr. Umezaki, he, too, observed a like expression, one he hadn't seen on his companion's face during their whole trip—a heartfelt look of ease and acceptance. "We have found what we wanted to find," he said, spotting his reflection in Mr. Umezaki's glasses.

"Yes, I believe we have."

"It is a truly simple thing, really—yet it affects me so, and I am at a loss to explain why."

"I share your feeling."

Mr. Umezaki bowed, righting himself almost immediately. Just then, it was as if he had something urgent to express, but Holmes shook his head, dissuading him. "Let us savor the remainder of this moment in silence, shall we? Our elaborations might do an injustice to such a rare opportunity—and we don't want that, do we?"

"No."

"Good," said Holmes.

After that, neither spoke for a time. Mr. Umezaki finished the cigarette and lit another watching as Holmes stared into and felt and probed the prickly ash while chewing relentlessly at the end of his Jamaican. Nearby, the waves curled in on themselves, and the beachcombers could be heard drawing closer. Still, it was their agreement of silence that, later on, formed a vivid impression within Holmes's mind (the two men there by the ocean, by the prickly ash, in the dunes, on an ideal spring day). Had he attempted imagining the inn where they'd stayed—or the streets they'd walked together, the buildings passed along the way—very little of substance would have materialized. Even so, he retained images of the sandy hills, the sea, the shrub, and the companion who had lured him to Japan. He remembered their brief speechlessness, and, as well, he remembered the strange sound wafting from the beach—faint at first, then growing louder, an attenuated voice and droning, sharply played chords—ending their mutual silence.

"It's a *shamisen* performer," said Mr. Umezaki, standing to peek over the wild grass, his chin tickled by stems.

"A performer of what?" Holmes grabbed his canes.

"A *shamisen*—it's like a lute."

With Mr. Umezaki's aid, Holmes rose alongside him, gazing past the wild grass. They spied a long, thin procession of children up the shore, moving slowly southward in the direction of the beach-combers; at its head walked a wild-haired man in a black kimono, plucking a three-stringed instrument with a large pick (the middle and index fingers of one hand pressing against the strings).

"I've known his sort before," said Mr. Umezaki after the procession had streamed by. "They're beggars who play for food or money. Most are accomplished—they actually do quite well in the bigger cities."

Like those entranced with the Pied Piper, the children trailed the man closely, listening while he sang and played for them. When the procession reached the beachcombers, it stopped, as did the singing and playing. The procession disbanded, and the children encircled the musician, finding places to sit in the sand. Joining the children, the beachcombers untied the ropes around their bundles, shrugging off their loads, and came to kneel or stand behind the youngsters. Once everyone was settled, the *shamisen* performer began—singing in a lyrical yet narrative style, his high-toned voice interspersed with chords that gave a kind of electric vibration.

Mr. Umezaki lazily tilted his head to one side, looking at the beach, and then, almost as an afterthought, said, "Should we go hear him?"

"I believe we must," replied Holmes as he stared at the gathering.

But they didn't hurry from the dunes, for Holmes had to gaze upon the shrub a final time, yanking several leaves and depositing them into a pocket (the samples eventually getting misplaced some-where en route to Kobe). Before crossing the beach, his eyes required a few lingering seconds on the prickly ash. "Haven't met the likes of you," he told the plant, "and I won't ever again, I fear—no—"

Then Holmes could depart, pushing through the wild grass with Mr. Umezaki, making his way onto the beach, where soon he sat among the beachcombers and the children, listening as the *shamisen* performer sang his stories and tugged strings (a partially blind man, he would learn, who had traveled Japan mostly by foot). Gulls dipped and glided overhead, seemingly buoyed by the music, while a ship grazed the horizon, sailing for port; all of it—the perfect sky, the engrossed audience, the stoic performer, the alien music, and the subdued ocean—Holmes could see with total clarity, fixing on that scene as the pleasant apex of his journey. What remained thereafter, however, flashed through his mind like glimpses of a dream: the procession re-forming in the late afternoon, the half-blind musician leading the entire group along the beach, guiding his followers between burning pyres of driftwood; the procession finally entering the thatched-roofed *izakaya* near the sea, greeted inside by Wakui and his wife.

Sunshine radiated the paper-covered windows; the shadows of tree branches were fuzzy and black. *Shimonoseki, last day, 1947,* Holmes had written on a napkin, which he then tucked away as a reminder of that afternoon. Like Mr. Umezaki, he was on his second beer. Sold out already, Wakui had informed them, of the special cake created with prickly ash. He'd make do anyway, cooling himself within the *izakaya.* He'd enjoy some drinks for a while, and the knowledge of what had been found. There, in the late day, as he drank with Mr. Umezaki, he saw the solitary shrub, thriving beyond the city, insect-pestered, a spiky thing, lacking beauty but still unique and useful—somehow not too different from himself, he was amused to think.

Patrons were filing into the *izakaya,* summoned by the shamisen music played at the end of the bar. The children were going home, faces sunburned, clothes sandy, waving bye to the performer and thanking him. "His name is Chikuzan Takahashi—he walks here yearly, Wakui says—and the children stick to him like flies." But the special cakes were sold out, so it was beer and soup for the wandering musician, and Holmes, and Mr. Umezaki. The boats were unloading their haul. Fishermen were shuffling down the streets, arriving at the open doors of the establishment, breathing the inviting aroma of alcohol, which hit them like a calming breeze. Even now the setting sun was beckoning the evening, and Holmes felt—was it in the second or third or fourth drink, in the finding of the prickly ash, in the music of a spring day?—a sense of something complete, ineffable yet replete, as in the gradual waking from a full night's sleep.

Mr. Umezaki lowered his cigarette, leaned forward across the table, and said as softly as he could, "If you'll allow me, I wish to thank you."

Holmes looked at Mr. Umezaki as if he were a nuisance. "What on earth for? It should be I thanking you. It has been a splendid experience."

"But if you'll only allow me . . . You've shed light on one quandary of my life—perhaps I haven't received every answer I've sought, but you've given me more than enough—and I thank you for assisting me."

"My friend, I assure you I have no idea what you're speaking of," Holmes said stubbornly.

"It's important I say it, that's all. I promise not to speak of it again."

Holmes toyed with his glass, at last saying, "Well, if you are so grateful, you might better display it by replenishing my cup, for it appears I'm running low."

Then Mr. Umezaki's gratefulness overtook him—in more ways than one—and he promptly ordered another round, and soon another, and another—smiling throughout the evening for no obvious reason, asking questions about the prickly ash as if he was suddenly interested, conveying his cheer to patrons who glanced at him (bowing and nodding and hoisting his glass). Even intoxicated, he was quick on his feet, helping Holmes stand up once they had finished their drinks. And the next morning, while riding the train destined for Kobe, Mr. Umezaki maintained his gregarious, mindful bearing—grinning and relaxed in his seat, apparently untroubled by the same hangover that plagued Holmes—indicating sights along the route (a temple concealed behind trees, a village where a famous feudal battle had occurred), periodically asking, "Are you feeling okay? Do you need anything? Should I open the window?"

"I am quite all right, really" was Holmes's grumbled answer; how, in those moments, he missed the hours of reserve that had previously marked their travels. Still, he was aware of return trips being always more tedious than a voyage's beginning (the initial departure, in which everything then encountered was wonderfully singular, and each subsequent destination offering a multitude of discoveries); so whenever heading back, it was better to nap as much as possible, slumbering while miles subtracted and his oblivious body raced toward home. But stirring repeatedly in his seat, cracking his eyelids and yawning into his hand, he became conscious of that overly attentive face, of that unending smile hovering nearby.

"Are you feeling okay?"

"I am quite all right."

Never before had Holmes imagined he'd welcome the sight of Maya's unforgiving expression, or that, upon arriving in Kobe, the normally affable Hensuiro might convey less enthusiasm than the overreaching Mr. Umezaki. Yet for all the annoying grins and disingenuous vigor, Holmes suspected Mr. Umezaki's intentions were, at the very least, honorable: In order to create a favorable impression during his guest's final days there, to eliminate the aura of his own erratic moods and unhappiness, he wanted himself recognized as a changed man—as someone who had benefited from Holmes's confidence, and as someone who would be forever appreciative for what he now believed was the truth.

This change, however, wouldn't transform Maya. (Had Mr. Umezaki even told his mother what he'd learned, Holmes wondered, or did she even care?) She avoided Holmes if possible, hardly acknowledging his presence, grunting her disdain as he sat down at her table. Ultimately, it made no difference whether Holmes's tale of Matsuda was shared with the woman or not, for the knowing would be no more comforting than the unknowing. Either way, she'd continue blaming him (the reality of the situation having little consequence, naturally). Moreover, the latest revelations would only suggest that Holmes had inadvertently sent Matsuda off to be cannibalized and, as a result, her surviving son lost his father (a devastating blow to the boy, which, in her mind, had deprived him of a sufficient male role model and turned him away from any woman's love other than her own). Regardless of which lie she chose—the contents of a letter sent ages ago by Matsuda, or the story told to Mr. Umezaki late one night—Holmes knew she'd despise him nonetheless; it was pointless expecting otherwise.

Even so, his last days in Kobe were pleasurable, although surely uneventful (several tiring walks around the city with Mr. Umezaki and Hensuiro, drinks after supper, early to bed). The details of what had been said or done or exchanged was beyond his memory's retrieval, and instead it was the beach and the dunes that filled the gap. And yet, having grown wary of Mr. Umezaki's attentiveness, he took from Kobe a feeling of true affection for Hensuiro—the young artist gripping at his elbow without any ulterior motives, graciously inviting Holmes into his studio room, showing his paintings (the red skies, the black landscapes, the contorted blue-gray bodies) while modestly casting his stare down to the paint-spattered floor.

"It's quite—I don't know—modern, Hensuiro."

"Thank you, *sensei,* thank you—"

Holmes studied an unfinished canvas—ravaged, bony fingers clawing desperately outward from beneath rubble, in the foreground an orange tabby cat gnawing apart its own hind paw—then he studied Hensuiro: the sensitive, almost shy brown eyes, the kind, boyish face.

"Such a gentle soul, I think, with such a harsh outlook—it is difficult reconciling the two."

"Yes—I thank you—yes—"

But among the finished pieces leaning against the walls, Holmes came to stand before a work that was different from Hensuiro's other paintings: a formal portrait of a handsome young man in his early to mid-thirties, posing against a backdrop of dark green leaves, and wearing a kimono, with *hakama* trousers, *haori* coat, *tabi* socks, and geta clogs.

"Now who is this?" asked Holmes, unsure at first if it was a self-portrait he was seeing, or perhaps even Mr. Umezaki in his younger days.

"This my bro-ther," Hensuiro said, and as best he could, he explained that his brother was dead—but not because of the war or some great tragedy. No, he indicated by moving an index finger across his wrist, his brother had killed himself. "This woman he loves—you know—like this, too." He slashed at his wrists again. "My only bro-ther—"

"A double suicide?"

"Yes, I think so."

"I see," said Holmes, bending for a closer look at the subject's oil-colored face. "It is a lovely painting. I like this one very much."

"Honto ni arigato gozaimas, sensei—thank you—"

Later, in the minutes prior to his departure from Kobe, Holmes felt an unusual desire to hug Hensuiro good-bye, except he resisted doing so, offering only a nod and the tap of a cane against the man's shin. It was Mr. Umezaki, however, who stepped forward on the train station platform, bringing his hands to Holmes's shoulders, bowing before him at the same time, saying, "It's our hope to see you again someday—perhaps in England. Perhaps we can visit you."

"Perhaps," said Holmes.

Afterward, he boarded the train, claiming a window seat. Outside, Mr. Umezaki and Hensuiro remained on the platform, looking upward at him, but Holmes—disliking sentimental departures, that often overwrought need to make the most of a parting—avoided their stares, busying himself with situating his canes, stretching out his legs. Then, as the train began pulling from the station, he glanced briefly to where the two had been standing, and frowning, he saw that they had already gone. Not until approaching Tokyo would he find those gifts that had been secreted into his coat pockets: a small glass vial containing a pair of Japanese honeybees; an envelope with Holmes's name written on it, containing haiku from Mr. Umezaki.

> *My insomnia—*
> *someone cries out while asleep,*
> *the wind answers him.*

> *Searching in the sand,*
> *twisting and turning, the dunes*
> *hide the prickly ash.*

> *A shamisen plays*
> *as dusk ushers forth shadows—*
> *trees embraced by night.*

> *The train and my friend*
> *have gone—summer beginning,*
> *springs' query fulfilled.*

While the origins of the haiku were certain, Holmes was perplexed by the vial when holding it near his face, contemplating the two dead honeybees sealed within—one mingling upon the other, their legs intertwined. Where had it come from? Tokyo's urban apiary? Somewhere along his travels with Mr. Umezaki? He couldn't say for sure (any more than he could explain most of the oddments that ended up in his pockets), nor could he envision Hensuiro collecting the bees, placing them carefully into the vial before slipping them inside his coat, where they lurked among scraps of paper and tobacco shreds, a blue seashell and grains of sand, the turquoise-colored pebble from Shukkei-en Garden, and a single prickly-ash seed. "Where did I find you? Think. . . . " No matter how he tried, he couldn't remember the vial coming into his possession. Still, he'd obviously gathered the dead bees for a reason—likely as research, maybe as a memento, or, possibly, as young Roger's present (a gift for tending the beeyard during his absence, of course).

And again, two days following Roger's funeral, Holmes saw himself read over the handwritten haiku, the page discovered under stacks of paper on his desk; fingertips at the creased edges, his body slumped forward in the chair, a Jamaican between his lips and smoke twisting toward the ceiling; saw himself set the page down sometime later, inhale the fumes, exhale through his nostrils, look at the window, look at the hazy ceiling. Saw the risen smoke float like wisps of ether. Then saw himself riding on that train, coat and canes in his lap, past diminishing countryside, past the outskirts of Tokyo, beneath bridges erected above the railroad tracks. Saw himself on a Royal Navy ship, amid enlisted men as they watched him, sitting or eating by himself, a relic from an age that had dismantled itself. Avoiding most conversation, the seafaring meals and the monotony of travel being a strain on retention. Returning to Sussex—Mrs. Munro had found him napping within the library. Going afterward to the beeyard, giving Roger the vial of honeybees. "This was meant for you. *Apis cerana japonica*—or perhaps we'll simply call them Japanese honeybees. How's that?" "Thank you, sir." He saw himself awaken in darkness, listening to his own gasps, feeling his mind had at last deserted him, but finding it still intact by daylight and cranking to life like some outmoded apparatus. And as Anderson's daugh-

ter brought him his breakfast of royal jelly spread upon fried bread
and asked him, "Has Mrs. Munro sent any word yet?" he saw himself shake his head, saying, "She has sent nothing."

But what of the Japanese honeybees? he deliberated now, reaching for his canes. Where did the boy keep them? he wondered, standing while glancing at the window—seeing the overcast, gray
morning that had proceeded from the night, stifling the dawn as he
had worked at his desk.

Where exactly has he put you? he thought when finally exiting
the farmhouse, the spare key to the cottage pressing against his
palm, enclosed in a hand wrapped about a cane's handle.

21

As storm clouds spread above the sea and his property, Holmes unlocked Mrs. Munro's living quarters, shuffling inside to where the drapes had been drawn, and the lights were kept off, and the woodsy barklike smell of mothballs obscured whatever else he inhaled. Each three or four steps, he paused, peering ahead into the darkness, and readjusted his grip on the canes, as if anticipating some vague, unimaginable form to spring out at him from the shadows. He continued forward—the taps of his canes falling less heavily, less wearily than his footsteps—until trudging past Roger's open doorway, entering the only cottage room that wasn't sealed wholly from daylight. Then, for the first and last time, he found himself among the boy's few possessions.

He took a seat at the edge of Roger's neatly made bed, looking over the general surroundings. The schoolbag hanging from the closet doorknob. The butterfly net standing in a corner. Eventually, he stood, wandering slowly about the room. The books. The *National Geographic* magazines. The rocks and seashells on the chest of drawers, the photographs and colorful drawings on the walls. The objects covering a student's writing desk: six textbooks, five sharpened pencils, drawing pens, blank paper—and the vial containing the two honeybees.

"I see," he said, lifting the vial, briefly staring at the contents (the creatures being undisturbed within, remaining as they had when he discovered them on the Tokyo-bound train). He lowered the vial to the desktop, making sure its placement was in no way changed. How methodical the boy had been, how precise—everything arranged, everything aligned; the items occupying the nightstand were also ordered: scissors, a bottle of rubber cement, a large scrapbook with an unadorned black cover.

And soon it was the scrapbook that Holmes took into his hands. Sitting again upon the bed, leisurely turning the pages, he examined the intricate collages depicting wildlife and forests, soldiers and war, ultimately bringing his gaze to the desolate image of the former prefectural government building in Hiroshima. When at last finishing with the scrapbook, the weariness he had carried since dawn seized him completely.

Outside, the diffusive sunlight grew suddenly dimmer.

Slender branches scraped against the windowpanes, almost noiselessly.

"I don't know," he uttered incomprehensibly, there on Roger's bed. "I don't know," he said again, lowering himself to the boy's pillow and shutting his eyes, the scrapbook pressed against his chest. "I haven't a clue."

He drifted away after that, though not into the sort of sleep that came from total exhaustion, or even a restless slumber in which dreams and reality were interlaced, but, rather, a torpid state submerging him into a vast stillness. Presently, that expansive, downreaching sleep delivered him elsewhere, tugging him from the bedroom where his body rested. For more than six hours, he was gone—his breathing steady and low, his limbs neither altering positions or flinching. The midday thunder cracks were inaudible to his ears, and he didn't perceive the storm blowing across his land, the tall grass bending wildly toward the ground, the stinging, hard drops of rain wetting the soil; with the storm's passing, he didn't sense the front door swinging back, sending a gust of cool rain-fresh air through the main room, along the corridor, into Roger's bedroom.

But Holmes felt the chill touch his face and neck, urging him awake like cold palms pushing gently upon his skin. "Who's there?" he mumbled when stirring. Cracking his eyelids, he stared at the nightstand (scissors, rubber cement). His gaze shifted minutely, fixing on the corridor beyond: that murky passage between the brightness of the boy's bedroom and the open front door, where, after several ascertaining seconds, he realized someone now waited in its shadows, motionless and facing him, silhouetted by the light coming from behind. The rushing air faintly ruffled clothing, flapping the hem of a dress. "Who is it?" he asked, not yet capable of sitting up. And only when the figure receded—gliding backwards, it seemed, stepping to the entryway—did she become visible. He watched while she brought a suitcase inside before closing the front door—once again steeping the cottage with darkness, vanishing as quickly as she had appeared. "Mrs. Munro—"

She materialized, gravitating toward the boy's bedroom, her head floating like a formless white sphere amid a pitch background; yet the darkness itself was not of one shade, and looked as if it were fluctuating and swaying beneath her: the fabric of her dress, Holmes suspected, the attire of mourning. Indeed, it was a black dress she wore, fringed with lace and austere in design; her skin was pallid, and bluish circles were visible under her eyes (the grief had diminished her youthfulness—her face was haggard, her movements sluggish). Stepping across the threshold, she nodded without expression when approaching him, showing none of the agony he'd heard the day Roger died or the festering anger she'd displayed at the beeyard. Instead, it was something benign he sensed about her, something yielding and likely tranquilized. You cannot blame me anymore, he thought, or my bees—you've judged us wrongly, my child, and you've realized your mistake. Her pale hands reached down to him, gingerly extracting the scrapbook from his fingers. She avoided his stare, but he glimpsed her wide pupils at an angle, recognizing in them the same vacuous quality he had seen on Roger's corpse. Saying nothing, she returned the scrapbook to the nightstand, positioning it uniformly as the boy might have done.

"Why are you here?" asked Holmes after lowering his feet to the floor, pushing himself upright on the mattress, and sitting there. The moment he spoke, his face flushed with embarrassment, for she had found him resting inside her quarters, embracing her dead son's scrapbook; if anything, he knew the question should have been hers. Even so, Mrs. Munro didn't seem terribly disturbed by his presence, a factor that made him more uncomfortable. He glanced around, spotting his canes propped against the nightstand. "Wasn't expecting you home this soon," he heard himself say, absently fumbling to grasp the cane handles. "I trust your trip wasn't too taxing." Shamed with the superficiality of his own words, his face turned redder.

Mrs. Munro now stood in front of the writing desk, keeping her back to him (just as he sat on the bed, his back to her). She'd decided it was better for her at the cottage, she explained, and once Holmes heard the calm voice in which she addressed him, his uneasiness waned. "I've plenty here that needs dealing with," she said. "I've affairs that need settling—Roger's and mine."

"You must be famished," he said, readying his canes. "I will have the girl bring you something—or perhaps you would rather dine at my table?"

He wondered if Anderson's daughter had already finished the grocery shopping in town, and as he stood, Mrs. Munro answered from behind him: "I'm not hungry."

Holmes turned toward her, meeting her sidelong glare (those reluctant, empty eyes never quite focusing on him, allocating him to the periphery). "Is there anything you might want?" was all he could think to ask. "Can I do anything?"

"I'll take care of myself, thank you," she said, averting her eyes completely.

Then Holmes understood her true reason for returning so soon, and—as she began considering the objects on the desk, her arms unfolding beneath her breasts—he observed the profile of a woman who was debating how best to conclude another chapter of her life. "You will be leaving me, won't you?" he said abruptly, the words escaping his mouth in midthought.

Her fingertips roamed the desktop, brushing over drawing pens, touching the blank paper, pausing for a while on the polished woodgrain surface (the spot where Roger had completed homework, fashioned his elaborate drawings for the walls, and surely pondered his magazines and books). Even in death, she saw the boy sitting there, while she cooked and cleaned and busied herself off in the main house. And Holmes, too, had conceived of Roger at the desk—slumped forward, like himself, as the day shifted into night, the night into dawn. He wanted to share the vision with Mrs. Munro, telling her what he believed they'd both imagined, but instead he remained silent, anticipating the answer that finally passed confidently between her lips: "Yes, sir—I'll be going from you."

Of course you will, thought Holmes, as if sympathetic with her decision. Yet he felt so wounded by the assuredness of her answer that he stammered like someone pleading for a second chance: "Please, you needn't make such a rash choice—really—especially at this time."

"But it wasn't rash, you see. I've spent hours thinking about it—and it's impossible seeing it differently. There's little here of value anymore—just these things and nothing else." She picked up a red drawing pen, rolling it thoughtfully with her fingers and thumb. "No, it wasn't rash."

A breeze suddenly hummed at the window above Roger's desk, scraping branches on the glass. The breeze increased momentarily, rustling the tree outside, tapping the branches harder against the panes. Dejected by Mrs. Munro's response, Holmes sighed with resignation, then asked, "And where will you go, to London? What will become of you?"

"I honestly don't know. I don't feel my life matters one way or the other."

Her son was dead. Her husband was dead. She was speaking as one who had buried those she cherished the most, and, in doing so, had placed herself within their graves. Holmes recalled a poem he'd read during his youth, that single line which had haunted his childhood: *I shall go beyond alone, so you may seek me there.* Overwhelmed by her complacent desperation, he stepped toward her, saying, "Of course it matters. To relinquish all hope is to relinquish everything—and you mustn't do that, my dear. In any case, you have an obligation to persevere, if you don't, your love for the boy won't endure."

Love: It was a word Mrs. Munro had never heard him utter. She gave him a sidelong glance, stopping him with the coldness of her stare. Then, as if to avoid the issue, she gazed again at the desktop, saying, "I've learned quite a lot about these."

Holmes saw that she was reaching for the vial of honeybees. "Have you indeed?" he remarked.

"These are Japanese—gentle and shy insects, right? Not like them ones of yours, ain't that so?" She set the vial in the palm of her hand.

"You are correct. You have done your research." He was surprised by the small amount of knowledge Mrs. Munro possessed, but he frowned when she had nothing further to say (her eyes remaining on the vial, fixed on the dead bees inside). Unable to bear the silence, he continued: "They are rather remarkable creatures—timid, as you say—although industrious in killing off a foe." He told her that the Japanese giant hornet hunted various species of bees and wasps. Once a hornet had discovered a nest, it left a secretion to mark the location; the secretion then signaled other hornets in the area to congregate and attack the colony. Japanese honeybees, however, could detect the hornet's secretion, allowing them to prepare for the imminent assault. As the hornets entered the nest, the honeybees would surround each attacker, enveloping it with their bodies and subjecting it to a temperature of forty-seven degrees Celsius (too hot for a hornet, perfect for a honeybee). "They really are fascinating, aren't they?" he concluded. "I chanced upon an apiary in Tokyo, you know—was fortunate enough to witness the creatures firsthand."

Sunlight broke through the clouds, illuminating the curtains. Just then, Holmes felt wretched for having launched into a speech at such an inappropriate moment (Mrs. Munro's son was in a grave, but all he could offer her was a lecture on Japanese honeybees). Burdened by helplessness, he shook his head at his own stupidity. And as he contemplated an apology, she placed the vial on the desktop, her voice trembling with emotion. "It's meaningless—it ain't human, the way you talk—none of it is human, just science and books—things stuck in bottles and boxes. What have you ever known about loving anyone?"

Holmes bristled at the caustic, hateful tone—the pointed, contemptuous emphasis in her hushed voice—and struggled to compose himself before replying. Then he realized his hands were clutching the canes, and that his knuckles had become white: You have no idea, he thought. Releasing an exasperated sigh, he loosened his grip on the canes and shuffled back to Roger's mattress. "I am surely not as rigid as that," he said, taking a seat at the bed's foot. "At least I don't wish to think I am—but how could I convince you otherwise? And what if I told you my passion for the bees didn't evolve from any branch of science or from the pages of books—would you find me less inhuman?"

Keeping her stare on the vial, she didn't respond, nor did she move.

"Mrs. Munro, I fear my advanced age has produced some diminishment of retention, as you are, no doubt, completely aware. I often misplace things—my cigars, my canes, sometimes my own shoes—and I find things in my pockets that mystify me; it's rather amusing and horrifying at the same instant. There are also periods when I cannot remember why I have gone from one room into another—or even fathom the sentences I have just written at my desk. Yet many other things are indelibly etched within my paradoxical mind. For example, I can recall being eighteen with the utmost clarity—very tall, lonely, an unhandsome Oxford undergraduate—spending evenings in the company of the don who lectured on mathematics and logic—a prim, fussy, disagreeable man, a resident of Christ Church like myself—someone you might know well as Lewis Carroll—but whom I knew as the Reverend C. L. Dodgson, an inventor of fantastic mathematical and word puzzles—and ciphers, to my infinite interest—his sleight-of-hand and paper-folding tricks are as vivid to me now as they were then. As well, I can see the pony I kept as a boy—and myself riding it on the Yorkshire moorland, getting gladly lost in an ocean of heather-covered waves. There are many such scenes in my head, and all are easily accessible. Why they remain and others flit away, I cannot say.

"But let me share something further about myself, for I feel it is relevant. When you look upon me, I believe you find a man incapable of feeling. I am more at fault for that perception than you are, my child. You have only known me in my declining years, sequestered out here and within my apiary. If I choose to speak at any length, I usually talk of the creatures. So I won't blame you for thinking too ill of me. In any case, until the age of forty-eight, I had scarcely a passing interest for bees and the world of the hive; however, by my forty-ninth year, I could think of nothing else. How do I explain it?" He inhaled, shutting his eyes for a second, then he continued: "You see, there was a woman under my investigation—she was younger, rather strange to me, but alluring—and I found myself preoccupied with her—it is not something I have ever fully understood. Our time together was fleeting—less than an hour, really—and she knew nothing about me—and I knew very little about her, except that she enjoyed reading books, and strolling and loitering around flowers—so I strolled with her, you see, among flowers. The details of the case are unimportant, aside from the fact that eventually she was gone from my life—and, as inexplicable as it was, I felt something essential had been lost, creating a void inside me. And yet—and yet—she began manifesting in my thoughts—existing in a lucid moment, which was as insignificant as when it had originally occurred, but which, soon thereafter, presented itself once again to me and hasn't left me." He fell silent, his eyes squinting, as if he were conjuring the past.

Mrs. Munro glanced back at him, grimacing slightly. "Why are you telling me this? What does this have to do with anything?" When she spoke, her unblemished face showed creases on her forehead, the deep-set lines being the most expressive thing about her. But Holmes wasn't looking toward her; his gaze had drifted to the floor, transfixed by something only he could envision.

It was of minor consequence, he told her—even as Mrs. Keller revealed herself to him, stretching her gloved hand outward through time. There in the Physics and Botanical Society park, she had brought her fingers to the echium and the *atropa belladonna*—the horsetail and the feverfew—and now she cupped an iris in her palm. Withdrawing her hand, she noticed that a worker bee had strayed onto her glove. But she didn't flinch, shaking the creature away, or crush it in her fist; instead, she pondered it closely, doing so with apparent reverence (a curious grin, affectionate whispers uttered beneath her breath). The worker bee, in turn, stayed upon her palm—not busying itself, or burying its stinger into her glove—as if regarding her the same.

"It is impossible to give an accurate view of such an intimate communion, the likes of which I haven't witnessed since," Holmes said, raising his head. "In all, the episode lasted perhaps ten seconds, certainly no more than that; then she saw fit to release the creature, setting it loose on the very flower from where it had come. Yet this brief and simple transaction—the woman and her hand and the creature she held without distrust—propelled me headfirst into what has become my greatest preoccupation. You see, it wasn't exacting, calculating science, my dear—it isn't as meaningless as you suggest."

Mrs. Munro kept her eyes on him: "But that's hardly true love, is it?"

"I have no understanding of love," he said miserably. "I have never made claim that I do." And regardless of who or what had ignited the fascination, he knew his solitary life's pursuit relied completely on scientific methods, that his ideas and writings weren't intended for the sentiments of the layman. Still, there was the golden throng. The gold of flowers. The gold of pollen dust. The miracle of a culture that had sustained its way of living—century after century, age after age, aeon after aeon—proving how adept its insect commonwealth was in overcoming the problems of existence. The self-reliant community of the hive, in which not a single dispirited worker relied upon human dispensation. The partnership of man and bees, relished solely by those who tended the fringes of the bees' world and safeguarded the evolution of their complex realms. The measure of peace discovered in the harmony of the insects' murmuring, soothing the mind and providing assurance against the confusion of a changing planet. The mystery and the astonishment and the deference, and accentuating that, the late-afternoon sunlight permeating the beeyard with colors of yellow and orange: all of it experienced and valued by Roger, he had no doubt. More than once, while at the apiary together, Holmes had recognized wonder on the boy's face, the sight of it consuming him with a sensation he couldn't readily express. "Some might call it a kind of love—if they so choose." His expression shifted to one of sorrow and dejection.

Mrs. Munro realized he was weeping almost imperceptibly (the tears welling in his eyes, dripping down his cheeks and into his beard). However, the tears ended as quickly as they'd begun, and Holmes brushed the wetness from his skin, sighing. Finally, he heard himself say, "I wish you would reconsider—it would mean a great deal to me if you'd stay on," but Mrs. Munro refused to speak and, instead, glanced around at the drawings on the wall, as if he weren't there. Holmes lowered his head again. I deserve as much, he thought. The tears started welling—then stopped.

"Do you miss him?" she asked plainly enough, at last breaking her silence.

"Of course I do" was his immediate answer.

Her gaze had traveled over the drawings, pausing on a sepia-tinted photograph (Roger cradled as an infant in her arms while her young husband stood proudly beside them). "He admired you, he did. Did you know that?" Holmes raised his head, nodding with a gesture of relief as she turned toward him. "It was Roger who told me about them bees in the jar. He mentioned everything you'd told him about them; he told me everything you said."

The hushed, caustic tone had vanished, and Mrs. Munro's sudden need to address him directly—the softness in her melancholy voice, her stare meeting his stare—made Holmes feel that she had somehow absolved him. Yet he could only listen and nod, looking narrowly at her.

With her anguish becoming evident, she searched his morose, withered face. "What am I supposed to do now, sir? What am I without my boy? Why'd he have to die like that?"

But Holmes could think of nothing affirming to tell her. Yet her eyes implored him, as if they wanted one thing: to be given something of value, something resolute and beneficial. In that moment, he doubted if there could be any mental state more relentlessly cruel than the desiring of real meaning from circumstances that lacked useful or definitive answers. Moreover, he knew he couldn't fabricate an appeasing falsehood to ease her suffering, as he'd done for Mr. Umezaki; nor could he fill in the blanks and create a satisfactory conclusion, like Dr. Watson had often done when writing his stories. No, the truth itself was too clear and undeniable: Roger was dead, a victim of misfortune.

"Why'd it have to happen, sir? I must know why—"

She spoke like so many before her had—those who had sought him out in London, and the ones who years later had intruded on his retirement in Sussex—requesting his help, beseeching him to alleviate their troubles and restore order to their lives. If only it were that easy, he thought. If only every problem was guaranteed a solution.

Then the perplexity that signified periods when his mind couldn't grasp its own ruminations cast its shadow over him, but he managed to articulate himself as best he could, solemnly saying, "It seems—or rather—it's that sometimes—sometimes things occur beyond our own understanding, my dear, and the unjust reality is that these events—being so illogical to us, devoid of whatever reason we might attach to them—are exactly what they are and, regrettably, nothing else—and I believe—I truly believe that that is the hardest notion for any of us to live with."

Mrs. Munro stared at him for a while, as if she had no intention of responding; then, smiling bitterly, she said, "Yes—it is." In the silence that followed, she faced the desk again—the pens, the paper, the books, the vial—and straightened all she had previously touched. When finished, she turned to him, saying, "Excuse me, but I'm needing my sleep—it's been an exhausting few days."

"Would you stay with me tonight?" Holmes asked, concerned for her and prompted by a feeling that told him she shouldn't be alone. "Anderson's girl is doing the cooking, although you will find her meals are far from appetizing. And I am sure there're clean sheets in the guest room."

"I'm comfortable here, thank you," she said.

Holmes considered insisting she accompany him, but already Mrs. Munro was gazing past him, peering into the darkened corridor. Her hunched, determined body and head, her wide pupils—full and black, ringed by faint circles of green—had now disregarded his presence, pushing him aside. She had entered Roger's room without speaking, so he imagined that she would exit in the same way. Yet when she started for the door, he intercepted her, seizing her hand, stopping her from going forward.

"My child—"

But she didn't pull herself away, nor did he attempt to inhibit her further; he simply held her hand as she gripped his, neither saying more or looking upon the other—his palm against her palm, their regards communicated in the gentle mutual pressure of fingers—until, nodding once, she slipped free and proceeded on through the doorway, soon fading down the corridor, leaving him to navigate the darkness by himself.

After a while, he rose to his feet and, not looking back, went from Roger's bedroom. In the corridor, his canes tapped in front of him as if guiding a blind man (behind was the brightness of the boy's room, ahead was the dimness of the cottage, and somewhere beyond him was Mrs. Munro). Coming into the entryway, he fumbled for the doorknob, clasped it, and, with some effort, opened the door. But the outside light stunned his vision, preventing him from advancing for a moment; and it was as he stood there, squinting his eyes, inhaling the rain-saturated air, that the sanctuary of the beeyard—the peacefulness of his apiary, the tranquillity he felt while sitting among those four rocks—beckoned him. He took a steadfast breath before starting, still squinting when he stepped to the path. Along the way, he paused, searching his pockets for a Jamaican, but he found only a box of matches. That's all right, he thought, resuming his walk, his shoes squishing in mud, the high grass on either side of the path glistening with moisture. Nearing the beeyard, a reddish butterfly fluttered by him. Another butterfly followed, as if in pursuit—and another. Once the last butterfly had passed, his eyes surveyed the beeyard, settling on the rows of hives and then the grassy spot that concealed the four rocks (everything now dampened, sodden and subdued by raindrops).

So he continued onward instead, heading for where his property met the sky, and the sheer white earth fell perpendicularly beneath the farmhouse and flower gardens and Mrs. Munro's cottage—its strata showing the evolution of time and jagging beside the meager trail that wound to the beach, while each layer indicated history's uneven progress, gradually transforming, persistent nonetheless, with fossils and tendril-like roots pressed between them.

As he began his descent upon the trail (legs coaxing him forward, the marks of his canes dotting the wet, chalky ground), he listened to the waves breaking against the shore, that distant rumble and hiss and brief silence afterward, like the initial dialect of creation before human life had been conceived. The afternoon breeze and the coursing of the ocean meshed in accord, as he observed—there beyond the shore, miles away—the sun reflected on the water and rippled among the currents. With every passing minute, the ocean grew increasingly radiant, the sun seemingly rising from its depths, the waves curling in expanding hues of orange and red.

But it all appeared so remote, so abstract and foreign to him. The more he watched the sea and sky, the more removed it felt from humanity; and this was why, he reasoned, mankind was at such odds with itself—this detachment being the inevitable by-product of a species accelerating way ahead of its own innate qualities, and that fact consumed him with an immense ruefulness he could hardly contain. Still, the waves broke, the cliffs loomed high, the breeze carried the smell of salt water, and the storm's aftermath tempered the summer's warmth. Proceeding down the trail, the desire to be a part of the original, natural order stirred inside him, the wish to escape the trappings of people and the meaningless clamor that heralded its self-importance; this need was set in him, surpassing everything he treasured or believed was true (his many writings and theories, his observations on a vast number of things). Already the heavens were wavering as the sun declined; the moon, too, occupied the sky while reflecting the sun's light, and hung there obscurely like a transparent half circle in the blue-black firmament. Briefly, he considered the sun and the moon—that hot, blinding star and that frigid, lifeless crescent—finding himself made content by how each one traveled in an orbit with its own motion, yet both were somehow essential to the other. The words sprang to his mind even as the source was forgotten: *The sun must not catch up the moon, nor does the night outstrip the day.* And at last—just as it had happened again and again for him while going along that winding trail—dusk approached.

When he reached the trail's midpoint, the sun had dipped toward the horizon, spilling its rays across the tide pools and scree below, mixing its light with deep-edged shadows. After easing himself to the overlook bench, he set his canes aside, peering downward at the shore—then the ocean, then the shifting, endless sky. A few lingering storm clouds remained in the distance, sporadically flashing within like lightning bugs, and several seagulls, which seemed to cry out at him, swam around one another, swaying deftly upon the breeze; underneath them, the waves were orangish and murky and also shimmering. Where the trail crooked, angling for the beach, he noticed clusters of new grass and riots of bramble, but they were like outcasts banished from the fertile land up above. Then he thought he heard the sound of his own breathing—a sustained low rhythm, not unlike the droning of wind—or was it something else, something emanating from nearby? Perhaps, he mused, it was the faint murmuring of the cliffs, the vibrations of those immeasurable seams of earth, of the stones and roots and soil stating its permanence over man as it had done throughout the ages; and it was addressing him now like time itself.

He closed his eyes.

His body slackened: Weariness was running through his limbs, keeping him on the bench. Don't move, he told himself, and envision the things that are durable. The wild daffodils and the herb beds. The breeze rustling in the pines, as it had since before his birth. A tingling sensation began on his neck, a vague tickling among the hairs of his beard. He lifted a hand, raising it slowly from his lap. The giant thistles snaked upward. The purple buddleias were in bloom. Today it had rained, wetting his property, soaking the ground; tomorrow the rain would return. The soil was made more fragrant after the downpour. The profusion of azaleas and laurel and rhododendrons shuddered in the pastures. And what's this? His hand captured the sensation, the tickling going from his neck into his fist. His breathing had grown shallow, but his eyes opened anyway. There, revealed in the unfurling of his fingers, it flitted about with the skittish movements of a common housefly: a lone worker bee, its pollen baskets full; a straggler far from the hives and foraging on its own. Remarkable creature, he thought, watching as it danced upon his palm. Then he shook his hand, sending it into the air—envious of its speed and how effortlessly it took flight into such a mutable, inconsistent world.

22

An Epilogue

Even after all this time, I am overcome with a heavy heart while taking up my pen to write these last paragraphs regarding the circumstances in which Mrs. Keller's life was cut short. In a disconnected and, as I now feel certain, a thoroughly unreliable manner, I have attempted to present some record of my rare connection to the woman, from the first glimpse of her face in a photograph, up to the afternoon which, at last, offered some fleeting insight into her mien. It was always my intention to have concluded there, at the Physics and Botanical Society, and to relate nothing of that event which has since fashioned a strange void in my mind—

which the gradual passing of forty-five years has yet to fully appease or displace.

However, my pen has been compelled on this dark night by my desire to report as much as possible, lest my rapidly faltering retention chooses, without my acquiescence, to soon banish her elsewhere. Fearing that inevitability, I feel I have no choice but to present the details just as they occurred. As I recall, there was a single brief account in the public press on the Friday following her departure from the Physics and Botanical Society park, appearing in an early edition of the *Evening Standard*; it seemed from its placement in the paper to have been judged an event of minor importance, and the account of it ran as follows:

A tragic railway accident occurred this afternoon on the tracks near St. Pancras Station, which involved a locomotive engine and culminated in the death of one woman. Engineer Ian Lomax, of the London & North Western Railway line, was surprised to see a woman with a parasol walking towards the oncoming engine at half past two. Unable to stop the locomotive before it could reach her, the engineer signalled with the engine's whistle, but the woman remained on the tracks and, making no noticeable attempt to save herself, was struck down. The force of the engine's impact shattered her body, and she was thrown a good distance from the tracks. Examination of the unfortunate woman's belongings later identified her as Ann Keller of Fortis Grove. Her hus-

band, who is said to be inconsolable, has made no official state-
ment yet as to why she may have strayed onto the tracks, although
the police are making private enquiries in an attempt to determine
the reasons.

Such are the only facts known concerning the violent end of Mrs.
Ann Keller. Even so, while it has already stretched into too great a
length, I shall prolong this narrative by mentioning how—on the
morning after learning of her death—I donned my facade of eyeglasses and false moustache with unsettled hands, how I regained my
composure while going by foot from Baker Street to the house on
Fortis Grove, of how the front door was slowly opened for me and all
I could see beyond was Thomas R. Keller's listless visage framed by
the darkness which loomed behind him. He appeared neither dismayed nor heartened by my arrival, nor did my disguise register any
questioning look from him. I immediately detected a harsh whiff
of brandy de Jerez—La Marque Speciale, to be precise—reeking
strongly from him when he uttered flatly, "Yes, please come in." But
the little which I wished to share with the man was left unspoken
for the moment—as I then followed him silently through rooms
where the curtains remained drawn, past a staircase, and into a study
which was illuminated by a single lamp; its glow was cast over two
chairs and, between them, a side table holding two bottles of the very
spirit I had smelled upon his breath.

And here it is that I miss John more than ever. With clever details and hyperbole verging on grandeur, he could transfigure a mundane story, which is the measure of a writer's true talent, into a thing of interest. Yet when I forge my own story, I have no real ability to paint in such lavish but refined strokes. I will, however, do my utmost to draw as vivid a portrait as is possible of that pallor of grief which had descended upon my client: For even while I sat near Mr. Keller, conveying to him my deepest expressions of sympathy, he said almost nothing in reply, but kept motionless, his stubbled chin upon his breast, sunk in the gravest stupor. His vacant, inanimate stare was fixed on the floor; with one hand clutching an arm of the chair, he kept the other wrapped tightly around the neck of a brandy bottle— yet in his debilitated state he was incapable of lifting the bottle from the side table to his mouth.

Nor did Mr. Keller behave as I imagined he would; he assigned no blame for her death, and when I absolved his wife of any wrongdoing, my words sounded hollow and unimportant. What did it matter, then, if she had not been taking covert armonica lessons, or that Madame Schirmer had been unfairly judged, or that his wife had, for the most part, been honest with him? Still, I imparted the few bits of information that she had withheld, explaining about Portman's tiny garden oasis, the books borrowed from the shelves, the music lessons which played to her as she read. I mentioned the back gate which led her into the alley behind the shop. I mentioned the aimlessness of her strolling—along footpaths, down narrow avenues, beside railway tracks—and how she managed to guide herself to the Physics and

Botanical Society. All the same, there was no reason to bring up Stefan Peterson, or to point out that my client's wife had spent a late afternoon in the company of one whose pursuit of her was less than noble.

"But I don't understand it," said he, stirring in the chair and turning his miserable gaze towards me. "What made her do it, Mr. Holmes? I don't understand."

I had repeatedly asked myself the same question, yet found myself at a loss to hit upon an easy answer. I patted him kindly on the leg; then I looked into his bloodshot eyes, which, as if wounded by my stare, moved wearily again to focus on the floor.

"I cannot say with any degree of certainty. I really cannot say."

It might well have been that several explanations existed, but I had already tried test after test in my mind and nothing convincing presented itself. There was the possible explanation of the pain of losing her unborn children being too much of a burden to bear. There was the explanation that the supposed power of the armonica's tones had exerted some control over her fragile psyche, or that she was driven mad by the injustices of life, or that she had some unknown disease which caused her madness. I could find no other solutions which were as adequate, so these became the explanations which I had spent hours sifting through and balancing against one another— without a satisfactory end.

For a time, I settled on madness as the more plausible conclusion. The restless, obsessive preoccupation with the armonica suggested something psychoneurotic about her nature. The fact that she had once locked herself in an attic for hours and created music to summon her unborn only gave strength to the idea of insanity. On the other hand, this woman who read romance literature on park benches, who showed great empathy for the flowers and creatures of gardens, seemed at peace with herself and the world around her. It is not impossible, however, for the mentally disturbed to betray any number of behavioural contradictions. Yet she showed no outward signs of being deranged. Indeed, there was hardly anything about her which hinted at a woman capable of walking headlong toward an approaching train; for if that had been the case, why, then, had she displayed such an infatuation for all that lived, flourished, and thrived in the spring? Again, I could not reach a conclusion which made sense of the facts.

There remained, however, a final theory, which seemed rather likely. Plumbism was, in those days, barely an uncommon ailment, especially since lead could be found in dinnerware and utensils, candles, water pipes, the leading of windows, paint, and pewter drinking vessels. Without question, lead would also be found in the armonica's glass stemware and the paint applied to each bowl as a means to differentiate the notes. I have long suspected that chronic lead poisoning was the cause of Beethoven's illnesses, deafness, and ultimate death, for he, too, devoted hours to the mastering of the armonica's glasses. Therefore, the theory was a strong one—so strong that I had determined to prove its validity. But what soon became apparent was that Mrs. Keller carried none of the symptoms of acute or chronic plumbism; she had no staggering gait, or seizures, or colic, or decreased intellectual functioning. And while she could have acquired lead poisoning by never having touched an armonica, I understood that the general malaise she experienced early on had been eased somewhat by the instrument and not compounded by it. Furthermore, her very hands dismissed that initial suspicion; they were lacking of blemishes or the blue-black discolourment which would have been seen nearest the fingertips.

No, I had finally concluded, she was never mad or ill, nor was she despairing to the point of insanity. She had, for reasons unknown, simply extracted herself from the human equation and ceased to be; doing so, perhaps, as some contrary means of survival. And even now I wonder if creation is both too beautiful and too horrible for a handful of perceptive souls, and if the realisation of this opposing duality can offer them few options but to take leave of their own accord. Beyond that, I can give no other explanation which may strike closer to the truth of the matter. Still, it has never been a conclusion I have wanted to live comfortably with.

As it happened, I was finishing this analysis of his wife when Mr. Keller eased forwards in the chair, his hand sliding limply down the bottle's length to rest palm upwards on a corner of the side table. But for once, his grim, haggard features had softened and there was a gentle breathing which rose from his chest. Too much grief and too little sleep, I was sure. Too much brandy. So I remained for a while, indulging myself with a glass of La Marque Speciale—then another—rising to go only when the liqueur flushed my cheeks and blunted the melancholy which had saturated my entire being. Soon I would cross the rooms of the house, seeking the sunlight which was seen faintly along the edges of those pulled curtains—although not until I retrieved Mrs. Keller's photograph from an overcoat pocket and, with some reluctance to do so, placed it in the lax palm of my client's outstretched hand. After that, I made my exit without looking back, traversing the space between darkness and light as swiftly as possible, jettisoning myself into an afternoon which persists in my memory just as bright and blue and cloudless as it was on that long-ago day.

But I was not yet willing to return to Baker Street; rather, on that sunny spring afternoon, I set off towards Montague Street, savouring the experience of strolling along the thoroughfares Mrs. Keller had known so well. And all the while, I imagined what might await me when I stepped into Portman's garden. In time, I found myself there— having passed through the empty shop, along the shadowy aisles, out the back—at the garden's centre where the small bench was encircled by the boxwood hedge. I paused to admire the view, surveying the perennial beds and the roses along the perimeter wall. There was a slight breeze, and looking beyond the hedge, I observed the foxglove and geraniums and lilies swaying. Presently, I seated myself upon the bench and waited for the armonica to play. I had brought with me several of John's Bradley cigarettes, and removing one from my waistcoat,

I began to smoke while listening for the music. And it was as I stayed there, peering at the hedge, relishing the scents of the garden, which mixed not unfavourably with the tobacco, that a tangible feeling of longing and isolation began to stir within me.

The breeze increased in strength, but only for a moment. The hedge shuddered wildly; the perennials wavered this way and that. The breeze settled, and in the ensuing quiet, I realised that the music would not, while the day dimmed, play for the likes of me. How regrettable that that alluring instrument, whose strains were so possessing, so richly emblematic, would fail to arouse me as before. How could it ever be the same? She had taken her life; she had gone. And what did it matter if, eventually, everything was to be lost, vanquished, or if there existed no ultimate reason, or pattern, or logic to all which was done on the earth? For she was not there, and yet I remained. Never had I felt such incomprehensible emptiness within myself, and just then, as my body moved from the bench, did I begin to understand how utterly alone I was in the world. So with dusk's fast approach, I would take nothing away from the garden, except that impossible vacancy, that absence inside which still had the weight of another person—a gap which formed the contour of a singular, curious woman who never once beheld my true self.

SOURCES OF ILLUSTRATIONS

The three illustrations in *A Slight Trick of the Mind* were originally printed in *New Observations on the Natural History of Bees,* by Francis Huber (London: W. & C. Tait, and Longman, Hurst, Rees, Orme, and Brown, 1821).

CANON▌▌GATE.tV

CHANNELLING GREAT CONTENT

WATCH

INTERVIEWS, TRAILERS, ANIMATIONS, READINGS, GIGS

LISTEN

AUDIO BOOKS, PODCASTS, MUSIC, PLAYLISTS

READ

CHAPTERS, EXCERPTS, SNEAK PEEKS, RECOMMENDATIONS

DISCOVER

BLOGS, EVENTS, NEWS, CREATIVE PARTNERS

SHOP

LIMITED EDITIONS, BUNDLES, SECRET SALES

THE SECOND
OLD HOUSE
CATALOGUE

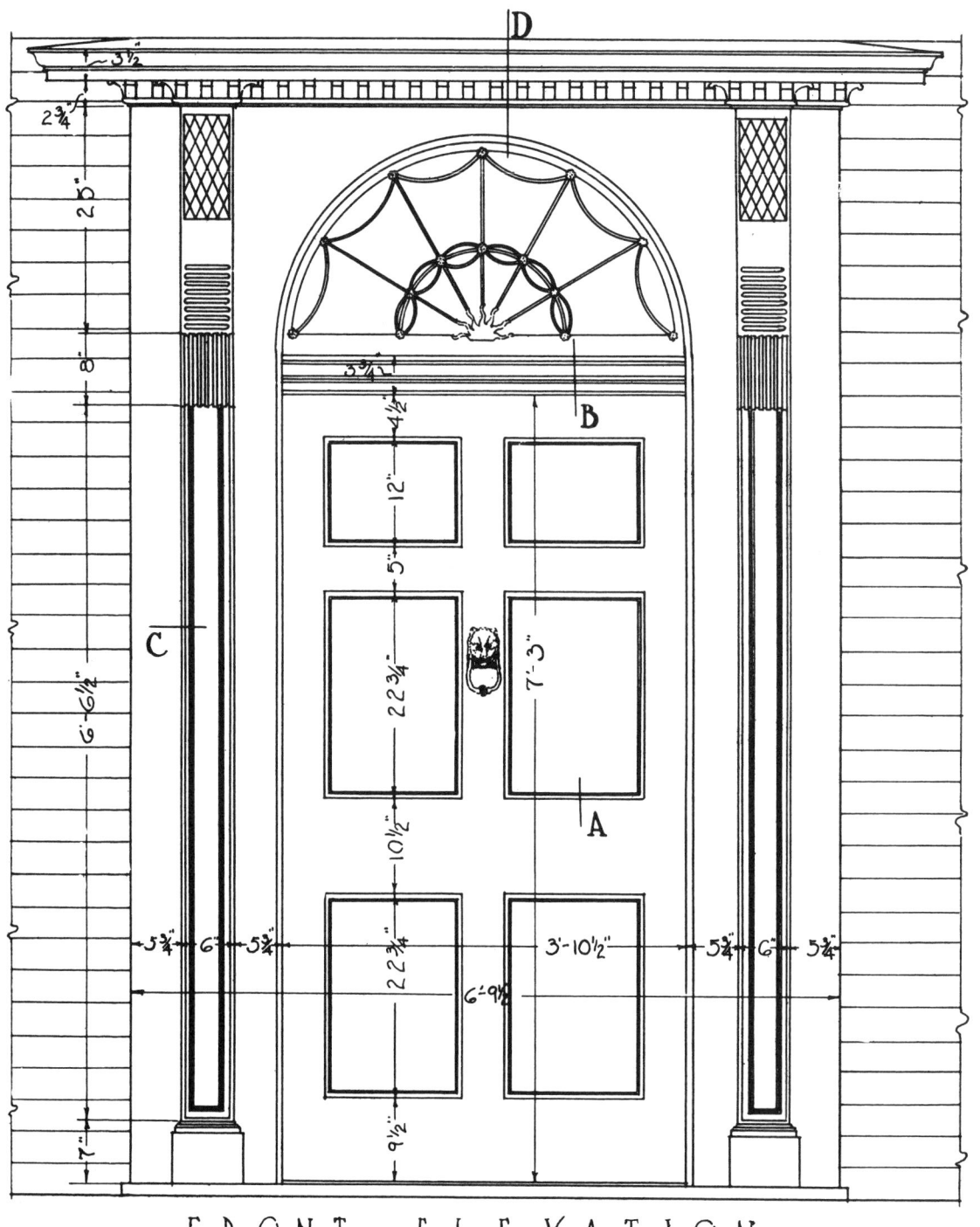

FRONT ELEVATION
SCALE ½" = 1'-0"

THE SECOND
OLD HOUSE
CATALOGUE

2,000 Completely New and Useful Products,
Services, and Suppliers For Restoring,
Decorating, and Furnishing the Period House—
From Early American to 1930s Modern.

Compiled by Lawrence Grow

BONANZA BOOKS
NEW YORK

Library of Congress Cataloging in Publication Data

Grow, Lawrence.
    The second old house catalogue.

    Bibliography: p.
    Includes index.
    1. Historic buildings—United States—
Conservation and restoration—Catalogs.
I. Title.
TH3411.G763   1982   728.3'7'028802947   81-21789
                                      AACR2

ISBN: 0-517-371626

h g f e d c b a

Contents

Foreword

The Second Old House Catalogue is not a replacement for *The Old House Catalogue* but a complete new book in itself. Some of the same suppliers of fine period materials will be found in this volume, but the products featured are different from those listed in *The Old House Catalogue*. Also included are companies and craftsmen that are brand new, many reaching out for the first time to the ever-growing band of old-house enthusiasts. These suppliers are found in all parts of North America and in the British Isles.

The first book is "a modest step toward meeting the real needs of old-house owners and those who would like to take part in the growing movement to retrieve the livable past." This book is no less modest an undertaking. It reflects the increasing diversity and energy present in the preservation/restoration movement of the last few years. Much more space has been devoted to basic structural needs as well as to period lighting fixtures and alternative heating sources.

Once again we have refrained from listing electricians, plumbers, and most building contractors. Experts in these areas are best located on the local level where they are best known by reputation. Few will travel long distances and are therefore limited in their services to specific geographic areas. What has been increased in this volume, however, are the listings for regional restoration specialists who may be able to help with everything from pre-purchase inspection of an old structure to its rebuilding and furnishing. And we have even included some contractors who specialize in building fine period homes according to traditional construction methods.

To further aid the person who wishes to use some of the best in period-style fabrics and papers and finds the wholesale market difficult to enter, two appendices have been added to the book. The first is a list of department stores across the United States that feature materials from Scalamandré and Brunschwig & Fils in their decorating departments. (Fabrics and papers from other manufacturers listed in the book are generally available from the companies themselves or through various retail outlets.) The second appendix provides a listing of regional chapters of the American Society of Interior Designers. To seek such professional advice, contact one of the chapters for assistance in selecting an experienced designer, who may be able to help you in selecting hard-to-get fabrics and papers.

Numerous people have freely contributed their suggestions in the making of *The Second Old House Catalogue*. Chief among them are the hundreds of craftsmen and manufacturers who make the "old-house" market as imaginative and quality conscious as it is. Without this willingness of producers to discuss their products openly, it would be impossible to proffer any objective recommendations or advice on their use. Those to whom we especially owe our thanks are Adriana Scalamandré Bitter and Serena Hortian of Scalamandré, Murray Douglas of Brunschwig

& Fils, Mary Ellen Fuller of Schumacher, Bill Grage of The Decorators Supply Corp., Gary Kray of San Francisco Victoriana, and Kenneth Lynch of Kenneth Lynch & Sons.

Experts in the preservation field are busy every hour of the day engineering the salvation of the past. We are particularly grateful, then, for the advice given us by the following people in our travels across the country: Al Chambers, Historic American Buildings Survey, Washington, D.C.; Dana Crawford, Larimer Square, Denver; William Cross, Cultural Heritage Program, Pasadena, Calif.; John Frisbee, West Coast Office, National Trust for Historic Preservation, San Francisco; Wilbert Hasbrouck, Historic Resources, Inc., Chicago; Cheryl Krieger, Midwest office, National Trust for Historic Preservation, Chicago; Clay Lancaster, architectural historian, Nantucket, Mass.; Barbara Sudler, Historic Denver; Jay Turnbull, The Foundation for San Francisco's Architectural Heritage; and Joseph, Olga, and Annette Valenta, artisans *par excellence*, Chicago.

An undertaking this complex could not have been undertaken without the assistance of members of the Main Street Press staff, in particular Richard Rawson who compiled information for several sections of the book. For special help with English materials, Alexandra Artley of the Architectural Press, Ltd., London, is owed our thanks. These, too, should go to Sally Held of Allanheld, Osmun & Co., for shepherding the manuscript through a complicated and tiring typesetting process.

"They Don't Touch Real Flowers"

In 1978 a resident of Flemington, New Jersey, reported to the local newspaper that artificial flowers left on his wife's grave were continually being stolen. Each day he would bring a new plastic bouquet to the cemetery, and each night it would disappear. Finally, he hit upon a solution to this unhappy dilemma: In place of plastic posies, he decorated the grave with honest-to-goodness growing things from the garden, for, in his own words, "They don't touch real flowers." So it has been with buildings in America for as long as anyone can remember. Most won't "touch real flowers": only the plastic. Old houses are therefore claimed only by Time, by those with taste and love, and—far too frequently—by the wrecker's ball.

All too often the ersatz is preferred to the real. It is the plastic which is still the most popular today. It is "new," easy to keep clean (so they say), and appears everlasting. Why then bother with materials that show age and cannot be considered up-to-date in any sense of the word? Why not just keep replacing the old and perishable with something of seeming permanence? As a Michigan realtor was heard to proclaim to a potential client: "For heaven's sake, you don't want a *used* house, do you?"

Well, maybe they and we and you *do*. Certainly lots of other people feel the same way—increasing numbers of them. The solution of "real flowers" is one that is enormously appealing at a time when new houses cost more than old, and present-day building materials fail to provide necessary protection from noise, heat, and dirt. To no one's surprise, an official of the Cleveland Wrecking Company reported in *The New York Times* that "new buildings are not as solidly constructed as they used to be." (He was rather downcast about this, naturally.) On a number of occasions, in fact, he had witnessed a wrecking ball bounce off a wall without even making a dent.

Unfortunately, many old houses—however well constructed—fall to the ground without a wrecker's help. They are merely left to die on their own without even a decent burial. America's cities and countryside are literally strewn with these gaping hulks. Everyone knows about the South Bronx, but perhaps closer to home are abandoned frame farmhouses or sagging and disfigured row houses. At a time when the average new home costs $50,000 to build, it seems particularly sad that the past should be allowed to decay. Improvement of the old, however, has not been encouraged on either aesthetic or economic grounds. Dependence on the property tax in most parts of the country has meant that fixing-up the old results in a higher assessment. And if a building has any historical value whatsoever, the taxable value will be raised even higher.

A Welsh friend of ours living in West Virginia always reported to the local tax assessor that the fine Italian Renaissance portraits in his home were ancestral paintings since those of "family" were not subject to personal property taxes. Ancestral or not, we need similar protection for legitimate architectural preservation of the past. Such legislative assistance is coming slowly. Hopefully, the property tax will continue to be challenged for its retrogressive and inequitable features. The Tax Reform Act of 1976 provides special relief for those whose properties are listed on the National Register of Historic Places or are located in one of the 150 historic districts throughout the country. Rehabilitation projects undertaken in these areas must be approved by the United States Department of Interior "as being consistent with the historic character of such property," a fair and necessary condition. Such legislation enables both investors in income-producing properties and private home owners to claim an accelerated depreciation deduction in their federal income tax for capital expenses incurred in rehabilitation. The effect is to make building restoration as financially attractive as new construction. In fact, it now can be more economical for an old building to be rebuilt than for it to be torn down.

Economic improvements such as these are the result of dedicated work by volunteers and professionals in the preservation field. Some are among the over 125,000 members of the National Trust for Historic Preservation; others are involved with the work of the Victorian Society, the Back-to-the-City Movement, and several thousand preservation and historical societies at the regional and local level. Increasingly the concern is with the general architectural environment in which we live and not with just *the* historic house or office building. *Recycling* is the key word these days: Waste not and want not in a time of dwindling resources, including money. This is all to the good. Preservation has for too long stood aloof from the movement to save the natural environment.

No one believes that everything can or should be saved. Not only are most buildings put up before World War II without architectural merit, but many are not even salvageable. And we cannot become so blinded by the old that we are insensitive to the new and adventuresome. Rather, what needs to be retained and reused are those buildings—homes, offices, stores, churches, schools—which are structurally sound and reflect something of the style and texture of our past, whether they be showplaces or not. Shopping malls on superhighways do not take the place of downtowns made up of unique but complementary shops and offices of different styles and sizes. It is perhaps the diversity and the personal scale that we miss most, whether consciously or not. A contributor to *The New York Times* wrote recently about the sad changes to his home town, Lyndhurst, New Jersey. "This may be the most significant type of change in all small communities: The destruction of elegant, beautiful and friendly—but economically outdated—old homes and their replacement with unesthetic but more functional buildings."

One can only hope that the future will not be as bleak as this writer suggests. The sanctity of landmark zoning has just been upheld by the United States Supreme Court in the Grand Central Terminal case. Aesthetic considerations have thus been given standing with those of health and safety. If we can begin to untangle some of the socio-economic restraints inherent in our system of taxation which so hinder the preservation of some fabric of the real past, then a start can also be made on winning the battle against the fast-food mentality in architectural design. This is a matter of public education, and it will be a Sisyphean task. The desire to destroy and begin anew runs deep in the American grain. As our friend, the professional wrecker, put it (this time with glee): "I've torn down every structure known to man—high rises, tenements, churches, banks. Every building is fun."

Understanding the heritage of the past is the only way to gain appreciation of it. The effects of the Victorian period are enormously popular these days—stained-glass windows, Tiffany-style lamps, exuberant paisley and Morris prints, sturdy pieces of turned oak. In fact, a reading of current home-fashion magazines indicates that the traditional passion for all things "Colonial" is being challenged at last. Is there some way to channel this love for century-old styles into tangible action? Or is this revival to be only a cosmetic one of the sort played out in the latest boutique or café-restaurant?

The matter of knowledge of architectural styles is so basic that we begin *The Second Old House Catalogue* with it once again. The following illustrated survey of American architecture is simplified, but suggestive. It is conveniently divided into Colonial, early nineteenth-century, mid-Victorian, and late-Victorian categories. The examples shown are representative in enough ways to suggest the general outline of exterior and interior architectural treatment. In no way, however, should they be taken as the final word on any particular period. They are meant to lead one into a much deeper consideration of the special character and feeling which define a true period style and which make it something of real value.

All the illustrations are from the archives of the Historic American Buildings Survey, a National Park Service unit which has diligently and imaginatively documented our architectural past since 1933.

Colonial

Nathaniel Macy House
Nantucket, Massachusetts

built prior to 1745

Simplicity itself is personified in the Nathaniel Macy House. A braced-frame structure with a central chimney, it was moved to its present location in 1745 from another site. Perhaps this is when a lean-to kitchen was added to the original structure which had a kitchen and parlor on the first floor and two chambers above. A third and later addition, a modern kitchen, can be seen at the far left. It is with additions of this sort that rectangular Colonial houses assumed a saltbox profile. Clapboard and shingles form a solid sheathing for the frame, and standing out from the wall are neatly framed 9-on-9 sash windows. The classical entrance is the only bow to high-style elegance.

Many of the first New England homes were built of only two rooms, and most have a massive central chimney rather than chimneys at the gable ends. Little or no ornamentation was applied in the cornice or on other structural elements. The vast majority of buildings throughout the Colonies were built of wood, the most available and inexpensive of materials. There are, however, vast regional differences in the use of various kinds of lumber. Oak in New England was soon replaced by pine for both exterior and interior use, as it was in Nantucket.

Both the first and second floors of the Macy house are clearly outlined in these plans drawn in 1969. The original core of the building is seen at the left. Each principal first-floor room measures 14′ 6¾″ by approximately 17′. There is, of course, a large fireplace in each. The second story was originally reached by a narrow staircase to the left of the front door. With the addition of the lean-to, interior space was almost doubled. A third fireplace and a new oven were integrated into the center chimney, and a second set of stairs—these of the closet variety—lead to a basement and up to the second floor. The third (attic) floor is still only reached through the original section. The house was restored after 1934, but modernization has occurred primarily at the back of the building and includes new dormer windows to make the rear portion of the second floor more liveable.

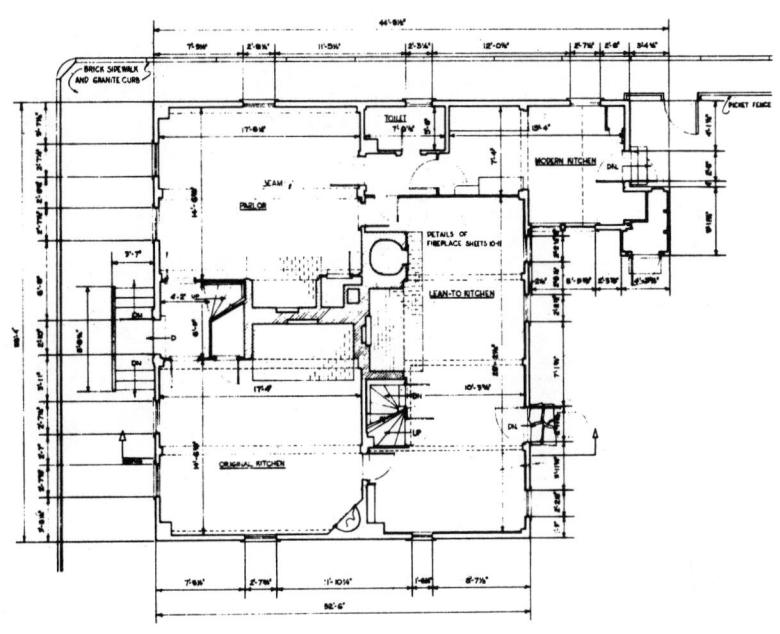

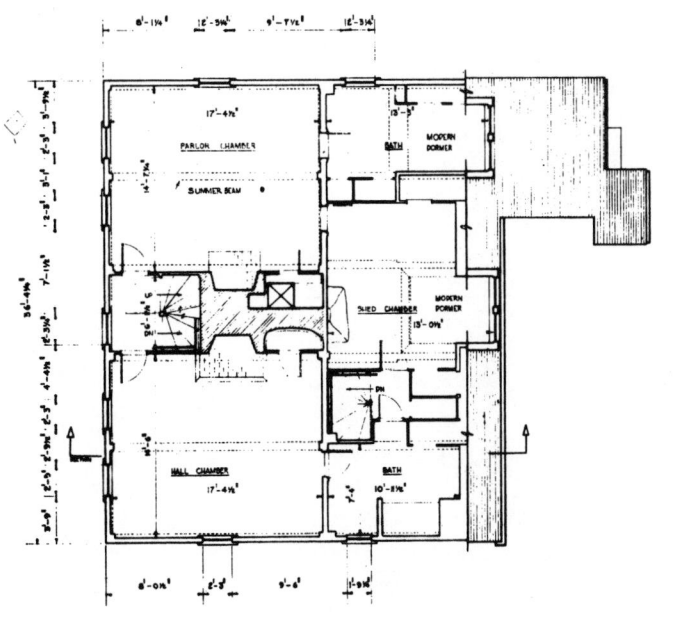

The front hall stairway is but a simple step and riser affair, a "tightwinder" in architectural parlance. The paneling is seen to be nothing more than stained pine boards with strips of lath covering the joints. The two-paneled door is to be found in other rooms in this section.

This is the original kitchen fireplace and is set in a paneled room end of a sort commonly found in many Colonial homes. The mantel is merely a carved series of mouldings. The hearth is very deep and extends into the room which is floored in pine. As can be noted, the floor has been covered with hooked and Oriental area rugs. The ceiling is low and the beams have been left exposed. The door to the left appears to lead to a storage area underneath the front stairs.

Early 19th Century/Federal

Robinson-Schofield House
Madison, Indiana

built c. 1820-21

The Federal style in America was introduced in the late 1700s. It derives in large part from the work of Robert Adam, an English architect and designer who influenced such American architects as Charles Bulfinch and Asher Benjamin. By the time of the settlement of Indiana, buildings in this style were to be found in all East Coast towns and cities of consequence. It is a much more restrained and dignified building form than that of the late Colonial or Georgian and perhaps more suitable to the new republic which was taking shape on the frontier of the Old Northwest Territory.

A chimney is situated at each end of the two-story building. The roof is typically low-pitched and ends in a simple cornice of brick. The windows and front entrance are slightly recessed below semicircular arches. Local legend has it that the home was the site of the founding of the Grand Lodge Free and Accepted Masons of Indiana in 1818. If so, the building, or some portion of it, must be somewhat older than can be documented.

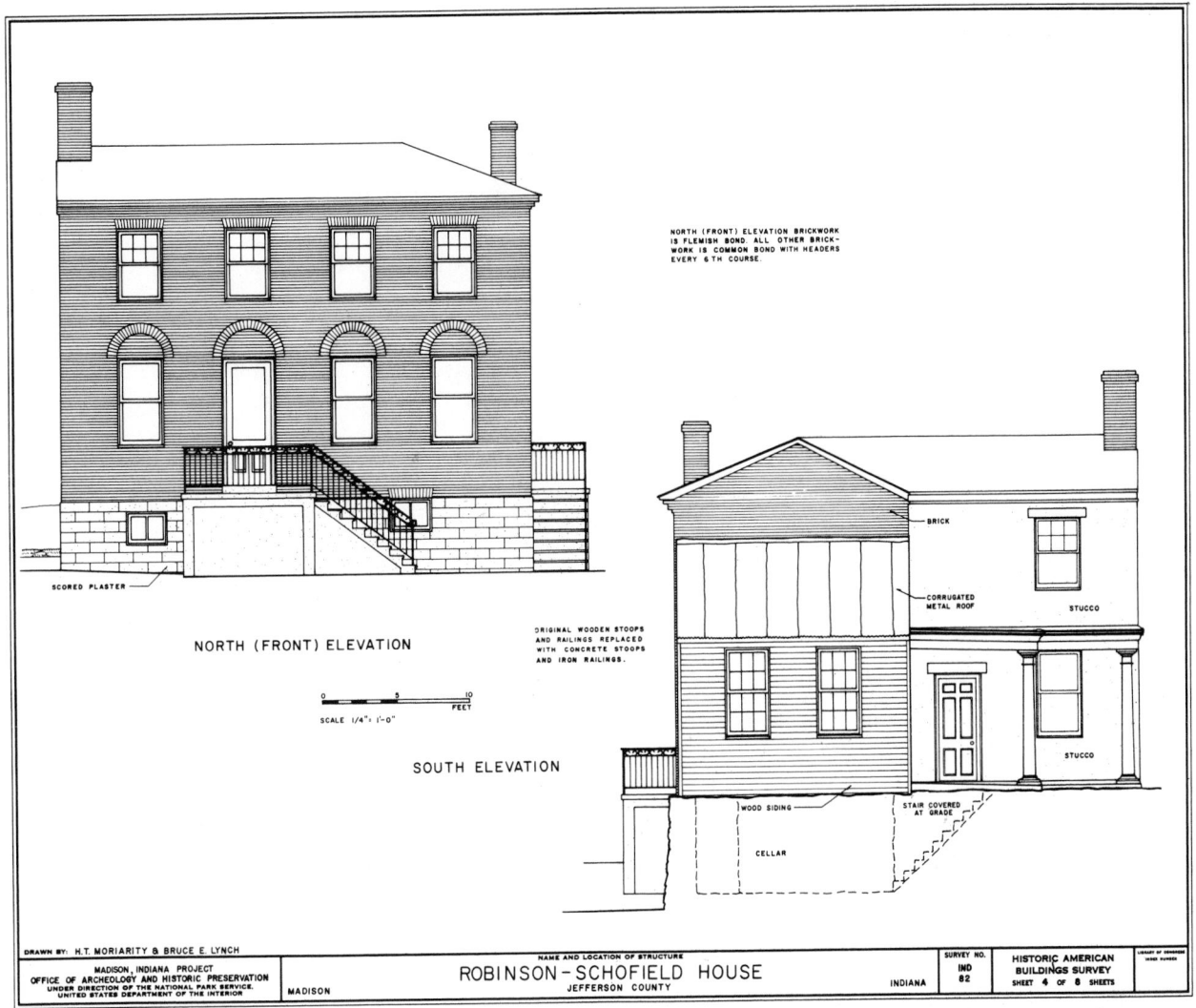

NORTH (FRONT) ELEVATION BRICKWORK IS FLEMISH BOND. ALL OTHER BRICK-WORK IS COMMON BOND WITH HEADERS EVERY 6TH COURSE.

BRICK

CORRUGATED METAL ROOF

STUCCO

SCORED PLASTER

NORTH (FRONT) ELEVATION

ORIGINAL WOODEN STOOPS AND RAILINGS REPLACED WITH CONCRETE STOOPS AND IRON RAILINGS.

SCALE 1/4"=1'-0"
0 5 10 FEET

SOUTH ELEVATION

WOOD SIDING

STAIR COVERED AT GRADE

CELLAR

STUCCO

DRAWN BY: H.T. MORIARITY & BRUCE E. LYNCH

MADISON, INDIANA PROJECT
OFFICE OF ARCHEOLOGY AND HISTORIC PRESERVATION
UNDER DIRECTION OF THE NATIONAL PARK SERVICE.
UNITED STATES DEPARTMENT OF THE INTERIOR

MADISON

NAME AND LOCATION OF STRUCTURE

ROBINSON-SCHOFIELD HOUSE
JEFFERSON COUNTY

INDIANA

SURVEY NO.
IND
82

HISTORIC AMERICAN
BUILDINGS SURVEY
SHEET 4 OF 8 SHEETS

The measured drawing shows the front (north) and rear (south) elevations of the Robinson-Schofield House. The front brickwork is of Flemish bond, and all brickwork elsewhere is of common bond with headers occurring every sixth course. Both the front and side cement stoops with iron railings are replacements for wooden stoops and wooden railings. The odd shape of the front roof line can be explained by studying the rear elevation. The house is L-shaped. The original el probably consisted of only one room, and that now designated as the dining room may have been the kitchen. A study of the first-floor plan makes this even more clear. An L-shaped porch fills the rear right side of the building.

Although many Federal style buildings were built of wood, especially in New England, brick was the medium which was increasingly used. This is as true of homes and public buildings in Kentucky, Indiana, and Ohio as it was of such Eastern cities as Charleston, Baltimore, Philadelphia, and New York. These buildings were considered fireproof, at least in relation to wooden structures, and were required by statute in some cities which had suffered great property losses in devastating fires. A brick building was also considered a more substantial one for a citizen of some standing in the community.

The first-floor plan gives some idea of the interior make-up of the Robinson-Schofield House. Unfortunately, interior photos do not exist. The formal entrance to the house is found on the side rather than at the front. The stairway to the basement and the second floor is slightly more than a tightwinder. The rooms are generously spaced, and most certainly ceilings were lowered to cover structural beams. The placement of windows, doors, and fireplaces in the rooms now designated parlor, living room, and dining room is much more formal and regular than that found in the majority of Colonial houses. This structural regularity is quite typical of Federal-style buildings. The succeeding popular architectural style, the Greek Revival, was to stress this even more emphatically. Not until the mid-nineteenth century would there be a widespread popular retreat into the more eccentric and irregular forms of Gothic and Victorian.

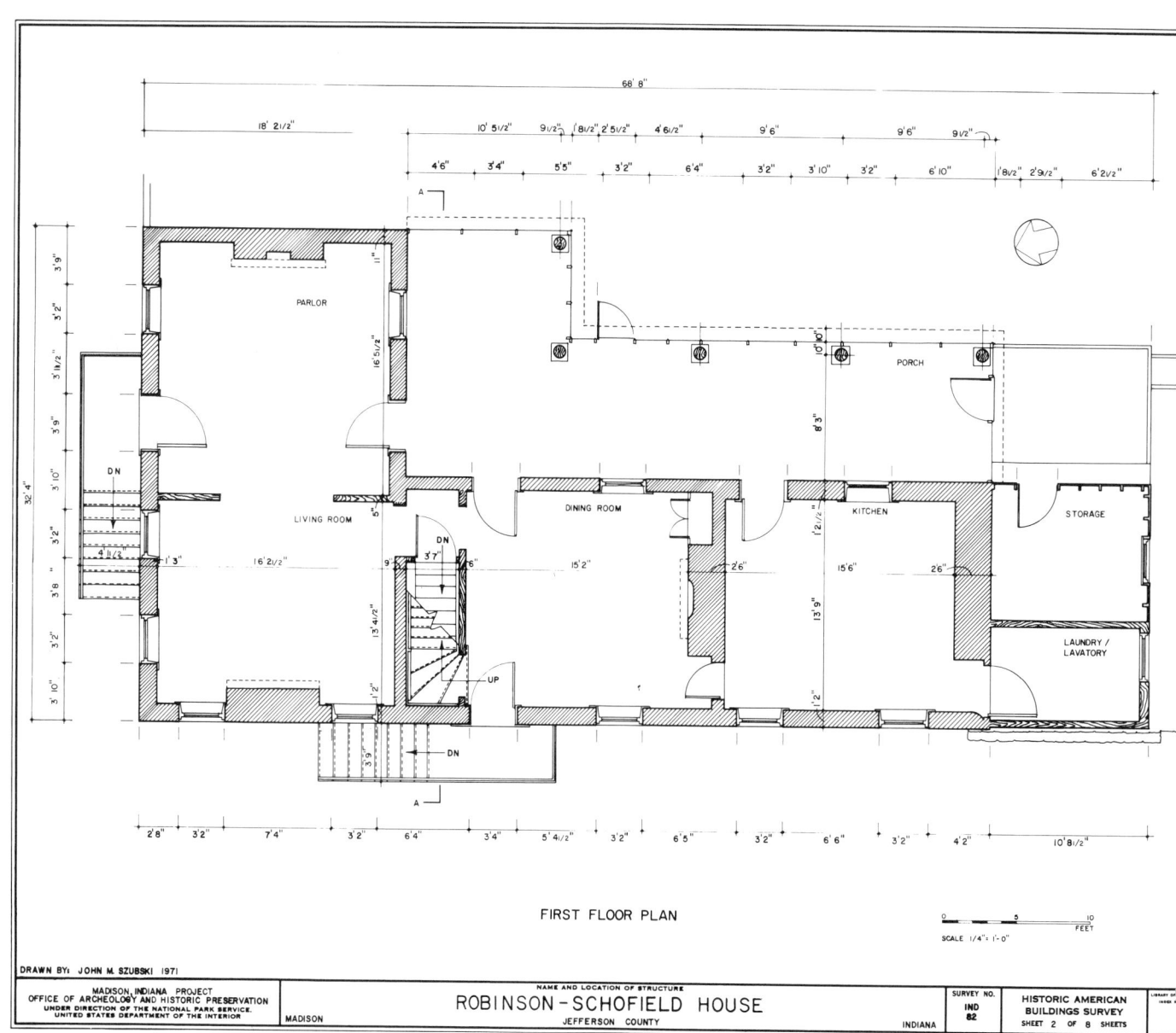

FIRST FLOOR PLAN

SCALE 1/4": 1'-0"

DRAWN BY: JOHN M. SZUBSKI 1971

MADISON, INDIANA PROJECT
OFFICE OF ARCHEOLOGY AND HISTORIC PRESERVATION
UNDER DIRECTION OF THE NATIONAL PARK SERVICE.
UNITED STATES DEPARTMENT OF THE INTERIOR

MADISON

NAME AND LOCATION OF STRUCTURE
ROBINSON – SCHOFIELD HOUSE
JEFFERSON COUNTY
INDIANA

SURVEY NO.
IND
82

HISTORIC AMERICAN
BUILDINGS SURVEY
SHEET 2 OF 8 SHEETS

Mid-Victorian

Morris-Butler House
Indianapolis, Indiana

built in 1864

John D. Morris's fine Victorian manse is attributed to architect Dietrich Bohlen of Indianapolis. In 1881 it was sold to Noble C. Butler and remained in his family's possession until 1964 when the Historic Landmarks Foundation of Indiana acquired it for use as a house museum. The building combines many of the popular architectural forms of the mid-nineteenth century—an Italianate tower, Second Empire mansard roof, arched window heads and entryways of Romanesque Revival inspiration. It is a massive building of brick and stone of rich textures and fine proportions.

The main entrance to the house is through the towering center pavillion. Here there is nothing fussy or gloomy to depress those with a distaste for the Victorian. The arched entryway is gracefully shaped and appropriately decorated with a sculpted keystone. The recessed double entrance doors have etched glass decoration and in style repeat the rhythmic arch of the exterior.

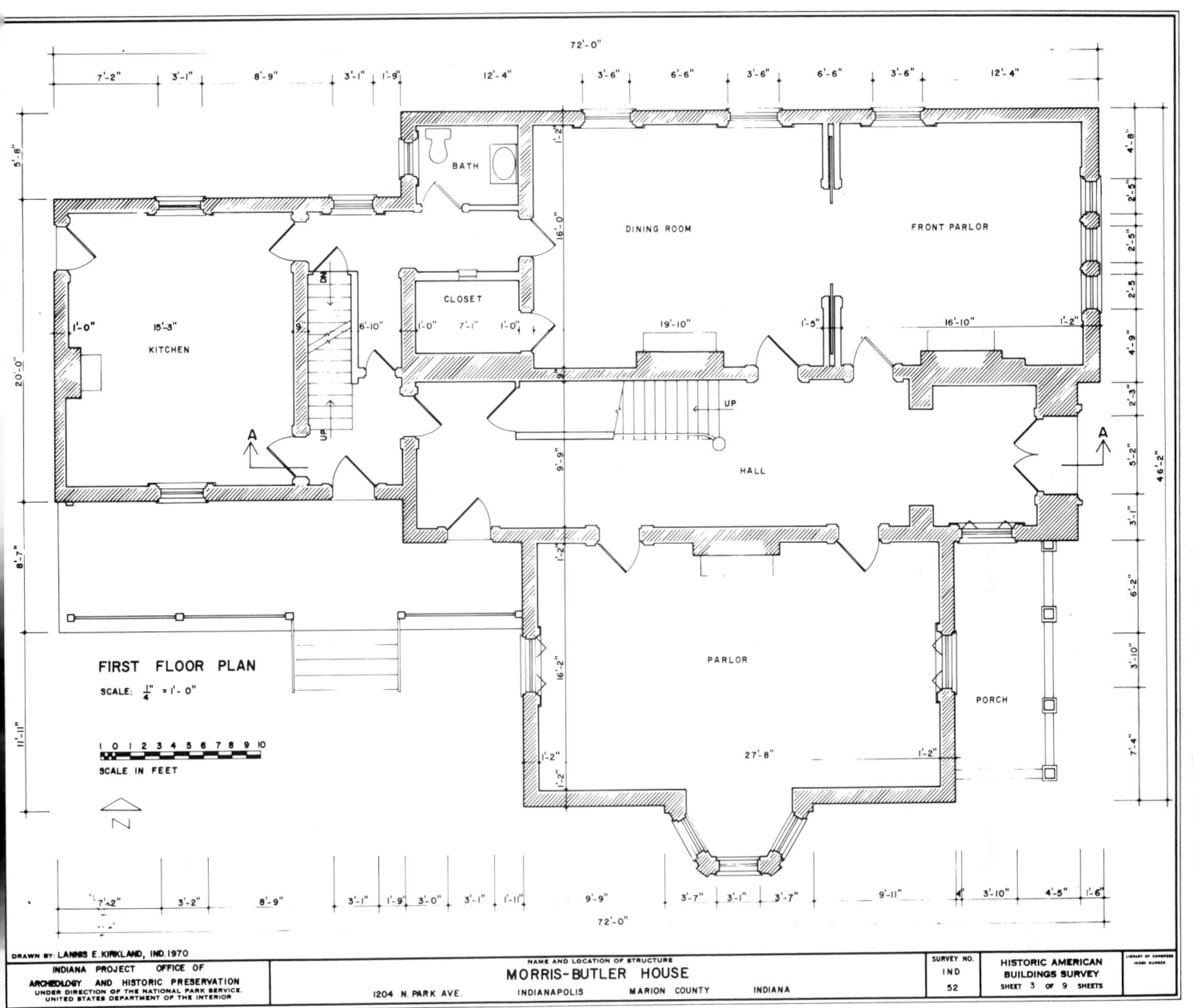

FIRST FLOOR PLAN

SCALE: $\frac{1}{4}"$ = 1'- 0"

SCALE IN FEET

DINING ROOM

FRONT PARLOR

BATH

CLOSET

KITCHEN

HALL

UP

PARLOR

PORCH

DRAWN BY: LANNIS E. KIRKLAND, IND. 1970

INDIANA PROJECT OFFICE OF ARCHEOLOGY AND HISTORIC PRESERVATION
UNDER DIRECTION OF THE NATIONAL PARK SERVICE.
UNITED STATES DEPARTMENT OF THE INTERIOR

NAME AND LOCATION OF STRUCTURE
MORRIS-BUTLER HOUSE
1204 N. PARK AVE. INDIANAPOLIS MARION COUNTY INDIANA

SURVEY NO. IND 52

HISTORIC AMERICAN BUILDINGS SURVEY
SHEET 3 OF 9 SHEETS

LIBRARY OF CONGRESS HABS NUMBER

The first floor plan says a great deal about the leisurely pace of life of the wealthy Victorian. The principal rooms are appropriate for entertainment; the main hall and vestibule stretch over 35 feet. Dining room and front parlor may be opened up to each other by means of sliding doors. The large main parlor is pleasantly fitted with a bay window, a feature popular in homes since the 1840s. The staircase, of course, is suitably grand for such a fine town mansion. Some sense of the height of the rooms can be gained from the two photos on the following two pages. Note that the fireplace provides the focal point of interest in each of the three principal rooms. Even though it was no longer used for burning wood, it remained an organizing design principle.

The view from the foyer is splendid in the extreme. Ornate chandeliers hung from ornamental plaster rosettes; a heavy marble-topped pier table, a writing table, and upholstered chairs and settee appear right in place. Note also the painted motifs on the inside of the archway between foyer and hall and in the far corners of the hall ceiling.

The main parlor is the most extensively appointed room in the house, yet the effect is not one of clutter or vulgarity. The gilded mirror is hardly an exercise in restraint, but neither this object nor the marble mantel seem out of keeping in a room of this style and size. Only the crystal chandelier can rival these elements in elegant beauty. The furniture is typical of the second half of the nineteenth century—highly carved and liberally upholstered. The richly ornamented ceiling and cornice in white, as well as the subdued carpeting, serve to soften what could be a stiff atmosphere. Brocade has been lavished at the window, which is topped with a tasseled lambrequin. A fine lace liner serves as a permanent filter of light. Note that this room was also used for musical entertainment.

Late Victorian

John H. Houghton House
Austin, Texas

built in 1886–87

One of the great glories of old Austin *was* this towering Queen Anne/Victorian Romanesque mansion; it was demolished in 1973. Mr. Houghton was a very prominent man, and the architect he chose, James Wahrenberger, was similarly well-known in central Texas. The roof line is the most interesting feature of the house with its numerous projections and imaginatively placed windows. In a state of disrepair when this photograph was taken, the building had obviously lost some of its details, particularly those of the conical and pyramidal-roofed towers. The hideous shapeless pile behind the Houghton mansion is typical of the "progress" that overtook it.

The detail of the center tower roof perfectly illustrates the lavish and eclectic
use of building materials.

The floor plan shows how extremely complex the form of the Victorian structure had become by the late nineteenth century. The dining room has an octagonal shape; the music room makes use of the circular space of the corner tower, perhaps providing a stage for performers; the hallway not only reaches straight back from the vestibule but also turns to form a grand stair hall. The parlor and ballroom are more regular spaces, but both these rooms extend into an enclosed porch. Only the service areas, neatly separated from the rest of the house, appear to be at all conventional.

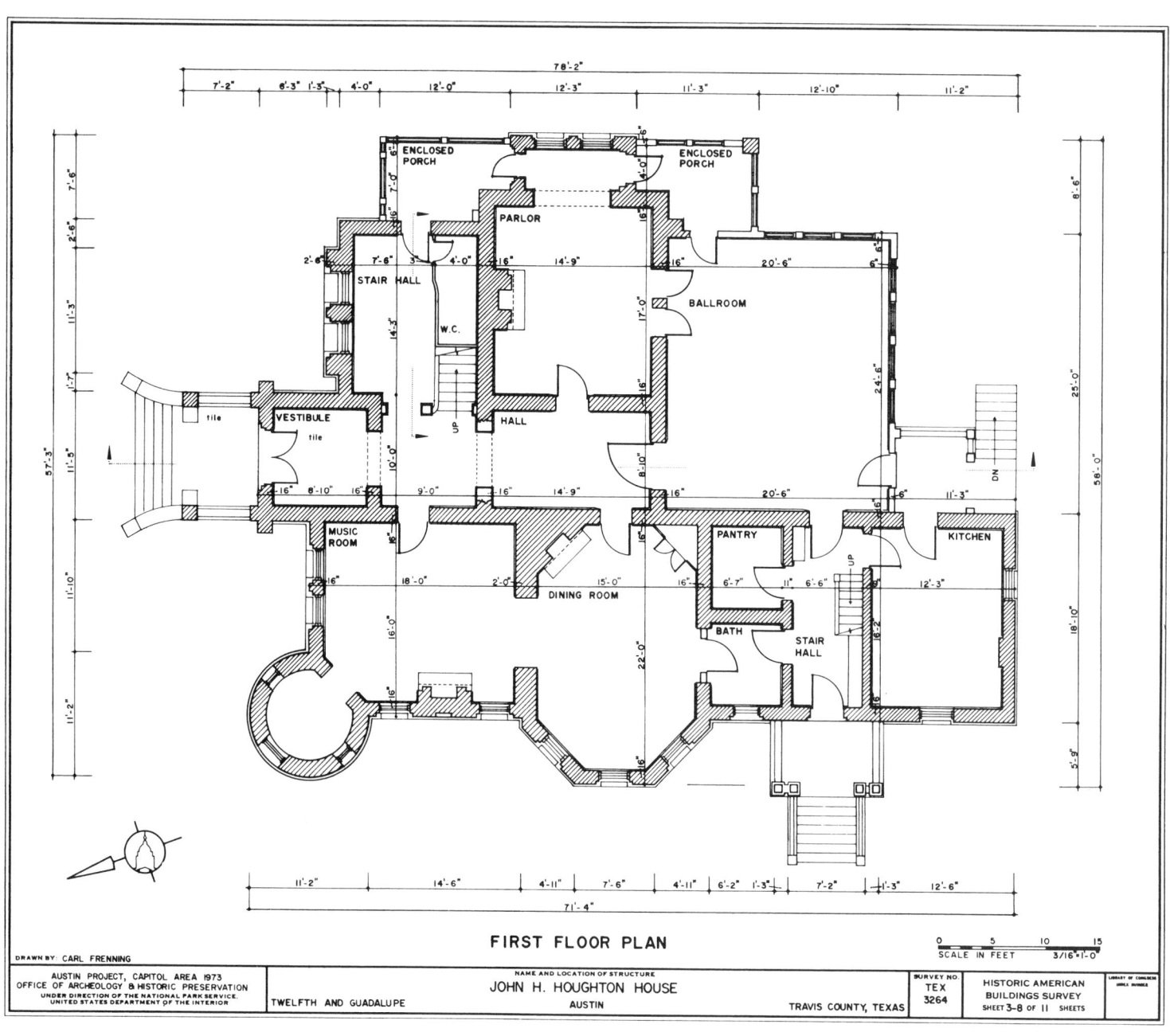

FIRST FLOOR PLAN

SCALE IN FEET   3/16"=1'-0"

DRAWN BY: CARL FRENNING

AUSTIN PROJECT, CAPITOL AREA 1973
OFFICE OF ARCHEOLOGY & HISTORIC PRESERVATION
UNDER DIRECTION OF THE NATIONAL PARK SERVICE.
UNITED STATES DEPARTMENT OF THE INTERIOR

TWELFTH AND GUADALUPE

NAME AND LOCATION OF STRUCTURE
JOHN H. HOUGHTON HOUSE
AUSTIN

TRAVIS COUNTY, TEXAS

SURVEY NO.
TEX
3264

HISTORIC AMERICAN
BUILDINGS SURVEY
SHEET 3-8 OF 11 SHEETS

Only this one built-in cupboard in the dining room remained to be photographed before the building was torn down. Particularly interesting is the combination of classical and Gothic motifs. Presumably the original furnishings would have been similarly eclectic.

Raised-panel front entrance door by Townsend H. Anderson;
hand-forged thumb latch by Robert Bordon. *See* page 41.

I Structural Products & Services

Structural materials are by definition the most important components in any house—new or old. In substance, they provide a structure's form; in design, they define its style. First and foremost, a building must be structurally sound. Load-bearing walls will settle with age, and joists and rafters may show some stress, but as long as these elements are not badly out of line, rotted, or diseased, problems of a structural sort can be kept to a minimum. Future deterioration may be prevented by the use of collar beams, extra supports, and careful attention to any moisture problems in the foundation or roof. The secondary structural elements—windows, doors, siding, paneling, decorative columns, steps, chimneys and fireplaces, railings and balusters—are more likely to require frequent attention. And these are also the elements which may have changed the most with age. It is somewhat difficult to change the basic structural framework of a house, but stylistic modifications were easier and less expensive to make. It is with these secondary structural appurtenances that most restoration work is concerned.

This first and most important section of *The Second Old House Catalogue* covers a great deal of the structural territory. It is primarily concerned with those elements which define a house style. Such items as structural beams are not ignored, but the basic work of re-building a house or restoring it to its original form is the business of a skilled contractor with knowledge of building technology past and present. There are few home owners who will attempt such work. Catalogued in this chapter are some of the best professionals to consult.

Supplies of antique building materials are becoming somewhat more difficult to obtain. Since old-house living has become a popular option, there has been a natural tendency for prices to rise with the decrease in available resources. It was once a relatively easy matter to find what you needed—shutters, doors, complete stairways—in junk or salvage yards. Anyone who became active in preservation work in the 1950s knows that there was a surfeit of old materials on hand thanks to the misguided efforts of so-called "planners" to renew our cities and towns and to transform the countryside with interstate expressways. Progress of this sort has slowed down to a rush hour crawl. Even the new highways are now becoming antique, and, if taxpayers continue to revolt, they may just stay that way.

What has been "lost" in antique materials in the 1970s has been gained in quality reproduction work. Educational and cultural institutions have assisted in the revival of traditional craft skills among the young and their preservation among the elderly. The restoration craftsmen of the first half of the twentieth century were a hardy but small band, and we all owe them a great debt of gratitude for keeping alive a small fire of practical antiquarianism. It is easy to laugh at the pretension of so much early restoration work of an upper-class sort, but without it we would be lost today. The new housewrights, blacksmiths, woodworkers, and masons have learned from their courtly peers the value of graceful old age.

Now that the preservation cause has swelled to movement importance, however, one must be on guard. Beware the prophet bearing false witness, or, in this case, the supplier pushing bogus goods. The "old" look is "in"—from early Colonial to late Victorian. There is no local, state, or national consumer protection agency to blow the whistle on "authentic" reproductions. And more and more people are choosing to visit a large-scale plastic recreation park than such a careful recreation of the past as Colonial Williamsburg or the period rooms of Winterthur. The temptation grows greater to substitute surface appearances for goods of long-lasting quality. Read on and you will discover that no one needs to accept the second-rate in houses any more than they do today in automobiles or clothing, and especially not when it comes to something as important as the very fabric of an old house.

Primary Materials

Good basic structural materials can be as hard to come by as well-made doors and windows. Real wood—as opposed to laminated composition—has escalated some 20% in price within the past year alone. Hopefully, the home restorer will not need vast quantities of lumber and will be able to make do with supplies readily available in his area—whether antique or newly sawed. Quality stone is just as "pricey." And there are bogus varieties which just won't pass muster. Stone-like blobs of some polymer are sold across the country under several different commerical names. They are called, of course, "authentic" and "faithful reproductions." It would be better to gather your own fieldstones one-by-one in the country on weekends than to create such an instant horror.

We can offer several sources for new and old wood in case you cannot locate supplies nearby. Structural stone is more regional in distribution and variety, and, of course, extremely expensive to ship any long distance. Whether it be for Colorado sandstone, Illinois limestone, Connecticut brownstone, Pennsylvania fieldstone, or any other regional variant, visit your nearest quarry or stone supplier. Masons can also help you to locate sources or supply.

Paneling

Both Simpson and Potlatch offer new solid-wood planks. Simpson features redwood paneling as well as pine, alder, Douglas fir, cedar, and juniper. Most of these are available in tongue and groove patterns which vary from 4″ to 10″ in width and do not appear to have been smeared with a laminate. The Townsend wall planks from Potlatch are less natural in appearance than those of Simpson because of treatment with a alkyd-urea finish which is baked on. But there is much greater variety in hardwoods—walnut, various oaks, ash, cypress, cottonwood, pecan, and cherry. Most of the woods are ½″ thick and measure from 4″ to 8″ in width.

You may wish to send for Potlatch's "Designer's Kit" of 14 samples, $5. Both Simpson and Potlatch products are distributed throughout North America.

Simpson Timber Co.
900 Fourth Ave.
Seattle, Wash. 98164
(206) 292-5000

Potlatch Corporation
Wood Products, Southern Division
P.O. Box 916
Stuttgart, Ark. 72160
(501) 673-1606

Those fortunate enough to live in old homes built of California redwood—an extremely durable material—and who are thinking of restoring or just preserving a building of such timber will find the literature offered by the California Redwood Association especially helpful. There are over 100 "idea booklets," technical data sheets, and bulletins distributed through architects, builders, and dealers. Ask one of them to show you what they have, or write:

California Redwood Association
617 Montgomery St.
San Francisco, Calif. 94111

If you can't abide the commercially-available lumbers, then there are specialists you can turn to for help. Wagon House Cabinetmaking is one of these and will make up walnut, cherry, oak, or ash paneling to order. This firm is also a specialist in random-width oak flooring.

The Wagon House Cabinetmaking, Inc.
Box 149
Mendenhall, Penn. 19357
(215) 388-6352

Diamond K. supplies old clapboards of 5″ widths. These are gray-brown, naturally-weathered boards which do not require stain or a sealer. Barnwood of weathered Eastern pine is also available and comes in golden brown, silver gray, or weathered red shades. Both clapboards and barnwood are priced at $1.50 a square foot.

Literature available.

Diamond K. Co., Inc.
130 Buckland Rd.
South Windsor, Conn. 06074
(203) 644-8486

Period Pine of Georgia was featured in the first *Old House Catalogue,* and so many readers responded favorably that we must report more good news. The pine—Virgin Longleaf Yellow Heart of Pine—which the company salvages and resaws, is now available not only for flooring and paneling, but can be made into wainscoting, chair rails, doors, mantels, mouldings, or can be supplied as beams. This is an extremely hard, clear antique wood that was largely timbered off by 1900. That which has replaced it, however, does not have exactly the same quality. The original trees were between 150-500 years old at the time they were cut.

Literature available.

Period Pine
P.O. Box 77052
Atlanta, Ga. 30309
(404) 876-4740

Don't be frightened off by the Weird Wood label. This is a product line begun by Green Mountain Cabins, and they may have what you need for replacing or patching small sections of paneling. You will want square edge stock, round edge, or a combination thereof. These shapes are available in white pine, butternut, cherry, sugar or rock maple, and yellow birch in various widths and grades. Everything will be done to see that you get as close a match to your old wood as is humanly possible.

Brochure available.

Weird Wood
Green Mountain Cabins, Inc.
Box 190
Chester, Vt. 05143
(802) 875-3535

Custom paneling will be executed by Accent Walls in whatever wood a customer specifies. This California firm will also provide custom-order wainscoting of the old-fashioned grooved variety and has some recycled lumber available as well.

Flyer available with stamped, self-addressed envelope.

Accent Walls
1565 The Alameda
San Jose, Calif. 95126
(408) 293-3082

For those seeking custom-order paneling of the most elegant sort, Architectural Paneling is the right answer. This firm is noted for its finely-executed wood interiors in the best of materials and traditional English and French styles. The contract division handles much more than panels; wainscoting, bookcases, mouldings,

doors, and mantels are designed and executed—if so desired—in their entirety.

Brochure and color slides available, $3.50.

Architectural Paneling, Inc.
979 Third Ave.
New York, N.Y. 10022
(212) 371-9632

Beams

Such structural members connote rusticity. For many people, they practically define an "old house" style. Unfortunately, a goodly number of such wooden supports should never be exposed; the original builders knew this and provided a plaster ceiling. If most of the beams are indeed worthy of display, however, you may want to make them visible. By doing so you will at least automatically raise the height of the room, a not inconsequential achievement in a low-ceilinged Colonial interior that has to be lived in by today's considerably taller folk. And if you need to replace a few beams or are completely restoring a primitive country interior, there are sources of supply available. There is no need to depend on the fake, "wood-like" timbers of styrofoam teture which are purveyed in too many lumber yards.

The Broad-Axe Beam Co. derives its name from the chisel-bladed instrument seen being used in the picture above. This method of hewing timber is one of several traditional steps taken by the firm to insure that its products are correctly produced. Two types of beams —structural and decorative—are available in white pine. Structural beams are available sawed one side or hewed four sides, and are approximately 7½″ x 7½″ in lengths of 8′, 12′, 14′, and 16′. These are available at $3.75 a linear foot. The decorative beam is a structural beam sawed in half lengthwise and measures approximately 3½″ x 7½″. The same lengths as for the structural are available at $2.75 a linear foot.

All the beams are air-dried for a period of at least six months, a process which assures that the lumber will gain in strength and properly shrink on the squared dimension. Broad-Axe will also undertake custom hewing jobs, including hardwood timbers, but they remind the customer that quality lengths greater than 24′ are difficult to find and are expensive. In addition, they require much more drying time.

Illustrated literature available, $1.

Broad-Axe Beam Co.
R. D. 2, Box 181-E
Brattleboro, Vt. 05301
(802) 257-0064

Most of Diamond K.'s beams are of the decorative sort. These are made from pine or spruce and are available in two grades: A at $2 a linear foot, 6″ x 6″ or 4″ x 6″ up to 30′ in length; and B, $1 a linear foot, 4″ x 4″ or 3″ x 5″ up to 15′ in length.

Hand-hewn structural beams of chestnut and pine can be ordered, and roughly 50% of these antique timbers will show peg and notch marks. The price of $5 a linear foot covers an 8″ x 8″ timber of up to 30′ in length.

Literature available.

Diamond K. Co., Inc.
130 Buckland Rd.
South Windsor, Conn. 06074
(203) 644-8486

A wide variety of decorative ceiling beams are available from Guyon, Inc. They do not stipulate exactly what type of timber is used, but it is cut and sawed in Lancaster County, Pennsylvania. Sizes range from 4″ x 6″ to 8″ x 10″, and prices vary from $1.70 a linear foot to $9.35. Beams can be rough sawn or hewn on one side or three sides. All are given a linseed oil stain in one of 66 colors that you choose unless you request that the beams be left natural. The price is reduced 5% for no stain.

Literature available, $1.

Guyon, Inc.
65 Oak St.
Lititz, Penn. 17543
(717) 626-0225

Doors

Perhaps no feature in an old house attracts more attention than a well-crafted front door. Considerably more care has been traditionally lavished on these openings than on any other, and their very style and execution can determine the ultimate success of a restoration project. Fortunately, most old doors—if removed at one time—were saved. Nearly every supplier of antique house parts has a supply of different sizes and models available. These suppliers are listed later in this chapter. If, however, you must start anew, here are some leads to follow.

Walter E. Phelps is an individual craftsman who undertakes various types of architectural reproduction woodwork, including doors. He uses traditional methods of joinery and construction and works only from precise measured drawings or an exact sample.

Walter E. Phelps
Box 76
Williamsville, Vt. 05362
(802) 348-6347

Alan Amerian is an expert maker of custom raised panel and carved doors. His four-man shop makes use of select woods.

Literature available.

Amerian Woodcarving
282 San Jose Ave.
San Jose, Calif. 95125
(408) 294-2968

Bel-Air is a producer of commerical carved doors for entryways. Few of their models in solid mahogany or fir are appropriate for pre-Victorian houses, but they are certainly suitable for some later period homes. Illustrated is the "Heritage" model with a leaded glass design of tulips.

Literature available.

Window Frames and Sashes

Windows are often a problem in an old house. Frames and sashes may have severely deteriorated over the years. If they cannot be adequately reconditioned, you have no alternative but to replace them. And it is quite unlikely that you will be able to use any sort of standard window that is commercially available. If you do not have a carpenter/woodworker in the area who can custom make what you need, all is not lost. There are competent firms that specialize in producing period window materials.

Maurer and Shepherd is one of the experts to consult. The firm makes Colonial-style small-pane windows, sashes, and frames. Mortise and tenon joinery is the method they follow in this carpentry work. Illustrated is a window that has been framed in this manner with 12 on 12 lights. Maurer and Shepherd will also undertake custom reproduction work in any other style you can name.

Bel-Air Door Co.
P.O. Box 829
Alhambra, Calif. 91802
(213) 576-2545
California toll free only outside Los Angeles (213) area:
1-800-242-4400

Homes in the Spanish Colonial or Mission style have special stylistic requirements, and these apply to doors as well. Spanish Pueblo Doors was founded over twenty years ago to meet the needs of a special group of home owners who, contrary to popular impression, are to be found almost everywhere in North America and not just in the Southwest. The company offers twenty basic reversible designs in quality-grade Ponderosa pine and Philippine mahogany. Each door is handmade and hand-finished, with each panel and samll part being cut, carved, and sanded separately. All doors are built from 1¾″ lumber. Custom-made doors are also available in such woods as red alder, red oak, and black walnut. Prices for the regular models range from $181.50 to $236; for custom-ordered, $219 to $468.75. Illustrated is regular style No. 160.

Literature available.

Spanish Pueblo Doors, Inc.
P.O. Box 2517, Wagon Rd.
Santa Fe, N.M. 87501
(505) 471-0811

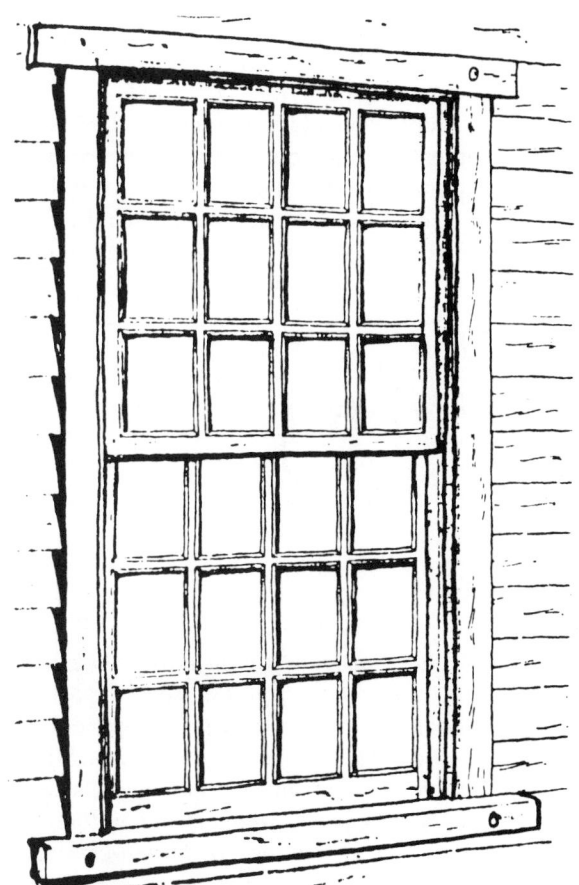

Literature available.

Maurer & Shepherd, Joyners
122 Naubuc Ave.
Glastonbury, Conn. 06033
(203) 633-2383

Michael Brofman is a very versatile woodworker. Although his company bears the name "Colonial," he enjoys working with more than plain rectangles. Quarter-circle, half-circle, full-circle, and Gothic triangle segment sash and frames are made to order.

Literature available.

Michael's Fine Colonial Products
22 Churchill Lane
Smithtown, N.Y. 11787
(516) 543-2479 after 6 p.m.

Expert advice is yours from the Preservation Resource Center. Their standard window sash is suitable for homes built from roughly the late eighteenth to the first decades of the nineteenth century. They can probably help you with other styles as well.

Data sheet, $1.

Preservation Resource Center
Lake Shore Rd.
Essex, N.Y. 12936
(518) 963-7305

If you can possibly save old windows, by all means do so. Replacements for antique glass panes are nearly impossible to find. Walter Phelps is one of a number of craftsmen who offers sash conservation, including glazing. It is delicate, precise work if properly executed, but very satisfying results may be achieved.

Walter E. Phelps
Box 76
Williamsville, Vt. 05362
(802) 348-6347

Shutters

Many architectural antiques supply houses carry a good stock of these traditional trappings. Search first in these haunts, catalogued separately in this chapter, before you turn to someone who can make them anew. Shutters were once used only for shutting out the outside and were, in essence, an early form of storm window. Now that a second layer of window or double-glazing has become customary, the utilitarian value of shutters has been replaced by decorative considerations. Shutters, however, may be hung so that in almost any situation they can be closed whenever desired, therefore providing an extra layer of insulation. If our winters are indeed growing colder each year, use of such devices may be one of the best investments we can make.

Michael Brofman is one woodworker who makes raised panel shutters. These are constructed of $1^{1}/_{16}''$ white pine, and range in size from 2'0" x 2'7" to 3' x 5'7". Prices vary from approximately $36 to $67. Different sizes and styles are also made to order.

Literature available.

Michael's Fine Colonial Products
22 Churchill Lane
Smithtown, N.Y. 11787
(516) 543-2479

Glass

If we stop to think of glass at all in an old house, we probably only have an image of the clear variety used in windows. So standard have materials become in the twentieth century, that we are frequently surprised by the exception. Glass was once a luxury, and even that used for simple windows was used sparingly—if at all— in the seventeenth and early eighteenth centuries. But by the middle of the nineteenth century, various varieties of glass came into vogue, and their use multiplied at least through the 1920s. Stained, leaded, beveled, etched, chipped—the techniques were many and the effects quite stunning.

The atmospheric effects produced by using a decorative glass are widely admired today. In fact, many of the so-called restored commercial areas of our cities are awash in stained glass. Mediocre copies are widely available and are sometimes pawned off as the real thing to the unknowing. Yet there is much that is good in this renaissance of period-glass design. A recent exhibition at Los Angeles's Design Center graphically proved that there are a considerable number of contemporary artists who are skilled in this medium.

Judson Studios has been providing fine leaded-glass designs since the turn of the century and is heartily recommended by preservation experts in the Los Angeles area. Repair work, the creation of new designs, and traditional lead glass designs are undertaken by the firm.

The Judson Studios
200 S. Avenue 66
Los Angeles, Calif.
(213) 255-0131

Penco Studios is another expert designer and manufacturer of leaded-glass windows and has been in business since 1892. It divides its products into four categories: entry sidelights, general patterns, transoms, and miscellaneous windows. The Penco catalog features more than 100 standard patterns which can be used for various purposes. Illustrated are just a few of these.

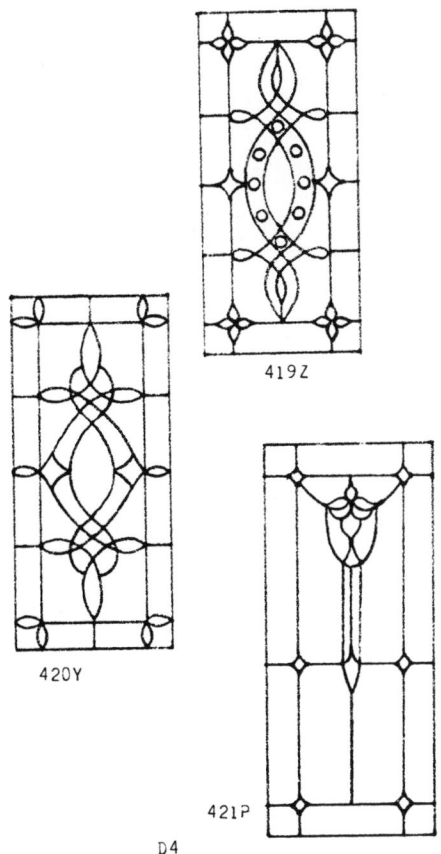

419Z

420Y

421P

D4

Penco will make any of these patterns (or others on a custom-order basis) with colored and/or beveled glass. The company has also developed a method of producing insulated leaded-glass windows by using an exterior protective sheet of glass and a vacuum seal.

Catalog available, $2.

Penco Studios
1110 Baxter Ave.
Louisville, Ky. 40404
(502) 459-4027

The artisans at Virtu work within the tradition of stained glass but seek to extend it with original new work. Much of this may be most appropriate for period interiors. One of the group's designs is illustrated here. Traditional patterns in leaded and copper-foiled stained glass can be produced as well.

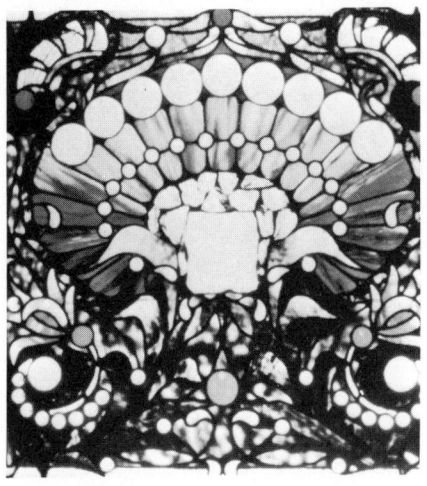

Virtu
P.O. Box 192
Southfield, Mich. 48037
(313) 357-1250

Cherry Creek provides hand- and machine-beveled glass for stained-glass artists, but can supply the home owner with standard blanks in many different sizes—which may be all that is necessary except for the framing. Two samples of the company's work are shown here along with an example of a hand-beveled

custom window panel. Standard pieces are made in a clear glass, but there are other colors and finishes of interest—bronze, mirror, frosted, miter, and something termed "glue chip." This last process—available on both plate and beveled glass—involves the use of animal glue and glass, a combination which produces a fern-like pattern. Such an appearance was popular in the early 1900s.

Catalog available.

Cherry Creek Ent., Inc.
937 Santa Fe Drive
Denver, Colo. 80204
(303) 892-1819

Era Victoriana specializes in antique American stained and beveled-glass windows. Many of these have required restoration, a process with which the firm is very familiar. This is an important source for windows, transoms, arches, skylights, and door panels that you should not overlook. Illustrated are two of their finest pieces, that below termed "Venus de Milo."

Illustrated brochure available, $1.25.

Era Victoriana
P.O. Box 9683
San Jose, Calif. 95157
(408) 296-5560

Bernard Gruenke of the Conrad Schmidt Studios is highly recommended by Chicago-area restorers. He will produce mosaics and beveled and frosted glass.

Bernard E. Gruenke, Jr.
Conrad Schmidt Studios
2405 S. 162nd St.
New Berlin, Wis. 53157
(414) 786-3030

Century is a good Texas outlet for clear or colored beveled plate glass. The glass used ranges from ¼″ to ¾″ in thickness. Various bevel widths are offered.

Price list available.

Century Glass Inc.
1417 N. Washington Ave.
Dallas, Tex. 75204
(214) 823-7773

Glass decorating and sculpturing have been specialties of Carved Glass and Signs in the New York area. They can duplicate sandblasted decorative glass and chipped glass panels and will undertake stained-glass work.

Carved Glass and Signs
767 E. 132nd St.
Bronx, N.Y. 10454
(212) 649-1266

Ceiling Materials

Metal ceilings have become almost as ubiquitous as stained glass. As is the way with architectural decoration, what was considered unbelievably dowdy, if not downright tacky at one time, is proclaimed ultra-chic a generation or two later. The story is somewhat the same with decorative plaster ceilings, but since these are extremely expensive undertakings, they have not achieved the same widespread popularity. Fortunately, suppliers who can provide new ceilings of both types, and craftsmen who can restore the old, are still very much with us.

AA-Abbingdon Ceiling Co is one of the two main suppliers of metal ceilings. These are available in 24" x 96" pieces. One of these plates contains 64 repeating designs or plates; most include only sixteen or four. A few are of one overall design. Illustrated are plates #507 (top) and #200 (bottom).

AA-Abbingdon also supplies the necessary sheet-metal moulding to finish off the ceiling.

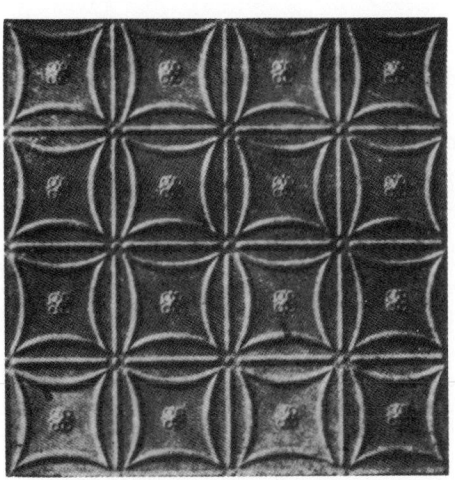

Brochure available.

AA-Abbingdon Ceiling Co., Inc.
2149 Utica Ave.
Brooklyn, N.Y. 11234
(212) 236-3251

Shanker ceilings are identical to those of AA-Abbingdon, but this firm—a manufacturing source rather than just a supplier—also offers handsome metal cornices which nicely finish off a late nineteenth-century interior. These, of course, do not have to be used only with metal ceilings. Cornice designs #807 (top) and #906 (bottom) are illustrated.

Literature available.

Barney Brainum-Shanker Steel Co., Inc.
70–32 83rd St.
Glendale, N.Y. 11227
(212) 894-5581

The design and fabrication of plaster ceiling ornaments has been a specialty of Decorators Supply for many years. The demand for these is obviously very limited, but the individual ornaments are part of the company's regular offerings and can be supplied on demand for either new or restored work. The ceiling design illustrated is termed "Louis XIV."

Catalog available, $1.

The Decorators Supply Corp.
3610–12 S. Morgan St.
Chicago, Ill. 60609
(312) 847-6300

Felber Studios is one of the last firms that will undertake the design, execution, and installation of an ornamental plaster ceiling. In the first *Old House Catalogue* we presented their "Haddon Hall Modified" design, and here is a second, "Hopewood Inn." Like the

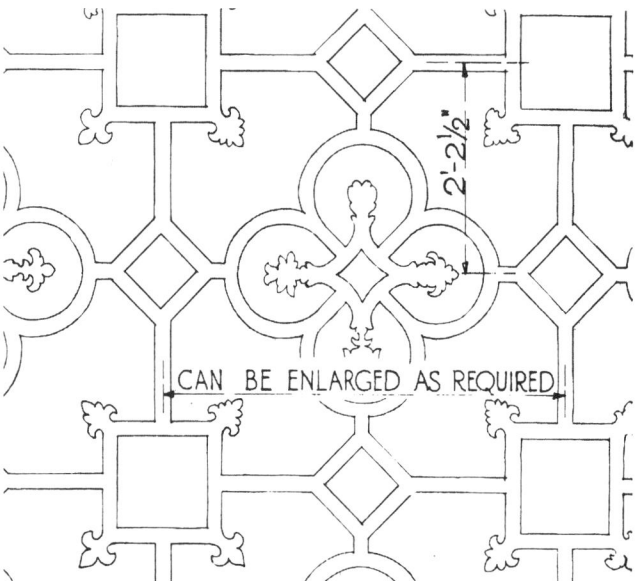

other, it is a Tudor design appropriate for a grand English Tudor mansion of the sort built between the turn of the century and the 1930s.

Felber also performs another most useful service—the reconstruction of antique plaster.

Catalog available.

Felber Studios
P.O. Box 551, 110 Ardmore Ave.
Ardmore, Penn. 19003
(215) MI2-4710

Roofing Materials

The importance of a particular roofing material and style is usually not appreciated until a new roof—of very different texture and appearance—replaces the old. This is especially true on those buildings of nineteenth-century style—French mansard, Queen Anne or Stick, and Spanish Colonial—which make use of either special materials or feature unusual multi-level roof treatments. The kind of shingling used on the exterior of many Victorian buildings, for instance, was continued on sloping façades which terminated in a flat or only slightly pitched roof. These shingles of various shapes are not always easy to find today. The terra-cotta tiles employed for homes in the Spanish Colonial or Mission style are similarly difficult to locate. Concrete imitations have taken their place.

Other kinds of materials—such as shakes and slate used for period buildings, including many pre-Victorian—have been more successfully imitated. There is still no real substitute for slate in either appearance or durability, but this has become prohibitively expensive. Fiberglass shingles are a considerable improvement on the first asphalt fire- and windproof materials and are worth the extra cost.

San Francisco Victoriana has provided San Francisco-area residents with traditional-cut cedar shingles for some time and is now offering these nationally. It is about time! These are needed just as badly in Boston and St. Louis as they are on the West Coast. Illustrated are the six different patterns available.

Included in their Book of Architectural Mouldings, *$1.*

San Francisco Victoriana
606 Natoma St.
San Francisco, Calif. 94103
(415) 864-5477

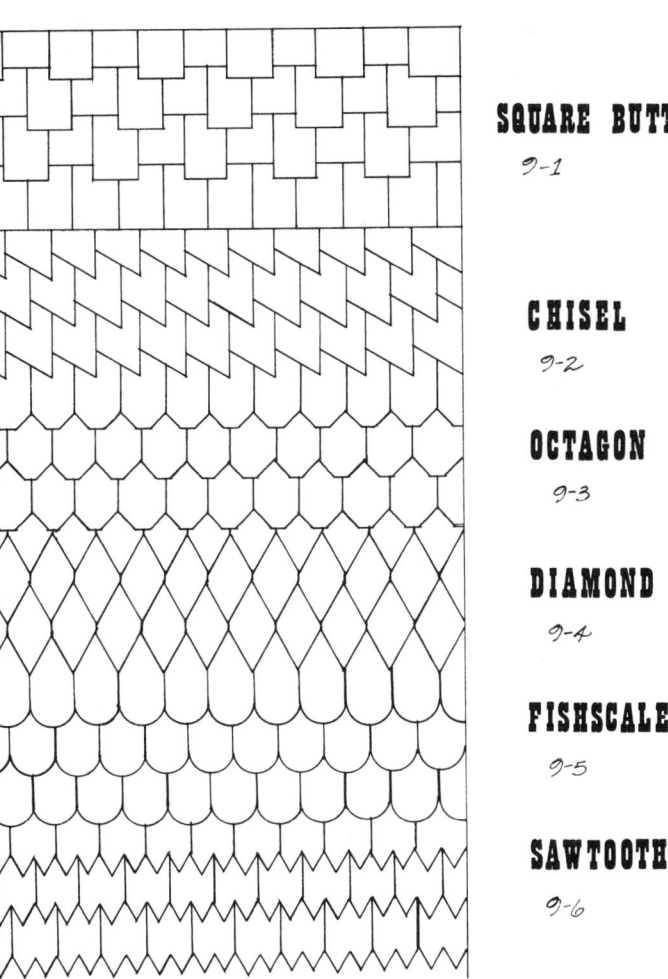

SQUARE BUTT
9-1

CHISEL
9-2

OCTAGON
9-3

DIAMOND
9-4

FISHSCALE
9-5

SAWTOOTH
9-6

more buildings are destroyed in future years. The only good that can come out of such urban warfare is a new supply of antique materials—a cold comfort, indeed.

Smith & Son Roofing
1360 Virginia Ave.,
Baldwin Park, Calif.
(213) 337-1524

Polyurethane Substitutes

Some purists may object to the inclusion of such an artificial material in a book devoted to honest, traditional materials and workmanship. We beg to disagree. A good number of molded forms available in modern polymers are useful for small-scale work of minor importance. Exactly how appropriate they might be for a particular purpose, however, is a matter which only the individual can determine. In any case, we feel that we have an obligation to announce their availability and to leave final aesthetic judgments to the prospective buyer. Bear in mind that products under discussion are not of the bogus "wood-like" sort being pushed commercially by too many major building suppliers.

Fypon, Inc. produces what they call "entrance systems" which feature pilasters, crossheads, and pediments for entryways. There are three product lines available—Eagle, Cardinal, and Sparrow—which reflect not differences in style but of quality and cost. All Fypon materials are made of high-density polyurethane which can be handled in much the same manner as structural millwork.

Literature available.

Fypon, Inc.
108 Hill St.
Stewartstown, Penn. 17363
(717) 993-2593

Dana-Deck offers machined and handsplit Western Red Cedar shakes. Both varieties have been treated with a fire retardant and are available in several sizes. The company· also supplies Western Red Cedar shingles for walls, mansards, and regular roofs. These come in ten fancy butt patterns—diagonal, half cove, diamond, round, hexagon, octagon, arrow, square, fish scale, and sawtooth.

Contact your local lumber dealer for supplies of these materials, or get in touch with Dana-Deck for help in this regard.

Dana-Deck, Inc.
P.O. Box 78
Orcas, Wash. 98280
(206) 376-4531 or 4787

The advantages of using polymers—they are molded in one piece, lightweight, and resistant to rot or insects—have been fully capitalized by Focal Point. The disadvantages—lack of precise details and texture—have been reduced as much as they probably can be. This firm does not attempt to create massive effects in the material, but rather concentrates on such features as domes, niches, ceiling medallions, and mouldings, the last category being one that is covered in the second section of this book. The domes and niches particularly interest us because these architectural elements are

Smith & Son Roofing warehouses handmade tiles of the sort suitable for Spanish-style dwellings. Just how long the supply will last probably depends on how many

extremely expensive and difficult to achieve in natural materials. The Focal Point dome is illustrated here.

Brochure available.

Focal Point, Inc.
4870 South Atlanta Rd.
Smyrna, Ga. 30080
(401) 351-0820

Cleaning of Façades

Ever since the advent of the automobile, America (and the rest of the civilized world) has been getting dirtier and dirtier. Masonry buildings blacken; structures of wood just turn a grimy gray. Perhaps the recent imposition of stringent pollution controls will help matters considerably, but, frankly, we have little hope that the air will become that clean. The pollution of the past may not have been quite so bad for buildings—except in coal-mining towns—but it, too, was noxious. Today we are more conscious of the filth around us, and of the immense damage that has been caused to the natural and man-made environment by the instruments of modern living. Now it is up to modern industry to provide ways for alleviating the damage, and it can be done. Sandblasting was considered the efficient method of wiping away the grime until the effects of blasting away brick and stone façades became clearly evident.

The pitted remains of once finely-surfaced brick and cut stone were hardly worth saving. Now there are chemical solutions which will clean much more effectively and leave the texture of a façade intact. They are also environmentally safe to use in other ways.

Sermac Systems is just one of several national firms that use new methods of cleaning. They can handle any kind of masonry structure and have also devised safe and efficient ways of removing paint from wood, metal, and masonry. Only the most delicate façades of terracotta ornament are still liable to damage, but progress is being made in this area, too.

Brochure available.

Sermac Industrial Cleaning
P.O. Box 1684
Des Plaines, Ill. 60018
(312) 824-1810

House Inspection Services

Anyone seriously considering the purchase of any kind of house—new or old—should also consider asking an outside expert to evaluate the building's condition. Technical expertise of this sort is especially valuable if the soundness of an old house is in question. Many were built of much better materials than those used today, but maintenance may not have been followed with care. In any case, you do not want to find yourself in a Mr.-Blanding-Builds-His-Dream-House kind of situation, with walls tumbling around you from the time the deed is turned over. If you know a good contractor in the area, you may want to depend on his advice. And there are also restoration experts that can be contacted through local or regional preservation societies. Probably best of all, however, is someone who has been trained to inspect buildings. He could save you a great deal of money.

Guardian National House Inspection, Inc., is a group of such trained inspectors. Unfortunately, the company covers only a five state area—New York, New Jersey, Connecticut, Rhode Island, and Massachusetts. If you live outside this region, you still might want to contact them for advice as to how to find a good inspector. Many of the preservation/restoration services cataloged in the next section of this chapter can also provide professional assistance of this type.

Brochure available.

Guardian National House Inspection, Inc.
Box 31
Pleasantville, N.Y. 10570
(914) 769-6186
or

Guardian National House Inspection, Inc.
Box 115
Orleans, Mass. 02653
(617) 255-6609

Restoration Specialists

The old-house field has its jacks-of-all-trades, men and women who can provide professional advice and work of considerable value. Only a few such individuals or groups were written up in The Old House Catalogue. Their number, however, has expanded, and so has their importance as preservation becomes not only a cause but a full-fledged business. These are the kinds of people who may be able to advise you on preservation law and zoning, on tax benefits and liabilities, on structuralwork and interior design, and who may even be able to provide many of the materials needed for a project.

Townsend H. Anderson, House Joiner

If you ever become depressed about saving an old house, try to communicate with Townsend Anderson. The only trouble is that you probably will not be able to find him. He will be off in pursuit of another period braced-frame dwelling which can be carefully disassembled to join the three that he now has in storage. Anderson doesn't collect these buildings for the fun of it. He is in the business of reconstructing and restoring them for clients. He also designs and builds braced-frame buildings from new timbers, but, as he puts it, "within the parameters of classical proportion and finish. . . ."

Anderson produces all the interior and exterior millwork needed for his buildings, and this work is accomplished by hand. These materials are also available for customers not involved in one of the complete house projects.

Illustrated here are several examples of his work. The Cape Cod—before and after—was found in Northfield, Vermont, disassembled, moved, and rebuilt in Duxbury, Vermont. The hutch and hanging wall cabinet are found in one of his restored houses. Using new timbers, Anderson constructed the braced-framed barn with attached shed in South Duxbury, Vermont.

Catalog available, $1.

Townsend H. Anderson
R.D. 1, Box 44D
Moretown, Vt. 05660
(802) 244-5095

Arch Associates/Stephen Guerrant

This is a professional restoration, rehabilitation, and remodeling architectural firm serving the Chicago area. They can help with the location of restoration materials and provide a real-estate inspection service for a fixed fee.

Arch Associates/Stephen Guerrant
874 Greenbay Rd.
Winnetka, Ill. 60093
(312) 446-7810

A. W. Baker Restorations, Inc.

Anne Baker provides a badly-needed service—consultation *before* a restoration project is begun. She and her colleagues will work out a plan to be followed and, if necessary, will follow up with a local contractor once the project is underway. In addition, the firm is continuing with the business of dismantling fine old structures and the reconstruction of them on more permanent sites. Illustrated is preparation for the relocation of a seventeenth-century Cape and the actual journey itself.

A. W. Baker Restorations, Inc.
670 Drift Rd.
Westport, Mass. 02790
(617) 636-8765

John Conti

Every aspect of a period restoration project can be handled by John Conti—from research work to the supplying of proper period materials. He is skilled in the manner of a master carpenter/builder of old.

John Conti, Restoration Contractor
Box 189
Wagontown, Penn. 19376
(215) 384-0553

Wilbert R. Hasbrouck, FAIA

Bill Hasbrouck has received about every preservation award that can be given—for good reason. His work in the South Prairie Avenue section of Chicago has been of great importance. A visit to Glesner House, H. H. Richardson's greatest gift to Chicago, provides ample evidence that this preservation architect is one of the very best. He directs only the restoration of buildings of significant architectural merit and uses the best trained craftsmen.

Wilbert R. Hasbrouck, FAIA
Historic Resources
711 S. Dearborn
Chicago, Ill. 60605

Historic Boulevard Services

This firm provides a fine line of terra-cotta chimney pots which have been described in the section on fireplaces and heating. The owner, William L. Lavicka, is a consulting engineer with a contracting practice. His specialty is 1880–1900 buildings which require renovation and restoration. For this purpose he maintains a large stock of antique doors, trim, railings, and fireplace mantels.

William L. Lavicka
Historic Boulevard Services
1520 W. Jackson Blvd.
Chicago, Ill. 60607
(312) 829-5562

The House Carpenters

These enterprising individuals blend the best of the old with the new. Their specialty is traditional timber frames of select white pine and oak, hewn or hand planed, with mortise and tenon and dovetail joinery. This type of fine reproduction work is illustrated in the framing shown below.

At the same time, The House Carpenters fabricate and supply materials for the restoration of early homes—shingles and clapboards, doors and windows, paneling and flooring, mouldings and hardware. One of their seventeenth-century leaded sash designs is illustrated here.

Brochure available, $4.

The House Carpenters
Box 217
Shutesbury, Mass. 01072
(413) 253-7020

Housesmiths

As the following four photographs show, Housesmiths is very much in the timber-framing business. Stewart

43

Elliott and Eugenie Wallas have written a whole book on this traditional subject, and Elliott has just completed a follow-up volume, *The Timber Frame Planning Book*. But they do more than write. They will package a custom pre-cut frame and ship it *anywhere*. If you are thinking of a new house built along old lines, you might want to consider such a braced-frame structure. If so, suggest the Housesmith package to a contracter.

The Timber Framing Book, $9.95.
The Timber Frame Planning Book, $15.

Housesmiths
P.O. Box 416
York, Maine 03909
(207) 363-5551

David Howard, Inc.

This is another firm which specializes in braced-frame structures, and like the others, it works out of the New England area. The frames are of oak and are of the sort most compatible for a period-style home of the Colonial period. The firm does not do reproduction work, but, rather, brings traditional techniques to bear on new house construction.

Brochure available, $4.

David Howard, Inc.
P.O. Box 295
Alstead, N.H. 03602
(603) 835-2213

Howell Construction

Restoration of homes in the Middle Tennessee area has become a major business in recent years, and Howell Construction is one of the leading firms. They bring to any project a professional combination of building skills and design knowledge which is necessary in the preservation field.

Howell Construction
2700 12th Ave. S.
Nashville, Tenn. 37204
(615) 269-5659

International Consultants, Inc.

This is a high-level firm of consulting engineers with impressive experience in major industrial, commercial, and cultural projects. A few of the projects they have undertaken involve study of the restoration or adaptation of an historically significant structure. This is not a service for the individual home owner, but it might be a valuable one for a neighborhood complex.

International Consultants, Inc.
227 S. Ninth St.
Philadelphia, Penn. 19107
(215) 923-8888

Bruce M. Kriviskey, AIP

After serving over ten years with various public and private agencies, Bruce Kriviskey has begun his own consulting practice in urban planning and design, historic preservation, and neighborhood conservation. He is the former executive director of Historic Walker's Point, Inc., in Milwaukee.

Bruce M. Kriviskey, AIP
3048-A N. Shepard Ave.
Milwaukee, Wis. 53211
(414) 332-9073

Old Town Restorations, Inc.

St. Paul, Minnesota's Historic Hill District is the special concern of this consulting firm. They can help Twin Cities residents with advice on financing, historical information, the location of skilled contractors and craftsmen, and, most important, with architectural plans.

Old Town Restorations, Inc.
158 Farrington
St. Paul, Minn.
(612) 224-3857

Preservation Associates, Inc.

Valuable skills predicated on knowledge of antique building methods and architectural design are possessed by the two principals of Preservation Associates. They can custom make hand-riven oak roofing shingles, hewn beams, hand-planed mouldings and trim, doors and windows, and even build reproduction log houses; a photo of one such structure is included here.

Their consulting service is also valuable. They provide an inspection service as well as helpful guidance with historic sites surveys, state and national Register of Historic Places nominations, etc.

Brochure available.

Preservation Associates, Inc.
P.O. Box 202
Sharpsburg, Md. 21782
(301) 432-5466

Preservation Resource Group, Inc.

This organization is primarily an educational group that provides information and training for public and private preservation agencies. They could be of inestimable help in developing an effective local or regional program. PRG also assists private individuals with an evaluation of restoration plans.

Brochure available.

Preservation Resource Group, Inc.
5619 Southampton Dr.
Springfield, Va. 22151
(703) 323-1407

Rambusch

It is hard to imagine a more skilled group of artisans than that brought together at Rambusch. They are capable of creating superb reproductions in stained glass, metal, and wood. Decorative painting and mosaics are done with extreme faithfulness to period style. Among their recent commissions has been the restoration of Boscobel. Consultation, planning, and design are also among the services offered.

Brochure available.

Rambusch
40 W. 13th St.
New York, N.Y. 10011
(212) 675-0400

Restorations, Ltd.

Both minor structural work and major restoration projects will be undertaken by Restorations, Ltd. Attention is given to whatever details are important to doing a good job—whatever the scale. Dating of antique paint, masonry, and wallpaper is another one of the services offered.

Brochure available.

Restorations, Ltd.
Jamestown, R.I. 02835
(401) 423-0756

Restorations Unlimited, Inc.

This is a complete restoration contracting firm that provides advice and help on everything from beams and joists to wallpapers and paints. They have recently taken on a franchise for Rich Craft kitchens, one of the more adaptable of modern designs for period homes.

Restorations Unlimited, Inc.
24 W. Main St.
Elizabethville, Penn. 17023
(717) 362-3477

San Francisco Victoriana

A visit to the headquarters of Victoriana is a bit like making a pilgrimage to Canterbury, Rome, or Jerusalem. The founders started in 1972 to provide their beautiful city with the best possible advice and materials available in the restoration field. After completing several hundred projects, they say there is still much to learn. Undoubtedly there is, but they already know more about Victorian design than the rest of us put together. Victorian hardware, millwork, lighting fixtures, etched glass panels, plaster brackets and medallions—all are available here "with the least amount of compromise in authentic design or materials," as the company correctly states. Restoration projects are only undertaken in the Bay area, but the firm is beginning to reach out to serve the greater, national period materials market.

San Francisco Victoriana
606 Natoma St.
San Francisco, Calif. 94103
(415) 864-5477

The Valentas

The Valentas "live" restoration. You cannot fully appreciate the work of Frank Lloyd Wright or Henry Hobson Richardson without talking with this extraordinarily talented couple and their equally-skilled daughter. Their understanding of and ability to work with fine woods is not to be matched by any cabinetmaker. Glesner House and the Frank Lloyd Wright home and studio in Oak Park, Illinois, are two projects on which they have collaborated. They'd like to help everyone with a sincere interest in good workmanship of the past, but, if you are interested, you will probably have to wait some time for your turn.

The Valentas
2105 S. Austin Blvd.
Cicero, Ill. 60650

Architectural Antiques

Suppliers of what has become known as "architectural antiques" are becoming more numerous each year. It is too bad that businesses of this sort did not start much earlier—when whole sections of urban areas were cleared for "redevelopment." Denver and Atlanta alone could have supplied the rest of the country with an almost endless quantity of stained glass, millwork, hardware, mantels, used brick, and on and on. Today's secondhand building materials dealer has to search out quality goods in every possible nook and cranny. Some come in from England; others are found in depressed neighborhoods and in rural areas of the country that have not become fashionable and "picked over."

Some of the firms listed in the following pages are better known as wrecking companies or salvage yards. In the days when restoration was only a pleasant idea, the search for old-house parts often began here. Many such demolition and salvage wrecking companies still provide true treasures, but their days as suppliers are clearly limited. Except for a very few firms, they are not interested in one-of-a-kind pieces which require special handling.

Architectural Antiques/ L'Architecture Ancienne

This Canadian firm specializes in four main areas: stained-glass windows, with over 1,000 in stock; doors, including 400 of the carved variety; mantels, with at least 250 in stock at all times; and gingerbread millwork—cornices, brackets, and fretwork pieces by the hundreds. Twelve-thousand square feet of warehousing space is also filled with paneling, staircases, pillars, moulding, etc.

Stock is continually changing. If you have something particular in mind, Architectural Antiques will furnish pictures or sketches of what they have on hand.

Architectural Antiques/L'Architecture Ancienne
410 St. Pierre
Montreal, Quebec H2Y 2M2
Canada
(514) 849-3344

Berkeley Architectural Salvage

This is a traditional source of old-house supplies in the San Francisco/Oakland/Berkeley area. No details are available as to the kinds of materials in stock; nonetheless, it is well worth checking out.

Berkeley Architectural Salvage
2750 Adeline
Berkeley, Calif. 94703
(415) 849-2025

The Cellar

Antique building parts of all sorts can be found at The Cellar—newel posts, barn siding, metal fireplaces, entrance doors, wood-burning cookstoves, plaster wall ornaments, pedestal sinks, iron fencing. You name it and The Cellar can probably find it for you. Their direct-mail service can also help you with particular design problems.

Information sheet available.

The Cellar
384 Elgin St.
Ottawa, Ontario 2KP 1N1
Canada
(613) 238-1999

Felicity, Inc.

Located in three Tennessee towns, Felicity specializes in columns and carvings, stained- and cut-glass windows and doors, decorative hardware, mantels, and lighting fixtures.

Felicity, Inc.
600 Eagle Bend Rd.
Clinton, Tenn. 37716
(615) 457-5443

Felicity, Inc.
Cookeville Antique Mall
I-40
Cookeville, Tenn.

Felicity, Inc.
Thieves' Market
4900 Kingston Pike
Knoxville, Tenn. 37902
(615) 584-9641

Gargoyles, Ltd.

This is the Philadelphia area's leading architectural antiques supplier. Gargoyles is a particularly fine place for mantels, doors, lighting fixtures, and ornamental iron. Reproduction materials are also supplied, as are new metal ceilings.

Brochures available.

Gargoyles, Ltd.
512 S. Third St.
Philadelphia, Penn. 19147
(215) 629-1700

Great American Salvage Company, Inc.

This firm has sold primarily to commercial clients, but is now planning to enter the home restoration market. They are experts on lighting and restore the old and fabricate the new along traditional lines.

Great American Salvage Co., Inc.
901 E. Second St.
Little Rock, Ark. 72203
(501) 371-0666

Materials Unlimited

Reynold Lowe is a convert to preservation. A former wrecker, he saw the light when Ann Arbor's old Municipal League building was pulled down to be replaced by a plastic fast-food franchise. To make up for his errant past, he devotes all of his time to three acres of antiques and reclaimed architectural materials. Most of

these date from the period 1870–1900, but there are supplies of earlier and later items.

Materials Unlimited
4100 E. Morgan Rd.
Ypsilanti, Mich. 48197
(313) 434-4300

Pat's Antiques, Etc.

You'll have to visit Patrick McCloskey in Texas if you want to know exactly what is available for your old house. He has a 5,000 square foot barn full of beveled stained, and leaded glass, fireplace mantels, light fixtures and doors. At the present time, architectural antiques cannot be shipped from Smithville.

Brochures available with self-addressed, stamped envelope.

Pat's Antiques, Etc.
Highway 71 at Alum Creek
P.O. Box 777
Smithville, Texas 78957
(512) 237-3600

The Renovation Source, Inc.

This is a new company that provides consulting services and materials for the home owner. Some of the supplies are antiques; others are good reproductions.

The Renovation Source, Inc.
3512–14 N. Southport
Chicago, Ill. 60657
(312) 327-1250

Greg Spiess

Good solid antique building materials—windows, mantels, exterior doors—are a specialty here. Greg Spiess will also undertake repair work and custom reproduction.

Greg Spiess
216 E. Washington St.
Joliet, Ill. 60433
(815) 722-5639

Sunrise Salvage

Sunrise is one of those junkyards that any lover of old things can admire. "Junk" it may be to some, but for us, and thousands of residents of the Bay area, Sunrise is a good place in which to spend a Saturday afternoon. They specialize in old tubs and sinks, but can help you out with other materials, too.

Sunrise Salvage
2210 San Pablo Ave.
Berkeley, Calif. 94710
(415) 845-4751

United House Wrecking Co.

This is the place that calls itself a "junkyard with a personality." United House is the granddaddy of the East Coast salvage depots and an extraordinary place to visit. There are more than five acres of materials located within 30,000 square-feet of buildings.

Literature available.

United House Wrecking Co.
328 Selleck St.
Stamford, Conn. 06902
(203) 348-5371

Urban Archaeology

Leon Schecter has been tracking down architectural decoration throughout the New York area during the past few years and beating the wreckers to the punch. He's just opened up his own store full of capitals, gates, keystones, stoves, streetlamps, stained-glass windows, and more.

Urban Archaeology
137 Spring St.
New York, N.Y. 10013
(212) 431-6969

Westlake Architectural Antiques

Carved doors, mantels, chandeliers, stained-glass panels—many of the trappings of the Victorian period can be found at Westlake. We've seen pictures of what parts of Austin *once* looked like, and thank heaven someone is at least recycling its past. On request, this firm will supply pictures and prices of particular kinds of items.

Westlake Architectural Antiques
3315 Westlake Dr.
Austin, Texas 78746
(512) 327-1110

The Wrecking Bar (Atlanta)

Over 12,000 square-feet are devoted to the display of architectural antiques. You name it, and The Wrecking Bar can probably come up with exactly what is needed or with a close match. There are doors and windows of all sorts, ornamental iron fencing, hardware and light-ing fixtures, mantels, pediments and pilasters. Most are American; some are European.

The Wrecking Bar
292 Moreland Ave., N.E.
Atlanta, Ga. 30307
(404) 525-0468

The Wrecking Bar (Dallas)

The founders of the Atlanta supply house moved on to new territory several years ago. This is an excellent source for antique materials of all sorts and living proof that not everyone in Big D is interested only in glass and steel.

Brochure available.

The Wrecking Bar, Inc.
2601 McKinney
Dallas, Texas 75204
(214) 826-1717

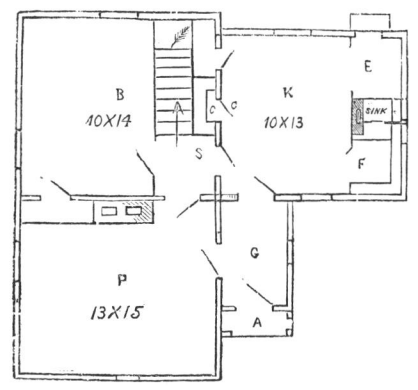

Other Sources of Structural Supplies and Services

Consult the List of Suppliers for addresses.

Paneling/Siding

Dale Carlisle
Craftsman Lumber
Dana-Deck
Driwood Moulding
Guyon
Old World Moulding

Doors

Allwood Door
Castle Burlingame
Simpson Timber
Spanish Pueblo Doors, Inc.

Windows

Blaine Window Hardware
Perkowitz Window Fashions

Shutters

Charles Walker Mfg.

Glass

Ball and Ball
Castle Burlingame
Cooke Art Glass Studio
Genesis Glass Ltd.
J. & R. Lamb Studios
Lead Glass Co.
Morgan Bockius Studios
Rococo Designs
Walton Stained Glass
Whittemore-Durgin Glass

Ceilings

Kenneth Lynch & Sons

Roofing

Celestial Design
Follansbee Steel
L. R. Lloyd
Structural Slate
Vermont Structural Slate

Cleaning

American Building Restoration

Inspection

Arch Associates/Stephen Guerrant
A. W. Baker
National Home Inspection Service of New England
Old House Inspection
Preservation Associates

Restoration Specialists

Bishop's Mill Historical Institute
R. H. Davis
KMH Associates
Jane Kent Rockwell
Raoul Savoie
Townscape
Jay Turnbull
Up Country Enterprises

Supply Houses

Antique Center
The Barn Peope
Castle Burlingame
Cleveland Wrecking
Yours & Mine Antiques

Two-story porch, Morris- Butler House, Indianapolis, Indiana.
Historic American Buildings Survey, 1970.

II Woodwork & Other Fittings

The making of decorative pieces for exterior and interior use in old houses has to be one of the most satisfying of occupations. From visits to workshops in San Francisco, Chicago, and New York, it seems evident to this writer that the business will never again be a large one, but that the future is bright for those who will learn traditional skills and master the fine art of producing period mouldings and ornamental devices in wood, plaster, stone, or metal.

Most of us are totally unaware of the small details which combine to define the structure of a period interior or exterior. By simply concentrating on specific elements—brackets, cornices, mouldings around doors and windows—a pattern of designs and of their imposition begins to appear. A Federal or Greek Revival house with columns and capitals or a Beaux Arts building embellished with many variations of the classical orders come readily to mind as probably the most prominent building styles which have relied heavily on a revival of sawn, carved, molded, or cast ornamentation of a structural kind. The elements which came into play in the Gothic Revival, Queen Anne, and the Romanesque Revival periods are more simply decorative. On many buildings of the twentieth century, decoration appears to be gratuitous, an attempt to warm up ever so slightly a frozen mass.

Now that the passion for the International Style is being codified in the architectural history books and Philip Johnson's justly famous glass house has been willed to the National Trust, there is the danger that there will be a new sort of revival—a grab-bag kind of camp mixing of traditional motifs. Style will continue to evolve and develop, and there is nothing anyone can do about it. But there is no such thing as "progress" when it comes to aesthetics, to design and its execution. Ornamentation cannot be simply borrowed from one form and transferred to another—with happy results. And what is poured of concrete or molded from fiberglass will hardly begin to approximate that of stone or terra cotta or even solid wood.

Traditional workers in the millwork, metal, and plaster ornamentation fields know that there are appropriate ways to do things and proper forms to follow. They are not without a willingness to try new ideas, to fashion something unique. Few can afford to be choosy. The number of firms which turn out period ornamentation has declined and declined until the last few years. Some didn't make it through the Depression. Decorative architectural elements can never be cost-efficient. But, fortunately, some of the best firms survived and are now being joined by new groups of younger craftsmen who are enthusiastic and dedicated in their work.

Elaborate mouldings are once again being used in interiors of both new and restored houses. The products of such firms as Decorators Supply in Chicago are being shipped from coast to coast. San Francisco Victoriana is offering its first full line of period architectural mouldings on a national basis. This is all to the good, and perhaps we shouldn't be quite so pessimistic about their misuse in kitsch revival interiors of the last decades of the 1900s. What seems monstrous to us now— atmospheric restaurants and boutiques loaded with plywood Victorian fretwork—may be considered merely a novelty or even quite innovative in 2025. There is no reason, however, why period materials should be manhandled in true restoration work. To bring a house back to its proper style is an exercise in careful documentation and imagination. The two approaches should complement each other. With a wide variety of decorative materials available from reputable sources, this kind of work can be accomplished with latitude allowed for personal taste and comfort, as well as for cost.

Wood Supplies

Although the concern of this section is with more than the fiber products suggested by the term "woodwork," a basic knowledge of the various kinds of woods available in the past for decorative architectural use is of real value. Some of these are hardwoods such as oak, cherry, maple, and mahogany. Others are soft varieties like pine or cedar. Pine has always been used in American homes, especially those of an early date. Historically, it has been widely available and easily cut. Supplies of some of the more unusual varieties are noted in the first section of the book. Redwood, an especially durable member of the pine family, became popular after discovery of vast tracts of it in the second half of the nineteenth century.

Hardwoods—always more costly than softwoods— have been traditionally used for decorative rather than structural purposes. There are, of course, exceptions to this general rule. In areas of North America where such woods as ash, cherry, oak, and maple have been plentiful, these have been used for such structural members as flooring, framing, and doors.

The supplies currently available from two firms illustrate the variety of traditional woods that can be used for restoration or reproduction work. From John Harra Wood & Supply: ash, chestnut (wormy), cherry, holly, Honduras mahogany, hard and soft maple, English brown oak, poplar, rosewood, teak, walnut, and others. This firm offers a lumber sample pack which includes $\frac{1}{4}''$ x 2'' x 6'' specimens of 25 different woods for a price of $18. Any woodworker undertaking a restoration would find this a valuable reference source.

Catalog available, $1.

John Harra Wood & Supply Co.
39 W. 19th St.
New York, N.Y. 10011
(212) 741-0290

David Short's Amherst Wood Working is another source for fine woods: ash, basswood, red birch, butternut, cherry, Honduras mahogany, maple, oak, rosewood, and walnut. Also available are such varieties as Atlantic white cedar, red cedar, yellow pine, and redwood.

Price list available.

Amherst Wood Working
Box 464, Sunderland Rd.
North Amherst, Mass. 01059
(413) 549-2806

Veneers

Veneers are of interest primarily to furniture makers, and Minnesota Woodworkers Supply Company is an excellent source to be consulted. The firm also offers a splendid assortment of inlays which may be called for in fine cabinetmaking. Veneers and inlays, however, can be of use to the home restorer who either does not wish to invest in expensive hardwood lumber or finds that veneer in bands or sheets would be more appropriate for his needs. Minnesota suppies 35 different veneers which vary in width from 4'' to 12''. They are shipped in 36'' lengths. It may be necessary to splice pieces together if you need more width than is available, but lengths over 36'' can be supplied. This firm also offers five basic hardwoods—cherry, walnut, birch, maple, Honduras mahogany, and white oak—if you wish to use only lumber.

Catalog available, $1.

Minnesota Woodworkers Supply Co.
21801 Industrial Blvd.
Rogers, Minn. 55374
(612) 428-4101

Mouldings

These forms are among the most useful materials offered today by manufacturers in the reproduction field. From simple to very complex, mouldings are found in almost every home as cornices, rails, bases, panels, or frames. The "higher" the house style, the more complex these forms become. By fitting one to another, rich and dramatic effects in woodwork were created during the Georgian and the high Victorian periods in domestic architecture.

Mouldings of wood, plaster, metal, and polyurethane are available today. Only the last-named material has no claim on authenticity. Some manufacturers of traditional millwork have suggested that producers of molded synthetic work be excluded from this book on the grounds that it is neither appropriate nor well executed. We believe they are wrong—in at least two cases.

Polyurethane Mouldings

Fypon produces six basic models—two crown dentil mouldings, two dentil mouldings, a surround moulding, and a ceiling moulding—which do not attempt fancy effects. The crown dentils and the ceiling mouldings are available in 16' lengths; the surround and simple dentil mouldings in 12'. In height, these mouldings vary in size from 1¾" to 7". According to the manufacturer, the material can be nailed, drilled, or sawed with field carpenter tools. The mouldings will not rot or warp and can be painted with oil-base or latex paints.

Fypon produces other forms as well, including pediments, mantels, window heads, sunbursts, acorns, brackets, and blocks.

Literature available.

Fypon, Inc.
Box 365, 108 Hill St.
Stewartstown, Penn. 17363
(717) 993-2593

Focal Point is a second major manufacturer making mouldings and other ornamental forms from polymers. Fourteen different mouldings may be examined in kit form. They are based on impressions from traditional wood or plaster models from the past.

Literature available.

Focal Point, Inc.
4870 S. Atlanta Rd.
Smyrna, Ga. 30080
(404) 351-0820

Wood Crown Mouldings

Traditional moulding patterns in wood are available from several manufacturers across the country who supply both retail outlets and individuals buying for themselves. Most of the mouldings are of pressed or embossed wood. KB Moulding is a representative dealer in the field. It offers many different crown mouldings which are of the sort to be used as the crowning or finishing element between wall and ceiling.

Catalog available, 25¢.

KB Moulding, Inc.
508A Larkfield Rd.
East Northport, N.Y. 11731
(516) 368-6009

San Francisco Victoriana's mouldings are of all-heart redwood. The patterns are based on historical models used between the years 1850 and 1920 in the United States. There are six different crown mouldings available, and a large assortment of other kinds which are catalogued later in this woodwork section. It is important to note that the full thickness of nineteenth-century mouldings has been maintained throughout the line. The crown mouldings are recommended for outside use, but presumably can also be employed in rooms of sufficient height.

Catalog available, $1.

San Francisco Victoriana
606 Natoma St.
San Francisco, Calif. 94103
(415) 864-5477

Carved Wood Mouldings

Deeply cut hardwood mouldings are the specialty of Bendix. Many of the designs are contemporary, but some may be useful for a Victorian interior. Bendix also supplies a plain crown moulding with dentils as well as other moulding forms which are covered under separate headings.

Catalog available, $1.

Bendix Mouldings, Inc.
235 Pegasus Ave.
Northvale, N.J. 07647
(201) 767-8888

Cornices

The equivalent of crown mouldings in wood have been produced for hundreds of years in plaster. Decorators Supply is one of the foremost manufacturers of such ornament in the world. The firm has hundreds of different ceiling cornices available, ranging from classical to the modern. Illustrated here, in order of appearance, are: the classic dentil (#1210), Gothic (#3495), Old English (#25114), Elizabethan (#25121), Colonial (#3454), Georgian (#25180), Louis XVI (#25183), and Sullivanesque (#3434).

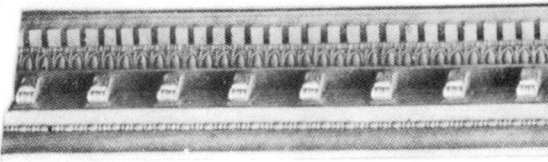

Catalog available, $1.

Decorators Supply Corp.
3610–12 S. Morgan St.
Chicago, Ill. 60609
(312) 847-6300

Felber Studios specializes·in custom work and in reconstruction of antique plaster. The cornices available from this company are exceptionally accurate copies of the antique. Of particular interest are the Old English or Tudor cornice mouldings which were used in many fine homes of the late nineteenth and early twentieth centuries. Felber has catalogued at least eighteen different styles.

Catalog available.

Felber Studios
110 Ardmore Ave.
Ardmore, Penn. 19003
(215) 642-4710

Casings

The interiors of most doors and windows require at least a simple frame known as a casing. This is a moulding which dresses up any structural opening and renders period interiors a great deal more interesting. Driwood Period Mouldings is one of the major suppliers of such basic woodwork. Illustrated, in order of appearance, are four of many styles available: a simple egg and dart design made up of two mouldings (#2138 and #2137, Assembly CA-7), a one-piece moulding which projects quite far—$2^3/_{16}''$ (#2061), a traditional bead design (#2120), and an acanthus pattern (#2108).

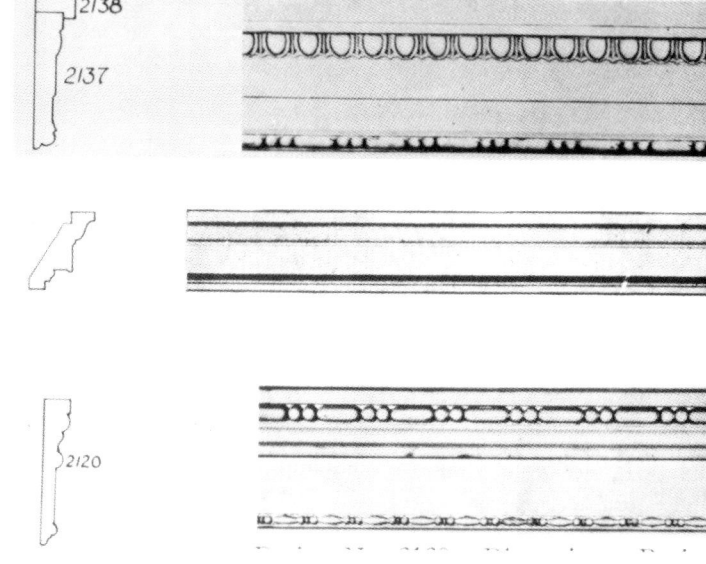

Casings are shipped in random lengths from 4' to 16', but you can request specific lengths. All are stocked in poplar. Work in other woods is done on a custom basis.

Catalog available, $1.

Driwood Moulding Co.
P.O. Box 1729
Florence, S.C. 29503
(803) 662-0541 or 669-2478

Old World casings are slightly more inventive, but no less traditional than those of Driwood. Illustrated are three examples of their work: an egg and dart and flower frieze pattern (#1061), a formal design of geometric patterns (#1042), and a simple casing which makes use of a rope moulding (#1092A). Many of these casings are appropriate for chair rails as well as windows and doors. Poplar is used by Old World, and their random lengths run from 8' to 16'.

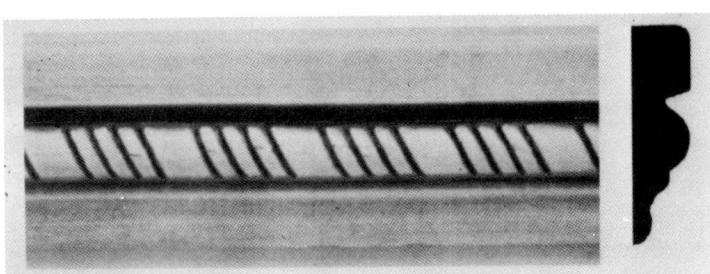

Catalog available.

Old World Moulding
115 Allen Blvd.
Farmingdale, N.Y. 11753
(516) 822-2280

Fretwork Mouldings

Fancy carved and embossed woodwork is frequently found in Victorian homes. This is sometimes termed "gingerbread," a term that refuses to die away. Bendix supplies three different embossed mouldings in hardwood and six overlay mouldings in complicated patterns in birch plywood.

Catalog available, $1.

Bendix Mouldings, Inc.
235 Pegasus Ave.
Northvale, N.J. 07647
(201) 767-8888

Exceptional fretwork panels are available from Victorian Reproductions. These are often used with open cut medallions and spandrils. They are made from oak, a wood especially popular in the late-Victorian period.

Literature available.

Victorian Reproductions
1601 Park Ave. S.
Minneapolis, Minn. 55404
(612) 338-3636

Wainscoting and Baseboard

There is usually no reason to contact a specialty firm for materials of this sort. The paneling of a lower part of a wall is usually no more difficult a job for the average woodworker/carpenter than any other type of panel work. Baseboarding is even simpler and may be only slightly more than a shoe moulding. But there are sometimes special requirements—especially in houses of the late nineteenth century—which call for an expert. The woodwork in a formal Victorian room can consist of as many as five or six components on one wall surface. Each must blend with the other in perfect proportion.

San Francisco Victoriana has mastered the skills and acquired the historical knowledge necessary to help the old-house restorer. In San Francisco alone, this firm has undertaken the restoration of over seventy homes. Their reputation has grown nationally, and they are prepared to provide redwood materials just about wherever they are needed.

There are two basic types of wainscoting available: 54″ tongue and groove (as illustrated in type F) and 72″ batten winscoting. San Francisco Victoriana can supply you with much information regarding these styles— when they were used in the San Francisco area and elsewhere, how they should be assembled and installed, what lengths are available, the number of components, etc.

Baseboards are much simpler in design and consist of no more than two units—a board and a cap. Several different styles are illustrated here from the Victoriana catalog. None extend up the wall more than a foot.

type D Baseboards

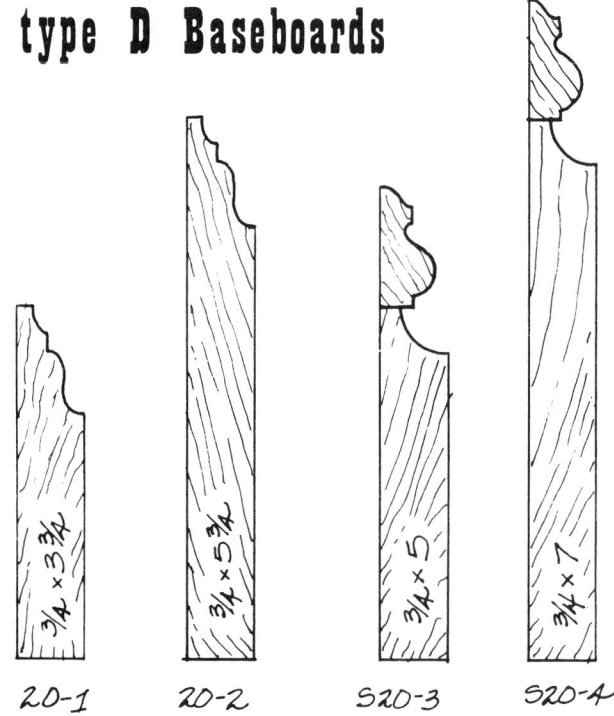

Book of Architectural Mouldings, $1.

San Francisco Victoriana
606 Natoma St.
San Francisco, Calif. 94103
(415) 864-5477

Carved Paneling

Paneling itself is dealt with in the first section of this book on structural materials. Although not properly construction work or in any way related to supporting walls, paneling has come to be regarded as an integral part of the basic fabric of a structure in the same manner as lath, or, as a more recent example, sheetrock. This leaves, then, only very special kinds of decorative paneling for consideration. Alan Amerian's hand-carved panels are carefully designed and wrought. Unfortunately, the photograph affords only a dim view of his work. Although rarely encountered in American homes, there is ample historical precedent for the use of

plaster

type F

highly decorative woodwork of this sort in homes built from the 1880s until the 1920s.

Amerian Woodcarving
282 San Jose Ave.
San Jose, Calif. 95125
(408) 294-2968

Wood Brackets, Incised Panels, Appliqué, and Corner Blocks

Most of these ornamental devices are sawn or molded and do not involve the considerable amount of time required by hand-carving. Nevertheless, they are out-of-the-ordinary kinds of items which call for skill and patience. Exterior porch and belt course brackets (which can also be used inside) are made of redwood by Hallelujah Redwood. Two of the basic designs are illustrated, the belt course being the simpler of the two.

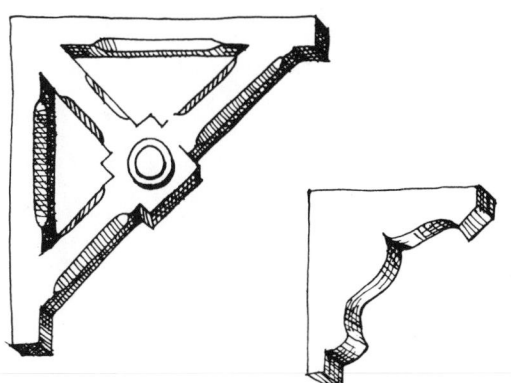

Incised panels and appliqués are other Hallelujah specialties which call for expertise. A sample of an appliqué block is seen at left; a panel at right.

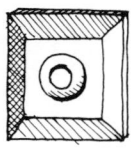

Catalog available, $1.

Hallelujah Redwood Products
39500 Comptche Rd.
Mendocino, Calif. 95460
(707) 937-4410

Corner blocks of various kinds are often found as part of door and window casings from the earliest Victorian buildings to those of the turn of the century. These are one-piece mouldings which incorporate circular patterns as simple as a bull's-eye and as fanciful as a rosette. Woodwork of this sort was standard fare in the 1800s. San Francisco Victoriana has helped us return to it.

Book of Architectural Mouldings available, $1.

San Francisco Victoriana
606 Natoma St.
San Francisco, Calif. 94103
(415) 864-5477

Composition Brackets and Capitals

To examine the catalog that Decorators Supply devotes to these elements is to lose momentarily a sense of time and place. What Kenneth Lynch has achieved in period metalwork, Decorators has more than supplied in wood fiber. Many home owners may have little reason to request such decorative pieces, but these pieces do exist and they are used in churches, theaters, government buildings, and in private residences of considerable scale and elegance. The illustrations can provide only a suggestion of the rich variety of forms and designs offered.

ters, several of which are illustrated. Other architectural antiques firms may be similarly stocked.

Brochures available.

Gargoyles, Ltd.
312 S. Third St.
Philadelphia, Penn. 19147
(215) 629-1700

Very simple new balusters are available through Bendix. The seven stock sizes—from 13″ to 30″ in length, and from 1⅜″ to 2½″ in diameter—are shown here.

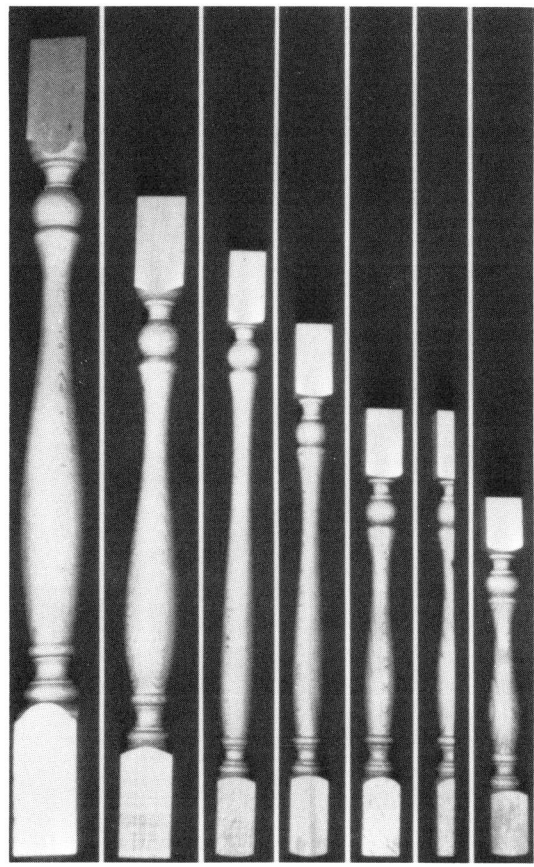

Catalog available, $1.

The Decorators Supply Corp.
3610-12 S. Morgan St.
Chicago, Ill. 60609
(312) 847-6300

Balusters

Turned rails known as balusters or banisters are often the victim of unruly children and shaky adults. These frail reeds are easy enough to split, but very difficult to repair. Gargoyles has a limited supply of antique balus-

Catalog available, $1.

Bendix Mouldings, Inc.
235 Pegasus Ave.
Northvale, N.J. 07647
(201) 767-8888

Metal Ornaments

This is Kenneth Lynch territory. No one can offer more than he, and the best we can do is to illustrate some of the many varieties of brackets and modillions, shells and shields, panel ornaments such as wreaths and garlands, scrolls, crestings, mitres, rosettes, urns and balusters, capitals, drops, and pinnacles. Then there are finials, pediments, eagles, gargoyles and caryatids, bows, festoons, ribbons.

At the same time, we should mention that Lynch can also provide metal mouldings which could be used to great effect with the stamped metal ceilings catalogued in the first section of this book on structural materials.

A book, Architectural Sheet Metal, *cataloguing 2,000 items, is available in paperback, $2.50.*

Kenneth Lynch & Sons
78 Danbury Rd.
Wilton, Conn. 06897
(203) 762-8363

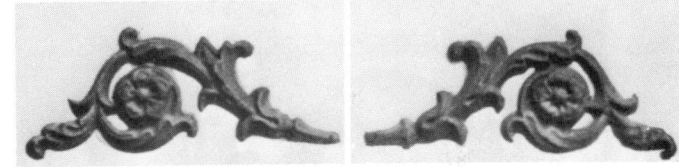

Plaster Ornaments

You've seen these before—on late nineteenth-century buildings in cities throughout the country. They were made of stone or of terra cotta, and many have either been ripped to the ground or fallen victim to pollution. Artist Pat Dunn is making copies in plaster, and you may prefer to keep these indoors. Illustrated is a design termed "Renaissance Man."

Catalog available, $1.50.

Architectural Ornaments
P.O. Box 115
Little Neck, N.Y. 11363
(212) 321-4159

Decorators Supply's plaster ornaments are truly splendid. Their castings are made of hard plaster of Paris which has been reinforced with hemp fiber and steel rods when necessary. As with Kenneth Lynch's products, they are nearly impossible to catalog. Every possible nuance of style appears to be represented—Classical, Gothic, Byzantine, Renaissance, Elizabethan, Tudor, Colonial, Victorian, Art Nouveau and even Art Moderne. There are grilles, rosettes, centers, panels, festoons, shields, wreaths, pineapples, eagles, urns, shells, columns, ribbons, pediments, corner decorations.

Catalog on plaster ornaments available, $1.

The Decorators Supply Corp.
3610–12 S. Morgan St.
Chicago, Ill. 60609
(312) 847-6300

Felber Studios is a more limited, but no less accomplished manufacturer of plaster ornaments. Including the ceilings and cornices, there are over 8,000 models to choose from. That should be enough for anyone. Niches and shells, centers, and cartouches are among their stock offerings.

Catalog available.

Felber Studios
110 Ardmore Ave.
Ardmore, Penn. 19003
(215) MI2-4710

Such different plaster ornaments as rosettes, corbels, and modillions are reproduced by the Larimer Dry Goods Co. There are twenty different rosette styles. The firm also makes available six different cresting styles cast in either iron or aluminum.

Catalog available, $1.

Larimer Dry Goods Co.
Attn.: RLC/RS
P.O. Box 17491 T.A.
Denver, Colo. 80217

In addition to their fine redwood work, San Francisco Victoriana is also a supplier of plaster brackets and centerpieces, including rosettes. Ornamentation of this sort may be needed in any late-Victorian building which has been substantially altered. When ceilings have been lowered or otherwise changed for modern lighting, much of the past may have become obliterated.

Price list available.

San Francisco Victoriana
606 Natoma St.
San Francisco, Calif. 94103
(415) 864-5477

Wood and Wood Fiber Ornamentation

Nearly every supplier of millwork offers some sort of decorative embellishment which will enrich a period interior. Decorators Supply's wood fiber carvings duplicate in large part what is offered in plaster, but those of wood are especially useful for mantels, cabinets, and such architectural details as pediments. Hallelujah

Redwod products offers strips of repeating ornament which would be useful as edging on shelves. San Francisco Victoriana and Driwood Period Mouldings supply plate rail mouldings. Driwood also has window drapery cornices in six different styles; the "Jenny Lind" is illustrated here.

Consult previous entries for addresses or see List of Suppliers.

Other Suppliers of Woodwork Materials

See List of Suppliers for addresses.

Lumber

Bangkok Industries
Castle Burlingame
Albert Constantine & Son
Craftsman Lumber
Harris Manufacturing
MacBeath Hardwood

Veneers

Architectural Paneling
Bangkok Industries
Albert Constantine & Son
Janovic/Plaza
Noel Wise Antiques

Crown Mouldings

Architectural Paneling
Decorators Wholesale Hardware

J. di Christina & Sons
Driwood Moulding
House of Moulding
Old World Moulding
Walter E. Phelps
Preservation Resource Center

Carved Wood Mouldings

Minnesota Woodworkers Supply

Casings

Driwood Moulding
Old World Moulding
San Francisco Victoriana

Wainscoting and Baseboard

Accent Walls
Bendix Mouldings
Castle Burlingame
Craftsman Lumber
Driwood Moulding
Guyon, Inc.
Maurer & Shepherd
Old World Moulding

Balusters/Railings/Spindles

California Wood Turning
Haas Wood and Ivory Works
Hallelujah Redwood Products
Minnesota Woodworkers Supply
Walter E. Phelps
Preservation Resource Center

Metal Cornices

AA Abingdon Ceiling
Barney Brainum-Shanker Steel
Guilfoy Cornice Works

Plaster Ornamentation

Gianetti Studios

Wood and Wood Fibre Ornaments

Bendix Mouldings
K.B. Moulding
Minnesota Woodworkers Supply

Columns and Capitals

Hartmann Sanders
A. F. Schwerd Manufacturing
Western Art Stone

III Hardware

Hardware is a fascinating and endless subject to explore. Locks, latches, pulls, and hinges are among the most functional objects in any house and can be among the most decorative. Unless hardware is of a bright, brassy sort, however, few people are going to stop to exclaim over basically utilitarian pieces of metal. Good hardware remains semi-hidden and should blend in with the general style of the dwelling itself.

Quality material lies at the heart of the hardware problem. Today it is difficult to find solid brass, heavy iron, and substantial carved wood fixtures. The best of the metal is hand-forged. The worst is stamped out in a thin manner. Pieces of wood are sometimes little more than composition. Until fairly recently, one could depend on the services of a local hardware supplier, but stores of this type are quickly disappearing to be replaced by supermarkets offering only a limited selection of second-rate materials. If you are fortunate enough to live in an area where a true-to-life hardware dealer can still make a livelihood, by all means strike up a friendship. But what to do in those many places where you are on your own?

Buy through the mail, visit wrecking yards, sift through the junk at secondhand furniture stores, ask antique dealers to help you find old architectural and furniture hardware. There is a surprising amount of stuff "out there." Hardware is less likely to have been thrown away and lost forever than other building supplies. Because of its weight and substance, it is also less likely to have decomposed with age. Rust remover may be all that it takes to make an old piece useful again.

Commercial imitations of period hardware are immensely popular. Most are not worth the metal from which they are formed. As Henry and Ottalie Williams wrote in a pioneer work on restoring old houses, "Labored imita-tion is worse than frank and honest indifference to authenticity." Nevertheless, the "rustic" look in imitations is favored today. This might be, for instance, an iron hinge which has been "aged" by hammering and then painted a jet black. When applied to a door or cabinet, such a bogus antique stands out like the proverbial sore thumb. Once paint began to be used in the interior of a house during the early to mid-eighteenth century, authentic hardware of this sort was painted over. It did not dominate the pieces to which it was attached. This is not true, of course, of doorknobs or knockers of brass or even of some iron latches. Many latches, however, as this writer has discovered in his own house, were routinely painted in the past.

To add insult to injury, hardware appropriate for a Colonial-style dwelling—strap hinges of various sorts, sliding door bolts, Suffolk latches—is frequently used on later-style buildings. Hardware styles kept pace with technology—even in the simple blacksmith's shop—and forms common to one age gave way to "improvements" of another. Thus, the strap hinge was replaced by the H and H-L; the Suffolk latch by Blake's cast-iron model. Only in the deepest recesses of the countryside did practice lag far behind technology.

Until recently no one bothered too much with Victorian reproduction hardware; it was too easily found in junk yards, barns, and attics; even as recent in time as two years ago, very few reproduction hardware suppliers carried it in their catalogs. Now such quality firms as Ball and Ball, Horton Brasses, and Pfanstiel Hardware devote considerable space to such wares. The use of period hardware is slowly growing more sophisticated. The number of trained metalsmiths is also on the increase. The village blacksmith was deserving of poetic praise. Although his day will never come again, his tradition of good workmanship is worthy of being maintained.

Architectural Hardware

Almost every part of an old house is fitted with some sort of hardware, and many areas contain objects of iron, brass, or bronze which are made by blacksmiths or metalsmiths. A few well-maintained homes may still have examples of the original hardware on doors and windows. In most places, however, locks have been changed, latches removed, and hinges may have rusted away. If old hardware is still in place, every attempt should be made to recondition it. If this fails, a careful reproduction can be installed in its place. A number of suppliers can give you what you need at nominal prices.

Hinges

Hinges in mid-eighteenth-century homes (and on into the 1800s) were usually painted the same color as the door, and were less obtrusive than they are today. Common types include these H and H-L, foliated H, cross garnet, and butterfly hinges. All are offered in various sizes by Newton Millham.

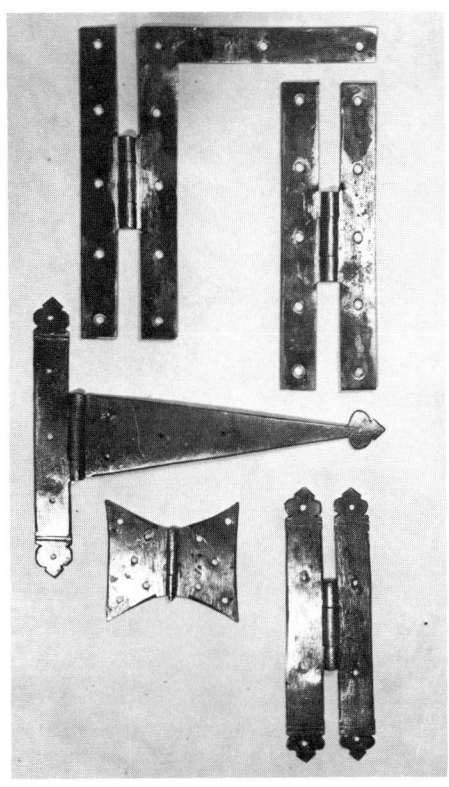

Brochure, $1.

Newton Millham-Star Forge
672 Drift Rd.
Westport, Mass. 02790
(617) 636-5437

Nearly everyone would like to find antique strap hinges. It is a relatively easy job to "antique" a reproduction, so be extra careful. The Cellar has some true antiques in stock, and so do other architectural antiques firms. Many originals were made of purer iron than today's reproductions and have resisted rust surprisingly well.

Information sheet available.

The Cellar
384 Elgin
Ottawa, Ontario
Canada
(613) 238-1999

Reproduction brass hinges are to be found at Horton Brasses, one of the traditional New England manufacturers of hardware. These should be used only where little stress is likely to occur. Larger iron strap hinges are also available. A 13″ butt type is $13.50 a pair.

Catalog available, $1.25.

Horton Brasses
P.O. Box 95, Nooks Hill Rd.
Cromwell, Conn. 06416
(203) 635-4400

Knobs

Various kinds of knobs can be bought separately from locks. Round and oval reproductions in brass and porcelain are available from Baldwin. Pfanstiel's line of new materials is far more ornate and includes some unusual decorative items, including very elaborate handles.

Brochures are available from Baldwin, 50¢.

Baldwin Hardware
841 Wyomissing Blvd.
Reading, Penn.
(215) 777-7811

Catalog available, $2.

H. Pfanstiel Hardware Co.
Jeffersonville, N.Y. 12748
(914) 482-4445

Antique knobs are still in plentiful supply, especially in the warehouses of such architectural antiques collectors as Materials Unlimited.

Materials Unlimited
4100 Morgan Rd.
Ypsilanti, Mich. 48197
(313) 434-4300

Knockers

There is nothing quite so ludicrous as a huge traditional brass knocker on a modern ranch house front door. This practice reminds us that decorative hardware is frequently misused. It is one of those "touches" which seem irresistible to the pretentious.

Large brass knockers of whatever variety are appropriate for only relatively high-style homes of the Colonial or Georgian style. More modest dwellings may have iron knockers. Many late-Victorian structures make use of pulls for mechanical bells.

The ever-popular Federal eagle knocker is cast in bronze by Steve Kayne. It is 8½″ x 3¾″ and sells for $20. Another bronze piece is in the form of a ring. Without the stud, it can be used as a door pull. It is priced at $12.

Catalogs available, $2.

Steve Kayne
17 Harmon Pl.
Smithtown, N.Y. 11787
(516) 724-3669

Dare we call this a striking object? This unique knocker is worked from polished steel. Robert Griffith will undertake a similar project only on a custom commission basis.

Robert Griffith, Metalsmith
16 S. Main St.
Trucksville, Penn. 18708
(717) 696-2395

A rather unusual knocker is sold by the Victorian supply house of Ritter and Son. It is a kissing couple—one partner on the doorplate, the other on the ring. Their busses can be heard through a closed door. The price is $5.

Catalog available, $1.

Ritter and Son Hardware
46901 Fish Rock Rd.
Anchor Bay (Gualala), Calif. 95445
(707) 884-3363

Latches/Bolts

Door latches of the eighteenth century reflect the creativity of local smiths who performed infinite variations on original English designs. Increasing numbers of very competent metalsmiths are now hammering out their own expressions for the trade in reproductions. The modern smiths are producing hardware which is appropriate for both public buildings and homes. Some of the ware is hand-forged; some is stamped out and then worked. The lore of the latch is rich and complex. Regional differences are considerable, and need to be studied by the serious student.

The bean latch was a common style throughout the Colonies and was still being made in the early 1800s. The illustrated version comes from Newton Millham's Star Forge and can be made in 6, 7, 8, and 9″ lengths.

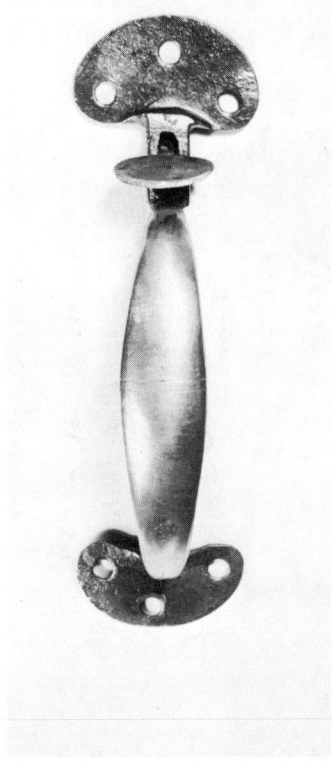

A more sophisticated, and therefore less common, device in the eighteenth century was the spring latch. Millham forges these in several sizes. The oval knob is made of brass.

This backlatch has a locking feature which holds the bar in the notch of the strike. The original piece was made in central Massachusetts in the mid-1700s.

Brochure available, $1.

Newton Millham-Star Forge
672 Drift Rd.
Westport, Mass. 02790
(617) 636-5437

Generally, thumb latches of an early period were called Suffolk latches, as opposed to Norfolk, and are distinguished by the wide, flattened portions at both ends of the handle called "cusps." Robert Griffith reproduces this early Suffolk for $45.

Door bolts provided greater security than latches in Colonial times. The same is true today. But don't be afraid to sacrifice authenticity for safety. If a reproduction is appropriate, Griffith's designs range from very simple to decorative. These examples sell for $25, $35, and $45.

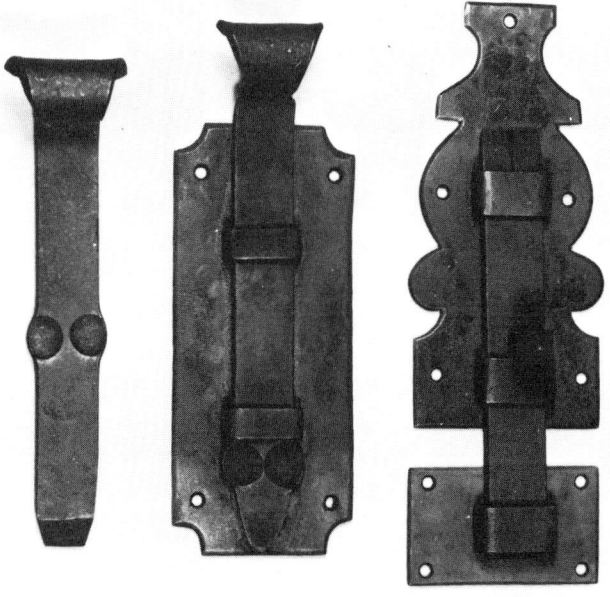

Catalog available, $1.

Robert Griffith, Metalsmith
16 S. Main St.
Trucksville, Penn. 18708
(717) 696-2395

Richard E. Sargent is another accomplished artisan. He produces a thumb latch which has arrowhead-shaped cusps. It's about 7″ long, and its $25 price includes nails and back group.

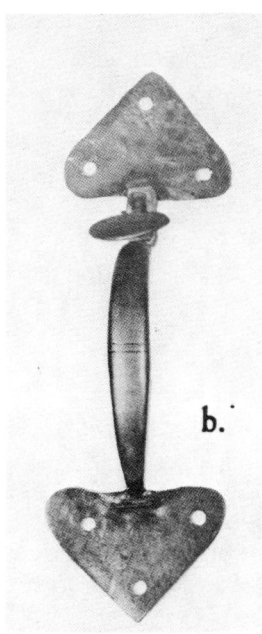

Catalog available, $2.

Richard E. Sargent
Hartland Forge
Box 83
Hartland Four Corners, Vt. 05049
(802) 436-2537

Complete latch sets are available for $13.50 from Horton Brasses. Each piece has a smooth finish and is painted flat black.

Catalog available, $1.25.

Horton Brasses Co.
Box 95, Nooks Hill Rd.
Cromwell, Conn. 06416
(203) 635-4400

Letter Plates

Noel Wise has both a wrought-iron and a solid-brass letter plate. Your choice will probably depend on the door's other hardware. The iron plate is rather ornate and sells for $17.50; the brass is priced at $30.

Catalog available, $1.

Noel Wise Antiques
6503 St. Claude Ave.
Arabi, La. 70032
(504) 279-6896

Locks

There are hundreds, if not thousands, of varieties of locks used in the past, and a goodly number are still kicking around. While other parts of an old house were quickly disposed of, there was a reluctance to toss out something as intricate and useful as a lock. Many antiques dealers stock these quite routinely. And there are reproductions galore.

Outwardly, the brass rim locks produced by Baldwin resemble the Colonial originals from which they were copied. Internally, the locks have been adapted to conform to contemporary security needs. Nevertheless, the locks are still operated with a skeleton key.

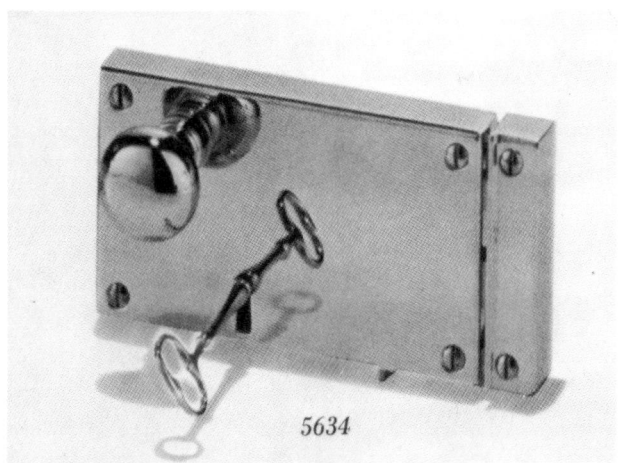

5634

Brochures, 50¢.

Baldwin Hardware
841 Wyomissing Blvd.
Reading, Penn. 19603
(215) 777-7811

Sash Lifts

It's a rarity to find a Victorian flush-mounted sash lift without several coats of paint on it. These are removed easily enough. But if the lift itself is missing, you can turn to several manufacturers for a reproduction. Ball and Ball has brass copies 3″ x 1⅜″ for $18.50 each.

Catalog available, $2.

Ball and Ball
463 W. Lincoln Hwy.
Exton, Penn. 19341
(215) 363-7330

Shutter Hardware

Shutter fasteners, or dogs, are utterly simple in function, but our forebears could not resist embellishing them on the forge. The four shown here were fashioned by Newton Millham. They are typical of shutterdogs found from New England down through the Mid-Atlantic states.

Brochure, $1.

Newton Millham-Star Forge
672 Drift Rd.
Westport, Mass. 02790
(617) 636-5437

Snow Guards

Snow guards, snow brakes, snow birds—whatever you choose to call them—perform both decorative and practical functions. They are attractive additions to almost any roof line and serve to break the fall of snow. Architectural antiques dealers usually stock the originals. Kenneth Lynch is surely the leading reproduction manufacturer in the field. His stock includes a score of different designs, such as the classic eagle, 5″ high and 6″ wide. It comes in cast brass, bronze, lead, or iron. According to Mr. Lynch, the iron model is bought mostly by collectors.

Lynch has a special brochure available on all models.

Kenneth Lynch & Sons.
Box 488, 78 Danbury Rd.
Wilton, Conn. 96897
(203) 762-8363

Bathroom Hardware and Fixtures

We remain adamantly opposed to dolling up the bathroom. If you already have a room which is fitted out with antique fixtures that work, keep them in place. They may require some cleaning up, perhaps even a new application of porcelain. Or if the bathroom in your new old house is in complete shambles, you will have to start anew and might as well consider something that fits the general decor. But if you are fortunate enough to have a perfectly fine modern bathroom, leave it as it is, adding only a bit here and there to take away the medicinal look. For some strange reason, the bathroom can become the kitsch-est room in the house, new or old. Perhaps it is our modern tendency to spray away any evidence of natural human functions. In any case, please don't tart up the john with a wicker throne for a toilet or covers for everything in sight.

Toilet Seats

Don't laugh. It can be hard to find a good seat that won't crack or slide away underneath you. The new foam jobs are not to be believed. They are hardly better than the plastic seats which yellow and crack in a wink.

Northwood, New Hampshire, seems to be the wooden toilet seat capital of America. Here you can find two firms—Shepherd Oak Products and Fife's Woodworking & Manufacturing Co.—that specialize in sturdy seats. Those from Fife are available in oak ($39.50), pine ($35), or mahogany ($58). You must specify light or dark in each case. Brass hinges are supplied. Shepherd Oak provides both a regular—illustrated here—

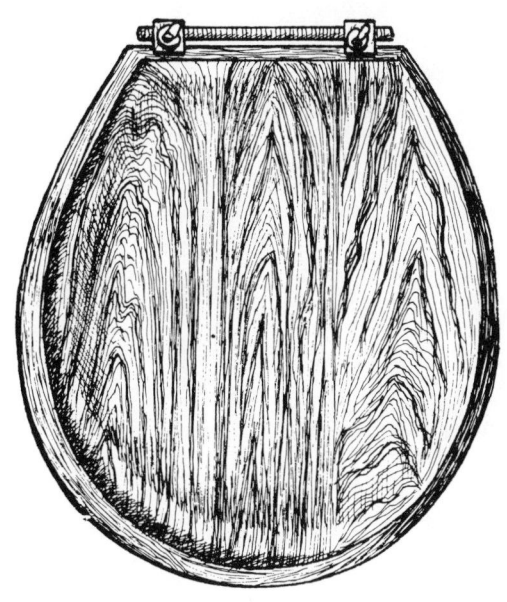

and an elongated seat for $53 and $58, respectively. These are of golden dark oak, and come with brass or chrome hinges and brass mounting screws.

Literature supplied by both firms.

Shepherd Oak Products
P.O. Box 27
Northwood, N.H. 03261
(603) 942-8148

Fife's Woodworking & Mfg. Co.
Rte. 107
Northwood, N.H. 03261
(603) 942-8339

A California firm, Heads Up, also supplies solid oak seats which will fit all standard toilets.

Brochure available.

Heads Up, Inc.
3201 W. MacArthur Blvd.
Santa Ana, Calif. 92704
(714) 549-8903

Toilets

If your bathroom has to be reconstructed, you might want to consider installing a pull chain toilet. Remember, these fixtures are not very silent. But they are efficient. An old-fashioned toilet of this sort will use only two gallons of water a flush, rather than eight. Sunrise Specialty outlets have the new reproductions, and Sunrise Salvage stocks the old originals. The new model #1 has an oak box which is fitted with a copper tank liner and an oak seat fitted to a porcelain base. All the fittings are brass.

Sunrise Specialty provides a brochure and has two showrooms:

Sunrise Specialty
The Galleria
101 Kansas St., Rm. 224
San Francisco, Calif. 94103
(415) 552-4148

Sunrise Specialty
8705 Santa Monica Blvd.
Los Angeles, Calif. 90069
(213) 652-3741

Sunrise Salvage
2210 San Pablo Ave.
Berkeley, Calif. 94710
(415) 845-4751

Restoration and Reincarnation Co. offers a useful service to residents of the San Francisco area. They will resurface an old toilet, bathtub, sink, or other fixture in your home or apartment. The charge for a toilet is $125 and up; a sink, $100 and up; and a tub, $250 or more. The firm also re-surfaces wall tile.

Literature available.

Restoration & Reincarnation Co.
250 Austin Alley
San Francisco, Calif. 94109
(415) 495-3233

Hardware

The hardware required for an old-style sink may not be any less drippy if it is antique, but it may be more fitting. Without a doubt, paper holders, bars, and rings of wood or solid brass will be sturdier and more attractive than those of plastic or lucite.

Broadway Supply Company features several different lines of bathroom hardware in their "Heritage Collection." In the "Old Dominion Suite" there are solid brass towel bars in three sizes (18, 24, and 30″), a towel ring, and robe hook. The toothbrush and tumbler holder, soap dish, and paper holder are of solid brass and porcelain.

Literature available.

Broadway Supply Company
7421 Broadway
Kansas City, Mo. 64114
(816) 361-3674

Shepherd Oak's basic accessory fixtures are of solid oak and can be too much of a good thing, but they are plain as can be and appear to be indestructible.

Shepherd Oak Products
P.O. Box 27
Northwood, N.H. 03261
(603) 942-8148

The fixtures for sinks, tubs and showers which Sunrise Specialty features are of a very clean, handsome sort. Those for a sink are available in three basic types— widespread, 4″ center, or single-hole mixers—and are either all brass or a combination of china and brass.

Brochure available.

Sunrise Specialty
The Galleria
101 Kansas St., Rm. 224
San Francisco, Calif. 94103
(415) 552-4148

Sunrise Specialty
8705 Santa Monica Blvd.
Los Angeles, Calif. 90069
(213) 652-3741

Tubs and Sinks

Most people appreciate a good-sized tub and an amply proportioned wash basin. Those of an antique variety are usually considerably larger than modern versions. This is an especially curious situation when you realize that people are larger today and really do require larger fixtures. Instead, we are being squeezed down.

The National House Inn manufactures three types of cultured marble sinks which date in style from c. 1900— old enough to be interesting. One is a drop-in ($65), a second a corner top with integral bowl ($75), and the third a rectangular top with integral bowl ($95). Illustrated is the self-rimming drop-in model. All bowls measure 14″ in diameter.

Literature available.

The National House Inn
102 South Parkview
Marshall, Mich. 49068
(616) 781-7374

Heads Up's Bristol model wall-mounted oak sink with china bowl is an attractive, unfussy fixture. Above it in the illustration can be seen the "Concord" recess mounting medicine cabinet of oak and mirrored glass. The hardware for the sink is your responsibility.

Brochure available.

Heads Up, Inc.
3201 W. MacArthur Blvd.
Santa Ana, Calif. 92704
(714) 549-8903

Sunrise Specialty features this oak-rimmed clawfoot antique in their literature. How many others like it exist

today, no one knows. But there are are thousands of standard free-standing tubs to be found in salvage yards and through period architectural antiques specialists. If you are on the West Coast, you might start first with Sunrise. If not, then get in touch with one of a number of firms, including United House Wrecking Co. (Stamford, Conn.), Rotar Services (Dallas, Texas), Cleveland Wrecking Co. (offices across the country), and P & G New & Used Plumbing Supply Co. (Brooklyn, N.Y.). *See* List of Suppliers for addresses.

Furniture Hardware

Proper pulls, escutcheons, latches, hinges or other hardware fittings for furniture are made by both individual craftsmen and large companies. The demand is so great that there is ample room for both stamped and forged pieces. The focus here, however, is on the better handcrafted pieces. In most cases, they do not have to be custom made, but are readily available in various sizes. Until recently, it has been somewhat difficult to find reproduction Victorian ware, but that, too, is now commonly available.

Latches

Colonial period closet and cupboard latches are one specialty of Steve Kayne. There are two basic kinds—pigtail and knob—which are of solid cast brass. They are priced from $3 to $4 a set, depending on the type and on the size (which ranges from 3″ to 7″).

Catalogs available on Colonial hardware, $2.

Steve Kayne
17 Harmon Pl.
Smithtown, N.Y. 11787
(516) 724-3669

Ritter & Son offer a Victorian latch set of the sort that would be found on an ice box. Either righthand or lefthand sets are available, and each is made of solid brass and priced at $7.95.

Catalog available, $1.

Ritter & Son Hardware
46901 Fish Rock Rd.
Anchor Bay (Gualala), Calif. 95445
(707) 884-3363

Pulls/Drops

Ball and Ball has been making traditional William and Mary, Queen Anne, Chippendale, Hepplewhite, and French-style pulls and drops for many, many years. Illustrated is a series of the William and Mary fittings, dated c. 1860 to 1710. All, of course, are "brasses" made of real brass. They vary greatly from style to style in thickness. The hardware for mounting each differs as well.

There are many standard designs to choose from. If you are trying to match a particular type, then Ball and Ball insists that you send them an actual sample: "Whenever copies are required, please send your BEST plate as the sample, since the copies will be cast from it. . . ."

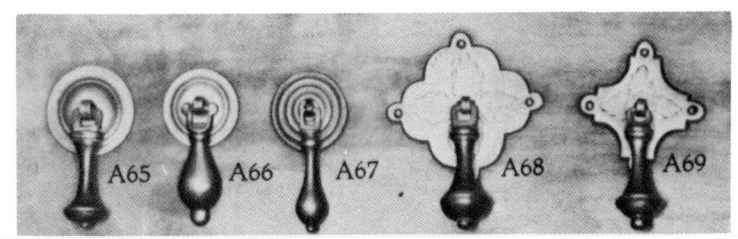

Drops and pulls of various styles, many of them appropriate for high-style French furniture, are available through Noel Wise Antiques. All of the hardware is solid brass and is offered in an antique or polished finish. These are reproduction pieces.

Ritter & Son offers the best cast and stamped late-Victorian dresser pulls that we have seen. They also supply bin pulls. A selection of some of their cast pull designs is illustrated here. They are of solid brass.

Horton Brasses is one of the last traditional New England hardware manufacturers and supplies many essential needs. Colonial-style pieces are their specialty, but they are also very strong in Victorian hardware of the mid- to late-nineteenth century. Illustrated, in order of appearance, is a Victorian tear drop, a Victorian drawer pull, a Hepplewhite drawer pull, and a Chippendale drawer pull. All are of brass, the tear drop being of wood with a stamped brass back plate.

DP-1

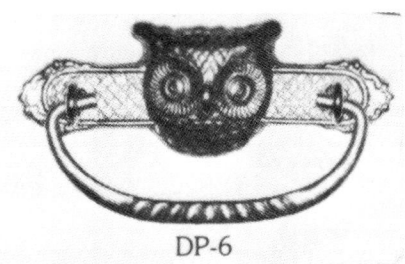

DP-6

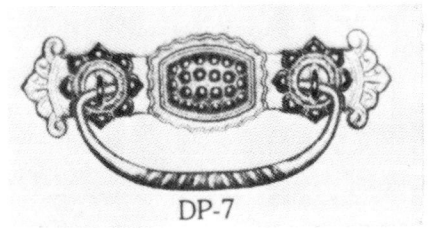

DP-7

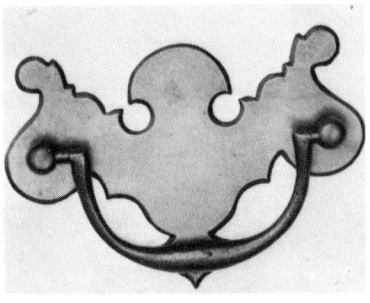

Catalog available, $1.25.

Horton Brasses
P.O. Box 95, Nooks Hill Rd.
Cromwell, Conn. 06416
(203) 635-4400

Knobs

Knobs of various sorts are useful for cupboards and drawers—antique or otherwise. Much country-style furniture has nothing but plain wood knobs, and, if you need replacements or additions, it might be simpler to ask a local woodworker to make them up. But there are other sorts, too, and you can contact Ball and Ball regarding their supply of original striped brown "Bennington" knobs. These are not reproductions, and the supply is dwindling. Ball and Ball is also a good source for glass, "compression bronze," and china-decorated knobs of the mid- to late 1800s. The reproduction of a "compression bronze" knob of the sort originally made by the Russell and Erwin Company is illustrated here.

Catalog available, $2.

Ball and Ball
463 W. Lincoln Hwy.
Exton, Penn. 19341
(215) 363-7330

Noel Wise Antiques supplies reproductions of stamped hollow and solid-brass knobs which are most suitable for Sheraton and early nineteenth-century pieces. The stamped brass face or rosette of each is very simple, but then most were.

Catalog available, $1.

Noel Wise Antiques
6503 St. Claude Ave.
Arabi, La. 70032
(504) 279-6896

Escutcheons and Roses

An escutcheon is used to frame a lock, and includes a keyhole. A rose is most often fitted to the outside of a cylinder—whether in a door or piece of furniture. Most door or furniture pulls come with roses. But they are available separately from H. Pfanstiel Hardware in quite wide variety. Three of the designs are illustrated here. As the manufacturer points out, "they provide the only effective and inexpensive means of converting old or commercial 'run of the mill' door hardware. These will eliminate the additional expense for carpentry work in plugging the old cylindrical lock hole which was previously a deterrent due to cost." The same principle holds for their use as replacements on furniture.

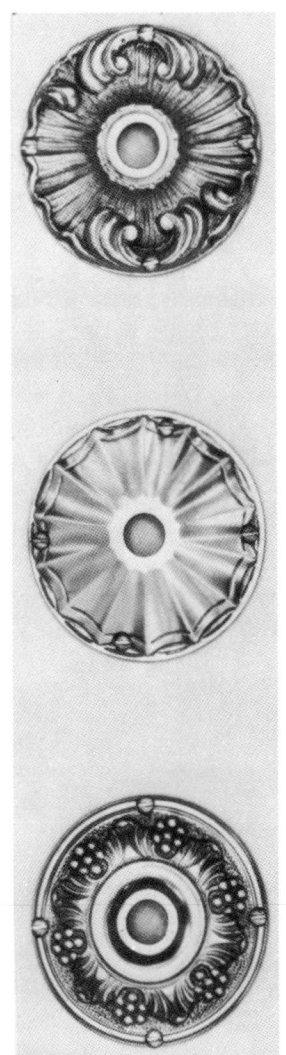

Catalog available, $2.

H. Pfanstiel Hardware Co., Inc.
Jeffersonville, N.Y. 12748
(914) 482-4445

Escutcheons of all sorts are available from Horton, but the Victorian styles are especially interesting. Several are illustrated, and each has a matching pull.

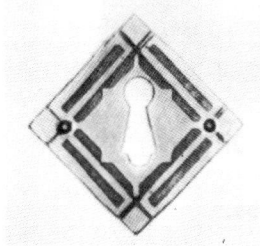

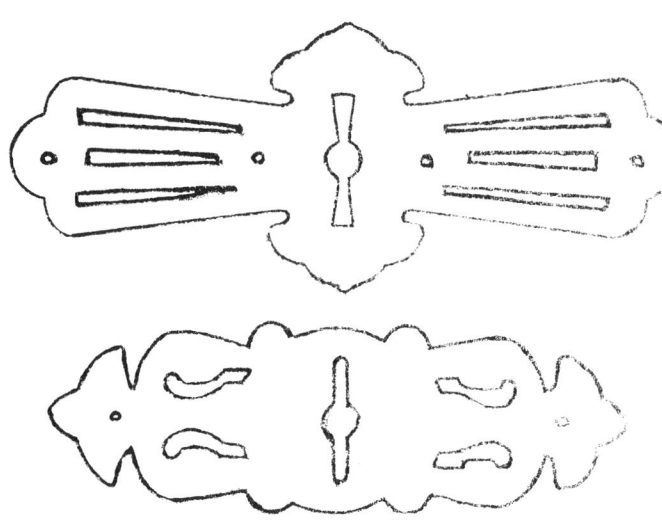

locks, a label holder, and a cast card frame pull. Carved drawer pulls of unfinished walnut are also available.

Catalog available, $1.

Noel Wise Antiques
6503 St. Claude Ave.
Arabi, La. 70032
(504) 279-6896

Catalog available, $1.25.

Horton Brasses
P.O. Box 95, Nooks Hill Rd.
Cromwell, Conn. 06416
(203) 635-4400

Kitchen and Miscellaneous Hardware

Blacksmiths and other traditional metalworkers produce a great number of useful objects which are also attractive to the kitchen and other areas of an old house. Some are hand-forged originals which cannot be found in hardware stores.

Hinges

Hinges for such different kinds of furniture as a slant front desk, tall case clock, a butler's tray, and a blanket chest are made by Ball and Ball. Stylistically, there are square, H and H-L, rattail, strap, harpischord, and butterfly hinges. Some are semi-handmade of iron; most are stamped or cast from brass.

Catalog available, $2.

Ball and Ball
463 W. Lincoln Hwy.
Exton, Penn. 19341
(215) 363-7330

Utensil and Pot Racks

Racks for the hanging of pots can be made in almost any size by an experienced blacksmith. J. R. Wallin offers two standard models, a round rack ($37) 20″ in diameter and a half-round ($32) which is 25″ wide. He also

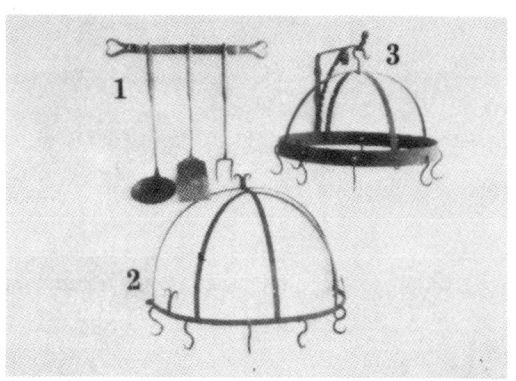

Roll-Top Desk Hardware

This is hardware of a very special sort, and Noel Wise Antiques can supply you with special escutcheons of solid brass, the designs of which are illustrated here—

custom makes other sizes and shapes. Illustrated here with the racks is his cooking utensil set ($35).

Catalog available, $2.

Wallin Forge
Rte. 1, Box 65
Sparta, Ky. 41086
(606) 567-7201

Robert Griffith is an accomplished metalsmith and primarily produces pieces of wrought iron. Most of his work is custom order only, including this handsome utensil rack.

Robert Griffith, Metalsmith
16 S. Main St.
Trucksville, Penn. 18708
(717) 696-2395

Trivets

No object is more folksy than a trivet. Those sold in gift shops are usually not worth their weight in iron, if, indeed, they contain any. Robert Griffith's stock trivet is a reproduction of an eighteenth-century wrought-iron Pennsylvania object. It is available in a black forge finish ($40) or polished ($50), as illustrated.

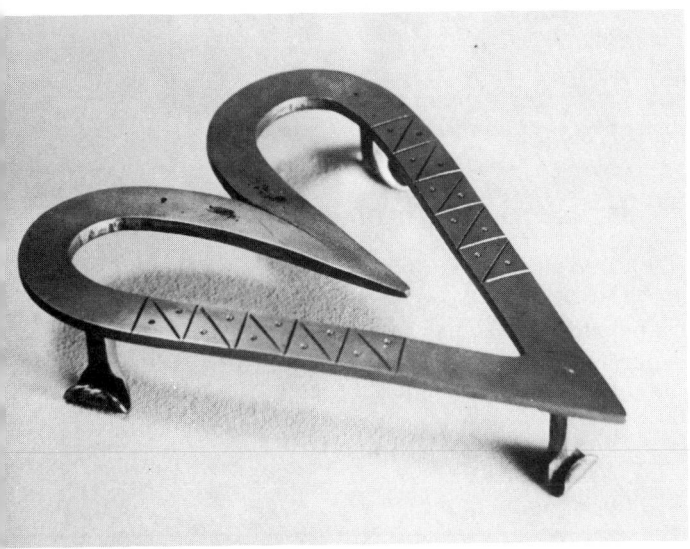

Robert Griffith, Metalsmith
16 S. Main St.
Trucksville, Penn. 18708
(717) 696-2395

Toasters

Newton Millham forges a number of different toaster models, but this is the most interesting. It is based on an eighteenth-century design and holds bread between finely twisted retainers and bent "flowers." When toasted, the bread has an unusual "brand."

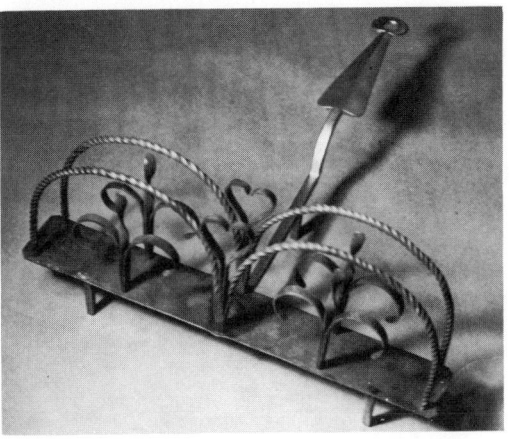

Catalog available.

Newton Millham-Star Forge
672 Drift Rd.
Westport, Mass. 02790
(617) 636-5437

Skewers, Fork, and Spoon

Inventive hand-forged hardware is the specialty of Steve Kayne. He is particularly interested in producing

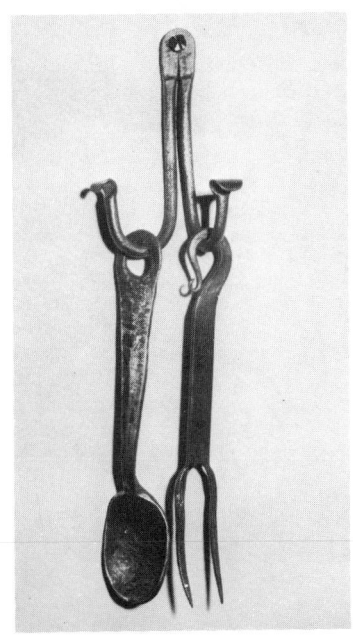

primitive Colonial pieces which can be used at home or out-of-doors. Illustrated are an eating fork and spoon on a hook rack and six skewers on a holder. The utensils are of the sort carried by soldiers many years ago.

Catalogs available, $2.

Steve Kayne
17 Harmon Pl.
Smithtown, N.Y. 11787
(516) 724-3669

Hooks

These most useful of small objects are produced by almost every blacksmith working today and serve a multitude of purposes. R. Hood & Co. offers a rugged 8″ wall hook for hanging plants ($7.50), a simple 4″ curled hook for attaching to the wall ($2), 5″ beam hooks which are either pointed for driving into the wood or drilled for screwing or nailing ($2.50), and a 4½″ ceiling hook ($2.75) which is flattened at the top for underside attachment. All are hand-forged of iron.

Literature available; send stamped and self-addressed envelope.

R. Hood & Co.
Heritage Village
Meredith, N.H. 03253
(603) 366-2200

Ritter & Son's hat hooks, some illustrated here, are of solid brass. The most interesting are of Victorian design, and all are well fashioned. These range in price from $1.35 to $4.50.

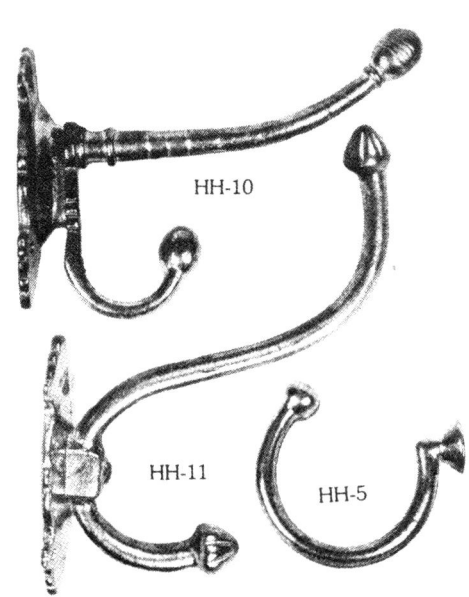

HH-10

HH-11

HH-5

Catalog available, $1.

Ritter & Son Hardware
46901 Fish Rock Road
Anchor Bay (Gualala), Calif. 95445
(707) 884-3363

Among the special hooks made by Steve Kayne are those used to hang a musket or rifle. There is also a hook or spike which can be used for hanging a lantern from a tree or beam, a trammel hook which can be raised and lowered, and a spice hook from which herbs, spices, and tobacco were hung in the barn.

Catalogs available, $2.

Steve Kayne
17 Harmon Pl.
Smithtown, N.Y. 11787
(516) 724-3669

Brackets and Other Hangers

Pete Taggett makes wall hangers of many varieties. Some can be used for plants or lighting fixtures; a few may be appropriate for signs. All are hand-forged iron.

Catalog available, $1.

Pete Taggett
Box 15
Mt. Holly, Vt. 05758
(802) 259-2452

Hand-crafted wrought-iron brackets are available from G. W. Mount, Inc. The plainest are made for shelves and are drilled both for wall mounting and shelf fastening. These reach out either 6, 8, or 12″.

Brochure available.

G. W. Mount, Inc.
P.O. Box 306
576 Leyden Rd.
Greenfield, Mass. 01301
(413) 773-5824

Nails, Keepers, Staples

Illustrated is a wide variety of fasteners made by blacksmith Newton Millham. Hardware of this sort was once a stock item in any hardware or general store. It is too expensive to use extensively, but you may find that it is suitable for replacement purposes here or there.

Catalog available, $1.

Newton Millham-Star Forge

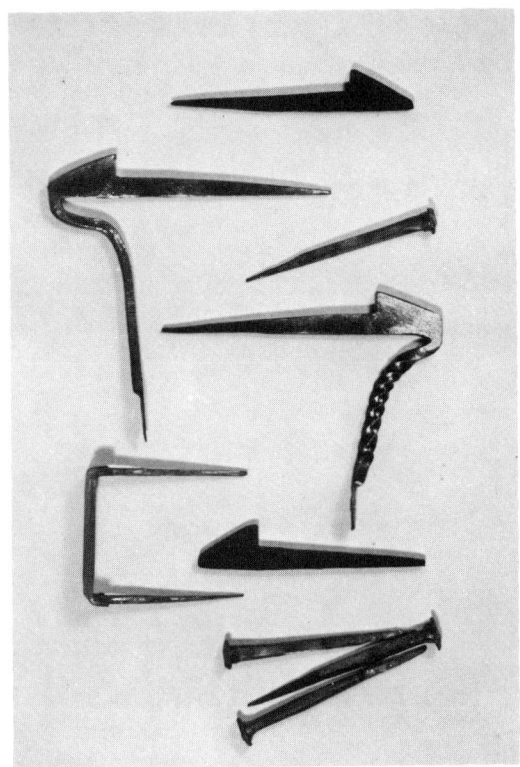

672 Drift Rd.
Westport, Mass. 02790
(617) 636-5437

Don't forget the Tremont Nail Co. This firm was written up extensively in the first *Old House Catalogue* and is the major supplier of old-style cut nails—cut spike, masonry, foundry, common siding, finish, clout, box, hinge, slating—and on and on. The company has been in business since 1819.

Literature available.

Tremont Nail Co.
P.O. Box 111
Wareham, Mass. 02571
(617) 295-0038

Tools

If you've looked through a tool supplier's catalog, you've probably found dozens of handy gadgets for performing tasks you never thought of doing. Did you know that you could get a hand-held tool for turning your own bed springs? Indispensable! But even the strangest devices can often mean the difference between a quality job and a merely adequate one. There are several excellent sources for quality mail-order tools. It might be worthwhile to peruse the catalogs, if only for the fun of it. We wager that you'll wind up buying something that you really needed all along.

For example, Brookstone sells giant rubber bands. They are perfect for clamping together chair legs for glueing, because they don't go limp like cords or cloth straps and they resist slippage on uneven surfaces. Beechwood carpenter's mallets, chamfering spoke shaves, shavehooks, carbide drills for glass, tap and die sets for threading dowels—all have their specific functions and have either proved their worth over generations or have become available through advanced technology.

Catalog available.

The Brookstone Co.
127 Vose Farm Rd.
Peterborough, N.H. 03458
(603) 924-7181

Veneering supplies and all the necessary paraphernalia can be ordered from the Minnesota Woodworker's Supply Company. They have special tools like joint and strip cutters, punches, saws, and rollers. Their upholstery equipment includes a complete collection of necessary and helpful gadgets such as needles, spline chisels, and ripping tools. Minnesota also supplies clamps, hand screws, sanding devices, knives, plug cutters, and dado sets.

Catalog available, $1.

Minnesota Woodworker's Supply Co.
21801 Industrial Blvd.
Rogers, Minn. 55374
(612) 428-4101

Albert Constantine is also big on veneering and offers materials, kits, tools and many how-to books on a variety of crafts. Many of this supplier's tools can be found in any good hardware store, but not so the specialty items.

Catalog available, 50¢.

Albert Constantine and Son, Inc.
2050 Eastchester Rd.
Bronx, N.Y. 10461
(212) 792-1600

Hardware from the Woodcraft Supply Corp. should be of particular interest to carpenters and joiners, because this is such a good source for traditional tools. They have broad axes, hatchets, heads, bark spuds, and peaveys which are essential to log cabin builders. The collection of carving and turning tools is outstanding.

Catalog available, 50¢.

Woodcraft Supply Corp.
313 Montvale Ave.

Woburn, Mass. 01801
1-800-225-1153

What Woodcraft doesn't have for log cabin building, Frog Tool Co. probably does. The two-man saw and the pit saw are just two examples. Frog also offers dozens of full-length books and manuals from carpentry to blacksmithing.

Catalog available, 50¢.

Frog Tool Co., Ltd.
541 N. Franklin St.
Chicago, Ill. 60610
(312) 644-5999

The nineteenth-century format of the Cumberland General Store's catalog is as fetching as the items they sell. The tool sections are especially strong in logging, joinery and blacksmith needs. Anyone seeking basic tools for country living should turn to Cumberland.

Catalog available, $3.

Cumberland General Store
Rte. 3, Box 479
Crossville, Tenn. 38555
(615) 243-0063

Furniture and cabinetmakers might want to take note of the Universal Clamp Company's products. Their mini-clamp treats each joint individually, and this feature eliminates the need for cumbersome pipe clamps. The Porta-Press frame and door jig is lightweight and keeps the work square and flat.

Send large stamped, self-addressed envelope for free information.

Universal Clamp Co.
6905 Cedros Ave.
Van Nuys, Calif. 91405
(213) 780-1015

Other Sources for Hardware

Consult List of Suppliers for addresses.

Architectural

Hinges

Ball and Ball
Broadway Supply
Cohasset Colonials
Robert Griffith
R. Hood & Co.
San Francisco Victoriana
Wallin Forge
Williamsburg Blacksmith

Knobs

Broadway Supply
The Cellar
R. Hood & Co.
Ritter & Son
San Francisco Victoriana

Knockers

Ball and Ball
Horton Brasses
G. W. Mount
Period Furniture Hardware
Pfanstiel Hardware

Latches

Ball and Ball
R. Hood & Co.
Horton Brasses
Steve Kayne

Period Furniture Hardware
Wallin Forge

Letter plates

Baldwin

Locks

Ball and Ball
Folger Adam
Newton Millham
Period Furniture Hardware
San Francisco Victoriana
Noel Wise

Shutter Hardware

Ball and Ball
Steve Kayne
Period Furniture Hardware
Wallin Forge
Wrightsville Hardware

Window Hardware

Blaine Window Hardware
Period Furniture Hardware
Ritter & Son

Bath Hardware

Toilets

Heads Up
P & G New & Used Plumbing Supply

Faucets/Taps and Accessories

Bona
Kohler Co.
Materials Unlimited
Pfanstiel Hardware
P & G New & Used Plumbing Supply

Tubs and Sinks

Broadway Supply Co.
Kohler Co.
Mayfair China
Period Furniture Hardware

Furniture Hardware

Escutcheons and Roses

Period Furniture
Noel Wise

Hinges

Robert Griffith

Horton Brasses
Steve Kayne
Minnesota Woodworkers Supply
Period Furniture Hardware
Richard E. Sargent

Knobs

Horton Brasses
Minnesota Woodworkers Supply
Period Furniture Hardware

Latches

Ball and Ball
Robert Griffith
R. Hood & Son
Horton Brasses
Period Furniture Hardware

Pulls/Drops

Broadway Supply
Albert Constantine & Son
Steve Kayne
Minnesota Woodworkers Supply
Period Furniture Hardware
Pfanstiel Hardware

Roll-Top Desk Hardware

Ball and Ball

Kitchen Hardware

Hooks

Broadway Supply
G. W. Mount
Richard E. Sargent
Pete Taggett

Toasters

Richard E. Sargent

Trivets

Steve Kayne

Utensil and Pot Racks

G. W. Mount
Pete Taggett

Miscellaneous

Nails/Staples

Ball and Ball
Cohasset Colonials
R. Hood & Son
Woodcraft

Raised-panel fireplace wall with "floating" mantel shelf by
Townsend H. Anderson. *See* page 41.

IV   Fireplaces & Heating

Everyone who wants to stop waste in our society—from the destruction of old houses to the leveling of hillsides on which they stand—agrees that energy is at the heart of the problem. Preservationists and environmentalists have a great deal in common, and in no area is this most strikingly illustrated than in heating. A recent Herblock cartoon showed a wreck of a Victorian house with a "for sale" sign outside. The real estate sign noted that the building contained four wood-burning fireplaces and went with an acre of woodland. The offering price *had* been $10,000; slapped over the old price was a new one, $100,000, and beneath this in large block letters was the simple word—"Sold."

Like any good cartoon, the point has been exaggerated, but not to the point of ineffectiveness. Wood can be used at least as a supplementary fuel in many homes. It is an almost infinitely renewable alternative source if used with care in small towns and in the country. Wood-lot management has never been practiced with much care in America, but we are learning quickly that there are ways to maintain a good stand and supply of wood. In those cities where the burning of wood is allowed, its effectiveness and availability is limited. Technology must come to the rescue with new devices that will generate energy from wind power, the sun, and the burning of waste materials.

Many old houses and buildings are already energy efficient. Their exterior walls are thick, and rooms are divided one from another with more than plasterboard. A good growth of trees serves as a windbreak, and the structure itself is positioned in a way that it does not bear the brunt of northwest winds. The building of a house in this manner was a common practice and no one needed a consulting engineer to come up with a plan for saving fuel and money. To site a house properly, to provide it with a cover, to construct it of solid materials which withstand heat loss—these were matters of common sense and experience. To do the same thing today with a new building is a very expensive proposition. Many of the best sites are gone, planting of bushes and trees runs into the thousands of dollars, *real* wood is at a premium. Therefore, we need our old buildings even more than ever before. What was $10,000 ten years ago *may* be approaching the $100,000 level in the late 1970s.

This is not to say that all old houses are as snug as a bug in a rug. Modern forms of insulation provide an extra security blanket. Just a small amount of material blown into an attic floor may save considerably on the winter fuel bill and also serve to keep the floor below cool during the summer. Windows must be kept properly caulked and covered with more than shutters. Some rooms, especially in large and high-ceilinged Victorian structures, should probably be sealed off in the winter and the heat concentrated in those areas where it is of most use.

Anyone who lives in a house or apartment that contains fireplaces will certainly want to use them. Despite all the talk about how inefficient they are in providing heat to a room, this writer's experience is that the temperature may rise as much as 10 degrees in a half hour in a moderately-sized area without the use of any sort of modern gadgets. A cast-iron fireback will help to reflect heat out into the room as will a properly-proportioned firebox or opening. A solid damper is, of course, necessary for proper draft and heat flow.

There are, however, appliances of recent origin which will cut down on heat loss up the chimney. One of these—a special grate—is covered in the following pages. Of course you can always convert your fireplace, as many nineteenth-century Americans did, for a Franklin-type stove. It does seem a shame to do this. Unless your fireplace is already merely a disreputable hole in the wall, think of keeping the fireplace and installing in addition a free-standing stove that can be vented either through the chimney flue or a new outlet.

Wood and coal-burning stoves are all the rage. Antique fixtures once sold for practically nothing as no one could even figure out what to do with them. Now they may bring as much as $2,000. Reproduction stoves are sold everywhere along with newer types of models, some of the best from Scandinavia, which have been engineered to produce more BTU's more efficiently. As with any new field of commercial endeavor, the rip-off artists are at work. Before buying any heating device—merely for warming up a room or for cooking—be sure that it is of solid construction, is safe to use and can be properly installed in the space you have in mind.

The center of focus in many period rooms was the hearth. The appointments and furnishings, therefore, were designed and arranged in relation to this structural "given." It is curious that in the last part of the twentieth century we are again returning to the central concern of keeping warm. If we can keep our old buildings standing, those of us lucky enough to live in them should have no trouble at all.

Antique Mantels

A handsome mantel properly finishes off almost any fireplace. Most mantels will surround the fireplace on three sides and effectively frame it in the manner of a picture, but mantels may also be nothing more than a series of mouldings which form a shallow shelf at the top. More elaborate are those which consist of a series of levels and sculpted projections which form a veritable console. Mantels in old houses may be of wood, quarried stone (such as marble), cast iron, or ornamental plaster. Not every period structure, of course, contains fireplaces which have been framed by a mantel. Some of the earliest fireplace walls are simply paneled room ends.

The supply of "used" or antique mantels is quite good. The mantel is one of the first features of an old house to be saved when demolition is the only prospect in sight. Mantels were also removed in the nineteenth century

when fireplace openings were closed up for the installation of stoves. More than one fortunate old-house owner has found these stored in a barn or the attic. Others have found them in wrecking yards or architectural antiques supply houses in their area.

The New York showroom of William Jackson always displays a variety of antique mantels, from early American pine to imported marble. (Do not confuse this friendly company with another of a similar name which boasts the sale of only eighteenth-century mantels for use in estate houses.) William Jackson provides a much wider selection and documents its resources in a handsome brochure. The company has also reproduced many of its fine acquisitions in its own workshops.

Wm. H. Jackson Co.
3 East 47th St.
New York, N.Y. 10017
(212) 753-9400

A growing number of architectural antiques supply houses stock mantels as a matter of course. Gargoyles is a virtual general store. It makes a point of maintaining a variety of styles—from carved Jacobean to Art Nouveau to stately marble mantels.

Gargoyles, Ltd.
512 S. 3rd St.
Philadelphia, Penn. 19147
(215) 629-1700

Materials Unlimited operates a salvage operation with a late-Victorian influence, much of their supply coming from doomed Midwestern sources.

Materials Unlimited
4100 Morgan Rd.
Ypsilanti, Mich. 48197
(313) 434-4300

The Renovation Source is an architectural consulting service that specializes in restoration of pre-1930 buildings. Among its other virtues, it is a good source of mantels.

The Renovation Source, Inc.
3512-14 Southport
Chicago, Ill. 60657
(312) 327-1250

You'll find a regional influence at Old Mansions which is welcome almost anywhere. Most of their mantels come from early New England homes.

Old Mansions Co.
1305 Blue Hill Ave.
Mattapan, Mass. 02126
(617) 296-0737

Westlake is based in Texas and offers some marble pieces which are most appropriate for Victorian homes—wherever they are found.

Westlake Architectural Antiques
3315 Westlake Dr.
Austin, Texas 78746
(512) 327-1110

Victor Carl's focus is limited to fine eighteenth-century French and English mantels with a price range of $600 to $5,000.

Victor Carl Antiques
841 Broadway
New York, N.Y. 10003
(212) 673-8740

The classic Georgian has a 3' x 4'6" opening. You must add 15% to its $450 price tag if you prefer oak or walnut.

Reproduction Mantels

Reproduction mantels can be constructed with as much fidelity as the craftsman and his customer choose to indulge. Almost every material used in the past is available today, and a number of firms employ craftsmen who have retained the skills of yesterday. An old-house owner may wish to duplicate the style of a mantel found in several rooms and missing in another. The same style was often used over and over within the same building or even the geographic area in which a woodworker was active. The apartment dweller may need a particular kind of mantel for a living room furnished in a period manner. And even the owner of a new home built with one of the manufactured fireplaces, such as the Heatilator, may decide to tie his modern fireplace into a traditional setting.

Catalog available, 50¢.

Decorators Supply Corporation
36100 S. Morgan St.
Chicago, Ill. 60609
(312) 847-6300

Reproduction mantels have been produced for years by Decorators Supply. They not only provide individual customers with any number of different styles, but also supply other dealers with their fine products.

Among the mantels which can be ordered are models in poplar and birch. The one illustrated, the Adam, sells for $410 and is shipped with a prime coat of paint. It has a 3'6" x 4'3" opening. Special sizes increase the price by 15%.

Constructed in what is termed a Williamsburg style, this Readybuilt poplar mantel and paneling combination is 8' high and 7'6" wide. Most of Readybuilt's mantels have a 50" x 37½" opening. This one sells for a reasonable $430. It is appropriate, of course, for only Colonial-period interiors.

Readybuilt lives up to its name in supplying mantels designed especially to fit metal prefabricated built-in

fireplaces. The model illustrated is 47″ wide and the legs can be cut off to accommodate hearth heights less than 39″. It is finished in prime white and sells for $87.45.

Catalog, $1.

The Readybuilt Products Co.
P.O. Box 4306
Baltimore, Md. 21223
(301) 233-5833

Alan Amerian executes a number of different styles— Colonial, Federal, Georgian, Greek Revival, and—for the home in a more European style—Louis XV and Italian Renaissance. Each mantel requires skillful carving. Woods such as oak, walnut, cherry, mahogany, bass, and poplar are used. The handsomely-carved piece shown here would dignify any mid-Victorian home.

Brochure available.

Amerian Woodcarving
282 San Jose Ave.
San Jose, Calif. 95125
(408) 294-2968

Fireplace Accessories

Supplies for the fireplace constitute a world of objects distinctly different from any other. Andirons, tools, firebacks, brooms, pots and pans, cranes, tiles for facing, grates, scuttles, bellows, match safes, screens—the list goes on and on. The skills of blacksmiths, foundry craftsmen, brass and copper metalworkers, and other artisans are called for to supply useful and attractive objects. Fortunately, the services of such individuals are widely available. The decorative appeal of fireplace accessories survived even when the necessity for their use ebbed away.

It is unnecessary in a book of this sort to provide souces for many of these very common objects which can be found in hardware and furniture stores and in antique shops. Rather, it is more useful to spotlight some of the high-quality manufacturers and to mention some of their most exceptional products.

The mythical dispensers of charm and beauty are framed in this 30″ x 37″ iron fireback from Steptoe & Wife. You'll need a fireplace of nearly Olympic proportions to accommodate it. But if the opening is that large, you will need the radiating effect of a cast-iron fireback in order to draw some of the heat into the room.

The "Castle Fire" suggests a medieval setting. You won't have to put it in the hearth of a long and narrow mead hall, however, because it's small enough (18″ wide, 11″ deep) for the most modest fireplace. Both the fireback and the grate are available only from this innovative Canadian firm.

Catalog available, $1.

Steptoe & Wife Antiques Ltd.
3626 Victoria Park Ave.
Willowdale, Ontario M2H 3B2
(416) 497-2989

Common sense dictates that some form of screening separate the fire from the room. Three-panel folding screens are very popular and are usually less expensive than permanently-mounted sliding curtains or recessed screens. But where to find well-made screens? Lemee's, a major supply house of fireplace accessories, sells several with brass tubular trim and handles. The extended width of each is 52″. Prices range from $24 to $109.50.

Keep a match holder near your stove or fireplace. You'll always have a light handy but in a place removed from children's hands. Lemee's has several to choose from. One depicts Venus and Cupid on two receptacles. It is cast iron and has a serrated edge for striking. The price is $4.40.

Although many fireplace accessories are just excess baggage to clutter up living space, some utensils can enhance the enjoyment and usefulness of the hearth. Iron skillets are fairly easy to come by, but kettles of cast iron are not as common. Those from Lemee are not to be confused with the thin models available in gift shops and used as planters. These are kettles and pots that can be hung from a crane or, if footed, kept steady on the fire surface. An eight-quart pot with lid sells for $21.95. A two-quart cast-iron bulge pot with a brass handle is $21.50.

Catalog available, 50¢.

Lemee's Fireplace Equipment
Rte. 28, 815 Bedford St.
Bridgewater, Mass. 02324
(617) 697-2672

Keep the handles of your fireplace tools within easy reach with this brass jamb hook. And the appropriate device for the business end of a poker, tong, and shovel is a tool stone. It is 7″ square, 1½″ thick, and indented and grooved to keep the tools from sliding along the hearth. Both of these items are available from Ball and Ball, a company better known for its furniture and architectural hardware. The jamb hook sells for $21.75 and is one of many models; the stone is unique and is priced at $19.50

Catalog available, $2.

Ball and Ball
463 W. Lincoln Highway
Exton, Penn. 19341
(215) 363-7330

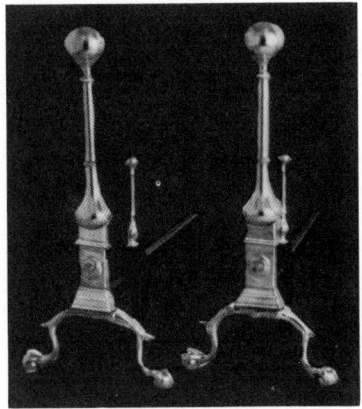

Andirons are as useful as the most modern of fireplace devices and can be found in every possible size and form. If you can't find an antique pair that will look right on the hearth, there are reproductions galore. These 20″ high solid-brass andirons are as handsome as any antique and carry the Historic Newport Reproduction label. They extend 21″. Virginia Metalcrafters makes them, and the price is handsome, too—$200. But, as the firm states about its whole line, "These products are intended for a discriminating clientele who appreciate craftsmanship 100 years behind the times." In this case, and we are grateful, they are about 200 years late.

Catalog available.

Virginia Metalcrafters
1010 E. Main St.
Waynesboro, Va. 22980
(703) 942-8205

As a purveyor of high-quality fireplace equipment since 1827, Wm. H. Jackson offers considerable flexibility when it comes to special needs. This 7″ high brass fender, for example, can be ordered in any length. Early fenders of this sort were imported from England, and American manufacture has always been limited.

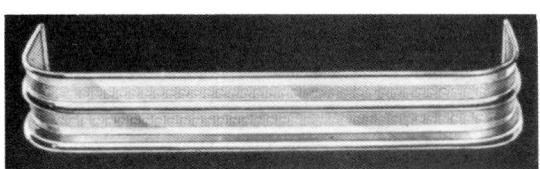

Jackson also does custom designs for tile facing. Six-inch square tiles are painted by the firm's own artist. These ceramic pieces range in price from $10 to $14 each. For someone seeking to duplicate or fill in an authentic design, Jackson's expertise is greatly appreciated.

Brochure available.

Wm. H. Jackson Co.
3 East 47th St.
New York, N.Y. 10017
(212) 753-9400

Several different kinds of grates have been devised in recent years that will send out more heat from the hearth. Some are complicated affairs that require closing up the fireplace is some manner and/or installing an electric fan. The Thermograte operates by natural convection only, and the manufacturers claim that it can double the heat output. The principle is a sound and simple one. A standard mild steel unit carries a two-year warranty against burn-out; the stainless steel model is guaranteed for five years. Various sizes are offered. Both models are known as "open grate." The company also makes an enclosed, glass door circulating air model. We suggest that you try the simpler first.

Literature available.

Thermograte Enterprises, Inc.
1639 Terrace Dr.

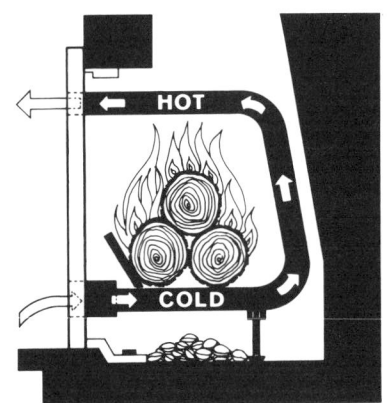

St. Paul, Minn. 55113
(612) 633-1376

Chimney Needs

Most chimneys just require a good cleaning every so often. Birds like to nest in them, and soot and creosote collect in amazing quantities. The danger of a chimney fire is always present, but, if the basic structure is maintained properly, the chance of this kind of misfortune is greatly lessened. Most home owners complain not of the dirt but of the chimney's draw. Some stacks are simply not high enough, and there is little that you can do about it without adding to them. Other chimneys are not topped properly, and a chimney pot or two may be the solution. In any case, call in an expert and don't try to remedy such problems as these yourself unless you are prepared to do the same for others.

All chimneys need cleaning, but you needn't call on an expert if you can learn to use one of Kristia's chimney brushes from Norway. If you are successful at it, you may have discovered a lucrative new career. These days chimney sweeps are even being written up in *The New York Times*. Kristia's instruction book ($1) lists the names of sweeps across the country. None of them force a pine tree through the chimney or load shotgun shells with rocksalt to blast away the soot. They prefer the Kristia brushes which come in several sizes.

Literature available.

Kristia Associates
343 Forest Ave.
P.O. Box 1118
Portland, Me. 04104
(207) 772-2821

Another enterprising firm, Self-Sufficiency Products, manufactures the brush illustrated here. This is suitable for cleaning out both a fireplace chimney or a metal chimney used for a stove. The tool is priced at $49.95.

Brochure available.

Self-Sufficiency Products
Environmental Manufacturing Corp.
P.O. Box 126
Essex Junction, Vt. 05452

There is more to the chimney pot than aesthetic appeal. It improves the draft and minimizes downdrafts. It also helps keep out the rain. A chimney pot can even be stuck on a non-functioning chimney to improve the roofscape, if that strikes your fancy. Historic Boulevard Services has a line that ranges in price from $37 to $109. The pots are clay and are available in six styles which are designed to fit various needs. They measure 2½ to 3 feet high, weigh 80 to 150 pounds, and are ½" to 1" thick.

Brochure available.

Historic Boulevard Services
1520 W. Jackson Blvd.
Chicago, Ill. 60607
(312) 829-5562

Heating Stoves

Even if we don't have winters like that of 1976–77 and 1977–78 during the next few years, oil and gas prices will continue to rise. The sale of free-standing and fireplace stoves will continue to increase. What was once a staple in the cabin has now become a part of the surburban and country home. Those who live in old houses are in a better position to make use of these devices. Older homes have more flues that can be used for venting purposes. Such buildings are also likely to contain more room for appliances of this sort.

The hard sell approach, as we've already observed, is gaining in momentum. Stove shops are becoming as popular as tennis centers, and one competitor is nudging another. As long as the boom is on, you might as well profit from it. More and more of the consumer and home magazines are paying attention to the stampede to wood. Read the literature carefully, and look for Underwriter's Laboratory approval. Above all, make sure that you will have an adequate supply of wood or coal on hand (some stoves will burn both) when the time comes, and that you will have the time to keep the home fires burning.

Today's wood-burning stoves must be as practical as they are good-looking. If you have to choose between these two criteria, by all means opt for the practical. In this case, you have the best of two worlds. Illustrated is a reproduction of the Victorian De Dietrich & Co.

stove. Its ornate exterior surrounds an internal baffling system and draft control for efficiency. An ash removal pan is slung under a full-width firebox. The upper chamber is a heating oven. The top, when lifted off, reveals a burner and warming area. This is model AL-77; six other models are available.

Brochure, free; catalog, 25¢.

The Burning Log (Eastern Office)
P.O. Box 438
Lebanon, N.H. 03766
(603) 448-4360

or

The Burning Log (Western Office)
P.O. Box 8519
Aspen, Colorado 81611
(303) 925-8968

Like all other Shaker products, the stove is a model of simplicity. In this case, however, simpler may not be better if you're looking for a major rather than supplementary source of heat. It doesn't have a draft control like the more sophisticated designs. If efficiency is not uppermost, then this 20″ high stove will work just fine.

Catalog available, $2.50.

Guild of Shaker Crafts
401 W. Savidge St.
Spring Lake, Mich. 49456
(616) 846-2870

Mohawk's Tempwood II woodstove uses a downdraft principle to achieve an efficient 55,000 BTU/hr. rating. Vents direct air down and around the logs for complete combustion. Since the only access is through the lid on top, ash removal is best left to a vacuum cleaner.

Literature available, including a booklet entitled Wood Energy, *$1.*

Mohawk Industries Inc.
173 Howland Ave.
Adams, Mass. 01220
(413) 743-3648

Le Petit Godin also boasts charm and efficiency. It comes in two sizes, the larger of which generates an estimated 32,000 BTU/hr. when stoked with coal. The gasketed fire door has a mica window and a spin-wheel draft control. The steel body is lined with firebrick and can be loaded through the top. It can also be used with wood. The top, fire door, and base are of enameled cast iron available in several colors—cedar green, sand, brown, and black. All in all, a Victorian beauty of Gallic esprit and dispatch.

Literature available.

Bow and Arrow Imports
14 Arrow St.
Cambridge, Mass. 02138
(617) 354-1459

There are several advantages to parlor stoves from Vermont Castings. A baffling system allows the doors to be removed for viewing the fire without filling the house with smoke. Logs up to 24″ can be loaded from the side or the front in the "Defiant" model. As an airtight stove it develops 55,000 BTU/hr. and can burn from 12 to 14 hours. A thermostat enables a constant temperature to be maintained. The "Defiant" is priced at $545.

The "Vigilant" is smaller than the "Defiant," but shares its efficiency. The top lid opens for loading. The design

of the smoke chamber prevents you from getting a face full of smoke when it's up. An automatic thermostat controls the air supply. These Vermonters have learned to be inventive when it comes to heat. The "Vigilant" is yours for $445.

Catalog available, $1.

Vermont Castings, Inc.
Box 126, Prince St.
Randolph, Vt. 05060
(802) 728-3355

The Fisher design, one of the best known in the heating industry, has a secondary combustion chamber to get the most out of gases released from burning wood. The bi-level top can be used for cooking at two temperatures. The "Baby Bear," shown here, is only 15½″ wide, 29″ long, and accommodates 18″ logs. The construction is of steel plate.

Brochure available.

Fisher Stoves International
P.O. Box 10605
Eugene, Ore. 97440

Many of the newest wood stove designs, like the Schrader, are made from heavy steel plate. This material tolerates a higher temperature than cast iron. Schrader manufactures a compact model with an aluminum alloy door. The maker claims that over 250,000 homes are already being heated with their stoves.

Brochure available.

Schrader Wood Stoves and Fireplaces
724 Water St.
Santa Cruz, Calif. 95060
(408) 425-8125

In an effort to capitalize on utter simplicity, Shenandoah markets a line of "basic" wood stoves like the model R-55 shown here. It is an airtight 18″ diameter steel cylinder lined with firebrick. The air flow is thermostatically controlled.

Brochure available.

Shenandoah Manufacturing Co., Inc.
P.O. Box 839
Harrisonburg, Va. 22801
(703) 434-3838

The folks at All Nighter Stove Works are rightfully proud of the Underwriters Laboratories seal of approval on four of their wood-burners. The heftiest stove, the "Big Mo'," is a firebrick-lined front-loader capable of handling logs up to 30″. There are three other proportionately smaller versions. All are available with an optional electric blower attachment for the hot-air convection system. Another optional feature is the hot-water extraction cylinder which fits around the flue and can supplement an existing hot water heater.

Brochure available.

All Nighter Stove Works, Inc.
80 Commerce St.
Glastonbury, Conn. 06033
(203) 633-3640

Grampa's Wood Stoves specializes in restoring and selling turn-of-the-century wood- and coal-burning ranges and parlor stoves. They use only authentic parts which they will also sell if an adequate description of the part needed accompanies a request.

Parlor stoves such as the "Round Oak" and "Century Oak" are part of Grampa's everchanging inventory.

Literature available.

Grampa's Wood Stoves
P.O. Box 492
Ware, Mass. 01082
(413) 967-6684

Cooking Stoves

Some of the heating stoves described above also serve for simple cooking purposes. A tea kettle or coffee pot was often kept warm on the top of the parlor stove, and perhaps more than one pre-TV dinner was served from the top of a pot belly. Those who have used wood- or coal-burning ranges and ovens swear that they are easy to use and maintain. Most modern housewives or their cooking husbands—in an old house or not—wouldn't want one anywhere near the kitchen. As long as electricity and gas can be obtained at reasonable prices and manufacturers of modern appliances continue to improve their efficiency, there may be little reason to fuss over an old-fashioned model. A stove of this sort is certainly perfect for a summer kitchen or to be used in the country when—as still happens—the lines are down.

The "Victor Jr." cooking range has been re-introduced. Production was halted in 1966 just before "back to nature" and "energy crisis" became household terms. This is a wood-burning cast-iron stove designed to provide even heat throughout or just a hot top surface. Options include a warming oven and a five-gallon water reservoir. Be sure of your wood supply before you depend on this one.

Literature available.

Home and Harvest, Inc.
4407 Westbourne Rd.
Greensboro, N.C. 27401

One of the best-known lines of wood stoves comes from Norway, where both wood and frigid weather are common. The "Lumberjack" is a cast-iron stove for

cooking and heating. Logs are placed so that they burn slowly, like a cigar.

Jotul's kitchen stove (#404) comes with a front grate for firing with coke or coal. It is a little on the small side, but it would be fine for a cabin in the woods or in a summer kitchen.

Book available, $1.

Jotul
Kristia Associates
Box 1118, 343 Forest Ave.
Portland, Me. 04102
(207) 772-2821

Grampa's Wood Stoves, as mentioned earlier, specializes in the real thing—antique stoves. The imposing "Roseland Royal" looks almost as it did when it left the foundry. The "Home Comfort" is similarly well preserved. A reservoir attached to it keeps water hot for bathing and shaving.

Literature available.

Grampa's Wood Stoves
P.O. Box 492
Ware, Mass. 01082
(413) 967-6684

those intended for the fireplace. Again, Jotul has anticipated your needs. Pete Tagget, a blacksmith, has made several handy utensils, and will supply them for Jotul and other stoves. They come in lengths of 24″ and 36″ with either a wall hanger or floor stand in which to hold them.

Pete Taggett
The Blacksmith Shop
P.O. Box 115
Mt. Holly, Vt. 05758

Stove Accessories

Every one of the stoves described requires installation, and this means stove pipe and other fittings. Requirements are different for each model, and what will be needed at your house could be completely different from what the neighbor down the street needs. You should, however, be able to get most of the necessary materials from a hardware or building supplier. The stove makers themselves will assist you in every way that they can, and various retail outlets may provide installation and servicing.

Jotul is one of the companies that provides expert help in finding appropriate fittings and pipe. Thompson and Anderson, another Maine firm, manufactures pipe and accessories especially for Jotul products. If you have decided on a Jotul, you'll be referred to Thompson and Anderson.

Thompson and Anderson
53 Seavey St.
Westbrook, Me. 04092
(207) 854-2905

The kinds of tools used in stoves differ somewhat from

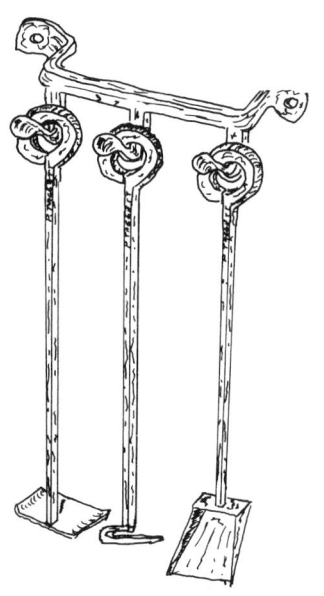

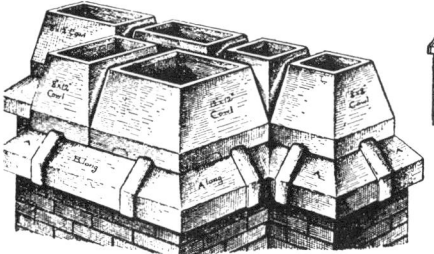

Other Sources for Fireplace and Heating Equipment

Consult the List of Suppliers for addresses.

Mantels/Antique

Architectural Antiques
Castle Burlingame
Eighteenth-Century Co.
Felicity, Inc.
Francis J. Purcell II
Greg Spiess
R. T. Trump & Co.
United House Wrecking
I. M. Wiese
Wrecking Bar

Mantels/New

Architectural Paneling
Black Millwork
European Marble Works
Felber Studios
Focal Point
Fypon
Old World Moulding

Stoves/Heaters

Atlanta Stove Works
Pfanstiel Hardware
Portland Franklin Stove Foundry
Washington Stove Works

Cooking Stoves

Cumberland General Store
Schrader Wood Stoves and Fireplaces
United House Wrecking
Washington Stove Works

Fireplace Accessories

Colonial Williamsburg, Craft House
Cumberland General Store
Robert Griffith
Steve Kayne
Newton Millham
George W. Mount
Period Furniture Hardware
Pete Taggett
Wallin Forge

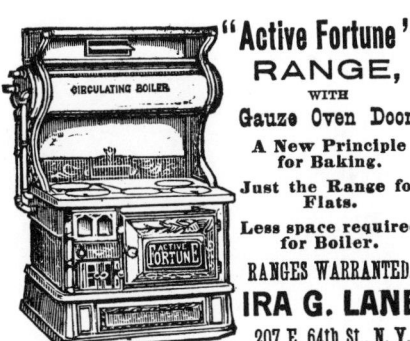

V Floors

One of the features most treasured by admirers of old houses is fine flooring. This may be of oak or pine or even a more exotic wood such as ash or chestnut. Oak was used widely in the Colonies, but the supply became limited and builders turned in the eighteenth century to pine—white in the North and yellow in the South. Like so many other things in an old house, economy and availability determined selection of materials as much as did aesthetic judgment. Oak continued to be used in the West when it was no longer easy to obtain in the East.

The earliest form of flooring was wide-board —from a foot to almost two feet. Not until the nineteenth century did narrow hardwood strip flooring or parquet come into popular use, and then only gradually. Mid-Victorian homes were unlikely to have random-width pine floors, and when remodeling a home (restoration was unthinkable at the time), the Victorians often laid the narrow over the wide and "crude" flooring. The new was easier to maintain and better held carpeting.

Before determining exactly what to do with flooring, the owner of any old house must determine exactly what the base consists of. Has one floor been laid over another? Or is what appears to be a second floor underneath merely a thinner arrangement of boards which closes the joints above? Examination of one small area could well save the restorer much time and effort. Since boards are laid from at least one joist to another, it should be possible to use several square feet of flooring in a room as typical of that remaining elsewhere. In order to do this, the homeowner may have to remove such artificial coverings as linoleum; this is a perfectly permissable operation. No one is likely to complain about the loss of what is almost always a badly-aged synthetic. Although linoleum has its devotees, this is one product of the unnatural past which we can do without.

Once the nature of the original flooring has been determined, the next step is to consider its treatment. Some boards may have to be replaced or pieces of wood relaid. The older the house, the harder it is to accomplish such tasks with success. Antique lumber is becoming more and more rare. Fortunately, the hardware with which it was attached— wooden pegs in many very early floors and hand- or machine-wrought nails on later—is being reproduced today. Attic floors may supply some of the replacement pieces; occasionally lumber from out buildings serves as well if of the proper thickness and wood. It is better to save such weathered wood, however, for more rustic purposes. Patterned wood floors can be much more easily repaired, but the cost is likely to be as great as for those which are earlier and wider.

You will thank your lucky stars if the floors have been covered with wall-to-wall carpeting or some other such material over the years. This will have prevented them from being gouged and scuffed to death. No doubt you will want to remove such a modern excrescence as soon as possible, despite what your more "up-to-date" neighbors may think. ("Do you mean to tell me," a prospective home buyer once asked this writer, "that there is no wall-to-wall carpeting? Just these old rugs?") But you must be prepared to live with the past—at least its minor accidents. Great gouges, sagging boards, nasty breaks, etc., must be removed, but if the old floor is to remain, you will have to accept scratches and unevenness. By all means, do *not* have the floors scraped or heavily sanded. This will remove much more that you wish, including the look of age. You might try a stain and linseed oil, and then a light wax (not acrylic) to see how well the surface can "come up" under normal circumstances. Then you may decide that some light sanding with a fine abrasive will be necessary here or there. Of course, if paint has been applied (and not paint of the sort used by home artists of earlier days which may have been original with the floor), you will need to turn to a good remover.

The beauty of an old floor may be enhanced with the use of a fine rug; one complements the other. Orientals of various sorts lead the most desirable list of coverings, but they are not as accurate a period furnishing for most pre-Victorian homes as a rag or hooked rug. A floorcloth or even straw matting may be truer to form. If you wish to be completely (historically) honest, bare floor would have to suffice. This may be fine for a museum, but most home owners will wish to warm up the floor beneath them. A coat of paint can be applied, but, better yet, a stencil design can be drawn. Representative stencil patterns can be bought and, if your ability is limited, even worked by an expert in your own home.

The assumption has been made that most old homes have wood floors. This may not be the case in those of Spanish Colonial design. Here tiles have been used most liberally. Unglazed Mexican tiles are available in most parts of the country. Better ceramic companies can supply you with authentic reproductions of Victorian tiles which are suitable for foyers and kitchens. Marble is always available for those able to pay the price. Slate, too, can be found almost everywhere. Substitutes for these in vinyl should be avoided if at all possible. If it seems the only alternative, then try a solid vinyl which has the thickness, color, and patina of the material it imitates.

Wood Flooring

Good lumber—used (antique) or new—is increasingly hard to find. Anyone who has built a house in the past two years knows how one must struggle to obtain redwood, and even cedar of quality. With a building boom at hand, supplies of solid pine (not merely plywood with a veneer) must be ordered far in advance of the time when it will be needed. Barn siding disappears almost as rapidly as the time taken to bulldoze an old red barn to the ground.

Supplies of old lumber may be found—if you keep looking—in most areas of North America where old houses abound. Reading the classified sections of local newspapers may prove more useful than following the columns of The Old-House Journal *or* Yankee. *A recent issue of one such weekly* The Hunterdon County Democrat *(New Jersey), carried three listings. The word is out: people do want old lumber for new and period homes. Look first, then, close to home. And if you can't find what you need there, start searching farther afield.*

Don't, please, fall for imitations. Floors have to be solid and what is mistakenly used for paneling is, fortunately, not sturdy enough to lie beneath the feet. But there are still ways to be tripped up. For example, some flooring manufacturers produce boards that are already "pegged," that is, they have what looks like a row of pegs stamped on them. You'll know they are not functional, and so will everyone else. Besides, only the very earliest of Colonial houses are likely to have floors that were pegged to the joists rather than nailed.

The atmosphere you wish to create will, of course, dictate the choice of flooring. Too often, the budget is the final arbiter. Wide-pine flooring of more recent vintage might be most appropriate for your project. It can be used—if properly matched—for patching where necessary.

Guyon mills shiplapped pine boards in widths of 6, 8, and 10″. Factory-stained, they run 88¢ per board foot.

You can order wider planks (up to 21″) from Dale Carlisle. He air dries the wood two years and will plane them if requested.

Craftsman Lumber sells pine planks as wide as 24″.

Maurer and Shepherd stock hand-planed, shiplapped pine and oak flooring.

Guyon, Inc.
650 Oak St.
Lititz, Penn. 17543
(717) 626-0225

Dale Carlisle
Rte. 123
Stoddard, N.H. 03464
(603) 446-3937

Craftsman Lumber Co.
Maid St.
Groton, Mass. 01450
(617) 448-6336

Maurer and Shepherd, Joyners
122 Naubuc Ave.
Glastonbury, Conn. 06033
(203) 633-2383

Antique Wood Flooring

Diamond K reclaims hard pine flooring in widths up to 20″. One side of this antique stock is planed so no sanding or waxing is necessary.

Literature Available

Diamond K
130 Buckland Rd.
South Windsor, Conn. 06074
(203) 644-8486

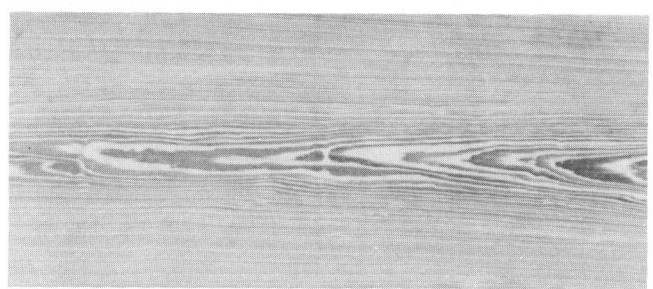

Probably the most sought-after antique flooring is old growth southern yellow pine. The last stands were felled early in this century and used for New England shipbuilding, bridges, and mill construction. The original wood becomes available as the old structures are dismantled. Outfits like The House Carpenters resaw and mill the valuable timber into 13/16″ tongue and groove.

Catalog available, $4.

The House Carpenters
Box 217
Shutesbury, Mass. 01072

Period Pine sells three grades of custom milled planing of southern yellow pine in widths of 4″ to 12″.

Brochure available.
Period Pine
P.O. Box 77052
Atlanta, Ga. 30309
(404) 876-4740

Inlaid Floors

For homes of the Victorian period and beyond, the use of inlaid woods can add distinction to residential foyers, living rooms, libraries, and dining rooms. The Lincoln series from Wood Mosaic is ¾″ tongue-and-groove white or red oak with an antique finish. It sells for $3.65 a square foot and is preassembled in 24″ x 24″ sections.

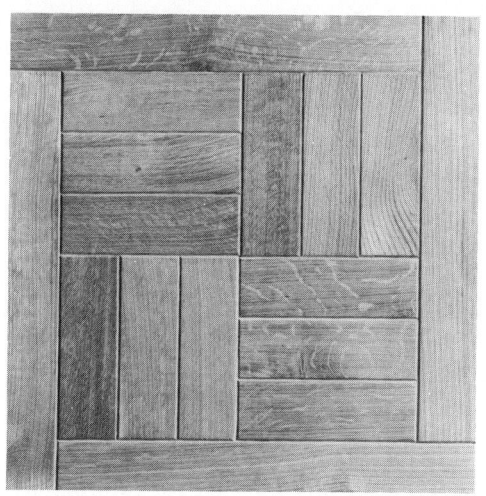

Brochure available.

Wood Mosaic
P.O. Box 21159
Louisville, Ky. 40221
(502) 363-3531

Another supplier of modern parquet flooring is the Harris Manufacturing Co. There are more than sixty patterns, wood species, and finishes to choose from. Some are available prefinished and will save time in installation. One of their new products, however, strikes us as especially appropriate for period interiors—Chaucer BondWood—and this is left unfinished. Each of the 13⁷/₁₆″ x 13⁷/₁₆″ panels is hand assembled at the factory. The flooring is available in ⁵/₁₆″ solid Angelique (Guiana teak), black walnut, white oak, and red oak.

Catalog available.

Harris Manufacturing Co.
783 E. Walnut St.
Johnson City, Tenn. 37601
(615) 928-3122

Ceramic Tiles

Tiling has always been an expensive way to cover a floor, except in those parts of the Southwest and West where clay products have been widely available. Southern Californians say that Mexico is still the place to go for the widest and most inexpensive assortment of glazed and unglazed tiles, but they are reluctant to give away their sources. As for other forms—Italian, Minton-style Victorian pieces, and the kind of institutional tiles used in the early years of this century—you must be willing to search high and low unless price is no problem. A few of the better salvage/wrecking/architectural antiques outfits may be able to find antique tiles for you.

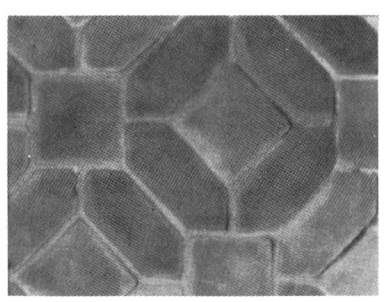

For the most part, commercially-available American ceramic tiles are exceptionally hideous, or, as Evelyn Waugh might have put it, "sick-making." The palette seems limited to the pastels, and patterns are similarly pale. If you search long enough, however, you may just find a modern pattern in ceramic tile which will enhance your period surroundings. Do-it-yourself kits should be avoided like the plague as the adhesives and grouts supplied are frequently as durable as toothpaste.

Flint and Terra Cotta

A variety of glazed and unglazed "primitive" tiles are available from American Olean. "Flint," in shades of black and brown, and a ruddy "Terra Cotta" have textured surfaces suitable for interior uses. Each can be ordered in several shapes and sizes.

"Murray Quarry Tile" is made from shale and fire clays in seven earth tones. A variety of shapes contributes to individualized patterns. All are ½″ thick and are recommended for indoor applications.

Literature available.

American Olean Tile Co.
1000 Cannon Ave.
Lansdale, Penn. 19446
(215) 855-1111

Cerreto Grande and Gascogne

To Europe you may have to go for your tile needs—via an American distributor. The vividness and clarity of ceramic tiles can create startling visual effects. Country Floors imports over 500 tile patterns from many countries. The sunny "Cerreto Grande" is an Italian design. The earthy "Gascogne" pattern is a classic French import.

Catalog available, $2.

Country Floors
300 East 61st Street
New York, N.Y. 10021
(212) 758-7414

Villeroy & Boch

Remember when you could eat out in a gleaming white ceramic-tiled restaurant? Most of these establishments are gone, but the look from the early years of this century is back again. The sanitary glare of white glazed tiles is enlivened with diagonally set squares in this flooring from Villeroy & Boch. It could brighten a residential kitchen and give it a correct period tone.

Villeroy & Boch also imports tiles with the early flavor of the Iberian peninsula. These are especially fitting in Spanish Colonial surroundings if Mexican products do not suit your taste.

Literature available.
Villeroy & Boch
912 Riverview Dr.
Totowa, N.J. 07512
(201) 256-7710

Delft for the Hearth

Tiling can also be used in another floor "area"—the hearth of a fireplace. Delft blue tiles have framed such spaces for generations. Typical tile designs are flowers, landscapes, and animals, but anything can be ordered since all patterns are hand-painted. The 4¼" x 4¼" windmill pattern, for example, is $4.75.

Catalog available.

Delft Blue
P.O. Box 103
Ellicott City, Md. 21043
(301) 624-4083

Vinyl Flooring

Yes, we'll admit it. We're prepared to bend a bit on this synthetic. Natural fibers are to be preferred everywhere in an old house, but there have to be compromises. Solid vinyl is one of the acceptable one—if limited in use to those areas of the house such as a kitchen, foyer, or bathroom where traffic is heavy and water sometimes a problem. Specifically excluded, however, is the vinyl asbestos tile which is most often urged on the consumer as a cheaper alternative. It is in every way. It has neither the look nor the wear of quality.

Kentile Solid Vinyl

Kentile makes several handsome solid vinyl patterns which do not strain to be authentic. They are simply attractively designed and worked. None have the real warmth or texture of natural stone or ceramic tile, but they are of appealing colors and are subdued underfoot. One such tile is "Terresque," an approximation of unglazed Mexican tiles, and the second is "Barre Slate," as its name indicates, a reproduction of slate. It comes in four different shades. Both patterns are ⅛" thick. "Terresque" comes in 9" x 9" squares; "Barre Slate" in 12" x 18" pieces.

These very simple patterns are by far the most successful in the Kentile line for the old house. Those which attempt to duplicate marble, brick, parquet, and other more complicated patterns are merely imitative.

Literature available from most flooring dealers.

Kentile Floors
58 Second Ave.
Brooklyn, N.Y. 11215
(212) 768-9500

Stone Materials

The use of natural stone for flooring has been limited in the past and will continue to be the exception in the future. Simply, it costs too much. Stone presents another problem—its unevenness. Only the smoothest quarried rock, such as marble, presents a relatively uniform surface, and it, of course, is the most expensive of all. Stone floors are most often encountered in the basement of old houses, especially in those houses built into a bank. This material may be of the crudest sort such as fieldstone or a semi-smooth sort such as slate. Here, too, one often finds brick, a ceramic material.

Marble Modes

If you can afford real marble for a foyer, by all means indulge yourself. And if you need to replace pieces, these can be found in various colors and patterns. Marble is often used for thresholds, and almost any building supply house can provide this. For more ambitious projects, you may decide to go directly to a quarry or to such a firm as Marble Modes. It has a wide selection of marble in tile form for residential and commercial use. Marble is an excellent investment. Not only is it rich in color and texture, but it is durable and easily maintained. The same thing can not be said for a material which is increasingly used as a substitute—travertine.

Literature available.

Marble Modes, Inc.
15–25 130th St.
College Point, N.Y. 11356
(212) LE 9-1334

Stenciled Floors

From marble to stenciled floors is an enormous leap in style and price. As mentioned in the introduction to this section, stenciling has been applied to wood floors for at least 125 years. It was not a common practice in Colonial America. At that time designs were applied freehand by itinerant decorators. In the nineteenth century stencil artists began to vend their wares. Sometimes the entire floor area was covered with flourishes and geometric patterns and, at others, only a simple border was applied. All of this was done in imitation of high-style interiors which would have contained inlaid flooring and fine carpets. Later in the nineteenth century, floors were even painted in simulation of marble graining.

Stenciled Interiors

S. Tarbox is one of a number of students of the stenciling art and has gathered a considerable collection of historically accurate designs. Custom designing and restoration work is also included in the firm's repertory. *Literature available.*

Stenciled Interiors
Hinman Lane
Southbury, Conn. 06488
(203) 264-8000

Floor Coverings

The covering of floor areas seems a simple task—until you start to do it. The assumption is that some sections of flooring will be left uncovered and that modern "piles" will be eschewed. Something in the shag family

has no place in a period interior. The appearance is all wrong, and the maintenance of such rugs has proved to be very difficult. Synthetic fibers do not hold up well in the wash and practically shrivel up if put in a drier. If you must have something soft and fluffy, then consider a sheepskin or other animal fiber.

Orientals are almost always appropriate in formal areas of the house. In the eighteenth century they were rare and most probably were used to cover tables or as wall hangings. Nevertheless, they can be employed without shame by the old-house owner, especially one who lives in a late-Victorian or twentieth-century home. No Persian carpets (Western Turkey) should be used in Colonial homes. These were not introduced in the United States until the 1870s. Most of the Orientals now on the market date from the end of the 1800s and early 1900s. Rugs of this sort are expensive but exceedingly good investments. Dealers in such material are found in every area of North America.

Simpler floor coverings will be used in most areas of an old house. These may be braided, hooked, or stitched rugs made of cotton and/or wool. Sometimes a small percentage of synthetic fiber (10 to 20%) may be mixed in, but not enough to render the rug artificial looking or difficult to maintain. In recent years there has been a virtual renaissance in hand rug making, and the techniques used do not vary that much from those followed in the past. There are also sources for antique rag rugs.

Antique Rag Rugs

You can still get the original antiques at more than affordable prices. The Kelter-Malce partnership has recently sold an 18' square rug from Connecticut for $550. That's a lot of rug for the dollar. Mr. Malce thinks old rag rugs are still underpriced.

Kelter-Malce
361 Bleecker St.
New York, N.Y. 10014
(212) 989-6760

Ford Museum Hooked Rugs

Designs on homemade hooked rugs were often patterned after motifs on other fabrics such as needlepoint and stencil designs found on chair backs. This is a reproduction from Mountain Rug Mills and is sold through The Henry Ford Museum and Greenfield Village where the original can be found.

A Gothic influence appears in this repetititve pattern also from Mountain Rug Mills and the Michigan museum and historical village.

Catalog available, $2.50.

Henry Ford Museum and Greenfield Village
20900 Oakwood Blvd.
Dearborn, Mich. 48121
(313) 271-1620

Sunflower Rag Rug

Pilgrim's Progress is one good mail-order source for reasonably-priced, versatile, and good-looking rag rugs. Their cotton objects can be custom designed to fit specific needs. The *Sunflower* measures 2'6" by 4' and sells for $39.

Catalog available, 75¢.

Pilgrim's Progress, Inc.
Penthouse
50 West 67th St.
New York, N.Y. 10023
(212) 580-3050

All-Wool Rag Rugs

Kay and Ron Loch have retained traditional weaving techniques in their Bucks County shop. They create all-wool rag rugs in any size up to 15' wide. A typical 8' x 10' rug is $295.

Literature available.

Heritage Rugs
Lahaska, Penn. 18931
(215) 794-7229

Throw Rugs

Banjos and fiddles are still more popular than electric guitars in Knott County, Kentucky. Hard times have left life simple, but have not diminished the quality of what talented fingers can create. Local hands also produce charming back-stitched throw rugs in your choice of colors. Custom sizes are available up to 54" wide. A 2' x 3' rug is $20. That illustrated is cotton with cotton/rayon blend pattern thread.

Literature available.

Quicksand Crafts
Vest, Ky. 41772
(606) 785-5230

Strip Rug

This is a sturdy handwoven wool strip rug with a sturdy Irish linen warp and braided ends. It can be made in any size and almost any color. It is sold for $6 a square foot.

Sample available, $2.

Diane Jackson Cole
9 Grove St.
Kennebunk, Me. 04043
(207) 846-5662

Braided Rugs

One of the charms of handcrafting is that when something is finished it is not machine-perfect. Individuality persists in the hit-or-miss designs of braided rugs. Adams and Swett's brochure tells us that their "Country Home" rugs are "handsewn by the wives and families of Japanese rice farmers in their homes." Their best quality rug is priced at $384 for an 8' x 10', and is made of 90% wool. It is suggested that you order a small size first so that you can gauge the quality and appearance.

Literature available.

Adams & Swett
380 Dorchester Avenue
Boston, Mass. 02127
(617) 268-8000

Do-It-Yourself

You can help carry on the Colonial braided rug tradition by doing it yourself. Country Braid House will sell the necessary materials and will even start the first few rows if you want. Or you can buy one already made. Their rugs are wool and are sold either in random colors or as a planned pattern of circular colored bands. Any size is possible. They will be glad to quote a price if you tell them the size and whether you want it round, oval, or long and narrow.

Literature available.

Country Braid House
Clark Rd.
Tilton, N.H. 03276
(603) 286-4511

Braid-Aid markets a complete line of rug braiding and hooking materials, designs, and instructions.

Catalogs available: $1 for book of instructions and patterns, $1 for materials and accessories.

Braid-Aid
466 Washington St.
Pembroke, Mass. 02359
(617) 826-6091

Heirloom Patterns

Although Scandanavia probably gave us the hooked rug, early New England and Canadian designs elevated it to an art of considerable value. Traditional patterns are generally crude floral, animal, or geometric designs. Today the art thrives in craft programs and homes throughout the country. Heirloom Rugs is an especially valuable resource for hundreds of unique patterns. The "Star Diamond" is a charming old quilt pattern and sells for $5. The "Sailcloth Primitive" is a copy of an old rug made by a sailor. The pattern sells for $8.50 and measures 29" x 69"

Catalog of patterns available, $1.

Heirloom Rugs
28 Harlem St.
Rumford, R.I. 02916
(401) 438-5672

Floorcloths

Manufacture of the types of material used in many Colonial homes has just recently been revived. Thanks to the diligent research of historians in the decorative arts, we know much more today about such matters as floorcloths. As has been explained, Orientals and other woven rugs were luxuries that very few people could afford. Even in the best of homes, painted canvas often took the place of textiles on the floor.

Craftswomen

Reproducing an eighteenth-century floorcloth is a time-consuming process. Carol Maicone and Linda La Bove begin with heavy cotton canvas. After each of several coats of hand-mixed paint has been applied and sanded, the surface is ready for the actual design. The pattern is then stenciled and/or painted freehand. The floorcloth then goes through a lengthy varnishing and drying process. The resulting finish is guaranteed for ten years against abrasion and deterioration.

Floorcloths from Craftswomen come in any length and are seamless up to a width of ten feet. Shown here are the "Checkerboard," "Chevron," and "Diamond" designs. The "Tree of Life" is an adaptation of a traditional quilt pattern.

Catalog available.

Craftswomen
Box 715
Doylestown, Penn. 18901
(215) 822-1025

Carpets

While purists in restoration rightfully question the use of Orientals in Colonial-style interiors, they do understand that they, along with such machine-woven carpets as Wiltons, Axminsters, and handwoven needlepoints, have a place in the post-Colonial home. In the 1890s even Sears and Montgomery Ward were offering their versions of Axminster and Brussels carpets. Large rugs or carpets became almost as popular as the widely and cheaply-produced wallpapers of the time. It is not true that the Victorians covered every inch of space in their homes with something, but they did pad out their manses quite comfortably. Severe expanses of wood flooring were not admired then as they are in sophisticated circles today.

Stark Carpets

Decorators and designers have been employing the services of Stark Carpet Corporation for over forty years. Amongst the stock items are these 12′ wide Wilton carpets from the Bouclé Collection. A 6¾″ stripe border is optional.

JACKS NAVY BLUE
JACKS HUNTER GREEN JACKS LIME GREEN
JACKS NATURAL JACKS TETRE NEGRE
FRENESI NAVY BLUE
MARTINIQUE NATURAL
LARGE ROMAIN NAVY BLUE

Boston's recently restored Harrison Gray Otis House, built in 1795, retains much of its original spirit through the use of carefully selected reproduction materials. For the front entry, a velvet cut pile, "Lozenge Directoire," was chosen from Stark.

Literature available. Full catalog available to designers, decorators, and architects, $10.

Stark Carpet Corp.
979 Third Avenue
New York, N.Y. 10022
(212) PL2-9000

Scalamandré Carpets

Through the Victorian period, Wilton carpets were among the most preferred of European imports. Scalamandré is now a major purveyor of these English-made cut-loop pile rugs.

The "Peel" is a mid-Victorian pattern of two colors woven of 80% wool and 20% nylon.

Five colors harmonize in the "Turner," another mid-Victorian reproduction from England.

104

The term "Axminster" referred originally to the town in England where the rugs were made. By the nineteenth century it came to be used for any British carpet with a "Turkish-knot" weave. Scalamandré offers thirteen patterns in Persian, Turkish, Victorian, and contemporary styles.

Scalamandré's Savannah Collection represents a community's successful effort to preserve a valued past and a manufacturer's dedication to faithfully reproducing it. The "Savannah Parlour" is 100% wool and is available in either cut pile or loop pile. The 100% wool "Savannah Adam," like the "Parlour," is reproduced from the original in the historic city's Werm's House. Both carpets are available with coordinating fabric and wallpaper if so desired.

Literature available. See special list of retail outlets, Appendix A.

Scalamandré
950 Third Avenue
New York, N.Y. 10022
(212) 361-8500

Straw, Sisal, Hemp, Rush, Coir Matting

Natural fibers such as these can be woven into useful and attractive forms for the purpose of covering floors. In Colonial times straw was used in the house and the barn. Without suggesting that you should turn your floors over to mooing creatures, let it be said that mats of various grasses and fibers are just as fitting a flooring material as floorcloths. These were used most frequently in upstairs bedrooms, that is, in less formal areas of the house.

Material of this sort is often sold by very contemporary home furnishing shops. Some flooring suppliers may also have it. It is ironic but true that lovers of simple, primitive things are attracted to old houses of a simpler era and to the most contemporary of structures. Reproduction Shaker furniture can be found in both kinds of homes; so, too, is rush matting.

Conran's

Conran's is a trendy and recent addition to New York. They offer sisal mats which are as natural in the city as they are in the country. Also available is tough coconut coir matting from India at about $9 a yard. Rush tile mats, shown here, are sewn together to make an attract-

ive floor covering. A 3' x 6' section is $10.85. All these things were made from natural grasses and can be wonderfully effective and fitting in a primitive or modern application.

Brochure available, 25¢.

Conran's
The Market at Citicorp Center
160 East 54th St.
New York, N.Y. 10022
(212) 371-2225

Other Sources of Flooring Materials

Consult the List of Suppliers for Addresses.

Wood Flooring

Accent Walls
Amherst Wood-Working
Bangkok Industries
Blair Lumber
Bruce Hardwood
Castle Burlingame

Dana-Deck & Laminates
William J. Erbe
John Harra
Nassau Flooring
New York Flooring
I. Peiser Floors
Simpson Timber
Wagon House
Weird Wood

Wood Flooring/Antique

The Cellar
Eighteenth-Century Co.
Period Pine
Wrecking Bar

Ceramic Flooring

Country Floors
Elon Inc.
Vanderlaan Co.
Western States Stone
Wrecking Bar

Stone Flooring

Delaware Quarries
Materials Unlimited
Structural Slate
Vermont Marble

Hand-Molded Brick

Old Carolina Brick Co.

Stenciling

New York Flooring
Megan Parry
Rambusch Decorating
Wall Stencils by Barbara

Braided, Hooked, and Rag Rugs

S. & C. Huber

Floorcloths

Floorcloths, Inc.

Carpets and Rugs

S. M. Hexter
Charles Jacobsen
Kenmore Carpet
Kent-Costikyan
Rosecore Carpet
F. Schumacher

107

VI   Lighting

Old habits are hard to kick. And in the case of lighting, they are expensive to maintain. We are speaking of the average American's tendency to overlight interior spaces. Despite the energy crisis and the ever-increasing cost of electric power, lights still burn too brightly across the country. The successful use of lighting fixtures in a period interior requires restraint and common sense.

What should be lit? Passageways and stairs, certainly. Artificial light for reading or other close work is often needed during the day as well as at night. Special lights for special requirements—whether it be washing dishes or shaving in the morning—are a must. Closets must be provided with some form of illumination. These are the main "can't do without" areas of modern living. To light a house as it might have been illuminated in the 1750s or 1850s is an exercise in futility and pretense. The conveniences of the electric age allow us to work and rest in relative comfort. We need these improvements to offset the discomforts of the bureaucratic, depersonalized, hectic time in which we live.

Even the utility companies, however, are urging conservation. Bulbs with lower wattage will serve perfectly well and are especially good for period-style interiors. The day may even come when a light bulb will last at least several years rather than a few months. The technology is available to produce them. Expertise is also available for those who can afford to disguise sources of modern illumination. This does not mean wiring a butter churn or coffee mill (Yes, it has been done—all too frequently), but paying the extra dollar for dimmers, batteries, and adapters which adjust the voltage to subdued levels. And since at least the 1920s, light has been used in an indirect manner, boxed in or otherwise hidden in the walls or ceiling. In addition, small spots of a very contemporary design can be used effectively in a period interior.

For most of us, these tricks of the master electrician are too expensive and quite beyond our real needs. Few old houses are "master wired" so that outlets can be opened up with ease almost anywhere. Unless the house is to be rewired, we usually are stuck with the given. Even wires (well-insulated) may have to be exposed here and there. The cost of channeling these into the wall (especially a stone wall) is nearly prohibitive. Since rewiring is beyond the scope of most home remodelers or restorers, careful thought must be given first to exactly what *has* to be lighted electrically. After this had been determined, consideration should be given to appropriate fixtures. There is a fairly plentiful supply of antique fixtures which have been wired for electricity and can be used in Colonial and early Victorian rooms as well as a goodly number of early electric or combination gas and electric fixtures which are appropriate for homes of the 1890–1930 vintage. In addition, one can find a wide assortment of quality reproduction fixtures which may serve the need for light quite admirably. The number of manufacturers of such devices seems to increase each year. It has become more difficult, however, to sort out the good from the bad.

Since the Bicentennial there has been a quickening of the Colonial "fever." The chandelier has become *de rigueur* in the lighting field. Most are used inappropriately. The more elaborate they are, the less plausible they appear in what is the average Colonial-style dwelling, a very simple structure. What lighted Carpenters' Hall in Philadelphia or Faneuil Hall in Boston is probably not the right thing for the Cape Cod on Rural Route 1. Hanging fixtures of wood, tin, and iron are more likely to suit the need for lighting in a dining room or center hall than those of silver, crystal, brass, or even pewter.

Except in Victorian structures fitted for gas

lighting, ceiling fixtures are more likely the exception than the rule. It is better, then, to make use of wall sconces, bracketed lanterns, even picture lights. Combined with carefully arranged table and floor lamps, these wall fixtures will sufficiently light up a period interior. As for lamps, porcelain ginger jars, glass kerosene or oil fixtures, large wooden candlesticks, and toleware columns have long provided handsome bases. The handy home owner can even adapt these himself. Floor lamps are a more difficult problem. The type of wrought-iron candlestand offered in the following pages by Essex Forge (and by other such lighting houses) is one solution. It has been a popular fixture since the early years of electricity and a convenient and appropriate one. There is a decent supply of such lamps in secondhand and antiques shops throughout the country.

Not every light need be an electric one, of course. Gas has had a renaissance in recent years but is becoming increasingly expensive to use. The lowly candle remains available at a relatively low cost. If used with restraint, such tapers provide a muted glow which enhances any well-furnished period interior. If of the dripless variety, they can be employed in hanging fixtures to great effect. Remember only that our pre-electric ancestors used them sparingly because of their cost.

Antique Lighting Fixtures

True period lighting fixtures of an early age are the province of fine antiques dealers and collectors. Rush-lights, crusies, Argand lamps, and Sandwich glass whale oil lamp bases command very high prices. They are not, however, impossible to find or to use. Some of these fixtures can be electrified; others only make sense as candle- or oil-burning vessels. Somewhat easier to lo-cate are the kerosene lamps, gas fixtures, combination gas and electric devices, and early electric fixtures. Some "junk" dealers have specialized in their retrieval from doomed structures and effectively recycled them for new use. Increasingly, however, such later fixtures are being handled by special dealers. In those parts of the

country where Victorian architecture is the norm and does not play second fiddle to Colonial, they are easier to come by.

Jo-El Shop

Bringing an old fixture back to life is often a labor of love. John Beglin sometimes spends more than forty hours rejuvenating a single antique. His Jo-El Shop is crammed with his collection of Victoriana and turn-of-the-century fixtures. Many are gas and early electric lights.

Catalog and other information available, $2.

John A. Beglin
Jo-El Shop
7120 Hawkins Creamery Rd.
Laytonsville, Md. 20760
(301) 253-3951

Yankee Craftsman

Increased interest in the restoration of period homes has encouraged some craftsmen to specialize in renewing old fixtures. The process demands technical and artistic skills as well as a feel for the era that produced the original. Yankee Craftsman offers a restoration service and executes custom designs, too. The firm maintains a sizable stock of antique fixtures. If you are looking for a specific type that they might have, Yankee Craftsman will send a photo and information at no charge. Seen here is one view of the shop and a restored chandelier.

Yankee Craftsman
357 Commonwealth Rd.
Wayland, Mass. 01778
(617) 653-0031

Gargoyles, Ltd.

Much of the Gargoyles, Ltd. collection is original. Most of the pieces date from the nineteenth and early twentieth centuries. This chandelier is solid brass and spans 24".

No catalog as of yet, but brochures are available on specific kinds of items.

Gargoyles, Ltd.
512 South Third St.
Philadelphia, Pa. 19147
(215) 629-1700

The Wrecking Bar

Some of us just have to have the "real thing." In many cases, the original has not been reproduced. The Wrecking Bar has a sizable collection of antique lighting devices, including these sconces, some of which have been electrified.

Literature on particular kinds of items available.

The Wrecking Bar of Atlanta, Inc.
292 Moreland Ave., N.E.
Atlanta, Ga. 30307
(404) 525-0468

John Kruesel

John Kruesel's collection of original devices spans two centuries. He specializes in pieces fueled with whale oil, gas, kerosene, gas/electric combinations, and early electric fixtures.

No catalog available, but please write for information.

John Kruesel
R. R. 4
Rochester, Minn. 55901
(507) 288-5148

Brasslight

Owner Steve Kaniewski prides himself on personal service. If he doesn't have the desired fixture in his collection, he keeps the request on file until he locates it. His specialty is Victoriana. Antiques only, please.

Write for information on various kinds of fixtures.

Stephen Kaniewski
Brasslight
2831 S. 12th St.
Milwaukee, Wis. 53215
(414) 672-0938

London Ventures

Some firms specialize in collecting, restoring, and selling Victorian era fixtures. London Ventures deals strictly with these originals, many of which are of European provenence. All have been electrified and lacquered to preserve their sheen. A new listing of available pieces appears quarterly.

Quarterly catalog, $1
London Ventures Co.
2 Dock Square
Rockport, Mass. 01966
(617) 856-7161

Candleholders

The simplest of lighting fixtures are those which hold and burn candles. Rushlights, of course, are even more venerable, but their use is best left to antiquarians. Although candles have risen in price in recent years (along with everything else), they can still provide an economical means for throwing just the right amount of light on the dinner table and in other places where 20/20 vision is not a prerequisite.

There are a thousand and one ways in which the candle can be held. Antique sticks are still widely available, and there is no reason to recommend the use of reproduction glass, ceramic, pewter, or other antique metal fixtures. Candesticks were produced in all forms for use in the kitchen, living room or parlour, and bedroom. Some can be carried from room to room and are equipped with a wide drip pan. Others are fragile columns which are best left in one place. The candelabra is probably the most romantic of the candle-burning devices, and with its varied numbers of branches can provide a surprising amount of light. Sconces, especially those equipped with reflectors, can also throw off much in the way of candlepower. These wall fixtures are covered in another section of this chapter.

The several candle-burning devices shown here are of the unusual sort not so easily encountered or come by. Each is a traditional form and illustrative of the fine reproduction work which is being done today.

Hanging Candleholders

The candle is an ideal source of light. It consumes itself and leaves no residue, only a stump to be removed. Since the invention of the braided wick in 1825, it has needed little or no tending. The hanging candleholder is also a simple device that lends mobility to a solitary light. Its pleasant curves and twisted shaft were commonplace in the eighteenth century. It can hook over the back of a chair, hang on a hook, or be carried. Robert Griffith is a gifted artisan who creates this and many other pieces at his coal-fired forge. It is priced at $20.

Catalog available, $2.

Robert A Griffith, Metalsmith
16 Main St.
Trucksville, Pa. 18708

Another authentic candleholder is available from the Craft Program of the Henry Ford Museum and Greenfield Village. The metalsmiths there turn out a 9″ model that is identical to a wrought-iron ancestor of 1750.

Catalog available, $2.50.

Henry Ford Museum and Greenfield Village
20900 Oakwood Blvd.
Dearborn, Mich. 48121
(313) 271-1620

Candlestand

One of the more important and affordable improvements in domestic lighting in the eighteenth century was the adjustable candlestand. It often consisted of a tall spindle mounted on a sturdy tripod. Candleholders were affixed to a crosspiece which could be snubbed up and down the spindle to the desired height. A 20″ high table version is crafted by Wallin Forge for $45.

Catalog available, $2; charge deducted from first order.

Wallin Forge
R. R. 1, Box 65
Sparta, Ky. 41086
(606) 567-7201

Chandeliers

Chandeliers, as noted in the introduction to this chapter, are often used for the wrong reason—to make fancy what was originally simple. Handsome fixtures of brass and of silver were used in Colonial America, and a vast majority of them came from the foundries of England. Magnificent fixtues could be found in churches, town halls, and in the homes of the very wealthy. In most homes, however, the chandelier was nothing more than a form of hanging light, and might have been made of wood or tin. Not until the nineteenth century, and well into it, could any sizeable number of people afford to use more elaborate fixtures which made use of crystal or etched glass. The Victorian chandelier can be a very fancy affair. Even the most utilitarian of late nineteenth century gas/electric combinations or electric fixtures display a delightful play of shape and decoration.

Of several or many branches, this form of lighting device is designed to dispel the shadows in a large area of almost any room. Since they are suspended from the ceiling, however, chandeliers must be wired in a special manner. The wire is sometimes carried through a metal shaft (as with many Victorian fixtures), or threaded through a link of chain which is attached to a canopy. In either case, a chandelier requires just the right-sized canopy cover for the outlet and the proper hardware to attach this to the ceiling and the chain or shaft to canopy and outlet.

Since almost any kind of reproduction chandelier is likely to be a major purchase, the buyer is urged to determine his electrical needs very carefully. Length of chain or shaft is also critical. Almost any reproduction, of course, can be made as a candle-burning fixture. With more than a few holders, such a light will provide quite sufficient light for dining.

Gas and Electric Chandeliers

Classic Illumination of San Francisco is a sophisticated manufacturer of honest and handsome Victorian light-ing fixtures. Their products are offered directly from the firm or through several suppliers listed below.

The years of transition from gas to electricity are captured in gasoliers which have been equipped for the best of both worlds. The Victorian home owner of the period may have impressed his neighbors by flirting with the future but could not fully part with the dependable past. "The Merchant Street" is a four-light gasolier suitable for the proper Victorian parlor.

A lofty hall, bath or kitchen might be the spot for a two-arm electric chandelier, the "National Hotel." It need not be the focal point of a room's symmetry, as might be expected of a multi-branched fixture.

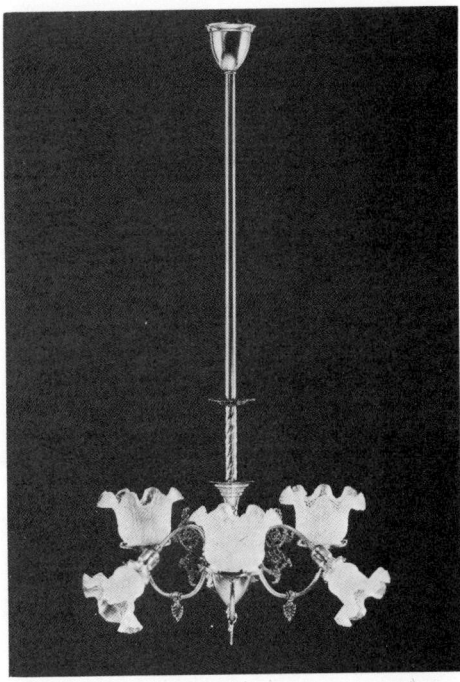

The three-and-three electric/gas combination is typical of Classic Illumination's level of achievement. Each detail reflects the spirit and form of the original. All the work from this firm comes with standard size sockets and modern electrical wiring for easy installation. For the traditionalist, gas pipe fittings are available upon request at no extra cost.

Catalog available, $2.

The Classic Illumination
P.O. Box 5851
San Francisco, Calif. 94101
(415) 527-5106

Classic Illumination fixtures are also available from the following distributors: San Francisco Victoriana, 606 Natoma, San Francisco, Calif. 94103 (415-429-5477) and Victorian Reproductions, 1601 Park Avenue South, Minneapolis, Minn. 55404 (612-338-3636).

Seven-Arm Chandelier

Richard Scofield combines the skills of an artisan and the rigors of a scholar. His lighting fixtures are individually-crafted reproductions. The Period Lighting Fixtures catalog is also a reference source on the origin, selection, and installation of his pieces. Scofield's research has led him to write a book on early American lighting.

Period Lighting's repertoire includes this handsome seven-arm chandelier. Most fixtures can be ordered in pewter, aged tin, and painted finishes. The pewter option is the hand-rubbed result of a careful dipping process. The candle covers are made with real beeswax.

Catalog available, $2.

Period Lighting Fixtures
1 Main St.
Chester, Conn. 06412
(203) 526-3690

Dutch Colonial Chandelier

The Delft influence in Holland, England, and North America has persisted for over three hundred years. Here it is expressed in this elegant solid brass chandelier.

Free brochure.

Dutch Products and Supply Co.
14 S. Main St.
Yardley, Pa. 19067
(215) 493-4873

Six-Arm Chandelier and Billiard Light

The quality tradition of Lester H. Berry has been carried on since the turn of the century. Over the years the firm has imported some of the finest European lighting devices. Their craftsmen have expertly recreated many of these pieces since many countries have restricted export of rare creations. The spirit of the eighteenth-century artisan has been strictly adhered to in these recreations. Each fixture is individually made. All parts are brass castings. The chandelier arms are held to the shaft with pins and are removable. The six-arm brass chandelier illustrated here has been reproduced from a rare French model of the eighteenth century. Unwired, it sells for $631; $48 additional is charged for wiring.

Gentlemen of noble bearing have played billiards in one form or another for centuries. Louis XIV played it for exercise after dinner. Here is a light worthy of the

noble tradition from Lester H. Berry. Note that this is termed a "light" and not a chandelier. It was probably called a chandelier in the eighteenth century; after that time the French adopted the term "lustre."

Catalog available, $3.
Lester H. Berry
1108 Pine St.
Philadelphia, Pa. 19107
(215) 923-2603

Wrought-Iron Chandeliers

Kenneth Lynch's craftsmen can do almost anything with metal. They produce a staggering array of products. Their wrought-iron chandeliers are rugged and unique. This hand-forged example can have as few as six lights or as many as sixteen, depending on its diameter. It can be finished in old iron or half-polished iron.

The second linear design can be lengthened to order. Lynch's craftsmen are accustomed to following the specifications of the customer.

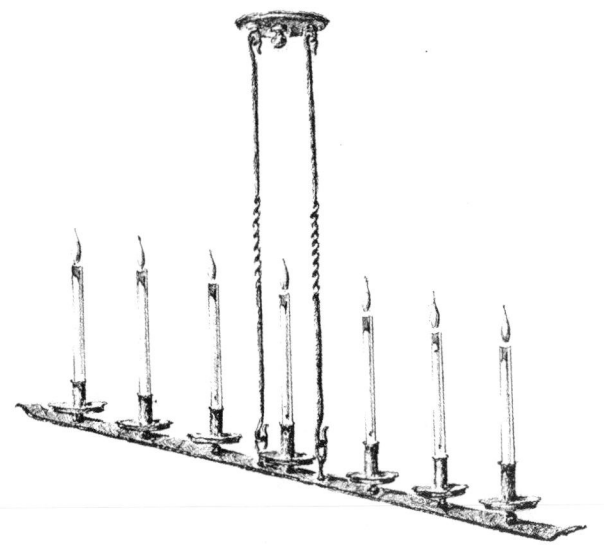

Catalog available, $3.50.

Kenneth Lynch & Sons
78 Danbury Rd.
Wilton, Conn. 06897
(203) 539-0532

Small Hall Chandelier

Wasley Lighting manufactures early American and traditional pieces of other sorts. They have just introduced this compact, handsome model (10″ diameter). You can get it in polished brass, antique brass, or pewter. It is equally appropriate in the dining room, foyer, or parlor. The list price is $101.40.

Catalog available, $2.50.

Wasley Lighting Division
Plainville Industrial Park
Plainville, Conn. 06062
(203) 747-5586

Sunburst Chandelier

Not many interiors are suited for a chandelier this fanciful. It illustrates the temptation facing the home

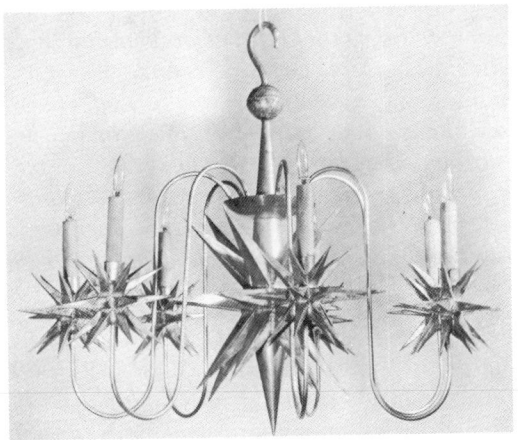

restorer seeking striking but appropriate furnishings. If you have the room in which to display such a dazzling fixture, be our guest. It is available from Gates Moore. The light from seven candles plays delightfully on these painstakingly-wrought sunbursts. The chandelier spreads across 26″ and comes with a ceiling canopy. It sells for $500.

Catalog available, $2.

Gates Moore
River Rd., Silvermine
Norwalk, Conn. 06850
(203) 847-3231

Moravian Tin Chandelier

The Mercer Museum's collection includes a chandelier of primitive Moravian design. Its radiant arms hold six candles. The pierced tin center is a bit like a Revere lantern in design. The chief difference is that the chandelier's light source surrounds the center instead of emanating from it.

Brochure available, 50¢.

The Mercer Museum Shop
Bucks County Historical Society
Pine and Ashland
Doylestown, Pa. 18901
(215) 345-0737

Table Lamps

Table lamps are a dime a dozen. Truly handsome fixtures of this sort are very rare. Frankly we've had it with bean pots and crocks for bases. Another cliché is the candle mold. Why not try something that was intended to hold an electric, gas, oil, or kerosene fixture, or even a candle? Bases for kerosene or whale oil table lamps can be simple or fancy affairs, slender glass sticks with graceful fonts or marble, ormolu, and crystal confections. Shades may be pierced tin, a heavy paper, or luxurious silk. The general style of a room will determine in large part what is appropriate in lamp style. The best rule seems to be: let it be a functioning fixture, not a purely decorative one, and choose a form that is fitting for a lamp.

Among the thousands of models to choose from are such standards as brass desk lamps, "Gone With the Wind" lamps (ironically not introduced until after the Civil War), cut-glass parlor lamps, molded and cut

girandoles, small chamber lamps of glass, tin, pewter, and brass, and various "student" lamps. In most cases, one needn't turn to a reproduction manufacturer to find what you need. For the very special, however, you may choose to contact such a firm as Royal Windyne, Ltd.

Victorian Brass

This distinctive solid brass table lamp could accent a rich Victorian study *and* provide useful light. Royal Windyne sells this and other period styles with accurate reproduction glass shades. A tarnish-preventing lacquer is applied unless you're a traditionalist who would rather buff than switch. The fixture sells for $82.50.

Catalog available, $1.

Royal Windyne Ltd.
Box 6622
Richmond, Va. 23230
(804) 355-5690

Floor Lamps

Floor lamps, as noted in the introduction to this chapter, are old-fashioned fixtures, and most are horrendously designed. There is no reason to go out of your way searching for something you can live with. Floor lamps aren't necessary in most cases, yet they are handy things to have behind a large upholstered chair used for reading. What is termed a "bridge" lamp has been around for years, and may do the trick.

Bridge Lamp

Originally this was a candlestand. Electrified, the 52″ fixture commends itself to lighting up awkward corners and can hover conveniently over the back of an easy chair. The harp moves up and down on the iron spindle and turns a full 360 degrees. It sells for $49.50 from Essex Forge.

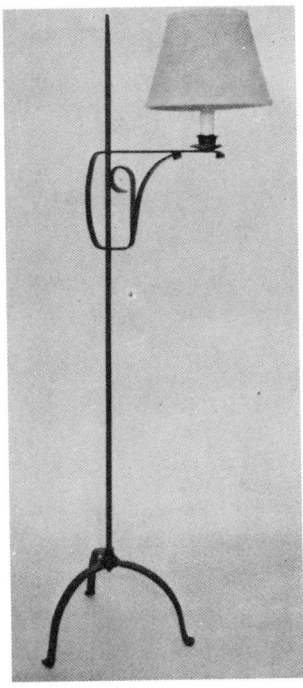

Catalog available, $1.

The Essex Forge
1 Old Dennison Rd.
Essex, Conn. 06426
(203) 767-1808

Hanging Lamps

Hanging lamps are not used as frequently as chandeliers in many period-style homes, but in many ways are more fitting. These are less expensive to buy and to maintain. For a small room, they may present the proper scale. In a narrow hall- or entryway a hanging lamp can provide just the right amount of light. Styles vary greatly—from Colonial period glass globes to late Victorian electric "gasoliers."

Glass Lamp and Smoke Bell

Ball and Ball reproductions hang in Independence Hall, Philadelphia. The brass they use is solid and the glass is off-hand blown lead crystal. The objects copied by the firm are of the sort found in the better homes of late

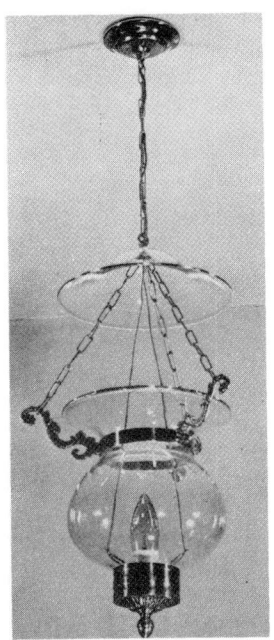

eighteenth and nineteenth-century America. Illustrated here is a pear-shape lamp and smoke bell. There are several different models but all hang on 6″ of chain from a canopy. The fixture is priced at $215.

Catalog available, $2.

Ball and Ball
463 West Lincoln Highway
Exton, Pa. 19341
(215) 363-7330

Oil Lamp

Saturday evening guests might have sat in the glow of this oil lamp as they discussed the shocking news of Lee's surrender at Appomatox. Its wood-polished crys-

117

tals, colorfully painted decoration, and brass trimmings combine perfectly with the glass font and shade. This classical "Lightyear" interpretation is supplied by the MarLe Company and sells for $405. MarLe is also a manufacturer of other kinds of traditional fixtures which are not part of the "Lightyear" line.

Catalog available, $1.

MarLe Company
170 Summer St.
Stamford, Conn. 06901
(203) 348-2645

Ceiling Canopy

All hanging lanterns, lights, lamps, or chandeliers require an appropriate piece of hardware from which to suspend them. A ceiling canopy is usually provided by the manufacturer along with the fixture. If such is not available, you might consider this model which, like the others, fits a universal ceiling adapter. Although it is of Spanish descent, its hammered look will suit most iron fixtures. It is priced at $4.95.

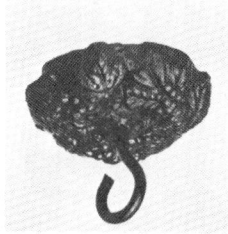

Catalog available, $1.

Mexico House
Box 970
Del Mar, Calif. 92014

Oil and Kerosene-Burning Lamps

Oil and kerosene-burning lamps are being used today indoors and out. If handled with normal care, there is no reason why such fixtures should not be as safe to use as an electric lamp. A surprising amount of light is given off by many of the models. There are a number of producers of modern and reproduction lamps.

"Northeaster"

The kerosene-burning "Northeaster" is substantially unchanged since the days when whaling fleets rounded Nantucket. It is made on Cape Cod with traditional techniques. Each fixture is solid copper and bears the signature of its maker, John Kopas.

Brochure available.

Copper Antiquities
Cummaquid P.O.
Cummaquid, Mass. 02637
(617) 775-7704

"Mary Light"

The "Mary Light" is a high-quality rendition of the old kerosene-fueled standby. It comes in hand-rubbed solid copper or brass. For the same $39, you can get this lamp wired for electric operation. But why not try the real thing?

Catalog available, $2.

Heritage Lanterns
Dept. OH78
Sea Meadows Lane
Yarmouth, Maine 04096
(207) 846-3911

Pottery and Betty Lamps

Until the mid-nineteenth century, hand-thrown pottery lamps were a common fixture in North American homes. The mass production of pressed glass made this labor-intensive piece virtually obsolete. Now interest in traditional crafts is bringing us back to older forms. Sturbridge Yankee Workshop makes a 17″ high fixture which comes with wick and crystal hurricane. The oil reservoir is hand-glazed with black and brown striations. It is priced at $28.50.

The same firm also produces a betty lamp reproduction. The betty was truly a lamp for the people. It made its way from Western Europe to America where it was often crafted by village smiths as an affordable alternative to the more exotic, ornamented fixtures of the gentry. Many of today's reproductions are designed to hold candles instead of oil and a wick. This is the case with Sturbridge's wrought-iron model. It is 7½″ high and sells for $4.95.

A *two-year subscription to the Sturbridge Yankee Workshop catalog (quarterly issues) is available for 50¢.*

Sturbridge Yankee Workshop
Dept. OHC
Sturbridge, Mass. 01566
(617) 347-7176 or 765-5550

Lamp Brackets

The natural place—and a safe one—for an old lamp may not be the mantle or a shelf. A lamp bracket combines convenience and safety. It can be mounted almost anywhere. A pin on the end of the bracket fits into the wall mount and allows it to pivot. This one is cast iron and comes in raw metal or black finish.

Literature available.

Wrightsville Hardware Co.
N. Front St.
Wrightsville, Pa. 17368
(717) 252-1561

Lanterns

For some reason lanterns seem to be the most popular of lighting forms. These convenient fixtures are often very portable, and they have been carried by soldiers, miners, country doctors, heroes and villains for hundreds of years. Lanterns are most often used today as postlights, and this is a pity. They may be conveniently hung by the door against a wall or suspended from the ceiling. Indoors or out, designed to fend off drafts or the wind, simple to carry or to hang, they provide an attractive and practical alternative means of lighting. Most lanterns—reproduction or antique—have been electrified, but they can be used or altered for the burning of candles.

"The Essex"

Lanterns from The Essex Forge are solid copper. The "Essex," seen here, is one of a pair that frames the entrance to Essex, Connecticut's Griswold Inn. At 21″ high, this lantern can take the measure of any early American doorway. By adding a fourth pane of glass and a collar, its can also perch atop a lampost.

Catalog available, $1.

The Essex Forge
Old Dennison Rd.
Essex, Conn. 06426
(203) 767-1808

119

"The Castille"

If you are into Spanish Colonial, Mexico House has a striking array of lighting fixtures at reasonable prices. Some are embellished with wrought-iron leaves and curlicues. Here is the "Castille," a 15″ high wall-mounted lamp. It lists for $20.95 or two for $37.

Catalog available, $1.

Mexico House
Box 970
Del Mar, Calif. 92014

Tall Lantern

This tall (18″) lantern can be mounted on a wall and comes in copper or pewterlure, a metal with the satiny sheen of real pewter. We'd rather stick with the copper.

Brochure available.

Copper Antiquities
Cummaquid P.O.
Cummaquid, Mass. 02637
(617) 775-7704

"Wall Huggers"

Many exterior wall-mounted lanterns might also be suitable for indoor use if they were only a little thinner. Newstamp has an attractive line of "wall huggers" that help solve the problem of overextension. Their smallest model is 5¾″ wide and extends only 4¾″ from the wall. It is solid copper and sells for $47.50 in hand-rubbed copper or brass finishes or $42.50 in satin black.

Catalog available, $2.

Newstamp Lighting Co.
227 Bay Rd.
North Easton, Mass. 02356
(617) 238-7071

"Welcome" and "Octagon" Lanterns

A trio of electric candles cast their light through the huge front panel of the "Welcome Lantern." The hous-

ing is tin and is pierced on the sides and front of the hood. It measures 21″ high, 13″ wide, and 7″ deep. The fixture is available in black and sells for $95 if electrified; $80 with candles.

The "Octagon Lantern" is a stately design. The pierced tin top creates a pattern on the ceiling. It comes with two feet of chain and a ceiling canopy. Electrified, it sells for $125.

Catalog available, $1.

Hurley Patentee Lighting
R.D. 7, Box 98A
Kingston, N.Y. 12401
(914) 331-5414

E.G. Washburne Lanterns

The ubiquitous lantern was born out of the need to protect and reflect a source of light. The accommodation of these requirements to period styles has produced

enormous variety and gives them almost universal appeal. E. G. Washburne markets a series of hanging and wall-mounted lanterns of eighteenth-century simplicity. Their copper housings take on a distinguished patina and will weather any storm.

Catalog available.

E. G. Washburne & Co.
85 Andover St., Rte. 114
Danvers, Mass. 01923
(617) 774-3645

"Hanging Lamp with Door"

The lamps from Washington Copper Works share unique features. First of all, many of them would be considered lanterns. More important, an aesthetically pleasing copper conduit houses the wire that enters the socket. A copper bug screen keeps out the moths. Each light is numbered and initialed. Their "Hanging Lamp with Door" is both graceful and practical. Thick copper wire runs diagonally down from each corner for a spiral effect. The lamp/lantern comes is a variety of sizes and prices. The largest, at $170, is 18″ wide and 28″ high.

Catalog available, $1.

The Washington Copper Works
Serge Miller, Proprietor
Washington, Conn. 06793
(703) 868-7527

Postlights

The postlight has become as ubiquitous a modern accessory as the cutely decorated mailbox. Nevertheless, this fixture may be a useful one, especially for the country or suburban house. Beside lighting the way to the door, it provides a cheerful welcome to the night visitor. Lanterns were once hung from posts to accomplish the same aims. In the electric age, the practice has only become more uniform. As an alternative to the flood-lit look of Alcatraz, increasingly common in these security-conscious days, the postlight is definitely to be preferred.

The electrified or gas-lit lantern is the proper form, but globes of various sorts are also historically accurate. The buyer of a post and a light must be conscious of several matters. Make sure that the light is of the right scale for the setting; a tiny or too large lantern will appear ridiculous. Also make sure that both elements are of sturdy construction. Changing bulbs, for instance, can be a hazardous business, especially if you have to lean over a stepladder to perform the operation. Last, be certain that the light is suitable for outdoor use and that it and the post have been properly weatherproofed.

Early Pennsylvania Design

This postlight is a copy of an early Pennsylvania design. The original was made of tinned sheet iron. The reproduction is antiqued solid brass and will surely outlast all of us. It sells for $175.

Brochure available, 75¢.

American Period Lighting Fixtures
The Saltbox
2229 Marietta Pike
Lancaster Pa. 17603
(717) 392-5649

and the following two authorized sales locations: 608 N. Greene St., Greensboro, N.C. 27401 (919-273-8758), and 216 W. Maxwell St., Lexington, Ky. 40508 (606-254-1265).

Welsbach Lighting

Welsbach patented the first of the "Boulevard" series in 1899. It became a standard fixture in American cities. Although the glass type is still available, a vandal resistant model has been developed that has metal or polycarbonate domes and globes. Despite this allowance for contemporary criminal mores, the spirit of the original line has been retained.

Welsbach's free brochure does not do justice to their line of uncatalogued items such as gas burners, chimneys, mantles, glass ware, electric conversion kits and more.

The firm uses a variety of foundry techniques to create durable and attractive posts. Some are spun, tapered, or extruded aluminum, while others are cast in aluminum or iron. One model has an upper section of wood.

Welsbach's pier bases are cast aluminum and are consistent in style with their Victorian heritage. They can be fairly simple or quite ornate.

Literature available.

Welsbach Lighting Inc.
240 Sargent Dr.
New Haven, Conn. 06511
(203) 789-1710

Sconces

Sconces provide the most natural appearance of artificial light. Used with candles, they are truly antique in appearance. But even those wired for electricity can carry the true look of the past. While no reproduction can be "authentic," it can aim toward a convincing verisimilitude. Most sconces are relatively simple fixtures to fashion. And good models are in plentiful supply. Providing for their wiring is a more complicated matter.

Combined Gas and Electric

Gas and electric combinations found their expression in wall sconces as well as chandeliers. Classic Illumination reproduces several fine examples, including one that, when viewed from the front, looks like a sine wave length. One end has an electric socket which points downward. To the other end is affixed a filigreed key and above that is a gas jet. Complementary shade combinations add another another dimension to this solid brass fixture.

Catalog available, $2.

The Classic Illumination
P.O. Box 5851
San Francisco, Calif. 94101
(415) 527-5106

Classic Illumination fixtures are also available from the following distributors: San Francisco Victoriana, 606 Natoma, San Francisco, Calif. 94103 (415-429-5477) and Victorian Reproductions, 1601 Park Avenue South, Minneapolis, Minn. 55404 (612-338-3636).

Williamsburg Sconce

Among Williamsburg's architectural treasures is the Peyton Randolph House. It sits in shaded serenity off the Green. Of particular note are its series of paneled rooms, considered the best in Williamsburg. Hanging from one of these walls is the original dark mahogany sconce from which this reproduction is copied for Williamsburg by Victorius, Inc. The curved glass front slides up for access to the candle. It measures 18″ by 13⅝″ and with this Balister candlestick sells for $273.50.

Catalog available, $4.95.

Colonial Williamsburg
Craft House
Williamsburg, Va. 23185
(804) 229-1000

Brass "Hands"

Whether these heavy cast-brass hands served as inspiration for Bram Stoker is a matter of conjecture. A left and

right hand is available. Each extends 11½″ from a 7″ diameter back plate. You can buy one for $149. A pewter or silver finish is available at additional cost.

Catalog available, $3.

Lester H. Berry
1108 Pine St.
Philadelphia, Pa. 19107
(215) 923-2603

Antique Tin

Antique American tin sconces rarely reveal their age, but it is widely accepted that the ones with circular reflectors are among the oldest. This reproduction has the popular channeled sunburst design. It is an object in the Old Sturbridge Village collection and sells for $18.50.

Catalog available.

Virginia Metalcrafters, Inc.
1010 East Main St.
Waynesboro, Va. 22980
(703) 942-8205

Gates Moore

To the Gates Moore people, electrification of authentic reproductions is an unfortunate necessity—but they make no apologies for their workmanship. The electric wires, for example, are as unobtrusive as possible. No modern bolts or fasteners show in any fixture. All metal parts are bent or crimped with simple hand tools. These

faithful reproductions come in distressed tin, pewter coat, or painted finish. Prices range from $20 for the diamond-shaped sconce to $45 for the twin candle.

Catalog available, $2.

Gates Moore
River Rd., Silvermine
Norwalk, Conn. 06850
(203) 847-3231

Reflector Sconce

Like all Hurley Patentee reproductions, the original of this unusual sconce is a museum-quality piece. The glass-enclosed reflectors are of antique leaded tin and are framed in wood. Wired, it sells for $70; subtract $10 for candle power.

Catalog available, $1.

Hurley Patentee Lighting
R.D. 7, Box 98A
Kingston, N.Y. 12401
(914) 331-5414

Supplies

True devotees of the art of lighting will find that their need for various supplies and replacement parts is never ending. Almost every reproduction lighting house carries a number of such items in its regular inventory. And even the once-in-a-lifetime home restorer may find that he will need to call on them for help.

Prisms

Crystal prisms have a way of breaking or disappearing over the years. Replacements may be elusive. Luigi Crystal imports several types that range in price from 50¢ to $2.50 each. Styles include pendalogue (tear drop), spear, Colonial, frog, and "U" drop.

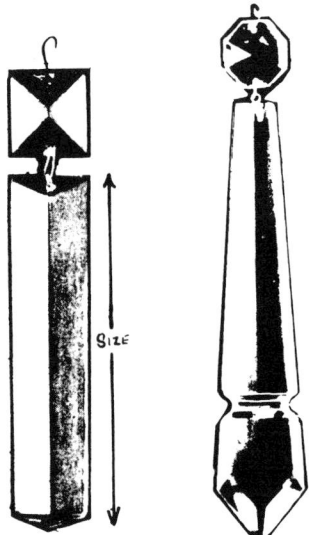

Catalog available, 25¢.

Luigi Crystal
7332 Frankford Ave.
Philadelphia, Pa. 19136
(215) 338-2978

Candle Covers

The Saltbox ("American Period Lighting Fixtures") offers off-white candle covers for electric fixtures in either 4″ or 6″ heights. The drippings add a touch of authenticity.

Catalogue available, 75¢.

American Period Lighting Fixtures
The Saltbox
2229 Marietta Pike
Lancaster, Pa. 17603
(717) 392-5649

and the following two authorized sales locations: 608 N. Greene St., Greensboro, N.C. 27401 (919-273-8758) and 216 W. Maxwell St., Lexington, Ky. 40508 (606-254-1265).

Tiffany Lamp Kits

Tiffany lamps are beautiful luxuries. The originals are stored in museums and prized by lucky collectors. For those of us less fortunate, there are reproductions. Better yet, if we are so inclined and skilled, there are kits. Tiffany's famous Wisteria lampshade, for example, which is now valued at over $33,000, can be bought in kit form for $47.50. Coran-Sholes has just about anything a professional artisan or rank amateur could want. Their kits include all the necessary materials such as precut glass, lead cames, solder, electrical and hanging hardware, *and* complete instructions.

Catalog available, $1.

Coran-Sholes
509 East Second St.
South Boston, Mass. 02127
(617) 268-3780

Gas Shades

Gas shades are often as delicate as flowers. Names like Diamond-Daisy and Snowflake suggest their character. Craftsmen have enhanced their fanciful form with intricate etching, pressing, and frosting. There are so many styles that one can be found to fit the personality of almost any room or its inhabitants. The shades are exact reproductions and range in price from $10 to $15.

Quarterly catalog, $1.

London Ventures Co.
2 Dock Square
Rockport, Mass. 01966
(617) 856-7161

Other Sources of Lighting Fixtures

Consult the List of Suppliers for addresses.

Antique Fixtures

Jerome W. Blum
The Cellar
Florence Maine
Materials Unlimited
Mrs. Eldred Scott
Westlake Architectural Antiques

Candleholders

Baldwin Hardware
Ball and Ball
Lester H. Berry
Historic Charleston Reproductions (Mottahedeh)
Colonial Williamsburg (Virginia Metalcrafters)
Copper Antiquities
Gates Moore
Guild of Shaker Crafts
Hurley Patentee Lighting
Steve Kayne
Mercer Museum Shop
Mexico House
George W. Mount
Period Furniture Hardware
Sturbridge Yankee Workshop
Washington Copper Works
Wasley Lighting

Chandeliers

Alcon Lightcraft Co.
American Period Lighting Fixtures (The Saltbox)
Authentic Designs
Ball and Ball
Colonial Williamsburg (Virginia Metalcrafters)
Copper Antiquities
Essex Forge
Robert Griffith
Heritage Lanterns
Hurley Patentee Lighting
Lightyear (MarLe)
Luigi Crystal
Mexico House
Newstamp Lighting
Packard Lamp Co., Inc.
Period Furniture Hardware
Spanish Villa
William Spencer
William Stewart & Sons
Sturbridge Yankee Workshop
Village Lantern
Wallin Forge
Washington Copper Works

Floor Lamps

Cohasset Colonials
Magnolia Hall
Rainbow Art Glass Corp
Sturbridge Yankee Workshop

Hanging Lamps
(including wall-mounted lamps)

American Period Lighting Fixtures (The Saltbox)
Authentic Designs
Lester H. Berry
Colonial Williamsburg (Virginia Metalcrafters)

Dahlman-Clift Lamps
Essex Forge
Gates Moore
Heritage Lanterns
Hurley Patentee Lighting
Magnolia Hall
Mexico House
Newstamp Lighting
Period Furniture Hardware
Royal Windyne Ltd.
Spanish Villa
William Spencer
Sturbridge Yankee Workshop
Wallin Forge
Washington Copper Works

Oil/Kerosene Lamps

Faire Harbour Boats (Aladdin)
Sturbridge Yankee Workshop
Washington Copper Works
Wasley Lighting

Table Lamps

Classic Illumination
Colonial Williamsburg (Virginia Metalcrafters)
Henry Ford Museum and Greenfield Village (Norman Perry)
Hurley Patentee Lighting
Luigi Crystal
Magnolia Hall
Ephraim Marsh
Mercer Museum Shop
Sturbridge Yankee Workshop
Wasley Lighting

Lanterns

American Period Lighting Fixtures (The Saltbox)
Copper House
Essex Forge
Gates Moore
Heritage Lanterns
Kenneth Lynch & Sons
Mercer Museum Shop
Period Lighting Fixtures
William Stewart & Sons
Sturbridge Yankee Workshop
Village Lantern
Wasley Lighting
Welsbach Lighting

Postlights

American Period Lighting Fixtures (The Saltbox)
Copper House
Gates Moore
Heritage Lanterns
Kenneth Lynch & Sons
Mexico House

Newstamp Lighting
Period Lighting Fixtures
William Spencer
Washington Copper Works
Wasley Lighting

Sconces

American Period Lighting Fixtures (The Saltbox)
Authentic Designs
Ball and Ball
Copper Antiquities
Essex Forge
Heritage Lanterns
Horton Brasses
Mexico House
Newton Millham
Newstamp Lighting
Period Furniture Hardware
Shaker Workshops
Spanish Villa
William Spencer
William Stewart & Sons
Sturbridge Yankee Workshop
Pete Taggett
Wasley Lighting

Supplies

B. &. P. Lamp Supply
Classic Illumination
Colonial Lamp & Supply
Hurley Patentee Lighting
Kenneth Lynch & Sons
Rainbow Art Glass
Welsbach Lighting

ELECTRIC LIGHT AND COMBINATION GAS FIXTURES.

MANUFACTURED BY EDISON GENERAL ELECTRIC CO.

Fixture & Decorative Bronze Dept.

"Chinoiserie Tree Cotton Print," Brunschwig & Fils, The
Winterthur Collection (#7237.04).

VII Fabrics

Fabric coverings are useful as well as decorative materials for the old house. Not only can they enhance a period interior and give it character, but they can help to insulate the inside from the outside elements and hide that which is not particularly attractive. The Victorians used to paper everything over. Today we have the nuisance of adhesive papers that successfully simulate just about everything *except* the intended material, and provide neither protection nor aesthetic value. Fabrics, too, can be an "easy way out" to a particular decorating dilemma. "Cover it" may seem the best advice at the time when you discover that a window sash is rotting away or that the previous owner has changed the height of one window of a series so that it no longer matches the others. But try to make structural improvements first. Fabrics should properly enhance whatever they cover whether it be furniture, a wall, or a window. Now that we have a wealth of reproduction historical textiles at hand, there is no reason why they should not be given the prominence that a budget will allow for.

A return to natural fiber materials is underway. This is a welcome change from the emphasis on synthetics which supposedly offered permanent pleats and colors. Cotton is back "in" again as is wool. Prices that once seemed grossly inflated for natural fabrics are being matched in artificial materials. Such synthetics can be mixed with natural fibers in a truly useful way; the stretched-out, shiny look of double-knit, however, is best left back in the recent past along with the yellowish rayon of the '50s and '60s. Claims of durability were misleading, and the cleaning of chemically-produced fibers was often a mystery that not even the best dry cleaner could solve. The best argument for natural fabrics is their natural look and texture. When mixed with similar natural building marials and furnishings, they not only seem to be right and fitting, they *are* right and fitting.

Fabrics are used primarily for window hangings and for upholstery. In both cases the past has much to recommend. Summer and winter curtains, slip covers and upholstery—these again make sense. Winter curtains were of a heavy sort that served to protect the room from cold. In the summer, sheer organdy or lace or thin cotton filtered out some light, but generally allowed for the flow of air. Slip covers had a cooling effect and protected furniture from the dirt and dust of the warm season. In winter, heavier upholstery material provided a welcome soft and warm cushion. It may not be possible to provide a double set of materials for all rooms in the house, but thought should be given to using two sets of curtains in at least the kitchen, if not the living room. Over the long run, such materials will more than pay for themselves. They will, of course, last twice as long as something which is used all year round.

Reproduction fabrics based on documents found in old homes and museums have been popular for many years. Their number continues to increase with demand. Less exact copies known as "adaptations" are also encountered. The diligent research will find that there is probably at least one reproduction fabric for each year of the period from 1700 to 1850. That is, if your house dates from 1838, you can find a material that was either introduced or was popularly used that year. This is not to say that you should use such a fabric, but merely to point out what a big and exacting business the reproduction of historic fabrics has become. Fabrics, however well manufactured, do not last more than several generations before they begin to disintegrate. Antique textiles can be purchased today, but most have to be used so gingerly that they might as well be framed and displayed as the antiques they are.

The most important recent change in the reproduction fabric business has been the new emphasis on Victorian-period materials. Although we tend to forget or ignore this fact, most of American building dates from the mid- to late-nineteenth century. Boston and Charleston have many more Victorian structures than Colonial. So, too, did Williamsburg and Philadelphia's Society Hill before these buildings were torn to the ground. San Francisco may lavish more love on its Victorian buildings than any other American city, but similar houses exist from coast to coast, and fortunately they are being discovered.

There are not many shortcuts available to the buyer of good period fabrics. Some are sold only through interior designers and the decorating departments of large retail outlets. For those who can afford to follow such paths, the way is relatively easy. Professional help and advice is always the best investment. The alternative is to seek out the increasing number of fabric lines which are sold both through design services and other retail outlets. The persistent and intelligent shopper may even find that very appropriate textiles may be found in surplus or remnant stores. The most fortunate buyer of all is the one who possesses not only the energy to track down good material, but the skill with which to upholster or to work it up at home into curtains, slip covers, hangings, etc.

Curtain and Drapery Materials

Four natural fibers—cotton, wool, silk, and flax—provide the best of materials for window, wall, and bed hangings. All of these basic fibers are often combined with man-made fibers such as rayon polyester. Some curtain material, of course, is totally synthetic, and the majority of such textiles is unsuitable for use in period interiors. The initial expense of a synthetic may be less, but now even this advantage is disappearing with the great advance in basic petrochemical costs. In any case, synthetics are not good long-term investments. On the simplest level, compare a feather pillow with one filled with polyurethane foam after several years of use. The former, if properly cared for, will puff up and remain useful; the foam-rubber filling will have begun its process of disintegration, and you may find that something resembling shredded wheat is all that remains between you and the mattress.

Fabrics are available in a bewildering variety of patterns, materials, and finishes. Fabric lines, like those of wallpaper, are in a constant state of change. For this reason, it is well worth checking remnant outlets in your area; discontinued items may be of considerable interest and value to you. Matching fabrics and papers are still popular. In many cases, however, use of one pattern at the windows and the same in upholstery, bed hangings, etc., can amount to overkill. Although it may be proper to make use of one good fabric in several different ways (our ancestors were similarly economical), it is questionable whether the design motif should be carried out in a paper identical to the fabric selected. Slightly different but coordinated patterns may be the best approach.

Suppliers and manufacturers are listed in alphabetical order.

Laura Ashley

Traditional patterns found in Welsh patchwork quilts and other Victorian fabrics form the country look favored by this design and manufacturing firm located in Wales. The cotton fabrics are mainly small prints with floral or geometric designs. They are just being introduced in North America.

Laura Ashley, Inc.
714 Madison Ave.
New York, N.Y. 10021

Brunschwig & Fils

A glazed chintz is a tightly-woven cotton fabric that has been given a high finish through weaving or through the addition of resins. "Antibes" (#17147.00) is reproduced exactly as designed by Jean-Ulric Tournier in Alsace, France, c. 1845. The document itself is to be found in the Musée Historique de Tissus in Mulhouse. The original was block printed; the reproduction has been hand-screen printed, and is available in six color combinations.

A second glazed chintz, "China Dream" (#6637.01), is appropriately based on watered silk bed hangings in the White and Gold Room at the Henry Francis du Pont Winterthur Museum. The original French pattern is dated 1775–1800. Also 100% cotton, the adaptation is available in the original cream color and four other shades.

Crewel embroidery has been popular for many years and was once one of the simpler ways to decorate woolen material. "Indigo Crewel" (#7328.04) is a hand-screen printed adaptation of an eighteenth-century American curtain panel in wool needlework. The original is found in the Hampton Room of the Winterthur Museum. The effect of hand-embroidery can never be exactly duplicated in a printed fabric, but this design, worked in 57% linen and 43% cotton, is quite effective. The original colors are blue shades and these and four other colorways are offered.

Brunschwig & Fils fabrics are sold through interior designers and decorating services of department stores. Consult appendixes A and B for further information on these sources. Further information may be secured from:

Brunschwig & Fils, Inc.
979 Third Ave.
New York, N.Y. 10022
(212) 838-7878

S. M. Hexter

Eighteenth-century floral patterns from England and France are among the most traditional of designs. They are suitable for elegant interiors of that time *and* of the twentieth century. "Aldbury" is a 100% cotton screen print introduced for the first time in 1977 and is based on an English document. It is available in six different color combinations: crimson and Canton blue, Nanking blue and camel, sorrel and plum, carmine and copper, burnt umber and stone, and Kent grey and wheat.

"Sylvia" is a glazed chintz developed from drawings found in the antique sketchbooks of Oberkampf, and was originally produced in the factory at Jouy, France, during the mid-eighteenth century. It is offered in biscuit and Canton blue, canary and platinum, peach-bloom and cayenne, white and crimson, and ivory and blue.

"Aesop's Fable" is typical of the documentary prints in cotton popular in America during the early 1800s. Hexter's rendition is based on original material found in the archives of the Henry Ford Museum and is available in spice, Canton blue, raisin, loganberry, and black.

The kind of prints used in French provincial country houses are not that different from those found in rural America during the nineteenth century. "Emilie" is an aptly-named 100% cotton fabric that evokes pastoral simplicity and is offered in nine different colors: brick, blueberry, eggplant, navy, cherry, flagstone blue, cocoa, country blue, and gingersnap.

132

Water lilies are a motif which occur frequently in printed textiles of the late 1800s. "1889" is based on a French document of that year and is a most appropriate 100% cotton design for any Victorian interior which reflects a passion for things Oriental and aesthetic. There are nine shades available: cinnabar, pewter, peachbloom, mauve, powder blue, tender taupe, sand beige, celadon, and cornsilk.

The luscious peonies of the "Wyndham" screen print would be welcome in any home where there is a love for the naturalistic and floral. In contrast to the florals of

the mid-eighteenth century, this fabric is alive with sharply rendered realistic detail. It is based on an English design and is offered in gem blue and coral, navy blue and moonbeam, espresso and pink, umbre and beach, and forest green and blush.

Hexter has showrooms in New York, Atlanta, Boston, Chicago, Cincinnati, Dallas, Denver, Detroit, Honolulu, Los Angeles, Miami, Minneapolis, Philadelphia, Phoenix, Portland, San Francisco, Seattle, St. Louis, Toronto, and London, England, or may be contacted at:

S. M. Hexter Co.
2800 Superior Ave.
Cleveland, Ohio 44114
(216) 696-0146

Old Stone Mill

"Baroda" is typical of the designs from India which were brought to America in the eighteenth-century via England. This is an adaptation from a fragment which survived the wear and tear of the years.

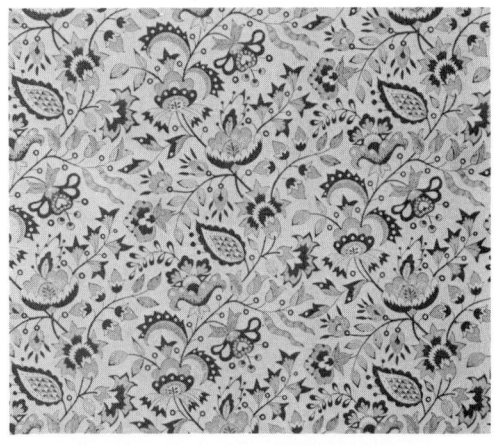

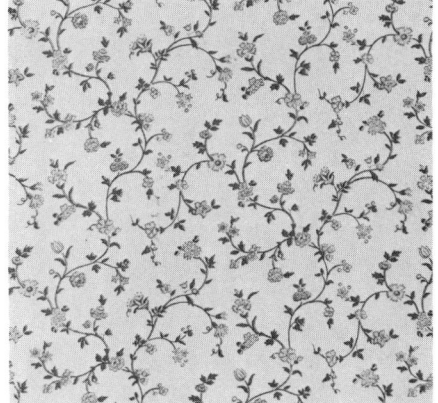

"Mademoiselle" is reproduced from an original block-printed toile de Jouy manufactured at the famous French *manufacture royale* from the mid-1700s to the early nineteenth century. This factory was a source for a number of wealthy Americans of the period.

Brochure available.

Old Stone Mill Corp.
Adams, Mass. 01220
(413) 743-1015

Scalamandré

Do not let Scalamandré's reputation for expensive quality frighten you away. There are fabrics here of real value and substance which will not break your pocketbook. And there are many about which you (and I) can dream or view—in the White House and other important historic mansions from coast to coast. All of the fabrics are sold through decorating departments or interior designers; and by consulting the information contained in appendices A and B, you may find that using a middleman is not such a difficult task as it may appear to be.

A cotton "Monk's Cloth" (#4010) is one of the reasonably-priced materials which Scalamandré has to offer. It is, of course, the solid pattern formed by a weaver. It can be dyed in one of many colors, and such material is most appropriate for curtains in a simple country interior.

"Coverlet Damask" (#7699-1), another 100% cotton, is also a simple material and uses only one color. It does not have the richness associated with jacquard-woven fabrics such as damasks, but the pattern is a pleasing one and not inappropriate.

Toiles of French origin were used in Colonial and early nineteenth-century homes in America. The fabric illustrated (#6708-1) is a copy of one used in the Betty Lewis bedroom at Kenmore, Fredericksburg, Virginia. It is of one color and of 100% cotton.

The "Directoire Toile" print (#6423) is a more complicated pattern made with two screens. It is representative of fabrics used in the early 1800s in fine homes up and down the East Coast. It is 100% cotton.

134

Italian Renaissance designs of great complexity and beauty slowly made their way in the New World. This is a silk damask (#97178) which was designed by Franco Scalamandré and used for draperies in the State Dining Room of the White House. It is a mixture of gold and cream and has to be custom-ordered.

"Werms House Diamond" (#6446) from Scalamandré's new Historic Savannah Collection is a geometric glazed cotton chintz of the sort that would have been used in

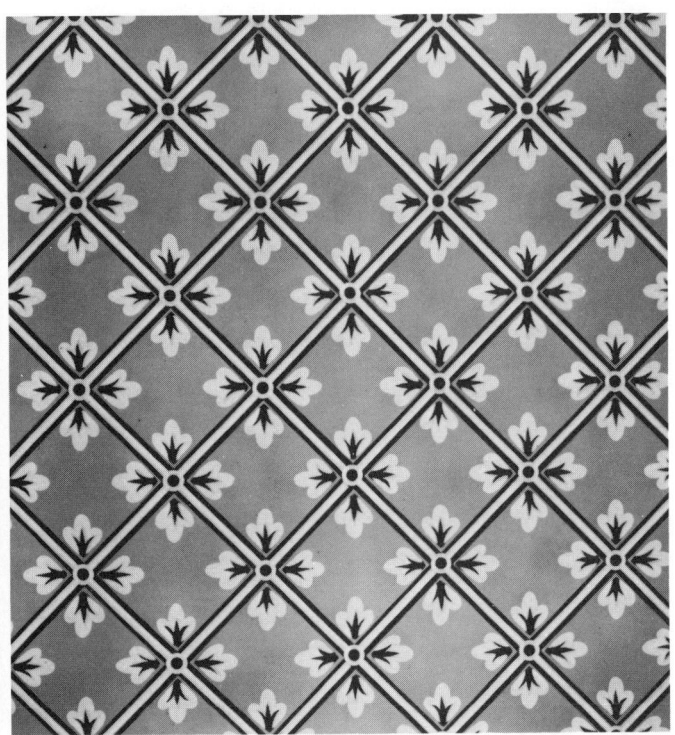

less than White House surroundings. It is a design adapted from the boiserie effect achieved in the first floor library ceiling of Werms House.

A wallpaper in the Sorrell-Weed House in Savannah was the source for this documentary design in the Adams or Federal style. "Sorrel-Weed House" (#6450), part of the Historic Savannah Collection, is made of 100% duck cotton.

Scalamandré
950 Third Ave.
New York, N.Y. 10022
(212) 361-8500

Schumacher

To many, the name Schumacher is only slightly less forbidding than that of Scalamandre. The initiated, however, realize that the firm has been associated with Colonial Williamsburg and many fine other historical institutions for some years and is really quite approachable. As with other high quality fabric manufacturers, there is a considerable variety of materials available in a wide price range. Many of the Schumacher fabrics can be found in retail outlets throughout North America.

"Phillipsburg Manor Resist" (#65555) is from the Sleepy Hollow Collection and is typical of the one-color patterns produced in the Colonies by primitive craftsmen during the early to mid-eighteenth century. The term

"Raleigh Tavern" (#178160 series), "Williamsburg Liner Stripe" (#63110 series), and "Pleasures of the Farm" (#50428) are from the Colonial Williamsburg collection of documented reproductions. These are seen, respectively, from top to bottom. The first is a "resist" block print in 70% linen and 30% cotton; the second, 100% cotton; and the third, a pastoral scene of 100% cotton.

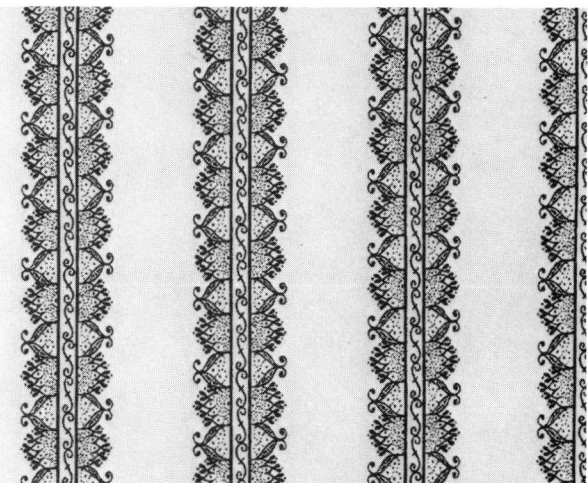

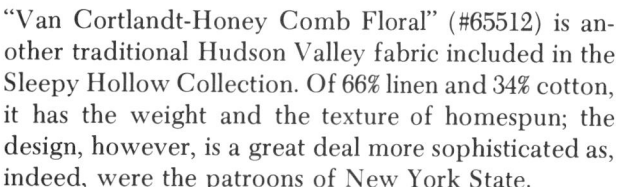

"Van Cortlandt-Honey Comb Floral" (#65512) is another traditional Hudson Valley fabric included in the Sleepy Hollow Collection. Of 66% linen and 34% cotton, it has the weight and the texture of homespun; the design, however, is a great deal more sophisticated as, indeed, were the patroons of New York State.

A shiny glazed 100% cotton—"Peplum Liner" (#67570) —might have been found in a late Colonial or an early 1800s interior. It is from the Smithsonian Institution Collection.

Few of Schumacher's fabrics are clearly designated for use in Victorian interiors, but many can be so utilized. Designer John Hargreaves has provided a new translation of a turn-of-the-century Tiffany-style brocade design in 100% cotton. "Topiary" (#69870 series) is a rich, colorful pattern of unusual interest. It is available in deep spruce, Braque brown, dove gray, shadow peach, and cathedral blue.

"Noailles (#64874) is yet another glazed 100% cotton print and is part of the Historic Newport Collection. As befits the social graces of this important seaport city, this is a particularly graceful and delicate design. It has been worked in several colors.

"Lagos" (#69830 series) is an adaptation of an eighteenth-century Portuguese design by Virginia Bowen, A.S.I.D., in 100% linen. Complex effects of this sort were employed in all the late-Victorian decorative arts—from wall and floor tiles to wallpapers to fabrics. The colors are also typical of the earthy tones favored at the time. Schumacher has given them Portuguese names: Algarve coral and sage, Tagus blue and brass, Oporto slate and brick, Litoral turquoise and beige, Portugal terra cotta and smoke, Marinha green and yellow.

"Ardebil" (#69890) is inspired by an antique Persian rug and is printed on "union" linen cloth and cotton. The design is that of Ruth Strachan Cole, A.S.I.D., and would have excited the interest of decorators in the 1880s and '90s. The colors are deep shades of the sort used in rugs from the Middle East.

F. Schumacher & Co.
939 Third Ave.
New York, N.Y. 10022
(212) 644-5943

Silk Surplus

Residents of the New York City area are fortunate in having three outlets of Silk Surplus to visit. Close-outs and fabrics which are termed "off-colors" are available here along with a large quality line made for sale only in these stores. Many famous names, including Scalamandré, can be found. Business is simply cash and carry. Silk Surplus is one good reason for making a trip to the Big Apple and its environs.

Silk Surplus
223 E. 58th St.
New York, N.Y. 10022
(212) 753-6511

Silk Surplus
843 Lexington Ave.
New York, N.Y. 10021
(212) 879-4708

Silk Surplus
449 Old Country Rd.
Westbury, N.Y. 11590
(516) 997-7469

Albert Van Luit

Almost all of Van Luit's fabrics are highly-colored dramatic prints of cotton or linen. Many would be suitable for mid- to late-Victorian interiors in which floral designs were not at all uncommon. The most interesting fabrics are those in the "Initial Collection," and the dyes used for the colors are obviously extremely receptive to the fibers that form their ground. "Merivale Lane," a 100% cotton, is just one of these colorful fabrics.

Catalog available, 50¢.

Albert Van Luit & Co.
4000 Chevy Chase Dr.
Los Angeles, Calif. 90039
(213) 245-5106

Watts & Co.

Watts' fabrics are of museum quality and in design are a continuation of work begun by the founders of the company during the Victorian era. These reflect tremendous interest in and understanding of Gothic Revival taste. Thomas Garner was the designer of "Gothic," which Watts has recently reproduced in rose and in blue

silk. The high altar frontal at St. Thomas Church, New York, is suitably adorned with a second Watts' fabric, "Gainford," illustrated here below "Gothic." A very special manufacturer for very special needs.

Catalog available, $2.

Watts & Co. Ltd.
7 Tufton St.
Westminster, London
SWIP 3QB England

Waverly

To move from Watts to Waverly is to return to the world in which we all live today, and as the photographs illustrate, the fabrics provide an atmosphere which combines good taste with good sense.

The Old Sturbridge Village Collection provides both interest and quality for the old-house buyer. "Draper Chintz" (#684621) is a glazed 100% cotton of muted,

subtle colors. It is an English floral design and has been named after one of the early merchants of Boston, Horace Draper.

"Fiske Stencil" (#682061) is based on a traditional stencil design. Colors are soft and the pattern is rendered in the somewhat off-hand fashion expected of stencil art. Both this fabric and that illustrated below it, "Village Strip" (#681221), are of 100% cotton. Each is recommended for use in early to mid-nineteenth century interiors.

"French Paisley" (#683972) is also included in the Sturbridge group and is a 100% glazed cotton. Subdued it is not, but paisleys with very exuberant colors and lively patterns were popular from the 1850s on. Queen Victoria even draped a paisley shawl around her royal shoulders.

Waverly Fabrics
58 W 40th St.
New York, N.Y. 10018
(212) 644-5900

Upholstery Fabrics

Material used for covering furniture is of necessity of heavier weight and weave. Printed cottons can be used, but are best reserved for slip covers. Combinations of cotton and linen provide more durability, and pure wool probably the most of all. There are, of course, damasks, brocades, and velvets which are more complicated weaves and are therefore better material for upholstery—regardless of the base fiber used. 100% silk appears on only the finest pieces of period furniture. Horsehair was commonly used in the Victorian era and can be supplied today by many upholsterers or fabric manufacturers.

In recent years upholstery fabrics have been routinely covered with a protective synthetic covering. This is better than slip covering the furniture in sheets of clear vinyl, but these modern chemical shields against spills may make cleaning a fabric more difficult. Drinks will roll off, but dirt and food will inevitably find their way to the surface. Natural, untreated fibers can be cleaned of such "debris," but fibers which have been coated with a repellent lose their elasticity and endurance.

Ephraim Marsh

The company's business is primarily furniture, but it does supply hand-worked India crewel. Designs are stitched in wool against a hand-woven cotton ground. Four patterns are available—"Tree of Life, Floral," "Tree of Life with Bird," "Shalamar," and "Floral." Crewel embroidery for upholstery became popular during the eighteenth century and was later superseded by more precise and complicated forms of needlework.

Ephraim Marsh Co.
Box 266
Concord, N.C. 28025
(704) 782-0814

Scalamandré

"Song of India" (#96356) crewel is made in that country of 50% cotton and 50% wool. It is a higher grade of material than that generally available from American supply houses and therefore of more lasting quality.

Resist designs can also be used for upholstery purposes. "French Resist" (#6410) is an adaptation from a document in the Metropolitan Museum's textile collection and is made of 44% linen and 56% cotton. Not as primitive in appearance as the Colonial American designs, it might be used in both late Colonial and early Victorian interiors. The material comes in seven different colors.

"Flowers of India" appears handmade because of the uneven lines of the contiguous octagonal shapes. This is, however, machine-made material from India of 60% cotton and 40% wool and is available with coordinate border strips. Despite its intentional irregularities, the quite systematic design can be used in the manner of high-style needlework.

Linen made in Belgium (#L-13) has the nubby, substantial texture which flatters country-style furniture. It is also a material well-suited for simple curtains in either contemporary or early Colonial interiors. Scalamandré imports a basic natural and white cloth which will serve several purposes.

The "Amsterdam" novelty stripe (#9638) is an even stronger weave of 15% cotton and 84% linen which is made in Belgium. Although it features a small flower design, the overall effect is one of formality and neatness that would be suitable for relatively high-style American Federal furniture.

Scalamandré is famous for its 100% silk and combination silk upholstery materials which have been used in the White House and in other famous buildings. "French Empire Medallion" (#97347) is a damask of 31% silk and 69% cotton made at their Long Island City plant. The design is most appropriate for early- to mid-nineteenth-century interiors.

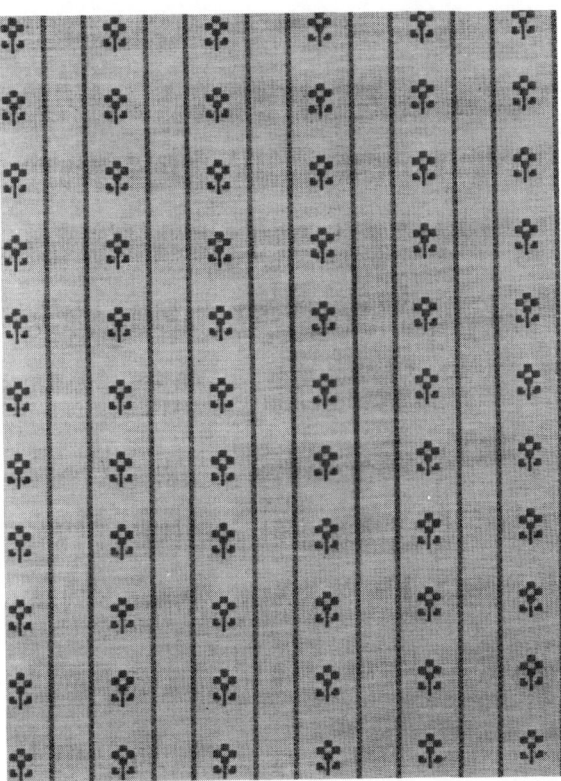

Reproduction of a Scotch ingrain wool fabric is extraordinarily difficult and expensive. "William Morris Bird" (#97373) was woven on Scalamandré's Scotch ingrain loom especially for the William Morris Society. Most fabric reproductions can be manufactured at less cost than the originals would be today, but, in this case, it would have been easier to start completely anew. The material *could* be used for small upholstery purposes but more than likely no one will really want this ruined by contact with the human body. It really belongs on the wall with other fine compositions.

Consult appendices A and B for further information regarding outlets for Scalamandré products, or contact:

Scalamandré Silks, Inc.
950 Third Ave.
New York, N.Y. 10022
(212) 361-8500

Schumacher

Schumacher's fabrics provide a constant source of materials for professional upholsterers and furniture craftsmen. The range of designs is unusually broad, and most are widely available.

"Stencil Flowers" (#66624) is a Colonial Williamsburg adaptation of a traditional eighteenth-century design. It is woven of 66% linen and 34% cotton.

Some fabrics can be reversed with good effect. "Sunnyside Floral" (#35356) is one of these. It is a very handsome 100% cotton of considerable weight and texture. "Sunnyside" was Washington Irving's home and the fabric is part of Schumacher's Sleepy Hollow Restoration Collection. So, too, is "Sunnyside Stripe" (#35400), seen below. The pattern is that found in ticking, but the effect is of an elegant formal cloth.

"Marseilles" (#36334) from the South Street Seaport Museum Collection, is an even more formal stripe, perfect for many period rooms of the 1800s.

Schumacher fabrics can be seen in showrooms around the country and are sold through numerous retail outlets. For further information, contact:

F. Schumacher & Co.
939 Third Ave.
New York, N.Y. 10018
(212) 644-5900

Trimmings

These are the little extras that can insure successful use of period window handings and upholstery. They are especially important for a high-style interior whether that be Georgian Colonial, Federal, Greek Revival, or Victorian.

Stroheim & Romann

This major supplier of fabric trimmings imports over fifty-three designs from Italy. These have to be hand-woven, a meticulous kind of work that calls for nimble fingers and steel nerves.

The firm's products are distributed throughout North America. For further information regarding sources, contact:

Stroheim & Romann
155 East 56th St.
New York, N.Y. 10022
(212) 691-0700

Scalamandré

Handmade trimmings and tiebacks are produced in America, too—primarily at this firm's Long Island City plant. Illustrated in the following two photographs are braid, gimp, tassels, fringes, and frogs. These by no means exhaust the Scalamandré repertoire.

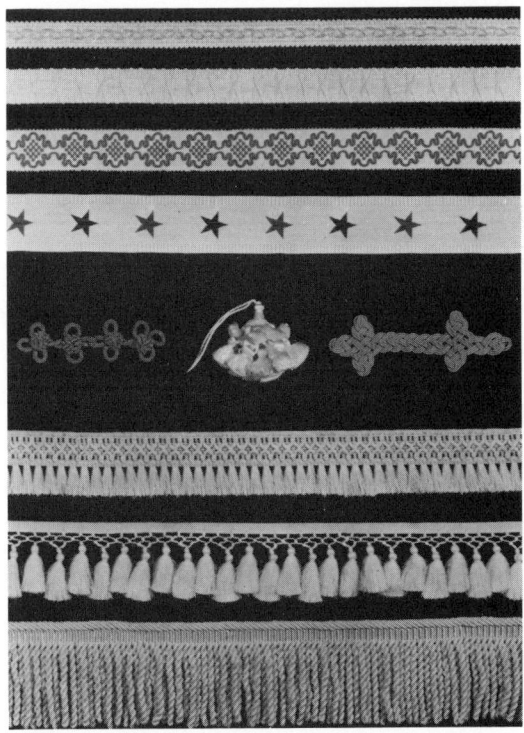

Available through interior design firms and decorating departments. For further information, contact:

Scalamandré Silks, Inc.
950 Third Ave.
New York, N.Y. 10022
(212) 361-8500

Raw Materials

The weaving and printing of fabrics is not only the concern of large-scale manufacturers. Increasingly, small companies of craftsmen have established themselves in this field. Since they are masters of the arts of spinning, dyeing, and weaving—and, frequently of block printing—they understand full well what went into the production of textiles one- or two-hundred years ago. Old-house devotees fortunate enough to have the leisure time and talent to pursue any or all phases of clothmaking may want to contact one or more of the following suppliers of materials.

Hearthside

This firm is best known for its quilting supplies and calicoes. It also supplies 100% virgin wool, grown and spun at Christopher Sheep Farm in New England. This is available in natural undyed shades or in heather tones.

Catalog and sample cards available.

Hearthside Mail Order
Box 127
West Newbury, Vt. 05085

Mercer Museum Shop

Homespun flax for the making of linen cloth is offered at $1.25 a hank.

Mercer Museum Shop
Bucks County Historical Society
Pine and Ashland Sts.
Doylestown, Penn. 18901
(215) 345-0737

S. & C. Huber

The S. & C. Huber farm is a "center for early country arts." Here one can take classes in spinning, weaving, stenciling, quilting, braiding, paper-making, and needlepoint. Other "country" craft skills are also developed in one-day workshops. All the tools and materials needed for such activities are also available, and these may be ordered by mail. Huber stocks various fibers for spinning, weaving, and dyeing—wool, flax, cotton, silk cocoons, camel's down, and hair. The same yarns— already spun—are available, or you can purchase the woven fabrics. These you can have them dye for you or you may buy the dyes and do it yourself. All the dyes are natural and of vegetable composition with the exception of the cochineal bug.

Catalog available, 50¢.

S. & C. Huber, Accoutrements
82 Plants Dam Rd.
East Lyme, Conn. 06333
(203) 739-0772

Sunflower Studio

Constance La Lena is an exceptional weaver and dyer of yard goods and period clothing. We are not in the practice of reprinting our suppliers' literature, but there is only one way of doing justice to the Sunflower Studio work. Illustrated is an insert from the catalog, giving a

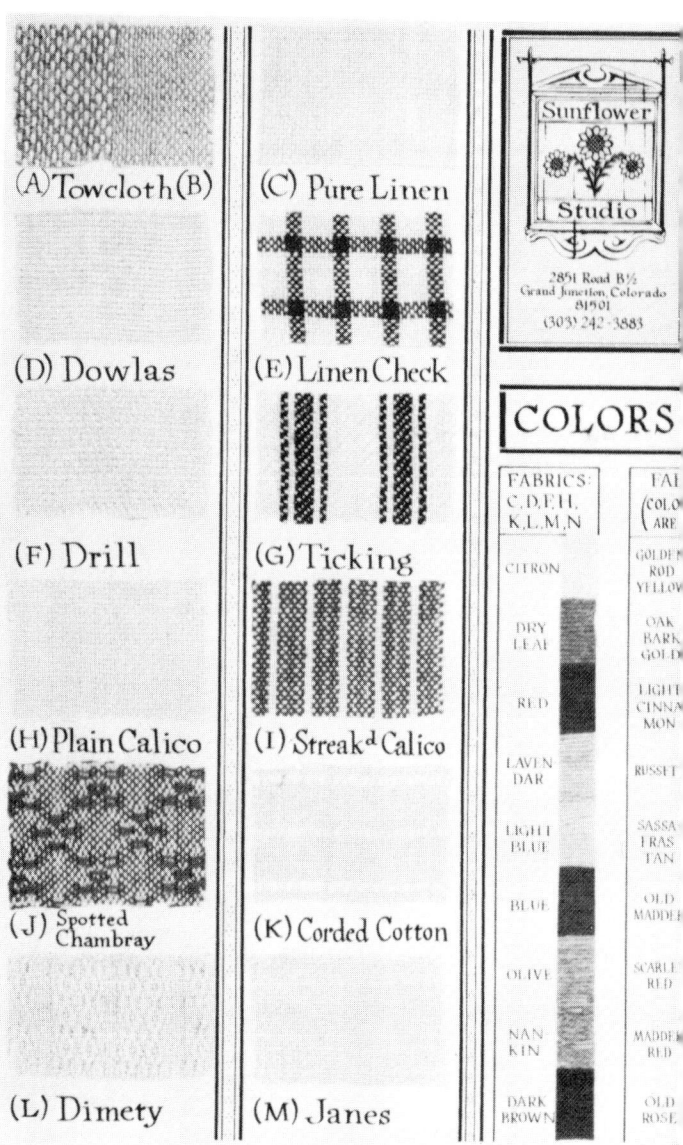

144

complete rundown of the fabrics available and the colors in which they can be dyed—if so desired. Unfortunately, we cannot reproduce this in color.

Swatches of the actual cloth may be ordered at 35¢ each or 3 for $1. The price is automatically credited to any order.

Catalog available, $2.

Constance La Lena
Sunflower Studio
2851 Road B½
Grand Junction, Colo. 81501
(303) 242-3883

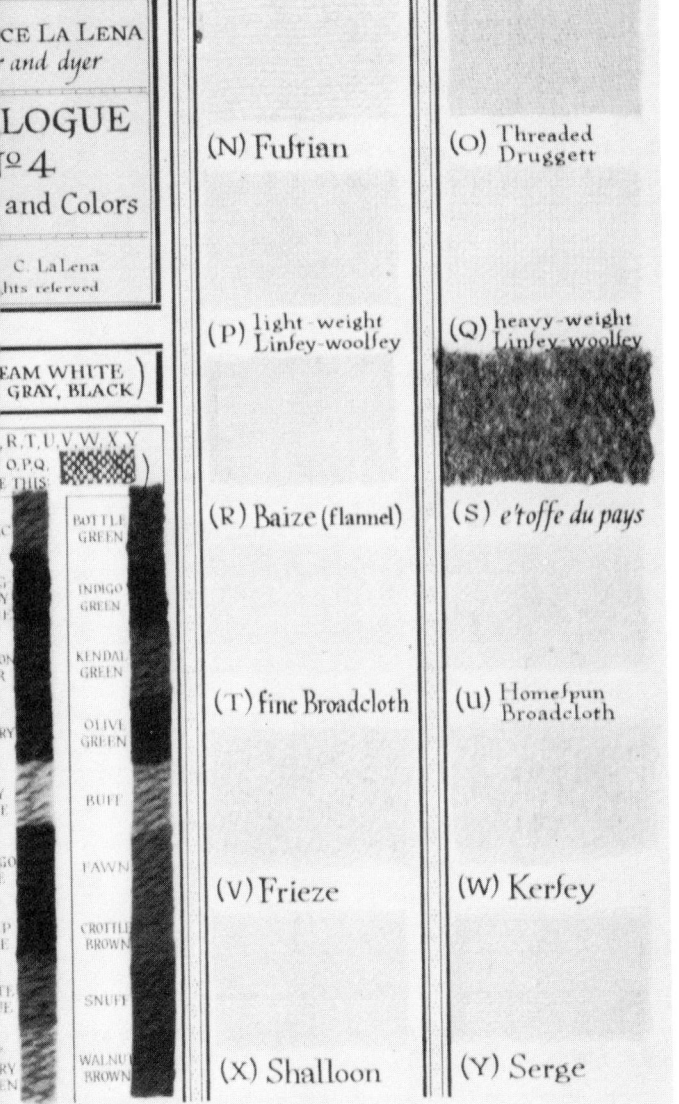

Ready-Mades and Kits

Ready-made curtains, throws, quilts, blankets, and wall hangings are a godsend if sent from a divinely-inspired person. The run-of-the-mill standard items found in many fabric or craft shops may suit some purposes, but are often not of the proper cut or material for period use. It may not be necessary, however, to special-order or have custom-made "standard" items from another era. There are craftsmen who can do the job for you as part of their daily routine. Of course if you are at all talented, you may decide to work on your own patterns and weaves.

Braid-Aid

Although best known for their rug braiding and hooking supplies, Braid-Aid also stocks crewel embroidery and needlepoint accessories and kits. These are handy for making chair seats, footstool and piano bench covers, and bell pulls.

Catalog available, $1.

Braid-Aid
466 Washington St.
Pembroke, Mass. 02359
(617) 826-6091

Carol Brown

If you can't make your way to Putney, Vermont—a trip well worth making—then write to Carol Brown who stocks Irish tweeds and other natural fiber fabrics. Her principal supplier is Avoca Handweavers, a firm known for its rare and beautiful wools. Bedspreads and wall hangings can be made to almost any size. But there are also cottons by the yard. Samples can be sent if you make a specific request.

Carol Brown
Putney, Vt. 05346
(802) 387-5875

Cohasset Colonials

Curtains in two styles—Brewster and Boston—are made of special plain woven fabrics or printed cottons from Waverly. The curtains are simple panels which may be hung from wide tabs (Brewster style) or from brass rings on rods (Boston style).

Decorator packs of 25 fabric samples are available for $4, with this charge credited to orders of $10 or more. General catalog available, 50¢.

Cohasset Colonials
Cohasset, Mass.
(617) 383-0110

Diane Jackson Cole

Handweaving of a special sort is undertaken by Diane Jackson Cole. A 100% virgin wool coverlet, illustrated here, is one of two stock items, and it is available in a range of color blends at $200 for a twin size, $250 for a

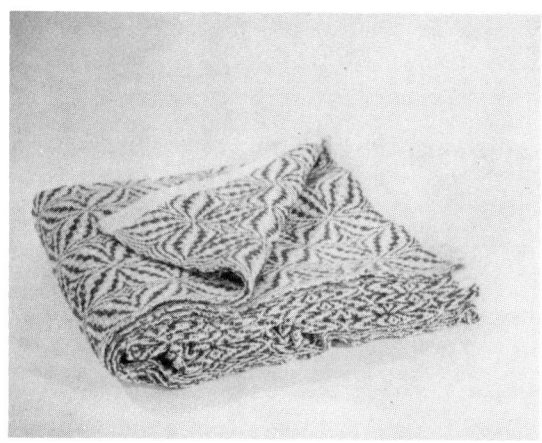

double, and $300 for king. A sample of fabric and color choice will be sent for a charge of $2. Once you have seen the work, you will understand why it is so special.

Diane Jackson Cole
9 Grove St.
Kennebunk, Me. 04043
(207) 457-1289

Country Curtains

This well-known firm has not let success go to its head. Most of their work is done in a mill overlooking the Housatonic and is not jobbed out to others. New additions are made to the basic line from time to time. A tab curtain of cotton and polyester with a wild rose stripe is one such new feature. These are available in varying

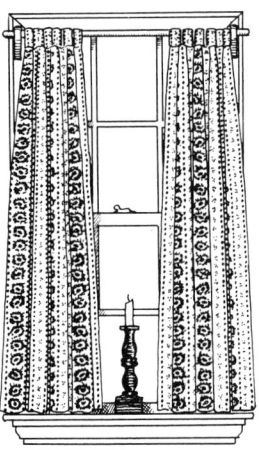

lengths—25, 30, 36, 45, 54, 63, 72, and 81 inches (lengths include the tabs). Prices range from $11 a pair to $17.50.

Catalog available.

Country Curtains
Stockbridge, Mass. 01262
(413) 298-5565

The Designing Woman

Drapery treatments of all periods are the specialty of this St. Louis custom design studio. Standard designs are not available. If you are interested in what they might be able to do, be sure to write precisely regarding your requirements.

The Designing Woman
705 Rivermont Dr.
St. Louis, Mo. 63137
(314) 869-5362

Down Home Comforts

Comforters, featherbeds, and covers for both are carefully crafted by this firm to your specifications. Down and feathers are used exclusively in the products, and good cotton fabrics are standard. Bed and special pillows are also available. And if you can find a way of getting old comforters, featherbeds, and pillows to Vermont, they will remake them for you.

Down Home Comforts
P.O. Box 281
West Brattleboro, Vt.
(802) 348-7944

Gurian's

Gurian's is truly the crewel king, as its literature proclaims. In addition to the many patterns of yard goods available, there are also finished crewel chair seats and backs as well as pillows, bedspreads, and tablecloths.

Brochure and one swatch, 50¢.

Gurian's
276 Fifth Ave.
New York, N.Y. 10001
(212) MU9-9696

The Pilgrim's Progress

Two Elizabethan designs—"Strawberry and Acorn Vine" and "Tree of Life"—are available in crewelwork kits. These are adaptations from embroidery designs found in the collection of the Folger Shakespeare Library. The kits contain 100% Persian wool yarns, hand-printed linen, needle, and instructions. The historical background of the design is also explained. The 18" x 18" squares are suitable for stool and chair covers.

Brochures available.

The Pilgrim's Progress
Penthouse
50 W. 67th St.
New York, N.Y. 10023
(212) 580-3050

Quicksand Crafts

Handwoven bedspreads are one specialty of this Appalachian concern. Split corners are included for poster beds, and corner-"pleat" inserts are available for beds with standard frames. The spreads are woven of a natural-colored mercerized cotton with an ivory pattern.

Literature available.

Quicksand Crafts
Vest, Ky. 41772
(606) 785-5230

Jane Kent Rockwell

Custom-made period draperies and bed hangings are expertly produced by Jane Kent Rockwell in her interior decoration shop. She can also assist with other fabric designs, wallpapers, hardware, lighting fixtures, and decorative plasterwork.

Jane Kent Rockwell, Interior Decorations
48-52 Lincoln St.
Exeter, N.H. 03833
(603) 778-0406

Southern Highland Handicraft Guild

Coverlets, quilts, and knotted and fringe trimmings are among the traditional crafts worked by members of the Southern Highland Handicraft Guild.

Brief literature available.

Southern Highland Handicraft Guild
P.O. Box 9545
Asheville, N.C. 28805
(704) 298-7928

Other Suppliers of Fabric Materials

Consult List of Suppliers for complete addresses.

Curtain/Drapery Materials

Bailey and Griffin
Barclay Fabrics
Norton Blumenthal
Carol Brown
China Seas
Clarence House
Connaissance Fabrics
A. L. Diament
S. & C. Huber
Lee/Jofa
Stroheim & Romann
Richard E. Thibaut

Upholstery Materials

China Seas
Clarence House
Gurian's
S.M. Hexter
Lee/Jofa
Stroheim & Romann

Trimmings

Barclay Fabrics
Bergamo Fabrics
Norton Blumenthal
Clarence House
Conso Products
F. Schumacher
Standard Trimmings
Tolland Fabrics

Ready-Made Materials

Appalachian Fireside Crafts
Constance Carol
Colonial Williamsburg (Bates)
Homespun Weavers
Mather's
Museum of Fine Arts Shop, Boston
New Hampshire Blankets
Quaker Lace Co.

Bedroom, Frensham Hill, Farnham, Surrey, England, as photographed in 1901
by Bedford Lemere. Courtesy, The Architectural Press, London.

VIII Paints & Papers

Materials that add decorative appeal to a surface and also help to protect it are widely available from many sources. More and more documented papers and paints, as well as period stencil patterns, are emerging each year. Research into and duplication of such late nineteenth-century materials as Lincrusta Walton—a composition paper based on linseed oil—Japanese "leather paper," and "ingrain" paper are well underway, and soon these, too, will be commercially available. The main problem facing the home restorer, then, is not a dearth of suitable materials, but how to choose from among the wealth of patterns and textures being offered.

Any old house will have been painted or papered several times, perhaps many times. An honest restoration will aim for exact or close duplication of materials from a particular period. If your house dates from the 1820s, for instance, you may decide to return it to that simple era and not a later one. This means that you will probably have to bypass the layers of Victorian decoration in search of the first decorative scheme. Layer upon layer of wallpaper may have to be removed (and carefully preserved, *at least* in fragment form) until you come to some semblance of the true age. The same process is required for discovering original paint colors—methodical chipping away of coat after coat, and—if possible, an analysis of each layer. There are several books which will aid you in this time-consuming but potentially rewarding work, and these are listed in the bibliography.

Most people will have neither the time nor the money, and probably not the inclination, to pursue such meticulous detective work. Their interest is in an approximation of a period style. Just what period to choose—if an old house is, indeed, an antique one—will be determined by the general stylistic characteristics of the structure itself. If a house from the 1870s is predominantly in the Second Empire mansard architectural style, it would make sense to consider panel sets or "fresco papers" of French inspiration for a front parlor. On the other hand, the walls of the parlor in a high-style Queen Anne residence of the same decade might have been covered in the latest William Morris or other complicated English-style print. Rather than vertical panels, the walls would be divided into three horizontal sections: a frieze above, filler below, and dado below the level of a chair rail, with each of the three sections separated from the others by a border.

Well-printed multi-color papers can be a very expensive acquisition. Fortunately, these are better made today than they were twenty-five or one-hundred years ago. Although the use of synthetic coatings is discouraged in other areas of restoration, here such a chemical process is welcomed. Adhesives are also improved, but must be used with care on certain kinds of materials. It is good to keep in mind the fact that wallpapers of the past were often cheaply manufactured and sold. Covering a surface was often no more expensive than painting it. Unless you are attempting a precise restoration job, there is no more need to bear the heavy expense of custom papers or limited-edition work than there was a century ago. Appropriate designs of every period are available at moderate cost. In the following pages, we have attempted to list only documented papers. Designs based on motifs found on porcelain, furniture, or other materials not akin to wallpaper have been excluded.

Application of paint is now the easiest way to radically change the appearance of an interior or exterior space. There are various sorts available from primitive skimmed milk mixtures and lead-based oils to modern latex and alkyd. It is difficult to recommend one rather than another. How they are to be used will determine the appropriate medium.

Paint colors are a somewhat simpler matter than wallpaper patterns. Even the major manufacturers have recognized the need for historical shades. What is fitting in New England, however, may not be right in North Carolina or Utah. Definite regional characteristics have developed over the years, and these are most marked in the oldest of the old homes. When mixing of paints was a matter of combining locally available mineral pigments, a great deal was left to chance. Not until the late nineteenth century and the introduction of manufacturers' books with paint chips did any sort of uniformity in colors begin to emerge.

The tendency to overemphasize color contrasts—particularly on the exterior of a building—is a problem of the 1960s when the whole world seemed to explode in psychedelic shades. At this time many highly ornamented Victorian houses were given a two or three-tone job that offends the eye only a decade later. There has been some move away from this practice since. More and more home owners are following the advice of such a critic as Gervase Wheeler, who wrote in 1855: "Cornices, window dressings, verandah mouldings, etc., might be made more prominent by coloring them a shade darker than the main building, although *this step must be taken with great caution so as not to divide the house by stripes, or produce too marked a line of contrast*"(italics added for emphasis).

Stenciling is an appealing and popular way of decorating a surface whether it be a wall or a floor. Designs of this sort can be transferred to paper or directly to the surface itself. A small number of historical homes in America contain examples of such work, and the remnants are to be treasured and, if worn, carefully restored. For the most part, original stencil decoration was applied from the early to mid-nineteenth century, and not during the Colonial period. At that time, freehand painted decoration—murals, friezes—was more common. This took the place of prohibitively expensive imported Chinese and scenic papers. In the late nineteenth century, painted rather than stenciled decoration again became popular. Ironically, this was not because of its cheapness, but rather because artists could embellish structural details more lavishly with paint than could be done with paper. Even many Victorian home owners who could afford marble and fine woods chose instead to have walls marbleized and grained.

Paints

It is not economically feasible to reproduce paint chips in a book of this sort. Hopefully, the evocative names of many of the hues offered for sale in thousands of outlets across the country will be sufficient to stir up interest. There are many variations of such standard shades as Penn Red, Federal Blue, and Bayberry Green in the lexicon of paints appropriate for Colonial-style buildings; special colors for Victorian houses are much more limited, and their manufacture has not been systematized to any degree. Not even San Francisco claims to have a paint manufacturer specializing in Victorian colors. Some of the following listings, however, may provide leads in this regard.

These listings by no means exhaust the supply of manufacturers. Such firms as Devoe (Historic Charleston), Finnaren & Haley (Historic Philadelphia colors), Glidden-Durkee, Cohasset Colonials, Pittsburgh Paints, Martin-Senour (Williamsburg), and the Guild of Shaker Crafts are covered in the first Old House Catalogue. These are listed at the end of this chapter under "Paints" and the interested person can either contact the company directly or check with one of his area paint suppliers.

Munsell Color Notation System

Before choosing a period paint color, you may want to do some basic research on the colors used at different periods in your own home. As explained in the introduction, this can be a complicated and time-consuming procedure. But it is one of the aspects of old-house restoration which is most challenging and rewarding. Familiarity with and use of the Munsell Color notation system would be of great help. Samples found throughout the house can be compared with the chips found in the Munsell Book of Color available in either glossy finish ($400) or matte finish ($325). The book is made up of 40 constant hue charts bound in 2 ring binders and the chips are removable. With the proper color codes noted (each hue is given its own color notation), a painter (or you yourself) can have proper paints mixed.

For those of us who neither need nor want to make such a large investment, Munsell can provide custom color standards when one submits a sample to them. The cost of this technical service varies and fees are quoted on request.

Brochure available.

Munsell Color
2441 N. Calvert St.
Baltimore, Md. 21218
(301) 243-2171

Old-Fashioned Milk Paints

Milk paint has been made for hundreds of years and may have been applied in your house in the eighteenth or nineteenth century. It is available again today from the Old-Fashioned Milk Paint Co. There are eight colors—Barn Red, Pumpkin, Mustard, Bayberry, Lexington Green, Soldier Blue, Oyster White, and Pitch Black—available in pints, quarts, or gallons. These are powdered paints made from milk products and mineral fillers to which water will have to be added. The paints are most often used for furniture and adhere especially well to wood surfaces, but they can be used for plaster walls as well. The makers suggest that a linseed or lemon oil be used lightly over the surface after painting, a procedure which will give depth and eliminate any chalky look.

Brochure and color card available.

The Old-Fashioned Milk Paint Co.
Box 222
Groton, Mass. 01450
(617) 448-6336

Fuller-O'Brien has a full range of historical colors appropriate for Colonial or Victorian-style homes in the East, South, Middle West, or West, and these are included in what is known as the "Heritage Color Collection." Their paints are especially popular in the San Francisco area. The "Colonial" colors do not differ significantly from those available from other companies, but among the later period shades are Santa Fe Tan, Arizona Tan, Oregon Pass, Sutter's Mill, Prairie, and Yankee Gold—all variations on earthy browns; Donner Pass, Iron Kettle, Pony Express, and Gold Rush—subtle grays; and Spanish Pink and Colony Buff—soft pink browns. Despite their "Western"-sounding names, such shades might well be appropriate for Victorian exteriors or interiors wherever they may be found.

The company has a number of brochures available on its products. That on the "Heritage Color Collection" includes color chips and is free. There are more ambitious decorating guides which also may be ordered for a nominal cost. For further information, contact the nearest office of The O'Brien Corporation:

450 East Grand Ave.
South San Francisco, Calif. 94080

2001 West Washington Ave.
South Bend, Ind. 46634

P.O. Box 864
Brunswick, Ga. 31520

Ox-Line

Ox-Line colors are of the vibrant sort favored by many decorators working in a contemporary vein; some are quite appropriate for period uses. These are deep, rich colors available in low lustre, semi-gloss, and high-gloss finishes in latex. In many ways, they reproduce the look of early lead-based oils. Among the colors possible for interior use are Old Pewter, Oyster White, Pongee, Williamsburg Red, Beaver Brown, True Blue, and Yew Green.

Brochure available with color chips.

Ox-Line
Lehman Bros. Corp.
115 Jackson Ave.
Jersey City, N.J. 07304
(201) 434-1882

Turco

Turco's line of buttermilk paints are already mixed with water. There are eight colors to choose from—a mixing white, Raw Muslin, Blueberry, Brick Dust, Azurite, Green Olive, Golden Ochre, and Raw Umber. These are suitable for furniture or structural purposes, although, as with any milk-based paint, adhesion may be a problem unless the surface is properly prepared. The company's oil base finish, lead-free paints are extremely handsome mixtures. Their use, along with the buttermilk, is suitable only for Colonial period sytles. There are two basic lines—"Old Sturbridge" reproduction colors and "Old Colonial." Both offer superb quality and value.

Free brochures with color chips.

Turco Coatings Incorporated
Wheatland & Mellon Sts.
Phoenixville, Penn. 19460
(215) 933-7758

Pratt & Lambert

Pratt & Lambert's "Calibrated Color" system may yield just the right shade for a mid- to late-Victorian period interior. The firm's "Permalize" house and trim finish line can also be "calibrated" to furnish you with a proper exterior paint. There are eight hundred and eighty colors available for almost every possible kind of use. Historic Denver, the nation's largest community preservation group, has used Pratt & Lambert paints for some of their preservation projects.

Literature available from local dealers, or contact:

Pratt & Lambert
625 Washington
Carlstadt, N.J. 07072
(201) 935-6200

Stains/Varnishes

Staining would seem to be a simple matter—even more so than painting—but proper work requires knowledge of woods and of suitable shades for historical structures. The use of a stain and/or varnish is to enhance and protect the natural qualities of the material and not to hide its imperfections or disguise its inferiority. Nothing seems worse than the application of dark oak and mahogany stains on pine, even though you may discover that "it was done in the past." Mistakes were made then, too. The Victorians were especially good at imitating various grains. It is a mistake, however, to consider the second half of the nineteenth century as one of gloomy, dark coloring. Oak may not be your favorite wood, but it can have a true golden glow to it. Mahogany and rosewood should be prized for their durability and natural beauty. Anyone fortunate enough to live in a home containing redwood will appreciate its extraordinary strength; it is almost impervious to disease. But all woods have to be cared for and given some sort of protective coating. This may be merely a stain such as a weathering oil, often used with cedar. Oiling and then waxing wood is one of the earliest known procedures for preservation. It can work as well on walls as it does on flooring. Regular stains, however, will still be necessary for at least touch-ups and for replacement woods.

California Redwood

The California Redwood Association has prepared a very useful data sheet (number 4B1-1) on redwood exterior finishes—from bleaching oil to paint to light-bodied stains. Paint, of course, is the most commonly used finish for period houses of the sort found up and down the West Coast. But there is no reason why stains of a soft effect can not be as successfully used as period paint colors. The Association also has available two other data sheets entitled "Brand List of Redwood Exterior Finishes" (4B1-2) and "Redwood Interior Finishes" (4B2-1).

California Redwood Association
617 Montgomery St.
San Francisco, Calif. 94111

Cabot

Cabot stains are known for their quality. The "Old Virginia Tints," solid color stains, are particularly useful products for the period home. These oil-base finishes were developed originally for use on shingles and shakes but are just as appropriate and effective with siding, clapboards, and other rough-sawed wood. There are some extremely attractive shades available—Cavalier Gray, Sequoia Red, Powhattan Red, Spruce Blue, Highland Rose, Sagebrush Gray, Coast Guard Gray, Cordovan Brown—which would melt the heart of the preservation purist. Such stains can be used over previously painted surfaces and, according to the manufacturer, will provide much more protection than a similar color paint. There are, of course, other Cabot stains, including the three-in-one stain wax, the stain wax, the transparent stain, and semi-transparent and creosote stains.

Brochures with color samples available.

Samuel Cabot, Inc.
1 Union St.
Boston, Mass. 02108
(617) 723-7740

Martin-Senour

Martin-Senour also produces full-color exterior wood stains which find use on period structures. Their alkyd stains are preferable to those of latex for use on siding because of greater durability.

Brochure on exterior wood stains available from local dealers.

Martin-Senour Co.
1370 Ontario Ave., N.W.
Cleveland, Ohio 44113
(216) 566-3140

Turco

Turco supplies paste wood stains and a clear paste varnish for interior use, especially for furniture. The stains are available in eight wood shades which closely approximate those found in aged lumber. None give that glossy polyurethane look which can spoil even the best reproduction and destroy an antique.

Card with samples available.

Turco Coatings, Inc.

Wheatland & Mellon Streets
Phoenixville, Penn. 19460
(215) 033-7758

Painted Decoration/Stenciling

Freehand decoration has become immensely popular in recent years. Much of it, unfortunately, is badly executed. It is neither inventive nor striking, but rather smacks of cuteness. Stencil patterns are often similarly cliché "artistic" touches. No amount of new decoration of this sort can possibly make up for sagging floors, weakened walls, or just plain ugly woodwork. New painted decoration of any sort should be used sparingly—even in Victorian homes where ceilings, cornices, and walls may have sported festoons of flowers and prancing nymphs. In the eighteenth century and earlier, wall murals and designs painted on floors often took the place of more expensive papers and carpets. If these have survived over the years, they have acquired a mellow patina of age. Their preservation is important and requires the services of a true art conservator. Stenciled patterns of the early to mid-nineteenth century may have also acquired antique status. There are experts on the proper handling of such motifs, a few of which are listed below. Wall and ceiling decoration of the late-Victorian period should also command respect, and there are those who can touch it up, repaint lost motifs, and give it a new lease on a longer life with the use of modern materials.

Stenciled Interiors

Sandra Tarbox is a Connecticut artist and expert on American stenciling. Both original stencil designs suited to the fancy of a home owner or one of a number of historically faithful patterns can be applied to any area of the house where they are deemed appropriate. Frescoes and fireboards are also included in her specialized work.

Ms. Tarbox's modus operandi, according to a recent issue of *American Preservation*, does not differ that much from the itinerant artists of the nineteenth century: "I get a call from someone working on a restoration project. I go. I stay until I'm finished. . . . The people pay me room and board and a pittance, and then I leave."

The cost is only $2 to $5 a foot, not very much for an artist who has studied her subject with as much care as has this one.

Brochure available, 50¢.

Stenciled Interiors
Hinman Lane

Southbury, Conn. 06488
(203) 264-8000

Megan Parry

Megan Parry is another such dedicated person. She has written a book, *Stenciling* (Van Nostrand Reinhold, 1977, $12.95) which handsomely documents her skill and knowledge. Many of her designs are modern and not suitable for period interiors, but she is perfectly capable of working in a traditional manner with documented patterns. And she is willing to travel. She will also provide material for the homebody who wants to do it himself.

Catalog of designs and price list, $1.

Megan Parry
1727 Spruce
Boulder, Colo. 80302
(303) 444-2724

Stencil Specialty Co.

For the home craftsman/artist who has the ability to execute fine work, there are some basic tools which will come in handy for the purpose of wood graining. These are rollers, combs, and grainers of good construction. Also available from the Stencil Specialty Co. are pouncing wheels which are useful to cut stencil patterns.

Literature available.

Stencil Specialty Co.
377 Ocean Ave.
Jersey City, N.J. 07305
(201) 333-3634

D. B. Wiggins

D. B. Wiggins is an itinerant artist who will paint, plaster, and stencil period interiors. Jack-of-all-trades of this sort were common in the glory days of stenciling. He works by day or by contract.

D. B. Wiggins
Hale Rd.
Tilton, N.H. 03276
(603) 286-3046

Thomas Bisesti

Tom Bisesti is a talented and enthusiastic painter of murals. He both restores and executes elaborate designs. Most of his work has been done in Victorian-period dwellings, and he enjoys working in tempera or in oil. New work may be done directly on plaster or on canvas which is then glued to a surface. European craftsmen who executed such painting in the late nineteenth century have long since disappeared from the scene. It is good to know that their skills have not been lost completely.

Thomas A. Bisesti
409 Oakland St.
Springfield, Mass. 01108
(413) 739-4583

Papers

Thanks to technology introduced in the mid-1800s, wallpapers of an almost infinite variety have been produced over the past 130 years. The quality of these papers has varied greatly as has their price. Simple designs produced on high-speed presses are much less expensive than the hand-screened or blocked prints. Every extra bit of handwork means that much more in labor costs. In-between in price are the papers which are run on smaller presses and involve three or four colors and more subtle designs than those printed on high-speed equipment. More time can be taken on a slower press to check color registration and proper inking.

As has been mentioned earlier, wallpapers were scarce in Colonial times because most had to be imported. This is not to say that Colonial-style homes built at a later time did not make use of such materials—imported or domestically-produced. With the end of the Revolution, the trade in fine papers from England and France steadily increased. By the mid-nineteenth century, domestically-produced papers were to be found in many American homes. Most were run off on steam-powered presses with cylinders carrying raised printing surfaces. This machinery was improved almost every year, and, in the last decades of the nineteenth century, wallpaper was being used for everything from ceilings to baseboards. To redecorate then was to repaper.

Manufacturers of fine reproduction papers and of designs appropriate for period interiors are not difficult to find. Even the papers produced by such firms as Schumacher, Scalamandré, and Brunschwig & Fils, which are sold primarily through interior designers, can be found in the decorating departments of major department stores, and good paint and building supply outlets will offer a good supply of pattern books which can be consulted. The problem, once again, is one of selection, and even the most experienced interior designer will admit to having difficulty from time to time on this score. There is so much that is offered and worthy of

consideration. Only if you are seeking to duplicate an antique paper will you find that your choices are limited. There are at least a thousand such documented papers available, and one of these might perfectly match the one you are seeking. If not, your only alternative will have to be custom work, an assignment that any one of several firms will be glad to undertake for a set minimum amount of material. The cost, of course, will be terribly high.

Exact reproductions of antique papers are usually commissioned only by museums or historical home associations. There is no reason why we cannot also use them if they are indeed appropriate for our purposes, and a number of manufacturers have been licensed to produce historically-accurate papers. Some of these are noted in the following listings. But don't forget the more common "undocumented" papers or adaptations of traditional designs. Whether they will "work" or not depends entirely on their intrinsic quality and suitability.

Producers of wallpapers and some of their designs that may serve your needs—documented or not—are given in alphabetical order.

Laura Ashley, Inc.

This is a firm based in Carno, Wales, which is known for its textiles. It is now planning to open an outlet in New York which will offer wallpapers as well. The traditional designs are simple country-style geometrics and florals. Colors are soft and pleasing.

Laura Ashley, Inc.
714 Madison Ave.
New York, N.Y. 10021

Bassett & Vollum, Inc.

George M. Funke is a talented antiquarian and craftsman who has done much to bring Galena, Illinois, alive with the spirit that it knew in the days of its most famous citizen—Ulysses S. Grant. His home, "Orrin-Smith," is open for private tours by prearrangement, and it is here that some fine papers and other antique materials are on display. Illustrated are three rooms from the house.

Bassett & Vollum once acted as the United States representative of a prestigious French wallpaper firm that was forced to destroy its wood blocks during the Second World War and afterward did not resume operation. The American distributor was given permission, however, to reproduce the French papers, and the bedroom pictured here contains a Louis Philippe design border which was part of the original collection. The striped paper is one of Funke's original designs which blends handsomely with the border.

The walls of a small front parlor or reception room are covered with another of Funke's designs, and it is called, naturally, "Medal of Honor," since the primary design element is a repeating design of Napoleonic medals. The third room—the drawing room—is papered with a border frieze, side wallpaper, and base in a reproduction of an original hand-blocked document found in Versailles, France. The original design is thought to date from 1840–50, and that of the unusual frieze features an American Indian chief with full headdress.

Bassett & Vollum, Inc.
217 N. Main St.
Galena, Ill. 61036
(815) 777-2460

Brunschwig & Fils

Brunschwig & Fils has supplied some of the leading museums in the country with the best in reproduction wallpapers. These are manufactured overseas and are among the higher-priced papers available for period restorations. Sometimes, however, there is no possible substitute for precisely rendered reproduction work.

"Reveillon Tulips" (#1159.06) is a reproduction of an eighteenth-century block-printed design from the French workshop of Reveillon. It is now available as a screen print in the original reds and greens on blue. There are also four other color combinations or "colorways" available. A high-style design of exceptional beauty, it would be appropriate for a similarly sumptuous Georgian-period town house or country mansion.

"Maize" (#1139.06) is a mannered, but naturalistic, design which features corn ears, tassels, and the swan of the Empress Josephine. The reproduction has been made from an early nineteenth-century French block-printed document and was originally colored in shades of gray or *grisaille*. Four other color combinations are available. This is a simply superb paper for a Federal or Adams-style American interior of elegant restraint and lines.

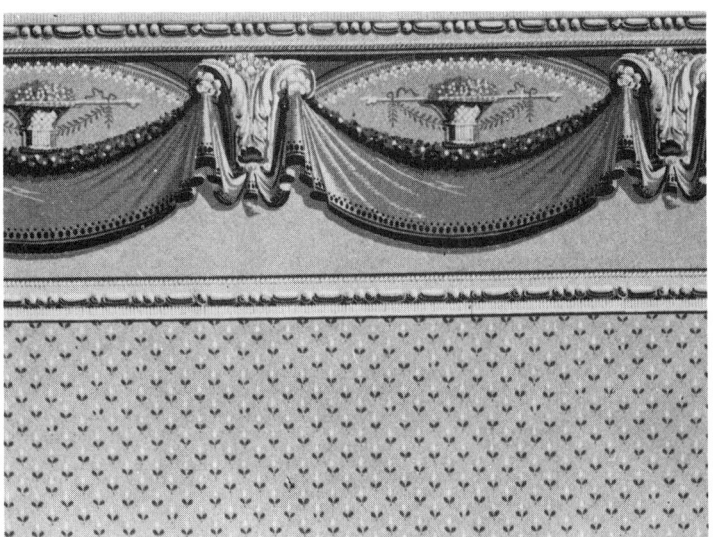

Another well-chosen design for a late eighteenth and early nineteenth-century interior would be the "Alexandria Frieze and Side Wall" (#1151.06). The term "side wall" is used to describe the larger section of paper below the cornice frieze. The original colors are a striking blue and white; five other combinations have also been printed. The side wall has an accompanying border that can be used as a simple stripe, as a dado, or to frame a door.

Owners of Victorian homes will welcome the "Bosphore Border" and companion side wall of scattered pink clover (#1154.06 for border, #1153.06 for "Bosphore Semis" side wall). The original red and green block-printed border of knotted swags, fringe, and tassels is brilliantly colored in the Napoleon III style, c. 1870, and so is the reproduction. A smaller border of tassel fringe (#1155.06) may also be ordered.

For further information regarding Brunschwig & Fils papers, see Appendix A and B, or contact:

Brunschwig & Fils, Inc.
979 Third Ave.
New York, N.Y. 10022
(212) 838-7878

Cole & Son

This firm is one of the imaginative English manufacturers of late nineteenth-century designs—a very high period, indeed, in wallpaper design. They are able to reproduce these designs from original blocks.

Cole has traditionally supplied dignified, tasteful wallpapers a bit less frenzied than those designed by

William Morris and his colleagues. This company is a superb source for borders and friezes of a delicate sort. A splendid example of a satin-ribbon border is seen in the frontispiece photograph to this section on paints and papers. Cole also produces gold and white borders appropriate for Greek Revival interiors, trompe l'oeil borders, and quite exprensive hand-painted borders of wild English flowers such as "Wild Rose" and "Rose & Pansy."

Cole and Son (Wallpapers), Ltd.
P.O. Box 4BU
18 Mortimer St.
London W1A 4BU
England

S. M. Hexter

The kind of research necessary to produce historically-accurate reproduction papers has been diligently and imaginatively done by the staff at Hexter. Some of their papers are based on documents at the Henry Ford Museum and Greenfield Village; others are adapted from designs found in Europe and the Far East.

Many of the earliest papers brought to America incorporated designs from the Far East. "Calcutta" and "Ceylon" are two companion designs included in Hexter's "West Winds Collection" of wall coverings and related fabrics. "Ceylon" is seen to the left with "Calcutta" on the right and lower left wall. These papers are pre-trimmed, pre-pasted, and strippable vinyl and are available in four colors—brick, yellow, sunset, and blue-peach.

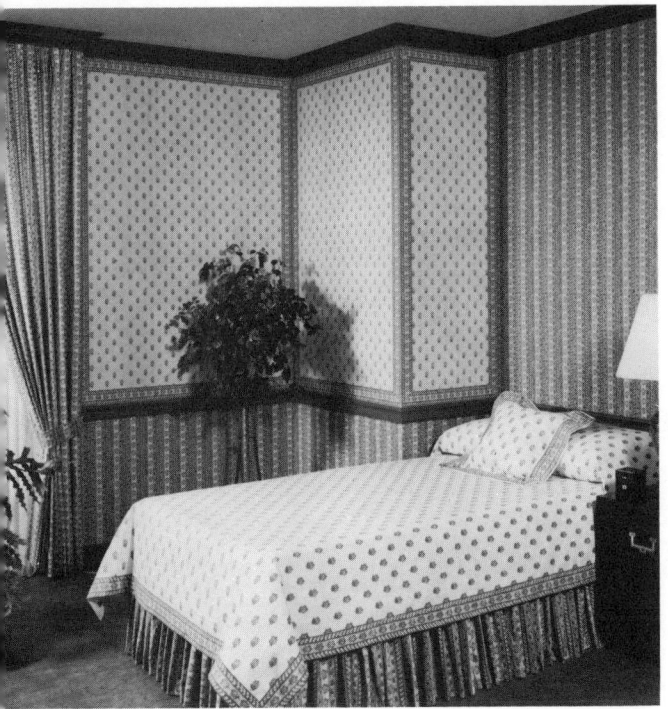

Two other highly decorative papers of Far Eastern design origin are the "Balinesian Garden" and "Balinesian Wave"; the former is also seen in a companion fabric while the Wave is well-suited for border use. Both designs are produced in blue/beige, taupe, green, and "sunrise."

Hexter has showrooms in New York, Atlanta, Boston, Chicago, Cincinnati, Dallas, Denver, Detroit, Honolulu, Los Angeles, Miami, Minneapolis, Philadelphia, Phoenix, Portland, San Francisco, Seattle, St. Louis, Toronto, and London, England, or may be contacted at:

S. M. Hexter Co.
2800 Superior Ave.
Cleveland, Ohio 44114
(216) 696-0146

Jones & Erwin

"American Fancy" will delight anyone who admires the quality of early stencil designs. This is a copy of an early wallpaper removed from an abandoned house in Maine. The original color is blue on white; the reproduction paper comes in seven other colorings as well.

The company produces good copies of William Morris prints. Seen at left is "Poppy," c. 1881; center, "Bruges," c. 1888; and right, "Sunflower," c. 1879.

"Portsmouth Pineapple" has been named in honor of the carved pineapple design to be found on doorways in that old New Hampshire city. A copy of the original paper, c. 1810, was found on a hatbox. (Objects of this sort were often covered in papers). Its vigor and strong colors (rust-pink pineapples and dark green leaves on a blue-green background) is evidence that not all early nineteenth-century designs were of a restrained neo-classical sort. Jones & Erwin has copied the document in its original colors and in five other combinations.

Jones & Erwin, Inc.
232 E. 59th St.
New York, N.Y. 10022
(212) 759-3706

Open Pacific Graphics

Open Pacific Graphics is an innovative restoration and custom wallpaper firm that has supplied materials for historical projects in British Columbia and California and in private homes. Their 150 designs—dating from 1860 to 1910—are reproduced by the silk screen process and are available in rolls of 36 square feet which are usually produced 20″ wide x 20′ long. Prices for these range from $20 (for one color) to $60 a roll (for eight colors); an exceptional bargain, we think, for Victorian-period papers. They are not vinyl, but may be given a protective finish. And they are not pre-pasted but must be hung in the traditional manner.

A similar swirled design, but one that suggests stenciling, is that illustrated below and used in the Hale House restoration, Los Angeles. It is called "Palm."

Reproduction Art Nouveau wallpaper designs are extremely difficult to find, but Open Pacific Graphics offers this example and others.

More traditional Victorian papers are the "Craigflower Manor," c. 1860, seen at left, and a floral panel with roses and decorative oval, seen at right.

Sample patterns sent on request; full sample book, $40.

Open Pacific Graphics
#43 Market Square
Victoria, British Columbia
Canada
(604) 388-5233

Reed "Early American Homes"

Documented papers from American homes dating from 1707 to 1880 form the basis of the Reed, Ltd. collection. Most of these are of English or French origin and many reflect the taste of the wealthy.

The building that served as Washington's Headquarters at Valley Forge is a simple, sober fieldstone building typical of those to be found in rural areas of the Delaware Valley. It is by no means a mansion and has been sparely furnished by curators of the National Park Service. The upstairs sitting room, used by Martha Washington when she visited the camp, is papered with a simple design featuring sprigs of greenery in diamond outlines on a vellum ground. It is a pleasant and airy design for such a cold, sparse interior.

The Faulkner House in Acton, Massachusetts, is a 1707 Colonial of traditional style and was once part of a complex of mills and farmland. It is a rather grand house for its time, and in the mid-eighteenth century the bed chamber over the garrison room was papered in an English hand-block design featuring connecting medallions of classical figures in charcoal and white on a stone-grey ground. This has been expertly reproduced

by Reed from samples. The same paper was also originally used in the House of Seven Gables, Salem.

The entire "Early American Homes" line has been researched and documented by Charles S. Freeman, A.S.I.D.

The complete line of historic papers is fully illustrated in a booklet, "Early American Homes," $4.50; the firm also has available a free brochure.

Reed Wallcoverings
550 Pharr Rd.
Atlanta, Ga. 30318
(404) 873-6363

Sanderson and Sons, Ltd.

This firm is yet another English manufacturer of Victorian and Edwardian papers, and probably the best known of all. Papers can be printed from the original blocks used in the past, and, therefore, are really much more than "reproductions."

Sanderson and Sons is *the* source for Morris papers, most of which are available in at least two color combinations. Among the designs of William and May Morris are: "Chrysanthemum," "Horn Poppy," "Bruges," "Bachelor's Button," "Sunflower," "Fritillary," "Net," "Willow," "Poppy," "Borage," "Pink and Rose," "Bird and Anemone," "Marigold," and Honeysuckle." Sanderson can also supply an earlier design by Owen Jones, "Ewan," and such early twentieth-century patterns as "Teazel" designed by C. F. A. Voysey, and a deco paper, "Decco-Nova," adapted from a design by William Odell.

All of these papers are part of the "Heritage Collection" and are hand-printed. They must be hand-trimmed before hanging.

Arthur Sanderson & Sons, Ltd.
Berners St.
London W1A 2JE
England

Saxon Paint and Home Care Centers

Wallpapers designed for use in Adler & Sullivan's great 1887 Auditorium Theater in Chicago were reproduced several years ago in a limited run of 400 bolts. Each bolt is equal to 1½ rolls or 49 square feet; this measures out to 7 running yards by a 28-inch width.

The two geometric papers which reflect so superbly the architectural firm's mastery of structural form are "Spi-

ral" and "Oak Leaf." All proceeds from their sale are donated to the Illinois Arts Council Foundation.

For further information regarding availability of the papers, write:

ArchiCenter
111 South Dearborn
Chicago, Ill. 60603
(312) 782-1776

Scalamandré

Scalamandré has more than earned its reputation as the premier American supplier of quality documented papers for museums, historical associations, and private individuals who have had the foresight and good fortune to invest in what is a complex and expensive restoration undertaking. Scalamandré, as with some other high-quality manufacturers, sells only through interior designers and decorating departments in major retail outlets. In this respect, the reader will find the appendixes concerning these two areas particularly helpful if trying to track down Scalamandre materials.

The firm has recently introduced its Historic Savannah Collection of papers and fabrics. These date from the first half of the nineteenth century and considerably enlarge Scalamandré's offerings in post-Colonial period styles. "Savannah Fleur de Lis" is just one of the papers and is an interpretation of the French symbol. The document was found in Savannah, but the design was originally used in the Vander Horst House, Kiawah Island, South Carolina.

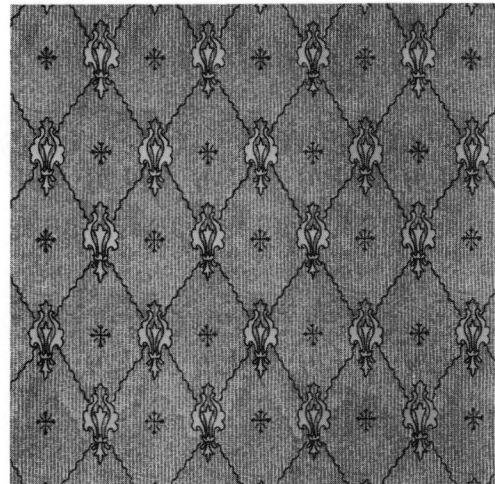

The Werms House is one of Savannah's best, and it is here that this elegant border (#81087) with floral sprigs was found. It has been reproduced just as it was. A coordinating fabric (#6428) transposes the same small groups of flowers into an allover pattern with a stripe motif.

Papers made for the recent restoration of the Barton House (Ranching Heritage Center) at Texas Tech University in Lubbock amply illustrate the variety of Victorian materials that Scalamandré has available. Only in the past ten years have wallpaper manufacturers given serious study to the later Victorian period, and their work in documenting eighteenth- and early nineteenth-century papers has provided them with the research know-how and tools for technical analysis which are a necessity for accurate reproduction. Illustrated in the order of their appearance are: #8115-1, a floral botanical design in shades of purple and green against a brown striped ground which has the appearance of stenciling; #8110-1, soft pink and white morning glories with white flowers and vines in shades of green against either light beige or resist areas of silver; #81104-1, a remarkably heavy Art Nouveau design in two shades of brown which gives the appearance of a Japanese "leather paper."

Information regarding prices and availability of papers is best secured from interior design firms or decorating departments of major stores listed in Appendix B. If further information is needed, contact:

Scalamandré
950 Third Ave.
New York, N.Y. 10022
(212) 361-8500

F. Schumacher

Schumacher offers considerable variety to the consumer—both in price and in design. Although best known for its textiles, the firm has available striking and useful papers. One of these was used on the cover of the first *Old House Catalogue* and requests for information about it were received by this writer. It is a simple, inexpensive print (#2825) known as "Amherst" and is part of the Mayflower Legacy Collection II. It is available in several colors, barn red being one of the most suitable for Colonial-style interiors.

"Truro" is another simple print (#2852) which might be used to handsome effect in a foyer, stairwell, or other small area. It is from the Gramercy Park Collection VIII and can be found in an ultramarine ground with red and white flowers. Both this paper and "Amherst" can be ordered through any well-equipped paint and paper store.

"French Damask" (Side wall #555-161, Group B) is a Warner Wallcovering available through Schumacher and is part of The Art Institute of Chicago Collection. It is pre-pasted and has a vinyl acrylic coating. Papers based on damask designs were used for many, many years to simulate high-style fashion.

"Chrysanthemum" (#5309A) is from the Pierre Frey Collection, Paris, and is a particularly suitable paper for homes of the 1880s and '90s which may have been influenced by what was known as the "Anglo-Japanese" style. This is a much more regular design than many produced at the time, but it is typical of the naturalistic Oriental exuberance which was translated in both fabrics and papers. Schumacher also manufactures a 100% cotton glazed fabric of the same design.

For further information regarding Schumacher papers, you may contact your local wallpaper outlet, a design firm or department, or Schumacher itself.

F. Schumacher & Co.
939 Third Ave.
New York, N.Y. 10022
(212) 644-5900

Thomas Strahan Company

The Strahan firm will soon be celebrating 100 years of fine craftsmanship. Since the beginning, the emphasis has been on reproduction of traditional American wall coverings. Since the company is located in the Boston area, there is a definite New England flavor to its products which in no way detracts from their usefulness in other parts of the country.

"Ipswich" was uncovered when the Ross House of Ipswich, Massachusetts, was torn down in 1933. The original was probably a French paper and it depicts America, in the figure of Washington, celebrating the victory over the British in the Revolution; Britannia weeps at left.

The "Samuel Sargent Chintz" comes from the Sargent-Robinson Homestead in Gloucester, Massachusetts. Although the house itself dates from c. 1690, the paper was probably first used in the mid-eighteenth century.

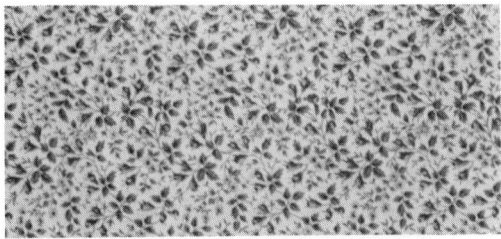

An old Newport, Rhode Island, mansion once used by Washington as headquarters contained this scenic paper. It is known as "Rochambeau" because Washington received the French military commander at this spot in July of 1780. The vignettes are thought to be of Spanish strolling players, the forerunners of modern circus performers.

Strahan papers are widely available through dealers across the country.

Thomas Strahan Co.
121 Webster Ave.
Chelsea, Mass. 02150
(617) 884-6220

Albert Van Luit & Co.

The Van Luit papers are exceptionally luxurious renderings of high-style designs. Many of these are of Oriental inspiration and could be suitable for late Victorian interiors. Other wall coverings are more traditional patterns which originated in eighteenth-century France or England.

"Campagne" is a scenic paper, a pleasant pastoral of the sort that became popular in the second half of the eighteenth-century and again during the Colonial Revival period of 1890–1930. Scenics, as they are called, are most often used in an entrance hall or in a dining room where they will not be hidden by heavy furniture.

A silk wall covering at the Palace of Versailles provided the inspiration for this fanciful pattern. A few extremely well-off Colonists may have used watered silks on their walls; most people turned to papers which cost a great deal less.

"Indienne" is a copy of a printed cotton imported by one of the East India companies in the eighteenth century. Here it is seen used in a contemporary kitchen, and it greatly softens the starkly modern and utilitarian lines. Certainly it could be used in other areas of almost any period house—with restraint. As is apparent, a little goes a long way.

Van Luit wall coverings are available from retailers and interior designers from coast to coast.

Various catalogs available, each 50¢.

Albert Van Luit & Co.
4000 Chevy Chase Dr.
Los Angeles, Calif. 90039
(213) 245-5106

Watts & Co.

This English firm is best known for its ecclesiastical furnishings, but according to *The Times* of London, they "also have a marvelous collection of Victorian designs for wallpaper and fabric, which are still printed by hand from the original carved pear wood blocks." Some of these designs were created by architect Augustus Pugin and are in the best tradition of the Victorian Gothic revival style. Some of Pugin's designs, thought to be lost, were rediscovered in 1975 and added to the Watts selections.

"Pugin Triad" is one of the rediscovered papers, a very felicitous composition which was recently used in a Victorian arts exhibition held at the Delaware Art Museum. Papers are produced by using specially-mixed colors which are then blocked on to the paper by hand and allowed to dry naturally before proceeding with another blocking. The minimum order for any of the Watts papers is 10 rolls. A roll measures 11 yards long and 21″ wide. Delivery (not including shipping) takes three months from receipt of order.

The patterns "Birds" and "Pear" appear to be just as imaginative as those of William Morris. Such extravagant compositions will have to be used with great care, but undoubtedly will dramatically set off any surface they adorn.

Brochure describing and showing available patterns, $2.

Watts & Co., Ltd.
7 Tufton St., Westminster
London, SW1P 3QB
England

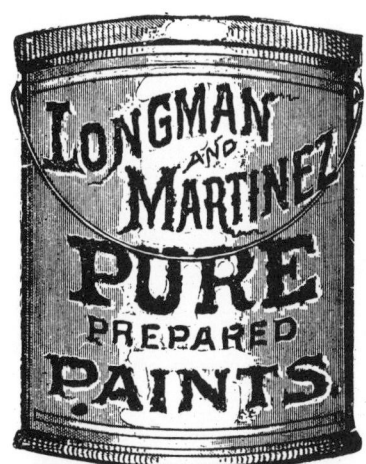

SOLD UNDER GUARANTEE.
Composed of only the Most Costly and Finest Materials.
ACTUAL COST LESS THAN $1.25 PER GAL.

Other Suppliers of Paints, Papers, and Stains

Consult the List of Suppliers for addresses.

Paints

Ameritone Paint
Cohasset Colonials
Devoe
Finnaren & Haley
Glidden-Durkee
Guild of Shaker Crafts
Janovic/Plaza
Kwal Paints
Maine Line Paints
Miss Kitty's Keeping Room Kolors
Benjamin Moore
Pittsburgh Paints
Sherwin-Williams

Stains and Varnishes

H. Behlen & Bros.
Cohasset Colonials
Gaston Wood Finishes
Glidden-Durkee

Painting, Decorating and Stenciling Services

Craftswomen
Pamela S. Friend
John L. Seekamp
Wall Stencils by Barbara
Roy Wingate

Papers

Birge Co.
Louis W. Bowen
Clarence House
Inez Croom
Jack Denst Designs
A. L. Diament
Katzenbach & Warren
Last's Paint & Wallpaper
Old Stone Mill
Nancy McClelland
Richard E. Thibaut
Waterhouse Wall Hangings

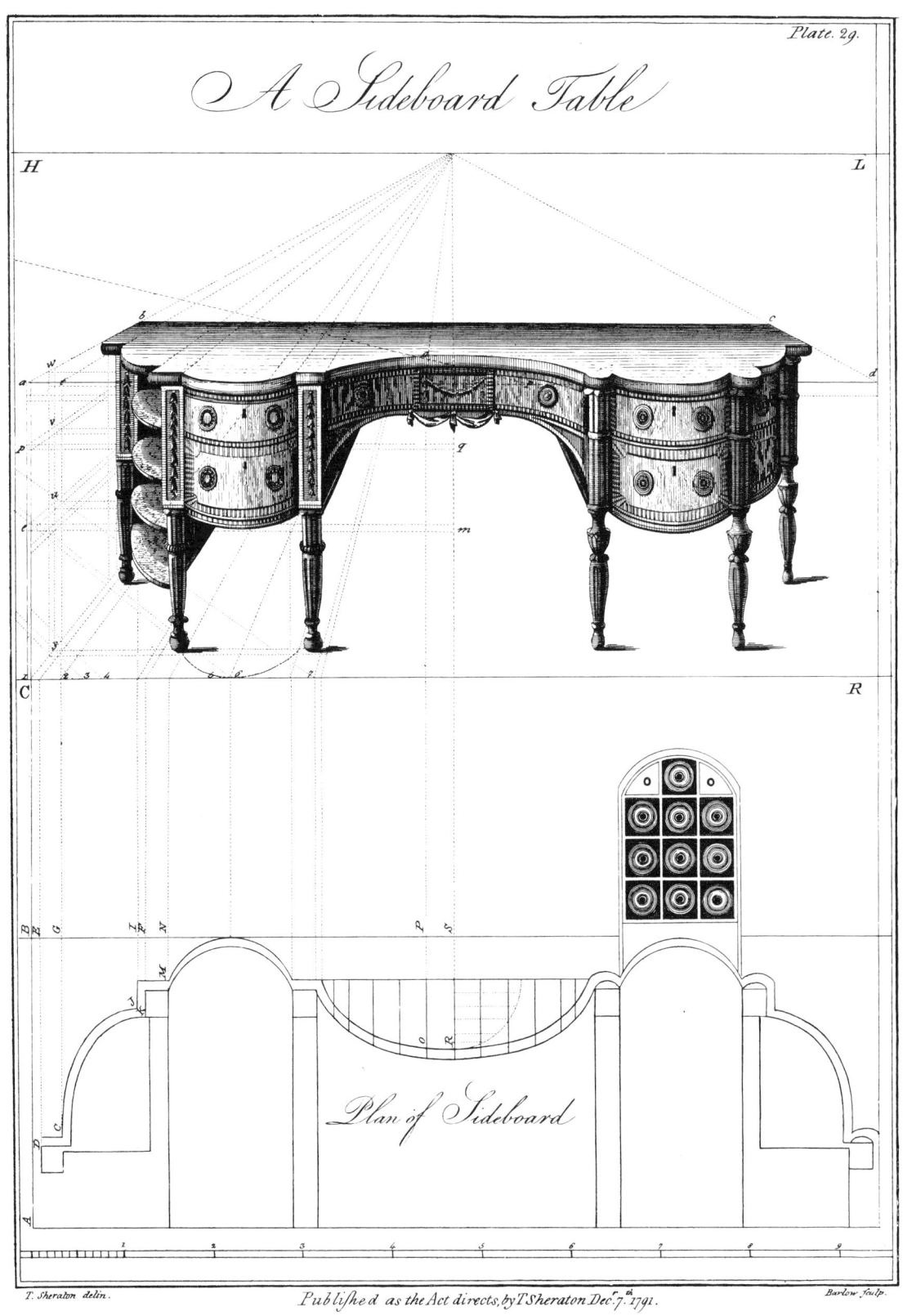

A Sideboard Table

Plan of Sideboard

T. Sheraton delin.

Publishe d as the Act directs, by T Sheraton Decr 7. 1791.

Barlow sculp.

Plate LVIII, Thomas Sheraton, *The Cabinet-Maker and Up-holsterer's Drawing-Book*, London, c. 1793.

IX   Furniture

Proper and imaginative furnishing of any period interior—whether it be found in a house or apartment—requires the utmost in patience and resourcefulness. This is not merely a matter of decoration. Rather, it is an exercise in design, in bringing together utility and aesthetic appeal. The basic structural character of the space itself will determine to a large extent the kinds of furnishings that will be fitting. There is no sense, for example, in cramming a low-ceilinged salt box with massive high-style furniture. Similarly, a late-Victorian Queen Anne residence can look rather preposterous if filled with primitive pine pieces from the Colonial period.

Whatever period appearance is called for, the guiding rule in selection of furnishings must be quality. Objects should not only be useful ones, but those which are of sound construction and which make proper use of woods, fabrics, and metals. Furnishing an interior should not be a chance to "show-off" with spectacular effects but, rather, an opportunity to provide a pleasing space for living which appears natural or fitting. Very little furniture of modern making—whatever the period style—will meet these requirements, as they partake of a construction and finish which is singularly graceless and lacking in proper proportions. Mass-produced furniture is today, for the most part, a mere shadow of a more substantial past and carries only the veneer of age. It is stamped out in assembly-line fashion, and sugar-coated with stains, varnish, and even plastic lamination. The end result is schlock of the first order. This writer's objection is not to the use of furniture of modern manufacture per se, but to that which is produced and packaged in an inappropriate manner, and often at a higher cost than the antique. Whatever you buy should not only be of correct design (and this can be checked easily enough by referring to models available in books and museums), but hopefully be of antique "potential."

The same rules of preservation which apply to buildings are appropriate for furnishings of such dwellings. Therefore, it is to the antiques and used furniture markets that one should first turn for materials. This can be a lifelong search and a rewarding activity. By no means does such old furniture have to be more expensive than new. Great objects will always be the passion of the privileged investor/collector. Simpler pieces—of which there are millions to be found—can be added to family heirlooms at relatively low cost. Despite the current fad for the "antique," most Americans will continue to choose the new and shiny and throw out the old. For members of the old house counterculture, this sad situation is a happy one.

Let's face it; *all* kinds of furniture are expensive today. It may not be possible to completely furnish a home in "old" pieces of the same style. Indeed it may not be desirable to do so. Only model rooms in historic houses or museums may be frozen in a particular time frame. In the best of such institutions, there has been an attempt in recent years to introduce a feeling for the movement of time and style by mixing complementary but different pieces representative of two or three generations of people.

Furniture craftsmen are on the increase. These are cabinetmakers who understand and practice the fine art of designing, shaping, joining, and finishing graceful objects. Many work alone; others have joined together in workshops; a few form the backbone of such reproduction furniture firms as Baker and Kittinger. They are to be found everywhere in North America, and this section of *The Second Old House Catalogue* can only provide a tiny sampling of their products. These are experts and their time and the materials they work with are very valuable. Accordingly, the prices they must charge are high. The average old-house owner will use their services infrequently, especially if he has a good eye for antique or "used" furniture. For certain basic types of furniture which are given heavy use—beds, chairs, even tables—and for replacement reproductions which can not be found elsewhere, today's craftsmen provide a most useful service. Customers stung by the high price of the bill will at least have the comfort of knowing that they have bought something which will appreciate in value rather than deteriorate with age.

Beds

Comfortable and properly-sized antique beds are difficult to find. Nothing is worth a sleepless night spent in the throes of a constricting frame and lumpen mattress. There are dealers who specialize in old beds, and such objects can be restored if not remodeled. But it may not be worth the effort and expense required to adapt the past to present needs, especially if this means providing for several members of the household. Of all the pieces of furniture we live with, beds are the most physically used and abused. And since most of us are considerably larger than our ancestors, we may need to call on the services of reproduction craftsmen or manufacturers.

Brass Beds

The Bedpost offers a dazzling array of brass beds suitable for Victorian interiors, and most of them are available in the standard sizes. A double bed with headboard and footboard ranges in price from $444 to over $1,100. All are solid brass. Mattresses and box springs are not included. The firm will also custom design a king or queen-size bed in brass.

If you already have a brass bed and are looking for post caps, finials, cannonballs, or tubing, the Bedpost has quite a selection. Number 15 is $6.50; number 1 is $10.

Literature available.

The Bedpost
R.D. 1, Box 155
Pen Argyl, Penn. 18072
(215) 588-3824

The company has three retail outlets (in Montgomeryville, Zionsville, and Bangor, Penn., but all correspondence should be addressed to the Penn Argyl address.
dress.

Rope Beds

A tradition of furniture-making began with the founding of Bishop Hill, Illinois, in the 1840s. Swedish pietists settled on the edge of the prairie frontier and built a prosperous community on faith and hard work. At first, their handiwork reflected the simplicity of their religious observances. Unlike the Shakers, however, these new Americans found that some ornamentation made their work more saleable. The settlers were finally absorbed by the great All-American melting pot, but their tradition of good workmanship has been continued by craftsmen such as Lehlan Murray. He has been commissioned by the State of Illinois to make eight cannonball rope beds for the restoration of Bishop Hill's Bjorklund Hotel. A standard single mattress will fit its maple frame. The bed can be delivered to your door for $1,160.

Lehlan Murray
Box 18
Bishop Hill, Ill. 61419

"Rice Bed"

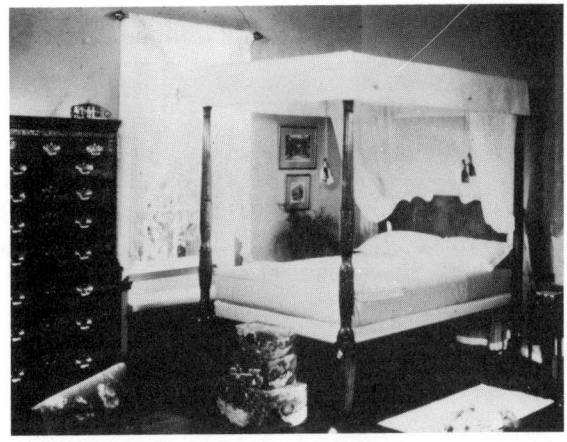

Historic Charleston Reproductions introduced its new "Rice Bed" in 1977, and it is made by Baker. It derives its name from the delicate carving of rice stalks on the posts, symbolizing the important place of the rice trade in eighteenth-century Charleston. Baker has faithfully reproduced this mahogany bed which was given as a gift to a new bride at Middleton Place House. It measures 64″ wide x 87¾″ deep x 91¾″ high and is available through select retail outlets. Be forewarned; it is expensive, and has to be.

Further information is available, along with a catalog, $4, from,

Historic Charleston Reproductions
51 Meeting St.
Charleston, S.C. 29401
(803) 723-1623

Field and Pencil-Post Beds

The influence of Thomas Sheraton was considerable at the turn of the eighteenth century The turned posts of this field bed by the craftsmen from the Country Bed Shop are available in maple or cherry. Other options include a canopy frame, box spring brackets or rope, a variety of headboard styles, and varying sizes. The bed sells for $580 as illustrated here.

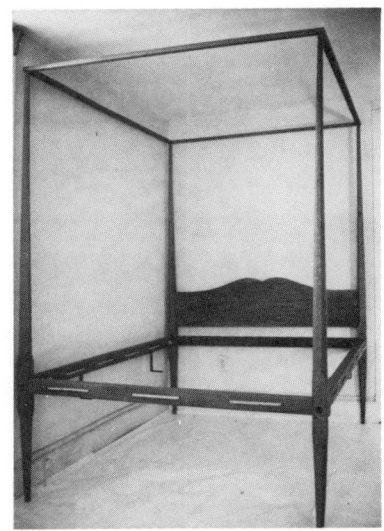

Country Bed Shop also offers a pencil-post bedstead of a style that made its appearance in the seventeenth century. Its fine, attenuated lines make it the utmost in simplicity. It is priced at $550 but is sold with a number of options such as four different lower post styles, which may raise the price.

Catalog available, $2.

Country Bed Shop
Box 222
Groton, Mass. 01450
(617) 448-6336

Low-Post Bed

Cabinetmaker Thomas Moser makes a low-post bed which is 33″ to the top of the headboard. As illustrated, it is a straightforward design of handsome proportions. The twin size (39″ wide x 74″ long) sells for $385; full size (54″ wide x 74″ long), $422; and queen, (60″ wide x 80″ long), $473. Rollers are an additional $20.

Catalog available, $2.

Thos. Moser, Cabinet Makers
Cobb's Bridge Road
New Gloucester, Maine 04260
(207) 926-4446

Chairs

When it comes to chairs, as with beds, there can be little compromise. We need solid, well-balanced, and comfortable objects on which to sit. Whether the activity is reading a book or dining, one wants to rest with ease and not with the fear of splintering underneath. Unfortunately, many antique chairs are not only unstable, they are downright backbreaking. Some may have been designed with shorter people or less bulk in mind. Antique chairs are to be preferred in the home if they do fulfill our real needs. Many can be reconditioned (joints strengthened, seats replaced, upholstery redone and even frames rebuilt), and every attempt should be made to reuse the old. But when your patience is at an end, consider turning to one of many fine reproduction chair makers. Some can also expertly reproduce a chair that is missing from a set.

Queen Anne Armchair

The ancestor of this Queen Anne armchair was made in Philadelphia in the mid-eighteenth century. Its ample seat and downward curving arms make it extremely comfortable. Master craftsman Robert Whitley has reproduced the original in every detail. This gifted artist has achieved considerable renown for his competence in the field. Many of his commissions have been to reproduce pieces for incomplete antique sets.

Brochure, $1.

The Robert Whitley Studio
Laurel Road
Solebury, Penn. 18963
(215) 297-8452

Ladder-Back Chair

Over 2,000 Appalachian craftsmen are represented and served by the non-profit Southern Highland Handicraft Guild. The organization maintains high quality standards and markets through its own merchandising program. This ladder-back chair is produced by a Guild craftsman who has lost none of his ancestral skills.

The Guild operates four retail stores—in Asheville and Blowing Rock, North Carolina, and Bristol, Virginia— where a wide variety of products are displayed. It also sponsors annual Craftsman's Fairs in Asheville, and Gatlinburg, Tennessee. For information on these outlets and the fairs, contact the Guild headquarters.

Brief literature available.

Southern Highland Handicraft Guild
P.O. Box 9545
Asheville, N.C. 28805
(704) 298-7928

Bow-Back and Pressback Chairs

Chairs suitable for use in the dining room or kitchen of a Victorian-period home are in the process of being "rediscovered." Some supply of real antiques is still available at moderate prices, and secondhand stores are a good place to start looking. If you are not successful, you might want to consider the many models produced by American Woodcarving.

The bow-back has retained its popularity through the years. An unfinished chair costs $43; finished, it sells for $55.

The more ornamental pressback features turned members and a carved back. You can get it for $86 unfinished or $106 for a finished piece.

 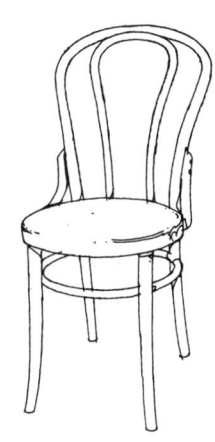

Literature available.

American Woodcarving
282 San Jose Ave.
San Jose, Calif. 95125

Corset Back Armchair

The students and master craftsmen at Berea College must meet high standards of quality. They specialize in careful early American and Colonial reproductions. Each piece is made from select or better walnut, cherry, or mahogany.

The "Corset Back Armchair" is descended from the provincial French *chaise a capucine*, a simple open-back chair found in monastic dwellings in the seventeenth century. The seat is available in corn shuck or Sudan grass. The chair is priced at $235 in mahogany or walnut; $220 in cherry. Berea also produces an armless model of the same form which sells for $195 in cherry and $210 in mahogany or walnut.

Catalog available.

Berea College
Student Craft Industries
Berea, Ky. 40404
(609) 986-9341

Swivel Armchair

Unlike many mass-producers of furniture, Ephraim Marsh does not go in for atmospheric photographs and slick promotional copy. The company sells a full line of eighteenth and nineteenth-century style furniture at very reasonable prices. No one claims that they are "authentic" reproductions. But they are honest, and that is more important since only an antique can be authentic.

The swivel armchair could be found, at one time or another, in every office in the country. Now it's not as common, and, if you can't find such a desk chair in a secondhand store, Marsh can help you out. The seat height and reclining tension are adjustable. This one is $128.

Catalog available, $1.

Ephraim Marsh Co.
Box 266
Concord, N.C. 28025
(704) 782-0814

Continuous Armchair

Thomas Moser's "continuous armchair" is a comfort to sit in and a pleasure to view. The sturdy turned legs are made of rock maple and the spindles are white ash. The

continuous arm and leg supports are fashioned from cherry. Mechanical and design patents are pending on this unique chair—an antique for the future. It is sold for $240.

Catalog available, $2.

Thos. Moser, Cabinet Makers
Cobb's Bridge Rd.
New Gloucester, Maine 04260
(207) 926-4446

Morris Chair

This is William Morris's century-old response to what he thought was the shoddy machine-made furniture of his day. A lot of it *was* shoddy, but this isn't. The Morris chair is a solid and eminently functional reproduction from Greystone Upholstery, and available only from them. It is made of grained oak and available in five

different finishes. The back reclines to four different positions, and the standard upholstery is either a synthetic "homespun" or Naugahyde. Better yet, send them your own upholstery fabric and they will perform the work at no extra charge.

Flyer available.

Greystone Upholstery Corp.
502 Clewell St.
Fountain Hill, Penn. 18015
(215) 691-0140

Cafe Chair and M Chair

Michael Thonet is best remembered for his bentwood rocker (*see* section on rockers), but his greatest success came when he designed this cafe chair for the mass market. Since 1876 it has sold over 50 million copies. The only real change has been in the seat, which is now available in padded vinyl in addition to natural cane or veneer.

The Thonet firm is also responsible for the introduction of Mies van der Rohe's "M Chair" (c. 1930). One of the first to utilize the natural resilience of steel in furniture design, Mies's designs are as appropriate for homes of the 1920s or '30s as they are for the most contemporary apartment of today. These are designs which have become antique in the best sense of that word.

Further information regarding Thonet chairs may be supplied by designers and decorators. *See* list of AISD chapters, Appendix B.

The following Thonet showrooms may also be able to provide information:

Thonet
A Simmons Company
Decorative Arts Center
305 East 63rd St.
New York, N.Y. 10021

Thonet
A Simmons Company
600 World Trade Center
2050 Stemmons Freeway
Dallas, Texas 75258

Thonet
A Simmons Company
11-100 Merchandise Mart
Chicago, Ill. 60654

Thonet
A Simmons Company
Los Angeles Home Furnishings Mart
Space 756
1933 South Broadway
Los Angeles, Calif. 90007

Rockers

The rocker provides a very simple human pleasure—sitting and gently moving to one's own rhythm. It is a homely pleasure, and one that has appealed to the down-home in all of us. Presidents—including Lincoln, Kennedy, and Carter—have enjoyed rocking away troubles. It is a movement from childhood and, often, of old age. No home is truly a castle without one of these chairs with curved runners. There are hundreds of varieties from the historic Boston rockers of the midnineteenth century to the weird contraptions on platforms invented by mad Victorians and updated in the twentieth century by kitsch purveyors. For our taste, the simpler the better. Be sure that what you get is sturdy; the pitching movement can create problems for the energetic of all ages.

Brumby Rocker

Jimmy Carter has made the Brumby rocker famous. Five new oak rockers were delivered to the White House last year and are finding good use on the Truman balcony. The chair has been around for over a century and is noted for its balance and superb rock. The handwoven seat and back make the rocker cool and comfortable. Carol Melson, whose husband revived the

Brumby works in 1972, is quoted in *The New York Times*: "Reproduction is not a term I would use. It's really a continuation of a broken production, a continuation from where they left off 30 years ago, using the same craftsmen, the same design and the same machines."

The demand is great for these new "antiques," but you may be able to convince the firm to make one for you—at $208—by contacting their retail outlet.

Literature available.

*The Rocker Shop
1421 White Circle, N.W.
P.O. Box 12
Marietta, Ga. 30061
(404) 427-2618*

Gliding Rocker

A more complicated rocker—a gliding one—is made by Ephraim Marsh. It moves on a platform in a smooth, easy fashion, and is less cumbersome than many of its Victorian cousins. The wood is maple, and the chair itself weighs 55 lbs. You won't want to move it around from room to room, but at least you'll know that it won't rock away.

Catalog available, $1.

*Ephraim Marsh Co.
Box 266
Concord, N.C. 28025
(704) 782-0814*

Goose Neck Rocker

Berea's craftsmen produce an unusual goose neck rocker with a caned seat. The spindles and front legs are turned, and the tall caned back is contoured. Back and seat are connected by downward sloping, looped arms. It sells for $465 in mahogany or walnut; $425 in cherry.

Catalog available.

Berea College
Student Craft Industries
Berea, Ky. 40404
(606) 986-9341

Bentwood Rocker

The bentwood rocker is perhaps the most elaborate expression of Michael Thonet's experiments with steam-bent beechwood. This is imported by Thonet and is available in several colors. It features a natural cane seat and back.

Further information regarding the Thonet rocker may be supplied by designers and decorators. *See* list of AISD chapters, Appendix B. Also refer to the listing for Cafe and M chairs for addresses of the company's showrooms.

Chests/Boxes

Long, low wooden chests are perfect for storing many things—from blankets to firewood. The fine antique pieces such as Pennsylvania-German decorated chests and the Pilgrim Century chests of New England have long since departed the common man's scene; these are now prized and priceless objects. Simple storage chests or boxes of nineteenth-century manufacture remain to be found, but because of their utility, the supply is diminishing rapidly. Some persons have turned to old trunks and cases as an alternative. As attractive as some of these containers may be, they really belong in a storage room and not at the foot of the bed or beside the hearth.

Wood Box

Guyon, Inc. makes a Pennsylvania wood box which is just over 4' wide and 22" high. It is not too big for other uses such as a toy box or hope chest. The box is made of pine appropriately enough and has a hinged lid at the top.

Literature available, $2.

Guyon, Inc.
65 Oak St.
Lititz, Penn. 17543
(717) 626-0225

Blanket Chest

This is a mahogany blanket chest which may someday become a treasured heirloom. Its builder, Craig Nutt, began his career restoring antiques and now recreates them with traditional techniques. The chest measures 30" x 18" x 18". Not only are the joints hand-dovetailed, but all the hardware—including lock and key—is made by hand.

Literature available.

Craig Nutt Fine Wood Works
2308 Sixth St.
Tuscaloosa, Ala. 35401
(205) 759-3142

Cupboards/Cabinets

As with chests, these useful pieces of furniture are being put up for sale one day and sold the next. When houses were without large closets, furniture of this sort was highly valued for practical purposes. Again today, with housing costs sky-rocketing and space at a premium, cupboards and cabinets are being viewed with a renewed interest. The antiques market should be searched diligently before turning to the reproduction craftsmen.

Storage Cupboard and Cabinet

At a height of 74″, this tin cupboard from Bittersweet can hold a lot of tin goods. Handcrafted of pine, all the joints are mortise and tenon to assure maximum strength.

Whether or not you preserve your own jams and jellies or put up other canned goods, you can probably find many uses for this handsome storage cabinet. It stands 45″ x 23″ x14″ and is made of pine.

Brochure available, 25¢.

Bittersweet
P.O. Box 5
Riverton, Vt. 05668
(802) 485-8562

Open Cupboard

Charles Thibeau of the Country Bed Shop has designed and will make this handmade open cupboard. It is a copy of an eighteenth-century New England piece. The cupboard measures 12″ x 32″ x 68″ and is fashioned from pine.

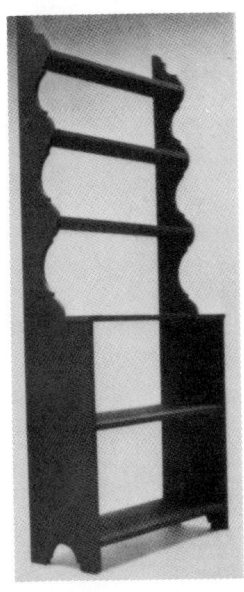

Catalog available, $2.

Country Bed Shop
Box 222
Groton, Mass. 01450
(617) 448-6336

Pie Safe

Pie safes are "hot items" in the country antiques market these days, and you will be lucky to find one at all. If you don't want to take time to search for the absolutely real thing, Old Timey Furniture Co. can help you. It would take a good day or two to fill this pie safe with fresh baked goods, and a big, hungry family to empty it. But, then, it is also useful—with punched tin paneled doors for ventilation—for preserves and canned goods. The wood is pine. The measurements are 78″ x 36″ x 13″.

Literature available, $1.50.

Old Timey Furniture Co.
Smithfield, N.C. 27577
(919) 965-6555

Tables

The need for a table becomes evident when you reach out in thin air to deposit a book or are left holding a precarious dinner plate at an informal buffet supper. No one seems to have enough tables, at least of the right size. Purchase of something as large as a reproduction dining table or even one for the kitchen is not strongly recommended. A trestle table is included in the listings; the price of this sort of primitive piece has become prohibitive in the antiques market. Most kinds of tables, however, can be purchased more cheaply "used" than new. You wouldn't want to disgrace your dining room with one of the period "sets" manufactured by hundreds of second-rate concerns that claim to produce authentic reproductions. For the most part, these are clunky designs which are fashioned from nameless woods. Only the brand name of the plastic lamination used on the top is announced with pride.

But there are good *reproductions of smaller pieces for those who need them.*

Lyre Table

Magnolia Hall is renowned for Victorian reproduction furniture. The two-drawer mahogany lyre table, shown here, is claimed to be the manufacturer's best-selling end table. It has a carved lyre base and an urn on the stretcher. The marble top is 18″ x 14″. It sells for $189.95. Have you priced the real thing lately? If so, you may decide to shop down South.

Subscription to three illustrated catalogs published each year, $1.

Magnolia Hall
726 Andover
Atlanta, Ga. 30327
(404) 256-4747

End Table

Lehlan Murray of the Bishop Hill restoration in Illinois has fashioned this simple table of white spruce. It can be delivered to you for $200. It would be suitable for use almost anywhere in the house.

Lehlan Murray
Box 18
Bishop Hill, Ill. 61419

Side Table

Brian Considine draws many of his design ideas from Shaker sources. The inspiration for this side table in

maple and pine, a common combination of woods, is a Shaker prototype. Considine also makes a similar table with turned legs. The measurements of the top are 24″ x 19″.

Literature available.

Brian Considine, Cabinet Maker
Post Mills, Vt. 05058

Candlestand

This cherry candlestand or "round stand" is a particularly fine rendition from The Guild of Shaker Crafts. It

is just a shade over 2′ tall; the top's diameter is 16″. Used alongside an easy chair, it will easily carry a small lamp. You can, of course, use it simply with a candlestick. The price is $65.

Catalog available, $2.50.

Guild of Shaker Crafts
401 W. Savidge
Spring Lake, Mich. 49456
(616) 846-2870

Pie-Crust Table

A Philadelphia Chippendale pie-crust table is a valuable antique; Craig Nutt makes a very fine reproduction. A table of this sort was found only in the most elegant home and was used for the serving of tea. The reproduction's carved mahogany top tilts and revolves on a "birdcage" mechanism and is supported by a claw-footed tripod. This 28½″ diameter table sells for $700

but its size, and presumably its price, can be scaled down if requested.

Literature available.

Craig Nutt Fine Wood Works
2308 Sixth St.
Tuscaloosa, Ala. 35401
(205) 759-3142

Ice Cream Parlor Furniture

Not since the 1920s has oak and wrought-iron ice cream parlor furniture been so popular. Crown of Fairhope is one of several companies that supply a set of two chairs and a table for $$99.50. These are shipped in "knock-down" condition and the supplier claims that they can be assembled in minutes. Stools, bought in sets of two, are $22.50 each.

Catalog available, $1.

Crown of Fairhope
P.O. Drawer G
Fairhope, Ala. 36532
(205) 928-2300

Pedestal Base

Pedestals for tables intended for indoor or outdoor use are often very difficult to find. Objects as varied as old sewing machine bases and washstands have been used as substitutes. Here is the real thing, a nineteenth-

century cast-iron base as used in cafes throughout the world. It is coated with a zinc chromate primer and a second coating of rust-inhibitive coloring. The price is $73.

Brochure available.

Santa Cruz Foundry
P.O. Box 831, 738 Chestnut St.
Santa Cruz, Calif. 95060

Trestle Table

Reproductions of trestle tables have multiplied each year as the supply of antique pieces declines. Here is a simple rendition in 2″ pine. Old Timey Furniture makes it in lengths of up to 84″.

Literature available, $1.50.

Old Timey Furniture Co.
Smithfield, N.C. 27577
(919) 965-6555

Hall Settees/Settles/Benches

Informal furniture of this sort can be used in many areas of an old house—in a living room, front hall, front porch, or a bedroom. It is furniture made for the use of more than one person, perhaps as many as three people. It is not meant to be as comfortable as an easy chair, but there is no reason why a bench or settle should not be inviting indoors or out. The settle or bench (the terms are almost synonymous) was used in old inns and hotels; the settee of the sort listed here was a precursor of the sofa, but without upholstery. All three kinds of furniture were used in all kinds of North American homes during the eighteenth and early nineteenth centuries. They weren't excluded from the mansions of the gentry as being too common. And, today, the same situation applies, making the supply of antique pieces somewhat limited.

Foyer Settees

Bishop White lived right across the green from Independence Hall during the important years of the eighteenth century. Two settees from his foyer have been copied in detail by Frederick Duckloe's craftsmen, a firm in business since 1859. Nineteen turned hickory spindles rise from a poplar plank seat and are connected by an 80″ ash steam-bent back. The arms are solid cherry. The original pair was made by Philadelphia craftsman John Letchworth during the Revolutionary period.

Literature available.

Frederick Duckloe & Bros., Inc.
Portland, Penn. 18351
(717) 897-6172

Shaker Bench

In a Shaker community a pine bench like this would have been used principally in the dining room. There is no reason why it can not be placed in other rooms—depending on the overall style of furnishings. Placed against the wall, it will serve the needs of even those with lower back trouble—a common American affliction of the twentieth century. The seat is 9½″ x 48″.

Catalog available, $2.50.

Guild of Shaker Crafts
401 W. Savidge
Spring Lake, Mich. 49456
(616) 846-2870

Estate Bench

Attractive benches for use out in the open are extremely difficult to find today—antique or reproduction. Too many home owners have opted for something salvaged

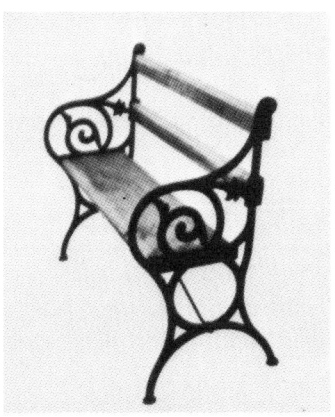

from a city park, often a bench that has been encased in cement. Santa Cruz Foundry makes a 5-foot "Estate" bench which will complement any well-tended grounds. The seat and back are Douglas fir prefinished with Danish oil stain. The wrought-iron ends come in black or forest green. You might want to anchor the legs in some manner as lawn furniture of this sort can disappear in even broad daylight. The bench is priced at $147.

Literature available.

Santa Cruz Foundry
P.O. Box 831, 738 Chestnut St.
Santa Cruz, Calif. 95060

Custom Furniture

Nearly all of the craftsmen listed in these pages will undertake commissions. They particularly enjoy the opportunity to create a one-of-a-kind object. If you are trying to complete a set of chairs or want to exactly duplicate a particular piece, these craftsmen will guide you along the way. Such work is terribly expensive and may take some time to complete.

Up Country Enterprise

Up Country Enterprise is a limited edition producer of furniture in the English and colonial Philadelphia traditions. Each piece is undertaken as a distinct entity; there is no mass production of any parts. Only when an order is received does the work begin. Up Country also engages in custom projects which may involve reproduction of an antique, adaptation of a design, or execution of an original design.

Literature available.

Up Country Enterprise
Old Jaffrey Rd.
Peterborough, N.H. 03458
(603) 924-6826

D. R. Millbranth

D. R. Millbranth has moved his shop from Maryland to New Hampshire and there will continue to make custom-ordered furniture. His specialty is Chippendale as well as primitive pieces.

D. R. Millbranth, Cabinetmaker
Center Rd., RR 2, Box 462
Hillsboro, N.H. 03244
(603) 464-5244

Kits/Plans

Fortunate is the woman or man skilled as a woodworker. Plans and kits are available to those who, unlike this writer, paid attention to the shop teacher at school and were smart enough to know early that working with the hands can be a rewarding experience. For the very skilled, plans may provide sufficient guidelines for constructing handsome pieces of furniture. For others, kits may be the answer.

Woodcraft Supply

If you have the notion to build your own Windsor chair or Boston rocker, Woodcraft Supply has a package of plans, assembly notes, material lists, and an 8" x 10" photo of the original—all for $8 each. Their 160-page book, *Windsor Chairmaking*, a step-by-step guide, is also recommended and sells for $10.25.

Catalog available, 50¢.

Woodcraft Supply Corp.
313 Montvale Ave.
Woburn, Mass. 01801
1-800-225-1153

Shaker Workshops

You can get good quality furniture kits from Shaker Workshops. The woods are northern hardwoods and pine. Each kit contains all you will need to complete the project except a hammer and screw driver. The classic straight chair sells for $45. The slats are secured with pegs, not nails. The seats come in your choice of colored fabric tape.

When its leaves are down, this table takes up very little space. With raised leaves, it is 38″ wide. You can order lengths of from 4′ to 7′. Prices range from $300 to $330.

Catalog available.

Shaker Workshops, Inc.
14 Bradford St.
Concord, Mass. 01742
(617)369-1790

Cohasset Colonials

Cohasset Colonials is another firm which offers well-made kits. Here is a slant-top desk with a rock maple lid which drops forward as a writing surface. It is 27″ wide and 19″ deep and has a drawer in the frame. It costs $140.

This half round table has a radius of 18″. The maple top is supported by tapered maple legs. It stands 28½″ high and sells for $34.

Here is a Shaker tray kit for $52. It makes a great serving tray, but can be used in other ways. It folds up nicely and takes up very little space. The top is 30″ x 19″ x 2½″.

Catalog available, 50¢.

Cohasset Colonials
Cohasset, Mass. 02025
(617) 383-0110

Ford Museum & Greenfield Village

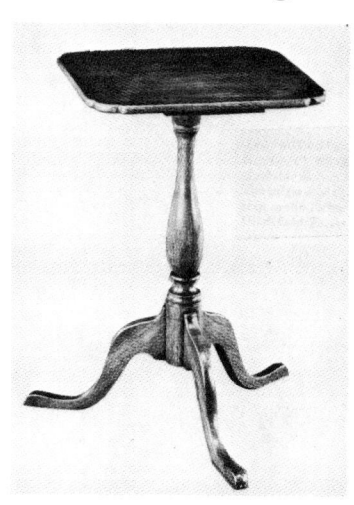

The original candle table from which this is copied is part of the Edison Collection at Greenfield Village. The Bartley Collection reproduces a number of pieces in kit form for the museum complex. The kits include all the things necessary to complete assembly and finishing.

Catalog available, $2.50.

Henry Ford Museum and Greenfield Village
20900 Oakwood Blvd.
Dearborn, Mich. 48121
(313) 271-1620

Crown of Fairhope

Assembled but unfinished pieces cost considerably less than finished. For instance, a finished $74.95 sculptured back chair can be bought unfinished for $59.95 from Crown of Fairhope. Similar bargains are available from manufacturers and retailers across the country. A basic course on finishing and refinishing furniture could be an excellent investment.

Catalog available, $1.

Crown of Fairhope
795 Nichols Ave.
P.O. Drawer G
Fairhope, Ala. 36532
(205) 928-2300

Odds and Ends

Reproduction craftsmen produce an almost endless number of objects in all sizes, shapes, and forms. Some are expert makers of looking glasses, spinets, swings, and such accessories as fern stands and hall trees.

Brumby Rocker

The Brumby Rocker people also produce a porch swing. Mortise and tenon joints make this oak swing sturdy, and an arched back makes it relaxing.

Literature available.

The Rocker Shop
1421 White Circle, N.W., P.O. Box 12
Marietta, Ga. 30061

(404) 427-2618

Wrought-Iron Corner Rack

Mexico House can supply many of the decorative requirements of a Spanish-style residence. Your plants will have room to grow in this wrought-iron corner rack. It's just over 5' tall and weighs only 20 pounds. The price is $39.95.

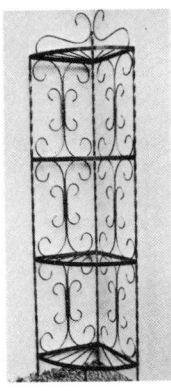

Catalog available, $1.

Mexico House
Box 970
Del Mar, Calif. 92014

Dressing Stand

Earlier and European forms of the dressing stand were often ornately carved and veneered. They were designed to display a lady's jewelry rather than to provide a place for its storage. Berea's craftsmen make a very modest stand. Only 9" deep, it has a drawer on each side of a tiltable mirror and is meant to perch atop a dressing table. It is available for $260 in cherry or $267 in mahogany or walnut.

Catalog available.

Berea College
Student Craft Industries
Berea, Ky. 40404
(606) 986-9341

Spinet Harpsichord

If your bank account matches your taste for elegance and your eighteenth-century music room is without an instrument, you may be interested in a spinet harpsichord. Frank Rockette is a scholar-craftsman who meticulously builds an instrument which he believes has "considerable investment value due to the integrity of workmanship." The woods are exotic, the brass hardware is cast to his molds, and even the varnish is made in the shop.

Frank Rockette
Strawberry Banke Museum
Box 300
Portsmouth, N.H. 03801

Looking Glasses

Stephen Franklin carves 200-year-old looking glasses out of 150-year-old wood. He recreates four Chippendale styles in varying degrees of fanciness. These are available from a simple fretwork model to one with a gilt phoenix and carved side drapes and scrolls.

Literature available.

Stephen Franklin
Box 717
Buckingham, Penn. 18912

Supplies

Most of the basic supplies for refinishing and maintaining furniture are available at your local hardware store. Items of particular interest are listed herewith. You may want to recommend them to retailers in your area.

Lemon Oil and Tung Oil

Fine furniture is made to last, but it must be cared for. You can use lemon oil as often as you dust. It replaces the natural oils in the wood. Paint and hardware stores sell some varieties, or it can be ordered from a specialty firm such as The Hope Company. Hope sells a variety of refinishing products, too. They are the only source for 100% tung oil in the United States.

Literature available.

The Hope Co.
2052 Congressional Dr.
St. Louis, Mo. 63141
(314) 432-5697

Caning Kits

The old wooden rocker in the garage is not beyond hope. Perhaps all it needs is a new seat. The Newell Workshop stocks all kinds of cane, tools, and instructions so that even a beginner can do a perfect job. Caning kits are $4; refills are $2. It might be wise to send them a sample of the old cane to be sure the right size is in your kit.

It takes about two pounds of cord to restring an average chair. Newell stocks a twisted kraft cord which resembles natural rush. It also has a strong cord made out of Oriental sea grass. This is similar to natural rush except that the twisted strands are raised instead of flat.

Literature available.

Newell Workshop
19 Blaine Ave.
Hinsdale, Ill. 60521

Pressed Fibre Seats

An inexpensive alternative to caning is the pressed fibre seat. This is an appropriate form for many late-Victorian pieces. The seat is strong and relatively easy to install. The style shown here is 12¾″ square and sells for $5.45.

Literature available.

Peco
P.O. Box 777
Smithville, Texas 78957
(512) 237-3600

Other Furniture Sources

Consult the List of Suppliers for addresses.

Beds

Bedlam Brass Beds
Berea College
Brass Bed Co. of America
Colonial Williamsburg
Davis Cabinet
Guild of Shaker Crafts
Magnolia Hall
Ephraim Marsh
Old Timey Furniture
Reid Classics
Townshend Furniture

Chairs

Cane Farm
Historic Charleston Reproductions (Baker)
Colonial Williamsburg (Kittinger)
Brian Considine
Country Bed Shop
Crown of Fairhope
Frederick Duckloe
Davis Cabinet
Guild of Shaker Crafts
Hitchcock Chair
Ernest Lo Nano
Magnolia Hall
Louis Maslow & Son
Nichols & Stone
Sturbridge Yankee Workshop

Chests/Boxes

Berea College
Colonial Williamsburg (Kittinger)
Brian Considine
Guild of Shaker Crafts
Magnolia Hall
Ephraim Marsh
D. R. Millbranth
Thomas Moser
Old Timey Furniture
Townshend Furniture

Cupboards/Cabinets

Berea College
Guyon
Magnolia Hall
Ephraim Marsh
Thomas Moser

Craig Nutt
Restorations Unlimited
Sturbridge Yankee Workshop

Looking Glasses/Mirrors

Berea College
Colonial Williamsburg (Friedman Brothers)
Brian Considine
Holmes Co.
Magnolia Hall
Ephraim Marsh
Rococo Designs

Rockers

Guild of Shaker Crafts
Sturbridge Yankee Workshop
Townshend Furniture
Robert Whitley

Settees/Settles/Benches

Bittersweet
Historic Charleston Reproductions (Baker)
Country Bed Shop
Guyon
Lennox Shop
Magnolia Hall
Ephraim Marsh
D. R. Millbranth
Thomas Moser
Old Timey Furniture
Townshend Furniture

Tables

American Woodcarving
Bittersweet
Historic Charleston Reproductions (Baker)
Colonial Williamsburg (Kittinger)
Country Bed Shop
Ephraim Marsh
Mexico House
Thomas Moser
Townshend Furniture
Robert Whitley

Customwork

Bittersweet
Brian Considine
Country Bed Shop
Noelwood
Craig Nutt
Robert Whitley

Kits/Plans

Albert Constantine & Sons
Furniture Designs
Minnesota Woodworkers
Peerless Rattan & Reed

X   Accessories

Maintaining the structural integrity of an old house is enough of a job without having to worry about suitable furnishings and accessories. It is understandable, then, that professionals in the building restoration business show little enthusiasm for the extras which make a house a home. These can be provided later if the owner is so inclined—and most are. This is why the first chapter of this book is devoted to structural needs and the very last to accessories. This organization of material serves to emphasize that the decorative values of old-house living are secondary to those of environment and structure. To merely embellish a crumbling building is about the same as painting a corpse before a viewing. Yet this is done in many renovation/decorating projects, and only the effect of "life," rather than its substance, is achieved. At worst, such a gussied up house becomes only a Hollywood set.

There are many reasons for this simplistic approach: the surface attractiveness of coverups such as paints, papers, and fabrics; a lack of interest in and knowledge of building technology; and, perhaps most important, economic limitations which preclude the kind of major structural work of returning a house to its original state and keeping it that way. If we don't have the time to do the work, we may not be able to afford to have someone else come in and perform it. Unless governmental aid is forthcoming in the form of tax breaks or outright grants for a truly historic home, there has to be some sort of compromise between past and future. While we may not be able to achieve period perfection (or even want to), we can at least get the props right and make sure that they are something more than a faint imitation of historic reality. There is no reason why the everyday objects we live with should not be as fitting and attractive as the house in which they are kept.

That is why space is properly devoted here to such a subject as accessories. Without pursuing antiquarian interests to an eccentric extreme, those who have learned to love living in a period setting should enjoy making use of other aspects of the material past—brooms made of straw that do not fall apart on first sweeping; fans that can cool a room almost as effectively as (and much more cheaply than) air conditioners; furniture and ornaments which make a porch or lawn as attractive a space for living as the inside of a house; pottery dishes that will not disintegrate when placed in the oven. There are other utilitarian benefits to be had from the craftsmanship of the past. But added to the tangible rewards must be the aesthetic. It is just plain nice to have attractive, well-made objects at hand whether we can explain their function or not. They are the immediate comforts of a good life.

Since we are bombarded daily with appeals to spend our hard-earned money on one piece of junk after another, there needs to be a constant sorting out of the good from the bad. It doesn't take very long to discover that most of the mail can be thrown into the fire. As George Funke, proprietor of Bassett & Vollum in Galena, Illinois, wrote this writer in a description of his historic house, "The stove is excellent for burning third class mail, too." He has the right attitude. You can't stop time, but neither do you need to fall victim to every fad and fancy for "the latest." We believe that the objects described in the following listings are not of the fleeting variety. Even the old-fashioned sugar cone used for table decoration has aesthetic appeal which has somehow survived the years.

Most of these secondary items for the old house are made by individual craftsmen and not large suppliers. (We have attempted to steer clear of ye olde gift shoppes and other such emporiums which often serve more nostalgic syrup than material substance). In the pages following are representative craftsmen who are producing objects that may become antiques of the future, regardless of the style in which they are working. A well-designed and crafted object will always retain intrinsic and extrinsic value.

Handmade Baskets

Baskets made of white oak splints are the specialty of Ken and Kathleen Dalton. They work and draw their materials from deep within the hills of southeastern Tennessee. Illustrated are round rib baskets from bushel size to those appropriate for eggs.

Brochure available.

Coker Creek Crafts
P.O. Box 95
Coker Creek, Tenn. 37314
(615) 261-2157

Similar kinds of baskets are produced by members of the Southern Highland Handicraft Guild. These are by Charlotte Tracy and illustrate stages of construction.

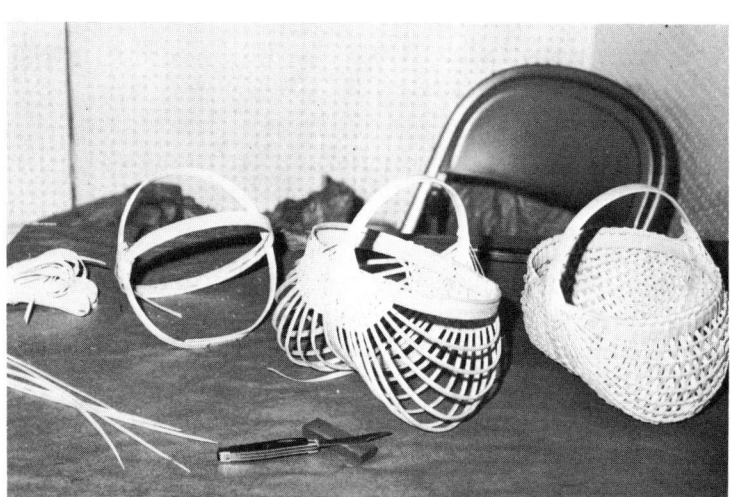

For further information, contact:

Southern Highland Handicraft Guild
P.O. Box 9545
Asheville, N.C. 28805
(704) 298-7928

Baskets of almost every sort can be found at the Cumberland General Store and through their mail order service. These are made of New England hardwood and are of the following kinds: bread, shopping, market, pie and cake, bicycle, produce, egg, feed, and fireplace grate.

Catalog available, $3.

Cumberland General Store
Rte. 3
Crossville, Tenn. 38555
(615) 484-8481

Boxes for Storage

Various kinds of wood boxes that fasten to the wall (such as those for knives or for candles) are handy containers to have around any house—old or not. The Candle Cellar & Emporium manufactures boxes of this sort in their workshop. They also have an adaptation of a workman's tool box (13¾ x 4 x 9½″) which can be used for holding garden tools, candles, mail, etc.

Brochure available, 25¢.

The Candle Cellar & Emporium
1914 North Main St.
Fall River, Mass. 02720
(617) 679-6057

The Shakers designed and produced some of the most beautiful and functional of wood containers. Several of these are now available from the Guild of Shaker Crafts. One especially handsome container is a dining room "deep tray" of pine with dovetailed corners. The original was used in the New Lebanon Ministry dining room for carrying water glasses. A berry box in pine is another appealing design. These were used for gathering and storing berries and nuts as well as herbs.

Catalog available, $2.50.

Guild of Shaker Crafts
401 W. Savidge St.
Spring Lake, Mich. 49456
(616) 846-2870

Brooms

Have you tried to buy a *real* broom recently? If so, you will appreciate knowing that old-fashioned brooms of straw *can* be found. In this illustration, Larry Kear, a member of the Southern Highland Handicraft Guild, is displaying his talents.

For further information, contact:

Southern Highland Handicraft Guild
P.O. Box 9545
Asheville, N.C. 28805
(704) 298-7928

Clocks

Unless you are a devotee of fine cabinetmaking and a precision jeweler, an antique clock may not be worth

the fuss. Most are notoriously unreliable instruments, and parts are sometimes hard to find. Millions of clocks were mass produced during the nineteenth century in much the same way that automobiles are manufactured today. Naturally, there are a goodly number of lemons. The handsome reproductions from The Royal Windyne Collection are made to last. Illustrated is the "Winthrop" model which strikes on the half hour and counts on the hour. It need be wound only once a month. The case is solid wood and the pendulum and hardware are of brass.

Catalog available, $1.

Royal Windyne Ltd.
Dept. OHC
Box 6622
Richmond, Va. 23230
(804) 355-5690

Fans

The New York Times recently noted that city dwellers are amazed to learn that country and suburban people depend little on air conditioners; in the country most people simply turn on a fan—unless, of course, they live in the midst of the Sun Belt or in a tropical rain forest. Although it is not easy to live in a modern house or apartment without air conditioning, old-house dwellers can more easily rely on the cooling effectiveness of an electric fan, especially if their houses are well-insulated. The Cumberland General Store catalog features seven standard ceiling fans with non-adjustable wood or metal blades. They also feature the "Adaptair Option" which they recommend for cathedral ceilings. The blades are adjustable so that air can be pulled up or down.

Catalog available, $3.

Cumberland General Store
Rte. 3
Crossville, Tenn.
(615) 484-8481

The Royal Windyne brass-appointed turn-of-the-century ceiling fans were featured in the first *Old House Catalogue.* We are repeating them here because we feel that they represent reproductions which are made with the quality of antiques. They are available in 39″ and 53″ diameter sizes. According to the manufacturer, the Royal Windyne models use only as much electricity as a light bulb—about 90 watts; the average room air conditioner consumes 1,566.

Catalog available, $1.

Royal Windyne Ltd.
Dept. OHC
Box 6622
Richmond, Va. 23230
(804) 355-5690

Fences

Fences don't always make good neighbors, but they may help to keep the pets in place and certainly do dress up the yard. Americans were frequently exhorted in the 1800s to improve and extend fencing so that the countryside would present a neat, prosperous appearance. And just as frequently, this advice was ignored by the majority of country dwellers. Those living in small and large towns or cities, however, were more likely to enclose their properties. Many of these fences—urban or rural—have not survived the years in very good shape and need replacement or at the least considerable refurbishing.

The extraordinary firm of Kenneth Lynch & Sons is best known for its garden ornaments and weather vanes. Owner Kenneth Lynch, however, is very interested in fences and is preparing a new book on them, *To Keep In, To Keep Out*. He is ready to help you with at least two kinds of fencing—wrought-iron and stone—and can also supply gates.

Kenneth Lynch & Sons, Inc.
Box 488
78 Danbury Rd.
Wilton, Conn. 06897
(203) 762-8363

Old Mansions Co., an architectural firm, is particularly interested in preserving period iron work. It stocks iron fencing and window guards. You can probably find brackets, crestings, and other decorative pieces here too.

Literature available.

Old Mansions Co.
1305 Blue Hill Ave.
Mattapan, Mass. 02126
(617) 296-0737 or 296-0445

Fountains, Urns, and Vases

Cast-iron urns in the Victorian and the Regency styles are expertly prepared by Steptoe & Wife. These can be placed on cast-iron plinths or used on other sorts of bases, as well as on the ground itself. Remember that these are hefty numbers weighing approximately 66 pounds.

Catalog available, $1.

Steptoe & Wife Antiques Ltd.
3626 Victoria Park Ave.
Willowdale, Ontario
M2H 3B2 Canada

A wide variety of fountains, urns, and vases in cast iron is available from Robinson Iron. This is a firm that values the past and makes a sincere effort to document all the period materials it produces. The "Venetian Fluted Urn" is an exact replica of one produced before

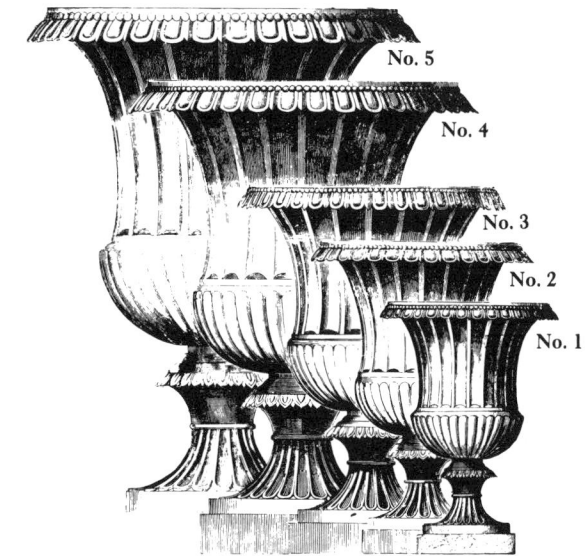

the Civil War. The Robinson catalog points out that "the top 'bowl' of the urn is made in a single piece. Only a master molder can make the urn bowl in one piece and even the masters have a failure rate of roughly 50%. Of course the technology for significantly reducing the failure rate is available, but this would require noticeable pattern modifications. We at Robinson have an intense desire to keep this particular tradition alive and well." Amen.

Literature available.

Robinson Iron
Robinson Rd.
Alexander City, Ala. 35010
(205) 234-3429

Garden ornaments of every possible sort in stone, lead, and wrought iron are indisputably Kenneth Lynch's eminent domain. There is no way to describe the riches which are available from his firm. You might want to inquire about the *Encyclopedia of Garden Ornaments*, a treasure trove of information that is available for $25. There are other books as well which are less costly and perhaps will suit your needs.

Kenneth Lynch & Sons, Inc.
78 Danbury Rd.
Wilton, Conn. 06897
(203) 762-8363

Garden Furniture

Some outdoor furniture has been discussed in the furniture section of this book, but the subject is one that is appropriate for "accessories" as well. The garden or lawn area of a home is probably the last concern when it comes to "furnishing," and it probably should be. As in the past, however, the outdoors can serve as a second living area—at least in the summer months—if properly planned and planted. Most old houses are generously endowed with trees and shrubs which may need only periodic maintenance to preserve their form. To place attractive garden furniture amidst them is an inviting prospect.

Tennessee Fabricating Co. mixes the new and the old. Its classic sets of tables, chairs, and settees are of ornamental metal but are cast in the patterns of the past.

Brochure available.

Tennessee Fabricating Co.
2366 Prospect
Memphis, Tenn. 38106
(901) 948-3354

About any style bench you can think of has been made by Kenneth Lynch. These are made of wrought iron, wood, cast iron, cast stone, marble, and granite. Many of the designs would suit the grounds of fine eighteenth and nineteenth-century homes.

A special catalog (book #9074) is available just on benches, $2.50 for paperback; $5 for hardcover.

Kenneth Lynch & Sons, Inc.
78 Danbury Rd.
Wilton, Conn. 06897
(203) 762-8363

Steptoe & Wife supply only cast-iron furniture of English Victorian design; tops of tables may be of aluminum or wood. Illustrated here is the Colebrookdale-style table and matching chairs. Naturally, you won't want to lug these from pace to place. The table weighs approximately 60 pounds and each of the chairs, 44.

Catalog available, $1.

Steptoe & Wife Antiques, Ltd.
3626 Victoria Park Ave.
Willowdale, Ontario
M2H 3B2 Canada

Metalware— Common and Rare

Antique metalware is avidly sought by collectors. Early pewter, silver, copper, and brass bring extremely high prices, so high, in fact, that the supply of fine materials is extremely limited. Even good tinware is becoming scarce. There are, however, craftsmen making very fine reproductions which may be even more appropriate for everyday wear. Deanne F. Nelson is one of these. She is a goldsmith and silversmith working at the historic Swedish colony of Bishop Hill, Illinois. She makes sterling porringer shown here. The design on the handle is taken from an 1840 Bishop Hill hymnal cover. Its price is only $45.

Deanne F. Nelson
Box 43
Bishop Hill, Ill. 61419

Historic Charleston's pewter is made by Gorham. A porringer, bowls, and plates found in the historic 1739 William Elliott House form the collection of reproduction pieces. Modern pewter is lead-free and thus perfectly safe for serving of food.

Catalog available, $4.

Historic Charleston Reproductions
51 Meeting St.
Charleston, S.C. 29401
(803) 723-1623

Craftsmen at Greenfield Village and the Henry Ford Museum produce their own pewter pieces. The form and detail of antique models are faithfully reproduced. Such pieces as a wall candle sconce, candleholder, candle extinguisher, chamberstick, and a porringer are carefully hand-shaped and finished.

Catalog available, $2.50.

Henry Ford Museum and Greenfield Village
20900 Oakwood Blvd.
Dearborn, Mich. 48121
(313) 271-1620

William Stewart is a traditional tinsmith who has done work for the National Park Service and many historical groups and museums. He uses tinplate which is custom dipped exactly to the specifications used in the past. Stewart is a purist and will not make "adaptations." If it is cups or coffee pots or various sorts of table and kitchen ware that you are seeking, this is the man you should contact.

William Stewart & Sons
708 N. Edison St.
Arlington, Va. 22203
(703) 841-1776

Mirrors

Rococo Designs has slowly expanded its line of acid-etched, bevelled glass mirrors of late Victorian design. Earlier forms of mirrors or looking glasses are not hard to find as antiques or reproductions. The manufacture of late nineteenth-century accessories, however, is a relatively recent phenomenon and the buyer has every reason to be skeptical about the honesty and quality of such pieces. There is a lot of shlock being peddled which has nothing but a weak nostalgic appeal. That is not true of the designs from Rococo or of the execution of them.

Catalog available, $1.50.

Rococo Designs
417 Pennsylvania Ave.
Santa Cruz, Calif. 95062
(408) 423-2732

The Holmes Co. produces traditional eighteenth-century furnishings, including two mirrors or looking glasses. One is a hand looking glass with mother-of-pearl inlay in the handle; the second is a Chippendale wall mirror. Both are made of fine Honduras mahogany to which a soft gloss finish is applied. Neither have the hard, shiny look of a second-rate reproduction, a look which often is the result of an attempt to cover up an inferior wood.

Catalog available.

The Holmes Co.
P.O. Box 382
York, Penn. 17405
(717) 846-6807

Pottery

Good pottery containers of various sorts are not that easy to find. There is a great amount of work available that is interesting, but not really historically accurate. And there is also the vast quantity of hand-crafted ware that is thrown haphazardly from kilns everywhere in the country. The following firms are sources for attractive, useful reproductions that should stand considerable wear.

Beaumont Heritage Pottery produces only salt-glazed stoneware which varies in color from tan to grey with variations of brown tones. All the wares are handmade and can be treated as roughly as Pyrex. The designs in cobalt blue, as illustrated here, are carefully rendered. Potter Jerry Beaumont's group of craftsmen produces pitchers, jugs, covered jars, crocks, flowerpots, mixing and serving bowls, candle holders, mugs, steins, pie plates, spice jars, spoon holders, butter tubs, and water glasses.

Literature available.

Beaumont Heritage Pottery
Box 300, Atkinson St.
Portsmouth, N.H. 03801
(603) 431-5284

Spongeware in a color termed "Swedish blue" is most appropriately produced at the Colony Pottery in Bishop Hill, Illinois, by craftsmen Steve and Linda Holden. A pitcher set is illustrated here and includes a 1½ quart pitcher, four 8 oz. mugs, a creamer, and a sugar bowl. The interior and collar of each piece is glazed a glossy Albany slip brown. The exterior is a waxy white with decoration "sponged" in blue. The seven pieces are priced at $40. An extraordinary value.

Also available from the Holdens is a set of twelve

ceramic spice jars with corks included. Each has a capacity of approximately 4 oz. The set is offered for $50; individual containers are $5 each.

Colony Pottery
Box 18
Bishop Hill, Ill. 61419

Stoneware and earthenware have been traditionally produced in the Jugtown area of North Carolina for over two-hundred years. The wares are of exceptional quality, with the orange-glazed earthenware containers being the most original to the region. Local clays are used, and these are of a reddish-orange. Most of the pieces, however, have a brown, blue, or gray glaze. There is an almost endless number of forms available—jugs, pitchers, noggins, vases, bowls, plates, teacups, pots, jars, and candle holders. Illustrated is a salt-glazed stoneware pitcher. The photograph is by Charles Tompkins.

Catalog available.

Jugtown Pottery
Rte. 2
Seagrove, N.C. 27341
(919) 464-3266

Plates with sgraffito decoration have been produced by the Pennsylvania Germans for many years. This tradition has been continued by several craftsmen, including Dorothy E. Long. She signs and dates her pieces which are made for the Philadelphia Museum of Art's Museum Shop after originals in the institution's collection. These are of red clay with pale yellow, green, and brown decoration. The glaze used is non-lead, and the ware is ovenproof and dishwasher safe. Each is roughly 10″ in diameter.

Illustrated at left is "Bird" ($66), patterned after a dish by Henry Roudebush, a potter active from 1804–16 in Montgomery County, Pennsylvania. The inscription translates as "I am afraid that my ugly daughter will get no husband." Above it is "Tulip" ($60), a plate copied from one by Johannese Neesz which was made in Tyler's Port, Montgomery County, in 1826. The translation on this reads: "I am made of potter's thoughts. When I break, I will be gone." At lower right is "Flowers" ($48), which is patterned after a plate thought to have been made by Johann Drey in Heidelberg Township, Lebanon County, c. 1800. When ordering, add $2.50 for cost of handling and shipping.

Catalog available.

The Museum Shop
Dept. OH
Philadelphia Museum of Art
P.O. Box 7858
Philadelphia, Penn. 19101
(215) 763-8100

Blue Hill is one of Maine's most handsome coastal villages. Rowantrees is very much a part of the pastoral scene. Founded in 1934 by Adelaide Pearson, it has been continued by Laura Paddock and, now, by one of her students, Sheila Varnum. You may find the brown-glazed, ovenproof beanpot of special use. There is also a wide selection of dinnerware.

Brochure available.

Rowantrees Pottery
Blue Hill, Me. 04614
(207) 374-5535

Venetian Blinds

Metal or plastic Venetian blinds are the norm these days, and wooden blinds are antique items. Norton Blumenthal decided that the situation needed to be changed and has arranged for the manufacture of blinds in clear-stained cedar or pine which are held by either nylon strings or tapes of cotton or rayon. Since they have to be custom-ordered, they are expensive. But after you root around the second-hand stores, you may find that there is no alternative but to start anew.

Norton Blumenthal, Inc.
979 Third Ave.
New York, N.Y. 10021
(212) 752-2535

Silhouettes

Silhouette cutting is one of the lost arts that has come alive again. The Laughons are masters of the techniques used to produce convincing heads and full-length portraits, as well as family groups with their house in the background. Itinerant silhouette artists once provided the home with appealing and relatively inexpensive portrait work. The Laughons do not amble around the countryside, but they will execute silhouettes from clear side-view photos or slides, as well as from life.

H. & N. Laughon
8106 Three Chopt Rd.
Richmond, Va. 23229
(804) 288-7795

Sugar Cones

These are not the variety available at the corner ice cream store, but rather giant inverted cones which are wrapped in blue paper. They are used for late eighteenth-century table centerpieces. You can see such copies at the Winterthur Museum.

Canada & Dom
Sugar Ltd.
P.O. Box 490
Montreal 3,
Quebec, Canada

Sundials

For any kind of sundial, turn to Kenneth Lynch. He has a whole catalog/book ($2.50 in paperback) devoted to nothing but lead, stone, and wrought-iron devices. Ilustrated is #3525, a design of Fairfield stone with gilded lead numerals and a gnomon of bronze.

Kenneth Lynch & Sons, Inc.
78 Danbury Rd.
Wilton, Conn. 06897
(203) 762-8363

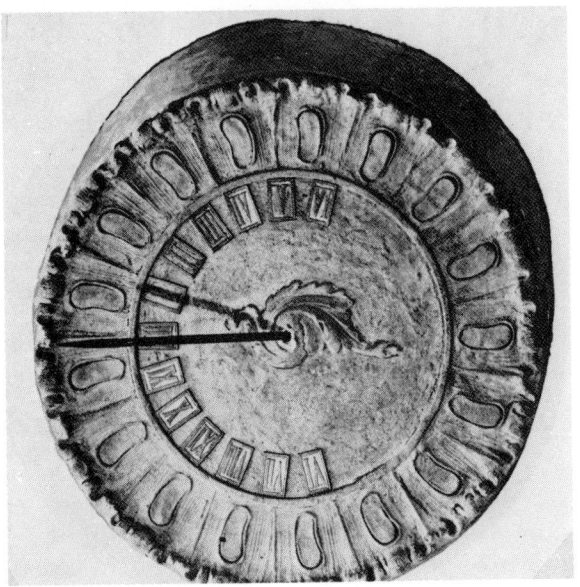

Tiles

Antique faience Delft tiles cannot be lavished as freely as other materials for floors and walls. But you may want to replace squares or introduce them in a fireplace facing or a small foyer area. Helen Williams is your expert, and, as she points out, only tiles made before 1800 are of the true hand-painted, tin-glazed variety. She has an extensive collection of these, and each measures roughly 5″ square. The most expensive are seventeenth-century blue and white designs with various scenes, animals, figures, etc. Those with tulips run $50 each. More affordable are eighteenth-century squares in solid white ($4) and tortoise shell ($9) or marble design ($8). Helen Williams also has some stock of antique English Liverpool transfer tiles and antique Spanish and Portuguese squares in blue and in polychrome. Illustrated are seventeenth-century blue designs.

Literature available.

Helen Williams/Rare Tiles
12643 Hortense St.
North Hollywood, Calif. 91604
(213) 761-2756

Weather Vanes

Although no longer used primarily for readings of wind direction, vanes serve an ornamental purpose for which no one need apologize. Not every old house or out-building should sport such an ornamental device, but some structures, particularly barns or the kind of attached or detached sheds once used for carriages and now automobiles, demand such attention. Vanes should be very securely affixed to a base, not only because they are buffeted by the elements, but also for security reasons. Whether antique or not, they are among the favorite objects of hit-and-run burglars.

Bruce Coutu of The Copper House handmakes copper vanes which are good reproductions of original models. He has a variety of styles and sizes available.

Catalog available, $1.

Bruce Coutu
The Copper House
Rte 4
Epsom, N.H. 03234
(603) 736-9792

E. G. Washburne vanes are handmade from their original cast-iron molds. Illustrated is one of the most typical of American designs, the galloping horse known as the "Kentucky." A complete vane includes a number of items other than the hammered figure. You must count on a steel spire, brass collar, large and small copper balls, and brass cardinals or letters.

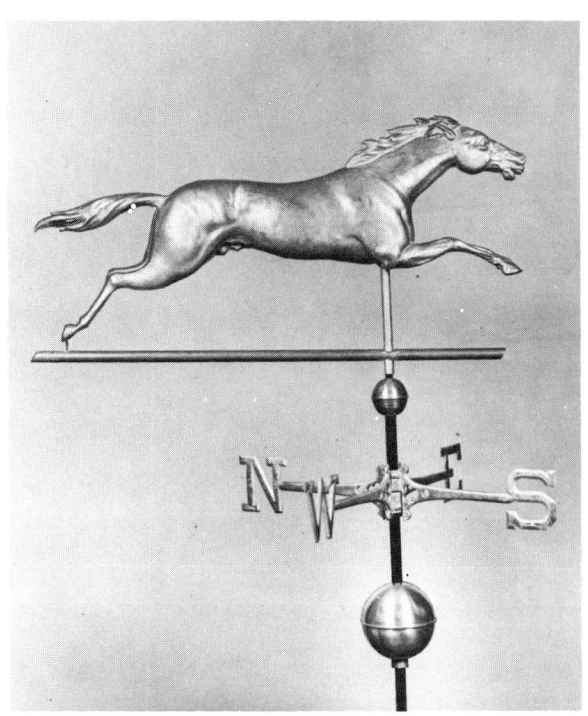

Literature available.

E. G. Washburne & Co.
85 Andover St., Rte. 114
Danvers, Mass. 01923
(617) 774-3645

Kenneth Lynch can provide you with a vane from almost any period and style—English, French, or American. Although often thought just a Colonial art form, vane making flourished in America and overseas throughout the nineteenth century. Some of the later ones are more properly called "bannerets." Illustrated is design #2504 in solid aluminum. Lynch also produces vanes in copper and other metals.

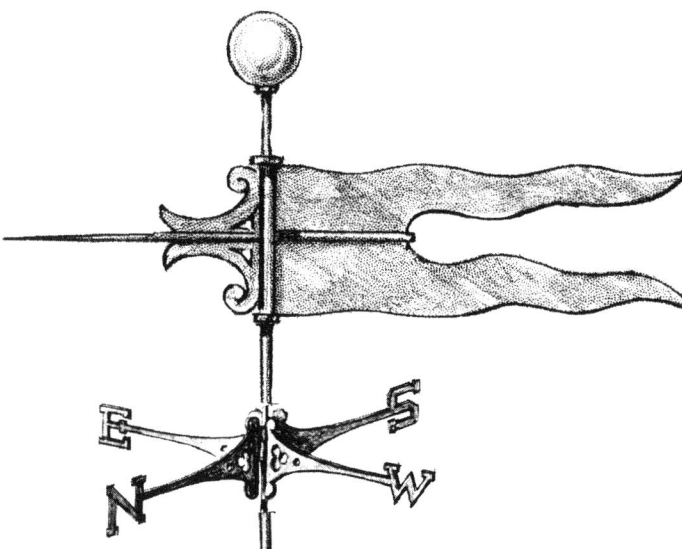

Catalog/book available, $2.50 paperback.

Kenneth Lynch & Sons, Inc.
78 Danbury Rd.
Wilton, Conn. 06897
(203) 762-8363

Woodenware

Wood bowls, plates, mugs, and utensils were the basics used in many Colonial kitchens; finer materials of china or pewter were used only in prosperous households. S. & C. Huber has faithfully reproduced basic containers and spoons—10½″ and 7″ plates, salt cellars, and hand-carved spoons. They are made of solid maple.

Catalog available, 50¢.

S. & C. Huber, Accoutrements
82 Plants Dam Rd.
East Lyme, Conn. 06333
(203) 739-0772

Fans

Gargoyles
United House Wrecking

Fences

The Cellar
Coker Creek Crafts
Gargoyles
Materials Unlimited
Renovation Source
Tennessee Fabricating
Wrecking Bar (Atlanta)

Fountains, Urns, Vases

Erkins Studios
Wrecking Bar (Dallas)

Garden Furniture

Gargoyles
Magnolia Hall

Kitchen Utensils

Bailey's Forge
Southern Highland Handicraft Guild

Metalware

Craft House, Williamsburg

Mirrors

The Cellar
Craft House, Williamsburg
Gargoyles
Magnolia Hall
Reale Mirror

Pottery

Henry Ford Museum & Greenfield Village
Craft House, Colonial Williamsburg

Shades

Perkowitz Window Fashions

Weather Vanes

Bailey's Forge
Cape Cod Cupola
J. W. Fiske Architectural Metals

Other Sources for Accessories

Consult List of Suppliers for addresses.

Baskets

Cane & Basket Supply
Guild of Shaker Crafts
West Rindge Baskets

Clocks

Henry Ford Museum & Greenfield Village
Magnolia Hall
R. Jesse Morley, Jr.
Seth Thomas
Trotman Clock
Weird Wood (kits)

Appendix A

The following is a list of retail outlets—arranged by state—carrying both Brunschwig & Fils and Scalamandre fabrics and papers. The majority of stores have branch outlets that may also supply these materials.

Levy's
El Con Center
Tucson, Ariz. 85702

Bullock's
7th and Hill Sts.
Los Angeles, Calif. 90014

Macy's San Francisco
Stockton and O'Farrell
San Francisco, Calif. 94108

W & J Sloane
216 Sutter
San Francisco, Calif. 94108

Denver Dry Goods
16th and California
Denver, Colo. 80201

May Co.-D & F
16th and Tremont Pl.
Denver, Colo. 80201

Woodward & Lothrop
10th and 11th, F and G Sts., N.W.
Washington, D.C. 20013

Blums of Boca
2980 N. Federal Highway
Boca Raton, Fla. 33432

Burdines
22 E. Flagler
Miami, Fla. 33131

Rich's, Inc.
Lenox Square
3393 Peachtree Rd., N.E.
Atlanta, Ga. 30326

Bonwit Teller
875 N. Michigan Blvd.
Chicago, Ill. 60611

Marshall Field & Co.
111 N. State St.
Chicago, Ill. 60690

Hochschild's
Howard and Lexington Sts.
Baltimore, Md. 21201

Hutzler's
212 N. Howard
Baltimore, Md. 21201

Filene's
426 Washington St.
Boston, Mass. 02101

Jordan Marsh
450 Washington St.
Boston, Mass. 02107

J. L. Hudson's
1206 Woodward
Detroit, Mich. 48211

Dayton's
700 On The Mall
Minneapolis, Minn. 55402

B. Altman & Co.
361 Fifth Ave.
New York, N.Y. 10016

Bloomingdales
1000 Third Ave.
New York, N.Y. 10022

W. &. J. Sloane
Fifth Ave., and 38th St.
New York, N.Y. 10018

The Higbee Co.
Public Square
Cleveland, Ohio 44113

Lazarus
S. High and W. Town
Columbus, Ohio 43216

Strawbridge & Clothier
8th and Market
Philadelphia, Penn. 19105

John Wanamaker
13th and Market Sts.
Philadelphia, Penn. 19101

Kaufmann's
Fifth and Smithfield
Pittsburgh, Penn. 15219

Dillard's
200 Houston
Fort Worth, Texas 76102

Joske's
4925 Westheimer
Houston, Texas 77027

Miller and Rhoads
517 E. Broad
Richmond, Va. 23219

The Bon Marche
4th and Pine
Seattle, Wash. 98101

Appendix B

Interior Designers

The design of any period interior is a serious matter of some expense. Although the work itself may be enjoyable and rewarding, it is not something which can be accomplished without expertise. *The Second Old House Catalogue* assists you to "do-it-yourself," but every home or apartment has special requirements which cannot be anticipated or documented in a book. If you feel that you need further assistance and can afford to enlist a professional, it would be best to contact a member of the American Society of Interior Designers. Many of the members have a thorough knowledge of period design. They are also in a position to obtain hard-to-get materials which are not generally available to the public—in particular, fabrics and special papers.

The following is a list of the ASID chapters throughout the United States. If you don't have a particular designer in mind, you might want to contact a chapter president or office regarding qualified professionals in period decoration in your area.

Alabama

Jim Mezrano, ASID
James Mezrano Associates
2841 Culver Rd.
Birmingham, Ala. 35223
(205) 879-4606

Arizona North

Mabel L. Helmick, ASID
1638 E. Cinnabar Ave.
Phoenix, Ariz. 85021
(602) 943-3837

Arizona South

Ronald C. Schuyler, ASID
Barrows
2800 E. Broadway
Tucson, Ariz. 85716
(602) 326-2479

California-Los Angeles

ASID California-Los Angeles Chapter
8687 Melrose Ave.
Los Angeles, Calif. 90069
(213) 652-2485

California-North

ASID California-North Chapter
300 Broadway
San Francisco, Calif. 94133
(415) 989-5363

California-Orange County

Daunine Vining, ASID
Daunine Vining & Associates
180 E. Main St., 140-A
Tustin, Calif. 92680
(714) 832-9855

California-Palm Springs

Marion Gardiner, FASID
370 Via Lola
Palm Springs, Calif. 92262
(714) 325-4496

California-Pasadena

Willis K. Hedrick
Willis Hedrick Interiors
441 S. Madison Ave.
Pasadena, Calif. 91101
(213) 796-5448

California-Peninsula

ASID California Peninsula Chapter
1612 El Camino Real
Menlo Park, Calif. 94025
(415) 323-3358

California-San Diego

Charles R. Wayland, ASID
Southwest Office Interiors
7480 Convoy St.
San Diego, Calif. 92110
(714) 565-7622

Carolinas

Howard R. Munroe, Jr., ASID
Carl Barnes Antiques and Interiors
2536 Reynolds Rd.
Winston-Salem, N.C. 27106
(919) 723-3594

Colorado

Victoria Degette, ASID
3113 E. Third Ave.
Denver, Colo. 80206
(303) 399-0280

Connecticut

Joan M. Arnold, ASID
Arnold-Brown
859 Post Rd.
Darien, Conn. 06820
(203) 655-2220

Florida-North

G. Dale Everett, ASID
1101 N.W. 39th Ave, A3
Gainesville, Fla. 32601
(904) 373-2566

Florida-South

Tulane Kidd, Jr., ASID
Tulane Kidd Interiors, Inc.
335 N. Federal Highway
Boca Raton, Fla. 33432
(305) 395-2848

Georgia

ASID Georgia Chapter
The Merchandise Mart, Suite 14A10
Atlanta, Ga. 30303
(404) 525-3778 (answering service)

Hawaii

Mary F. Philpotts, ASID
649 Sheridan St.
Honolulu, Hawaii 96814
(808) 947-1815

Illinois

ASID Illinois Chapter
620 Merchandise Mart
Chicago, Ill. 60654
(312) 467-5080

Indiana

Sallie Rowland, ASID
5619 E. 38th St.
Indianapolis, Ind. 46218
(317) 546-2451

Louisiana

John Eskew Campbell, ASID
P.O. Drawer 7087
Alexandria, La. 71306
(318) 445-0398

Maryland

Vicki Wenger, ASID
Rte. 1, Box 390
Old Annapolis Rd.
Frederick, Md. 21701
(301) 336-7600

Michigan

Frederick A. Sargent, ASID
Smith, Hinchman & Grylls Assoc.
455 W. Fort St.
Detroit, Mich. 48226
(313) 964-3000

Minnesota

Michael Johns Hopkins, ASID
1912 Franklin Ave., S.E.
Minneapolis, Minn. 55414
(612) 373-2073

Missouri-East

J. Randall Choate, ASID
618 S. Hanley
St. Louis, Mo. 63105
(314) 862-4520

Missouri-West/Kansas

Diane Wake Vogel, ASID
In Touch
7323 W. 97th St.
Overland Park, Kans. 66212
(913) 341-3702

Nebraska-Iowa

Leslie Berry, ASID
1146 S. 32nd St.
Omaha, Neb. 68105
(402) 341-8666

New England

F. Raymond Strawbridge, ASID
North House
West Main Rd.
Little Compton, R.I. 02837
(401) 635-2708

New Jersey

Stephen Greenberger, ASID

P.O. Box 427M
Morristown, N.J. 07960
(201) 538-4000

New Mexico

Ronald W. Nelson, ASID
3431 Florida N.E.
Albuquerque, N.M. 87110
(505) 881-3203

New York-Metropolitan

ASID New York-Metropolitan Chapter
950 Third Ave.
New York, N.Y. 10022
(212) 421-8765

New York State

Robert C. Frisch, ASID
Zausmer-Frisch Assoc.
219 Burnet Ave.
Syracuse, N.Y. 13203
(315) 475-8404

Ohio-North

Sheila Conner, ASID
The Dray Company
1154 E. Market St.
Warren, Ohio 44482
(216) 399-1843

Ohio-South/Kentucky

Robin A. Schmidt, ASID
Scoa Industries, Inc.
35 N. 4th St.
Columbus, Ohio 43215
(614) 221-5421

Oklahoma

Sydney Jane Winn, ASID
J. Richard Blissit Interiors
5550 S. Lewis, Suite 27
Tulsa, Okla. 74105
(918) 749-7711

Oregon

ASID Oregon Chapter
519 S.W. 3rd, Dekum Building
Portland, Ore. 97204
(503) 223-8231

Pennsylvania-East

Bernard Halkin, ASID
2104 Chestnut St.
Philadelphia, Penn. 19103
(215) 567-6364

Pennsylvania-West

Anne H. Ruben, ASID
Parke Interiors
4919 Centre Ave.
Pittsburgh, Penn. 15213
(412) 681-1313

Potomac (Washington, D.C., Northern Virginia)

John Richard Miller, FASID
6001 Joyce Dr.
Camp Springs, Md. 20031
(301) 423-8364

Tennessee

Dottie Sanders, ASID
Dottie Sanders Interior Design
160 S. McLean at Union
Memphis, Tenn. 38104
(901) 274-9263

Texas

ASID Texas Chapter
4007 Dallas Trade Mart
2100 Stemmens Freeway
Dallas, Texas 75207
(214) 748-1541

Texas-Gulf Coast

ASID Texas Gulf Coast Chapter
2607 Waugh
Houston, Texas 77006
(713) 526-6407

Utah

Bert F. Vieta, ASID
Gayl Baddeley Assoc.
430 E. South Temple
Salt Lake City, Utah 84111
(801) 532-2435

Virginia

Janet E. Kane, ASID
Janet Kane Interiors
1773 Parham Rd., Suite 202
Richmond, Va. 23229
(804) 320-2212

Washington State

ASID Washington State Chapter
107 S. Main St.
Seattle, Wash. 98104
(206) 624-0432

Wisconsin

Marie E. Crowley, ASID
Porter's
301 6th St.
Racine, Wis. 53403
(414) 633-6363

List of Suppliers

A

AA Abbington Ceiling Co.
2149 Utica Ave.
Brooklyn, N.Y. 11234

Accent Walls
1565 The Alameda
San Jose, Calif. 95126

Adams & Swett
380 Dorchester Ave.
Boston, Mass. 02127

Alcon Lightcraft Co.
1424 W. Alabama
Houston, Texas 77006

All-Nighter Stoves Works, Inc.
80 Commerce St.
Glastonbury, Conn. 06033

Allwood Door
345 Bayshore Rd.
San Francisco, Calif. 94124

Amerian Woodcarving
282 San Jose Ave.
San Jose, Calif. 95125

American Building Restoration, Inc.
9720 S. 60th St.
Franklin, Wis. 53132

American Olean Tile Co.
1000 Cannon Ave.
Lansdale, Penn. 19446

Ameritone Paint Co.
18414 S. Santa Fe. Ave.
Long Beach, Calif. 90810

Amherst Woodworking
P.O. Box 464
North Amherst, Mass. 01059

Townsend H. Anderson
House Joiner
R.D. #1, Box 44D
Moretown, Vt. 05660

Antique Center
6519 Telegraph Ave.
Oakland, Calif. 94609

Appalachian Fireside Crafts
Box 276
Booneville, Ky. 41314

Arch Associates/Stephen Guerrant,
AIA
874 Green Bay Rd.
Winnetka, Ill. 60093

ArchiCenter
111 S. Dearborn
Chicago, Ill. 60603

Architectural Antiques
410 St. Pierre
Montreal, Quebec H2Y 2M2
Canada

Architectural Ornaments
P.O. Box 115
Little Neck, N.Y. 11363

Architectural Paneling, Inc.
979 Third Ave.
New York, N.Y. 10022

Laura Ashley, Inc.
714 Madison Ave.
New York, N.Y. 10021

Atlanta Stove Works, Inc.
P.O. Box 5254
Atlanta, Ga. 30307

Authentic Designs, Inc.
330 E. 75th St.
New York, N.Y. 10021

B

B & P Lamp Supply, Inc.
Box #P-300
McMinnville, Tenn. 37110

Bailey and Griffin
1406 E. Mermaid Lane
Philadelphia, Penn. 19118

Bailey's Forge
221 E. Bay St.
Savannah, Ga. 31401

A. W. Baker Restorations, Inc.
670 Drift Rd.
Westport, Mass. 02790

Baldwin Hardware Mfg.
841 Wyomissing Blvd.
Reading, Penn. 19603

Ball and Ball
463 W. Lincoln Highway
Exton, Penn. 19341

Bangkok Industries, Inc.
1900 S. 20th St.
Philadelphia, Penn. 19145

Barclay Fabrics Co., Inc.
7120 Airport Highway, Box 650
Pennsauken, N.J. 08101

The Barn People
Star Rte. 44
West Windsor, Vt. 05037

Barney Brainum-Shanker Steel
  Co., Inc.
70–32 83rd St.
Glendale, N.Y. 11227

Bassett & Vollum, Inc.
217 N. Main St.
Galena, Ill. 61036

Bates Fabrics, Inc.
1431 Broadway
New York, N.Y. 10018

Beaumont Heritage Pottery
Box 300, Atkinson St.
Portsmouth, N.H. 03801

Bedlam Brass Beds
19–21 Fair Lawn Ave.
Fair Lawn, N.J. 07410

The Bedpost
R.D. 1, Box 155
Pen Argyl, Penn. 18072

H. Behlen & Bros.,
P.O. Box 698
Amsterdam, N.Y. 12010

Bel-Air Door Co.
P.O. Box 829
Alhambra, Calif. 91802

Bendix Mouldings, Inc.
235 Pegasus Ave.
Northvale, N.J. 07647

Berea College
Student Craft Industries
Berea, Ky. 40404

Bergamo Fabrics, Inc.
969 Third Ave.
New York, N.Y. 10022

Berkeley Architectural Salvage
2750 Adeline
Berkeley, Calif. 94703

Lester H. Berry
1108 Pine St.
Philadelphia, Penn. 19107

The Birge Co.
390 Niagara St.
Buffalo, N.Y. 14202

Thomas A. Bisesti
409 Oakland St.
Springfield, Mass. 01108

Bishop's Mill Historical Institute
P.O. Box 150
Edgmont, Penn. 19028

Bittersweet
Rte. 12, P.O. Box 5
Riverton, Vt. 05668

Black Millwork Co., Inc.
Lake Ave.
Midland Park, N.J. 07432

Blaine Window Hardware, Inc.
1919 Blaine Dr.
Hagerstown, Md. 21740

Blair Lumber Co., Inc.
Rte. 1
Powhatan, Va. 23139

Jerome W. Blum
Ross Hill Rd.
Lisbon, Conn. 06351

Norton Blumenthal, Inc.
979 Third Ave.
New York, N.Y. 10022

Morgan Bockius Studios, Inc.
1412 York Rd.
Warminster, Penn. 18974

Bona
2227 Beechmont Ave.
Cincinnati, Ohio 45230

Bow & Arrow Imports
14 Arrow St.
Cambridge, Mass. 02138

Louis W. Bowen, Inc.
979 Third Ave.
New York, N.Y. 10022

Braid-Aid
466 Washington St.
Pembroke, Mass. 02359

Brass Bed Co. of America
1933 S. Broadway
Los Angeles, Calif. 90007

Brasslight
2831 S. 12th St.
Milwaukee, Wis. 53215

The Broad-Axe Beam Co.
R.D. 2, Box 181-E
W. Brattleboro, Vt. 05301

Broadway Supply Co.
7421 Broadway
Kansas City, Mo. 64114

Brookstone Co.
127 Vose Farm Rd.
Petersboro, N.H. 03458

Carol Brown
Putney, Vt. 05346

Bruce Hardwood Floors
P.O. Box 16902
Memphis, Tenn. 38116

Brunschwig & Fils, Inc.
979 Third Ave.
New York, N.Y. 10022

The Burning Log (Eastern Office)
P.O. Box 438
Lebanon, N.H. 03766

The Burning Log (Western Office)
P.O. Box 8519
Aspen, Colo. 81611

C

Samuel Cabot, Inc.
1 Union St.
Boston, Mass. 02108

California Redwood Assoc.
617 Montgomery St.
San Francisco, Calif. 94111

California Wood Turning
25 Lyon St.
San Francisco, Calif. 94117

Canada & Dom Sugar, Ltd.
P.O. Box 490
Montreal 3, Quebec
Canada

The Candle Cellar & Emporium
1914 N. Main St.
Fall River, Mass. 02720

The Cane Farm
Rosemont, N.J. 08556

Cane & Basket Supply Co.
1283 S. Cochran Ave.
Los Angeles, Calif. 90019

Cape Cod Cupola Co.
North Dartmouth, Mass. 02747

Victor Carl Antiques
841 Broadway
New York, N.Y. 10003

Dale Carlisle
Rte. No. 123
Stoddard, N.H. 03464

Constance Carol
P.O. Box 899
Plymouth, Mass. 02360

Carved Glass & Signs
767 E. 132 St.
Bronx, N.Y. 10454

Castle Burlingame
R.D. 1, Box 352
Basking Ridge, N.J. 07920

Celestial Design
1239 Blake St.
Berkeley, Calif. 94702

The Cellar, Antique Building Parts
384 Elgin
Ottawa, Ontario
Canada

Century Glass, Inc.
1417 N. Washington Ave.
Dallas, Texas 75204

Cherry Creek Enterprises, Inc.
937 Santa Fe Dr.
Denver, Colo. 80204

China Seas, Inc.
149 E. 72nd St.
New York, N.Y. 10021

Clarence House
40 E. 57th St.
New York, N.Y. 10022

The Classic Illumination
P.O. Box 5851
San Francisco, Calif. 94101

Cleveland Wrecking Co.
2800 Third St.
San Francisco, Calif. 94107

Cleveland Wrecking Co.
3170 E. Washington Blvd.
Los Angeles, Calif. 90023

Cohasset Colonials
335 Ship St.
Cohasset, Mass. 02025

Coker Creek Crafts
P.O. Box 95
Coker Creek, Tenn. 37314

Diane Jackson Cole
9 Grove St.
Kennebunk, Me. 04043

Cole and Son (Wallpapers), Ltd.
P.O. Box 4BU
18 Mortimer St.
London, W1A 4BU
England

Colonial Lamp & Supply Co.
P.O. Box 867
McMinnville, Tenn. 37110

Colonial Williamsburg, Craft House
Box CH
Williamsburg, Va. 23185

Colony Pottery
Box 18
Bishop Hill, Ill. 61419

Connaissance Fabrics and Wallcoverings, Inc.
979 Third Ave.
New York, N.Y. 10022

Conran's
The Market at Citicorp Center
160 E. 54th St.
New York, N.Y. 10022

Brian Considine
Post Mills, Vt. 05058

Conso Products
261 Fifth Ave.
New York, N.Y. 10016

Albert Constantine and Son
2050 Eastchester Rd.
Bronx, N.Y. 10461

John Conti, Restoration Contractor
Box 189
Wagontown, Penn. 19376

Cooke Art Glass Studio
222 Diamond St.
San Francisco, Calif. 94114

Copper Antiquities
Cummaquid P.O.
Cummaquid, Mass. 02637

The Copper House
Rte. 4
Epsom, N.H. 03234

Coran Sholes Industries
509 E. 2nd St.
South Boston, Mass. 02127

Country Bed Shop
Box 222
Groton, Mass. 01450

Country Braid House
Clark Rd.
Tilton, N.H. 03276

Country Curtains
Stockbridge, Mass. 01262

Country Floors
300 E. 61st St.
New York, N.Y. 10021

Craftsman Lumber Co.
Maid St.
Groton, Mass. 01450

Craftswomen
Box 715
Doylestown, Penn. 18901

Inez Croom
55 E. 76th St.
New York, N.Y. 10021

Crown of Fairhope
759 Nichols Ave.
P.O. Drawer G
Fairhope, Ala. 36532

Cumberland General Store
Rte. 3
Crossville, Tenn. 38555

D

Dahlman-Clift Lamps
10930 W. Loomis Rd.
Franklin, Wis. 53132

Dana-Deck, Inc.
P.O. Box 78
Orcas, Wash. 98280

Davis Cabinet Co.
Box 5424
Nashville, Tenn. 38106

R. H. Davis, Inc.
Gregg Lake Rd.
Antrim, N.H. 03440

The Decorators Supply Corp.
3610 S. Morgan
Chicago, Ill. 60609

Delaware Quarries, Inc.
River Road
Lumberville, Penn. 18933

Delft Blue
P.O. Box 103
Ellicott City, Md. 21043

Jack Denst Designs, Inc.
6–117 Merchandise Mart
Chicago, Ill. 60654

The Designing Woman
705 Rivermont Dr.
St. Louis, Mo. 63137

Devoe Paint Division
Celanese Coatings
1 Riverfront Plaza
Louisville, Ky. 40402

A. L. Diament & Co.
P.O. Box 7437
Philadelphia, Penn. 19101

Diamond K. Co., Inc.
130 Buckland Rd.
South Windsor, Conn. 06074

J. di Christina & Sons
350 Treat Ave.
San Francisco, Calif. 94110

Down Home Comforts
P.O. Box 281
West Brattleboro, Vt. 05301

Driwood Moulding Co.
P.O. Box 1729
Florence, S.C. 29501

Frederick Duckloe & Bros.
Portland, Penn. 18351

Dutch Products & Supply Co.
14 S. Main St.
Yardley, Penn. 19067

E

The Eighteenth Century Co.
Haddam Quarter Rd.
Durham, Conn. 06422

Eighteenth Century Hardware Co.
131 E. 3rd St.
Derry, Penn. 15627

Elon, Inc.
964 Third Ave.
New York, N.Y. 10022

Era Victoriana
P.O. Box 9683
San Jose, Calif. 95157

William J. Erbe Co.
434½ E. 75th St.
New York, N.Y. 10021

Erkins Studios
14 E. 41st St.
New York, N.Y. 10017

The Essex Forge
1 Old Dennison Rd.
Essex, Conn. 06426

European Marble Works
661 Driggs Ave.
Brooklyn, N.Y. 11211

F

Faire Harbour Boats
44 Captain Pierce Rd.
Scituate, Mass. 02066

Felber Studios
110 Ardmore Ave., P.O. Box 551
Ardmore, Penn. 19003

Felicity, Inc.
600 Eagle Bend Rd.
Clinton, Tenn. 37716

Felicity, Inc.
Cookeville Antique Mall
I-40
Cookeville, Tenn. 38501

Felicity, Inc.
Thieves' Market

4900 Kingston Pike
Knoxville, Tenn. 37902

Fife's Woodworking & Mfg. Co.
Rte. 107
Northwood, N.H. 03261

Finnaren & Haley, Inc.
1300 N. 60th St.
Philadelphia, Penn. 19151

Fisher Stoves International
P.O. Box 10605
Eugene, Ore. 97440

J. W. Fiske Architectural Metals, Inc.
111–117 Pennsylvania Ave.
Paterson, N.J. 07053

Floorcloths, Inc.
109 Main St.
Annapolis, Md. 21401

Focal Point, Inc.
4870 S. Atlanta Rd.
Smyrna, Ga. 30080

Folger Adam Co.
Box 688
Joliet, Ill. 60434

Follansbee Steel Corp.
Follansbee, West Va. 26037

Henry Ford Museum and Greenfield
  Village Reproductions
20900 Oakwood Blvd.
Dearborn, Mich. 48121

Stephen Franklin
Box 717
Buckingham, Penn. 18912

Friedman Brothers Decorative Arts,
  Inc.
305 E. 47th St.
New York, N.Y. 10017

Pamela S. Friend
590 King St.
Hanover, Mass. 02339

Frog Tool Co., Ltd.
541 N. Franklin St.
Chicago, Ill. 60610

Fuller O'Brien Paints

The O'Brien Corp.
P.O. Box 864
Brunswick, Ga. 31520

Fuller O'Brien Paints
The O'Brien Corp
450 E. Grand Ave.
South San Francisco, Calif. 94080

Fuller O'Brien Paints
The O'Brien Corp.
2001 W. Washington Ave.
South Bend, Ind. 46634

Furniture Designs
1425 Sherman Ave.
Evanston, Ill. 60201

Fypon Inc.
Box 365, 108 Hill St.
Stewartstown, Penn. 17363

G

Gargoyles, Ltd.
512 S. 3rd St.
Philadelphia, Penn. 19147

Gaston Wood Finishes
P.O. Box 1246
Bloomington, Ind. 47401

Gates Moore
River Rd., Silvermine
Norwalk, Conn. 06850

Genesis Glass, Ltd.
700 N.E. 22nd Ave.
Portland, Ore. 97223

Giannetti Studios
3806 38th St.
Brentwood, Md. 20722

Glidden-Durkee
900 Union Commerce Bldg.
Cleveland, Ohio 44115

Grampa's Wood Stoves
Box 492
Ware, Mass. 01082

Great American Salvage Co., Inc.
901 E. 2nd St.
Little Rock, Ark. 72203

Greystone Upholstery Corp.
502 Clewell St.
Fountain Hill, Penn. 18015

Robert Griffith, Metalsmith
16 S. Main St.
Trucksville, Penn. 18708

Bernard E. Gruenke, Jr.
Conrad Schmidt Studios
2405 S. 162nd St.
New Berlin, Wis. 53157

Guardian National House Inspection
P.O. Box 31
Pleasantville, N.Y. 10570

Guardian National Home Inspection
Box 115
Orleans, Mass. 02653

Guilfoy Cornice Works
1234 Howard
San Francisco, Calif. 94005

Guild of Shaker Crafts
401 W. Savidge St.
Spring Lake, Mich. 49456

Gurian's
276 Fifth Ave.
New York, N.Y. 10001

Guyon, Inc.
65 Oak St.
Lititz, Penn. 17543

H

Haas Wood and Ivory Works
64 Clementine St.
San Francisco, Calif. 94105

Hallelujah Redwood Products
39500 Comptche Rd.
Mendocino, Calif. 95460

John Harra Wood & Supply Co.
39 W. 19th St.
New York, N.Y. 10011

Harris Manufacturing Go.
763 E. Walnut St.
Johnson City, Tenn. 37601

Hartmann Sanders Co.
1717 Arthur Ave.
Elk Grove Village, Ill. 60007

Wilbert R. Hasbrouck
Historic Resources
711 S. Dearborn
Chicago, Ill. 60605

Heads Up, Inc.
3201 W. McArthur Blvd.
Santa Ana, Calif. 92704

Hearthside Mail Order
Box 127
West Newbury, Vt. 05085

Heirloom Rugs
28 Harlem St.
Rumford, R.I. 02916

Heritage Lanterns
Dept. OH78
Sea Meadows Lane
Yarmouth, Me. 04096

Heritage Rugs
Lahaska, Penn. 18931

S. M. Hexter Co.
2800 Superior Ave.
Cleveland, Ohio 44114

Historic Boulevard Services
1520 W. Jackson Blvd.
Chicago, Ill. 60607

Historic Charleston Reproductions
105 Broad St.
Charleston, S.C. 29401

The Hitchcock Chair Co.
Riverton, Conn. 06065

The Holmes Co.
P.O. Box 382
York, Penn. 17405

Home and Harvest, Inc.
4407 Westbourne Rd.
Greensboro, N.C. 27406

Homespun Weavers
Ridge and Keystone Sts.
Emmaus, Penn. 18049

R. Hood & Co.

Heritage Village
Meredith, N.H. 03253

The Hope Co., Inc.
2052 Congressional Dr.
St. Louis, Mo. 63141

Horton Brasses
P.O. Box 95, Nooks Hill Rd.
Cromwell, Conn. 06416

The House Carpenters
Box 217
Shutesbury, Mass. 01072

House of Moulding
15202 Oxnard St.
Van Nuys, Calif. 91411

Housesmiths
P.O. Box 416
York, Maine 03909

David Howard, Inc.
P.O. Box 295
Alstead, N.H. 03602

Howell Construction
2700 12th Ave., S.
Nashville, Tenn. 37204

S. & C. Huber, Accoutrements
82 Plants Dam Rd.
East Lyme, Conn. 06333

Hurley Patentee Manor
R.D. 7, Box 98A
Kingston, N.Y. 12401

I

International Consultants
227 S. 9th St.
Philadelphia, Penn. 19107

J

William H. Jackson Co.
3 E. 47th St.
New York, N.Y. 10017

Charles W. Jacobsen
401 S. Salina St.
Syracuse, N.Y. 13201

Janovic/Plaza
1291 First Ave.
New York, N.Y. 10021

Jo El Shop
7120 Hawkins Creamery Rd.
Laytonsville, Md. 20760

Jones & Erwin, Inc.
232 E. 59th St.
New York, N.Y. 10022

The Judson Studios
200 South Avenue 66
Los Angeles, Calif. 90042

Jugtown Pottery
Rte. 2
Seagrove, N.C. 27341

K

Katzenbach & Warren, Inc.
950 Third Ave.
New York, N.Y. 10022

Steve Kayne, Blacksmith
17 Harmon Pl.
Smithtown, N.Y. 11787

KB Moulding, Inc.
508A Larkfield Rd.
East Northport, N.Y. 11731

Kelter-Mace
361 Bleecker St.
New York, N.Y. 10014

Kenmore Carpet Corp.
979 Third Ave.
New York, N.Y. 10022

Kent-Costikyan, Inc.
305 E. 63rd St.
New York, N.Y. 10022

Kentile Floors
58 Second Ave.
Brooklyn, N.Y. 11215

Kittinger Co.
1893 Elmwood Ave.
Buffalo, N.Y. 14207

KMH Associates, Inc.

The Dam Site
Ceresco, Mich. 49033

Kohler Co.
Kohler, Wis. 53044

Kristia Associates
343 Forest Ave., P.O. Box 1118
Portland, Me. 04104

Bruce M. Kriviskey, AIP
3048–A N. Shepard Ave.
Milwaukee, Wis. 53211

John Kruesel
R.R. 4
Rochester, Minn. 55901

Kwal Paints
3900 Joliet
Denver, Colo. 80239

L

J. R. Lamb Studios
151 Walnut St.
Northvale, N.J. 07647

Larimer Drygoods Co.
Attn. RLC/RS
P.O. Box 17491 T.A.
Denver, Colo. 80217

Last's Paint & Wallpaper
2813 Mission St.
San Francisco, Calif. 94110

H. & N. Laughon
8106 Three Chopt Rd.
Richmond, Va. 23229

William A. Lavicka
(see Historic Boulevard Services)

Lead Glass Co.
14924 Beloit Snodes Rd.
Beloit, Ohio 44609

Lee/Joffa, Inc.
979 Third Ave.
New York, N.Y. 10022

Lemees Fireplace Equipment
Rte. 28
Bridgewater, Mass. 02324

L. R. Lloyd Co.
Box 975
Uniontown, Penn. 15401

Ernest Lo Nano
S. Main St.
Sheffield, Mass. 01257

London Venturers Co.
2 Dock Sq.
Rockport, Mass. 01966

Luigi Crystal
7332 Frankford Ave.
Philadelphia, Penn. 19136

Kenneth Lynch & Sons
Box 488, 78 Danbury Rd.
Wilton, Conn. 06897

M

MacBeath Hardwood Co.
2150 Oakdale Ave.
San Francisco, Calif. 94124

Nancy McClelland, Inc.
232 E. 59th St.
New York, N.Y. 10022

Magnolia Hall
726 Andover
Atlanta, Ga. 30327

Florence Maine
113 W. Lane, Rte. 35
Ridgefield, Conn. 06877

Maine Line Paints
13 Hutchins St.
Auburn, Me. 14210

Marble Modes, Inc.
15–25 130th St.
College Point, N.Y. 11356

MarLe Company, Inc.
170 Summer St.
Stamford, Conn. 06901

Ephraim Marsh Co.
Box 266
Concord, N.C. 28025

The Martin-Senour Co.
1370 Ontario Ave., N.W.
Cleveland, Ohio 44113

Louis Maslow & Son, Inc.
979 Third Ave.
New York, N.Y. 10022

Materials Unlimited
4100 E. Morgan Rd.
Ypsilanti, Mich. 48197

Mather's
31 E. Main St.
Westminster, Md. 21157

Maurer & Shepherd, Joyners
122 Naubuc Ave.
Glastonbury, Conn. 06033

Mayfair China Corp.
142 22nd St.
Brooklyn, N.Y. 11232

Mercer Museum Shop
Bucks County Historical Society
Pine and Ashland
Doylestown, Penn. 18901

Mexico House
Box 970
Del Mar, Calif. 92014

Michael's Fine Colonial Products
22 Churchill Lane
Smithtown, N.Y. 11787

D. R. Millbranth, Cabinetmaker
Center Rd., R.R. 2, Box 462
Hillsboro, N.H. 03244

Newton Millham—Star Forge
672 Drift Rd.
Westport, Mass. 02790

Minnesota Woodworkers Supply Co.
Industrial Blvd.
Rogers, Minn. 55374

Miss Kitty's Keeping Room Kolors
Turkey Run
Box 117-A, Rte. 1
Clear Brook, Va. 22624

Mohawk Industries, Inc.
173 Howland Ave.
Adams, Mass. 01220

Benjamin Moore & Co.
Chestnut Ridge Rd.
Montvale, N.J. 07645

R. Jesse Morley, Jr.
88 Oak St.
Westwood, Mass. 02090

Thomas Moser, Cabinet Maker
Cobb's Bridge Rd.
New Gloucester, Me. 04260

Mottahedeh & Co.
225 Fifth Ave.
New York, N.Y. 10010

George W. Mount, Inc.
P.O. Box 306
576 Leyden Rd.
Greenfield, Mass. 01301

Munsell Color Products
2441 N. Calvert St.
Baltimore, Md. 21218

Lehlan Murray
Box 18
Bishop Hill, Ill. 61419

Museum of Fine Arts
Museum Shop
Boston, Mass. 02115

N

Nassau Flooring Corp.
P.O. 351, 242 Drexel St.
Westbury, N.Y. 11590

National Home Inspectors Service of
  New England, Inc.
2 Calvin Rd.
Watertown, Mass. 02172

The National House Inn
102 S. Parkview
Marshall, Mich. 49068

Deanne F. Nelson
Box 43
Bishop Hill, Ill. 61419

Newell Workshop
19 Blaine Ave.
Hinsdale, Ill. 60521

New Hampshire Blankets
Main St.
Harrisville, N.H. 03450

Newstamp Lighting Co.
227 Bay Rd.
North Easton, Mass. 02356

New York Flooring, Inc.
1733 First Ave.
New York, N.Y. 10028

Nichols & Stone
Gardner, Mass. 01440

Noelwood Handmade Furniture
123 Virginia St.
Elmhurst, Ill. 60126

Craig Nutt Fine Wood Works
2308 6th St.
Tuscaloosa, Ala. 35401

O

Old Carolina Brick Co.
Salisbury, N.C. 28144

Old-Fashioned Milk Paint Co.
Box 222
Groton, Mass. 01450

Old-House Inspection Co.
140 Berkeley Pl.
Brooklyn, N.Y. 11217

Old Mansions Co.
1305 Blue Hill Ave.
Mattapan, Mass. 02126

Old Stone Mill
Adams, Mass. 01220

Old Timey Furniture Co.
Smithfield, N.C. 27577

Old Town Restorations
158 Farrington
St. Paul, Minn. 55102

Old World Moulding & Finishing, Inc.
115 Allen Blvd.
Farmingdale, N.Y. 11735

Open Pacific Graphics
#43 Market Square
Victoria, British Columbia
Canada

Ox-Line Paints
Lehman Bros. Corp.
115 Jackson Ave.
Jersey City, N.J. 07304

P

P & G New and Used Plumbing
 Supply
818 Flushing Ave.
Brooklyn, N.Y. 11206

Packard Lamp Co., Inc.
67 E. 11th St.
New York, N.Y. 10003

Megan Parry
1727 Spruce
Boulder, Colo. 80302

Pat's Etc. Co. (PECO)
Highway 71 at Alum Creek
P.O. Box 777
Smithville, Texas 78957

Peerless Rattan & Reed Mfg. Co.
97 Washington
New York, N.Y. 10006

I. Peiser Floors
418 E. 91st St.
New York, N.Y. 10028

Penco Studios
1110 Baxter Ave.
Louisville, Ky. 40204

Period Furniture Hardware
123 Charles St.
Boston, Mass. 02114

Period Lighting Fixtures
Dept. OH78
1 Main St.
Chester, Conn. 06412

Period Pine
P.O. Box 77052
Atlanta, Ga. 30309

Perkowitz Window Fashions, Inc.
135 Green Bay Rd.
Wilmette, Ill. 60091

Norman Perry, Inc.
P.O. Box 90
Plymouth, N.H. 03264

Pfanstiel Hardware Co.
Hust Rd.
Jeffersonville, N.Y. 12748

Walter Phelps
Box 76
Williamsville, Vt. 05362

Philadelphia Museum of Art
The Museum Shop
P.O. Box 7646
Philadelphia, Penn. 19101

Pilgrim's Progress, Inc.
Penthouse
50 W. 67th St.
New York, N.Y. 10023

Pittsburgh Paints
PPG Industries, Inc.
1 Gateway Center
Pittsburgh, Penn. 15222

Portland Franklin Stove Foundry, Inc.
57 Kennebec St.
Portland, Me. 04104

Potlatch Corp.
Wood Products, Southern Division
P.O. Box 916
Stuttgart, Ark. 72160

Pratt & Lambert
625 Washington
Carlstadt, N.J. 07072

Preservation Associates, Inc.
P.O. Box 202
Sharpsburg, Md. 21782

Preservation Resource Center
Lake Shore
Essex, N.Y. 12936

Preservation Resource Group
5619 Southampton Dr.
Springfield, Va. 22151

Francis J. Purcell II
R.D. 2, Box 7
New Hope, Penn. 18938

Q

Quaker Lace Co.
4th St. and Lehigh Ave.
Philadelphia, Penn. 19133

Quicksand Crafts
Vest, Ky. 41772

R

Rainbow Art Glass Corp.
49 Shark River Rd.
Neptune, N.J. 07753

Rambusch Decorating Co.
40 W. 13th St.
New York, N.Y. 10011

The Readybuilt Products Co.
Box 4306, 1701 McHenry St.
Baltimore, Md. 21223

Reale Mirror Mfg. Co.
16–18 E. 12th St.
New York, N.Y. 10003

Reed Wallcoverings
550 Pharr Rd.
Atlanta, Ga. 30318

Reid Classics
P.O. Box 8383
3600 Old Shell Rd.
Mobile, Ala. 36608

The Renovation Source, Inc.
3513–14 N. Southport
Chicago, Ill. 60657

Restoration & Reincarnation
250 Austin Alley
San Francisco, Calif. 94109

Restorations, Ltd.
Jamestown, R.I. 02835

Restorations Unlimited
24 W. Main St.
Elizabethville, Penn. 17023

Ritter & Son
46901 Fish Rock Rd.
Anchor Bay (Gualala)
Calif. 95445

Robinson Iron
Robinson Rd.
Alexander City, Ala. 35010

The Rocker Shop
P.O. Box 12, 1421 White Circle, N.W.
Marietta, Ga. 30061

Frank Rockette
Strawberry Banke Museum
P.O. Box 300
Portsmouth, N.H. 03801

Jane Kent Rockwell, Interior
 Decorations
48–52 Lincoln St.
Exeter, N.H. 03833

Rococo Designs
417 Pennsylvania Ave.
Santa Cruz, Calif. 95062

Rosecore Carpet Co., Inc.
979 Third Ave.
New York, N.Y. 10022

Rotar Services
5007 W. Lovers Lane
Dallas, Texas 75209

Rowantrees Pottery
Union St.
Blue Hill, Me. 04614

Royal Windyne Ltd.
Box 6622, Dept. OHC
Richmond, Va. 23230

S

The Saltbox
2229 Marietta Pike
Lancaster, Penn. 17603

Arthur Sanderson & Sons, Ltd.
Berners St.
London W1A 2JE
England

San Francisco Victoriana
606 Natoma St.
San Francisco, Calif. 94103

Santa Cruz Foundry Co.
P.O. Box 831, 738 Chestnut St.
Santa Cruz, Calif. 94115

Richard E. Sargeant
Hartland Forge, Box 83
Hartland 4 Corners, Vt. 05049

Raoul Savoie
657 Prospect Blvd.
Pasadena, Calif. 91103

Scalamandré
950 Third Ave.
New York, N.Y. 10022

Schrader Wood Stoves & Fireplaces
724 Water St.
Santa Cruz, Calif. 95060

F. Schumacher & Co.
939 Third Ave.
New York, N.Y. 10022

A. F. Schwerd Mfg. Co.
3215 McClure Ave.
Pittsburgh, Penn. 15212

Mrs. Eldred Scott
The Riven Oak
Birmingham, Mich. 48012

John L. Seekamp
472 Pennsylvania
San Francisco, Calif. 94107

Self Sufficiency Products
Environmental Manufacturing Corp.
P.O. Box 126
Essex Junction, Vt. 05452

Sermac
P.O. Box 1684
Des Plaines, Ill. 60018

Shaker Workshops, Inc.
14 Bradford St.
Concord, Mass. 01742

Shenandoah Mfg. Co., Inc.
P.O. Box 839
Harrisonburg, Va. 22801

Shepherd Oak Products
Box 27
Northwood, N.H. 03261

Sherwin-Williams Co.
101 Prospect Ave., N.W.
Cleveland, Ohio 44101

Silk Surplus
223 E. 58th St.
New York, N.Y. 10022

Silk Surplus
843 Lexington Ave.
New York, N.Y. 10021

Silk Surplus
449 Old Country Rd.
Westbury, N.Y. 11590

Simpson Timber Co.
900 Fourth Ave.
Seattle, Wash. 98164

Smith & Son Roofing
1360 Virginia Ave.
Baldwin Park, Calif. 91706

Southern Highland Handicraft Guild
P.O. Box 9545
Asheville, N.C. 28805

Spanish Pueblo Doors, Inc.
P.O. Box 2517, Wagon Rd.
Santa Fe, N.M. 87501

Spanish Villa
2145 Zercher Rd.
San Antonio, Texas 78209

William Spencer
Creek Rd./Rancocas Woods
Mount Holly, N.J. 08060

Greg Spiess
216 E. Washington St.
Joliet, Ill. 60433

Standard Trimming Corp.
1114 First Ave.
New York, N.Y. 10021

Stark Carpet Corp.
979 Third Ave.
New York, N.Y. 10022

Stencil Specialty Co.
377 Ocean Ave.
Jersey City, N.J. 07305

Stencilled Interiors
Hinman Lane
Southbury, Conn. 06488

Steptoe and Wife Antiques, Ltd.
3626 Victoria Park Ave.
Willowdale, Ontario M2H 3B2
Canada

William Stewart & Sons
708 N. Edison St.
Arlington, Va. 22203

Thomas Strahan Co.
121 Webster Ave.
Chelsea, Mass. 02150

Stroheim & Romann
155 E. 56th St.
New York, N.Y. 10022

The Structural Slate Co.
Pen Argyl, Penn. 18072

Sturbridge Yankee Workshop
Dept. OHC
Sturbridge, Mass. 01566

Sunflower Studio
2851 Road B½
Grand Junction, Colo. 81501

Sunrise Salvage
2210 San Pablo Ave.
Berkeley, Calif. 94710

Sunrise Specialty
The Galleria
101 Kansas St., Rm. 224
San Francisco, Calif. 94103

Sunrise Specialty
8705 Santa Monica Blvd.
Los Angeles, Calif. 94710

T

Pete Taggett
The Blacksmith Shop
P.O. Box 115
Mt. Holly, Vt. 05758

Tennessee Fabricating Co.
2366 Prospect St.
Memphis Tenn. 38106

Thermograte Enterprises, Inc.
51 Iona Lane
St. Paul, Minn. 55113

Richard E. Thibaut
204 E. 58th St.
New York, N.Y. 10022

Seth Thomas
135 S. Main
Thomaston, Conn. 06787

Thompson & Anderson, Inc.
53 Seavey St.
Westbrook, Me. 04092

Thonet
A Simmons Co.
Decorative Arts Center
305 E. 63rd St.
New York, N.Y. 10021

Thonet
A Simmons Co.
600 World Trade Center
2050 Stemmons Freeway
Dallas, Texas 75258

Thonet
A Simmons Co.
11–100 Merchandise Mart
Chicago, Ill. 60654

Thonet
A Simmons Co.
Los Angeles Home Furnishings Mart
Space 756, 1933 S. Broadway
Los Angeles, Calif. 90007

Tolland Fabrics
1114 First Ave.
New York, N.Y. 10021

Townscape
30 Public Sq.
Medina, Ohio 44526

Townshend Furniture Co., Inc.
Rte. 30
Townshend, Vt. 05353

Tremont Nail Co.
P.O. Box 111
Wareham, Mass. 02571

Trotman Clock Co.
Box 71
Amherst, Mass. 01002

R.T. Trump & Co.
Bethlehem Pike
Flourtown, Penn. 19031

Turco Coatings, Inc.
Wheatland and Mellon Sts.
Phoenixville, Penn. 19460

Jay Turnbull, A.I.A.
2007 Franklin St.
San Francisco, Calif. 94109

U

United House Wrecking
328 Selleck St.
Stamford, Conn. 06902

Universal Clamp Co.
6905 Cedros Ave.
Van Nuys, Calif. 91405

Up Country Enterprise
Old Jaffrey Rd.
Peterborough, N.H. 03458

Urban Archaeology
137 Spring St.
New York, N.Y. 10012

V

The Valentas
2105 S. Austin Blvd.
Cicero, Ill. 60650

Vanderlaan Tile Co., Inc.
103 Park Ave.
New York, N.Y. 10017

VanHouten & Brick
Millwork and Building Hardware
920 Ocean St.
Santa Cruz, Calif. 95060

Albert Van Luit & Co.
4000 Chevy Chase Dr.
Los Angeles, Calif. 90039

Vermont Castings, Inc.
Box 126, Prince St.
Randolph, Vt. 05060

The Vermont Marble Co.
61 Main St.
Proctor, Vt. 05765

Vermont Structural Slate
Fair Haven, Vt. 05743

Victorian Reproductions
1601 Park Avenue S.
Minneapolis, Minn. 55404

Village Lantern
598 Union St.
N. Marshfield, Mass. 02059

Villeroy & Boch
912 Riverview Dr.
Totowa, N.J. 07512

Virginia Metalcrafters
1010 E. Main St.
Waynesboro, Va. 22980

Virtu
P.O. Box 192
Southfield, Mich. 48075

W

Wagon House Cabinetmaking
Box 149
Mendenhall, Penn. 19357

Charles Walker Mfg. Co.
189 13th St.
San Francisco, Calif. 94103

Wallin Forge
R.R. 1, Box 65
Sparta, Ky. 41086

Wall Stencils by Barbara
R.R. 2, Box 462, Center Rd.
Hillsboro, N.H. 03244

Walton Stained Glass
30 S. Central
Campbell, Calif. 95008

E. G. Washburne & Co.
85 Andover St.
Danvers, Mass. 01923

The Washington Copper Works
South St.
Washington, Conn. 06793

Washington Stove Works
P.O. Box 687
Everett, Wash. 98201

Wasley Lighting Division
Plainville Industrial Park
Plainville, Conn. 06062

Waterhouse Wallhangings
420 Boylston St.
Boston, Mass. 02116

Watts & Co., Ltd.
7 Tufton St., Westminster
London SW1P 3QB
England

Waverly Fabrics
58 W. 40th St.
New York, N.Y. 10018

Weird Wood
Green Mountain Cabins
Box 190
Chester, Vt. 05143

Welsbach Lighting, Inc.
240 Sargent Dr.
New Haven, Conn. 06511

Western Art Stone Co.
541 Tunnel Ave.
P.O. Box 315
Brisbane, Calif. 94005

Western States Stone
1849 East Slauson
Los Angeles, Calif. 90058

Westlake Architectural Antiques
3315 Westlake Dr.
Austin, Texas 78746

West Rindge Baskets
Box 24
Rindge, N.H. 03461

The Robert Whitley Studio
Laurel Rd.
Solebury, Penn. 18963

Whittemore-Durgin Glass Co.
P.O. Box 2065OH
Hanover, Mass. 02339

I. M. Wiese Antiquarian
Main St.
Southbury, Conn. 06488

D. B. Wiggins
Hale Rd.
Tilton, N.H. 03276

Helen Williams/Rare Tiles
12643 Hortense St.
North Hollywood, Calif. 91604

Williamsburg Blacksmith, Inc.
Buttonshop Rd.
Williamsburg, Mass. 01096

Roy Wingate
560 Green St.
San Francisco, Calif. 94123

Noel Wise Antiques
6503 St. Claude Ave.
Arabi, La. 70032

Woodcraft Supply Corp.
313 Montvale Ave.
Woburn, Mass. 01801

Wood Mosaic
P.O. Box 21159
Louisville, Ky. 40221

The Wrecking Bar
292 Moreland Ave., N.E.
Atlanta, Ga. 30307

The Wrecking Bar, Inc.
2601 McKinney
Dallas, Texas 75204

Wrightsville Hardware Co.
N. Front St.
Wrightsville, Penn. 17368

Y

Yankee Craftsman
357 Commonwealth Rd.
Wayland, Mass. 01778

Yours and Mine Antiques
10400 Sonoma Highway
Kenwood, Calif. 95452

Selected Bibliography

Benjamin, Asher. *American Builder's Companion.* 1827 edition. New York: Dover Publications, 1969.

Bicknell, A. J., and W. T. Comstock. *Victorian Architecture* (reprints of Bicknell's *Detail, Cottage, and Constructive Architecture* [1873] and Comstock's *Modern Architectural Designs and Details* [1881]). Watkins Glen, N.Y.: The American Life Foundation & Study Institute, 1978.

Bicknell, A. J. *Village Builder.* 1872 edition. Watkins Glen, N.Y.: The American Life Foundation & Study Institute, 1976.

Blumenson, John J.-G. *Identifying American Architecture.* Nashville, Tenn.: American Association for State and Local History, 1977.

Chippendale, Thomas. *The Gentleman & Cabinet-Maker's Director.* 3rd edition. New York: Dover Publications, 1966.

Condit, Carl W. *American Building: Materials and Techniques from the First Colonial Settlement to the Present.* Chicago: University of Chicago Press, 1968.

Cooke, Lawrence S. *Lighting in America, From Colonial Rushlights to Victorian Chandeliers.* Antiques Magazine Library. New York: Universe Books, 1976.

Curtis, Will, and Jane Curtis. *Antique Woodstoves, Artistry in Iron.* Ashville, Me.: Cobblesmith, 1975.

Devoe Paint Company. *Exterior Decoration.* Philadelphia: The Athaeneum of Philadelphia, 1976.

Downing, Andrew Jackson. *The Architecture of Country Houses.* 1850 edition. New York: Dover Publications, 1969.

Early American Life Society. *The Architectural Treasures of Early America*, 8 vols. New York: Arno Press, 1977. (The 150 monographs of the early 1900s have been compressed into this edited modern set. Get the originals if you can as the reproduction is poor in these copies.)

Eastlake, Charles. *Hints on Household Taste.* 4th edition. New York: Dover Publications, 1969.

Eiland, Murray L. *Oriental Rugs, A Comprehensive Guide.* Greenwich, Conn.: New York Graphic Society, 1973.

Fowler, John, and John Cornforth. *English Decoration in the Eighteenth Century.* London: Barrie & Jenkins, 1974.

Grow, Lawrence. *The Old House Catalogue.* New York: Universe Books, 1976.

Grow, Lawrence, comp. *Old House Plans.* New York: Universe Books, 1978.

Harris, Cyril M., ed. *Historic Architecture Sourcebook.* New York: McGraw-Hill, 1977.

Hayward, Arthur H. *Colonial and Early American Lighting.* New York: Dover Publications, 1962.

Hussey, E. C. *Home Building.* 1876 edition. Watkins Glen, N.Y.: The American Life Foundation & Study Institute, 1976.

Isham, Norman M. *Early American Houses and a Glossary of Colonial Architectural Terms.* New York: Da Capo Press, 1967.

Lipman, Jean, and Eve Meulendyke. *American Folk Decoration.* New York: Dover Publications, 1972.

Little, Nina Fletcher. *American Decorative Wall Painting: 1700–1850.* New York: E. P. Dutton & Co., 1972.

Loth, Calder, and Julius Toursdale Sadler, Jr. *The Only Proper Style, Gothic Architecture in America.* Boston: New York Graphic Society, 1975.

Maass, John. *The Victorian Home in America.* New York: Hawthorn Books, 1972.

McKee, Harley J. *Introduction to Early American Masonry, Stone, Brick, Mortar and Plaster.* Washington, D.C.: National Trust for Historic Preservation, 1973.

McRaven, Charles. *Building the Hewn Log House.* Hollister, Mo.: Mountain Publishing Services, 1978.

Montgomery, Florence M. *Printed Textiles, English and American Cottons and Linens 1700–1850*. A Winterthur Book. New York: The Viking Press, 1970.

Mumford, Lewis. *The Brown Decades: A Study of the Arts in America, 1865–1895*. New York: Dover Publications, 1955.

Mumford, Lewis. *Sticks and Stones: A Study of American Architecture and Civilization*. 2nd revised edition. New York: Dover Publications, 1955.

Palliser, Palliser & Co. *Palliser's New Cottage Homes and Details*. 1887 edition. Watkins Glen, N.Y.: The American Life Foundation & Study Institute, n.d.

Petit, Florence H. *America's Indigo Blues, Resist-Printed and Dyed Textiles of the Eighteenth Century*. New York: Hastings House, n.d.

Pettit, Florence H. *America's Printed and Painted Fabrics, 1600–1900*. Hastings House, 1970.

Pierson, William H., Jr. *American Buildings and Their Architects: The Colonial and Neoclassical Style*. Garden City, N.Y.: Doubleday and Co., 1970

Saylor, Henry H. *Dictionary of Architecture*. New York: John Wiley & Sons, 1952.

Scully, Vincent. *American Architecture and Urbanism*. New York: Frederick A. Praeger, 1969.

Seale, William. *The Tasteful Interlude, American Interiors Through the Camera's Eye, 1860–1917*. New York: Praeger Publishers, 1974.

Stanford, Deirdre, and Louis Reens. *Restored America*. New York: Praeger Publishers, 1975.

Stephen, George. *Remodeling Old Houses Without Destroying Their Character*. New York: Alfred A. Knopf, 1972.

Vaux, Calvert. *Villas and Cottages*. 2nd edition. New York: Dover Publications, 1970.

Wall, William E. *Graining: Ancient and Modern*. Revised edition by F. N. Vaderwalker. New York: Drake Publishers, 1972.

Waring, Janet. *Early American Stencils on Walls and Furniture*. New York: Dover Publications, n.d.

Whiffen, Marcus. *American Architecture Since 1780*. Cambridge, Mass.: The M.I.T. Press, 1969.

Williams, Henry L. and Ottalie K. *Old American Houses and How to Restore Them (1700–1850)*. New York: Doubleday, 1946. (The finest book yet written on the subject. Beg, borrow, or steal it.)

Index